Leigh Hunt

The Town

Its memorable characters and events

Leigh Hunt

The Town
Its memorable characters and events

ISBN/EAN: 9783337094287

Printed in Europe, USA, Canada, Australia, Japan

Cover: Foto ©Raphael Reischuk / pixelio.de

More available books at **www.hansebooks.com**

THE TOWN

ITS MEMORABLE CHARACTERS AND EVENTS

By LEIGH HUNT

WITH FORTY-FIVE ILLUSTRATIONS

A NEW EDITION

LONDON
SMITH, ELDER, & CO., 15 WATERLOO PLACE
1889

ADVERTISEMENT.

In this volume entitled "THE TOWN," the reader will find an account of London, partly topographical and historical, but chiefly recalling the memories of remarkable characters and events associated with its streets between St. Paul's and St. James's; being that part of the great metropolis which may be said to have constituted "THE TOWN" when that term was commonly used to designate London.

The present edition comprises the entire contents, unabridged, with the Illustrations.

CONTENTS.

INTRODUCTION.

CHAPTER I.

ST. PAUL'S AND THE NEIGHBOURHOOD.

CHAPTER II.

ST. PAUL'S AND THE NEIGHBOURHOOD.

CHAPTER III.

FLEET STREET.

CHAPTER IV.

THE STRAND.

CHAPTER V.

LINCOLN'S INN AND THE NEIGHBOURHOOD.

CHAPTER VI.

CHAPTER VII.

DRURY LANE, AND THE TWO THEATRES IN DRURY LANE AND COVENT GARDEN.

CHAPTER VIII.

COVENT GARDEN CONTINUED AND LEICESTER SQUARE.

CHAPTER IX.

CHARING CROSS AND WHITEHALL.

CHAPTER X.

WOLSEY AND WHITEHALL.

CHAPTER XI.

CHAPTER XII.

ILLUSTRATIONS.

ENGRAVED BY C. THURSTON THOMPSON, FROM DRAWINGS BY
J. W. ARCHER AND C. T. THOMPSON.

The Initial Letters and Tail-pieces designed by J. W. ARCHER and
    C. T. THOMPSON. (The Initial Letter to Chapter XII. represents
    the Conduit at St. James's.)

THE TOWN.

INTRODUCTION.

Different impressions of London on different passengers and minds—
Extendibility of its interest to all—London before the Deluge!—
Its origin according to the fabulous writers and poets—First his-
torical mention of it—Its names — British, Roman, Saxon, and
Norman London—General progress of the city and of civilisation—
Range of the Metropolis as it existed in the time of Shakspeare and
Bacon—Growth of the streets and suburbs during the later reigns—
"Merry London" and "Merry England"—Curious assertion respect-
ing trees in the city.

N one of those children's books which con-
tain reading fit for the manliest, and
which we have known to interest very
grave and even great men, there is a
pleasant chapter entitled *Eyes and no
Eyes*, or the *Art of Seeing*.* The two
heroes of it come home successively from a
walk in the same road, one of them having
seen only a heath and a hill, and the meadows by the water-
side, and therefore having seen nothing ; the other expatiating
on his delightful ramble, because the heath presented him
with curious birds, and the hill with the remains of a camp,
and the meadows with reeds, and rats, and herons, and king-
fishers, and sea-shells, and a man catching eels, and a glorious
sunset.

In like manner people may walk through a crowded city,
and see nothing but the crowd. A man may go from Bond
Street to Blackwall, and unless he has the luck to witness an
accident, or get a knock from a porter's burden, may be conscious, when he has returned, of nothing but the names of

* See Evenings at Home, by Dr. Aikin and Mrs. Barbauld.

B

those two places, and of the mud through which he has passed.
Nor is this to be attributed to dullness. He may, indeed, be
dull. The eyes of his understanding may be like bad
spectacles, which no brightening would enable to see much.
But he may be only inattentive. Circumstances may have
induced a want of curiosity, to which imagination itself shall
contribute, if it has not been taught to use its eyes. This is
particularly observable in childhood, when the love of novelty
is strongest. A boy at the Charter House, or Christ Hospital,
probably cares nothing for his neighbourhood, though stocked
with a great deal that might entertain him. He has been too
much accustomed to identify it with his schoolroom. We
remember the time ourselves when the only thought we had
in going through the metropolis was how to get out of it; how
to arrive, with our best speed, at the beautiful vista of home
and a pudding, which awaited us in the distance. And long
after this we saw nothing in London, but the book-shops
which have taught us better.

"I have often," says Boswell, with the inspiration of his great
London-loving friend upon him, "amused myself with thinking how
different a place London is to different people. They whose narrow
minds are contracted to the consideration of some one particular
pursuit, view it only through that medium. A politician thinks of it
merely as the seat of government in its different departments; a
grazier as a vast market for cattle; a mercantile man as a place where
a prodigious deal of business is done upon 'Change; a dramatic
enthusiast as the grand scene of theatrical entertainments; a man of
pleasure as an assemblage of taverns, &c. &c.; but the intellectual
man is struck with it as comprehending the whole of human life in
all its variety, the contemplation of which is inexhaustible."

It does not follow that the other persons whom Boswell
speaks of are not, by nature, intelligent. The want of
curiosity, in some, may be owing even to their affections and
anxiety. They may think themselves bound to be occupied
solely in what they are about. They have not been taught
how to invigorate as well as to divert the mind, by taking a
reasonable interest in the varieties of this astonishing world,
of which the most artificial portions are still works of nature
as well as art, and evidences of the hand of Him that made
the soul and its endeavours. Boswell himself, with all his
friend's assistance, and that of the tavern to boot, probably
saw nothing in London of the times gone by—of all that rich
aggregate of the past, which is one of the great treasures of
knowledge; and yet, by the same principle on which Boswell
admired Dr. Johnson, he might have delighted in calling to

mind the metropolis of the wits of Queen Anne's time, and of the poets of Elizabeth; might have longed to sit over their canary in Cornhill with Beaumont and Ben Jonson, and have thought that Surrey Street and Shire Lane had their merits, as well as the illustrious obscurity of Bolt Court. In Surrey Street lived Congreve; and Shire Lane, though nobody would think so to see it now, is eminent for the origin of the Kit-Kat Club (a host of wits and statesmen,) and for the recreations of Isaac Bickerstaff, Esq., of Tatler celebrity, at his *contubernium*, the Trumpet.

It may be said that the past is not in our possession; that we are sure only of what we can realise, and that the present and future afford enough contemplation for any man. But those who argue thus, argue against their better instinct. We take an interest in all that we understand; and in proportion as we enlarge our knowledge, enlarge, *ad infinitum*, the sphere of our sympathies. Tell the grazier, whom Boswell mentions, of a great grazier who lived before him—of Bakewell, who had an animal that produced him in one season the sum of eight hundred guineas; or Fowler, whose horned cattle sold for a value equal to that of the fee-simple of his farm; or Elwes, the miser, who, after spending thousands at the gaming table, would haggle for a shilling at Smithfield; and he will be curious to hear as much as you have to relate. Tell the mercantile man, in like manner, of Gresham, or Crisp, or the foundation of the Charter House by a merchant, and he will be equally attentive. And tell the man, *par excellence*, of anything that concerns humanity, and he will be pleased to hear of Bakewell, or Crisp, or Boswell, or Boswell's ancestor. Bakewell himself was a man of this sort. Boswell was proud of his ancestors, like most men that know who they were, whether their ancestors were persons to be proud of or not. The mere length of line flatters the brevity of existence. We must take care how we are proud of those who may not be fit to render us so; but we may be allowed to be anxious to live as long as we can, whether in prospect or retrospect. Besides, the human mind, being a thing infinitely greater than the circumstances which confine and cabin it in its present mode of existence, seeks to extend itself on all sides, past, present, and to come. If it puts on wings angelical, and pitches itself into the grand obscurity of the future, it runs back also on the more visible line of the past. Even the present, which is the great business of

life, is chiefly great, inasmuch as it regards the interests of
the many who are to come. and is built up of the experiences
of those who have gone by.   The past is the heir-loom of
the world.

Now in no shape is any part of this treasure more visible
to us, or more striking, than in that of a great metropolis.
The present is nowhere so present : we see the latest marks
of its hand.   The past is nowhere so traceable: we discover,
step by step, the successive abodes of its generations.   The
links that are wanting are supplied by history; nor perhaps
is there a single spot in London in which the past is not
visibly present to us, either in the shape of some old buildings
or at least in the names of the streets; or in which the absence
of more tangible memorials may not be supplied by the antiquary.   In some parts of it we may go back through the
whole English history, perhaps through the history of man,
as we shall see presently when we speak of St. Paul's Churchyard, a place in which you may get the last new novel, and
find remains of the ancient Britons and of the sea.   There,
also in the cathedral, lie painters, patriots, humanists, the
greatest warriors and some of the best men; and there, in
St. Paul's School, was educated England's epic poet, who
hoped that his native country would never forget her privilege of " teaching the nations how to live."   Surely a man
is more of a man, and does more justice to the faculties of
which he is composed, whether for knowledge or entertainment, who thinks of all these things in crossing St. Paul's
Churchyard, than if he saw nothing but the church itself, or
the clock, or confined his admiration to the abundance of
Brentford stages.

Milton, who began a history of England, very properly
touches upon the fabulous part of it ; not, as Dr. Johnson
thought (who did not take the trouble of reading the second
page), because he confounded it with the true, but, as he
himself states, for the benefit of those who would know how
to make use of it—the poets.   In the same passage he alludes
to those traces of a deluge of which we have just spoken, and
to the enormous bones occasionally dug up, which, with the
natural inclination of a poet, he was willing to look upon as
relics of a gigantic race of men.   Both of these evidences of
a remote period have been discovered in London earth, and
might be turned to grand account by a writer like himself.
It is curious to see the grounds on which truth and fiction

so often meet, without knowing one another. The Oriental writers have an account of a race of pre-Adamite kings, not entirely human. It is supposed by some geologists, that there was a period before the creation of man, when creatures vaster than any now on dry land trampled the earth at will; perhaps had faculties no longer to be found in connection with brute forms, and effaced, together with themselves, for a nobler experiment. We may indulge our fancy with supposing that, in those times, light itself, and the revolution of the seasens, may not have been exactly what they are now; that scme unknown monster, mammoth or behemoth, howled in the twilight over the ocean solitude now called London; or (not to fancy him monstrous in nature as in form, for the hugest creatures of the geologist appear to have been mild and grami-nivorous), that the site of our metropolis was occupied with the gigantic herd of some more gigantic spirit, all good of their kind, but not capable of enough ultimate good to be permitted to last. However, we only glance at these specu-lative matters, and leave them. Neither shall we say any-thing of the more modern elephant, who may have recreated himself some thousands of years ago on the site of the Chapter Coffee House; or of the crocodile, who may have snapped at some remote ancestor of a fishmonger in the valley of Dow-gate.

By the fabulous writers, London was called Troynovant or New Troy, and was said to have been founded by Brutus, great-grandson of Æneas, from whom the country was called Brutain, or Britain.

> For noble Britons sprong from Trojans bold,
> And Troynovant was built of old Troye's ashes cold.

(This is one of Spenser's fine old lingering lines, in which he seems to dwell on a fable till he believes it.) Brutus, having the misfortune to kill his father, fled from his native country into Greece, where he set free a multitude of Trojans, captives to King Pandrasus, whose daughter he espoused. He left Greece with a numerous flotilla, and came to an island called Legrecia, where there was a temple of Diana. To Diana he offered sacrifice, and prayed her to direct his course. The prayer, and the goddess's reply, as told in Latin by Gildas, have received a lustre from the hand of Milton. He gives us the following translation of them in his historical frag-ment:—

" Diva potens nemorum : "

" Goddess of Shades, and Huntress, who at will
    Walk'st on the rolling sphere, and through the deep,
    On thy third reign, the earth, look now ; and tell
    What land, what seat of rest, thou bidst me seek ;
    What certain seat, where I may worship thee,
    For aye, with temples vowed, and virgin quires."

" To whom, sleeping before the altar," says the poet, " Diana in a
vision that night, thus answered :—

" Brute, sub occasum solis : "

" Brutus, far to the west, in th' ocean wide,
    Beyond the realm of Gaul, a land there lies,
    Sea-girt it lies, where giants dwelt of old :
    Now void, it fits thy people. Thither bend
    Thy course : there shalt thou find a lasting seat ;
    There to thy sons another Troy shall rise,
    And kings be born of thee, whose dreaded reign
    Shall awe the world, and conquer nations bold."[*]

According to Spenser, Brutus did not find England cleared
of the giants. He had to conquer them. But we shall speak
of those personages when we come before their illustrious
representatives in Guildhall.

This fiction of Troynovant, or new Troy, appears to have
arisen from the word Trinobantes in Cæsar, a name given by
the historian to the inhabitants of a district which included
the London banks of the Thames. The oldest mention of the
metropolis is supposed to be found in that writer, under the
appellation of *Civitas Trinobantum*, the city of the Trinobantes ;
though some are of opinion that by *civitas* he only meant their
government or community. Be this as it may, a city of the
Britons, in Cæsar's time, was nothing either for truth or
fiction to boast of, having been, as he describes it, a mere
spot hollowed out of the woods, and defended by a ditch and
a rampart.

We have no reason to believe that the first germ of London
was anything greater than this. Milton supposes that so many
traditions of old British kings could not have been handed
down without a foundation in truth ; and the classical origin
of London, though rejected by himself, was not only firmly
believed by people in general as late as the reign of Henry
the Sixth (to whom it was quoted in a public document), but
was maintained by professed antiquaries,—Leland among
them.[†] It is probable enough that, before Cæsar's time, the

—————
[*] History of England, 4to. 1670, p. 11.
[†] We learn this from Selden's notes to the Polyolbion of Drayton.

affairs of the country may have been in a better situation than he found them ; and it is possible that something may have once stood on the site of London, which stood there no longer. But this may be said of every other place on the globe ; and as there is nothing authentic to show for it, we must be content to take our ancestors as we find them. In truth, nothing is known with certainty of the origin of London, not even of its name. The first time we hear either of the city or its apellation is in Tacitus, who calls it Londinium. The following list, taken principally from Camden, comprises, we believe, all the names by which it has been called. We dwell somewhat on this point, because we conclude the reader will be pleased to see by how many *aliases* his old acquaintance has been known.

Troja Nova, Troynovant, or New Troy.

Tre-novant, or the New City, (a mixture of Latin and Cornish).

Dian Belin, or the City of Diana.

Caer Ludd, or the City of Ludd.—These are the names given by the fabulous writers, chiefly Welsh.

Londinium.—*Tacitus, Ptolemy, Antoninus.*

Lundinium.—*Ammianus Marcellinus.*

Longidinium.

Lindonium, (Λινδόνιον).—*Stephanus* in his Dictionary.

Lundonia.—*Bede.*

Augusta.—The complimentary title granted to it under Valentinian, as was customary with flourishing foreign establishments.

Lundenbyrig.

Lundenberig.

Lundenberk.

Lundenburg.

Lundenwic, or wyc.

Lundenceastre (that is, London-*castrum* or camp).

Lundunes.

Lundene, or Lundenne.

Lundone.—Saxon names. Lundenceastre is Alfred the Great's translation of the Lundonia of Bede.

Luddestun.

Ludstoune.—Saxon translations of the Caer Ludd of the Welsh.

Londres.—French.

Londra.—Italian. The letter *r* in these words is curious.

It seems to represent the *berig* or *burgh* of the Saxons; *quasi* Londrig, from Londonberig; in which case *Londres* would mean London-borough.

The disputes upon the derivation of the word London have been numerous. In the present day, the question seems to be, whether it originated in Celtic British, that is, in Welsh, and signified "a city on a lake," or in Belgic British (old German), and meant "a city in a grove." The latest author who has handled the subject inclines to the latter opinion.* Mr. Pennant being a Celt, was for the " city on a lake," the Thames in the early periods of British history having formed a considerable expanse of water near the site of the present metropolis. *Llyn-Din* is Lake-City, and *Lun-Den* Grove-City. Erasmus, on the strength of those affinities between Greek and Welsh, which can be found between most languages, fetched the word from *Lindus*, a city of Rhodes; Somner, the antiquary, derived it from *Llawn*, full, and *Dyn*, man, implying a great concourse of people; another antiquary, from *Lugdus*, a Celtic prince; Maitland from *Lon*, a plain, and *Dun* or *Don*, a hill; another, we know not who, referred to by the same author, from a word signifying a ship and a hill†; Camden from *Llong-Dinas*, a City of Ships; and Selden, " seeing conjecture is free,"‡ was for deriving it from *Llan-Dien*, or the temple of Diana, for reasons which will appear presently. Pennant thinks that London might have been called Lake-City first, and Ship-City afterwards. The opinion of the editor of the *Picture of London* seems most plausible —that Lun-Den, or Grove-City was the name, because it is compounded of Belgic British, which, according to Cæsar, must have been the language of the district; and he adds, that the name is still common in Scandinavia.§ It may be argued, that London might have existed as a fortress on a lake before the arrival of settlers from Belgium; and that Grove-City could not have been so distinguishing a characteristic of the place as Lake-City, because wood was a great deal more abundant than water. On the other hand, all the rivers at that time were probably more or less given to overflowing.

* Picture of London, 1824, p. 3.
† These etymologies are to be found in Maitland's History and Survey of London. Fol. 1756. Vol. i. Book i.
‡ In the notes to Drayton's Polyolbion, Song viii.
§ There is a Lunden in Sweden, mentioned by Maitland, vol. i. *ubi sup.* It is the capital of the province of Schonen. Another town of the name is in Danish Holstein.

Grove-City might have been the final name, though Lake-City was the first; and the propensity to name places from trees, is still evident in our numerous Woot-tons, or Wood-towns, Wood-fords, Woodlands, &c. But of all disputes, those upon etymology appear the most hopeless. Perhaps the word itself was not originally what we take it to be. Who would suspect the word *wig* to come from *peruke; jour* from *dies; uncle* from *avus;* or that *Kensington* should have been corrupted by the despairing organs of a foreigner, into *Inhimthorp?* *

Whether London commenced with a spot cleared out in the woods by settlers from Holland, (Gallic Belgium,) as conjecture might imply from Cæsar, or whether the germ of it arose with the aboriginal inhabitants, we may conclude safely enough with Pennant, that it existed in some shape or other in Cæsar's time.

"It stood," says he, "in such a situation as the Britains would select, according to the rule they established. An immense forest originally extended to the river side, and even as late as the reign of Henry II. covered the northern neighbourhood of the city, and was filled with various species of beasts of chase. It was defended naturally by fosses, one formed by the creek which ran along Fleet Ditch; the other, afterwards known by that of Walbrook. The south side was guarded by the Thames; the north they might think sufficiently protected by the adjacent forest." †

In this place, then, seated on their hill, (probably that on which St. Paul's Cathedral stands, as it is the highest in London,) and gradually exchanging their burrows in the ground for huts of wicker and clay, we are to picture to ourselves our metropolitan ancestors, half-naked, rude in their manners, ignorant, violent, vindictive, subject to all the half-reasoning impulses—their bodies tattooed like South Sea Islanders — but brave, hospitable, patriotic, anxious for esteem — in short, like other semi-barbarians, exhibiting energies which they did not yet know how turn to account, but possessing, like all human beings, the germs of the noblest

* "We have one word," says Dr. Pegge, "which has not a single letter of its original, for of the French *peruke,* we got *periwig,* now abbreviated to *wig. Earwig* comes from *eruca,* as Dr. Wallis observes, *Anonymiana,* p. 56. The French word *jour* (day) comes from *dies,* through *diurnus, diurno, giorno;* so *giornale,* journal. *Uncle* is from *avus,* through *avunculus.* For *Inhimthorpe,* and other impossibilities, see Cosmo the Third's Travels through England, in the reign of Charles II."

† Pennant's London, third edition, 4to., p. 3.

capabilities. The accounts given of them by Cæsar and other ancient writers appear to be inconsistent, perhaps because we do not enough consider the inconsistencies of our own manners. According to their statements, the Britons had found out the art of making chariots of war, and yet had not learnt how to convert grain into flour, or to make a solid substance of milk. They rode, as it were, in their coaches, and yet had not arrived at the dignity of bread and cheese. Probably their chariots were magnified both in number and construction. The scythes which modern fancy has turned into proper haymaking sabres, and which some antiquaries have found so convenient for cutting through "a woody country" (a strange way of keeping them sharp), may have been nothing but spikes. We know not so easily what to say to the bread and cheese, except that in more knowing times people are not always found very ready to improve upon old habits, even with reasons staring them in the face; though, on the other hand, lest habits should be thought older than they are, and reformers be too impatient, it is worth while to consider, not how *long*, but how *short*, a period has elapsed (considering what a little thing a few centuries are in the progress of time) since in the very spot where a Briton sat half-naked and savage, unpossessed of a loaf or a piece of cheese, are to be found gathered together all the luxuries of the globe. Fancy the soul of an ancient Briton visiting his old ground in St. Paul's Churchyard, and hardly staring more at the church and houses, than at the bread in the baker's window, and the magic leaves in that of the bookseller. In one respect, an ancient City-Briton differed *toto cælo* with a modern. He would not eat goose! He had a superstition against it.

London, in Cæsar's time, was most probably a City of Ships; that is to say it traded with Gaul, and had a number of boats on its marshy river. Cæsar's pretence for invading England, was, that it was too good a provider for Gaul, and rendered his conquest of that country difficult. But it is doubtful whether he ever beheld or even alludes to the infant metropolis. His countrymen are supposed to have first taken possession of it about a hundred years afterwards, in the reign of Claudius. They had heard of a pearl-fishery, says Gibbon. At all events they found oysters; for Sandwich (Rutupium) became famous with them for that luxury.

It is not our design, in this Introduction, to give anything more than a sketch of the rise and growth of the metropolis; we shall leave the rest to be gathered as we proceed. Our intention is to go through London, quarter by quarter, and to notice the memorials as they arise; a plan, which, compared with others (at least if we are to judge of the effect which it has had on ourselves), seems to possess something of the superiority of sight over hearsay. When we read of events in their ordinary train, we pitch ourselves with difficulty into the scenes of action—sometimes wholly omit to do so; and there is a want of life and presence in them accordingly. When we are placed in the scenes themselves, and told to look about us—such and such a thing having happened in *that* house—*this* street being one in which another famous adventure took place, and *that* old mansion having been the dwelling of wit or beauty, we find ourselves comparatively at home, and enjoy the probability and the spectacle twice as much. We feel (especially if we are personally conversant with the spot) as if Shakspeare and Milton, Pope, Gay, and Arbuthnot, the club at the Mermaid, and the beauties at the court of White-Hall, were our next-door neighbours.

We shall take the reader, then, as speedily as possible among the quarters alluded to, and trouble him very little beforehand with dry abstracts and chronologies, or with races of men almost as uninteresting. The most patriotic reader of our history feels that he cares very little for his ancestors the Britons; of whom almost all he knows is, that they painted their skins, and made war in chariots. Nor do the Romans in England interest us more. They are men in helmets and short skirts, who have left us no memorial but a road or two, and an iron name. That is all that we know of them, and we care accordingly. Perhaps the Saxons, after having destroyed the Roman architecture as much as possible, and repented of it, took their own from what had survived. The greatest relic of Cæsar's countrymen in the metropolis was the piece of wall which ran lately south of Moorfields, in a street still designated as London Wall. The Romans had a vast material genius, not so intellectual as that of the Greeks, nor so calculated to move the world ultimately, but highly fitted to prepare the way for better impressions, by showing what the hand could perform; and as they built their wall in their usual giant style of solidity, it remained a long while to testify their magnificence. Small relics of it are yet to be seen in Little Bridge Street, behind Ludgate Hill; on the

north of Bull-and-Mouth Street, between that street and St.
Botolph's Churchyard; and on the south side of the Church-
yard of Cripplegate. There was another in the garden of
Stationer's Hall, but it has been blocked up.

ANCIENT BRITISH LONDON was a mere space in the woods,
open towards the river, and presenting circular cottages on
the hill and slope, and a few boats on the water. As it
increased, the cottages grew more numerous, and commerce
increased the number of sails.

ROMAN LONDON was British London, interspersed with the
better dwellings of the conquerors, and surrounded by a wall.
It extended from Ludgate to the Tower, and from the river to
the back of Cheapside.

SAXON LONDON was Roman London, despoiled, but retaining
the wall, and ultimately growing civilized with Christianity,
and richer in commerce. The first humble cathedral church
then arose, where the present one now stands.

NORMAN LONDON was Saxon and Roman London, greatly
improved, thickened with many houses, adorned with palaces
of princes and princely bishops, sounding with minstrelsy,
and glittering with the gorgeous pastimes of knighthood.
This was its state through the Anglo-Norman and Plantagenet
reigns. The friar then walked the streets in his cowl (Chaucer
is said to have beaten one in Fleet Street), and the knights
rode with trumpets in gaudy colours to their tournaments in
Smithfield.

In the time of Edward the First, houses were still built of
wood, and roofed with straw, sometimes even with reeds,
which gave rise to numerous fires. The fires brought the
brooks in request; and an importance which has since been
swallowed up in the advancement of science, was then given
to the *River of Wells* (Bagnigge, Sadler's, and Clerkenwell),
to the *Old Bourne* (the origin of the name of Holborn,) to
the little river Fleet, the Wall-brook, and the brook Lang-
bourne, which last still gives its name to a ward. The
conduits, which were large leaden cisterns, twenty in number,
were under the special care of the lord mayor and aldermen,
who, after visiting them on horseback on the eighteenth of
September, " hunted a hare before dinner, and a fox *after* it,
in the *Fields near St. Giles's.*"* Hours, and after-dinner
pursuits, must have altered marvellously since those days,
and the *body* of aldermen with them.

* Picture of London, p. 12

It was not till the reign of Henry the Fifth, that the city was *lighted at night*. The illumination was with lanterns, slung over the street with wisps of rope or hay. Under Edward the Fourth we first hear of *brick houses;* and in Henry the Eighth's time of *pavement in the middle of the streets*. The general aspect of London then experienced a remarkable change, in consequence of the dissolution of religious houses; the city, from the great number of them, having hitherto had the appearance " of a monastic, rather than a commercial metropolis."* The monk then ceased to walk, and the gallant London apprentice became more riotous. London, however, was still in a wretched condition, compared with what it is now. The streets, which had been impassable from mud, were often rendered so with filth and offal; and its homeliest wants being neglected, and the houses almost meeting at top, with heavy signs lumbering and filling up the inferior spaces, the metropolis was subject to *plagues* as well as fires. Nor was the interior of the houses better regarded. The people seemed to cultivate the plague. " The floors," says Erasmus, " are commonly of clay, strewed with rushes, which are occasionally renewed; but underneath lies unmolested an ancient collection of beer, grease, fragments of fish, &c., &c., and everything that is nasty."† The modern Englishman piques himself on his cleanliness, but he should do it modestly, considering what his ancestors could do ; and he should do it not half so much as he does, considering what he still leaves undone. It is the disgrace of the city of London in particular, that it still continues to be uncleanly, except in externals, and even to resist the efforts of the benevolent to purify it. But time and circumstance ultimately force people to improve. It was plague and fire that first taught the Londoners to build their city better. We hope the authorities will reflect upon this; and not wait for cholera to complete the lesson.

Erasmus wrote in the time of Henry the Eighth, when the civil wars had terminated in a voluptuous security, and when the pride of the court and nobility was at its height. Knighthood was becoming rather a show than a substance ; and the changes in religion, the dissolution of the monasteries, and

* Picture of London, p. 14. For a larger account of this and other matters briefly touched upon in the present introduction, see Brayley's London and Middlesex, vol. i. The spirit of them, however, will appear in our work, together with particulars hitherto unnoticed.
† Id. p. 13.

above all, the permission to read the Bible, set men thinking, and identified history in future with the progress of the general mind.   Opinion, accidentally set free by a tyrant, was never to be put down, though tyranny tried never so hard.   Poetry revived in the person of Henry Howard, Earl of Surrey; and, by a maturity natural to the first unsophisticated efforts of imagination, it came to its height in the next age with Shakspeare.   The monasteries being dissolved, London was become entirely the commercial city it has remained ever since, though it still abounded with noblemen's mansions, and did so till a much later period.   There were some in the time of Charles the` Second.   The manners of the citizens under Henry the Eighth were still rude and riotous, but cheerful; and manly exercises were much cultivated.   Henry was so pleased with one of the city archers, that he mock-heroically created him Duke of Shoreditch; upon which there arose a whole suburb peerage of Marquisses of Hogsdon and Islington, Pancras, &c.

In Elizabeth's time the London houses were still mostly of wood.   We see remains of them in the Strand and Fleet Street, and in various parts of the city.   They are like houses built of cards, one story projecting over the other; but unless there is something in the art of building, which may in future dispense with solidity, the modern houses will hardly be as lasting. People in the old ones could at least dance and make merry. Builders in former times did not spare their materials, nor introduce clauses in their leases against a jig.   We fancy Elizabeth hearing of a builder who should introduce such a proviso against the health and merriment of her buxom subjects, and sending to him, with a good round oath, to take a little less care of his purse, and more of his own neck.

In this age, ever worthy of honour and gratitude, the illustrious Bacon set free the hands of knowledge, which Aristotle had chained up, and put into them the touchstone of experiment, the mighty mover of the ages to come.   This was the great age, also, of English poetry and the drama.   Former manners and opinions now began to be seen only on the stage; intellect silently gave a man a rank in society he never enjoyed before; and nobles and men of letters mixed together in clubs.   People now also began to speculate on government, as well as religion; and the first evidences of that unsatisfied argumentative spirit appeared, which produced the downfall of the succeeding dynasty, and ultimately the Revolution, and all that we now enjoy.

The governments of Elizabeth and James, fearing that the greater the concourse the worse would be the consequences of sickness, and secretly apprehensive, no doubt, of the growth of large and intellectual bodies of men near their head-quarters, did all in their power to confine the metropolis to its then limits, but in vain.　Despotism itself, even in its mildest shape, cannot prevail against the spirit of an age; and Bacon was at that minute foreseeing the knowledge that was to quicken, increase, and elevate human intercourse, by means of the growth of commerce.　Houses and streets grew then as they do now, not so quickly indeed, but equally to the astonishment of their inhabitants; and the latter had reason to congratulate themselves on a pavement to walk upon; a luxury for which a lively Parisian, not half a century ago, is said to have gone down on his knees, when he came into England, thanking God that there was a country "in which some regard was shown to foot passengers."　In Charles the First's reign the suburbs of Westminster and Spitalfields were greatly enlarged, and the foundation of Covent Garden was commenced, as it now stands.　Symptoms of a future neighbourhood appeared also in Leicester Fields, though the place continued to be what the name imports, as late as the beginning of the last century.　The progress of building received a check from the Civil Wars, but only to revive with new spirit; and the great Fire—which was a great blessing—swallowed up at once both the deformity and the disease of old times, by widening the streets, and putting an end to the liability to pestilence.　London has not had a "*plague*" since, unless it be indigestion; which, however, is the great disease of modern sedentary times, and will never be got rid of, till we grow mental enough to have more respect for our bodies.

Towards the end of the reign of Charles the Second the metropolis began to increase in the direction of Holborn; Hatton Garden, Brook, and Greville Streets were built; and Ormond Street ran towards the fields.　In this and the following reigns the mansion-houses of the nobility on the river side began to give way to the private houses and streets, still retaining the name of the Strand.　Pall Mall and St. James's increased also; and Soho Square, on its first building, received the name of the Duke of Monmouth.　But particulars of that nature will be better noticed in the body of our work.　The nobility, gentry, and the wits, were now mixed up together. City taverns were still frequented by them; and city marriages began to be sought after, to mend the fortunes of the debauched cavaliers. Elizabeth's successor, James, was the first king who entered into anything like domestic familiarity with the monied men of the city. Charles the Second took " t'other bottle " with them (see the *Spectator*); and Lord Rochester played the buffoon on Tower Hill, as a quack doctor.

The streets about St. Martin's-in-the-fields and St. Giles's-in-the-fields, those of Clerkenwell, the neighbourhood of Old Street and Shoreditch, Marlborough Street, Soho, &c., successively arose in the time of Queen Anne, as well as a good portion of Holborn, beginning from Brook Street and including the neighbourhood of Bedford Street and Red Lion Square. St. Paul's, too, was completed as it now stands. This, and the succeeding times of the Hanover succession, were the times of Whig and Tory, of the principal wit-poets, of writers upon domestic manners, and of what may be called an ambition of good sense and reason,—" sense " being the favourite term in books, as " wit " had been in the age of Charles. Clubs were multiplied *ad infinitum* by the more harmless civil wars between Whig and Tory; and ale and beer brought the middle classes together, as wine did the rich. *Mug-house* clubs abounded in Long Acre, Cheapside, &c.; " where gentlemen, lawyers, and tradesmen used to meet in a great room, seldom under a hundred," if we are to believe the *Journey through England*, in the year 1724.

At the commencement of the last century the village of St. Mary-le-bone was almost a mile distant from any part of London; the nearest street being Old Bond Street, which scarcely extended to the present Clifford Street. Soon after the accession of George the First, New Bond Street arose, with others in the immediate neighbourhood, and the houses in Berkeley Square and its vicinity. Hanover Square and Cavendish Square were open fields in the year 1716. They were built about the beginning of the reign of George the Second, at which time the houses arose on the north side of Oxford Street, which then first took the name. The neighbourhood of Cavendish Square, and Oxford Market, Holles Street, Margaret Street, Vere Street, &c., are of the same date; and the grounds for Harley, Wigmore, and Mortimer Streets were laid out; the village and church of Mary-le-bone being still separated from them all by fields.

At the same period the legislature ordered the erection of the three parishes of St. George's Bloomsbury, St. Anne's Lime-house, and St. Paul's Deptford, London having, at that time, extended further in the last quarter than any other, by reason of the trade on the river.

So late, nevertheless, as this period, Fleet Ditch was a sluggish, foul stream, open as far as Holborn Bridge, and admitting small vessels for trade, coal barges, &c. It had become such a nuisance, that it was now arched over, and the late Fleet Market soon appeared on the covering. About the year 1737, the west end of the town was improved by the addition of Grosvenor Square and its neighbourhood.

The increase of the metropolis on all sides was in proportion to the length of the reign of George the Third. The space between Mary-le-bone was filled in ; Southwark became a mass of houses united with Westminster ; and new towns rather than suburbs, appeared in all quarters ; some with the names of towns, as Camden and Somers Town ; to which have been added, since the death of that prince, Portland Town ; a good half of Paddington, now joined with Kilburn ; a world of new streets between Paddington and Notting Hill ; Notting Hill itself including Shepherd's Bush ; another new world of streets, called Belgravia, between Knightsbridge and Pimlico ; others out by Peckham and Camberwell, including Clapham and Norwood ; and others again on the east, reaching as far as the skirts of Epping Forest ! Indeed, every village which was in the immediate and even the remote neighbourhood of London, and was quite distinct from one another at the beginning of the reign of George the Third, is now almost, if not quite, joined with it, including Highgate and Hampstead themselves on the north, Norwood on the south, Turnham Green and Parson's Green on the west, and Laytonstone on the east. The whole of this enormous mass of houses now presents us, more or less, in all quarters, with handsome streets, and even with squares ; and the two sides of the river are united by a series of noble bridges. New churches also have risen in every direction ; and though the architecture is none of the best, they contribute to a general air of neatness and freshness, which the increase of education and politeness promises to keep up. There is an old prophecy that Hampstead is to be in the middle of London ; a pheno-menon that London would really seem inclined to bring about. But a metropolis must stop somewhere ; and the very causes

C

of its growth (we mean the facilities of carriage, &c.) will ultimately, perhaps sooner than is looked for, prevent it. Railways now allow numbers to reside at a distance, who a few years ago would have remained in London.

Ancient British London is conjectured to have been about a mile long, and half a mile wide. Modern London occupies an area of above eighteen square miles ; and all this space, deducting not quite two miles for the river, is filled up with houses and public buildings, with a population of perhaps two million of souls, and with riches from all parts of the globe. In this respect London may justly be said to be the "metropolis of the world ;" though Paris has the advance of it in some others.

During the reign of George the Third, the whole mind of Europe was shaken up more vehemently than ever by the French Revolution ; and, as the consequence is after such tempestuous innovations, men began to look about them, to see what had stood the test of it, and how they might improve their condition still farther. After a great many disputes, natural on all sides, and a singular proof of the omnipotence of public opinion over the most extraordinary military power, it may be safely asserted, that the essence of that opinion, or the intellectual part of it is secretly acknowledged as the great regulator of society, even by those who appear to regulate it themselves ; and who never show their sense to more advantage, than when they lead where they must have followed. This is the most remarkable era, perhaps, in the history of mankind ; and experiment, and promise, are of a piece with it. Everybody is now more or less educated; the extension of the graces of life does away with sordidness, and teaches people that men do not live by "bread alone;" there *is* a reading public, let the jealousies of secluded scholarship say what they will; the mighty hands which Bacon set free are in full action ; the Press reports and assists them, and utters a thousand voices daily, not to be put an end to by anything short of a convulsion of the globe. Time and space themselves are comparatively annihilated by the inventions of the steam-carriage and the electric telegraph. The corn-laws have gone, opening still wider the prospects of mankind; and improvements may be looked for in society, so much to the benefit of all classes, that the most reasonable observer will decline stating the amount of his expectations, lest they should be thought as extravagant, as old times would have thought the telegraph just mentioned, or the publication of those thousands of volumes a day called News-papers.*

A word or two more on health, and our modes of living. London was once called " Merry London," the metropolis of " Merry England." The word did not imply exclusively what it does now. Chaucer talks of the " merry organ at the mass." But it appears to have had a signification still more desirable—to have meant the best condition in which anything could be found, with cheerfulness for the result. Gallant soldiers were " merry men." Favourable weather was " merry." And London was " merry," because its in-habitants were not only rich, but healthy and robust. They had sports infinite, up to the time of the Commonwealth— races and wrestlings, archery, quoits, tennis, foot-ball, hurl-ing, &c. Their May-day was worthy of the burst of the season ; not a man was left behind out of the fields, if he could help it; their apprentices piqued themselves on their stout arms, and not on their milliners' faces ; their nobility shook off the gout in tilts and tournaments ; their Christmas closed the year with a joviality which brought the very trees in-doors to crown their cups with, and which promised admirably for the year that was to come. In everything they did, there was a reference to Nature and her works, as if nothing should make them forget her ; and a gallant re-cognition of the duties of health and strength, as the foundation of their very right to be fathers.

We are aware of the drawbacks that accompanied this physical wisdom; of the comparative ignorance of the people, and the abuses they suffered accordingly; of slaveries, and star-chambers; of plagues, fires, and civil wars; of the burnings in Smithfield; of the murderings of wretched old women, supposed to be witches; and of other domestic superstitions, of which we are, perhaps, now-a-days unable to calculate the mischief. Surely we desire to see no more of them; and we are heartily willing that the same progress of thought which has swept them away, should have done us *a dis-service meanwhile*, which *more thinking* shall put an end to.

---

* Since this paragraph was written, the wonderful events have taken place in France, which have so agitated the whole of Europe, and which promise to open a new epoch in human history. May all benefit from them, as we believe all may, without real injury to any one !

Far are we from desiring to go back. But we would hasten the time when reflection shall recover the good for us, without bringing back the evil. And this surely it may. This it must—for real knowledge could not make its progress without it. The labour would not end in the reward. It has been supposed, that the poorer orders cannot have their enjoyments again—cannot have their old Christmas, for example, unless the rich supply them with the means of enjoyment, and so renew their charter of dependence. But this is to suppose that times are not changing in other respects, and that knowledge is not spreading. Riches and poverty themselves are modified by the progress of society; means are increased, however, to their apparent detriment at first, among the poor; and the knowledge of enjoyment becomes no longer confined to the rich, any more than the enjoyment of knowledge. Men may surely learn how to stouten their legs, as well as to improve their stockings. Now of all pleasures, those are the cheapest which are bought of nature—such as air and exercise, and manly sports; and though we allow that the poor, in order to relish them, must be free from the melancholier states of poverty, it is desirable *meanwhile* that the dispensers of knowledge should assist in hastening more cheerful times by preparing for them, and that all classes should be told how much the cultivation of their bodily health increases the ability, both of rich and poor, to get out of their troubles. You may steep a *gipsey* in trouble, and he shall issue out of it laughing. It would not be easy to do this with an epicurean, or a fund-holder, or with one of the parish poor; but neither need any one despair; for neither can the might of mechanical inventions, nor the greater might of opinion, be put down, whether in their first awful issuing forth, or in their final beneficence. And he that shall keep this oftenest in his mind, and be among the first to prepare for their enjoyment, by administering what helps he can to the encouragement of manly exercises among us, will assist in reviving the good old epithets of "merry England," and "merry London," *in a sense they never have had yet*. The progress of society has put an end to the melancholy absurdity of inquisitions, and star-chambers, and civil wars. The ground, therefore, is more clear for us to make England merrier in all respects than she was before. These things, we are aware, must result from other changes; but the changes themselves are in the reasonable and inevitable course of events.

As a link of a very pleasing description between old times and new not unconnected with what we have been speaking of, we shall conclude our introduction by observing, that there is scarcely a street in the *city* of London, perhaps not one, nor many out of the pale of it, from some part of which the passenger may not discern a *tree*. Most persons to whom this has been mentioned have doubted the accuracy of our information, nor do we profess hitherto to have ascertained it; though since we heard the assertion, we have made a point of endeavouring to do so whenever we could, and have not been disappointed. The mention of the circumstance generally creates a laughing astonishment, and a cry of "impossible!" Two persons, who successively heard of it the other day, not only thought it incredible as a general fact, but doubted whether half a dozen streets could be found with a twig in them; and they triumphantly instanced "Cheapside," as a place in which it was "out of the question." Yet in Cheapside is an actual, visible, and even ostentatiously visible tree, to all who have eyes to look about them. It stands at the corner of Wood Street, and occupies the space of a house. There was a solitary one the other day in St. Paul's Churchyard, which has now got a multitude of young companions. A little child was shown us a few years back, who was said never to have beheld a tree but that single one in St. Paul's Churchyard. Whenever a tree was mentioned, she thought it was that and no other. She had no conception even of the remote tree in Cheapside! This appears incredible; but there would seem to be no bounds, either to imagination or to the want of it. We were told the other day, on good authority, of a man who had resided six-and-thirty years in the square of St. Peter's at Rome, and then for the first time went inside the Cathedral.

There is a little garden in *Watling Street!* It lies completely open to the eye, being divided from the footway by a railing only.

In the body of our work will be found notices of other trees and green spots, that surprise the observer in the thick of the noise and smoke. Many of them are in churchyards. Others have disappeared during the progress of building. Many courts and passages are named from trees that once stood in them, as Vine and Elm Court, Fig-tree Court, Green-arbour Court, &c. It is not surprising that *garden-houses*, as they were called, should have formely abounded in Holborn, in

Bunhill Row, and other (at that time) suburban places. We notice the fact, in order to observe how fond the poets were of occupying houses of this description. Milton seems to have made a point of having one. The only London residence of Chapman which is known, was in Old Street Road; doubtless at that time a rural suburb. Beaumont and Fletcher's house, on the Surrey side of the Thames (for they lived as well as wrote together), most probably had a garden: and Dryden's house in Gerard Street looked into the garden of the mansion built by the Earls of Leicester. A tree, or even a flower, put in a window in the streets of a great city (and the London citizens, to their credit, are fond of flowers,) affects the eye something in the same way as the hand-organs, which bring unexpected music to the ear. They refresh the common-places of life, shed a harmony through the busy discord, and appeal to those first sources of emotion, which are associated with the remembrance of all that is young and innocent. They seem also to present to us a portion of the tranquillity we think we are labouring for, and the desire of which is felt as an earnest that we shall realise it somewhere, either in this world or in the next. Above all, they render us more cheerful for the performance of present duties; and the smallest seed of this kind, dropt into the heart of man, is worth more, and may terminate in better fruits, than anybody but a great poet could tell us.

CHAPTER I.

ST. PAUL'S, AND THE NEIGHBOURHOOD.

The Roman Temple of Diana—The first Christian Church—Old St. Paul's—Inigo Jones's Portico—Strange Usages of Former Times—Encroachments on the Fabric of the Cathedral—Paul's Walkers—Dining with Duke Humphrey—Catholic Customs—The Boy-Bishop—The Children of the Revels—Strange Ceremony on the Festivals of the Commemoration and Conversion of St. Paul—Ancient Tombs in the Cathedral—Scene between John of Gaunt and the Anti-Wickliffites — Paul's Cross—The Folkmote—The Sermons—Jane Shore—See-saw of Popery and Protestantism—London House—The Charnel—The Lollards' Tower—St. Paul's School—Desecration of the Cathedral during the Commonwealth—The present Cathedral —Sir Christopher Wren—Statue of Queen Anne.

S St. Paul's Churchyard is probably the oldest ground built upon in London, we begin our perambulations in that quarter. The cross which formerly stood north of the cathedral, and of which Stowe could not tell the antiquity, is supposed by some to have originated in one of those sacred stones which the Druids made use of in worship; but at least it is more than probable that here was a burial-ground of the ancient Britons; because when Sir Christopher Wren dug for a foundation to his cathedral, he discovered abundance of ivory and wooden pins, apparently of box, which are supposed to have fastened their winding sheets. The graves of the Saxons lay above them, lined with chalk-stones, or consisting of stones hollowed out: and in the same row with the pins, but deeper, lay Roman horns, lamps, lachrymatories, and all the elegancies of classic sculpture. Sir Christoper dug till he came to sand, and sea-shells, and to the London clay, which has since become famous in geology; so that the single history of St. Paul's Churchyard carries us back to the remotest periods of tradition; and we commence our book in the proper style of the old Chroniclers, who were not content, unless they began with the history of the world.

The Romans were thought to have built a Temple to Diana on the site of the modern cathedral, by reason of a number of relics of horned animals reported to have been dug up there.

Sir Christopher Wren asserts that there was no ground for the supposition. There was a similar story of a temple of Apollo at Westminster, built on the site of the present abbey, and said to have been destroyed by an earthquake. "Earthquakes," observed Sir Christopher, "break not stones to pieces; nor would the Picts be at that pains; but I imagine that the monks, finding the Londoners pretending to a Temple of Diana, where now St. Paul's stands (horns of stags and tusks of boars having been dug up in former times, and it is said also in later years), would not be behindhand in antiquity; but I must assert, that having changed all the foundations of old St. Paul's, and upon that occasion rummaged all the ground thereabouts, and being very desirous to find some footsteps of such a temple, I could not discover any, and therefore can give no more credit to Diana than to Apollo."*

Woodward, on the other hand, insisted on the Temple of Diana. He asserted, that a variety of the relics alluded to, in his own possession, were actually dug up on the spot, together with sacrificing vessels sculptured with beasts of chase, and with figures of Diana. In digging between the Deanery and Blackfriars a small brass figure of the goddess had also been found.†

Woodward was an enthusiast, eager to find what he fancied. Wren was willing to find also, but with cooler eyes. It is at the same time worth observing, that though Sir Christopher appears to have rejected the Pagan story with reason, he could not find it in his heart to refuse credit to the gratuitous traditions of old writers in favour of a Christian church "planted here by the Apostles themselves."‡ He calls the traditions "authentic testimony."

It is barely possible that the relics mentioned by Woodward might have been all dug up by the time Sir Christopher set about his inquiry; but let them have been what they might, they would have proved nothing in favour of a Roman Temple, *because the Romans never buried under their temples; neither did their legions remain long enough in this country to see the character of the place altered. It was sufficiently remarkable, that proofs had been discovered even of their burying there at all; for, at Rome, none but very extraordinary persons were suffered to be buried within the walls; and the Roman ceme-

* Parentalia, p. 290, quoted in the work next mentioned.
† Brayley's London and Middlesex, vol. i. p. 87.
‡ Parentalia, p. 27.

teries in England are proved to have been without them. It can only be accounted for on the supposition that, as no great men are so great as the great men of colonies, the Prefects and their officers at London decreed themselves an honour, which was to be attained at Rome by nothing short of the merits of a Fabricius or a Publicola.

The first authentic account of the existence of a Christian church on this spot is that of Bede, who attributes the erection of it to King Ethelbert, about the year 610, soon after his conversion by St. Augustine. The building, which was probably of wood, was burned down in 961, but was restored the same year—a proof that, notwithstanding the lofty terms in which it is spoken of by the old historian, it could not have been of any great extent. This second church lasted till the time of William the Conqueror, when it, too, was destroyed by a conflagration, which burned the greater part of the city. Bishop Maurice, who had just been appointed to the see, now resolved to rebuild the cathedral on a much grander scale than before, at his own expense. To assist him in accomplishing this object, the King granted him the stones of an old castle, called the Palatine Tower, which stood at the mouth of the Fleet River, and which had been reduced to ruins in the same conflagration. The Bishop's design was looked upon as so vast, that "men at that time," says Stowe, "judged it wold never have bin finished; it was then so wonderfull for length and breadth."* This was in the year 1087 ; and the people had some reason for their astonishment, for the building was not completed till the year 1240, in the reign of Henry the Third. Some even extend the date to 1315, which is two hundred and twenty-eight years after its foundation; but this was owing rather to repairs and additions than to anything wanting in the original edifice. The cathedral thus patched, altered, and added to, over and over again, with different orders and no orders of architecture, and partially burned, oftener than once, remained till the Great Fire of London, when it was luckily rendered incapable of further deformity, and gave way to the present.

It was, indeed, a singular structure, and used for singular purposes.

"The *exterior* of the building," says an intelligent writer, himself an architect, "presented a curious medley of the architectural style of

---

* Survey of London, p. 262. First edition.

different ages. At the western front Inigo Jones had erected a portico of the Corinthian order; thus diplaying a singular example of that bigotry of taste, which, only admitting one mode of beauty, is insensible to the superior claims of congruity. This portico, however, singly considered, was a grand and beautiful composition, and not inferior to any thing of the kind which modern times have produced: fourteen columns, each rising to the lofty height of forty-six feet, were so disposed, that eight, with two pilasters placed in front, and three on each flank, formed a square (oblong) peristyle, and supported an entablature and balustrade, which was crowned with statues of kings, predecessors of Charles the First, who claimed the honour of this fabric. Had the whole front been accommodated to Roman architecture, it might have deserved praise as a detached composition; but though cased with rustic work, and decorated with regular cornices, the pediment retained the original Gothic character in its equilateral proportions, and it was flanked by barbarous obelisks and ill-designed turrets.

" The whole of the exterior body of the church had been cased and reformed in a similar manner, through which every detail of antiquity was obliterated, and the general forms and proportions only left. The buttresses were converted into regular piers, and a complete cornice crowned the whole: of the windows, some were barely ornamented apertures, whilst others were decorated in a heavy Italian manner, with architrave dressings, brackets, and cherubic heads. The transepts presented fronts of the same incongruous style as the western elevation, and without any of its beauties." *

In its original state, however, old St. Paul's must have been an imposing building. Its extent at least was very great. The entire mass measured 690 feet in length, by 130 in breadth, and it was surmounted by a spire 520 feet high. The spire was of timber. It bore upon its summit not only a ball and cross, but a large gilded eagle, which served as a weather-cock. But the church having been nearly burned to the ground in June, 1561, owing to the carelessness of a plumber who left a pan of coals burning near some wood-work while he went to dinner, it was hastily restored without the lofty spire; so that in Hollar's engraving, given by Dugdale, of the building as it appeared in 1656, it stands curtailed of this ornament. Only the square tower, from which the spire sprang up, remains. " The old cathedral," says Mr. Malcolm, on the authority of a note with which he was furnished by the Rev. Mr. Watts, of Sion College, "did not stand in the same direc-tion with the new, the latter inclining rather to the south-west and north-east ; and the west front of the Old Church came much farther towards Ludgate than the present."†

It is of the Cathedral, as thus renovated, that Sir John Denham speaks in the following passage of his Cooper's Hill :—

> " That sacred pile, so vast, so high,
> That whether it 's a part of earth or sky,
> Uncertain seems, and may be thought a proud
> Aspiring mountain, or descending cloud ;
> Paul's, the late name of such a muse whose flight
> Has bravely reach'd and soar'd above thy height ;
> Now shalt thou stand, though sword, or time, or fire,
> Or zeal, more fierce than they, thy fall conspire,
> Secure, whilst thee the best of poets sings,
> Preserv'd from ruin by the best of kings."

" The best of poets " is his brother courtier Waller, who had some time before written his verses " Upon his Majesty's repairing of St. Paul's," in which he compares King Charles, for his regeneration of the Cathedral, to Amphion and other " antique minstrels," who were said to have achieved archi-tectural feats by the power of music, and who, he says,

> " Sure were Charles-like kings,
> Cities their lutes, and subjects' hearts their strings ;
> On which with so divine a hand they strook,
> Consent of motion from their breath they took."

---

* Fine Arts of the English School, quoted in Brayley, vol. ii. p. 217.
† Londinium Redivivum, iii., p. 134.

Jones's first labour, the removal of the various foreign
encumbrances that had so long oppressed and deformed the
venerable edifice, Waller commemorates by a pair of references
to St. Paul's history, not unhappily applied: he says the whole
nation had combined with his Majesty

> "to grace
> The Gentiles' great Apostle, and deface
> Those state-obscuring sheds, that like a chain
> Seem'd to confine and fetter him again;
> Which the glad Saint shakes off at his command,
> As once the viper from his sacred hand."

Denham's prediction did no credit to the prophetic reputation of poetry. Of the fabric which was to be unassailable
by zeal or fire the poet himself lived to see the ruin, begun
by the one and completed by the other; and he himself,
curiously enough, a short time before his death, was engaged
as the King's surveyor-general in (nominally at least) presiding over the erection of the new Cathedral—the successor
of the "sacred pile," of which he had thus sung the immor-
tality.

When Jones began the repairs and additions of which his
portico formed a part, in 1633, the rubbish that was removed
was carried, Mr. Malcolm informs us, to Clerkenwell fields,
where, he suggests, "some curious fragments of antiquity may
still remain."* The very beauty of this portico, surmounted
with its strange pediment and figures, and dragging at its back
that heap of deformity, completed the monstrous look of the
whole building, like a human countenance backed by some
horned lump. But this was nothing to the moral deformities
of the interior. Old St. Paul's, throughout almost the whole
period of its existence, at least from the reign of Henry the
Third, was a thoroughfare, and a "den of thieves." The
thoroughfare was occasioned probably by the great circuit
which people had been compelled to make by the extent of
the wall of the old churchyard—a circumference a great deal
larger than it is at present. There is a principle of familiarity
in the Catholic worship which, while it excites the devotional
tenderness of more refined believers, is apt to produce the
consequence, though not the feelings, of contempt among the
vulgar. Fear hinders contempt; but when license is mixed
with it, and the fear is not in action, the liberties taken are
apt to be in proportion. We have seen, in a Catholic chapel

* Londinium Redivivum. iii., p. 81.

in London, a milk-maid come into the passage, dash down her
pails, and having crossed herself, and applied the holy water
with reverence, depart with the same air with which she came
in. The next thing to setting down the pails, under the circumstances above mentioned, would have been to creep with
them through the church. Porters and loiterers would follow;
and by degrees the place of worship would become a place of
lounging and marketing, and intrigue, and all sorts of disorder. In the reign of Edward the Third, the King complains
to the Bishop that the "eating-room of the canons" had
"become the office and work-place of artisans, and the resort
of shameless women." The complaint turned out to be of no
avail; nor had the mandate of the Bishop a better result in the
time of Richard the Third, though it was accompanied with
the penalty of excommunication. An Act was passed to as
little purpose in the reign of Philip and Mary; and in the
time of Elizabeth the new opinions in religion seem to have
left the place fairly in possession of its chaos, as if in derision
of the old. The toleration of the abuse thus became a matter
of habit and indifference; and a young theologian, afterwards
one of the witty prelates of Charles the Second (Bishop Earle),
did not scruple to make it the subject of what we should now
call a "pleasant article."

"It must appear strange," says a note in Brayley's *London and
Middlesex* (vol. ii. p. 219), "to those who are acquainted with the
decent order and propriety of regulation now observed in our cathedral churches, and other places of divine worship, that ever such an
extended catalogue of improper customs and disgusting usages as
are noticed in various works, should have been formerly admitted to
be practised in St. Paul's church, and more especially that they should
have been so long habitually exercised as to be defended on the plea
of prescription.
"These nuisances had become so great, that in the time of Philip
and Mary the Common Council found it necessary to pass an act,
subjecting all future offenders to pains and penalties. From that act,
the church seems to have been not only made a common passage-way
for all—beer, bread, fish, flesh, fardels of stuffs, &c., but also for
mules, horses, and other beasts. This statute, however, must have
proved only a temporary restraint (excepting, probably, as to the
leading of animals through the church); for in the reign of Elizabeth,
we learn from *Londinium Redivivum* (vol. iii. p. 71), that idlers and
drunkards were indulged in lying and sleeping on the benches at the
choir door; and that other usages, too nauseous for description, were
also frequent."

Among the curious notices relating to the irreverent prac-
tices pursued in this church in the time of Elizabeth, collected

by Mr. Malcolm from the manuscript presentments on visita-
tions preserved at St. Paul's, are the following :—

"In the upper quier wher the comon [communion] table dothe
stande, there is much unreverente people, *walking* with *their hatts on
their heddes*, comonly all the service tyme, no man reproving them
for yt."

"Yт is a greate disorder in the churche, that porters, butchers, and
water-bearers, and who not, be suffered (in special tyme of service)
to carrye and recarrye whatsoever, no man withstandinge them, or
gainsaying them," &c.

"The notices of encroachments on St. Paul's, in the same reign, are
equally curious. The chantry and other chapels were completely
diverted from their ancient purposes; some were used as receptacles
for stores and lumber; another was a school, another a glazier's shop;
and the windows of all were, in general, broken. Part of the vaults
beneath the church was occupied by a carpenter, the remainder was
held by the bishop, the dean and chapter, and the minor canons.
One vault, thought to have been used for a burial-place, was converted into a wine-cellar, and a way had been cut into it through the
wall of the building itself. (This practice of converting church
vaults into wine-cellars, it may be remarked, is not yet worn out.
Some of the vaults of Winchester Cathedral are now, or were lately,
used for that purpose.) The shrowds and cloisters under the convo-
cation house, ' where not long since the sermons in foul weather were
wont to be preached,' were made 'a common lay-stall for boardes,
trunks, and chests, being lett oute unto trunk-makers, where, by
meanes of their daily knocking and noyse, the church is greatly dis-
turbed.' More than twenty houses also had been built against the
outer walls of the cathedral; and part of the very foundations was
cut away to make offices. One of those houses had literally a closet
dug in the wall; from another was a way through a window into a
wareroom in the steeple; a third, partly formed by St. Paul's, was
lately used as a *play-house;* and the owner of the fourth baked his
bread and *pies* in an *oven* excavated within a buttress."*

The middle of St. Paul's was also the Bond Street of that
period, and remained so till the time of the Commonwealth.
The loungers were called Paul's Walkers.

"The young gallants from the inns of court, the western and the
northern parts of the metropolis, and those that had spirit enough,"
says our author, "to detach themselves from the counting-houses in
the east, used to meet at the central point, St. Paul's; and from this
circumstance obtained the appellations of *Paul's Walkers*, as we now
say, *Bond-street Loungers*. However strange it may seem, tradition
says that the great Lord Bacon used in his youth to cry, *Eastward ho!*
and was literally a Paul's Walker."†

Lord Bacon had a taste for display, which was afterwards
exhibited in a magnificent manner, worthy of the grandeur
of his philosophy; but this, when he was young, might

* Londinium Redivivum. vol. iii., pp. 71, 73.
† Moser, in the European Magazine, July, 1807.

probably enough have been vented in the shape of an exube-
rance, which did not yet know what to do with itself. Who
would think that the late Mr. Fox ever wore red-heeled shoes,
and was a " buck about town ?"

But to conclude with these curious passages :—

" The Walkers in Paul's," continues our author, " during this and
the following reigns, were composed of a motley assemblage of the
gay, the vain, the dissolute, the idle, the knavish, and the lewd ; and
various notices of this fashionable resort may be found in the old plays
and other writings of the time. Ben Jonson, in his *Every man out of
his Humour*, has given a series of scenes in the interior of St. Paul's,
and an assemblage of a great variety of characters ; in the course of
which the curious piece of information occurs, that it was common to
affix *bills*, in the form of advertisements, upon the columns in the
aisles of the church, in a similar manner to what is now done in the
Royal Exchange : those bills he ridicules in two affected specimens,
the satire of which is admirable. Shakspeare also makes Falstaff say,
in speaking of Bardolph, 'I bought him in *Paul's*, and he'll buy me a
horse in Smithfield : if I could get me but a wife in the stews, I were
mann'd, hors'd, and wiv'd.' "

To complete these urbanities, the church was the resort of
pickpockets. Bishop Corbet, a poetical wit of the time of
Charles the First, sums up its character, as the " walke

" Where all our Brittaine sinners sweare and talk." *

Only one reformation had taken place in it since the complaint made by Edward the Third : no woman, at the time of
Earle's writing, was to be found there ; at least not in the
crowd. " The visitants," he says, " are all men without
exception."† A commonwealth writer insinuates otherwise;
but the visitation was not public. The practice of " walking
and talking" in St. Paul's appears to have revived under
James the Second, probably in connection with Catholic
wishes ; for there was an Act of William and Mary, by which
transgressors forfeited twenty pounds for every offence; and,
what is remarkable, the Bishop threatened to enforce this Act
so late as the year 1725 ; " the custom," says Mr. Malcolm,
" had become so very prevalent."‡

A proverb of " dining with Duke Humphrey," has survived to the present day, owing to a supposed tomb of
Humphrey, the good Duke of Gloucester, which was popular
with the poorer frequenters of the place. They had a custom
of strewing herbs before it, and sprinkling it with water.

* Poems. Gilchrist's edition, 1807, p. 5.
† Microcosmographie, quoted in Pennant.
‡ Anecdotes of the Manners and Customs of London during the
Eighteenth Century, vol. i. p. 281.

The tomb, according to Stow, was not Humphrey's, but that of Sir John Beauchamp, one of the house of Warwick. Men who strolled about for want of a dinner, were familiar enough with this tomb; and were therefore said to dine with Duke Humphrey.

While some of the extraordinary operations above-mentioned were going on (the intriguing, picking of pockets, &c.), the sermon was very likely proceeding. It is but fair, however, to conclude, that in the Catholic times, during the elevation of the host, there was a show of respect. We have heard a gentleman say, who visited Spain in his childhood, that he remembered being at the theatre during a fandango, when a loud voice cried out "*Dios*" (God); and all the people in the house, including the dancers, fell on their knees. A profound silence ensued. After a pause of a few seconds, the people rose, and the fandango went on as before. The little boy could not think what had happened, but was told that the host had gone by. The Deity (for so it was thought) had been sent for to the house of a sick man; and it was to honour him in passing, that the theatre had gone down on their knees. Catholics reform as well as other people, with the growth of knowledge, especially when restrictions no longer make their prejudices appear a matter of duty. We know not how it is in Spain at this moment, with regard to the devout interval of the fandango; but we know what would be thought of it by thousands of the offspring of those who witnessed it on this occasion; and certainly in no Catholic church now-a-days can be seen the abominations of old St. Paul's.

The passenger who now goes by the cathedral, and associates the idea of the inside with that of respectful silence and the simplicity of Protestant worship, little thinks what a noise has been in that spot, and what gorgeous processions have issued out of it.

Old St. Paul's was famous for the splendour of its shrine, and for its priestly wealth. The list of its copes, vestments, jewels, gold and silver cups, candlesticks, &c., occupies thirteen folio pages of the *Monasticon*. The side aisles were filled with chapels to different saints and the Virgin; that is to say, with nooks partitioned off one from another, and enriched with separate altars; and it is calculated, that, taking the whole establishment, there could hardly be fewer than two hundred priests. On certain holidays, this sacred multitude, in their richest copes, together with the lord mayor, aldermen, and city companies, and all the other parish priests of London, who carried a rich silver cross for every church, issued forth from the cathedral door in procession, singing a hymn, and so went through Cheapside and Cornhill to Leaden- hall, and back again. The last of these spectacles was for the peace of Guisnes, in 1546 ; shortly after which Henry the Eighth swept into his treasury the whole glories of Catholic worship—copes, crosses, jewels, church-plate, &c.—himself being the most bloated enormity that had ever misused them.

Among other retainers to the establishment, Henry sup- pressed a singular little personage, entitled the Boy-Bishop. The Boy-Bishop (*Episcopus Puerorum*) was a chorister annu- ally elected by his fellows to imitate the state and attire of a bishop, which he assumed on St. Nicholas's day, the sixth of December, and retained till that of the Innocents, December the twenty-eighth.

" This was done," says Brayley, " in commemoration of St. Nicholas, who, according to the Romish Church, was so piously fashioned, that even when a babe in his cradle he would fast both on Wednesdays and Fridays, and at those times was ' well pleased' to suck but once a-day. However ridiculous it may now seem, the Boy-Bishop is stated to have possessed episcopal authority during the above term ; and the other children were his prebendaries. He was not permitted to celebrate mass, but he had full liberty to preach ; and however puerile his dis- course; might have been, we find they were regarded with so much attention, that the learned Dean Colet, in his statutes for St. Paul's school, expressly ordained that the scholars shall, on ' every *Childermas* daye, come to Paule's Churche, and hear the Chylde Bishop's sermon, and after be at the hygh masse, and each of them offer a penny to the Chylde Bishop ; and with them the maisters and surveyors of the scole.' Probably," continues Mr. Brayley, " these orations, though affectedly childish, were composed by the more aged members of the church. If the Boy-Bishop died within the time of his prelacy, he was interred *in pontificalibus*, with the same ceremonies as the real diocesan ; and the tomb of a child-bishop in Salisbury Cathedral may be referred to as an instance of such interment." *

" From a printed church-book," says Mr. Hone, " containing the service of the boy-bishops set to music, we learn that, on the eve of Innocents'-day, the Boy-Bishop, and his youthful clergy, in their copes, and with burning tapers in their hands, went in solemn pro- cession, chanting and singing versicles, as they walked into the choir by the west door, in such order that the dean and canons went foremost, the chaplains next, and the Boy-Bishop with his priests in the last and highest place. He then took his seat, and the rest of the children disposed themselves on each side of the choir, upon the upper- most ascent, the canons resident bearing the incense and the book,

* London and Middlesex, vol. ii., p. 229.

and the petit-canons the tapers, according to the rubrick. Afterwards he proceeded to the altars of the Holy Trinity and All Saints, which he first censed, and next the image of the Holy Trinity, his priests all the while singing. Then they all chanted a service with prayers and responses, and, in the like manner taking his seat, the Boy-Bishop repeated salutations, prayers, and versicles; and in conclusion gave his benediction to the people, the chorus answering *Deo Gratias.*" *

The origin of customs is often as obscure as that of words, and may be traced with probability to many sources. Perhaps the boy-bishop had a reference, not only to St. Nicholas, but to Christ preaching when a boy among the doctors, and to the divine wisdom of his recommendations of a childlike simplicity. The school afterwards founded by Dean Colet was in honour of " the child Jesus." There was a school attached to the cathedral, of which Colet's was, perhaps, a revival, as far as scholarship was concerned. The boys in the older school were not only taught singing but acting, and for a long period were the most popular performers of stage-plays. In the time of Richard the Second, these Boy-Actors petitioned the King to prohibit certain ignorant and " inexpert people from presenting the History of the Old Testament." They began with sacred plays, but afterwards acted profane ; so that St. Paul's singing-school was numbered among the play-houses. This custom, as well as that of the boy-bishop, appears to have been common wherever there were choir-boys; and it doubtless originated, partly in the theatrical nature of the catholic ceremonies at which they assisted, and partly in the delight which the more scholarly of their masters took in teaching the plays of Terence and Seneca. The annual performance of a play of Terence, still kept up at Westminster school, is supposed by Warton to be a remnant of it. The choristers of Westminster Abbey, and of the chapel of Queen Elizabeth, (who took great pleasure in their performances), were celebrated as actors, though not so much so at those of St. Paul's. A set of them were incorporated under the title of Children of the Revels, among whom are to be found names that have since become celebrated as the fellow-actors of Shakspeare—Field, Underwood, and others. It was the same with Hart, Mohun, and others, who were players in the time of Cibber. It appears that children with good voices were sometimes *kidnapped* for a supply.† Tusser, who wrote the Five Hundred

* Ancient Mysteries described, &c., 1823, p. 195.

† *Purvey'd* is the word of Mr. Chalmers; who says, however, that he knows not on what principle the right of " purveying such children "

Points of Good Husbandry, is thought to have been thus pressed into the service; and a relic of the custom is supposed to have existed in that of pressing drummers for the army, which survived so late as the accession of Charles the First. The exercise of the right of might over children, and by people who wanted singers—an effeminate press-gang—would seem an intolerable nuisance; but the children were probably glad enough to be complimented by the violence, and to go to sing and play before a court.

Ben Jonson has some pretty verses on one of these juvenile actors:

> Weep with me, all you that read
> This little story;
> And know, for whom a tear you shed,
> Death's self is sorry.
>
> 'Twas a child that so did thrive
> In grace and feature,
> As heaven and nature seemed to strive
> Which owned the creature.
>
> Years he numbered, scarce thirteen,
> When fates turned cruel;
> Yet three filled zodiacs had he been
> The stage's jewel;
>
> And did act (what now we moan)
> Old men so duly,
> As, sooth, the Parcæ thought him one,
> He played so truly.
>
> Till, by error of his fate,
> They all consented;
> But viewing him since (alas! too late)
> They have repented;
>
> And have sought (to give new birth)
> In baths to steep him!
> But being so much too good for earth,
> Heaven vows to keep him.

This child, we see, was celebrated for acting old men. It is well known that, up to the Restoration, and sometimes afterwards, boys performed the parts of women. Kynaston, when a boy, used to be taken out by the ladies an airing, in his female dress after the play. This custom of males appearing as females gave rise, in Shakspeare's time, to the frequent introduction of female characters disguised; thus

was justified, "except by the maxim that the king had a right to the services of all his subjects." See Johnson and Steeven's Shakspeare, Prolegomena, vol. ii., p. 516.

presenting a singular anomaly, and a specimen of the gratuitous imaginations of the spectators in those days; who, besides being contented with taking the bare stage for a wood, a rock, or a garden, as it happened, were to suppose a boy on the stage *to pretend to be himself.*

One of the strangest of the old ceremonies, in which the clergy of the cathedral used to figure, was that which was performed twice a year, namely, on the day of the Commemoration and on that of the Conversion of St. Paul. On the former of these festivals, a fat doe, and on the latter, a fat buck, was presented to the Church by the family of Baud, in consideration of some land which they held of the Dean and Chapter at West Lee in Essex. The original agreement made with Sir William Le Baud, in 1274, was, that he himself should attend in person with the animals; but some years afterwards it was arranged that the presentation should be made by a servant, accompanied by a deputation of part of the family. The priests, however, continued to perform their part in the show. When the deer was brought to the foot of the steps leading to the choir, the reverend brethren appeared in a body to receive it, dressed in their full pontifical robes, and having their heads decorated with garlands of flowers. From thence they accompanied it as the servant led it forward to the high altar, where having been solemnly offered and slain, it was divided among the residentiaries. The horns were then fastened to the top of a spear, and carried in procession by the whole company around the inside of the church, a noisy concert of horns regulating their march. This ridiculous exhibition, which looks like a parody on the pagan ceremonies of their predecessors the priests of Diana, was continued by the cathedral clergy down to the time of Elizabeth.

The modern passenger through St. Paul's Churchyard has not only the last home of Nelson and others to venerate, as he goes by. In the ground of the old church were buried, and here, therefore, remains whatever dust may survive them, the gallant Sir Philip Sydney (the *beau ideal* of the age of Elizabeth), and Vandyke, who immortalised the youth and beauty of the court of Charles the First. One of Elizabeth's great statesmen also lay there—Walsingham—who died so poor, that he was buried by stealth, to prevent his body from being arrested. Another, Sir Christopher Hatton, who is supposed to have danced himself into the office of her

Majesty's Chancellor,* had a tomb which his contemporaries thought too magnificent, and which was accused of "shouldering" the altar. There was an absurd epitaph upon it, by which he would seem to have been a *dandy* to the last.

Stay and behold the mirror of a dead man's house,
Whose lively person would have made thee stay and wonder.
    *   *   *   *

When Nature moulded him, her thoughts were most on Mars;
And all the heavens to make him goodly were agreeing;
Thence he was valiant, active, strong, and passing comely;
And God did grace his mind and spirit with gifts excelling.
Nature commends her workmanship to Fortune's charge,
Fortune presents him to the court and queen,
Queen Eliz. (O God's dear handmayd) his most miracle.
Now hearken, reader, raritie not heard or seen;
This blessed Queen, mirror of all that Albion rul'd,
Gave favour to his faith, and precepts to his hopeful time;
First trained him in the stately band of pensioners;
    *   *   *   *

And for her safety made him Captain of the Guard.
Now doth she prune this vine, and from her sacred breast
Lessons his life, makes wise his heart for her great councells,
And so, *Vice-Chamberlain*, where foreign princes eyes
Might well admire her choyce, wherein she most excels.

He then aspires, says the writer, to "the highest subject's seat," and becomes

Lord Chancelour (measure and conscience of a holy king:)
Robe, Collar, Garter, dead figures of great honour,
Alms-deeds with faith, honest in word, frank in dispence,
The poor's friend, not popular, the church's pillar.
This tombe sheweth one, the heaven's shrine the other.†

The first line in italics, and the poetry throughout, are only to be equalled by a passage in an epitaph we have met with on a Lady of the name of Greenwood, of whom her husband says:—

"Her graces and her qualities were such
That she might have married a bishop or a judge;
But so extreme was her condescension and humility,
That she married *me*, a poor doctor of divinity;
By which heroic deed, she stands confest,
Of all other women, the phœnix of her sex."

Sir Christopher is said to have died of a broken heart, because his once loving mistress exacted a debt of him which he found it difficult to pay. It was common to talk of

---

* "His bushy beard, and shoe-strings green,
   His high-crown'd hat, and satin doublet,
   Mov'd the stout heart of England's queen,
      Though Pope and Spaniard could not trouble it."—GRAY.
† Maitland's History of London, vol. ii., p. 1170.

courtiers dying of broken hearts at that time; which gives
one an equal notion of the Queen's power, and the servility of
those gentlemen.   Fletcher, Bishop of London, father of the
great poet, was another who had a tomb in the old church,
and is said to have undergone the same fate.   It was he that
did a thing very unlike a poet's father.   He attended the
execution of Mary Queen of Scots, and said aloud, when her
head was held up by the executioner, " So perish all Queen
Elizabeth's enemies ! "   He was then Dean of Peterborough.
The Queen made him a bishop, but suspended him for marrying a second wife, which so preyed upon his feelings, that it
is thought, by the help of an immoderate love of smoking, to
have hastened his end — a catastrophe worthy of a mean
courtier.   He was well, sick, and dead, says Fuller, in a
quarter of an hour.   Most probably he died of apoplexy, the
tobacco giving him the *coup de grace.**

Dr. Donne, the head of the metaphysical poets, so well
criticised by Johnson, was Dean of St. Paul's, and had a
grave here, of which he has left an extraordinary memorial.
It is a wooden image of himself, made to his order, and representing him as he was to appear in his shroud.   This, for
some time before he died, he kept by his bed-side in an open
coffin, thus endeavouring to reconcile an uneasy imagination
to the fate he could not avoid.   It is still preserved in the
vaults under the church, and is to be seen with the other
curiosities of the cathedral.   We will not do a great man such
a disservice as to dig him up for a spectacle.   A man should
be judged of at the time when he is most himself, and not when
he is about to consign his weak body to its elements.

Of the events that have taken place connected with St.
Paul's, one of the most curious was a scene that passed in the
old cathedral between John of Gaunt and the Anti-Wickliffites.   It made him very unpopular at the time.   Probably,
if he had died just after it, his coffin would have been torn to
pieces; but subsequently he had a magnificent tomb in the
church, on which hung his crest and cap of state, together
with his lance and target.   Perhaps the merits of the friend
of Wickliff and Chaucer are now as much overvalued.   The
scene is taken as follows, by Mr. Brayley, out of Fox's Acts
and Monuments.

---

* The Bishop's second wife was a Lady Baker, who is said, by
Mr. Brayley, to have been young as well as beautiful, and probably did
not add to the prelate's repose.

" One of the most remarkable occurrences that ever took place within the old cathedral was the attempt made, in 1376, by the Archbishop of Canterbury and the Bishop of London, under the command of Pope Gregory the Eleventh, to compel Wickliff, the father of the English Reformation, to subscribe to the condemnation of some of his own tenets, which had been recently promulgated in the eight articles that have been termed the Lollards' Creed. The Pope had ordered the above prelates to apprehend and examine Wickliff; but they thought it most expedient to summon him to St. Paul's, as he was openly protected by the famous John of Gaunt, Duke of Lancaster; and that nobleman accompanied him to the examination, together with the Lord Percy, Marshall of England. The proceedings were soon interrupted by a dispute as to whether Wickliff should sit or stand; and the following curious dialogue arose on the Lord Percy desiring him to be seated:—

" *Bishop of London.*—' If I could have guessed, Lord Percy, that you would have played the master here, I would have prevented your coming.'

" *Duke of Lancaster.*—' Yes, he shall play the master here for all you.'

" *Lord Percy.*—' Wickliff, sit down! You have need of a seat, for you have many things to say.'

" *Bishop of London.*—' It is unreasonable that a clergyman, cited before his ordinary, should sit during his answer. He shall stand!'

" *Duke of Lancaster.*—' My Lord Percy, you are in the right! And for you, my Lord Bishop, you are grown so proud and arrogant, I will take care to humble your pride; and not only yours, my lord, but that of all the prelates in England. Thou dependest upon the credit of thy relations; but so far from being able to help thee, they shall have enough to do to support themselves.'

" *Bishop of London.*—' I place no confidence in my relations, but in God alone, who will give me the boldness to speak the truth.'

" *Duke of Lancaster* (*speaking softly to Lord Percy*).—' Rather than take this at the Bishop's hands, I will drag him by the hair of the head out of the court!' "*

Old St. Paul's was much larger than now, and the churchyard was of proportionate dimensions. The wall by which it was bounded ran along by the present streets of Ave Maria Lane, Paternoster Row, Old Change, Carter Lane, and Creed Lane; and therefore included a large space and many buildings which are not now considered to be within the precincts of the cathedral. This spacious area had grass inside, and contained a variety of appendages to the establishment. One of these was the cross. which we have alluded to at the beginning of this chapter, and of which Stow did not know the antiquity. It was called PAUL'S CROSS, and stood on the north side of the church, a little to the east of the entrance of Cannon Alley. It was around Paul's Cross, or rather in the space to the east

* London and Middlesex, vol. ii., p. 231.

of it that the citizens were wont anciently to assemble in Folkmote, or general convention — not only to elect their magistrates and to deliberate on public affairs, but also, as it would appear, to try offenders and award punishments. We read of meetings of the Folkmote in the thirteenth century; but the custom was discontinued, as the increasing number of the inhabitants, and the mixture of strangers, were found to lead to confusion and tumult. In after times the cross appears to have been used chiefly for proclamations, and other public proceedings, civil as well as ecclesiastical; such as the swearing of the citizens to allegiance, the emission of papal bulls, the exposing of penitents, &c., " and for the defaming of those," says Pennant, " who had incurred the displeasure of crowned heads." A pulpit was attached to it, it was not known when, in which sermons were preached, called Paul's Cross Sermons, a name by which they continued to be known when they ceased in the open air. Many benefactors contributed to support these sermons. In Stow's time the pulpit was an hexagonal piece of wood, " covered with lead, elevated upon a flight of stone steps, and surmounted by a large cross." During rainy weather the poorer part of the audience retreated to a covered place, called the shrowds, which are supposed to have abutted on the church wall. The rest, including the lord mayor and aldermen, most probably had shelter at all times; and the King and his train (for they attended also) had covered galleries.* Popular preachers were invited to hold forth in this pulpit, but the Bishop was the inviter. In the

* The active habits of our ancestors enabled them to bear these out-of-door sermons better than their posterity could ; yet, as times grew less hardy, they began to have consequences which Bishop Latimer attributed to another cause. " The citizens of Raim," said he, in a sermon preached in Lincolnshire, in the year 1552, "had their burying-place without the city, which, no doubt, is a laudable thing; and I do marvel that London, being so great a city, hath not a burial-place without, for no doubt it is an unwholesome thing to bury within the city, especially at such a time when there be great sickness, and many die together. I think, verily, that many a man taketh his death in Paul's Churchyard, and this I speak of experience; for I myself, when I have been there on some mornings to hear the sermons, have felt such an ill savoured unwholesome savour, that I was the worse for it a great while after; and I think no less, but it is the occasion of great sickness and disease."—Brayley, vol. ii., p. 315. After all, the Bishop may have been right in attributing the sickness to the cemetery. We have seen frightful probabilities of the same kind in our own time; and nothing can be more sensible than what he says of burial-grounds in cities.

reign of James the First, the lord mayor and aldermen ordered, that every one who should preach there, " considering the journies some of them might take from the universities, or else-where, should at his pleasure be freely entertained for five days' space, with sweet and convenient lodging, fire, candle, and all other necessaries, viz., from Thursday before their day of preaching, to Thursday morning following." * " This good custom," says Maitland, " continued for some time. And the Bishop of London, or his chaplain, when he sent to any one to preach, did actually signify the place where he might repair at his coming up, and be entertained freely." In earlier times a kind of inn seems to have been kept for the entertain-ment of the preachers at Paul's Cross, which went by the name of the *Shunamites' House.*

" Before the cross," says Pennant, " was brought, divested of all splendour, Jane Shore, the charitable, the merry concubine of Edward the Fourth, and, after his death, of his favourite, the unfortunate Lord Hastings. After the loss of her protectors, she fell a victim to the malice of crooked-backed *Richard.* He was disappointed (by her excellent defence) of convicting her of witchcraft, and confederating with her lover to destroy him. He then attacked her on the weak side of frailty. This was undeniable. He consigned her to the severity of the church: she was carried to the Bishop's palace, clothed in a white sheet, with a taper in her hand, and from thence conducted to the cathedral and the cross, before which she made a confession of her only fault. Every other virtue bloomed in this ill-fated fair with the fullest vigour. She could not resist the solicitations of a youthful monarch, the handsomest man of his time. On his death she was reduced to necessity, scorned by the world, and cast off by her hus-band, with whom she was paired in her childish years, and forced to fling herself into the arms of Hastings."

" In her penance she went," says Holinshed, " in countenance and pace demure, so womanlie, that albeit she were out of all araie, save her kertle onlie, yet went she so faire and lovelie, namelie, while the wondering of the people cast a comlie rud in her cheeks (of which she before had most misse), that hir great shame wan hir much praise among those that were more amorous of hir bodie, than curious of hir soule. And manie good folks that hated her living (and glad were to see sin corrected), yet pitied they more hir penance, than rejoiced therein, when they considered that the Protector procured it more of a corrupt intent than any virtuous affection."

" Rowe," continues Pennant, " has flung this part of her sad story into the following poetical dress; but it is far from possessing the moving simplicity of the old historian."†

---

* Maitland, vol. ii, p. 949.
† The reader, perhaps, will agree with us in thinking, that the last three lines of this poetry are unworthy of the rest, and put Jane in a theatrical attitude which she would not have effected.

Submissive, sad, and lonely was her look;
A burning taper in her hand she bore;
And on her shoulders, carelessly confused,
With loose neglect her lovely tresses hung;
Upon her cheek a faintish flush was spread;
Feeble she seemed, and sorely smit with pain;
While, barefoot as she trod the flinty pavement,
Her footsteps all along were marked with blood.
Yet silent still she passed, and unrepining;
Her streaming eyes bent ever on the earth,
Except when, in some bitter pang of sorrow,
To heaven she seemed, in fervent zeal, to raise,
And beg that mercy man denied her here.

" The poet has adopted the fable of her being denied all sustenance, and of her perishing with hunger, but that was not a fact. She lived to a great age, but in great distress and miserable poverty ; deserted even by those to whom she had, during prosperity, done the most essential services. She dragged a wretched life even to the time of Sir Thomas More, who introduces her story in his Life of Richard the Third. The beauty of her person is spoken of in high terms; 'Proper she was, and faire; nothing in her body that you would have changed, but if you would have wished her somewhat higher. Thus sai they that knew hir in hir youth. Albeit, some that now see hir, for she yet liveth, deem hir never to have been well visaged. Now is she old, leane, withered, and dried up : nothing left but shrivelled skin and hard bone ; and yet, being even such, whoso well advise her visage, might gesse and devise, which parts how filled, would make it a faire face.' " *

To these pictures, which are all drawn with spirit, may be added a portrait in the notes to Drayton's *Heroical Epistles,* referring to the one by Sir Thomas More.

" Her stature," says the comment, " was mean ; her hair of a dark yellow, her face round and full, her eye grey, delicate harmony being betwixt each part's proportion, and each proportion's colour ; her body fat, white, and smooth ; her countenance cheerful, and like to her condition. That picture which I have seen of her, was such as she rose out of her bed in the morning, having nothing on but a rich mantle, cast under her arm, over her shoulder, and sitting in a chair on which her naked arm did lie. What her father's name was, or where she was born, is not certainly known ; but Shore, a young man of right goodly person, wealth, and behaviour, abandoned her bed, after the King had made her his concubine."†

Richard, in the extreme consciousness of his being in the wrong, made a sad bungling business of his first attempts on the throne. The penance of Jane Shore was followed by Dr. Shawe's sermon at the same cross, in which the servile preacher attempted to bastardise the children of Edward, and to recommend the " legitimate" Richard, as the express image

* Some account of London, third edition, p. 394.
† Chalmers's British Poets, vol. iv., p. 91.

of his father.   Richard made his appearance, only to witness
the sullen silence of the spectators ; and the doctor, arguing
more weakness than wickedness, took to his house, and soon
after died.*

In the reign of the Tudors, Paul's Cross was the scene of
a very remarkable series of contradictions.   The government,
under Henry the Eighth, preached for and against the same
doctrines in religion.   Mary furiously attempted to revive
them ; and they were finally denounced by Elizabeth.
Wolsey began, in 1521, with fulminating, by command of the
Pope, against " one Martin Eleutherius" (Luther).   The
denouncement was made by Fisher (afterwards beheaded for
denying the King's supremacy) ; but Wolsey sate by, in his
usual state, censed and canopied, with the pope's ambassador
on one side of him, and the emperor's on the other.   During
the sermon a collection of Luther's books was burnt in the
churchyard ; "which ended, my Lord Cardinal went home
to dinner with all the other prelates."†   About ten years
afterwards the preachers at Paul's Cross received an order
from the King to "teach and declare to the people, that
neither the pope, nor any of his predecessors, were anything
more than the simple Bishops of Rome."   On the accession of
Mary, the discourses were ordered to veer directly round,
which produced two attempts to assassinate the preachers in
sermon-time ; and the moment Elizabeth came to the throne,
the divines began recommending the very opposite tenets, and
the pope was finally rejected.   At this Cross Elizabeth afterwards attended to hear a thanksgiving sermon for the defeat
of the Invincible Armada ; on which occasion a coach was
first seen in England—the one she came in.   The last sermon
attended there by the sovereign was during the reign of her
successor; but discourses continued to be delivered up to the
time of the Civil Wars, when, after being turned to account
by the Puritans for about a year, the pulpit was demolished

* "After which, once ended," says Stow, "the preacher gat him
home, and never after durst look out for shame, but kept him out of
sight like an owle; and when he once asked one that had been his
olde friende, what the people talked of him, all were it that his own
conscience well shewed him that they talked no good, yet when the
other answered him, that there was in every man's mouth spoken of
him much shame, it so strake him to the hart, that in a few daies
after, he withered, and consumed away."—Brayley, vol. i., p. 312.
† From a MS. in the British Museum, quoted by Brayley, vol. ii.,
p. 312.

by order of Parliament. The "willing instrument" of the
overthrow was Pennington, the lord-mayor. The inhabitants
who look out of their windows now-a-days on the northern
side of St. Paul's may thus have a succession of pictures
before their mind's eye, as curious and inconsistent as those
of a dream—princes, queens, lord-mayors, and aldermen,

A court of cobblers, and a mob of kings,

Jane's penance, Richard's chagrin, Wolsey's exaltation, clergymen preaching for and against the pope; a coach coming
as a wonder, where coaches now throng at every one's service;
and finally, a puritanical lord-mayor, who " blasphemed
custard," laying the axe to the tree, and cutting down the
pulpit and all its works.

The next appendage to the old church, in point of importance, was the Bishop's or London House, the name of which
survives in that of London House Yard. This, with other
buildings, perished in the Great Fire; and on the site of it
were built the houses now standing between the yard just
mentioned and the present Chapter House. The latter was
built by Wren. The old one stood on the other side of the
cathedral, where the modern deanery is to be found, only
more eastward. The bishop's house was often used for the
reception of princes. Edward the Third and his queen were
entertained there after a great tournament in Smithfield; and
there poor little Edward the Fifth was lodged, previously to
his appointed coronation. To the east of the bishop's house,
stretching towards Cheapside, was a chapel, erected by the
father of Thomas Becket, called Pardon-Church-Haugh,
which was surrounded by a cloister, presenting a painting of
the Dance of Death on the walls, a subject rendered famous
by Holbein.*

Another chapel called the Charnel, a proper neighbour to
this *fresco*, stood at the back of the two buildings just mentioned. It received its name from the quantity of human
bones collected from St. Paul's Churchyard, and deposited in
a vault beneath. The Charnel was taken down by the

---

* A Dance of Death (for the subject was often repeated) is a procession of the various ranks of life, from the pope to the peasant, each
led by a skeleton for his partner. Holbein enlarged it by the addition of a series of visits privately paid by Death to the individuals.
The figurantes, in his work, by no means go down the dance " with
an air of despondency." The human beings are unconscious of their
partners (which is fine); and the Deaths are as jolly as skeletons well
can be.

Protector Somerset about 1549, and the stones were employed in the building of the new palace of Somerset House. On this occasion it is stated that more than a thousand cart-loads of bones were removed to Finsbury Fields where they formed a large mount, on which three windmills were erected. From these Windmill Street in that neighbourhood derives its name. The ground on which the chapel stood was afterwards built over with dwellings and warehouses, having sheds before them for the use of stationers. Immediately to the north of St. Paul's School, and towards the spot where the churchyard looks into Cheapside, was a campanile, or bell-house ; that is to say, a belfry, forming a distinct building from the cathedral, such as it is accustomed to be in Italy. It was by the ringing of this bell that the people were anciently called together to the general assemblage, called the Folkmote. The campanile was very high, and was won at dice from King Henry the Eighth by Sir Miles Partridge, who took it down and sold the materials. On the side of the cathedral directly the reverse of this (the south-west), and forming a part of the great pile of building, was the parish church of St. Gregory, over which was the Lollards' Tower, or prison, infamous, like its namesake at Lambeth, for the ill-treatment of heretics.

" This," says Brayley, on the authority of Fox's Martyrology, " was the scene of at least one 'foul and midnight murder,' perpetrated in 1514, on a respectable citizen, named Richard Hunne, by Dr. Horsey, chancellor of the diocese, with the assistance of a bell-ringer, and afterwards defended by the Bishop Fitz-James and the whole body of prelates, who protected the murderers from punishment, lest the clergy should become amenable to civil jurisdiction. Though the villains, through this interference, escaped without corporal suffering, the King ordered them to pay 1,500*l.* to the children of the deceased, in restitution of what he himself styles the ' cruel murder.' "*

The clergy, with almost incredible audacity, afterwards commenced a process against the dead body of Hunne for heresy ; and, having obtained its condemnation, they actually burned it in Smithfield. The Lollards' Tower continued to be used as a prison for heretics for some time after the Reformation. Stow tells us that he recollected one Peter Burchet, a gentleman of the Middle Temple, being committed to this prison, on suspicion of holding certain erroneous opinions, in 1573. This, however, is, we believe, the last case of the kind that is recorded.

* Brayley, vol. ii., p. 320.

It remains to say a word of St. Paul's School, founded, as we have already mentioned, by Dean Colet, and destined to become the most illustrious of all the buildings on the spot, in giving education to Milton. We have dwelt more upon the localities of St. Paul's Churchyard than it is our intention to do on others.   The dignity of the birth-place of the metropolis beguiled us ; and the events recorded to have taken place in it are of real interest. Milton was not the only person of celebrity educated at this school.   Bentley, his critic, was probably induced by the like circumstance to turn his unfortunate attention to the poet's epic in after life, and make those gratuitous massacres of the text, which give a profound scholar the air of the most presumptuous of coxcombs.   Here also Camden received part of his education ; and here were brought up, Leland, his brother antiquary, the Gales (Charles, Roger, and Samuel), all celebrated antiquaries ; Sir Anthony Denny, the only man who had the courage and honesty to tell Henry the Eighth that he was dying ; Halley, the astronomer ; Bishop Cumberland, the great grandfather of the dramatist ; Pepys, who has lately obtained so curious a celebrity, as an annalist of the court of Charles the Second ; and last, not least, one in whom a learned education would be as little looked for as in Pepys, if we are to trust the stories of the times, to wit, John Duke of Marlborough.   Barnes was laughed at for dedicating his *Anacreon* to the duke, as one to whom Greek was unheard of ; and it has been related as a slur on the great general (though assuredly it is not so), that having alluded on some occasion to a passage in history, and being asked where he found it, he confessed that his authority was the only historian he was acquainted with, namely, William Shakspeare.

Less is known of Milton during the time he passed at St. Paul's School, than of any other period of his life. It is ascertained, however, that he cultivated the writing of Greek verses, and was a great favourite with the usher, afterwards master, Alexander Gill, himself a Latin poet of celebrity. At the back of the old church was an enormous rose-window, which we may imagine the young poet to have contemplated with delight, in his fondness for ornaments of that cast ; and the whole building was calculated to impress a mind, more disposed, at that time of life, to admire as a poet, than to quarrel as a critic or a sectary. Gill, unluckily for himself, was not so catholic. Some say he was suspended from his

mastership for severity ; a quality which he must have carried
to a great pitch, for that age to find fault with it ; but from
an answer written by Ben Johnson to a fragment of a satire of
Gill's, it is more likely he got into trouble for libels against
the court. Aubrey says, that the old doctor, his father, was
once obliged to go on his knees to get the young doctor pardoned, and that the offence consisted in his having written a
letter, in which he designated King James and his son, as the
" old foole and the young one." There are letters written in
early life from Milton to Gill, full of regard and esteem ; nor
is it likely that the regard was diminished by Gill's petulance
against the Court. In one of the letters, it is pleasant to hear
the poet saying, " Farewell, and on Tuesday next expect me
in London, among the booksellers." *

The parliamentary soldiers annoyed the inhabitants of the
churchyard, by playing at nine-pins at unseasonable hours—
a strange misdemeanour for that " church militant." They
hastened also the destruction of the cathedral. Some scaffolding, set up for repairs, had been given them for arrears of
pay. They dug pits in the body of the church to saw the
timber in ; and they removed the scaffolding with so little
caution, that great part of the vaulting fell in, and lay a heap
of ruins. The east end only, and a part of the choir continued to be used for public worship, a brick wall being raised
to separate this portion from the rest of the building, and the
congregation entering and getting out through one of the
north windows. Another part of the church was converted
into barracks and stables for the dragoons. As for Inigo
Jones's lofty and beautiful portico, it was turned into " shops,"
says Maitland, " for milliners and others, with rooms over
them for the convenience of lodging ; at the erection of which
the magnificent columns were piteously mangled, being
obliged to make way for the ends of beams, which penetrated
their centres." † The statues on the top were thrown down
and broken to pieces.

We have noticed the lucky necessity for a new church,
occasioned by the Great Fire. An attempt was at first made

* See Todd's Milton, vol. vii. ; Aubrey's Letters and Lives ; and
Ben Jonson's Poems. Gill's specimen of a satire is very bad, and the
great laureate's answer is not much better. The first couplet of the
latter, however, is to the purpose:—
    " Shall the prosperity of a pardon still
       Secure thy railing rhymes, infamous Gill?"
† History of London, vol. ii., p. 1166.

to repair the old building—the work, as we have already
mentioned, being committed to the charge of Sir John Denham (the poet), his Majesty's surveyor-general. But it was
eventually found necessary to commence a new edifice from
the foundation. Sir Christopher Wren, who accomplished
this task, had been before employed in superintending the
repairs, and was appointed head surveyor of the works in
1669, on the demise of Denham. Unfortunately, he had
great and ungenerous trouble given him in the erection of the
new structure ; and, after all, he did not build it as he wished.
His taste was not understood, either by court or clergy ; he
was envied (and towards the close of his life ousted) by inferior
workmen ; was forced to make use of two orders instead of
one, that is to say, to divide the sides and front into two
separate elevations, instead of running them up and dignifying
them with pillars of the whole height; and during the whole
work, which occupied a great many years, and took up a considerable and anxious portion of his time, not unattended
with personal hazard, all the pay which he was then, or ever
to expect, was a pittance of two hundred a-year. A moiety
of this driblet was for some time actually suspended, till the
building should be finished ; and for the arrears of it he was
forced to petition the government of Queen Anne, and then
only obtained them under circumstances of the most unhandsome delay. Wren, however, was a philosopher and a patriot;
and if he underwent the mortification attendent on philosophers and patriots, for offending the self-love of the shallow,
he knew how to act up to the spirit of those venerable names,
in the interior of a mind as elevated and well-composed
as his own architecture. Some pangs he felt, because he was
a man of humanity, and could not disdain his fellow-creatures ;
but he was more troubled for the losses of the art than his
own. He is is said actually to have shed tears when compelled to deform his cathedral with the side aisles—some say
in compliance with the will of the Duke of York, afterwards
James the Second, who anticipated the use of them for the
restoration of the old Catholic chapels. Money he despised,
except for the demands of his family, consenting to receive a
hundred a-year for rebuilding such of the city churches (a
considerable number) as were destroyed by the fire ! And
when finally ousted from his office of surveyor-general, he
said with the ancient sage, "Well, I must philosophise a little
sooner than I intended." (*Nunc me jubet fortuna expeditius*

philosophari). The Duchess of Marlborough, in resisting the claims of one of her Blenheim surveyors, said, " that Sir C. Wren was content to be dragged up in a basket three times a-week to the top of St. Paul's, at a great hazard, for 200*l.* a-year." But, as a writer of his life has remarked, she was perhaps "little capable of drawing any nice distinction between the feelings of the hired surveyor of Blenheim, and those of our architect, in the contemplation of the rising of the fabric which his vast genius was calling into existence: her notions led her to estimate the matter by the simple process of the rule of three direct; and on this principle she had good reason to complain of the surveyor." * The same writer tells us, that Wren's principal enjoyment during the remainder of his life, consisted in his being " carried once a year to see his great work; " " the beginning and completion of which," observes Walpole, " was an event which, one could not wonder, left such an impression of content on the mind of the good old man, that it seemed to recall a memory almost deadened to every other use." The epitaph upon him by his son, which Mr. Mylne, the architect of Blackfriars' bridge, caused to be rescued from the vaults underneath the church, where it was ludicrously inapplicable, and placed in gold letters over the choir, has a real sublimity in it, though defaced by one of those plays upon words, which were the taste of the times in the architect's youth, and which his family perhaps had learnt to admire.

> Subtus *conditur*
> Hujus ecclesiæ et urbis *conditor*
> Cn. Wren,
> Qui vixit annos ultra nonaginta,
> Non sibi sed bono publico.
> Lector, si monumentum requiris,
> Circumspice.

We cannot preserve the pun in English, unless, perhaps, by some such rendering as, " Here found a grave the founder of this church;" or " Underneath is founded the tomb," &c. The rest is admirable:

> "Who lived to the age of upwards of ninety years,
> Not for himself, but for the public good.
> Reader, if thou seekest his monument,
> Look around."

The reader *does* look around, and the whole interior of the

* Life of Sir Christoper Wren, in the Library of Useful Knowledge, No. 24, p. 27.

cathedral, which is finer than the outside, seems like a magnificent vault over his single body. The effect is very grand, especially if the organ is playing. A similar one, as far as the music is concerned, is observable when we contemplate the statues of Nelson and others. The grand repose of the church, in the first instance, gives them a mortal dignity, which the organ seems to waken up and revive, as if in the midst of the

<blockquote>"Pomp and threatening harmony,"*</blockquote>

their spirits almost looked out of their stony and sightless eyeballs. Johnson's ponderous figure looks down upon us with something of sourness in the expression; and in the presence of Howard we feel as if pomp itself were in attendance on humanity. It is a pity that the sculpture of the monuments in general is not worthy of these emotions, and tends to undo them.

A poor statue of Queen Anne, in whose reign the church was finished, stands in the middle of the front area, with the figures of Britain, France, Ireland, and America, round the base. Garth, who was a Whig, and angry with the councils which had dismissed his hero Marlborough, wrote some bitter lines upon it, which must have had double effect, coming from so good-natured a man.

> Near the vast bulk of that stupendous frame,
> Known by the Gentiles' great apostle's name,
> With grace divine great Anna's seen to rise,
> An awful form that glads a nation's eyes:
> Beneath her feet four mighty realms appear,
> And with due reverence pay their homage there.
> Britain and Ireland seem to own her grace,
> And e'en wild India wears a smiling face.
> But France alone with downcast eyes is seen,
> The sad attendant on so good a queen.
> Ungrateful country! to forget so soon
> All that great Anna for thy sake has done,
> When sworn the kind defender of thy cause,
> Spite of her dear religion, spite of laws,
> For thee she sheath'd the terrors of her sword,
> For thee she broke her gen'ral—and her word:
> For thee her mind in doubtful terms she told,
> And learn'd to speak like oracles of old:
> For thee, for thee alone, what could she more ?
> She lost the honour she had gain'd before;
> Lost all the trophies which her arms had won,
> (Such Cæsar never knew, nor Philip's son ;)

---

* Wordsworth.

Resign'd the glories of a ten years' reign,
And such as none but Marlborough's arm could gain:
For thee in annals she's content to shine,
Like other monarchs of the Stuart line.

Many irreverent remarks were also made by the coarser wits of the day, in reference to the position of her Majesty, with her back to the church and her face to a brandy shop, which was then kept in that part of the churchyard. The calumny was worthy of the coarseness. Anne, who was not a very clever woman, had a difficult task to perform; and though we differ with her politics, we cannot, even at this distance of time, help expressing our disgust at personalities like these, especially against a female.

CHAPTER II.

ST. PAUL'S AND THE NEIGHBOURHOOD.

The Church of St. Faith—Booksellers of the Churchyard—Mr. Johnson's—Mr. Newberry's—Children's Books—Clerical Names of Streets near St. Paul's—Swift at the top of the Cathedral—Dr. Johnson at St. Paul's—Paternoster Row—Panyer's Alley—Stationers' Hall—Almanacks—Knight-Riders' Street—Armed Assemblies of the Citizens—Doctor's Commons—The Heralds' College—Coats of Arms—Ludgate—Story of Sir Stephen Forster—Prison of Ludgate—Wyatt's Rebellion—The Belle Sauvage Inn—Blackfriars—Shakspeare's Theatre—Accident at Blackfriars in 1623—Printing House Square—The Times—Baynard's Castle—Story of the Baron Fitzwalter—Richard III. and Buckingham—Diana's Chamber—The Royal Wardrobe—Marriages in the Fleet—Fleet Ditch—The Dunciad.

E remember, in our boyhood, a romantic story of a church that stood under St. Paul's. We conceived of it, as of a real good-sized church actually standing under the other; but how it came there nobody could imagine. It was some ghostly edification of providence, not lightly to be inquired into; but as its name was St. Faith's, we conjectured that the mystery had something to do with religious belief. The mysteries of art do not remain with us for life, like those of Nature. Our phenomenon amounted to this:

"The church of St. Faith," says Brayley, "was originally a distinct building, standing near the east end of St. Paul's; but when the old cathedral was enlarged, between the years 1256 and 1312, it was taken down, and an extensive part of the vaults was appropriated to the use of the parishioners of St. Faith's, in lieu of the demolished fabric. This was afterwards called the church of St. Faith in the Crypts (*Ecclesia Sanctæ Fidei in Cryptis*) and, according to a representation made to the Dean and Chapter, in the year 1735, it measured 180 feet in length, and 80 in breath. After the fire of London, the parish of St. Faith was joined to that of St. Augustine; and on the rebuilding of the cathedral, a portion of the churchyard belonging to the former was taken to enlarge the avenue round the east end of St. Paul's, and the remainder was inclosed within the cathedral railing." *

The parishioners of St. Faith have still liberty to bury their dead in certain parts of the churchyard and the Crypts.

* Brayley, vol. ii., p. 303.

Other portions of the latter have been used as storehouses
for wine, stationery, &c.   The stationers and booksellers of
London, during the fire, thought they had secured a great
quantity of their stock in this place; but on the air being
admitted when they went to take them out, the goods had
been so heated by the conflagration of the church overhead,
that they took fire at last, and the whole property was
destroyed.   Clarendon says it amounted to the value of two
hundred thousand pounds.*

One of the houses on the site of the old episcopal mansion,
now converted into premises occupied by Mr. Hitchcock the
linendraper, was Mr. Johnson's the bookseller—a man who
deserves mention for his liberality to Cowper, and for the
remarkable circumstance of his never having seen the poet,
though his intercourse with him was long and cordial.   Mr.
Johnson was in conection with a circle of men of letters,
some of whom were in the habit of dining with him once a
week, and who comprised the leading polite writers of the
generation—Cowper, Darwin, Hayley, Dr. Aikin, Mrs. Barbauld, Godwin, &c.   Fuseli must not be ommitted, who was
at least as good a writer as a painter.   Here Bonnycastle
hung his long face over his plate, as glad to escape from
arithmetic into his jokes and his social dinner as a great
boy; and here Wordsworth, and we believe Coleridge,
published their earliest performances.   At all events they
both visited at the house.

But the most illustrious of all booksellers in our boyish
days, not for his great names, not for his dinners, not for
his riches that we know of, nor for any other full-grown
celebrity, but for certain little penny books, radiant with gold
and rich with bad pictures, was Mr. Newberry, the famous
children's bookseller, "at the corner of St. Paul's churchyard," next Ludgate Street.   The house is still occupied by
a successor, and children may have books there as formerly
—but not the same.   The gilding, we confess, we regret:
gold, somehow, never looked so well as in adorning literature.   The pictures also—may we own that we preferred the
uncouth coats, the staring blotted eyes, and round pieces of
rope for hats, of our very badly drawn contemporaries, to all
the proprieties of modern embellishment?   We own the
superiority of the latter, and would have it proceed and
prosper; but a boy of our own time was much, though his

* In his Life, vol. iii., p. 98. Edit. 1827.

coat looked like his grandfather's. The engravings probably were of that date. Enormous, however, is the improvement upon the morals of these little books; and there we give them up, and with unmitigated delight. The good little boy, the hero of the infant literature in those days, stood, it must be acknowledged, the chance of being a very selfish man. His virtue consisted in being different from some other little boy, perhaps his brother; and his reward was having a fine coach to ride in, and being a King Pepin. Now-a-days, since the world has had a great moral earthquake that set it thinking, the little boy promises to be much more of a man; thinks of others, as well as works for himself; and looks for his reward to a character for good sense and benefi- cence. In no respect is the progress of the age more visible, or more importantly so, than in this apparently trifling matter. The most bigoted opponents of a rational education are obliged to adopt a portion of its spirit, in order to retain a hold which their own teaching must accordingly undo : and if the times were not full of hopes in other respects, we should point to this evidence of their advancement, and be content with it.

One of the most pernicious mistakes of the old children's books, was the inculcation of a spirit of revenge and cruelty in the tragic examples which were intended to deter their readers from idleness and disobedience. One, if he did not behave himself, was to be shipwrecked, and eaten by lions; another to become a criminal, who was not to be taught better, but rendered a mere wicked contrast to the luckier virtue; and, above all, none were to be poor but the vicious, and none to ride in their coaches but little Sir Charles Grandisons, and all-perfect Sheriffs. We need not say how contrary this was to the real spirit of Christianity, which, at the same time, they so much insisted on. The perplexity in after life, when reading of poor philosophers and rich vicious men, was in proportion; or rather virtue and mere worldly success became confounded. In the present day, the profi- tableness of good conduct is still inculcated, but in a sounder spirit. Charity makes the proper allowance for all; and none are excluded from the hope of being wiser and happier. Men, in short are not taught to love and labour for themselves alone or for their little dark corners of egotism; but to take the world along with them into a brighter sky of improvement; and to discern the want of success in success itself, if not accompanied by a liberal knowledge.

The *Seven Champions of Christendom, Valentine and Orson.* and other books of the fictitious class, which have survived their more rational brethren (as the latter thought them-selves), are of a much better order, and, indeed, survive by a natural instinct in society to that effect. With many absurd-ities, they have a general tone of manly and social virtue, which may be safely left to itself. The absurdities wear out and the good remains. Nobody in these times will think of meeting giants and dragons; of giving blows that con-found an army, or tearing the hearts out of two lions on each side of him, as easily as if he were dipping his hands into a lottery. But there are still giants and wild beasts to en-counter, of another sort, the conquest of which requires the old enthusiasm and disinterestedness; arms and war are to be checked in their career, and have been so, by that new might of opinion to which every body may contribute much in his single voice; and wild men, or those who would become so, are tamed, by education and brotherly kindness, into orna-ments of civil life.

The neighbourhood of St. Paul's retains a variety of appel-lations indicative of its former connection with the church. There is Creed Lane, Ave-Maria Lane, Sermon Lane*, Canon Alley, Pater-Noster Row, Holiday Court, Amen Corner, &c. Members of the Cathedral establishment still have abodes in some of these places, particularly in Amen Corner, which is enclosed with gates, and appropriated to the houses of prebendaries and canons. Close to Sermon Lane is Do-little Lane; a vicinity which must have furnished jokes to the Puritans. Addle Street is an ungrateful corruption of Athelstan Street, so called from one of the most respectable of the Saxon kings, who had a palace in it.

We have omitted to notice a curious passage in Swift, in which he abuses himself for going to the top of St. Paul's. "To-day," says he, writing to Stella, "I was all about St. Paul's, and up at the top like a fool, with Sir Andrew Fountain, and two more; and spent seven shillings for my dinner, like a puppy." "This," adds the doctor, "is the

---

* Unless, indeed, we are to suppose, as has been suggested, that *Sermon* Lane is a corruption of *Sheremoniers* Lane, that is, the lane of the money clippers, or such as cut and rounded the metal which was to be coined or stamped into money. There was anciently a place in this lane for melting silver, called the *Blackloft*—and the Mint was in the street now called Old Change, in the immediate neighbourhood. See Maitland, ii., 880 (edit. of 1756.)

second time he has served me so : but I will never do it
again, though all mankind should persuade me—unconsidering
puppies ! " *   The being forced by richer people than one's
self to spend money at a tavern might reasonably be lamented;
but from the top of St. Paul's Swift beheld a spectacle, which
surely was not unworthy of his attention; perhaps it affected
him too much.   The author of Gulliver might have taken
from it his notions of little bustling humankind.

Dr. Johnson frequently attended public worship in St. Paul's.
Very different must his look have been, in turning into
the chancel, from the threatening and trampling aspect they
have given him in his statue.   We do not quarrel with his
aspect; there is a great deal of character in it.   But the contrast, considering the place, is curious.   A little before his
death, when bodily decay made him less patient than ever of
contradiction, he instituted a club at the Queen's Arms, in
St. Paul's Churchyard.   "He told Mr. Hook," says Boswell,
" That he wished to have a *City Club*, and asked him to
collect one; but, said he, don't let them be patriots." †   (This
was an allusion to the friends of his acquaintance Wilkes.)
Boswell accompanied him one day to the club, and found the
members "very sensible well-behaved men : " that is to say
Hook had collected a body of decent listeners.   This, however, is melancholy.   In the next chapter we shall see Johnson
in all his glory.

St. Paul's Churchyard appears as if it were only a great
commercial thoroughfare ; but if all the clergy could be seen
at once, who have abodes in the neighbourhood, they would
be found to constitute a numerous body.   If to the sable
coats of these gentlemen be added those of the practisers of
the civil law, who were formerly allied to them, and who live
in Doctors' Commons, the churchyard increases the clerkly
part of its aspect.   It resumes, to the imagination, something of the learned and collegiate look it had of old.   Paternoster Row is said to have been so called on account of
the number of Stationers or Text-writers that dwelt there,
who dealt much in religious books, and sold horn-books, or
A B C's, with the Paternoster, Ave-Maria, Creed, Graces,
&c.   And so of the other places above-named.   But it is more
likely that this particular street (as indeed we are told) was

---

* Letters to Stella, in the duodecimo edition of his works, 1775.
Letter vi., p. 43.
  † Boswell's Life of Johnson, eighth edition, vol. iv., p. 93.

named from the rosary or paternoster-makers ; for so they were called, as appears by a record of "one Robert Nikke, a paternoster-maker and citizen, in the reign of Henry the Fourth."

It is curious to reflect what a change has taken place in this celebrated *book-street*, since nothing was sold there but rosaries. It is but rarely the word Paternoster-Row strikes us as having a reference to the Latin Prayer. We think of booksellers' shops, and of all the learning and knowledge they have sent forth. The books of Luther, which Henry the Eighth burnt in the neighbouring churchyard, were turned into millions of volumes, partly by reason of that burning.

Paternoster-Row, however, has not been exclusively in possession of the booksellers, since it lost its original tenants, the rosary-makers. Indeed it would appear to have been only in comparatively recent times that the booksellers fixed themselves there. They had for a long while been established in St. Paul's Churchyard, but scarcely in the Row, till after the commencement of the last century.

"This street," says Maitland, writing in 1720, "before the fire o London, was taken up by eminent mercers, silkmen, and lacemen; and their shops were so resorted unto by the nobility and gentry in their coaches, that ofttimes the street was so stopped up, that there was no passage for foot passengers. But since the said fire, those eminent tradesmen have settled themselves in several other parts; especially in Ludgate Street, and in Bedford Street, Henrietta Street, and King Street, Covent Garden. And the inhabitants in this street are now a mixture of tradespeople, such as tire-women, or milliners, for the sale of top-knots, and the like dressings for the females."

In a subsequent edition of his history, published in 1755, it is added, "There are now many shops of mercers, silkmen, eminent printers, booksellers, and publishers."* The most easterly of the narrow and partly covered passages between Newgate Street and Paternoster Row is that called Panyer's Alley, remarkable for a stone built into the wall of one of the houses on the east side, supporting the figures of a pannier or wicker basket, surmounted by a boy, and exhibiting the following inscription :—

> "When you have sought the city round,
> Yet still this is the highest ground."

We cannot say if absolute faith is to be put in this asseveration ; but it is possible. It has been said that the top of St. Paul's is on a level with that of Hampstead.

* History of London, vol. ii., p. 925.

We look back a moment between Paternoster Row and the churchyard, to observe, that the only memorial remaining of the residence of the Bishop of London is a tablet in London-House Yard, let into the wall of the public house called the Goose and Gridiron. The Goose and Gridiron is said by tradition to have been what was called in the last century a " music house ;" that is to say, a place of entertainment with music. When it ceased to be musical, a landlord, in ridicule of its former pretensions, chose for his sign " a goose stroking the bars of a gridiron with his foot," and called it the Swan and Harp.*

Between Amen Corner and Ludgate Street, at the end of a passage from Ave-Maria Lane, " stood a great house of stone and wood, belonging in old time to John, Duke of Bretagne, and Earl of Richmond, cotemporary with Edward II. and III. After him it was possessed by the Earls of Pembroke, in the time of Richard II. and Henry IV., and was called Pembroke's Inn, near Ludgate. It then fell into the possession of the title of Abergavenny, and was called Burgavenny House, under which circumstances it remained in the time of Elizabeth. To finish the anti-climax," says Pennant, "it was finally possessed by the Company of Stationers, who rebuilt it of wood, and made it their Hall. It was destroyed by the Great Fire, and was succeeded by the present plain building."† Of the once-powerful possessors of the old mansion nothing now is remembered, or cared for ; but in the interior of the modern building are to be seen, looking almost as if they were alive, and as if we knew them personally, the immortal faces of Steele and Richardson, Prior in his cap, and Dr. Hoadley, a liberal bishop. There is also Mrs. Richardson, the wife of the novelist, looking as prim and particular as if she had been just chucked under the chin ; and Robert Nelson, Esq., supposed author of the Whole Duty of Man, and prototype of Sir Charles Grandison, as regular and passionless in his face as if he had been made only to wear his wig. The same is not to be said of the face of Steele, with his black eyes and social aspect ; and still less of Richardson, who, instead of being the smooth, satisfied-looking personage he is represented in some engravings of him (which makes his heartrending romance appear unaccountable and

* The Tatler. With notes historical, biographical, and critical 8vo. 1797. Vol. iv., p. 206.
† Pennant's London, p. 377.

cruel), has a face as uneasy as can well be conceived—flushed and shattered with emotion. We recognise the sensitive, enduring man, such as he really was—a heap of bad nerves. It is worth anybody's while to go to Stationers' Hall, on purpose to see these portraits. They are not of the first order as portraits, but evident likenesses. Hoadley looks at once jovial and decided, like a good-natured controversialist. Prior is not so pleasant as in his prints; his nose is a little aquiline, instead of turned up; and his features, though delicate, not so liberal. But if he has not the best look of his poetry, he has the worst. He seems as if he had been sitting up all night; his eyelids droop: and his whole face is *used* with rakery.

It is impossible to see Prior and Steele together, without regretting that they quarrelled: but as they did quarrel, it was fit that Prior should be in the wrong. From a Whig he had become a Tory, and showed that his change was not quite what it ought to have been, by avoiding the men with whom he had associated, and writing contemptuously of his fellow wits. All the men of letters, whose portraits are in this hall, were, doubtless, intimate with the premises, and partakers of Stationers' dinners. Richardson was Master of the Company. Morphew, a bookseller in the neighbourhood, was one of the publishers of the *Tatler;* and concerts as well as festive dinners used to take place in the great room, of both of which entertainments Steele was fond. It was here, if we mistake not, that one of the inferior officers of the Company, a humourist on sufferance, came in, one day, on his knees, at an anniversary dinner when Bishop Hoadley was present, in order to drink to the " Glorious Memory."* The company, Steele included, were pretty far gone; Hoadley had remained as long as he well could; and the genuflector was drunk. Steele, seeing the Bishop a little disconcerted, whispered him, " Do laugh, my lord ; pray laugh :—'t is *humanity* to laugh." The good-natured prelate acquiesced. Next day, Steele sent him a penitential letter, with the following couplet:—

> Virtue with so much ease on Bangor sits,
> All faults he pardons, though he none commits.

The most illustrious musical performance that ever took place in the hall was that of Dryden's Ode. A society for the annual commemoration of St. Cecilia, the patroness of music,

* Of William III.

was instituted in the year 1680, not without an eye perhaps
to the religious opinions of the heir presumptive who was
shortly to ascend the throne as James the Second. An ode
was written every year for the occasion, and set to music by
some eminent composer ; and the performance of it was followed by a grand dinner. In 1687, Dryden contributed his
first ode, entitled, "A Song for Saint Cecilia's Day," in
which there are finer things than in any part of the other,
though as a whole it is not so striking. Ten years afterwards it was followed by "Alexander's Feast," the dinner,
perhaps, being a part of the inspiration. Poor Jeremiah
Clarke, who shot himself for love, was the composer.* This
is the ode with the composition of which Bolingbroke is said
to have found Dryden in a state of emotion one morning, the
whole night having been passed, *agitante deo*, under the fever
of inspiration.

From Stationers' Hall once issued all the almanacks that
were published, with all the trash and superstition they kept
alive. Francis Moore is still among their "living dead men."
Francis must now be a posthumous old gentleman, of at least
one hundred and fifty years of age. The first blunder the
writers of these books committed, in their cunning, was the
having to do with the state of the weather; their next was to
think that the grandmothers of the last century were as
immortal as their title-pages, and that nobody was getting
wiser than themselves. The mysterious solemnity of their
hieroglyphics, bringing heaven and earth together, like a
vision in the Apocalypse, was imposing to the nurse and the
child ; and the bashfulness of their bodily sympathies no less
attractive. We remember the astonishment of a worthy
seaman, some years ago, at the claim which they put into

---

* The genius of Clarke, which, agreeably to his unhappy end, was
tender and melancholy, was unsuited to the livelier intoxication of
Dryden's feast, afterwards gloriously set by Handel. Clarke has been
styled the musical Otway of his time. He was organist at St. Paul's,
and shot himself at his house in St. Paul's Churchyard. Mr. John
Reading, organist of St. Dunstan's, who was intimately acquainted
with him, was going by at the moment the pistol went off, and upon
entering the house "found his friend and fellow-student in the agonies
of death." Another friend of his, one of the lay vicars of the cathedral, relates of him, that a few weeks before the catastrophe, Clarke
had alighted from his horse in a sequestered spot in the country,
where there was a pond surrounded by trees, and not knowing whether
to hang or drown himself, tossed up a piece of money to see which.
The money stuck in the earth edgeways. Of this new chance for
life, poor Clarke, we see, was unable to avail himself.

the mouth of the sign Virgo. The monopoly is now gone; almanacks have been forced into improvement by emulation; and the Stationers (naturally enough at the moment) are angry about it. This fit of ill humour will pass; and a body of men, interested by their very trade in the progress of liberal knowledge, will by and by join the laugh at the tenderness they evinced in behalf of old wives' fables. It is observable, that their friend Bickerstaff (Steele's assumed name in the *Tatler*) was the first to begin the joke against them.

Knight-Riders' Street (Great and Little), on the south side of St. Paul's Churchyard, is said to have been named from the processions of Knights from the Tower to their place of tournament in Smithfield. It must have been a round-about way. Probably the name originated in nothing more than a sign, or from some reference to the Heralds' College in the neighbourhood. The open space, we may here notice, around the western extremity of the Cathedral, was anciently used by the citizens for assembling together " to make shew of their arms," or to hold what was called among the Scotch "a *weapon shaw*." A complaint was made by the Lord Mayor and the Ward, in the reign of Edward I., against the Dean and Chapter for having inclosed this ground, which they insisted was "the soil and lay-fee of our lord the King," by a mud wall, and covered part of it with buildings.* The houses immediately to the west of Creed Lane and Ave-Maria Lane probably occupy part of the space in question.

Behind Great Knight-Riders' Street is Doctors' Commons, so called from the Doctors of Civil Law who dined together four days in each term. The Court of Admiralty is also there. The Admiralty judge is preceded by an officer with a silver oar. There is something pleasing in the parade of a civil officer, thus announced by a symbol representing the regulation of the most turbulent of elements.

The civil and ecclesiastical lawyers, who connect the law with the church, had formerly much more to do than they have at present. The proctors (or attorneys) are said to have been so numerous and so noisy in the time of Henry VII., that the judge sometimes could not be heard for them. They thrust themselves into causes without the parties' consent, and shouldered the advocates out of their business. The diminution of their body was owing to Cranmer. Doctors' Commons are of painful celebrity in the annals of domestic trouble.

* See Maitland, vol. ii., p. 949.

We have hardly perhaps among us a remnant of greater
barbarism than " an action for damages,"* whether considered
with a view to recompense or prevention. Doctors' Commons
bind as well as set loose. "Hence originates," says the
facetious Mr. Malcolm, "the awful scrap of parchment, bearing the talismanic mark of *John Cantuar* (the Archbishop of
Canterbury), which constitutes thousands of Benedicts the
happiest or most miserable of married men: in short, it is the
grand lottery of life, in which, fortunately, there are far more
prizes than blanks."† The community ought to be thankful
to Mr. Malcolm for this last piece of information, as there is
a splenetic notion among them to the contrary.

A history deeply interesting to human nature might be
drawn up from the documents preserved in this place; for
besides cases of personal infidelity, here are to be found others
of *infidelity religious*, of blasphemy, simony, &c., together
with romantic questions relative to kindred and succession ;
and here are deposited those last specimens of human strength
or weakness—last wills and testaments, together with cases in
which they have been contested. It was these records that
furnished us with accounts of the latest days of Milton; and
that set the readers of Shakspeare speculating why he should
make no mention of his wife, except to leave her his " second
best bed;"—a question most unexpectedly as well as happily
cleared up by Mr. Charles Knight, who shows that the bequest
was to the lady's honour. Of the practisers in the civil courts,
we can call to mind nothing more worthy of recollection than
the strange name of one of them, " Sir Julius Cæsar," and
the ruinous volatility of poor Dr. King, the Tory wit, who is
conjectured to have been the only civilian that ever went to
reside in Ireland, " after having experienced the emoluments
of a settlement in Doctors' Commons." The doctor unfortunately practised too much with the bottle, which hindered
him from adhering long to anything.

Behind Little Knight-Riders' Street, to the east of Doctors'
Commons, is the Heralds' College. A gorgeous idea of colours
falls on the mind in passing it, as from a cathedral window,

" And shielded scutcheons blush with blood of queens and kings."
                                                                Keats.

* Since this was written, the jurisdiction of the Ecclesiastical
Court in Doctors' Commons on matters of divorce has been transferred
to a new "Court of Divorce and Matrimonial Causes," sitting at
Westminster.

Londinium Redivivum, vol. ii., p. 473.

The passenger, if he is a reader conversant with old times, thinks of bannered halls, of processions of chivalry, and of the fields of Cressy and Poictiers, with their vizored knights, distinguished by their coats and crests ; for a coat of arms is nothing but a representation of the knight himself, from whom the bearer is descended. The shield supposes his body; there is the helmet for his head, with the crest upon it ; the flourish is his mantle ; and he stands upon the ground of his motto, or moral pretension. The supporters, if he is noble, or of a particular class of knighthood, are thought to be the pages that waited upon him, designated by the fantastic dresses of bear, lion, &c., which they sometimes wore. Heraldry is full of colour and imagery, and attracts the fancy like a " book of pictures." The Kings at Arms are romantic personages, really crowned, and have as mystic appellations as the kings of an old tale—Garter, Clarencieux, and Norroy. Norroy is King of the North, and Clarencieux (a title of Norman origin) of the South. The heralds, Lancaster, Somerset, &c., have simpler names, indicative of the counties over which they preside ; but are only less gorgeously dressed than the kings, in emblazonment and satin ; and then there are the four pursuivants, Rouge Croix, Rouge Dragon, Portcullis, and Blue Mantle, with hues as lively, and appellations as quaint, as the attendants on a fairy court. For gorgeousness of attire, mysteriousness of origin, and in fact for similarity of origin (a knave being a squire), a knave of cards is not unlike a herald. A story is told of an Irish King at Arms,* who, waiting upon the Bishop of Killaloe to summon him to Parliament, and being dressed, as the ceremony required, in his heraldic attire, so mystified the bishop's servant with his appearance, that not knowing what to make of it, and carrying off but a confused notion of his title, he announced him thus : " My lord, here is the King of Trumps."

Mr. Pennant says, that the Heralds' College " is a foundation of great antiquity, in which the records are kept of all the old blood in the kingdom." But this is a mistake. Heralds, indeed, are of great antiquity, in the sense of messengers of peace and war ; but in the modern sense, they are no older than the reign of Edward III., and were not incorporated before that of the usurper Richard. The house which they formerly occupied was a mansion of the Earls of Derby. It

* On the authority of Langton, Johnson's friend. See Memoirs, Anecdotes, &c., by Letitia Matilda Hawkins, vol. i., p. 293.

was burnt in the Great Fire, and succeeded by the present building, part of which was raised at the expense of some of their officers. As to their keeping records of " all the old blood in the kingdom," they may keep them, or not, as they have the luck to find them ; but the blood was old, before they had anything to do with it. Men bore arms and crests when there were no officers to register them. This, as a writer in the *Censura Literaria* observes, justly diminishes the pretension they set up, that no arms are of authority which have not been registered among their archives.

"If this doctrine," says he, " were just, the consequence would be, that arms of comparatively modern invention are of better authority than those which a man and his ancestors have borne from times before the existence of the College of Arms, and for time immemorial, supported by the evidence of ancient seals, funeral monuments, and other authentic documents. Surely this is grossly absurd; and the more absurd, if we consider that the heralds seem originally not to have been instituted for the manufacturing of armorial ensigns, but for the recording those ensigns which had been borne by men of honourable lineage, and which might, therefore, be borne by their posterity. Perhaps it would not be too much to presume, that it will be found on inquiry, that there are no grants of arms by the English Heralds of any very high antiquity; and that the most ancient which can be produced, either in the original or in well-authenticated copies, are of a date when the general use of seals of arms, circumscribed with the names and titles of the bearers, was wearing away."*

We learn from the same writer, that the value of " a painted shield of parchment" is fifty pounds. Of the spirit in which these things have been done, the reader may judge from a letter written by an applicant to one of the most respectable names in the college list. His object was to get the illegitimate coat of a female friend changed to one by which it was to appear she was not illegitimate. He offers five pounds for it ; and adds, that there is another friend of his, " an alderman's son, in Chester, whose great-grandfather was baseborn, whom I have bine treating with severall tymes about the alteration of his coat, telling him for 10^{li} and not under, it may be accomplished ; five he is willing to give, but not above ; if you please to accept of that sume, you may writt me a line or two. I desire that you will send the scroll down again, as soon as you can."†

* Censura Literaria, vol. iii., p. 254.
† Life, Diary, and Correspondence of Sir William Dugdale, by Hamper. Lond. 1827. Our memorandum has omitted the page. The letter was written to Dugdale by Randall Holme, a brother herald.

The truth is, that, except as far as their records go, and
as they can be turned to account in questions of kindred and
inheritance, the heralds are of no importance in modern times.
Nor have they anything to do with the spirit and first principles of the devices, of which they assume the direction.
We think this is worth notice, because heraldry itself, or at
least the discussion of coats of arms, of which most people
are observed to be fonder than they choose to confess, might
be reconciled to the progress of knowledge, or made, at any
rate, the ground of a pleasing and not ungraceful novelty.
To a coat of arms no man, literally speaking, has pretensions,
who is not the representative of somebody that bore arms
in the old English wars ; but when the necessity for military
virtue decreased, arms gave way to the gown; and *shields* had
honourable, but fantastic augmentations, for the peaceful
triumphs of lawyers and statesmen.   Meanwhile commerce
was on the increase, and there came up a new power in the
shape of pounds, shillings, and pence, which was to be represented also by its coat of *arms ;* how absurdly, need not be
added ; though the individuals who got their lions and their
shields behind the counter, were often excellent men, who
might have cut as great a figure in battle as the best, had
they lived in other times.   At length, not to have a military
coat was to be no gentleman ; and then the heralds fairly sold
achievements at so much the head.   They received their fees,
put on their spectacles, turned over their books like astro-
logers, and found that you were deserving of a bear's paw, or
might clap three puppies on your coach.   " Congreve," says
Swift, in one of his letters to Stella, " gave me a Tatler he
had written out, as blind as he is, for little Harrison.   'Tis
about a scoundrel that was grown rich, and went and bought
a coat of arms at the heralds', and a set of ancestors at Fleet
Ditch."   And this is the case at present.   Numbers of persons do not, however, stand on this ceremony with the heralds.
Many are content to receive their exploits, at half-a-guinea
the set, from pretenders who undertake to " procure arms ;"
and many more assume the arms nearest to their name and
family, or invent them at once ; naturally enough concluding,
that they might as well achieve their own glories, as buy them
of an old gentleman or a pedlar.
      Now arms were not originally given; they were assumed.
Men in battle, when armies fought pell-mell, and bodily
prowess was more in request than it is now, wished to have

F

their persons distinguished; and accordingly they put a device on their shield, or some towering symbol on their
helmet. This at once served to mark out the bearer, and to
express the particular sentiment or alliance upon which he
was to be understood as priding himself. The real spirit of
heraldry consisted, therefore, and must always consist, in distinguishing one person from another, and in expressing his
individual sentiments; and as the adoption of some device is
both an elegant exercise of the fancy, and acts as a kind of
memento to the conscience, tending to keep us to what we
profess, people who have no certain arms of their own, or who
do not care for them if they have, might not ungracefully or
even uselessly entertain themselves with doing, in their
own persons, what the old assumers of arms did in theirs;
that is to say, invent their own distinctions. The emblazonment might amuse their fancies, and be put in books, or elsewhere, like other coats of arms; and a little difference in
the mode of it could easily set aside the interference of the
heralds. People might thus express their views in life, or
their particular tastes and opinions; and the "science of
heraldry," which has been so much laughed at, not always
with justice, be made to accord with the progress of knowledge—or, at all events, with the entertaining part of it.

As to coats of arms really ancient, or connected with old
virtue, or with modern, we have already shown that we
are far from pretending to despise anything which indulges
the natural desire of mortality to extend or to elevate its
sense of existence. We have no respect for shields of no
meaning, or for bearers of better shields that disgrace them;
but we do not profess to look without interest on very old
shields, if only for the sake of their antiquity, much less
when they are associated with names,

Familiar in our mouths as household words.

The lions and stags, &c., of the Howards and Herberts, of the
Cavendishes, Russells, and Spencers, affect us more than those
of Cuvier himself, especially when we recollect they were
borne by great writers as well as warriors, men who advanced
not only themselves but their species in dignity. The most
interesting coats of arms, next to those which unite antiquity
with ability (that is to say, duration backward with duration
and utility in prospect), are such as become ennobled by
genius, or present us with some pleasing device. Such is
the spear of Shakspeare, whose ancestors are thought to have

won it in Bosworth field; * the spread eagle of Milton—a proper epic device : the flower given to Linnæus for a device when he was ennobled ; the philosophical motto of the great Bacon, *Mediocria firma* (Mediocre things firm—the Golden Mean) ; the modest, yet self-respecting one, first used, we believe, by Sir Philip Sydney, *Vix ea nostra voco* (I scarcely call these things one's own) ; and those other mottoes, taken from favourite classics, which argue more taste than antiquity. We are not sorry, however, for mere antiquity's sake, to recognise the ship of the Campbells; the crowned heart (a beautiful device) of Douglas ; and even the checquers of the unfortunate family of the Stuarts. They tell us of names and connections, and call to mind striking events in history. Indeed, all ancient names naturally become associated with history and poetry. The most interesting coat in Scottish heraldry, if we are to believe tradition, is that of Hay, Earl of Errol; whose ancestors, a couple of peasants, with their father, rallied an army of their countrymen in a narrow pass, and led them back victoriously against the Danes. Two peasants are the supporters of the shield. But unquestionably the most interesting sight in the whole circle of heraldry, British or foreign, if we consider the rational popularity of its origin, and the immense advance it records in the progress of what is truly noble, is that of the plain English motto assumed by Lord Erskine, *Trial by Jury.* The devices of the Nelsons and Wellingtons, illustrious as they are, are nothing to this ; for the world might relapse into barbarism, as it has formerly done, notwithstanding the exploits of the greatest warriors ; but words like these are trophies of the experience of ages, and the world could not pass them, and go back again, for very shame. It is the fashion now-a-days to have painted windows ; and a very beautiful fashion it is, and extremely worthy of encouragement in this climate, where the general absence of colours renders it desirable that they should be collected wherever they can, so as to increase a feeling of cheerfulness and warmth. When the sun strikes through a painted window,

* Another opinion, however, is that the spear had been given to one of his ancestors as having been a magistrate of some description. This supposition seems to be supported by the grant of arms to John Shakspeare in 1599, which has been printed by Mr. Malcolm. But Shakspeares in Warwickshire are as plentiful as blackberries, and perhaps the name originated in the stout arms of a whole tribe of soldiers.

it seems as if Heaven itself were recommending to us the
brilliance with which it has painted its flowers and its skies.
It is a pity we have no devices invented for themselves by
the great men of past times, otherwise what an illustrious
window would they make!   We should like to have presented the reader with such of the escutcheons above mentioned as have been created or modified in some respect by
their ennoblers; and to have shown him how different the old
parts now appear, with which the individuals had nothing to
do, compared with those of their own achievement, or adoption, even when nothing better than a motto.   Sir Philip's
motto almost rejects his coat.*   If all persons, ambitious of
good conduct and opinions, were to adopt our suggestion, and
assume a device of their own, windows of this kind might
abound among friends; and many of them would become as
interesting to posterity, as *such* "coats of arms" would, above
all others, deserve to be.

The most eminent names in the Heralds' College are
Camden, the great antiquary; Dugdale (whose merits, however, are questionable); King, a writer on political arithmetic; and Vanbrugh, the comic writer, who wore a tabard
for a short time, as Clarencieux.   Gibbon had an ancestor, a
herald, who took great interest in the profession.   He had
another progenitor, who, about the reign of James the First,
changed the scallop shells of the historian's coat " into three
ogresses or female cannibals, with a design of stigmatising
three ladies, his kinswomen, who had provoked him by an
unjust lawsuit."†   A good account of heraldry, its antiquities and its freaks, is a desideratum, and would make a
very amusing book.

We move westward from St. Paul's, because, though the
metropolis abounds with interest in every part of it, yet the
course this way is the most generally known; and readers
may choose to hear of the most popular thoroughfares first.

---

* *Vix ea nostra voco*—(as above translated).   The effect is stronger
if the whole passage is called to mind.   It is Ovid;

    Nam genus, et proavos, et quæ non fecimus ipsi,
    Vix ea nostra voco.—*Metamor.* lib. 13. v. 140.
    For birth, and rank, and what our own good powers
    Have earned us not, I scarcely call them ours.

Ovid, himself a man of birth, puts this sentiment in the mouth of
Ulysses, a king.   But then he was a king whose talents were above
his royalty.

† Life of Gibbon, in the Autobiography, vol i.

The origin of the word Ludgate is not known. The old opinion respecting King Lud has been rejected, and some think it is the same as word as Flud or Fludgate, meaning the Gate on the Fleet, Floet, or Flood, F being dropt, as in *leer* for Fleer, Lloyd for Floyd or Fluyd, &c. It may be so; but it is not easy to see, in that case, why Fleet Street should not have been called Lud Street. Perhaps the old tradition is right, and some ancient Lud, or Lloyd, was the builder of an "old original" gate, whether king or not. Its successor (which formerly crossed the street by St. Martin's church), was no older than the reign of King John. It was rebuilt in 1586, and finally removed in 1760. Pennant says, he remembered it "a wretched prison for debtors." The old chroniclers tell us a romantic story of a lord-mayor, Sir

Stephen Forster, who enlarged this prison, and added a chapel to it. He had been confined in it himself, and, begging at the grate, was asked by a rich widow what sum would purchase his liberty. He said, twenty pounds. She paid it, took him into her service, and afterwards became his wife. One of our old dramatists (Rowley), in laying a scene in this prison, has made use of the name of Stephen Forster in a different manner; and probably his story had a foundation in truth. According to him, Stephen, who had been a profligate fellow, was relieved by the son of his brother, with whom he was at variance. Stephen afterwards becomes rich in his turn, and seeing his brother become poor and thrust into the same prison, forbids his nephew Robert, whom he had adopted on that condition, to relieve his father. The nephew disobeys, and has the misfortune to incur the hatred of both uncle and parent, for his connection with either party, but ultimately finds his virtue acknowledged. The following scene is one of those in which these old writers, in their honest confidence in nature, go direct to the heart. The reader will see the style of begging in those days. Robert Forster, who has been cursed by his father, comes to Ludgate, and stands concealed outside the prison, while his father appears above at the grate, " a box hanging down."

Forster. Bread, bread, one penny to buy a loaf of bread, for the tender mercy.

Rob. O me! my shame! I know that voice full well;
I'll help thy wants, although thou curse me still.
　　　　　　　　　[He stands where he is unseen by his father.

Fors. Bread, bread, some Christian man send back
Your charity to a number of poor prisoners.
One penny for the tender mercy—　　　*[Robert puts in money.*
The hand of Heaven reward you, gentle sir!
Never may you want, never feel misery;
Let blessings in unnumbered measure grow,
And fall upon your head, where'er you go.

Rob. Oh, happy comfort! curses to the ground
First struck me; now with blessings I am crowned.

Fors. Bread, bread, for the tender mercy; one penny for a loaf of bread.

Rob. I'll buy more blessings: take thou all my store:
I'll keep no coin and see my father poor.

Fors. Good angels guard you, sir; my prayers shall be,
That Heaven may bless you for this charity.

Rob. If he knew me sure he would not say so:
Yet I have comfort, if by any means
I get a blessing from my father's hands.*

The prison of Ludgate was anciently considered to be not so much a place of confinement as a place of refuge, into which debtors threw themselves to escape from their creditors —" a keep, not so much of the wicked as of the wretched"— (" non sceleratorum carcer, sed miserorum custodia "), as it is expressed in a Latin speech which was addressed by the inmates to King Philip of Spain, when he passed through

* Lamb's Specimens of English Dramatic Poets, p. 147.

the city, in 1554, and which the celebrated Roger Ascham was employed to compose. As it does not appear, however, that the persons who took up their abode here were allowed to come out again until they had discharged their debts, the distinction attempted to be drawn seems to be a somewhat shadowy one. A writer, nevertheless, quoted by Maitland, who in 1659 published a description of the house in which he had himself been for a long time a resident, expresses great indignation against the authorities for having " basely and injuriously caused to be taken down" the old inscription, affixed by Sir Stephen Forster, of *Free Water and Lodging,* " and set up another over the outward street door with only these words engraven : *This is the* PRISON *of* LUDGATE."*
The prison of Ludgate stood on the south side of the street, and extended back till it almost joined a portion of the old London Wall, which ran nearly parallel to Ludgate Hill. About the year 1764 this wall is described as being eight feet and a half thick.† Bits of it (as before noticed) still remain in this neighbourhood.

At this gate a stop was put to the insurrection of Sir Thomas Wyatt against Queen Mary, at the time when her marriage with Philip was in contemplation. Sir Thomas was son of the poet who had been a friend of the Earl of Surrey, and a warm partisan of Anne Bullen. He led his forces up the Strand and Fleet Street in no very hopeful condition, after suffering a loss in his rear; and on arriving at Ludgate, found it shut against him, and strongly manned. The disappointment is said to have affected him so strongly, that he threw himself on a bench opposite the Bell-Savage Inn, and mourned the rashness of his hopes. He retired, only to find his retreat cut off at Temple Bar; and being summoned by a herald to submit, requested it might be to a gentleman; upon which his sword was received by a person of his own rank. He was beheaded. It is worth observing, that Mary, alarmed at this insurrection, had pretended, in a speech at Guildhall, that she would give up the marriage, provided it were seriously and properly objected to: she only called upon the citizens to stand by her against rebels. When the rebels, however, were put down, the marriage, though notoriously unpopular, was concluded.

The Bell-Savage is an inn of old standing. The name is

* Maitland, vol. i., p. 28.
† Malcolm, Londinium Redivivum, iv., p. 367.

now learnedly written over the front—Belle Sauvage. **The** old sign was a bell with a savage by it. Stow derived the name from Isabella Savage, who had given the house to the company of Cutlers; and most likely this was its origin ; but as the inn was formerly one of those in which plays were acted, and as the players had dealings with romance, and sign painters varied their hieroglyphics according to the whim of the moment, Pennant might have reasonably found one derivation in the *Spectator*, without objecting to the other. A sight of the passage to which he refers will leave the immediate derivation beyond all doubt. "As for the Bell-Savage," says Addison (for the paper is his), "which is the sign of a Savage Man standing by a Bell, I was formerly very much puzzled upon the conceit of it, till I accidentally fell into the reading of an old romance translated out of the French ; which gives an account of a very beautiful woman who was in a wilderness, and is called in the French *la belle Sauvage;* and is everywhere translated by our countrymen the Bell-Savage."* This was one of the inns at which the famous Tarlton used to perform. London has a modern look to the inhabitants ; but persons who come from the country find as odd and remote-looking things in it as the Londoners do in York or Chester; and among these are a variety of old inns, with corridors running round the yard. They are well worth a glance from anybody who has a respect for old times. The play used to be got up in the yard, and the richer part of the spectators occupied "the galleries."†

* Spectator, vol. i., No. 28.

† Malone, in his Historical Account of the English Stage, has an ingenious parallel between these inn-theatres and the construction of the modern ones. "Many of our ancient dramatick pieces," he observes, "were performed in the yards of carriers' inns, in which, in the beginning of Queen Elizabeth's reign, the comedians, who then first united themselves in companies, erected an occasional stage. The form of these temporary play-houses seems to be preserved in our modern theatre. The galleries in both are ranged over each other on three sides of the building. The small rooms under the lowest of these galleries answer to our present boxes; and it is observable, that these, even in theatres which were built in a subsequent period expressly for dramatick exhibitions, still retained their old name, and were frequently called *rooms* by our ancient writers. The yard bears a sufficient resemblance to the pit, as at present in use. We may suppose the stage to have been raised in this arena, on the fourth side, with its back to the gateway of the inn, at which the money for admission was taken. Thus in fine weather, a play-house, not incommodious, might have been formed." Reed's Edition of Johnson's and Steevens's Shakspeare, vol. iii., p. 73.

The wall in which Lud-gate stood was the occasion of the hill's having two names, which is still the case, the upper part, between the Bell-Savage and St. Paul's Churchyard, being called Ludgate Street, and only the rest Ludgate Hill. This latter portion went anciently by the name of Bowyers' Row, no doubt from its being principally inhabited by persons of that trade. On Ludgate Hill lived the cobbler whom Steele mentions as a curious instance of pride.* He had a wooden figure of a beau, who stood before him in a bending posture, humbly presenting him with his awl, or bristle, or whatever else his employer chose to put in his hand, after the manner of an obsequious servant. Steele seems to have thought the man mad; otherwise the conceit would have been an agreeable one. Ludgate Street, as if to keep up and augment the didactic reputation of the neighbourhood, was not long since the head-quarters of the Society for the Diffusion of Knowledge, at least as far as regarded their publications. And, curiously enough, the house was next door to old " Newberry's."

Between Ludgate Hill and the Thames, in the district more properly retaining the name, was the monastery of the Black Friars, an order of Dominicans, in which parliaments were sometimes held. The Emperor Charles V. was lodged in it when he visited Henry VIII., in 1522 ; and in a hall of the same building, seven years after, the cause was tried between Henry and his queen, Catherine. Shakspeare has given us the opening scene. In Elizabeth's time, the desecrated tenements and neighbourhood of Blackfriars became the resort of the world of fashion—a court end of the city ; and close at hand, on the site retaining the name of Play-house Yard, was the famous Theatre in Blackfriars, where Shakspeare's, Ben Jonson's, and Beaumont and Fletcher's plays were performed, and where many of them came out. It was what they called at that time a " private" theatre, the peculiarity of which is not exactly understood. All that is known of it is, that it was smaller than the public ones; but it was open to public admission. Perhaps a private theatre meant a theatre more select than the others, and frequented by politer company ; for such, at any rate, the present one appears to have been. It is conjectured also to have been a winter theatre, and its performances took place by candlelight. The gallants and ladies of the courts of Elizabeth and James took their dinner at noon,

* Tatler, No. 127.

and after riding or lute-playing till evening, went to their snug little theatre in the neighbourhood, to laugh or weep over the divine fancies of Shakspeare. Shakspeare himself must often have been on the spot; a certainty which an intellectual inhabtiant will be glad to possess. The theatre, at one time, was partly his property.

A part of the monastery of the Blackfriars was, in 1623, the scene of a frightful accident, which made a great noise at the time. Mr. Malcolm has enumerated several of the publications recording it; and from these it appears that on Sunday, the 5th of November in that year, a congregation of about three hundred individuals had assembled in a small gallery over the gateway of the lodgings of the French Ambassador in this building, in order to hear a sermon from a Jesuit, named Father Drury, who enjoyed considerable reputation as a preacher. Under the floor of the chamber where they were assembled was an empty apartment, and under that another, making together a height of twenty-two feet from the ground; and the floor itself, as it afterwards turned out, was mainly supported by a single beam, which in the centre was not more than three inches thick. The people had been in their seats for about half-an-hour, when this beam suddenly gave way, and the whole of them were instantly precipitated, mixed with the timber, plaster, and rubbish of the floors, into the vacant depth below. Drury, and another priest, named Redgate, were both killed, as were also a Lady Webbe, and the daughter of a Lady Blackstone, together with, it is supposed, between ninety and a hundred persons. Many more were seriously injured. " Several people," says Mr. Malcolm, "escaped in a very extraordinary manner, particularly Mrs. Lucy Penruddock, who was preserved by a chair falling hollow over her; and a young man, who lay on the floor, overwhelmed by people and rubbish, yet untouched by them, through the resting of fragments on each other, and thus leaving a space round him. In this horrible situation he had the presence of mind to force his way through a piece of the ceiling, and he shortly after had the indescribable happiness of assisting in the liberation of others."[*]   There were many persons, it would appear, foolish and wicked enough to represent this calamity as a token of the displeasure of heaven against the Roman Catholic faith. The pamphlets noticed by Mr. Malcolm are some of those that were published by

[*] Londinium Redivivum, ii., 375.

the parties in a violent controversy which raged for some time on the subject. The day on which this accident happened was long remembered under the name of the Fatal Vespers ; and the circumstance that it was the anniversary of the Gunpowder Plot was not forgotten by the judgment-mongers. Most of the bodies of those who were killed on this occasion were buried without either the ceremony of a funeral service, or the decency of a coffin or winding-sheet, in two large pits or trenches, dug, the one in the court before, and the other in the garden behind the house, in which the accident had taken place.

Printing-house Square, close to Playhouse-yard, marks out the site of the ancient King's Printing-House, whence bibles, prayer-books, and proclamations were issued. It was rebuilt in the middle of the last century, and became, according to Maitland, " the completest printing-house in the world." The king's printer now lives elsewhere ; but in the same spot is a house, which may be called the world's printing-house, seeing the enormous multitude of newspapers which the mighty giant of steam daily throws forth out of his iron lap, full of interest to all quarters of the globe. We need not say that we allude to the *Times* newspaper. There is knowing, in this and other instances, what bounds to put to human expectation, when mechanical and intellectual force are thus joined in a common object.

On the other side of the way, in Bridge Street, stood, and stands now, though hidden by the new houses, and much altered, the former palace of Bridewell, now known as a house of industry and correction. In ancient times the King used frequently to reside here ; and when such was the case, the courts of law sometimes attended him. The building, having fallen into decay, was restored about the year 1522, by Henry VIII. ; and here the attendants of the Emperor Charles V. were lodged while the emperor himself occupied the Blackfriars, a communication being formed between the two palaces by a gallery carried over the Fleet Ditch, and through the old city wall. Both Henry and Catherine, also, were lodged here, while the cause between them was proceeding at Blackfriars. In 1553 Edward VI. granted the palace, on the solicitation of Bishop Ridley, for the purposes to which it has been since applied ; an act of benevolence which was recorded, with more precision than elegance, in the following

lines under a portrait of his majesty, that used to hang near
the pulpit in the old chapel :—

> " This Edward of fair memory the sixth.
> In whom with greatness, goodness was commixt,
> Gave this Bridewell, a Palace in old times,
> For a chastising house of vagrant crimes."

Bridewell having been burnt down in the Great Fire was
rebuilt immediately after that calamity, and it has since been
frequently repaired, and partially renovated. Henry the
Eighth (" sturdy rogue !") would have been a fit personage
to lodge in it still, though under somewhat different circumstances.

One of the steep and gloomy descents from Thames Street
still preserves the name of Castle Street ; and immediately to
the west of this stood in ancient times, on the banks of the
river, a large building called Baynard's Castle. Baynard, by
whom it was originally erected in the eleventh century, was
one of the Conqueror's Norman followers. His descendant,
William Baynard, however, soon after the commencement of
the next century, forfeited his inheritance to the crown, by
which it was bestowed upon the family of Clare. The representative of this family, and the possessor of Baynard's Castle,
in the reign of King John, was the Baron Robert Fitzwalter,
a portion of whose history, as related by some of our old
chroniclers, gives an interest to the spot. Among the beauties
of the time, one of the fairest was Matilda, the daughter of
Fitzwalter. The licentious monarch, who may have seen her
at some high festival held in this very castle, was smitten,
after his fashion, by her charms ; but his suit was rejected with
indignation, both by herself and her father. His "love" now
turned into hatred and thirst of revenge ; he soon after
resorted to open force, and having first driven Fitzwalter to
seek refuge in France, easily got the unhappy girl into his
custody, and, if we are to believe the story, despatched her by
poison. He at the same time ordered Castle Baynard to be
demolished. · The next year the armies of the English and
French Kings lay encamped during a truce on the opposite
sides of a river in France, when an English knight, impatient,
as it would seem, of the bloodless inactivity that prevailed,
thought fit to challenge any one of the enemy who chose to
come forth and break a lance with him. It was not long
before a champion appeared making his way across the water,

who, unattended as he was, had no sooner reached the land, than he mounted a horse and rode up to meet his challenger. The duel took place in the sight of King John and his troops, but it did not last long : for both the English knight and his horse were thrown to the ground by the first thrust of his antagonist's spear, which was also broken to shivers in the shock. " By God's troth," exclaimed John, as he beheld this heroic exploit, " he were a king indeed who had such a knight." The words were caught by some of the bystanders, who had observed more narrowly than the monarch the figure of the unknown victor, and who suspected him to be no other than their old acquaintance, the Baron Fitzwalter. It was, in fact, no other. The next day, the praise which the King had bestowed upon his prowess being reported to him, he returned to the English camp, and throwing himself at the feet of his sovereign, was re-admitted to favour, and restored to all his former possessions and honours. We may observe, however, that this narrative is scarcely detailed with sufficient precision to entitle it to be received as a piece of authentic history, and that especially it does not seem to be very easy to reconcile some parts of it, as commonly given, with the ascertained dates and course of the events of King John's reign. This Robert Fitzwalter is placed by Matthew Paris at the head of his list of the Barons, who, in 1215, came armed in a body to the King, at the Temple, and made those demands which led to the concession of the Great Charter at Runnymede. Indeed, in the short military contest which preceded the King's sub-mission, Fitzwalter was appointed by his brother barons the commander-in-chief of their forces, and dignified in that capacity with the title of Marshal of the Army of God and of Holy Church. On his return to England, he is said to have rebuilt or repaired his castle in London which the King had thrown down, and the edifice continued for a long time to be the principal fortress within the city. The family of Fitz-walter, in consequence of their possession of Baynard's Castle, held the office of Chastilians and Bannerets, or Banner-bearers of London ; and the reader who is curious upon such matters may consult Stow, or those who have copied him, for an account of the rights, services, and ceremonial customs apper-taining to that dignity. The punishment of a person found guilty of treason within the banneret's jurisdiction is worth noticing : he was to be tied to a post in the Thames, at one of the wharfs, and left there for two ebbings and two flowings of the tide. After this, there was certainly little chance of his committing more treason.

It is not known how Baynard's Castle, and the privileges belonging to the lordship, got out of the hands of this family; but in 1428, in the reign of Henry the Sixth, the building, having been burned down, is stated to have been restored by Humphrey, Duke of Gloucester. After the duke's death it came once more into the possession of the crown; and here it was that the great council assembled in the beginning of March, 1461, which proclaimed the Earl of March King, by the title of Edward IV. It was here also, twenty-two years after, that the solemn farce was enacted in which Richard III. assumed the royal dignity on the invitation of Buckingham, and in obedience to the pretended wishes of the citizens.

Shakspeare has given this scene with an exact conformity, in all the matters of fact, to the narratives of the old chroniclers; the crafty Protector, it will be remembered, being made to present himself in the gallery above, supported by a bishop on each side, while Buckingham, the lord mayor, the aldermen, and the citizens, occupy the court of the castle below. Baynard's Castle was once more rebuilt in 1487, by Henry VII., with a view to its answering better the purpose of a royal palace; and the King occasionally lodged there. Some time after this we find the place in possession of the Earls of Pembroke, who made it their common residence; and it was here that the Earl of that name, on the 19th of July, 1553, about a fortnight after the death of Edward VI., assembled the council of the nobility and clergy, at which the determination was taken, on the motion of Lord Arundel, to abandon the cause of Lady Jane Grey, and to proclaim Queen Mary, which, accordingly, was instantly done in different parts of the city. This is supposed to have been the building which was destroyed in the Great Fire of 1666. It is represented in an old print of London as a square pile surrounding a court, and surmounted with numerous towers. A large gateway in the middle of the south side led to the river by a bridge of two arches and stairs. This ancient fortress was never rebuilt after the fire ; and its site has been since occupied by wharfs, timber-yards, workshops, and common dwelling-houses. The ward, however, in which it was situated, and which embraces also St. Paul's Churchyard, and nearly all the localities we have as yet noticed, still retains the name of the Ward of Baynard's Castle.

Upon Paul's Wharf Hill, to the north-east of Baynard's Castle, were a number of houses within a great gate, which are said by Maitland to have been designated, in the leases granted by the dean and chapter, as the *Camera Dianæ*, or Diana's Chamber, and to have been so denominated from a spacious building in the form of a labyrinth, constructed here by Henry II. for the concealment of the fair Rosamond Clifford. We need scarcely say that this tradition has all the air of a fable. The author we have just named, however, assures us that "for a long time there remained some evident testifications of tedious turnings and windings, as also of a passage under ground from his house to Castle Baynard ; which was no doubt the King's way from thence to the *Camera Dianæ*," * or the chamber of his " brightest Diana." What the testifications may in question really have amounted to, we cannot pretend to say ; but Diana, not being a family name, as in the case of another royal favourite, Diana of Poitiers, seems a strange one to have been given to the lady already christened by so poetical an appellation as Rosamond, and so different in her reputation from the chaste goddess. We should, for our parts, rather suppose that the dean and chapter had been moved to call the place Diana's chamber by some tradition, or a conceit of their own, connecting it with the temple of that goddess, said to have formerly stood on the site of the neighbouring cathedral; or if the name was really a very ancient one, and in popular use, it may perhaps be taken

* History of London, ii., 880.

as lending some slight confirmation to the notion of the actual existence of that heathen edifice, and may " help," as Iago phrases it, "to thicken other proofs that also demonstrate thinly." Diana's Chamber, however, may have been so called from its being hung with painted tapestry, representing some story of the goddess. Inigo Jones, by the way, is said by Lord Orford to be buried in the church of St. Bennet, Paul's Wharf, which stands immediately to the south of the spot where we now are, at the corner formed by the meeting of Thames Street and St. Bennet's Hill.

Another building which formerly existed in this neighbour-hood was the Royal Wardrobe. It occupied the site of the present Wardrobe Court, immediately to the north of the church of St. Andrew's and gave to the parish the name of St. Andrew's Wardrobe, by which it is still known. This building was erected about the middle of the fourteenth century, by Sir John Beauchamp, Knight of the Garter, a son of Guido, Earl of Warwick, by whose heirs it was sold to Edward III. Mr. Malcolm has printed some extracts from the Manuscript Account Book, since preserved in the Harleian collection, of a keeper of this Wardrobe, from the middle of April to Michaelmas 1481, (towards the close of the reign of Edward IV.), which are interesting and valuable as memorials, both of the prices and of the fashions of that time. During the period, of less than six months, over which the accounts extend, the sum of 1,174*l*. 5*s*. 2*d*. appears to have been received by the keeper, for the use of his office. Of this the most considerable portion seems to have been expended in the purchase of velvet and silks from Montpellier. The velvets cost from 8*s*. to 16*s*. per yard; black cloths of gold, 40*s*. ; what is called velvet upon velvet, the same; damask, 8*s*. ; satins, 6*s*. 10*s*. and 12*s*., camlets, 30*s*. a-piece ; and sarcenets for 4*s*. to 4*s*. 2*d*. Feather beds, with bolsters, " for our sovereign lord the King," are charged 16*s* 8*d*. each. A pair of shoes, of Spanish leather, double soled, and not lined, cost 1*s*. 4*d*.; a pair of black leather boots, 6*s*. 8*d*.; hats 1*s*. a-piece; and ostrich feathers, each 10*s*. The keeper's salary appears to have been 100*l*. per annum—that of his clerk 1*s*. a-day; and the wages of the tailors 6*d*. a-day each. The King sometimes lodged at the Wardrobe; on one of which occasions the washings of the sheets which had been used is charged at the rate of 3*d*. a pair. Candles cost 1*d*. a pound. All the money disbursed by the keeper of the wardrobe, how-

ever, was not expended in decorating the persons of his
Majesty and the royal household.   Among other items we find
20s. paid to Piers Bauduyn (or Peter Baldwin, as we should
now call him), stationer, "for binding, gilding, and dressing
of a book called Titus Livius;" for performing the same offices
to a Bible, a Froisard, a Holy Trinity, and the Government
of Kings and Princes, 16s. each; for three small French books,
6s. 8d.; for the Fortress of Faith, and Josephus 3s. 4d.; and
for what is designated "the Bible Historical," 20s.   So that
in those days, we see the binding a book was conceived to be a
putting of it into breeches, and the artist employed for that
purpose looked upon as a sort of literary tailor.

How impossible it would now be in a neighbourhood like
this, for such nuisances to exist, as a fetid *public* ditch, and
scouts of degraded clergymen asking people to " walk in and
be married !" Yet such was the case a century ago. At the
bottom of Ludgate Hill the little river Fleet formerly ran, and
was rendered navigable. Adjoining the site of Fleet Market is
Sea-coal Lane, so called from the barges that landed coal there;
and Turnagain Lane, at the bottom of which the unadvised passenger found himself compelled by the water to retrace his steps.
The water gradually got clogged and foul; and the channel
was built over and made a street, as we have noticed in our
introduction.   But even in the time we speak of, this had not
been entirely done. The ditch was open from Fleet Market
to the river, occupying the site of the modern Bridge Street ;
and in the market, before the door of the Fleet prison,
men plied in behalf of a clergyman, literally inviting people to
walk in and be married   They performed the ceremony inside
the prison, to sailors and others, for what they could get. It
was the most squalid of Gretnas, bearding the decency and
common-sense of a whole metropolis. The parties retired to a
gin shop to treat the clergyman; and there, and in similar
houses, the register was kept of the marriages. Not far from
where the Fleet stood is Newgate; so that the victims had
their succession of nooses prepared, in case, as no doubt it
often happened, one tie should be followed by the other.
Pennant speaks of this nuisance from personal knowledge.

" In walking along the streets in my youth," he tells us, "on the
side next this prison, I have often been tempted by the question, ' *Sir,
will you be pleased to walk in and be married.*' Along this most lawless
space was frequently hung up the sign of a male and female hand con-
joined, with *Marriages performed within,* written beneath. A dirty
fellow invited you in. The parson was seen walking before his shop; a

squalid, profligate figure, clad in a tattered plaid night-gown, with a fiery face, and ready to couple you for a dram of gin or roll of tobacco. Our great chancellor, Lord Hardwicke, put these demons to flight, and saved thousands from the misery and disgrace which would be entailed by these extemporary thoughtless unions."

This extraordinary disgrace to the city, which arose most likely from the permission to marry prisoners, and one great secret of which was the advantage taken of it by wretched women to get rid of their debts, was maintained by a collusion between the warden of the Fleet and the disreputable clergymen he became acquainted with. "To such an extent," says Malcolm, "were the proceedings carried, that twenty and thirty couple were joined in one day, at from ten to twenty shillings each;" and "between the 19th Oct., 1704, and the 12th Feb., 1705, 2,954 marriages were celebrated (by evidence), besides others known to have been omitted. To these neither licence nor certificate of banns were required, and they concealed, by private marks, the names of those who chose to pay them for it." The neighbourhood at length complained; and the abuse was put an end to by the Marriage Act, to which it gave rise.

Ludgate and Fleet ditch figure among the scenes of the Dunciad. It is near Bridewell, on the site of the modern Bridge Street, that the venal and scurrilous heroes of that poem emulate one another, at the call of Dulness, in seeing who can plunge deepest into the mud and dirt.

> "This labour past, by Bridewell all descend,
> (As morning prayer and flagellation end *),
> To where Fleet ditch, with disemboguing streams,
> Rolls the large tribute of dead dogs to Thames ;
> The king of dykes ! than whom no sluice of mud
> With deeper sable blots the silver flood.
> Here strip, my children ! here at once leap in ;
> Here prove who best can dash through thick and thin ;
> And who the most in love of dirt excel,
> And dark dexterity of groping well." †

This part of the games being over,

> "Through Lud's famed gates, along the well-known Fleet,
> Rolls the black troop and overshades the street ;
> Till showers of sermons, characters, essays,
> In circling fences whiten all the ways :
> So clouds replenished from some bog below,
> Mount in dark volumes and descend in snow."

---

* The whipping of the criminals in Bridewell took place after the church service.

† Dunciad, book ii., v. 269.

The "well-known Fleet" is the prison just mentioned, the side of which appears to have been visible at that time in Ludgate Hill, and where it was a joke (too often founded in truth) to suppose authors incarcerated.

"Few sons of Phœbus in the courts we meet ;
But fifty sons of Phœbus in the Fleet,"

says a prologue of Sheridan's. The Fleet having "rules," like the King's Bench, authors were found in the neighbourhood also. Arthur Murphy, provoked by the attacks of Churchill and Lloyd, describes them as among the poor hacks,

"On Ludgate Hill who bloody murders write,
Or pass in Fleet Street supperless the night."

Booksellers' shops were then common as now in Fleet Street and the Strand, in Paternoster Row, and St. Paul's Churchyard. This is pleasant to think of; for change is not desirable without improvement. One feels gratified, where difference is not demanded of us, in being able to have the same association of ideas with such men as Pope and Dryden, even if it be upon no higher ground than the quantity of books in Paternoster Row, or the circumstance that Ludgate Hill still leads into Fleet Street.

THE STONE IN PANYER ALLEY.

CHAPTER III.

FLEET STREET.

Burning of the Pope—St. Bride's Steeple—Milton—Illuminated Clock
—Melancholy End of Lovelace the Cavalier—Chatterton—Gene-
rosity of Hardham, of Snuff Celebrity—Theatre in Dorset Garden
—Richardson, his Habits and Character—Whitefriars, or Alsatia
—The Temple—Its Monuments, Garden, &c.—Eminent names con-
nected with it—Goldsmith dies there—Boswell's first Visit there to
Johnson—Johnson and Madame de Boufflers—Bernard Lintot—
Ben Jonson's Devil Tavern—Other Coffee-houses and Shops—
Goldsmith and Temple-bar—Shire Lane, Bickerstaff, and the
Deputation from the Country—The Kit-Kat Club—Mrs. Salmon—
Isaac Walton—Cowley—Chancery Lane, Lord Strafford, and Ben
Jonson—Serjeant's Inn—Clifford's Inn—The Rolls—Sir Joseph
Jekyll—Church of St. Dunstan in the West—Dryden's House in
Fetter Lane—Johnson, the Genius Loci of Fleet Street—His Way
of Life—His Residence in Gough Square, Johnson's Court, and
Bolt Court—Various Anecdotes of him connected with Fleet Street,
and with his favourite Tavern, the Mitre.

 E are now in Fleet Street, and pleasant
memories thicken upon us. To the left
is the renowned realm of Alsatia, the
Temple, the Mitre, and the abode of
Richardson; to the right divers abodes
of Johnson; Chancery Lane, with
Cowley's birth-place at the corner;
Fetter Lane, where Dryden once lived;
and Shire or Sheer Lane, immortal for the *Tatler*.

Fleet Street was, for a good period, perhaps for a longer
one than can now be ascertained, the great place for shows
and spectacles. Wild beasts, monsters, and other marvels,
used to be exhibited there, as the wax-work was lately; and
here took place the famous ceremony of burning the Pope,
with its long procession, and bigoted anti-bigotries. However, the lesser bigotry was useful, at that time, in keeping
out the greater. Roger North has left us a lively account of
one of these processions, in his *Examen*. It took place towards
the close of the reign of Charles the Second, when just fears
were entertained of his successor's design to bring in Popery.
The day of the ceremony was the birth-day of Queen Elizabeth, the 17th March.

"When we had posted ourselves," says North, "at windows
expecting the play to begin" (he had taken his stand in the Green

Dragon Tavern), "it was very dark ; but we could perceive the street to fill, and the hum of the crowd grew louder and louder ; and at length, with help of some lights below, we could discern, not only upwards towards the bar, where the squib-war was maintained, but downwards towards Fleet Bridge ; the whole street was crowded with people, which made that which followed seem very strange ; for about eight at night we heard a din from below, which came up the street, continually increasing till we could perceive a motion ; and that was a row of stout fellows, that came, shouldered together, cross the street, from wall to wall on each side. How the people melted away, I cannot tell ; but it was plain those fellows made clear board, as if they had swept the street for what was to come after. They went along like a wave; and it was wonderful to see how the crowd made way : I suppose the good people were willing to give obedience to lawful authority. Behind this wave (which, as all the rest, had many lights attending), there was a vacancy, but it filled apace, till another like wave came up ; and so four or five of these waves passed, one after another ; and then we discerned more numerous lights, and throats were opened with hoarse and tremendous noise ; and with that advanced a pageant, borne along above the heads of the crowd, and upon it sat an huge Pope, *in pontificalibus*, in his chair, with a seasonable attendance for state : but his premier minister, that shared most of his ear, was Il Signior Diavolo, a nimble little fellow, in a proper dress, that had a strange dexterity in climbing and winding about the chair, from one of the Pope's ears to the other.

"The next pageant was a parcel of Jesuits ; and after that (for there was always a decent space between them) came another, with some ordinary persons with halters, as I took it, about their necks ; and one with a stenterophonic tube, sounded 'Abhorrers! Abhorrers!' most infernally ; and, lastly, came one, with a single person upon it, which some said was the phamphleteer, Sir Roger L'Estrange, some the King of France, some the Duke of York ; but, certainly, it was a very complaisant, civil gentleman, like the former, that was doing what everybody pleased to have him ; and, taking all in good part went on his way to the fire."

The description concludes with a brief mention of burning the effigies, which, on these occasions, appear to have been of pasteboard.*

One of the great figurers in this ceremony was the doleful image of Sir Edmondbury Godfrey, a magistrate, supposed to have been killed by the Papists during the question of the plot. Dryden has a fine contemptuous couplet upon it, in one of his prologues ;—

"Sir Edmondbury first in woful wise,
Leads up the show, *and milks their maudlin eyes.*"

We will begin with the left side, as we are there already;

---

* See Walter Scott's edition of Dryden, vol. x., p. 372. "Abhorrers" were addressers on the side of the court, who had avowed "abhorrence" of the proceedings of the Whigs. The word was a capital one to sound through a trumpet.

and first let us express our thanks for the neat opening by
which St. Bride's church has been rendered an ornament to
this populous thoroughfare. The steeple is one of the most
beautiful of Wren's productions, though diminished, in consequence of its having been found to be too severely tried by
the wind. But a ray now comes out of this opening as we
pass the street, better even than that of the illuminated clock
at night time; for there, in a lodging in the churchyard, lived
Milton, at the time that he undertook the education of his
sister's children. He was then young and unmarried. He is
said to have rendered his young scholars, in the course of a
year, able to read Latin at sight, though they were but nine
or ten years of age. As to the clock, which serves to remind
the jovial that they ought to be at home, we are loth to object
to anything useful; and in fact we admit its pretensions; and
yet as there is a time for all things, there would seem to be a
time for time itself; and we doubt whether those who do not
care to ascertain the hour beforehand, will derive much benefit
from this glaring piece of advice.

"At the west end of St. Bride's Church," according to
Wood, was buried Richard Lovelace, Esq., one of the most
elegant of the cavaliers of Charles the First, and author of the
exquisite ballad beginning—

> "When Love with unconfined wings
> Hovers within my gates,
> And my divine Althea brings
> To whisper at my grates.

> "When I lie tangled in her hair,
> And fetter'd in her eye,
> The birds that wanton in the air,
> Know no such liberty.
> *   *   *   *

> "Stone walls do not a prison make,
> Nor iron bars a cage,
> Minds innocent and quiet take
> That for an hermitage."

This accomplished man, who is said by Wood to have been
in his youth "the most amiable and beautiful person that eye
ever beheld," and who was lamented by Charles Cotton as an
epitome of manly virtue, died at a poor lodging in Gunpowder Alley, near Shoe Lane, an object of charity.* He

* Aubrey says that his death took place in a cellar in Long Acre;
and adds, "Mr. Edm. Wylde, &c., had made a collection for him, and

had been imprisoned by the Parliament and lived during his imprisonment beyond his income. Wood thinks that he did so in order to support the royal cause, and out of generosity to deserving men, and to his brothers. He then went into the service of the French King, returned to England after being wounded, and was again committed to prison, where he remained till the King's death, when he was set at liberty. " Having then," says his biographer, " consumed all his estate, he grew very melancholy (which brought him at length into a consumption), became very poor in body and purse, and was the object of charity, went in ragged clothes, (whereas, when he was in his glory, he wore cloth of gold and silver,) and mostly lodged in obscure and dirty places, more befitting the worst of beggars than poorest of servants," &c.[*] " Geo. Petty, haberdasher in Fleet Street," says Aubrey, " carried 20 shillings to him every Monday Morning from Sir —— Manny, and Charles Cotton, Esq., for —— months: but was never repaid." As if it was their intention he should be I Poor Cotton, in the excess of his relish of life, lived himself to be in want ; perhaps wanted the ten shillings that he sent. The mistress of Lovelace is reported to have married another man, supposing him to have died of his wounds in France. Perhaps this helped to make him careless of his fortune : but it is probable that his habits were naturally showy and expensive. Aubrey says he was proud. He was accounted a sort of minor Sir Philip Sydney. We speak the more of him, not only on account of his poetry (which, for the most part, displays much fancy, injured by want of selectness), but because his connection with the neighbourhood probably suggested to Richardson the name of his hero in Clarissa. Grandison is another cavalier name in the history of those times. It was the title of the Duchess of Cleveland's father. Richardson himself was buried in St. Bride's. He was laid, according to his wish, with his first wife, in the middle aisle, near the pulpit. Where he lived, we shall see presently.

Not far from Gunpowder Alley, in the burying-ground of the workhouse in Shoe Lane, lies a greater and more unfortunate name than Lovelace—Chatterton. But we shall say more

given him money." But Aubrey's authority is not valid against Wood's. He is to be read like a proper gossip, whose accounts we may pretty safely reject or believe, as it suits other testimony.

† Wood's Athenæ Oxonienses, fol. vol. ii., p. 145.

of him when we come to Brook Street, Holborn. We have been perplexed to decide, whether to say all we have got to say upon anybody, when we come to the first place with which he is connected, or divide our memorials of him according to the several places. Circumstances will guide us; but upon the whole it seems best to let the places themselves decide. If the spot is rendered particularly interesting by the division, we may act accordingly, as in the present instance. If not, all the anecdotes may be given at once.

On the same side of the way as Shoe Lane, but nearer Fleet Market, was Hardham's, a celebrated snuff-shop, the founder of which deserves mention for a very delicate generosity. He was numberer at Drury Lane Theatre, that is to say, the person who counted the number of people in the house, from a hole over the top of the stage; a practice now discontinued. Whether this employment led him to number snuffs, as well as men, we cannot say, but he was the first who gave them their distinctions that way. Lovers of

"The pungent grains of titillating dust"

are indebted to him for the famous compound entitled "37." "Being passionately fond of theatrical entertainments, he was seldom," says his biographer, "without embryo Richards and Hotspurs strutting and bellowing in his dining-room, or in the parlour behind his shop. The latter of these apartments was adorned with heads of most of the persons celebrated for dramatic excellence; and to these he frequently referred in the course of his instructions."

"There is one circumstance, however, in his private character," continues our authority, "which deserves a more honourable rescue from oblivion. His charity was extensive in an uncommon degree, and was conveyed to many of its objects in the most delicate manner. On account of his known integrity (for he once failed in business, more creditably than he could have made a fortune by it,) he was often entrusted with the care of paying little annual stipends to unfortunate women, and others who were in equal want of relief; and he has been known, with a generosity almost unexampled, to continue these annuities, long after the sources of them had been stopped by the deaths or caprices of the persons who at first supplied them. At the same time he persuaded the receivers that their money was remitted to them as usual, through its former channel. Indeed his purse was never shut even to those who were casually recommended by his common acquaintance."*

This admirable man died in 1772; and by his will be-

* Baker's Biographia Dramatica. Reed's edition, 1782, vol. i., p. 207.

queathed the interest of 20,000*l.* to a female acquaintance, and at her decease the principal, &c., to the poor of his native city, Chichester.

Returning over the way we come to Dorset Street and Salisbury Court, names originating in a palace of the Bishop of Salisbury, which he parted with to the Sackvilles. Clarendon lived in it a short time after the Restoration. At the bottom of Salisbury Court, facing the river, was the celebrated play-house, one of the earliest in which theatrical entertainments were resumed at that period. The first mention we find of it is in the following curious memorandum in the manuscript book of Sir Henry Herbert, master of the revels to King Charles I. " I committed Cromes, a broker in Longe Lane, the 16th of Febru., 1634, to the Marsalsey, for lending a church robe with the name of *Jesus* upon it to the players in Salisbury Court, to present a Flamen, a priest of the heathens. Upon his petition of submission, and acknowledgment of his fault, I released him, the 17 Febru., 1634."*

It is not certain, however, whether the old theatre in Salisbury Court, and that in Dorset Garden, were one and the same; though they are conjectured to have been so. The names of both places seem to have been indiscriminately applied. Be this as it may, the house became famous under the Davenants for the introduction of operas and of a more splendid exhibition of scenery; but in consequence of the growth of theatres in the more western parts of the town, it was occasionally quitted by the proprietors, and about the beginning of the last century abandoned. This theatre was the last to which people went in boats.

In a house, "in the centre of Salisbury Square or Salisbury Court, as it was then called," Richardson spent the greater part of his town life, and wrote his earliest work, Pamela. Probably a good part of all his works were composed there, as well as at Fulham, for the pen was never out of his hand. He removed from this house in 1755, after he had written all his works; and taking eight old tenements in the same quarter, pulled them down, and built a large and commodious range of warehouses and printing offices. " The dwelling-house," says Mrs. Barbauld, " was neither so large nor so airy as the one he quitted, and therefore the reader will not be so ready, probably, as Mr. Richardson seems to

* Malone in the Prolegomena to Shakspeare, as above, vol. iii., p. 287.

have been, in accusing his wife of perverseness in not liking the new habitation as well as the old."* This was the second Mrs. Richardson. He calls her in other places his "worthy-hearted wife;" but complains that she used to get her way by seeming to submit, and then returning to the point, when his heat of objection was over. She was a formal woman. His own manners were strict and formal with regard to his family, probably because he had formed his notions of life from old books, and also because he did not well know how to begin to do otherwise (for he was naturally bashful), and so the habit continued through life. His daughters addressed him in their letters by the title of " Honoured Sir," and are always designating themselves as " ever dutiful." Sedentary living, eternal writing, and perhaps that indulgence in the table, which, however moderate, affects a sedentary man twenty times as much as an active one, conspired to hurt his temper (for we may see by his picture that he grew fat, and his philosophy was in no respect as profound as he thought it); but he was a most kind-hearted generous man; kept his pocket full of plums for children, like another Mr. Burchell; gave a great deal of money away in charity, very handsomely too; and was so fond of inviting friends to stay with him, that when they were ill, he and his family must needs have them to be nursed. Several actually died at his house at Fulham, as at an hospital for sick friends.

It is a fact not generally known (none of his biographers seem to have known of it) that Richardson was the son of a joiner, received what education he had (which was very little, and did not go beyond English), at Christ's Hospital.† It may be wondered how he could come no better taught from a school which had sent forth so many good scholars; but in his time, and indeed till very lately, that foundation was divided into several schools, none of which partook of the lessons of the others; and Richardson, agreeably to his father's intention of bringing him up to trade, was most probably confined to the writing-school, where all that was taught was writing and arithmetic. It was most likely here that he intimated his future career, first by writing a letter, at eleven years of age, to a censorious woman of fifty, who

* Correspondence of Samual Richardson, &c., by Anna Letitia Barbauld, vol. i., p. 97.

† Our authority (one of the highest in this way) is Mr. Nichols, in his Literary Anecdotes of the Eighteenth Century, vol. iv., p. 579.

pretended a zeal for religion ; and afterwards, at thirteen, by composing love-letters to their sweethearts for three young women in the neighbourhood, who made him their confidant. To these and others he also used to read books, their mothers being of the party ; and they encouraged him to make remarks ; which is exactly the sort of life he led with Mrs. Chapone, Miss Fielding, and others, when in the height of his celebrity. " One of the young women," he informs us, "highly gratified with her lover's fervour, and vows of everlasting love, has said, when I have asked her direction, ' I cannot tell you what to write, but (her heart on her lips) you cannot write too kindly ;' all her fear was only that she should incur a slight for her kindness." This passage, with its pretty breathless parenthesis, is in the style of his books. If the writers among his female coterie in after-life owed their inspiration to him, he only returned to them what they had done for himself. Women seem to have been always about him, both in town and country; which made Mrs. Barbauld say, very agreeably, that he " lived in a kind of flower-garden of ladies." This has been grudged him, and thought effeminate ; but we must make allowance for early circumstances, and recollect what the garden produced for us. Richardson did not pretend to be able to do without female society. Perhaps, however, they did not quiet his sensibility so much as they charmed it. We think, in his Correspondence, a tendency is observable to indulge in fancies, not always so paternal as they agree to call them; though doubtless all was said in honour, and the ladies never found reason to diminish their reverence. A great deal has been said of his vanity and the weakness of it. Vain he undoubtedly was, and vanity is no strength; but it is worth bearing in mind, that a man is often saved from vanity, not because he is stronger than another, but because he is less amiable, and did not begin, as Richardson did, with being a favourite so early. Few men are surrounded, as he was, from his very childhood,· with females ; and few people think so well of their species or with so much reason. In all probability too, he was handsome when young, which is another excuse for him. His vanity is more easily excused than his genius accounted for considering the way in which he lived. The tone of Lovelace's manners and language, which has created so much surprise in an author who was a city printer, and passed his life among a few friends between Fleet Street and a suburb, was caught, probably, not merely from Cibber, but from the famous profligate Duke of Wharton, with whom he became acquainted in the course of his business. But the unwearied vivacity with which he has supported it is wonderful. His pathos is more easily accounted for by his nerves, which for many years were in a constant state of excitement, particularly towards the close of his life; which terminated in 1761, at the age of seventy-two, with the death most common to sedentary men of letters, a stroke of apoplexy.* He was latterly unable to lift a glass of wine to his mouth without assistance.

At Fulham and Parson's Green (at which latter place he lived for the last five or six years), Richardson used to sit with his guests about him, in a parlour or summer-house, reading, or communicating his manuscripts as he wrote them. The ladies made their remarks; and alterations or vindications ensued. His characters, agreeably to what we feel when we read of them (for we know them all as intimately as if we occupied a room in their house), interested his acquaintances so far that they sympathised with them as if they were real; and it is well known that one of his correspondents, Lady Bradshaigh, implored him to reform Lovelace, in order " to save a soul." In Salisbury Court, Richardson, of course, had the same visitors about him; but the "flower-garden" is not talked of so much there as at Fulham. In the evening the ladies read and worked by themselves, and Richardson retired to his study; a most pernicious habit for a man of his bad nerves. He should have written early in the morning, taken good exercise in the day, and amused himself in the evening. When he walked in town it was in the park, where he describes himself (to a fair correspondent who wished to have an interview with him, and who recognised him from the description) as " short, rather plump, about five feet five

* "——Apoplexy cramm'd intemperance knocks
   Down to the ground at once, as butcher felleth ox;"—
says Thomson, in his Castle of Indolence. It was the death which the good-natured, indolent poet probably expected for himself, and which he would have had, if a cold and fever had not interfered; for there is an apoplexy of the head alone, as well as of the whole body; and men of letters who either exercise little, or work overmuch, seem almost sure to die of it, or of palsy; which is a disease analogous. It is the last stroke, given in the kind resentment of nature, to the brains which should have known better than bring themselves to such a pass. In the biography of Italian literati, "Mori' d' apoplessia"—(he died of apoplexy)—is a common verdict.

inches, fair wig, one hand generally in his bosom, the other a cane in it, which he leans upon under the skirts of his coat, that it may imperceptibly serve him as a support when attacked by sudden tremors or dizziness, of a light brown complexion, teeth not yet failing." "What follows," observes Mrs. Barbauld, "is very descriptive of the struggle in his character, between innate bashfulness and a turn for observation :"—"Looking directly forwards, as passengers would imagine, but observing all that stirs on either hand of him, without moving his short neck ; a regular even pace, stealing away ground rather than seeming to rid it ; a grey eye, too often overclouded by mistiness from the head, by chance lively, very lively if he sees any he loves ; if he approaches a lady, his eye is never fixed first on her face, but on her feet, and rears it up by degrees, seeming to set her down as so and so."*

Latterly Richardson attended little to business. He used even to give his orders to his workmen in writing; a practice which Sir John Hawkins is inclined to attribute to stateliness and bad temper, but for which Mrs. Barbauld finds a better reason in his bad nerves. His principal foreman also was deaf, as the knight himself acknowledges. Richardson encouraged his men to be industrious, sometimes by putting half-a-crown among the types as a prize to him who came first in the morning, at others by sending fruit for the same purpose from the country. Agreeably to his natural bashfulness, he was apt to be reserved with strangers. Sir John Hawkins tells us, that he once happened to get into the Fulham stage when Richardson was in it (most likely he got in on purpose); and he endeavoured to bring the novelist into conversation, but could not succeed, and was vexed at it. But Sir John was one of that numerous class of persons who, for reasons better known to others than to themselves,

"Deemen gladly to the badder end,"

as the old poet says ; and Richardson probably knew this pragmatical person, and did not want his acquaintance.

Johnson was among the visitors of Richardson in Salisbury Court. He confessed to Boswell, that although he had never much sought after anybody, Richardson was an exception. He had so much respect for him, that he took part with him in a preposterous undervaluing of Fielding, whom he described

* Correspondence, as above, vol. i., p. 177.

in the comparison as a mere writer of manners, and sometimes as hardly any writer at all. And yet he told Boswell that he had read his *Amelia* through "without stopping:" and according to Mrs. Piozzi she was his favourite heroine. In the comparison of Richardson with Fielding, he was in the habit of opposing the nature of one to the manners of the other; but Fielding's manners are only superadded to his nature, not opposed to it, which makes all the difference. As to Richardson, he was so far gone upon this point, in a mixture of pique and want of sympathy, that he said, if he had not known who Fielding was, "he should have taken him for an ostler." Fielding, it is true, must have vexed him greatly by detecting the pettiness in the character of Pamela. Richardson, as a romancer, did not like to have the truth forced upon him, and thus was inclined to see nothing but vulgarity in the novelist. This must have been unpleasant to the Misses Fielding, the sisters, who were among the most intimate of Richardson's friends. Another of our author's visitors was Hogarth. It must not be forgotten that Richardson was kind to Johnson in money matters ; and to use Mrs. Barbauld's phrase, had once " the honour " to be bail for him.

We conclude our notice, which, on the subject of so original a man, has naturally beguiled us into some length, with an interesting account of his manners and way of life, communicated by one of his female friends to Mrs. Barbauld. "My first recollection of him," says she, "was in his house in the centre of Salisbury Square, or Salisbury Court as it was then called; and of being admitted as a playful child into his study, where I have often seen Dr. Young and others ; and where I was generally caressed and rewarded with biscuits or *bonbons* of some kind or other ; and sometimes with books, for which he, and some more of my friends, kindly encouraged a taste, even at that early age, which has adhered to me all my long life, and continues to be the solace of many a painful hour. I recollect that he used to drop in at my father's, for we lived nearly opposite, late in the evening to supper ; when, as he would say, he had worked as long as his eyes and nerves would let him, and was come to relax with a little friendly and domestic chat. I even then used to creep to his knee and hang upon his words, for my whole family doated on him; and once, I recollect that at one of these evening visits, probably about the year 1753, I was standing by his knee when my mother's maid came to summon me to bed; upon which,

being unwilling to part from him and manifesting some reluct-
ance, he begged I might be permitted to stay a little longer;
and, on my mother's objecting that the servant would be
wanted to wait at supper (for, in those days of friendly intercourse and *real* hospitality, a decent maid-servant was the
only attendant at *his own* and many creditable tables, where,
nevertheless, much company was received), Mr. Richardson
said, ' I am sure Miss P. is now so much a woman, that she
does not want anyone to attend her to bed, but will conduct
herself with so much propriety, and put out her own candle
so carefully, that she may henceforward be indulged with
remaining with us till supper is served.'   This hint and the
confidence it implied, had such a good effect upon me that I
believe I never required the attendance of a servant afterwards
while my mother lived ; and by such sort of ingenious and
gentle devices did he use to encourage and draw in young
people to do what was right.   I also well remember the happy
days I passed at his house at North End; sometimes with my
mother, but often for weeks without her, domesticated as one
of his own children.   He used to pass the greatest part of the
week in town ; but when he came down, he used to like to
have his family flock around him, when we all first asked and
received his blessing, together with some small boon from his
paternal kindness and attention, for he seldom met us empty-
handed, and was by nature most generous and liberal.

" The piety, order, decorum, and strict regularity that prevailed in
his family were of infinite use to train the mind to good habits and to
depend upon its own resources.   It has been one of the means which,
under the blessing of God, has enabled me to dispense with the
enjoyment of what the world calls pleasures, such as are found in
crowds, and actually to relish and prefer the calm delights of retirement and books.   As soon as Mrs. Richardson arose, the beautiful
Psalms in Smith's Devotions were read responsively in the nursery,
by herself and daughters standing in a circle: only the two eldest
were allowed to breakfast with her and whatever company happened
to be in the house, for they were seldom without.   After breakfast,
we younger ones read to her in turns the Psalms and Lessons for the
day.   We were then permitted to pursue our childish sports, or to
walk in the garden, which I was allowed to do at pleasure; for, when
my father hesitated upon granting that privilege for fear I should
help myself to the fruit, Mrs. Richardson said, ' No, I have so much
confidence in her, that, if she is put upon honour, I am certain that
she will not touch so much as a gooseberry.'   A confidence I dare
safely aver that I never forfeited, and which has given me the power
of walking in any garden ever since, without the smallest desire to
touch any fruit, and taught me a lesson upon the restraint of appetite,
which has been useful to me all my life.   We all dined at one table,

and generally drank tea and spent the evening in Mrs. Richardson's parlour, where the practice was for one of the young ladies to read while the rest sat with mute attention round a large table, and employed themselves in some kind of needle-work. Mr. Richardson generally retired to his study, unless there was particular company.

"These are trifling and childish anecdotes, and savour, perhaps you may think too much of egotism. They certainly can be of no further use to you than as they mark the extreme benevolence, condescension, and kindness of this exalted genius, towards young people; for, in general society, I know *he* has been accused as being of few words and of a particularly reserved turn. He was, however, all his lifetime the patron and protector of the female sex. Miss M. (afterwards Lady G.) passed many years in his family. She was the bosom friend and contemporary of my mother ; and was so much considered as *enfant de famille* in Mr. Richardson's house, that her portrait is introduced into a family piece.

"He had many *protégées*;—a Miss Rosine, from Portugal, was consigned to his care; but of her, being then at school, I never saw much. Most of the ladies that resided much at his house acquired a certain degree of fastidiousness and delicate refinement, which, though amiable in itself, rather disqualified them from appearing in general society to the advantage that might have been expected, and rendered an intercourse with the world uneasy to themselves, giving a peculiar air of shyness and reserve to their whole address; of which habits his own daughters partook, in a degree that has been thought by some a little to obscure those really valuable qualifications and talents they undoubtedly possessed. Yet this was supposed to be owing more to Mrs. Richardson than to him; who, though a truly good woman, had high and Harlowean notions of parental authority, and kept the ladies in such order, and at such a distance, that he often lamented, as I have been told by my mother, that they were not more open and conversable with him.

"Besides those I have already named, I well remember a Mrs. Donellan, a venerable old lady, with sharp piercing eyes; Miss Mulso, &c., &c.; Secker, Archbishop of Canterbury; Sir Thomas Robinson (Lord Grantham), &c., &c., who were frequent visitors at his house in town and country. The ladies I have named were often staying at North End, at the period of his highest glory and reputation; and in their company and conversation his genius was matured. His benevolence was unbounded, as his manner of diffusing it was delicate and refined."[*]

Richardson was buried in the nave of St. Bride's Church ; and a stone was placed over his remains, merely recording his name, the year of his death, and his age. In this church were also interred Wynken de Worde, the famous printer ; the bowels of Sackville the poet, whom we shall presently have occasion to mention again ; and Sir Richard Baker, the author of the well-known book of English Chronicles. De Worde resided in Fleet Street.

Between Water Lane and the Temple, and leading out of

* Correspondence, &c., by Mrs. Barbauld, vol. i., p. 183.

Fleet Street by a street formerly called Whitefriars, which has been rebuilt, and christened Bouverie Street, is one of these precincts which long retained the immunities derived from their being conventual sanctuaries, and which naturally enough became as profane as they had been religious.   The one before us originated in a monastery of White Friars, an order of Carmelites, which formerly stood in Water Lane, and it acquired an infamous celebrity under the slang title of Alsatia.   The claims, however, which the inhabitants set up to protect debtors from arrest, seem to have originated in a charter granted to them by James I., in 1608.   For some time after the Reformation and the demolition of the old monastery, Whitefriars was not only a sufficiently orderly district, but one of the most fashionable parts of the city. Among others of the gentry, for instance, who had houses here at this period, was Sir John Cheke, King Edward VI.'s tutor, and afterwards Secretary of State.   The reader of our great modern novelist has been made almost as well acquainted with the place in its subsequent state of degradation and lawlessness, as if he had walked through it when its bullies were in full blow.   The rags of their Dulcineas hang out to dry, as if you saw them in a Dutch picture ; and the passages are redolent of beer and tobacco.   The sanctuary of Whitefriars is now extremely shrunk in its dimensions; and the inhabitants retain but a shadow of their privileges.   The nuisance, however, existed as late as the time of William III., who put an end to it; and the neighbourhood is still of more than doubtful virtue.   One alley, dignified by the title of Lombard Street, is of an infamy of such long standing, that it is said to have begun its evil courses long before the privilege of sanctuary existed, and to have maintained them up to the present moment.   The Carmelites complained of it, and the neighbours complain still.   In the Dramatis Personæ to Shadwell's play called the *Squire of Alsatia*, we have a set of characters so described as to bring us, one would think, sufficiently acquainted with the leading gentry of the neighbourhood; such as—

" *Cheatley*. A rascal, who by reason of debts dares not stir out of *White-fryers*, but there inveigles young heirs in tail, and helps them to goods and money upon great disadvantages; is bound for them, and shares for them till he undoes them. A lewd, impudent, debauch'd fellow, very expert in the *cant* about the town.

" *Shamwell*. Cousin to the Belfonds; an heir, who being ruined by Cheatley, is made a decoy-duck for others: not daring to stir out of

H

Alsatia, where he lives: is bound with Cheatley for heirs, and lives upon 'em a dissolute, debauched life.

"*Capt. Hackman.* A block-head bully of Alsatia; a cowardly, impudent, blustering fellow; formerly a sergeant in Flanders, run from his colours, retreated into White-fryers for a very small debt, where by the Alsatians he is dubbed a Captain, marries one that lets lodgings, sells cherry brandy, &c.

"*Scrapeall.* A hypocritical, repeating, praying, psalm-singing, precise fellow, pretending to great piety, a godly knave, who joins with Cheatley, and supplies young heirs with goods and money."

But Sir Walter, besides painting the place itself as if he had lived in it (vide *Fortunes of Nigel*, vol. ii.), puts these people in action, with a spirit beyond anything that Shadwell could have done, even though the dramatist had a bit of the Alsatian in himself—at least as far as drinking could go, and a flood of gross conversation.

Infamous, however, as this precinct was, there were some good houses in it, and some respectable inhabitants. The first Lord Sackville lived there; another inhabitant was Ogilby, who was a decent man, though a bad poet, and taught dancing; and Shirley another. It appears also to have been a resort of fencing-masters, which probably helped to bring worse company. They themselves, indeed, were in no good repute. One of them, a man of the name of Turner, living in White-friars, gave rise to a singular instance of revenge recorded in the State Trials. Lord Sanquire, a Scotch nobleman, in the time of James I., playing with Turner at foils, and making too great a show of his wish to put down a master of the art (probably with the insolence common to the nobility of that period), was pressed upon so hard by the man, that he received a thrust which put out one of his eyes. "This mischief," says Wilson, "was much regretted by Turner; and the baron, being conscious to himself that he meant his adversary no good, took the accident with as much patience as men that lose one eye by their own default use to do for the preservation of the other." "Some time after," continues this writer, "being in the court of the late great Henry of France, and the King (courteous to strangers), entertaining discourse with him, asked him, ' How he lost his eye:' he (cloathing his answer in a better shrowd than a plain fencer's) told him ' It was done with a sword.' The King replies, 'Doth the man live?' and that question gave an end to the discourse, but was the beginner of a strange confusion in his working fancy, which neither time nor distance could compose, carrying it in

his breast some years after, till he came into England, where
he hired two of his countrymen, Gray and Carliel, men of low
and mercenary spirits, to murther him, which they did with
a case of pistols in his house in Whitefriars many years
after."* For many years—read five—enough, however, to
make such a piece of revenge extraordinary. Gray and
Carliel were among his followers. Gray, however, did not
assist in the murder. His mind misgave him; and Carliel
got another accomplice, named Irweng. "These two, about
seven o'clock in the evening (to proceed in the words of
Coke's report), came to a house in the Friars, which Turner
used to frequent, as he came to his school, which was near
that place, and finding Turner there, they saluted one another;
and Turner, with one of his friends, sat at the door asking
them to drink; but Carliel and Irweng, turning about to cock
the pistol, came back immediately, and Carliel, drawing it
from under his coat, discharged it upon Turner, and gave
him a mortal wound near the left pap; so that Turner, after
having said these words, 'Lord, have mercy upon me! I am
killed,' immediately fell down. Whereupon Carliel and
Irweng fled, Carliel to the town, Irweng towards the river;
but mistaking his way, and entering into a court where they
sold wood, which was no thoroughfare, he was taken. Carliel
likewise fled, and so did also the Baron of Sanchar. The
ordinary officers of justice did their utmost, but could not
take them; for, in fact, as appeared afterwards, Carliel fled
into Scotland, and Gray towards the sea, thinking to go to
Sweden, and Sanchar hid himself in England."†

James, who had shown such favour to the Scotch as to
make the English jealous, and who also hated an ill-natured
action, when it was not to do good to any of his favourites,
thought himself bound to issue a promise of reward for the
arrest of Sanquire and the others. It was successful; and all
three were hung, Carliel and Irweng in Fleet Street, opposite
the great gate of Whitefriars (the entrance of the present
Bouverie Street), and Sanquire in Palace Yard, before Westminster Hall. He made a singular defence, very good and
penitent, and yet remarkably illustrative of the cheap rate at
which plebeian blood was held in those times; and no doubt
his death was a great surprise to him. The people, not yet

* Life and Reign of King James I., quoted in Howell's State Trials,
vol. ii., p. 745.
† State Trials, *ut supra*, p. 762.

H 2

enlightened on these points, took his demeanour in such good part, that they expressed great pity for him, till they perceived that he died a Catholic!

This and other pretended sanctuaries were at length put down by an Act of Parliament passed about the beginning of the last century. It is curious that the once lawless domain of Alsatia should have had the law itself for its neighbour; but Sir Walter has shown us, that they had more sympathies thar. might be expected. It was a local realisation of the old proverb of extremes meeting. We now step out of this old chaos into its quieter vicinity, which, however, was not always as quiet as it is now. The Temple, as its name imports, was once the seat of the Knights Templars, an order at once priestly and military, originating in the crusades, and whose business it was to defend the Temple at Jerusalem. How they degenerated, and what sort of vows they were in the habit of making, instead of those of chastity and humility, the modern reader need not be told, after the masterly pictures of them in the writer from whom we have just taken another set of ruffians. The Templars were dissolved in the reign of Edward II., and their house occupied by successive nobles, till it came into the possession of the law, in whose hands it was confirmed "for ever" by James I. We need not enter into the origin of its division into two parts, the Inner and Middle Temple. Suffice to say, that the word Middle, which implies a third Temple, refers to an outer one, or third portion of the old buildings, which does not appear to have been ever occupied by lawyers, but came into possession of the celebrated Essex family, whose name is retained in the street where it was situated, on the other side of Temple Bar. There is nothing remaining of the ancient buildings but the church built in 1185, which is a curiosity justly admired, particularly for its effigies of knights, some of whose cross legs indicate that they had either been to the Holy Land, or have been supposed to or vowed to go thither. One of the band is acertained to have been Geoffrey de Magnavile, Earl of Essex, who was killed at Benwell in Cambridgeshire, in 1148. Among the others are supposed to be the Marshals, first, second, and third Earls of Pembroke, who all died in the early part of the thirteenth century. But even these have not been identified upon any satisfactory grounds; and with regard to some of the rest, not so much as a probable conjecture has been offered.

As it is an opinion still prevailing, that these cross-legged knights are Knights Templars, we have copied below the

TOMBS OF KNIGHTS IN TEMPLE CHURCH.

most complete information respecting them which we have hitherto met with. And the passage is otherwise curious.*

* "It is an opinion which universally prevails with regard to those cross-legged monuments," says Dr. Nash, "that they were all erected to the memory of Knights Templars. Now to me it is very evident that not one of them belonged to that order; but, as Mr. Habingdon, in describing this at Alve church, hath justly expressed it, to Knights of the Holy Voyage. For the order of Knights Templars followed the rule of the Canons regular of St. Austin, and, as such, were under a vow of celibacy. Now there is scarcely one of these monuments which is certainly known for whom it is erected; but it is as certain, that the person it represented was a married man. The Knights Templars always wore a white habit, with a red cross on the left shoulder. I believe, not a single instance can be produced of either

The two Temples, or law colleges, occupy a large space of ground between Whitefriars and Essex Street; Fleet Street bounding them on the north, and the river on the south. They compose an irregular mass of good substantial houses, in lanes and open places, the houses being divided into chambers, or floors for separate occupants, some of which are let to persons not in the profession.   The garden about forty years ago was enlarged, and a muddy tract under it, on the side of the Thames, converted into a pleasant walk.   This garden is still not very large, but it deserves its name both for trees and flowers.   There is a descent into it after the Italian fashion, from a court with a fountain in it, surrounded with trees, through which the view of the old walls and buttresses of the Middle Temple Hall is much admired.   But a poet's hand has touched the garden, and made it bloom with roses above the real.   It is the scene in Shakspeare, of the origin of the factions of York and Lancaster.

the mantle or cross being carved on any of these monuments, which surely would not have been omitted, as by it they were distinguished from all other orders, had these been really designed to represent Knights Templars. Lastly, this order was not confined to England only, but dispersed itself all over Europe : yet it will be very difficult to find one cross-legged monument anywhere out of England; whereas they would have abounded in France, Italy, and elsewhere, had it been a fashion peculiar to that famous order.   But though, for these reasons, I cannot allow the cross-legged monuments to have been for Knights Templars, yet they had some relation to them, being the memorials of those zealous devotees, who had either been in Palestine, personally engaged in what was called the Holy War, or had laid themselves under a vow to go thither, though perhaps they were prevented from it by death. Some few, indeed, might possibly be erected to the memory of persons who had made pilgrimages there merely out of private devotion. Among the latter, probably, was that of the lady of the family of Mepham, of Mepham in Yorkshire, to whose memory a cross-legged monument was placed in a chapel adjoining to the one collegiate church of Howden, in Yorkshire, and is at this day remaining, together with that of her husband on the same tomb. As this religious madness lasted no longer than the reign of Henry III. (the tenth and last crusade being published in the year 1268), and the whole order of Knights Templars was dissolved by Edward II., military expeditions to the Holy Land, as well as devout pilgrimages there, had their period by the year 1312; consequently none of those cross-legged monuments are of a later date than the reign of Edward II., or beginning of Edward III., nor of an earlier than that of King Stephen, when these expeditions first took place in this kingdom."— *History and Antiquities of Worcestershire*, fol. vol. i., p. 31. Since Dr. Nash wrote, however, it has been denied that even the cross legs had any thing to do with crusades.

PLANTAGENET.

" Since you are tongue-ty'd, and so loth to speak.
In dumb significence proclaim your thoughts;
Let him that is a true born gentleman,
And stands upon the honour of his birth,
If he suppose that I have pleaded truth,
From off this brier pluck a white rose with me.

SOMERSET.

Let him that is no coward nor no flatterer,
But dare maintain the party of the truth,
Pluck a red rose from off this thorn with me.

WARWICK.

I love no colours; and, without all colour
Of base insinuating flattery,
I pluck this white rose with Plantagenet.

SUFFOLK.

I pluck this red rose with young Somerset;
And say withal I think he held the right."

There were formerly rooks in the Temple trees, a colony brought by Sir Edward Northey, a well-known lawyer in Queen Anne's time, from his grounds at Epsom. It was a pleasant thought, supposing that the colonists had no objection. The rook is a grave legal bird, both in his coat and habits; living in communities, yet to himself; and strongly addicted to discussions of *meum* and *tuum*. The neighbourhood, however, appears to have been too much for him; for, upon inquiring on the spot, we were told that there had been no rooks for many years.

The oldest mention of the Temple as a place for lawyers has been commonly said to be found in a passage of Chaucer, who is reported to have been of the Temple himself. It is in his character of the Manciple, or Steward, whom he pleasantly pits against his learned employers, as outwitting even themselves :

" A gentle manciple was there of a temple,
Of which achatours (purchasers) mighten take ensample,
For to ben wise in buying ot vitáille.
For whether that be paid, or took by taille,
Algate he waited so in his achate,
That he was ay before in good estate;
Now is not that of God a full fair grace,
That such a lewèd (ignorant) mannès wit shall pass
The wisdom of a heap of learned men ? " *

* Prologue to the Canterbury Tales. We quote no edition, because where we could we have modernised the spelling; which is a justice

Spenser, in his epic way, not disdaining to bring the home
liest images into his verse, for the sake of the truth in them,
speaks of—

> —— "those *bricky* towers
> The which on Thames' broad aged back do ride,
> Where now the studious lawyers have their bowers ;
> There whilom wont the Templar Knights to bide,
> Till they decayed through pride."*

The "studious lawyers," in their towers by the water side,
present a quiet picture. Yet in those times, it seems, they
were apt to break into overt actions of vivacity, a little
excessive, and such as the habit of restraint inclines people
to, before they have arrived at years of discretion.   In
Henry VIII.'s time the gentlemen of the Temple were addicted
to "shove and slip-groats,"† which became forbidden them
under a penalty; and in the age in which Spenser wrote, so
many encounters had taken place, of a dangerous description,
that Templars were prohibited from carrying any other
weapon into the hall (the dining room), "than a dagger or
knife,"—"as if," says Mr. Malcolm, "those were not more
than sufficient to accomplish unpremeditated deaths"‡ We
are to suppose, however, that gentlemen would not kill each
other, except with swords. The dagger, or carving knife,
which it was customary to carry about the person in those
days, was for the mutton.§

A better mode of recreating and giving vent to their

to this fine old author in a quotation, in order that nobody may pass
it over. With regard to Chaucer being of the Temple, and to his
beating the Franciscan in Fleet Street, all which is reported, depends
upon the testimony of a Mr. Buckley, who, according to Speght, had
seen a Temple record to that effect.

* Prothalamion.

† " Shove-groat, named also Slyp-groat, and Slide-thrift, are sports
occasionally mentioned by the writers of the sixteenth and seventeenth
centuries, and probably were analogous to the modern pastime called
Justice Jervis, or Jarvis, which is confined to common pot-houses, and
only practised by such as frequent the tap-rooms."—*Strutt's Sports
and Pastimes of the People of England*, 1828, chap. i., sect. xix. It is
played with halfpence, which are jerked with the palm of the hand
from the edge of a table, towards certain numbers described upon it.

‡ Londinium Redivivum, vol. ii., p. 290.

§ Sir John Davies, who was afterwards Lord Chief Justice of the
King's Bench, and wrote a poem on the Art of Dancing (so lively was
the gravity of those days !) "bastinadoed" a man at dinner in the
Temple Hall, for which he was expelled. The man probably deserved
it, for Davies had a fine nature ; and he went back again by favour
of the excellent Lord Ellesmere.

animal spirits, was the custom prevalent among the lawyers at that period of presenting masques and pageants. They were great players, with a scholarly taste for classical subjects; and the gravest of them did not disdain to cater in this way for the amusement of their fellows, sometimes for that of crowned heads. The name of Bacon is to be found among the "getters up" of a show at Gray's Inn, for the entertainment of the sovereign; and that of Hyde, on a similar occasion, in the reign of Charles I.

A masque has come down to us written by William Browne, a disciple of Spenser, expressly for the society of which he was a member, and entitled the *Inner Temple Masque*. It is upon the story of Circe and Ulysses, and is worthy of the school of poetry out of which he came. Beaumont wrote another, called the *Masque of the Inner Temple and Gray's Inn*. A strong union has always existed between the law and the belles-lettres, highly creditable to the former, or rather naturally to be expected from the mode in which lawyers begin their education, and the diversity of knowledge which no men are more in the way of acquiring afterwards. Blackstone need not have written his farewell to the Muses. If he had been destined to be a poet, he could not have taken his leave; and, as an accomplished lawyer, he was always within the pale of the *literæ humaniores*. The greatest practical lawyers, such as Coke and Plowdon, may not have been the most literary, but those who have understood the law in the greatest and best spirit have; and the former, great as they may be, are yet but as servants and secretaries to the rest. They know where to find, but the others know best how to apply. Bacon, Clarendon, Selden, Somers, Cowper, Mansfield, where all men of letters. So are the Broughams and Campbells of the present day. Pope says, that Mansfield would have been another Ovid. This may be doubted; but nobody should doubt that the better he understood a poet, the fitter he was for universality of judgment. The greatest lawyer is the greatest legislator.

The "pert Templar," of whom we hear so much between the reigns of the Stuarts and the late King, came up with the growth of literature and the coffee-houses. Every body then began to write or to criticise; and young men, brought up in the mooting of points, and in the confidence of public speaking, naturally pressed among the foremost. Besides, a variety of wits had issued from the Temple in the reign of

Charles and his brother, and their successors in lodging took
themselves for their heirs in genius. The coffee-houses by
this time had become cheap places to talk in. They were
the regular morning lounge and evening resource; and every
lad who had dipped his finger and thumb into Dryden's
snuff-box, thought himself qualified to dictate for life. In
Pope's time these pretensions came to be angrily rejected,
partly, perhaps, because none of the reigning wits, with the
exception of Congreve, had had a Temple education.

> "Three college sophs, and three pert Templars came,
>   The same their talents, and their tastes the same;
>   Each prompt to query, answer, and debate,
>   And smit with love of poetry and prate."*

We could quote many other passages to the same purpose,
but we shall come to one presently which will suffice for all,
and exhibit the young Templar of those days in all the glory
of his impertinence. At present the Templars make no more
pretensions than other well-educated men. Many of them
are still connected with the literature of the day, but in the
best manner and with the soundest views; and if there is no
pretension to wit, there is the thing itself. It would be endless to name all the celebrated lawyers who have had to do
with the Temple. Besides, we shall have to notice the most
eminent of them in other places, where they passed a greater
portion of their lives. We shall therefore confine ourselves
to the mention of such as have lived in it without being
lawyers, or thrown a grace over it in connection with wit and
literature.

Chaucer, as we have just observed, is thought, upon slight
evidence, to have been of the Temple. We know not who
the Mr. Buckley was, that says he saw his name in the
record; and the name, if there, might have been that of
some other Chaucer. The name is said to be not unfrequent
in records under the Norman dynasty. We are told by
Thynne, in his *Animadversions* on Speght's edition of the
poet's works (published a few years ago from the manuscript
by Mr. Todd, in his *Illustrations of Chaucer and Gower*),
that "it is most certain to be gathered by circumstances of
records that the lawyers were not in the Temple until towards
the latter part of the reign of King Edward III., at which
time Chaucer was a grave man, holden in great credit, and
employed in embassy." "So that methinketh," adds the

* Dunciad, book ii.

writer, "he should not be of that house; and yet, if he then were, I should judge it strange that he should violate the rules of peace and gravity in those years."

The first English tragedy of any merit, *Gorbuduc*, was written in the Temple by Thomas Norton and Thomas Sackville, afterwards the celebrated statesman, and founder of the title of Dorset. He was author of a noble performance, the *Induction for the Mirrour of Magistrates*, in which there is a foretaste of the allegorical *gusto* of Spenser. Raleigh was of the Temple; Selden, who died in Whitefriars; Lord Clarendon; Beaumont; two other of our old dramatists, Ford and Marston (the latter of whom was lecturer of the Middle Temple); Wycherly, whom it is said the Duchess of Cleveland used to visit, in the habit of a milliner; Congreve, Rowe, Fielding, Burke, and Cowper. Goldsmith was not of the Temple, but he had chambers in it, died there, and was buried in the Temple Church. He resided, first on the Library Staircase, afterwards in King's Bench Walk, and finally at No. 2, Brick Court, where he had a first floor elegantly furnished. It was in one of the former lodgings that, being visited by Dr. Johnson, and expressing something like a shame-faced hope that he should soon be in lodgings better furnished, "Johnson," says Boswell, "at the same time checked him, and paid him a handsome compliment, implying that a man of talent should be above attention to such distinctions. 'Nay, sir, never mind that : *Nil te quæsiveris extra.*'* (It is only yourself that need be looked for). He died in Brick Court. It is said that when he was on his deathbed, the landing-place was filled with inquirers, not of the most mentionable description, who lamented him heartily, for he was lavish of his money as he went along Fleet Street. We are told by one of the writers of the life prefixed to his works (probably Bishop Percy, who contributed the greater part of it), that "he was generous in the extreme, and so strongly affected by compassion, that he has been known at midnight to abandon his rest in order to procure relief and an asylum for a poor dying object who was left destitute in the streets." This, surely, ought to be praise to no man, however benevolent : but it is, in the present state of society. However, the offices of the good Samaritan are now reckoned among the things that may be practised as well as preached, without diminution of a man's reputation for common-sense ; and this is a great step.

* Boswell's Life of Johnson, eighth edit., 8vo. 1816, vol. iv., p. 27.

We will here mention, that Goldsmith had another residence
in Fleet Street. He wrote his Vicar of Wakefield in Wine
Office Court. Of the curious circumstances under which this
delightful novel was sold, various inaccurate accounts have
been given. The following is Boswell's account, taken from
Dr. Johnson's own mouth :—

"I received one morning," said Johnson, "a message from poor
Goldsmith, that he was in great distress, and as it was not in his power
to come to me, begging that I would come to him as soon as possible.
I sent him a guinea, and promised to come to him directly. I accordingly went to him as soon as I was dressed, and found that his landlady had arrested him for his rent, at which he was in a violent
passion. I perceived that he had already changed my guinea, and had
a bottle of Madeira and a glass before him. I put the cork into the
bottle, desired he would be calm, and began to talk to him of the
means by which he might be extricated. He then told me that he had
a novel ready for the press, which he produced to me. I looked into
it, and saw its merit; told the landlady I should soon return, and
having gone to a bookseller, sold it for sixty pounds. I brought
Goldsmith the money, and he discharged his rent, not without rating
his landlady in a high tone for having used him so ill."*

Johnson himself lived for some time in the Temple. It was
there that he was first visited by his biographer, who took
rooms in Farrar's Buildings in order to be near him. His
appearance and manners on this occasion, especially as our
readers are now of the party, are too characteristic to be
omitted. "His chambers," says Boswell, "were on the first
floor of No. 1, Middle Temple Lane—and I entered them with
an impression given me by the Rev. Dr. Blair, of Edinburgh,
who had been introduced to him not long before, and described
his having ' found the giant in his den,' an expression which,
when I came to be pretty well acquainted with Johnson, I
repeated to him, and he was diverted at this picturesque
account of himself. . . .

"He received me very courteously; but it must be confessed that
his apartment, and furniture, and morning dress, were sufficiently
uncouth. His brown suit of clothes looked very rusty; he had on a
little shrivelled unpowdered wig, which was too small for his head;
his shirt-neck and knees of his breeches were loose; his black
worsted stockings ill-drawn up; and he had a pair of unbuckled
shoes by way of slippers. But all these slovenly particularities were
forgotten the moment he began to talk. Some gentlemen, whom I
do not recollect, were sitting with him; and when they went away, I
also rose; but he said to me, "Nay, don't go.'—' Sir,' said I, ' I am
afraid that I intrude upon you. It is benevolent to allow me to sit
and hear you.' He seemed pleased with this compliment which I

* Boswell's Life of Johnson, eighth edit. 1816, vol. i., p. 398.

sincerely paid him, and answered, ' Sir, I am obliged to any man who visits me.' "* (He meant that it relieved his melancholy.)

It was in a dress of this sort, and without his hat, that he was seen rushing one day after two of the highest-bred visitors conceivable, in order to hand one of them to her coach. These were his friend Beauclerc, of the St. Albans family, and Madame de Boufflers, mother (if we mistake not) of the Chevalier de Boufflers, the celebrated French wit. Her re-report, when she got home, must have been overwhelming ; but she was clever and amiable, like her son, and is said to have appreciated the talents of the great uncouth. Beauclerc, however, must repeat the story :—

"When Madame de Boufflers," says he, "was first in England, she was desirous to see Johnson. I accordingly went with her to his chambers in the Temple, where she was entertained with his conversation for some time. When our visit was over, she and I left him, and were got into Inner Temple Lane, when all at once I heard a noise like thunder. This was occasioned by Johnson, who, it seems, on a little recollection, had taken it into his head that he ought to have done the honours of his literary residence to a foreign lady of quality ; and eager to show himself a man of gallantry, was hurrying down the stairs in violent agitation. He overtook us before we reached the Temple-gate, and brushing in between me and Madame de Boufflers, seized her hand and conducted her to the coach. His dress was a rusty-brown morning suit, a pair of old shoes by way of slippers, a little shrivelled wig sticking on the top of his head, and the sleeves of his shirt and the knees of his breeches hanging loose. A considerable crowd of people gathered round, and were not a little struck by his singular appearance." †

It was in the Inner Temple Lane one night, being seized with a fit of merriment at something that touched his fancy, not without the astonishment of his companions, who could not see the joke, that Johnson went roaring all the way to the Temple-gate ; where, being arrived, he burst into such a convulsive laugh, says Boswell, that in order to support himself he "laid hold of one of the posts at the side of the foot-pavement, and sent forth peals so loud, that in the silence of the night, his voice seemed to resound from Temple-bar to Fleet-ditch. This most ludicrous exhibition," continues his follower, "of the awful, melancholy, and venerable Johnson, happened well to counteract the feelings of sadness which I used to experience when parting from him for a considerable time. I accompanied him to his door, where he gave me his blessing." ‡

* Boswell's Life of Johnson, eighth edit. 1816, vol. i., p. 378.
† Ibid, vol. ii., p. 421.
‡ Ibid, vol. ii., p. 271.

Between the Temple-gates, at one time, lived Bernard Lintot, who was in no better esteem with authors than the other great bookseller of those times, Jacob Tonson. There is a pleasant anecdote of Dr. Young's addressing him a letter by mistake, which Bernard opened, and found it begin thus:— "That Bernard Lintot is so great a scoundrel."—"It must have been very amusing," said Young, "to have seen him in his rage : he was a great sputtering fellow." *

Between the gates and Temple-bar, but nearer to the latter, was the famous Devil Tavern, where Ben Jonson held his club. Messrs. Child, the bankers, bought it in 1787, and the present houses were erected on its site. We believe that the truly elegant house of Messrs. Hoare, their successors, does not interfere with the place on which it stood. We rather think it was very near to Temple-bar, perhaps within a house or two. The club-room, which was afterwards frequently used for balls, was called the Apollo, and was large and handsome, with a gallery for music. Probably the house had originally been a private abode of some consequence. The *Leges Convivales*, which Jonson wrote for his club, and which are to be found in his works, are composed in his usual style of elaborate and compiled learning, not without a taste of that dictatorial self-sufficiency, which, notwithstanding all that has been said by his advocates, and the good qualities he undoubtedly possessed, forms an indelible part of his character. "Insipida poemata," says he, "nulla *recitantur*" (Let nobody repeat to us insipid poetry); as if all that he should read of his own must infallibly be otherwise. The club at the Devil does not appear to have resembled the higher one at the Mermaid, where Shakspeare and Beaumont used to meet him. He most probably had it all to himself. This is the tavern mentioned by Pope :—

> "And each true Briton is to Ben so civil,
> He swears the Muses met him at the Devil."

It was in good repute at the beginning of the last century. "I dined to-day," says Swift, in one of his letters to Stella, "with Dr. Garth and Mr. Addison at the Devil Tavern, near Temple-bar, and Garth treated : and it is well I dine every day, else I should be longer making out my letters ; for we are yet in a very dull state, only inquiring every day after new elections, where the Tories carry it among the new

* Spence's Anecdotes, Singer's edit. p. 355.

members six to one. Mr. Addison's election has passed easy
and undisputed; and I believe if he had a mind to be chosen
king, he would hardly be refused."* Yet Addison was a
Whig. Addison had not then had his disputes with Pope
and others; and his intercourse, till his sincerity became
doubted, was very delightful. It is impossible to read of those
famous wits dining together and not lingering upon the occasion a little, and wishing we could have heard them talk.
Yet wits have their uneasiness, because of their wit. Swift
was probably not very comfortable at this dinner. He was
then beginning to feel awkward with his Whig friends; and
Garth, in the previous month of September, had written a
defence of Godolphin, the ousted Minister, which was unhand-
somely attacked in the *Examiner* by their common acquaintance
Prior, himself formerly a Whig.

There was a multitude of famous shops and coffee-houses
in this quarter, all of which make a figure in the *Tatler* and
other works, such as Nando's coffee-house; Dick's (still extant as Richard's); the Rainbow (which is said to have been
indicted in former times for the *nuisance* of selling coffee);
Ben Tooke's (the bookseller); Lintot's; and Charles Mather's,
alias Bubble-boy, the Toyman, who, when Sir Timothy
Shallow accuses him of selling him a cane "for ten pieces,
while Tom Empty had as good a one for five," exclaims,
"Lord! Sir Timothy, I am concerned that you, whom I took
to understand canes better than anybody in town, should be
so overseen! Why, Sir Timothy, yours is a true *jambee*, and
esquire Empty's only a plain dragon." †

The fire of London stopped at the Temple Exchange coffee-
house; a circumstance which is recorded in an inscription,
stating the house to have been the last of the houses burnt,
and the first restored. The old front of this house was taken
down about a century ago; but on its being rebuilt, the stone
with the inscription was replaced.

But we must now cross over the way to Shire Lane, which
is close to Temple Bar on the opposite side.

* Swift's Works, *ut supra*, vol. iv., p. 41.
† *Tatler*, No. 142. According to the author of a lively rattling
book, conversant with the furniture of old times, Arbuthnot was a
great amateur in sticks. "My uncle," says he, "was universally
allowed to be as deeply skilled in caneology as any one, Dr. Arbuthnot
not excepted, whose science on important questions was quoted even
after his death; for his collection of the various headed sticks and
canes, from the time of the first Charles, taken together, was unri-
valled."—*Wine and Walnuts*, vol. i., p. 242.

Here, "in ancient times," says Maitland, writing in the middle of the last century, "were only posts, rails, and a chain, such as are now at Holborn, Smithfield, and Whitechapel bars. Afterwards there was a house of timber erected across the street, with a narrow gateway, and an entry on the south side of it under the house." The present gate was built by Wren after the great fire, but although the work of so great a master, is hardly worth notice as a piece of architecture. It must be allowed that Wren could do poor things as well as good, even when not compelled by a vestry. As the last of the city gates, however, we confess we should be sorry to see it pulled down, though we believe there is a general sense that it is in the way. If it were handsome or venerable we should plead hard for it, because it would then be a better thing than a mere convenience. The best thing we know of it is a jest of Goldsmith's; and the worst, the point on which the jest turned. Goldsmith was coming from Westminster Abbey, with Dr. Johnson, where they had been looking at the tombs in Poets' Corner, and Johnson had quoted a line from Ovid:—

"Forsitan et nostrum nomen miscebitur istis."
(Perhaps, some day, our names may mix with theirs.)

"When we got to Temple Bar," says Johnson, "Goldsmith stopped me, pointed to the heads upon it, and slily whispered to me ('in allusion,' says Boswell, 'to Dr. Johnson's supposed political opinions, and perhaps to his own,')

"'Forsitan et nostrum nomen miscebitur *istis*.'"
(Perhaps, some day, our names may mix with *theirs*.)

These heads belonged to the rebels who were executed for rising in favour of the Pretender. The brutality of such spectacles, which outrage the last feelings of mortality, and as often punish honest mistakes as anything else, is not likely to be repeated. Yet such an effect has habit in reconciling men's minds to the most revolting, and sometimes the most dangerous customs, that here were two Jacobites, one of whom made a jest of what we should now regard with horror. However, Johnson must often have felt bitterly as he passed there; and the jesting of such men is frequently nothing but salve for a wound.

Shire Lane still keeps its name, and we hope, however altered and improved, it will never have any other; for here, at the upper end, is described as residing, old Isaac Bickerstaff, the Tatler, the more venerable but not the more delightful double of Richard Steele, the founder of English periodical literature. The public-house called the Trumpet, now known as the Duke of York, at which the Tatler met his club, is still remaining. At his house in the lane he dates a great number of his papers, and receives many interesting visitors ; and here it was that he led down into Fleet Street that immortal deputation of " twaddlers " from the country, who, as a celebrated writer has observed, hardly seem to have settled their question of precedence to this hour.*

In Shire Lane is said to have originated the famous Kit-Kat Club, which consisted of " thirty-nine distinguished noblemen and gentlemen, zealously attached to the Protestant succession of the house of Hanover." " The club," continues a note in Spence by the editor, " is supposed to have derived its name from Christopher Katt, a pastry-cook, who kept the house where they dined, and excelled in making mutton-pies, which always formed a part of their bill of fare ; these pies, on account of their excellence, were called Kit-Kats. The summer meetings were sometimes held at the Upper Flask on Hampstead Heath."†

"You have heard of the Kit-Kat Club," says Pope to Spence. " The master of the house where the club met was Christopher Katt; Tonson was secretary. The day Lord Mohun and the Earl of Berwick were entered of it, Jacob said he saw they were just going to be ruined. When Lord Mohun broke down the gilded emblem on the top of his chair, Jacob complained to his friends, and said a man who would do that, would cut a man's throat. So that he had the good and the forms of the society much at heart. The paper was all in Lord Halifax's handwriting of a subscription of four hundred guineas for the encouragement of good comedies, and was dated 1709, soon after they broke up. Steele, Addison, Congreve, Garth, Vanbrugh, Manwaring, Stepney, Walpole, and Pulteney, were of it ; so was Lord Dorset and the present Duke. Manwaring, whom we hear nothing of now, was the ruling man in all conversations; indeed, what he wrote had very little merit in it. Lord Stanhope and the Earl of Essex were also members. Jacob has his own, and all their pictures, by Sir Godfrey Kneller. Each member gave his, and he is going to build a room for them at Barn Elms."‡

It is from the size at which these portraits were taken (a three-quarter length), that the word Kit-Kat came to be applied to pictures. The society afterwards met in higher places; but humbleness of locality is nothing in these matters. The refinement consists in the company, and in whatever they

* Tatler, No. 86.
† Spence's Anecdotes, by Singer, p. 337.   ‡ Ibid.

I

choose to throw a grace over, whether venison or beef. The great thing is, not the bill of fare, but, as Swift called it, the "bill of company."

We cross to the south side of the street again, and come to Mrs. Salmon's. It is a curious evidence of the fluctuation of the great tide in commercial and growing cities, that, a century ago, this immortal old gentlewoman, renowned for her wax-work, gives as a reason for removing from St. Martin's-le-Grand to Fleet Street, that it was "a more convenient place for the coaches of the quality to stand unmolested."* Some of the houses in this quarter are of the Elizabethan age, with floors projecting over the others, and looking pressed together like burrows. The inmates of these humble tenements (unlike those of great halls and mansions) seem as if they must have had their heights taken, and the ceiling made to fit. Yet the builders were liberal of their materials. Over the way, near the west corner of Chancery Lane, stood an interesting specimen of this style of building, in the house of the famous old angler, Isaac Walton.

Walton's was the second house from the lane, the corner house being an inn, long distinguished by the sign of the Harrow. He appears to have long lived here, carrying on the business of a linen-draper about the year 1624. Another person, John Mason, a hosier, occupied one-half of the tenement. Walton afterwards removed to another house in Chancery Lane, a few doors up from Fleet Street, on the west side, where he kept a sempster's, or milliner's shop.

A great deal has been said lately of the merits and demerits of angling, and Isaac has suffered in the discussion, beyond what is agreeable to the lovers of that gentle pleasure. Unfortunately the brothers of the angle do not argue ingenuously. They always omit the tortures suffered by the principal party, and affect to think you affected if you urge them; whereas their only reason for avoiding the point is, that it is not to be defended. If it is, we may defend, by an equal abuse of reason, any amusement which is to be obtained at another being's expense; and an evil genius might angle for ourselves, and twitch us up, bleeding and roaring, into an atmosphere that would stifle us. But fishes do not roar; they cannot express any sound of suffering; and therefore the angler chooses to think they do not suffer, more than it is convenient to him to fancy. Now it is a poor sport that depends for

* Tatler, as above, vol. iv., p. 600.

its existence on the want of a voice in the sufferer, and of imagination in the sportsman. Angling, in short, is not to be defended on any ground of reflection; and this is the worst thing to say of Isaac; for he was not unaware of the objections to his amusement, and he piqued himself upon being contemplative.

Anglers have been defended upon the ground of their having had among them so many pious men; but unfortunately men may be selfishly as well as nobly pious; and even charity itself may be practised, as well as cruelty deprecated, upon principles which have a much greater regard to a man's own safety and future comfort, than anything which concerns real Christian beneficence. Doubtless there have been many good and humane men anglers, as well as many pleasant men. There have also been some very unpleasant ones—Sir John Hawkins among them. They make a well-founded pretension to a love of nature and her scenery; but it is a pity they cannot relish it without this pepper to the poor fish. Walton's book contains many passages in praise of rural enjoyment, which affect us almost like the fields and fresh air themselves, though his brethren have exalted it beyond its value; and his lives of his angling friends, the Divines, have been preposterously over-rated. If angling is to be defended upon good and manly grounds, let it; it is no longer to be defended on any other. The best thing to be said for it (and the instance is worthy of reflection) is, that anglers have been brought up in the belief of its innocence, and that an inhuman custom is too powerful for the most humane. The inconsistency is to be accounted for on no other grounds; nor is it necessary or desirable that it should be. It is a remarkable illustration of what Plato said, when something was defended on the ground of its being a trifle, because it was a custom. "But custom," said he, "is no trifle." Here, among persons of a more equivocal description, are some of the humanest men in the world, who will commit what other humane men reckon among the most inhuman actions, and make an absolute pastime of it. Let one of their grandchildren be brought up in the reverse opinion, and see what he will think of it. This, to be sure, might be said to be only another instance of the effect of education; but nobody, the most unprejudiced, thinks it a bigotry in Shakspeare and Steele to have brought us to feel for the brute creation in general; and whatever we may incline to think for the accommodation of our propensities,

there will still remain the unanswered and always avoided
argument, of the dumb and torn fish themselves, who die
agonised, in the midst of our tranquil looking on, and for no
necessity.

John Whitney, author of the *Genteel Recreation, or the
Pleasures of Angling*, a poem printed in the year 1700,
recommends the lovers of the art to bait with the eyes of fish,
in order to decoy others of the same species. A writer in the
Censura Literaria exclaims, "What a Nero of Anglers doth
this proclaim John Whitney to have been! and how unworthy
to be ranked as a lover of the same pastime, which had been
so interestingly recommended by Isaac Walton, in his *Contemplative Man's Recreation*."*

But Isaac's contemplative man can content himself with
impaling live worms, and jesting about the tenderness with
which he treats them—using the worm, quoth Isaac, "as if
you loved him." Doubtless John thought himself as good a
man as Isaac. He poetizes, and is innocent with the best of
them, and probably would not have hurt a dog. However,
it must be allowed that he had less imagination than Walton,
and was more cruel, inasmuch as he could commit a cruelty
that was not the custom. Observe, nevertheless, that it was
the customary cruelty which led to the new one. Why
must these contemplative men commit any cruelty at all ?
The writer of the article in the *Censura* was, if we mistake
not, one of the kindest of human beings, and yet he could see
nothing erroneous in torturing a worm. "A good man,"
says the Scripture, "is merciful to his beast.". Therefore
"holy Mr. Herbert" very properly helps a horse out of a
ditch, and is the better for it all the rest of the day. Are
we not to be merciful to fish as well as beasts, merely because
the Scripture does not expressly state it ? Such are the
inconsistencies of mankind, during their very acquirement of
beneficence.

On the other side of the corner of Chancery Lane was
born a man of genius and benevolence, who would not have
hurt a fly—Abraham Cowley. His father was a grocer;
himself, one of the kindest, wisest, and truest gentlemen that
ever graced humanity. He has been pronounced by one,
competent to judge, to have been "if not a great poet, a
great man." But his poetry is what every other man's
poetry is, the flower of what was in him; and it is at least so

far good poetry, as it is the quintessence of amiable and deep reflection, not without a more festive strain, the result of his sociality. Pope says of him—

> "Forgot his epic, nay pindaric art;
> Yet still we love the language of his heart."*

His prose is admirable, and his character of Cromwell a masterpiece of honest enmity, more creditable to both parties than the zealous royalist was aware. Cowley, notwithstanding the active part he took in politics, never ceased to be a child at heart. His mind lived in books and bowers—in the sequestered "places of thought;" and he wondered and lamented to the last, that he had not realised the people he found there. His consolation should have been, that what he found in himself was an evidence that the people exist.

Chancery Lane, "the most ancient of any to the west," having been built in the time of Henry the Third, when it was called New Lane, which was afterwards altered to Chancellor's Lane, is the greatest legal thoroughfare in England. It leads from the Temple, passes by Sergeants' Inn, Clifford's Inn, Lincoln's Inn, and the Rolls, and conducts to Gray's Inn. Of the world of vice and virtue, of pain and triumph, of learning and ignorance, truth and chicanery, of impudence, violence, and tranquil wisdom, that must have passed through this spot, the reader may judge accordingly. There all the great and eloquent lawyers of the metropolis must have been, at some time or other, from Fortescue and Littleton, to Coke, Ellesmere, and Erskine. Sir Thomas More must have been seen going down with his weighty aspect; Bacon with his eye of intuition; the coarse Thurlow; and the reverend elegance of Mansfield. In Chancery Lane was born the celebrated Lord Strafford, who was sent to the block by the party he had deserted, the victim of his own false strength and his master's weakness. It is a curious evidence of the secret manners of those times, which are so often contrasted with the licence of the next reign, that Clarendon, in speaking of some love-letters of this lord, a married man, which transpired during his trial, calls them "things of levity." What would he have said had he found any love letters between Lady Carlisle and Pym? Of Southampton Buildings, on the site of which lived Shakspeare's friend, Lord Southampton, we shall speak imme-

* Imitations of Horace, Ep. i., book ii.

diately; and we shall notice Lincoln's Inn when we come to
the Western portion of Holborn. But we may here observe,
that on the wall of the Inn, which is in Chancery Lane, Ben
Jonson is said to have worked, at the time he was compelled
to assist his father-in-law at his trade of bricklaying. In the
intervals of his trowel, he is said to have handled his Horace
and Virgil. It is only a tradition, which Fuller has handed
down to us in his *Worthies;* but tradition is valuable when
it helps to make such a flower grow upon an old wall.

Sergeants' Inn, the first leading out of Chancery Lane,
near Fleet Street, has been what its name implies for many
generations. It was occasionally occupied by the Sergeants
as early as the time of Henry the Fourth, when it was called
Farringdon's Inn, though they have never, we believe, held
possession of the place but under tenure to the bishops of
Ely, or their lessees. Pennant counfounds this inn with
another of the same name, now no longer devoted to the same
purpose, in Fleet Street.* Sergeants' Inn in Fleet Street was
reduced to ruins in the great fire, but was soon after rebuilt
in a much more uniform style than before. It continued
after this to be occupied by the lawyers in 1730, when the
whole was taken down, and the present court erected. The
office of the Amicable Annuitant Society, on the east side of
the court, occupies the site of the ancient hall and chapel.
All the judges, as having been Sergeants-at-law before their
elevation to the bench, have still chambers in the inn in
Chancery Lane. The windows of this house are filled with
the armorial bearings of the members, who, when they are
knighted, are emphatically *equites aurati* (knights made
golden), at least as far as rings are concerned, for they give
rings on the occasion, with mottoes expressive of their sentiments upon law and justice. As to the *equites,* learned
"knights" or horsemen (till "knight" be restored to its
original meaning—servant) will never be anything but an
anomaly, especially since the brethren no longer even ride to
the Hall as they used. The arms of the body of Sergeants
are a golden shield with an ibis upon it; or, to speak
scientifically, "Or, an Ibis proper;" to which Mr. Jekyll
might have added, for motto, "*In medio tutissimus.*" The
same learned punster made an epigram upon the oratory and
scarlet robes of his brethren, which may be here repeated

* Pennant, *ut supra*, p. 172.

without offence, as the Sergeants have had among them some
of the best as well as most tiresome of speakers:

> "The Sergeants are a grateful race ;
> Their dress and language show it ;
> Their purple robes from Tyre we trace,
> Their arguments go to it."

One of the customs which used to be observed so late as
the reign of Charles I. in the creation of sergeants, was for
the new dignitary to go in procession to St. Paul's, and there
to choose his pillar, as it was expressed. This ceremony is
supposed to have originated in the ancient practice of the
lawyers taking each his station at one of the pillars in the
cathedral, and there waiting for clients. The legal sage stood,
it is said, with pen in hand, and dexterously noted down the
particulars of every man's case on his knee.

Clifford's Inn, leading out of Sergeants' Inn into Fleet
Street and Fetter Lane, is so called from the noble family
of De Clifford, who granted it to the students-at-law in the
reign of Edward III. The word inn (Saxon, chamber),
though now applied only to law places, and the better sort
of public-houses in which travellers are entertained, formerly
signified a great house, mansion, or family palace. So
Lincoln's Inn, the mansion of the Earls of Lincoln; Gray's
Inn, of the Lords Gray, &c. The French still use the word
hôtel in the same sense. Inn once made as splendid a figure
in our poetry, as the palaces of Milton:

> "Now whenas Phœbus, with his fiery waine,
> Unto his inne began to draw apace ;"*

says Spenser; and his disciple Browne after him:

> "Now had the glorious sun tane up his inne."†

There are three things to notice in Clifford's Inn : its little
bit of turf and trees ; its quiet ; and its having been the
residence of Robert Pultock, author of the curious narrative
Peter Wilkins, with its Flying Women. Who he was, is not
known ; probably a barrister without practice ; but he wrote
an amiable and interesting book. As to the sudden and
pleasant quiet in this little inn, it is curious to consider what
a small remove from the street produces it. But even in the
back room of a shop in the main street, the sound of the carts
and carriages becomes wonderfully deadened to the ear ; and
a remove, like Clifford's Inn, makes it remote or nothing.

* Faerie Queen, book vi., canto iii.
† Britannia's Pastorals, book i., song iii.

The garden of Clifford's Inn forms part of the area of the
ROLLS, so called from the records kept there, in rolls of parchment.   It is said to have been the house of an eminent Jew,
forfeited to the crown ; that is to say, it was most probably
taken from him, with all that it contained, by Henry III.,
who made it a house for converts from the owner's religion.
These converted Jews, most likely none of the best of their
race (for board and lodging are not arguments to the scrupulous), appear to have been so neglected, that the number of
them soon came to nothing, and Edward III. gave the place to
the Court of Chancery to keep its records in.   There is a fine
monument in the chapel to a Dr. Young, one of the Masters,
which, according to Vertue, was executed by Torregiano,
who built the splendid tomb in Henry VII.'s Chapel.   Sir
John Trevor, infamous for bribery and corruption, also lies
here.   "Wisely," says Pennant, "his epitaph is thus confined : ' Sir J. T. M.R. 1717.'   "Some other Masters," he
adds, "rest within the walls; among them Sir John Strange,
but without the quibbling line,

> ' Here lies an honest lawyer, that is Strange.' "

Another Master of the Rolls, who did honour to the profession, was Sir Joseph Jekyll, recorded by Pope as an

> .   .   .   .   "odd old Whig,
> Who never changed his principles or wig."

When Jekyll came into the office, many of the houses were
rebuilt, and to the expense of ten of them he added, out of his
own purse, as much as 350*l.* each house ; observing, that
" he would have them built as strong and as well as if they
were his own inheritance."*   The Master of the Rolls is a
great law dignitary, a sort of under-judge in Chancery,
presiding in a court by himself, though his most ostensible
office is to take care of the records in question.   He has a
house and garden on the spot, the latter secluded from public
view.   The house, however, has not been used as a residence
by the present holder of the office or his predecessor.

Between Chancery and Fetter Lane is the new church of
St. Dunstan's in the West—a great improvement upon the old
one, though a little too plain below for the handsome fret-
work of its steeple.   The old building was eminent for the
two wooden figures of wild men, who, with a gentleness not
to be expected of them, struck the hour with a little tap of

* Londinium Redivivum, vol. ii., p. 279.

their clubs. At the same time they moved their arms and heads, with a like avoidance of superfluous action. These figures were put up in the time of Charles II., and were thought not to confer much honour on the passengers who stood "gaping" to see them strike. But the passengers might surely be as alive to the puerility as any one else. An absurdity is not the least attractive thing in this world. They who objected to the gapers, probably admired more things than they laughed at. It must be remembered also, that when the images were set up, mechanical contrivances were much rarer than they are now. Two centuries ago, St. Dunstan's Churchyard, as it was called, being the portion of Fleet Street in front of the church, was famous for its booksellers' shops. The church escaped the great fire, which stopped within three houses of it, and consequently was one of the most ancient sacred edifices in London. It was supposed to have been built about the end of the fourteenth century, but had undergone extensive repairs. Besides the clock with the figures, it was adorned by a statue of Queen Elizabeth, which stood in a niche over the east end, and had been transferred thither about the middle of last century from the west side of old Ludgate, which was then removed.

The only repute of Fetter Lane in the present days is, or was, for sausages. But at one time it is said to have had the honour of Dryden's presence. The famous Praise God Barebones also, it seems, lived here, in a house for which he paid forty pounds a year, as he stated in his examination on a trial in the reign of Charles II.* He paid the above rent, he says "except during the war:" that is, we suppose, during the confusion of the contest between the King and the Parliament, when probably this worthy contrived to live rent free. In this neighbourhood also dwelt the infamous Elizabeth Brownrigg, who was executed in 1767 for the murder of one of her apprentices. Her house, with the cellar in which she used to confine her starved and tortured victims, and from the grating of which their cries of distress were heard, was one of those on the east side of the lane, looking into the long and narrow alley behind, called Flower-de-Luce Court. It was some years ago in the occupation of a fishing-tackle maker.

Johnson once lived in Fetter Lane, but the circumstances of his abode there have not transpired. We now, however, come to a cluster of his residences in Fleet Street, of which

* See Malcolm's Londinium Redivivum, vol. iii., 453.

place he is certainly the great presiding spirit, the *Genius loci*. He was conversant for the greater part of his life with this street, was fond of it, frequented its Mitre Tavern above any other in London, and has identified its name and places with the best things he ever said and did.   It was in Fleet Street, we believe, that he took the poor girl up in his arms, put her to bed in his own house, and restored her to health and her friends ; an action sufficient to redeem a million of the asperities of temper occasioned by disease, and to stamp him, in spite of his bigotry, a good Christian.   Here, at all events, he walked and talked, and shouldered wondering porters out of the way, and mourned, and philosophised, and was "a good-natured fellow" (as he called himself), and roared with peals of laughter till midnight echoed to his roar.

"We walked in the evening," says Boswell, " in Greenwich Park. He asked me, I suppose by way of trying my disposition, 'Is not this very fine?' Having no exquisite relish of the beauties of nature, and being more delighted with the busy hum of men, I answered, 'Yes, sir; but not equal to Fleet Street.' *Johnson.* 'You are right, sir.' "*

Boswell vindicates the tastes here expressed by the example of a "very fashionable baronet," who, on his attention being called to the fragrance of a May evening in the country, observed, "This may be very well, but I prefer the smell of a flambeau at the playhouse."   The baronet here alluded to was Sir Michael le Fleming, who, by way of comment on his indifference to fresh air, died of an apoplectic fit while conversing with Lord Howick (the late Earl Grey), at the Admiralty.†   However, Johnson's *ipse dixit* was enough.   He wanted neither Boswell's vindication, nor any other.   He was melancholy, and glad to be taken from his thoughts; and London furnished him with an endless flow of society.

Johnson's abodes in Fleet Street were in the following order:—First, in Fetter Lane, then in Boswell Court, then in Gough Square, in the Inner Temple Lane, in Johnson's Court, and finally, and for the longest period, in Bolt Court, where he died.   His mode of life, during a considerable portion of his residence in these places, is described in a communication to Boswell by the Rev. Dr. Maxwell, assistant preacher at the Temple, who was intimate with Johnson for many years, and who spoke of his memory with affection.

* Boswell, *ut supra*, vol. i., p. 441.
† Malone, on the passage in Boswell, ibid.

"About twelve o'clock," says the doctor, "I commonly visited him, and found him in bed, or declaiming over his tea, which he drank very plentifully. He generally had a levee of morning visitors, chiefly men of letters ; Hawkesworth, Goldsmith, Murphy, Langton, Steevens, Beauclerk, &c., &c., and sometimes learned ladies ; particularly, I remember, a French lady of wit and fashion doing him the honour of a visit. He seemed to me to be considered as a kind of public oracle, whom everybody thought they had a right to visit and consult; and, doubtless, they were well rewarded. I never could discover how he found time for his compositions. He declaimed all the morning, then went to dinner at a tavern, where he commonly staid late, and then drank his tea at some friend's house, over which he loitered a great while, but seldom took supper. I fancy he must have read and wrote chiefly in the night; for I can scarcely recollect that he ever refused going with me to a tavern, and he often went to Ranelagh, which he deemed a place of innocent recreation.

"He frequently gave all the silver in his pocket to the poor, who watched him between his house and the tavern where he dined. He walked the streets at all hours, and said he was never robbed, for the rogues knew he had little money, nor had the appearance of having much.

"Though the most accessible and communicative man alive, yet when he suspected that he was invited to be exhibited, he constantly spurned the invitation.

"Two young women from Staffordshire visited him when I was present, to consult him on the subject of Methodism, to which they were inclined. 'Come (said he), you pretty fools, dine with Maxwell and me at the Mitre, and we will talk over that subject; which they did, and after dinner he took one of them on his knees, and fondled them for half an hour together."*

This anecdote is exquisite. It shows, that however impatient he was of having his own superstitions canvassed, he was loth to see them inflicted on others. He is here a harmless Falstaff, with two innocent damsels on his knees, in lieu of Mesdames Ford and Page.

In Gough Square, Johnson wrote part of his Dictionary. He had written the Rambler and taken his high stand with the public before. "At this time," says Barber, his servant, "he had little for himself, but frequently sent money to Mr. Shiels when in distress." (Shiels was one of his amanuenses in the dictionary.) His friends and visitors in Gough Square are a good specimen of what they always were—a miscellany creditable to the largeness of his humanity. There was Cave, Dr. Hawkesworth, Miss Carter, Mrs. Macauley (two ladies who must have looked strangely at one another), Mr. (afterwards Sir Joshua) Reynolds, Langton, Mrs. Williams (a poor poetess whom he maintained in his house), Mr. Levett (an

* Boswell, vol. ii., p. 117.

apothecary on the same footing), Garrick, Lord Orrery, Lord Southwell, and Mrs. Gardiner, wife of a tallow chandler on Snow-hill—" not in the learned way," said Mr. Barber, " but a worthy good woman." With all his respect for rank, which doubtless he regarded as a special dispensation of Providence, his friend Beauclerk's notwithstanding, * Johnson never lost sight of the dignity of goodness. He did not, however, confine his attentions to those who were noble or amiable ; though we are to suppose, that everybody with whom he chose to be conversant had some good quality or other ; unless, indeed, he patronised them as the Duke of Montague did his ugly dogs, because nobody would if he did not. The great secret, no doubt, was, that he was glad of the company of any of his fellow-creatures who would bear and forbear with him, and for whose tempers he did not care as much as he did for their welfare. And he was giving alms ; which was a catholic part of religion, in the proper sense of the word.

"He nursed," says Mrs. Thrale, in her superfluous style, " *whole nests* of people in his house, where the lame, the blind, the sick, and the sorrowful found a sure retreat from all the evils whence his little income could secure them; and commonly spending the middle of the week at our house, he kept his numerous family in Fleet Street upon a settled allowance ; but returned to them every Saturday to give them three good dinners and his company, before he came back to us on the Monday night, treating them with the same, or perhaps more, ceremonious civility, than he would have done by as many people of fashion, making the Holy Scripture thus the rule of his conduct, and only expecting salvation as he was able to obey its precepts." †

Johnson's female inmates were not like the romantic ones of Richardson.

" We surely cannot but admire," says Boswell, " the benevolent exertions of this great and good man, especially when we consider how grievously he was afflicted with bad health, and how uncomfortable his home was made by the perpetual jarring of those whom he charitably accommodated under his roof. He has sometimes suffered me to talk jocularly of his group of females, and call them his *seraglio*. He thus mentions them, together with honest Levitt, in one of his letters to Mrs. Thrale : ' Williams hates everybody ; Levett hates Desmoulins, and does not love Williams ; Desmoulins hates them both ; Poll loves none of them.' " ‡

Of his residence in Inner Temple Lane we have spoken

* Beauclerk, of the St. Alban's family, was a descendant of Charles II., whom he resembled in face and complexion, for which Johnson by no means liked him the less.

† Anecdotes of Samuel Johnson, &c.   Allman, 1822, p. 69.

‡ Boswell, vol. iii., p. 398.

before. He lived there six or seven years, and then removed to Johnson's Court, No. 7, where he resided for ten. Johnson's Court is in the neighbourhood of Gough Square. It was during this period that he accompanied his friend Boswell to Scotland, where he sometimes humorously styled himself " Johnson of that *ilk*" (that same, or Johnson of Johnson), in imitation of the local designations of the Scottish chiefs. In

JOHNSON'S HOUSE IN BOLT COURT.

1776, in his sixty-seventh year, still adhering to the neighbourhood, he removed into Bolt Court, No. 8, where he died eight years after, on the 13th December, 1784. In Bolt Court he had a garden, and perhaps in Johnson's Court and

Gough Square : which we mention to show how tranquil and removed these places were, and convenient for a student who wished, nevertheless, to have the bustle of London at hand. Maitland (one of the compilers upon Stow), who published his history of London in 1739, describes Johnson and Bolt Courts as having " good houses, well inhabited ;" and Gough Square he calls fashionable.*

Johnson was probably in every tavern and coffee-house in Fleet Street. There is one which has taken his name, being styled, *par excellence*, " Doctor Johnson's Coffee-house." But the house he most frequented was the Mitre tavern, on the other side of the street, in a passage leading to the Temple. It was here, as we have seen, that he took his two innocent theologians, and paternally dandled them out of their misgivings on his knee. The same place was the first of the kind in which Boswell met him. " We had a good supper," says the happy biographer, " and port wine, of which he then sometimes drank a bottle." (At intervals he abstained from all fermented liquors for a long time.) " The orthodox, high-church sound of the Mitre, the figure and manner of the celebrated Samuel Johnson, the extraordinary power and precision of his conversation, and the pride arising from finding myself admitted as his companion, produced a variety of sensations, and a pleasing elevation of mind beyond what I had before experienced."† They sat till between one and two in the morning. He told Boswell at that period that " he generally went abroad at about four in the afternoon, and seldom came home till two in the morning. I took the liberty to ask if he did not think it wrong to live thus, and not to make more use of his great talents. He owned it was a bad habit."

The next time, Goldsmith was with them, when Johnson made a remark which comes home to everybody, namely, that granting knowledge in some cases to produce unhappiness, " knowledge *per se* was an object which every one would *wish* to attain, though, perhaps, he might not take the trouble necessary for attaining it." One of his most curious remarks followed, occasioned by the mention of Campbell, the author

* Johnson's Court runs into Gough Square, " a place lately built with very handsome houses, and well inhabited by persons of fashion." —*Maitland's History and Survey of London*, by Entick, folio, 1756 p. 961.

† Boswell, vol. i., p. 384.

of the *Hermippus Redivivus*, on which Boswell makes a no less curious comment. "Campbell," said Johnson, "is a good man, a pious man. I am afraid he has not been in the inside of a church for many years; but he never passes a church without pulling off his hat. This shows that he has good principles." On which, says Boswell in a note, "I am inclined to think he was misinformed as to this circumstance. I own I am jealous for my worthy friend Dr. John Campbell. For though *Milton* could without remorse absent himself from public worship, *I* cannot."*

It was at their next sitting in this house, at which the Rev. Dr. Ogilvie, a Scotch writer, was present, that Johnson made his famous joke, in answer to that gentleman's remark, that Scotland has a great many "noble wild prospects." *Johnson.* "I believe, sir, you have a great many. Norway, too, has noble, wild prospects; and Lapland is remarkable for prodigious, noble, wild prospects. But, sir, let me tell you, the noblest prospect which a Scotchman ever sees is the high road that leads him to England!" "This unexpected and pointed sally," says Boswell, "produced a roar of applause. After all, however" (he adds), "those who admire the rude grandeur of nature, cannot deny it to Caledonia."†

Johnson had the highest opinion of a tavern, as a place in which a man might be comfortable, if he could anywhere. Indeed, he said that the man who could not enjoy himself in a tavern, could be comfortable nowhere. This, however, is not to be taken to the letter. Extremes meet; and Johnson's uneasiness of temper led him into the gayer necessities of Falstaff. However, it is assuredly no honour to a man, not to be able to "take his ease at his inn." "There is no private house," said Johnson, talking on this subject, "in which people can enjoy themselves so well as at a capital tavern. Let there be ever so great a plenty of good things, ever so much grandeur, ever so much elegance, ever so much desire that everybody should be easy, in the nature of things it cannot be: there must always be some degree of care and anxiety. The master of the house is anxious to entertain his guests; the guests are anxious to be agreeable to him; and no man, but a very impudent dog indeed, can as freely command what is in another man's house as if it were his own. Whereas, at a tavern, there is a general freedom from anxiety. You are sure you are welcome; and the more noise you

* Boswell, vol. i., p. 400.   † Id., p. 408.

make, the more trouble you give, the more good things you call for, the welcomer you are. No servants will attend you with the alacrity which waiters do, who are incited by the prospect of an immediate reward in proportion as they please. No, sir, there is nothing which has yet been contrived by man, by which so much happiness is produced, as by a good tavern or inn." He then repeated with great emotion Shenstone's lines :—

> " Whoe'er has travelled life's dull round,
> Where'er his stages may have been,
> May sigh to think he still has found
> The warmest welcome at an inn." *

" Sir John Hawkins," says Boswell in a note on this passage, " has preserved very few *memorabilia* of Johnson." There is, however, to be found in his bulky tome, a very excellent one upon this subject. " In contradiction to those who, having a wife and children, prefer domestic enjoyments to those which a tavern affords, I have heard him assert, that *a tavern chair was the throne of human felicity.* ' As soon ' (said he), ' as I enter the door of a tavern, I experience an oblivion of care, and a freedom from solicitude : when I am seated, I find the master courteous, and the servants obsequious to my call, anxious to know and ready to supply my wants : wine there exhilarates my spirits, and prompts me to free conversation, and an interchange of discourse with those whom I most love ; I dogmatise, and am contradicted ; and in this conflict of opinion and sentiments I find delight.' "

The following anecdote is highly to Johnson's credit, and equally worthy of every one's attention. " Johnson was known to be so rigidly attentive to the truth," says Boswell, " that even in his common conversation the slightest circumstance was mentioned with exact precision. The knowledge of his having such a principle and habit made his friends have a perfect reliance on the truth of everything that he told, however it might have been doubted if told by many others. As an instance of this I may mention an odd incident, which he related as having happened to him one night in Fleet Street. ' A gentlewoman' (said he) ' begged I would give her my arm to assist her in crossing the street, which I accordingly did ; upon which she offered me a shilling, supposing me to be the watchman. I perceived that she was somewhat in liquor.' This, if told by most people, would

* Boswell, vol. ii., p. 469.

have been thought an invention; when told by Johnson, it was believed by his friends, as much as if they had seen what passed." *

The gentlewoman, however, might have taken him for the watchman without being in liquor, if she had no eye to discern a great man through his uncouthness. Davies, the bookseller, said, that he "laughed like a rhinoceros." It may be added he walked like a whale; for it was rolling rather than walking. "I met him in Fleet Street," says Boswell, "walking, or rather, indeed, moving along; for his peculiar march is thus described in a very just and picturesque manner, in a short life of him published very soon after his death:—'When he walked the streets, what with the constant roll of his head, and the concomitant motion of his body, he appeared to make his way by that motion independent of his feet.' That he was often much stared at," continues Boswell, "while he advanced in this manner, may be easily believed; but it was not safe to make sport of one so robust as he was. Mr. Langton saw him one day, in a fit of absence, by a sudden start, drive the load off a porter's back, and walk forwards briskly, without being conscious of what he had done. The porter was very angry, but stood still, and eyed the huge figure with much earnestness, till he was satisfied that his wisest course was to be satisfied and take up his burden again." †

There is another remark on Fleet Street and its superiority to the country, which must not be passed over. Boswell, not having Johnson's reasons for wanting society, was a little overweening and gratuitous on this subject; and on such occasions the doctor would give him a knock. "It was a delightful day," says the biographer; "as we walked to St. Clement's Church, I again remarked that Fleet Street was the most cheerful scene in the world; 'Fleet Street,' said I, 'is in my mind more delightful than Tempè.' *Johnson.*—'Ay, sir, but let it be compared with Mull.'" ‡

The progress of knowledge, even since Johnson's time, has enabled us to say, without presumption, that we differ with this extraordinary person on many important points, without ceasing to have the highest regard for his character. His faults were the result of temperament; perhaps his good qualities and his powers of reflection were, in some measure, so too; but this must be the case with all men. Intellect

* Boswell, vol. ii., p. 455.   † Ibid. vol. iv., p. 77.
‡ Ibid. vol. iii., p. 327.

and beneficence, from whatever causes, will always command respect; and we may gladly compound, for their sakes, with foibles which belong to the common chances of humanity. If Johnson has added nothing very new to the general stock, he has contributed (especially by the help of his biographer) a great deal that is striking and entertaining. He was an admirable critic, if not of the highest things, yet of such as could be determined by the exercise of a masculine good sense; and one thing he did, perhaps beyond any man in England, before or since—he advanced, by the powers of his conversation, the strictness of his veracity, and the respect he exacted towards his presence, what may be called the personal dignity of literature. The consequence has been, not exactly what he expected, but certainly what the great interests of knowledge require; and Johnson has assisted men, with whom he little thought of co-operating, in setting the claims of truth and beneficence above all others.

East from Fetter Lane, on the same side of the street, is Crane Court—the principal house in which, facing the entry, was that in which the Royal Society used to meet, and where they kept their museum and library before they removed to their late apartments in Somerset House. The society met in Crane Court up to a period late enough to allow us to present to our imaginations Boyle and his contemporaries prosecuting their eager inquiries and curious experiments in the early dawn of physical science, and afterwards Newton presiding in the noontide glory of the light which he had shed over nature.

131

CHAPTER IV.

THE STRAND.

N going through Fleet Street and the Strand, we seldom think that the one is named after a rivulet, now running under ground, and the other from its being on the banks of the river Thames.   As little do most of us fancy that there was once a line of noblemen's houses on the one side, and that, at the same time, all beyond the other side, to Hampstead or Highgate, was open country, with the little hamlet of St. Giles's in a copse.   So late as the reign of Henry VIII. we have a print containing the vill a of Charing.   Citizens used to take an evening stroll to the well now in St. Clement's Inn.

In the reign of Edward III. the Strand was an open country

road, with a mansion here and there, on the banks of the river
Thames, most probably a castle or stronghold.   In this state
it no doubt remained during the greater part of the York and
Lancaster period.   From Henry VII.'s time the castles most
likely began to be exchanged for mansions of a more peaceful
character.   These gradually increased ; and in the reign of
Edward VI. the Strand consisted, on the south side, of a line
of mansions with garden walls ; and on the north, of a single
row of houses, behind which all was field.   The reader is to
imagine wall all the way from Temple Bar to Whitehall, on
his left hand, like that of Kew Palace, or á succession of
Burlington Gardens ; while the line of humbler habitations
stood on the other side, like a row of servants in waiting.

As wealth increased, not only the importance of rank
diminished, and the nobles were more content to recollect
James's advice of living in the country (where, he said, they
looked like ships in a river, instead of ships at sea), but the
value of ground about London, especially on the river side,
was so much augmented, that the proprietors of these princely
mansions were not unwilling to turn the premises into money.
The civil wars had given another jar to the stability of their
abodes in the metropolis ; and in Charles the Second's time
the great houses finally gave way, and were exchanged for
streets and wharfs.   An agreeable poet of the last century lets
us know that he used to think of this great change in going
up the Strand.

> "Come, Fortescue, sincere, experienc'd friend,
>   Thy briefs, thy deeds, and e'en thy fees suspend ;
>   Come, let us leave the Temple's silent walls ;
>   Me, business to my distant lodging calls ;
>   Through the long Strand together let us stray ;
>   With thee conversing, I forget the way.
>   Behold that narrow street which steep descends,
>   Whose building to the slimy shore extends ;
>   Here Arundel's fam'd structure rear'd its fame :
>   The street alone retains the empty name.
>   Where Titian's glowing paint the canvass warmed.
>   And Raphael's fair design with judgment charmed,
>   Now hangs the bellman's song ; and pasted here
>   The coloured prints of Overton appear.
>   Where statues breathed, the works of Phidias' hands.
>   A wooden pump, or lonely watch-house stands.
>   There Essex's stately pile adorned the shore,
>   There Cecil's, Bedford's, Villiers',—now no more."*

---

* Gay's Trivia, or the Art of Walking the Streets of London,
book ii.

As the aspect in this quarter is so different from what it was, and the quarter is one of the most important in the metropolis, we may add what Pennant has written on the subject:—

"In the year 1353, that fine street the Strand was an open highway, with here and there a great man's house, with gardens to the water's side. In that year it was so ruinous, that Edward III., by an ordinance, directed a tax to be raised upon wool, leather, wine, and all goods carried to the staple at Westminster, from Temple Bar to Westminster Abbey, for the repair of the road; and that all owners of houses adjacent to the highway should repair as much as lay before their doors. Mention is also made of a bridge to be erected near the royal palace at Westminster, for the conveniency of the said staple; but the last probably meant no more than stairs for the landing of the goods, which I find sometimes went by the name of a bridge.

"There was no continued street here till about the year 1533; before that it entirely cut off Westminster from London, and nothing intervened except the scattered houses, and a village, which afterwards gave name to the whole. St. Martin's stood literally in the fields. But about the year 1560 a street was formed, loosely built, for all the houses on the south side had great gardens to the river, were called by their owners' names, and in after times gave name to the several streets that succeeded them, pointing down to the Thames; each of them had stairs for the conveniency of taking boat, of which many to this day bear the names of the houses. As the court was for centuries either at the palace at Westminister, or Whitehall, a boat was the customary conveyance of the great to the presence of their sovereign. The north side was a mere line of houses from Charing-cross to Temple Bar; all beyond was country. The gardens which occupied part of the site of Covent Garden were bounded by fields, and St. Giles's was a distant country village. These are circumstances proper to point out, to show the vast increase of our capital in little more than two centuries."*

The aspect of the Strand, on emerging through Temple Bar, is very different from what it was forty years ago. "A stranger who had visited London in 1790, would on his return in 1804," says Mr. Malcolm, "be astonished to find a spacious area (with the church nearly in the centre) on the site of Butcher Row, and some other passages undeserving of the name of streets, which were composed of those wretched fabrics, overhanging their foundations, the receptacles of dirt in every corner of their projecting stories, the bane of ancient London, where the plague, with all its attendant horrors, frowned destruction on the miserable inhabitants, reserving its forces for the attacks of each returning summer."†

The site of Butcher Row, thus advantageously thrown

* Pennant, *ut supra*, p. 139.
† Londinium Redivivum, vol. iii., p. 397.

open, is called Pickett Street, after the alderman who projected the improvements. Unfortunately they turned out to
be on too large a scale ; that is to say, the houses were found
to be too large and expensive for the right side of the Strand
in this quarter; the tide of traffic between the city and Westminster flowing the other side of the way.   The consequence
is, that the houses are under-let, and that something of the old
squalid look remains in the turning towards Clement's Inn, in
spite of the pillared entrance.

Butcher Row, however squalid, contained houses worth
eating and drinking in.   Johnson frequented an eating-house
there; and, according to Oldys, it was "in returning from
the Bear and Harrow in Butcher Row, through Clare Market,
to his lodgings in Duke Street, that Lee, the dramatic poet,
overladen with wine, fell down (on the ground, as some say—
according to others, on a bulk), and was killed, or stifled in
the snow.   He was buried in the parish church of St. Clement
Danes, aged about thirty-five years."* "He was a very handsome as well as ingenious man," says Oldys, "but given to
debauchery, which necessitated a milk diet.   When some of
his university comrades visited him, he fell to drinking out of
all measure, which, flying up into his head, caused his face to
break out into those carbuncles which were afterwards observed there; and also touched his brain, occasioning that madness so much lamented in so rare a genius.   Tom Brown says,
he wrote, while he was in Bedlam, a play of twenty-five acts;
and Mr. Bowman tells me that, going once to visit him there,
Lee showed him a scene, 'in which,' says he, 'I have done a
miracle for you.'   'What's that?' said Bowman.   'I have
made you a good priest.'"

Oldys mentions another of his mad sayings, but does not
tell us with whom it passed.

> "I've seen an unscrewed spider spin a thought,
>   And walk away upon the wings of angels!"

"What say you to that, doctor?"   "Ah, marry, Mr. Lee, that's
superfine indeed.   The thought of a winged spider may catch sublime
readers of poetry sooner than his web, but it will need a commentary
in prose to render it intelligible to the vulgar."†

Lee's madness does not appear to have been melancholy,
otherwise these anecdotes would not bear repeating.   There
are various stories of the origin of it; but, most probably,

---

* Biographia Dramatica, from Oldys's MS. Notes on Langbaine.
† Censura Literaria, vol. i., p. 176.

he had an over-sanguine constitution, which he exasperated by intemperance. Though he died so young, the author of *A Satyr on the Poets* gives us to understand that he was corpulent.

> " Pembroke loved tragedy, and did provide
> For the butchers' dogs, and for the whole Bank-side :
> The bear was fed ; but dedicating Lee
> Was thought to have a greater paunch than he."*

This Pembroke, who loved a bear-garden, was the seventh earl of that title. His daughter married the son of Jefferies. Lee, on a visit to the earl at Wilton, is said to have drunk so hard, that "the butler feared he would empty the cellar." The madness of Lee is almost visible in his swelling and overladen dramas; in which, however, there is a good deal of true poetic fire, and a vein of tenderness that makes us heartily pity the author.

The social Boswell, in speaking of Johnson's eating-house in Butcher Row, does not approve of establishments of that sort. We shall see, by and by, that he was wrong.

" Happening to dine," says he, " at Clifton's eating-house in Butcher Row, I was surprised to see Johnson come in and take his seat at another table. The mode of dining, or rather being fed, at such houses in London, is well known to many to be peculiarly unsocial, as there is no ordinary or united company, but each person has his own mess, and is under no obligation to hold any intercourse with any one. A liberal and full-minded man, however, who loves to talk, will break through this churlish and unsocial restraint. Johnson and an Irish gentleman got into a dispute concerning the cause of some part of mankind being black. ' Why, sir (said Johnson), it has been accounted for in three ways : either by supposing that they are the posterity of Ham, who was cursed; or that God at first created two kinds of men, one black and another white ; or that, by the heat of the sun, the skin is scorched, and so acquires a sooty hue. This matter has been much canvassed among naturalists, but has never been brought to any certain issue.' What the Irishman said is totally obliterated from my mind ; but I remember that he became very warm and intemperate in his expressions; upon which Johnson rose, and quietly walked away. When he had retired, his antagonist took his revenge, as he thought, by saying, ' He has a most ungainly figure, and an affectation of pomposity unworthy of a man of genius.'"*

The ungainly figure might have been pardoned by the Irishman ; who, we suppose, was equally fiery and elegant. As to Johnson's pompous manner, the most excusable part of it originated, doubtless, in his having decided opinions. The rest may have been an instinct of self-defence, arising from

* State Poems, vol. ii., p. 143,
† Boswell, vol. i., p. 383.

the "ungainly figure," not without a sense of the dignity of
his calling. He certainly lost nothing by it, upon the whole.
At all events, one is willing to think the best of what was
accompanied by so much excellence. Affectation it was not;
for nobody despised pretension of any kind more than he did.
Johnson was a sort of born bishop in his way, with high
judgments and cathedral notions lording it in his mind; and
ex cathedrâ he accordingly spoke.

In Butcher Row, one day, Johnson met, in advanced life, a
fellow-collegian, of the name of Edwards, whom he had not
seen since they were at the university. Edwards annoyed
him by talking of their age. "Don't let us discourage one
another," said Johnson. It was this Edwards, a dull but good
man, who made that *naïve* remark, which was pronounced by
Burke and others to be an excellent trait of character:—"You
are a philosopher, Dr. Johnson," said he: "I have tried in
my time to be a philosopher; but, I don't know how, cheerfulness was always breaking in."*

Before we come to St. Clement's, we arrive, on the left-
hand side of the way, at Essex Street; a spot once famous
for the residence of the favourite Earl of Essex. We have
mentioned an Outer Temple, which originally formed a companion to the Inner and Middle Temples, the whole constituting the tenements of the knights. This Outer Temple
stretched beyond Temple Bar into the ground now occupied
by Essex Street and Devereux Court; and after being possessed (Dugdale supposes) by the Prior and Canons of the
Holy Sepulchre, was transferred by them, in the time of
Edward III., to the Bishops of Exeter, who occupied it till
the reign of Henry VI., and called it Exeter House. Sir
William Paget (afterwards Lord Paget) then had it, and did
"re-edify the same," calling it Paget Place. After this it
was occupied by the Duke of Norfolk, who was executed for
his dealings with Mary, Queen of Scots; then by Dudley,
Earl of Leicester, the favourite, who called it Leicester House,
and bequeathed it to his "son, Sir Robert;" and then by the
other favourite, Leicester's son-in-law, Essex, from whom it
retained the name of Essex House. It was occasionally
tenanted by men of rank till some time after the Restoration,
when it was pulled down, and the site converted into the present street and court. The only remnant of it supposed to
exist is the present Unitarian Chapel, which, before it became

* Boswell, vol. iii., p. 331.

such, was called Essex House, and latterly contained an auction room.*

The repose enjoyed in this precinct since the Restoration has been like silence after a succession of storms, for the house was of a turbulent reputation. The first bishop who had it after the Templars, being a favourite of Edward II., was seized by the mob, hurried to Cheapside, where they beheaded him, and then carried back a corpse, and buried in a heap of sand at his door. Lord Paget got into trouble, together with his friend the Duke of Somerset, who was accused of intending to assassinate Northumberland and others at this house. Norfolk possessed it while he formed his designs on Mary, Queen of Scots, for which he was brought to the scaffold; Leicester was always having some ill design or other—perhaps poisoned a visitor or so occasionally (for he is said to have thought nothing of that gentle expediency); and Essex made the house famous by standing a siege in it against the troops of his mistress. The siege was not long, nor any of his actions in the business very wise, though he was a man of an exalted nature. Essex got into his troubles partly from heat and ambition, partly from the inferior and more cunning nature of some of his rivals at court. There is no doubt that all these causes, together with his confidence in Elizabeth's inability to proceed to extremities, conspired to lead him into rebellion. His first offence that we hear of, next to a general petulance of manner, which the Queen's own mixture of fondness and petulance was calculated enough to provoke, was a quarrel with some young lords for her favour; the second, his joining the expedition to Cadiz without leave; and the third, his marriage with the daughter of Sir Francis Walsingham: for Elizabeth never thought it proper that her favourites should be married to any thing but her "fair idea."

His next dispute with her, which was on the subject of an assistant in the affairs of Ireland, to which he was going as

* Dugdale's Antiquities of Westminster. Heraldic MS. in the Museum, quoted in Londinium Redivivum (vol. ii., p. 282). Brydges's Collins's Peerage. Belsham's Life of Lindsey. We have been thus minute in tracing the occupancies of this house, from the interest excited by some of the members connected with it. Pennant says, upon the authority of the Sydney Papers, that Leicester bequeathed it to his son-in-law, which appears probable, since the latter possessed it. Perhaps the herald was confused by the name of Robert, which belonged both to son and son-in-law.

lord deputy, terminated in the singular catastrophe of his
receiving from her a box on the ear, with the encouraging
addition of bidding him "Go, and be hanged." It is said to
have been occasioned by his turning his back upon her. He
clapped his hand to his sword, and swore he would not have
put up with such an insult from her father. His fall is
generally dated from this circumstance, and it is thought he
never forgave it. But surely this is not a correct judgment :
for the blow which might have been intolerable from the hand
of a king, implied, in its very extravagance, something not
without flattery and self-abasement from that of a princess.
It was as if Elizabeth had put herself into the situation
of a termagant wife. The quarrel preceded the violence.
Essex went to Ireland against the rebels, but apparently with
great unwillingness, calling it, in a letter to the Queen, the
"cursedest of all islands," and insinuating that the best thing
that could happen both to please her and himself was the loss
of his life in battle. The conclusion of this letter is a remarkable instance of the mixture of romance with real life in those
days. It is in verse, terminating with the following pastoral
sentiment. Essex wishes he could live like·a hermit, " in
some unhaunted desert most obscure"—

> "From all society, from love and hate
>   Of worldly folk ; then should he sleep secure,
> Then wake again, and yield God every praise,
>   Content with hips and hawes, and bramble-berry ;
> In contemplation parting out his days,
>   And change of holy thoughts to make him merry.
> Who when he dies, his tomb may be a bush,
>   Where harmless robin dwells with gentle thrush.
>   Your Majesty's exiled servant,
>   " ROBERT ESSEX."

Think of this being a letter from a lord lieutenant of
Ireland to his sovereign! Warton says, from the evidence of
some sonnets preserved in the British Museum, that although
Essex was "an ingenious and elegant writer of prose," he
was no poet. There is an ungainliness in the lines we have
just quoted, and he was probably too much given to action to
be a poet; but there is something in him that relished of
the truth and directness of poetry, when he had to touch
upon any actual emotion. Poetry is nothing but the voluntary power to get at the inner spirit of what is felt, with
imagination to embody it. It was supposed that Essex's
enemies first got him into the office of lord lieutenant, and

then took advantage of his impatience under it to ruin him. He was accused of tampering with the rebels, and meditating his return into England with the troops under his charge; with a view to which object he is said to have described his army as a force with which he " would make the earth to tremble as he went." He came over, with the passion of an injured man, and presented himself before the Queen, who gave him a tolerable reception, but afterwards confined him to the house of the lord keeper. It was then, according to his confession before his death, that he first contemplated violent measures against the throne, though always short of treason. Before his liberation, he was soured by his ineffectual attempts to renew his facility of admission to the presence chamber; and he let fall an expression which his enemies greedily seized at, to wit, that the " Queen grew old and cankered, and that her mind was become as crooked as her carcase." This was exactly in his style, which was off-hand and energetic, with a gusto of truth in it. Meantime he began to have his friends about him more than ever, and to affect a necessity for it; and a summons being sent him to attend the council, he was driven by anger and fear to decline it, and to fortify himself in his house. His chief and most generous companion on this occasion was Henry, Earl of Southampton, the friend of Shakspeare. There was some little resistance; and the Lord Keeper, with the Lord Chief Justice and the Earl of Worcester, coming to summon him to his allegiance, he locked them up in a room, on pretence of taking care of their persons, and then sallied through Fleet Street into the city, where he expected a rising in his favour; for he was the most popular noble, perhaps, that England had ever seen, and the city had been disgusted by repeated levies on its purse, under pretence of invasions from Spain: though, according to Essex, Spain had never been so much in favour. The levies, in truth, were made against himself. He was disappointed: heard himself proclaimed a traitor by sound of trumpet in Gracechurch Street, and after a little more scuffling on the part of his adherents, returned by water from Queenhithe, and surrendered himself; being partly moved, he said, by the "cries of ladies." It is clear that he did not know what to be at. He expected, most likely, every moment, that the Queen's tenderness would interfere, fearful of seeing her once beloved favourite in danger. But the Cecils and others aided her good sense in keeping her quiet. Essex had certainly acted in a way incompatible with the duty of a subject, and such as no sovereign could tolerate. He was tried in Westminster Hall, and convicted of an intention to seize the court and the Tower, to surprise the Queen in her apartments, and then to summon a parliament for a "redress of grievances;" which, he said, should give his enemies " a fair trial." Southampton was acquitted, no doubt from a sense that he intended nothing but a romantic adherence to his friend.

How a man of Essex's understanding could give into these preposterous attempts, it would be difficult to conceive, if every day's experience did not show how powerful a succession of little circumstances is to bring people into situations which themselves might have least looked for. Essex evidently expected pardon to the last. When Lord Grey's name was read over among the peers who were to try him, he smiled and jogged the elbow of Southampton, for offending whom Grey had been punished. He was at his ease throughout the trial. He said to the Attorney-General (Coke), who had told him in the course of his speech that he should be " Robert the Last" of an earldom, instead of " Robert the First" of a kingdom—" Well, Mr. Attorney, I thank God you are not my judge this day, you are so uncharitable."

" *Coke.* Well, my lord, we shall prove you anon, what you are; which your pride of heart, and aspiring mind, hath brought you unto.
    Essex. Ah, Mr. Attorney, lay your hand upon your heart, and pray to God to forgive us *both.*"*

And when sentence was passed, though it is not true that he refused to ask for mercy, for he did it after the best fashion of his style, " kneeling (he said) upon the very knees of his heart," yet he seemed to threaten Elizabeth, in a tender way, with his resolution to die. She left him, like a politic sovereign, to his fate; but is thought never to have recovered it, as a friend. The romantic story of her visiting the Countess of Nottingham, who had kept back a ring which Essex sent her after his condemnation, of her shaking her on her deathbed, and crying out that " God might forgive, but she could not," is more and more credited as documents transpire. The ring, it is said, had been given to Essex, with a promise that it should serve him in need under any circumstances, if he did but send it. It is supposed that the non-appearance of it hurt the proud heart of Elizabeth, and

* Howell's State Trials, vol. i., p. 1343.

finally allowed her to let him die.   Yet she was a great sovereign, and might have suffered the law to take its course, with whatever sorrow.   She was jealous of her reputation with the old and cool-headed lords about her.   When the death, however, had taken place, she might have fancied otherwise.   Something preyed strongly on her mind towards her decease, which happened within two years after his execution.   She refused to go to bed for ten days and nights before her death, lying upon the carpet with cushions about her, and absorbed in the profoundest melancholy.   To be sure, this may have been disease.   A princess like Elizabeth, possessed of sovereign power, which had been sharply exercised on some doubtful occasions, might have had misgivings when going to die.   Two certain causes of regret she must have had for Essex.   She must have been well aware that she had alternately encouraged and irritated him over much; and she must have known that he was a better man than many who assisted in his overthrow, and that if he had been less worthy of regard, he probably would have survived her, as they did.

It may easily be imagined that Essex was a man for whom a strong affection might be entertained.   He excited interest by his character, and could maintain it by his language.   In everything he did there was a certain excess, but on the liberal side.   When a youth, he plunged into the depths of rural pleasures and books; he was lavish of his money and good words for his friends; he said everything that came uppermost, but then it was worth saying, only his enemies were not as well pleased with it as his friends, and they never forgot it: in fine, he was romantic, brave, and impassioned. He is so like a *preux chevalier*, that till we call to mind other gallant knights who have not been handsome, we are somewhat surprised to hear that he was not well made, and that nothing is said of his face but that it looked reserved—a seeming anomaly, which deep thought sometimes produces in the countenances of open-hearted men.   These were no hindrances, however, to the admiration entertained of him by the ladies; and he was so popular with authors and with the public, that Warton says he could bring evidence of his scarcely ever quitting England or even the metropolis, on the most frivolous enterprise, without a pastoral or other poetical praise of him, which was sold and sung in the streets.   He was the friend of Spenser, most likely of Shakspeare too,

being the friend of Southampton. Spenser was well acquainted
with Essex House. In his '*Prothalamion*,' published in 1596,
he has left interesting evidence of his having visited Leicester
there; and he follows up the record with a panegyric on
Leicester's successor, which was probably his first hint to
Essex that he was still in want of such assistance as he had
received from his father-in-law. The two passages taken
together render the hint rather broad, and such as would
make one a little jealous for the dignity of the great poet,
were not the manners of that time different in this respect
from what they are now. Speaking of the Temple, in the
lines quoted in our last chapter, he goes on to say—

> " Next whereunto there stands a stately place,
> Where oft I gayned giftes and goodly grace
> Of that great lord, which therein wont to dwell.
> Whose want too well now feels my friendless case :
> But, ah ! here fits not well
> Olde woes, but ioyes, to tell
> Against the bridale daye, which is not long :
> Sweet Themmes ! runne softly till I end my song.
>
> Yet therein now doth lodge a noble peer,
> Great England's glory, and the world's wide wonder,
> Whose dreadful name late through all Spaine did thunder,
> And Hercules' two pillars standing near
> Did make to quake and feare :
> Faire branch of honour, flower of chevalrie ;
> That fillest England with thy triumph's fame,
> Joy have thou of thy noble victorie."

Essex no doubt took the poet at his word, both for his panegyric and his hint : for it was he that gave Spenser his funeral
in Westminster, and he was not of a spirit to treat a great poet,
as poets have sometimes been treated—with neglect in their
lifetime, and self-complacent monuments to them after their
death.

We shall close this notice (in which we have endeavoured
to concentrate all the interest we could) of the once great and
applauded Essex, whose memory long retained its popularity,
and gave rise to several tragedies, with a letter of his to the
Lord Keeper Egerton, in which there is one of his finest sentiments expressed with his most passionate felicity. Egerton's
eldest son had accompanied Essex into Ireland, and died there,
which is the subject of the letter. As Spenser's death also
happened just before the earl set out for that country, at a
moment when he might have been of political as well as
poetical use to him (for Spenser was a politician, and had

been employed in the affairs of Ireland), Mr. Todd thinks, that among the friends alluded to, part of the regret may have been for him:

"Whatt can you receave from a cursed country butt vnfortunate newes? whatt can be my stile (whom heaven and earth are agreed to make a martyr) butt a stile of mourning? nott for myself thatt I smart, *for I wold I had in my hart the sorow of all my frends*, but I mourn that my destiny is to overlive my deerest frendes. Of y[r] losse yt is neither good for me to write nor you to reade. But I protest I felt myself sensibly dismembered, when I lost my frend. Shew y[r] strength in lyfe. Lett me, yf yt be God's will, shew yt in taking leave of the world, and hasting after my frends. Butt I will live and dy

"More y[r] lp's then any
"man's living.
"Essex."

"*Arbrackan, this last day of August*" [1599].

"Little,"* says Mr. Todd, "did the generous but unfortunate Essex then imagine, that the learned statesman, to whom this letter of condolence was addressed, would be directed very soon afterwards to issue an order for his execution. The original warrant, to which the name of Elizabeth is prefixed, is now in the possession of the Marquis of Stafford; and the queen has written her name, not with the firmness observable in numerous documents existing in the same and other collections, but with apparent tremor and hesitation."

In Essex House was born another Robert, Earl of Essex, son of the preceding, well known in history as general of the Parliament. He was a child when his father died; and was in the hands, first, of his grandmother, Lady Walsingham, and, secondly, of Henry Saville (afterwards Sir Henry), under whose severe discipline he was educated at Eton. We mention these circumstances, because they tended to keep him in that Presbyterian interest, which his father patronised out of a love of toleration and popularity. Perhaps, also, they did him no good with his wives; for he married two, and was singularly unfortunate in both. To the first, Lady Frances Howard, he was betrothed when a boy. He travelled, returned, and married her, with little love on his own side, and none on hers. Her connection with Car, Earl of Somerset, and all the infamy, crime, and wretchedness it brought upon her, are well known. Her best excuse, which is the ordinary one in cases of great wickedness (and it is a comfort to human nature that it is so), is, that she was a great fool. Her dislike of her first husband was not, perhaps, the least excusable part of her conduct, first, because she was a child like himself

---

* Todd's edit, of Spenser, vol. i., p. cxli.

when they were betrothed ; and secondly, because his second wife appears to have liked him no better.   The latter was divorced also.   After this, Essex took to a country retirement, and subsequently to an active part in the Civil Wars, during which his love of justice and affability to his inferiors rendered him extremely popular.   He was of equivocal service, however, to the Parliament.   He was a better general than politician, not of a commanding genius in any respect, and was suspected, not without reason, of an overweening desire to accommodate matters too much, partly out of ignorance of what the nature of the quarrel demanded, and partly from an affectation of playing the part of an amicable dictator for his own aggrandisement.   So the Parliament got rid of him by the famous self-denying ordinance.   Clarendon says, that when he resigned his commission, the whole Parliament went the day following to Essex House, to return him thanks for his great services ; but a late historian of the commonwealth says, there is no trace of this compliment on the journals.*   Next year they attended him to his grave. Essex's character was a prose-copy of his father's, with the love and romance left out.

Dr. Johnson, the year before he died, founded in Essex Street one of his minor clubs.   The Literary Club did not meet often enough for his want of society, was too distant, and perhaps had now become too much for his conversational ambition.   He wanted a mixture of inferior intellects to be at ease with.   Accordingly, this club, which was held at the Essex Head, then kept by a servant of Mr. Thrale, was of a more miscellaneous nature than the other, and made no pretension to expense.   One cannot help smiling at the modest and pensive tone of the letter which Johnson sent to Sir Joshua, inviting him to join it.   " The terms are lax, and the expenses light.   We meet thrice a-week ; and he who misses, forfeits two-pence."†   This stretch of philosophy seems to have startled the fashionable painter, who declined to become a member.   When we find, however, in the list the names of Brocklesby, Horsley, Daines Barrington, and Windham, Boswell has reason to say that Sir John Hawkins's charge of its being a " low ale-house association " appears to be sufficiently obviated.   But the names might have been subscribed out of civility without any further intention.   The club,

* Godwin's History of the Commonwealth, vol. i., p. 410.
† Boswell, vol. iv., p. 276.

nevertheless, was in existence when Boswell wrote, and went on, he says, happily. Johnson said of him, when he was proposed, " Boswell is a very *clubable* man."

In Devereux Court, through which there is a passage round into the Temple, is the Grecian Coffee House, supposed to be the oldest in London. We should rather say the revival of the oldest, for the premises were burnt down and rebuilt. The Grecian was the house from which Steele proposed to date his learned articles in the *Tatler*.

In this court are the premises of the eminent tea-dealers, Messrs. Twining, the front of which, surmounted with its stone figures of Chinese, has an elegant appearance in the Strand. We notice the house, not only on this account, but because the family have to boast of a very accomplished scholar, the translator of the *Poetics* of Aristotle. Mr. Twining was contemporary with Gray and Mason at Cambridge; and besides his acquirements as a linguist (for, in addition to his knowledge of Greek and Latin, he wrote French and Italian with idiomatic accuracy), was a musician so accomplished as to lead the concerts and oratorios that were performed during term-time, when Bate played the organ and harpsichord. He was also a lively companion, full of wit and playfulness, yet so able to content himself with country privacy, and so exemplary a clergyman, that for the last forty years of his life he scarcely allowed himself to be absent from his parishioners more than a fortnight in a year.

The church of St. Clement Danes, which unworthily occupies the open part of the Strand, to the west of Essex Street, was the one most frequented by Dr. Johnson. It is not known why this church was called St. Clement *Danes.* Some think because there was a massacre of the Danes thereabouts; others because Harold Harefoot was buried there; and others, because the Danes had the quarter given them to live in, when Alfred the Great drove them out of London, the monarch at the same time building the church, in order to assist their conversion to Christianity. The name *St. Clement* has been derived with probability from the patron saint of Pope Clement III., a great friend of the Templars, to whom the church at one time belonged. St. Clement's was rebuilt towards the end of the century before last by Edward Pierce, under the direction of Sir Christopher Wren, but is a very incongruous ungainly edifice. Its best aspect is at

L

night-time in winter, when the deformities of its body are not
seen, and the pale steeple rises with a sort of ghastliness of
grandeur through the cloudy atmosphere. The chimes may
still be heard at midnight, as Falstaff describes having heard
them with Justice Shallow. If they did not execute one of
Handel's psalm-tunes, we should take them to be the very
same he speaks of, and conclude that they had grown hoarse
with age and sitting-up; for to our knowledge they have lost
some of their notes these twenty years, and the rest are
falling away. A steeple should set a better example.

A few years back, when the improvements on the north
side, in this quarter, had not been followed by those on the
south, Gay's picture of the avenue between the church and
the houses was true in all its parts. We remember the
" combs dangling in our faces," and almost mourned their
loss for the sake of the poet.

> " Where the fair columns of St. Clement stand,
> Whose straiten'd bounds encroach upon the Strand ;
> Where the low penthouse bows the walker's head,
> And the rough pavement wounds the yielding tread ;
> Where not a post protects the narrow space,
> And, strung in twines, combs dangle in thy face ;
> Summon at once thy courage, rouse thy care,
> Stand firm, look back, be resolute, beware.
> Forth issuing from steep lanes, the collier's steeds
> Drag the black load ; another cart succeeds ;
> Team follows team, crowds heap'd on crowds appear,
> And wait impatient till the road grow clear."

Everybody can testify to the truth of this description. A
little patience, however, is well repaid by the sight of the
noble creatures dragging up the loads. The horses of the
colliers and brewers of London are worth notice at all times
for the magnificence of their *build*. Gay proceeds to other
particulars, now no longer to be encountered. He cautions
you how you lose your sword ; and adds a pleasant mode of
theft, practised in those times :—

> " Nor is the flaxen wig with safety worn :
> High on the shoulder, in a basket borne,
> Lurks the sly boy, whose hands, to rapine bred,
> Plucks off the curling honours of thy head."*

---

* Trivia ; or the Art of Walking the Streets of London, book iii.
Of a similar, and more perplexing facetiousness was the trick of
extracting wigs out of hackney coaches. " The thieves," says the
Weekly Journal (March 30, 1717), " have got such a villanous way
now of robbing gentlemen, that they cut holes through the backs of

Clement's Inn is named from the church. The device over the gate, of an anchor and the letter C, is supposed to allude to the martyrdom of St. Clement, who is said to have been tied to an anchor and thrown into the sea, by order of the Emperor Trajan.

" The hall is situated on the south side of a neat but small quadrangle. It is a Tuscan diminutive building, with a very large Corinthian door, and arched windows, erected in 1715. Another irregular area is surrounded by convenient houses, in which are the possessor's chambers. Part of this is a pretty garden, with a kneeling African, of considerable merit, supporting a dial, on the eastern side."*

In Knox's *Elegant Extracts* are some lines on this negro, which have often been repeated :—

> " In vain, poor sable son of woe,
>   Thou seek'st the tender tear ;
> For thee in vain with pangs they flow ;
>   For mercy dwells not here.

> From cannibals thou fledst in vain ;
>   Lawyers less quarter give ;
> The first won't eat you till you're slain,
>   The last will do't alive."

This inn, like all the other inns of court, is of great antiquity. Dugdale states it to have been an inn of Chancery in the reign of Edward II. Some have conjectured, according to Mr. Moser, " that near this spot stood an inn, as far back as the time of King Ethelred, for the reception of penitents who came to St. Clement's Well; that a religious house was in process of time established, and that the church rose in consequence." Be this as it may, the holy brotherhood was probably removed to some other institution; the Holy Lamb, an inn on the west side of the lane, received the guests; and the monastery was converted, or rather perverted, from the purposes of the gospel to those of the law, and was probably, in this profession, considered as a house of considerable antiquity in the days of Shakspeare; for he, who with

hackney coaches, and take away their wigs, or fine head-dresses of gentlewomen; so a gentleman was served last Sunday in Tooley Street, and another but last Tuesday in Fenchurch Street; wherefore this may serve as a caution to gentlemen and gentlewomen that ride single in the night-time, to sit on the fore-seat, which will prevent that way of robbing."—Malcolm's Anecdotes of the Manners and Customs of London during the Eighteenth Century, second edit., vol. i., p. 104.

* Londinium Redivivum, vol. ii.

respect to this kind of chronology may be safely quoted, makes in the second act of Henry IV. one of his justices a member of that society:—

"He must to the Inns of Court. I was of Clement's once myself, where they talk of Mad Shallow still."

A pump now covers St. Clement's Well. Fitzstephen, in his description of London, in the reign of Henry II., speaks of certain "excellent springs at a small distance" from the city, "whose waters are sweet, salubrious, and clear, and whose runnels murmur o'er the shining stones: among these," he continues, "Holywell, Clerkenwell, and St. Clement's Well may be esteemed the principal, as being much the most frequented, both by the scholars from the school (Westminster) and the youth from the city, when on a summer's evening they are disposed to take an airing."

Six hundred years and upwards have elapsed since Eitzstephen wrote. It is pleasant to think that the well has lasted so long, and that the place is still quiet.

The Clare family, who have left their name to Clare Market, appear to have occupied Clement's Inn during part of the reign of the Tudors. From their hands it reverted to those of the law. It is an appendage to the Inner Temple. We are not aware of any greater legal personage having been bred there, than the one just mentioned. Shallow takes delight in his local recollections, particularly of this inn. In one of the masterly scenes of this kind, Falstaff's corroboration of a less pleasant recollection, and Shallow's anger against the cause of it, after such a lapse of time, are very ludicrous.

"*Shallow.* Oh, Sir John, do you remember since we lay all night in the windmill in St. George's Fields ?

"*Fals.* No more of that, good Master Shallow, no more of that.

"*Shal.* Ha, it was a merry night. And is Jane Nightwork alive ?

"*Fals.* She lives, Master Shallow.

"*Shal.* She never could away with me.

"*Fals.* Never, never; she would always say she could not abide Master Shallow.

"*Shal.* By the mass. I could anger her to the heart. She was then a bonaroba. Doth she hold her own well ?—and had Robin Nightwork by old Nightwork, before I came to Clement's Inn.

"*Silence.* That's fifty-five years ago.

"*Shal.* Ha, Cousin Silence, that thou hadst seen that that this knight and I have seen ! Ah, Sir John, said I well ?

"*Fals,* We have heard the chimes at midnight, Master Shallow.

"*Shal.* That we have, that we have, that we have; in faith, Sir John, we have; our watchword was, *Hem, boys!* Come, let's to dinner: come, let's to dinner: Oh, the days that we have seen! Come, come."*

The sites of Arundel, Norfolk, Surrey, and Howard Streets (the last of which crosses the others), were formerly occupied by the house and grounds originally constituting the town residence of the Bishop of Bath and Wells, then of the Lord High Admiral Seymour, and afterwards of the Howards Earls of Arundel, from whom it came into possession of the Duke of Norfolk. It was successively called Bath's Inn (Hampton Place, according to some, but we know not why), Seymour Place, Arundel House, and Norfolk House. It was a wide low house, but according to Sully, who lodged in it when he was ambassador to James I., very convenient, on account of the multitude of rooms on the same floor.

In this house the Lord High Admiral, Thomas Seymour, brother of the Protector Somerset, in the reign of Edward VI., contrived to place the Princess (afterwards Queen) Elizabeth, with a design of possessing her person, and sharing her succession to the Crown. No doubt is entertained of these views by the historians. Elizabeth was not averse to him, though he had lately married the Queen Dowager (Catherine Parr); and some gossipping stories transpired of the evidences of their good-will. Catherine's death increased the suspicion, and she herself expressed it on her death-bed. Seymour's ambition, however, shortly brought him to the scaffold, and saved us from a King Thomas I., who would probably, as Pennant thinks, have been a very bad one.

We have mentioned the Countess of Nottingham who withheld from Elizabeth the ring sent her by Essex. It was in this house she died. Her husband was a Howard, and, probably, she was on a visit there. We take an opportunity, therefore, of relating the particulars of that romantic story, as collected by the accurate Dr. Birch, and repeated in the *Memoirs of the Peers of England during the reign of James I.* " The following curious story," says the compiler of this work, " was frequently told by Lady Elizabeth Spelman, great granddaughter of Sir Robert Carey, brother of Lady Nottingham, and afterwards Earl of Monmouth, whose curious memoirs of himself were published a few years ago by Lord Corke."

" When Catherine, Countess of Nottingham, was dying (as she did, according to his lordship's own account, about a fortnight before Queen Elizabeth), she sent to her Majesty to desire that she might

---

* Second Part of Henry IV. act 3. sc. 2.

see her, in order to reveal something to her Majesty without the discovery of which she could not die in peace. Upon the Queen's coming, Lady Nottingham told her, that, while the Earl of Essex lay under sentence of death, he was desirous of asking her Majesty's mercy, in the manner prescribed by herself, during the height of his favour; the Queen having given him a ring, which being sent to her as a token of his distress, might entitle him to her protection. But the earl, jealous of those about him, and not caring to trust any of them with it, as he was looking out of his window one morning, saw a boy, with whose appearance he was pleased; and engaging him by money and promises, directed him to carry the ring, which he took from his finger and threw down, to Lady Scroope, a sister of the Countess of Nottingham, and a friend of his lordship, who attended upon the Queen; and to beg of her that she would present it to her Majesty. The boy, by mistake, carried it to Lady Nottingham, who showed it to her husband, the admiral, an enemy of Lord Essex, in order to take his advice. The admiral forbid her to carry it, or return any answer to the message; but insisted upon her keeping the ring.

"The Countess of Nottingham, having made this discovery, begged the Queen's forgiveness; but her Majesty answered, ' *God may forgive you, but I never can,*' and left the room with great emotion. Her mind was so struck with the story that she never went into bed, nor took any sustenance from that instant, for Camden is of opinion, that her chief reason for suffering the earl to be executed, was his supposed obstinacy in not applying to her for mercy."*

"In confirmation of the time of the countess's death," continues the compiler, "it now appears from the parish register of Chelsea, extracted by Mr. Lysons (*Environs of London*, vol. ii., p. 120), that she died at Arundel House, London, February 25, and was buried the 28th, 1603. Her funeral was kept at Chelsea, March 21st; and Queen Elizabeth died three days afterwards."

Clarendon gives a singular character of this house and its master when it was in possession of Thomas Howard, Earl of Arundel. He says that the earl

"Seemed to live, as it were, in another nation, his house being a place to which all people resorted, who resorted to no other place; strangers, or such as affected to look like strangers, and dressed themselves accordingly. He was willing to be thought a scholar, and to understand the most mysterious parts of antiquity, because he made a wonderful and costly purchase of excellent statues whilst in Italy and in Rome (some whereof he could never obtain permission to remove out of Rome, though he had paid for them), and had a rare collection of medals. As to all parts of learning, he was almost illiterate, and thought no other part of history so considerable as what related to his own family, in which, no doubt, there had been

---

* Birch's Negotiations, pp. 206, 207, quoted in the work above mentioned, p. 189. Whenever we quote from any authorities but the original, I beg the reader to bear in mind, first, that we always notice our having done so; and, secondly, that we make a point of comparing the originals with the report. Both Monmouth and Birch, for example, have been consulted in the present instance.

some very memorable persons. It cannot be denied that he had in his own person, in his aspect and countenance, the appearance of a great man, which he preserved in his gait and motion. He wore and affected a habit very different from that of the time, such as men had only beheld in pictures of the most considerable men; all which drew the eyes of most, and the reverence of many, towards him, as the image and representative of the ancient nobility, and native gravity of the nobles, when they had been most venerable; but this was only his outside, his nature and true humour being much disposed to levity and delights, which indeed were very despicable and childish."

The marbles here mentioned, now at Oxford, were collected at Arundel House. This character from the pen of Clarendon has been thought too severe. Perhaps the earl had given the noble historian a repulse when he was nothing but plain Mr. Hyde; for personal resentments of this sort are apparent in his writings. The last Duke of Norfolk but one, who wrote anecdotes on the Howard family, asks how the man who collected the Oxford marbles could be the slave of such family self-love as Clarendon describes, and how it was that he held the first places in the state, and the most important commissions abroad. It is well-known, however, that a man may do all this, and yet be more fortunate than wise. Arundel was certainly proud, if not dull; and the proudest men are not apt to be the brightest. It was he that, in a dispute with Lord Spenser, in the Upper House, when the latter spoke of the treason of the earl's ancestors, said, " My lord, my lord, while my ancestors were plotting treason, yours were keeping sheep." He little thought that his marbles would help to bring about a time, when an historian, by no means indifferent to rank and title, should regard a romantic poem as the "brightest jewel" in a ducal coronet, and that coronet be a Spenser's. *

At the south-west corner of Norfolk Street lived at one time the famous Penn, who from being a coxcomb in his youth became a Quaker and a founder of a state. However, his coxcombry was a falling-off from early seriousness. His father was a rough admiral, who could not for the life of him conceive why his son should relapse into a preciseness so unlike the rest of the world, and so unfitted to succeed at court. Voltaire says,† that young Penn (for he was little more than twenty years of age) appeared suddenly before his

* We allude to the celebrated saying of Gibbon respecting the Fairy Queen.

† In his Letters on the English Nation. But we quote from memory.

father in a Quaker dress, and to the old man's astonishment
and indignation said, without moving his hat, "Friend Penn,
how dost thee do?" But, according to more serious biographers, the change was not so sudden. The hat, however,
was a great matter of contention between them, the admiral
wishing to stipulate that his son should uncover to the King
(Charles II.), the King's brother, and himself; but Penn
having recourse to "fasting and supplication," found that
his hat was not to be moved. These were the weaknesses of
a young enthusiast. His enthusiam remained for greater
purposes; but he is understood to have grown wiser with
regard to the rest, though he continued a Quaker for life.
Penn, though a legislator, never seems to have given up a
taste for good living. His appearance in the portraits of
him, notwithstanding his garb, is fat and festive; and he
died of apoplexy.

In the same house, we believe, that had been occupied by
Penn*, resided an author who must not be passed over in a
work of this kind; to wit, the indefatigable and honest
antiquary, Dr. Birch. He came of a Quaker stock. Birch
astonished his friends by going a great deal into company;
but the secret of his uniting sociality with labour, was his
early rising. This, which appears to be one of the main
secrets of longevity, ought to have kept him older, for he died
at the age of sixty-one: but he was probably festive as well
social, and should have taken more exercise. Being a bad
horseman, he was thrown on the Hampstead road, and killed
on the spot; but the doctors were uncertain whether apoplexy
had not a hand in the disaster. In speaking of Birch, nobody
should omit a charming billet, written to him by his first
wife, almost in the article of death. The death took place
within a year after their marriage, and was accelerated by
childbed.

"This day I return you, my dearest life, my sincere hearty thanks
for every favour bestowed on your most faithful and obedient wife.
    "*July* 31, 1729."   "HANNAH BIRCH."*

In Norfolk Street, for upwards of thirty years, lived
Dr. Brocklesby, the friend and physician of Dr. Johnson.
Physicians of this class may, *par excellence*, be styled the

* We conclude so from our authorities in both instances. Mr.
Malcolm's Londinium Redivivum, vol. iii., p. 398.
† See his life in Chalmers's General Biographical Dictionary, vol. v.,
p. 280.

friends of men of letters. They partake of their accomplishments, understand their infirmities, sympathise with their zeal to do good, and prolong their lives by the most delicate and disinterested attentions. Between no two professions has a more liberal and cordial intimacy been maintained than between literature and medicine. Brocklesby was an honour to the highest of his calling.

"In the course of his practice," we are told that "his advice, as well as his purse, was ever accessible to the poor, as well as to men of merit who stood in need of either. Besides giving his advice to the poor of all descriptions, which he did with an active and unwearied benevolence, he had always upon his list two or three poor widows, to whom he granted small annuities ; and who, on the quarter-day of receiving their stipends, always partook of the hospitalities of his table. To his relations, who wanted his assistance in their business or professions, he was not only liberal, but so judicious in his liberalities as to supersede the necessity of a repetition of them. To his friend Dr Johnson (when it was in agitation amongst his friends to procure an enlargement of his pension, the better to enable him to travel for the benefit of his health), he offered an establishment of one hundred pounds per year during his life; and upon Dr. Johnson's declining it (which he did in the most affectionate terms of gratitude and friendship), he made him a second offer of apartments in his own house, for the more immediate benefit of medical advice. To his old and intimate friend Edmund Burke, he had many years back bequeathed by will the sum of one thousand pounds; but recollecting that this event might take place (which it afterwards did) when such a legacy could be of no service to him, he, with that judicious liberality for which he was always distinguished, gave it to him in advance, '*ut pignus amicitiæ:*' it was accepted as such by Mr. Burke, accompanied with a letter, which none but a man feeling the grandeur and purity of friendship like him could dictate."[*]

If it be dangerous in the present condition of society, to incur pecuniary obligations, particularly for those who are more qualified to think than to act, and who may ultimately startle to find themselves in positions in which they can neither prove the benefit done them, nor the good feelings which allowed them to receive it, nobody can doubt the generosity of such a man as Brocklesby; who, so far from being a mere patron, jealous of being obliged himself, was equally as prepared to receive kindness as to show it. Proposing just before he died to go down to Burke's house at Beaconsfield, and somebody hinting to him the danger of being fatigued, and of lying out of his own bed,

[*] General Biographical Dictionary, 8vo., 1812, vol. vii.

he replied with his usual calmness, "My good friend, I perfectly understand your hint, and am thankful to you for it; but where's the difference, whether I die *at a friend's house*, at an inn, or in a postchaise? I hope I am every way prepared for such an event, and perhaps it is as well to elude the expectation of it." This was said like a man, and a friend. Brocklesby was not one who would cant about giving trouble at such a moment—the screen of those who hate to be troubled; neither would he grudge a friend the melancholy satisfaction of giving him a bed to die in. He better understood the first principles which give light and life to the world, and left jealousy and misgiving to the vulgar.

Dr. Brocklesby died at his house in the street above mentioned, and was buried in the churchyard. Lee was buried, "at St. Clement Danes;" probably, therefore, in the churchyard also. There are now in that spot some trees, by far the best things about the church. The reader may imagine them to shade the places where the poet and the physician lie.

Arundel or Norfolk House, after the great fire, became the temporary place of meeting for the Royal Society, previously to its return to Gresham College. It was pulled down on their leaving it, the century before last, and the streets before mentioned built in its room. They appear to have been favourite places of residence with persons connected with the drama. Congreve lived in Surrey Street, Mountford the player in Norfolk Street, Mrs. Bracegirdle in Howard Street, and Mrs. Barry somewhere near her.

Congreve died where he had lived (Jan. 29, 1728-9), after having been for several years afflicted with blindness and gout; of which, however, he seems to have made the best he could, by the help of good sense and naturally good spirits. If his wits ever failed him, it was in the propensity to a love of rank and fashion, which, in spite of all that he had seen in the world, never forsook him. It originated probably in the need he thought he had of them, when he first set out in life. The finest sense of men of his cast does not rise above a graceful selfishness. It was most probably in Surrey Street (for he had come to the "verge of life"), that he had a visit paid him by Voltaire, who has recorded the disgust given him by an ebullition of his foppery: for the Frenchman had a great admiration of him as a writer. "Congreve spoke of his works," says Voltaire, "as of trifles that were beneath him; and hinted to me, in our first conversation, that I should visit him upon no other foot than upon that of a gentleman, who led a life of plainness and simplicity. I answered, *that had he been so unfortunate as to be a mere gentleman,* I should never have come to see him ; and I was very much disgusted at so unseasonable a piece of vanity."* Our readers will admire the fineness of this rebuke.

But the most glaring instance of this propensity was his leaving the bulk of his fortune to a duchess, when he had poor relations in want of it.

" Having lain in state," says Johnson, "in the Jerusalem Chamber, he was buried in Westminster Abbey, where a monument is erected to his memory by Henrietta, Duchess of Marlborough, to whom, for reasons either not known or not mentioned, he bequeathed a legacy of about ten thousand pounds, the accumulation of attentive parsimony, which, though to her superfluous and useless, might have given great assistance to the ancient family from which he descended ; at that time, by the imprudence of his relation, reduced to difficulties and distress." †

" Congreve," says Dr. Young, " was very intimate for years with Mrs. Bracegirdle, who lived in the same street—his house very near hers; until his acquaintance with the young Duchess of Marlborough. He then quitted that house. The duchess showed me a diamond necklace (which Lady Di. used afterwards to wear), that cost seven thousand pounds, and was purchased with the money Congreve left her. How much better would it have been to have given it to poor Mrs. Bracegirdle !" ‡

Yet this dramatist, throughout his life, had had the good word of everybody. All parties praised him : all parties kept him in office (he had some places that are said to have pro-duced him twelve hundred a year): Pope dedicated his *Iliad* to him ; called him, after his death, *Ultimus Romanorum;* and added that " Garth, Vanbrugh, and he were the three most honest-hearted, real good men of the Kit-Kat Club !" §

The secret of this is, that Congreve loved above all things to be at ease, and spoke politicly of everybody. He had a bad opinion of mankind, as we may see by his comedies ; and he made the best of it, by conversing with them as if he took heed of their claws. The only person, we believe, that he ever opposed, was Collier, who attacked the stage with more spirit than elegance, and who was at enmity with the whole world of wit and fashion. We are far from thinking with Collier, that the abuses of the stage outweigh the benefit it does to the world ; nor do we think the world by any

* Letters on the English Nation.
† Life, in Chalmers's English Poets, p. 26.
‡ Spence's Anecdotes, p. 376.   § Idem, p. 46.

means so bad as Congreve supposed it, nor himself either : but it is useful to know the tendencies of those who have a habit of thinking otherwise.

Congreve's bequest created a good deal of gossip. Curll, the principal scandal-monger of those times, got up a catch-penny life of him, professing to be written by " Charles Wilson, Esq.," but supposed to be the work of Oldmixon. There is no relying upon Charles Wilson ; but, from internal evidence, we may take his word occasionally ; and we may believe him when he says that the duchess and her friends were alarmed at the threatened book. The picture which he draws of her manner has also an air like a woman of quality. She had demanded a sight of the documents on which the book was founded ; and being refused, asked what authority they had, and what pieces contained in it were genuine. " Upon being civilly told there would be found several essays, letters, and characters of that gentleman's writing," says Mr. Wilson, " she, with a most affected, extraordinary, dramatic drawl, cried out, ' Not one single sheet of paper, I dare to swear.' " * Mr. Wilson's own grand air in return is very amusing. He speaks of Arbuthnot's coming with " ex-presses," probably to Curll's ; and adds, that if he be despatched with any more, " he may, if he please, come to me, who am as easily to be found in Great Russell Street, Bloomsbury, *when in town*, as he is in Burlington Gardens.— Cha. Wilson."

Mr. Wilson's book opens with a copy of the will, in which 500*l*. are left among the Congreves ; about 500*l*. more to friends and domestics, &c. (not omitting 200*l*. to Mrs. Brace-girdle) ; and all the rest (with power to annul or increase the complimentary part of the legacies) to the Duchess of Marlborough. We know not that anybody could have brought forward grounds for objecting to this will, had the duchess been poor herself ; for his relations may or may not have have had claims upon him—relations, as such, not being of necessity friends, though it is generally fit that they should partake of the family prosperity. We except, of course, a man's immediate kindred, particularly those whom

* Memoirs of the Life, Writings, &c., of William Congreve, Esq., 1730, p. xi. Curll discreetly omits his name in the titlepage. [On reconsidering this interview (though we have no longer the book by us, and therefore speak from memory) we are doubtful, whether the lady was not Mrs. Bracegirdle, instead of the duchess.]

he has brought into the world. But here was a woman, rolling in wealth, and relatives neither entirely forgotten, nor yet, it seems, properly assisted. The bequest must, therefore, either have been a mere piece of vanity, or the consequence of habitual subjection to a woman's humours. The duchess was not ungrateful to his memory. She raised him, as we have seen, a monument ; and it is related in Cibber's *Lives of the the Poets*,* we know not on what authority, that she missed his company so much, as to cause "an image of him to be placed every day on her toilet-table, to which she would talk as to the living Mr. Congreve, with all the freedom of the most *polite* and *unreserved* conversation." There is something very ludicrous in this way of putting a case, which might otherwise be affecting. It is as if there had been a sort of polite mania on both sides.

Congreve's plays are exquisite of their kind, and the excessive heartlessness and duplicity of some of his characters are not to be taken without allowance for the *ugly ideal*. There is something not natural, both in his characters and wit ; and we read him rather to see how entertaining he can make his superfine ladies and gentlemen, and what a pack of sensual busybodies they are, like insects over a pool, than from any true sense of them as " men and women." As a companion he must have been exquisite to a woman of fashion. We can believe that the duchess, in ignorance of any tragic emotion but what was mixed with his loss, would really talk with a waxen image of him in a peruke, and think the universe contained nothing better. It was carrying wit and politeness beyond the grave. Queen Constance in Shakspeare makes grief put on the pretty looks of her lost child : the Duchess of Marlborough made it put on a wig and jaunty air, such as she had given her friend in his monument in Westminster Abbey. No criticism on his plays could be more perfect. Congreve's serious poetry is a refreshment, from its extreme insipidity and common-place. Everybody is innocent in some corner of the mind, and has faith in something. Congreve had no faith in his fellow-creatures, but he had a scholar's (not a poet's) belief in nymphs and weeping fauns ; and he wrote elegies full of them, upon queens and marquisses. If it be true that he wrote the character of Aspasia (Lady Elizabeth Hastings), in the *Tatler* (No. 42), he had indeed faith in something better ; for in that paper is not only given

* Lives of the Poets, &c., by Mr. Cibber and others, 1753.

an admiring account of a person of very exalted excellence,
but the author has said of her one of the finest things that a
sincere heart could utter ; namely, that "to love her was a
liberal education." We cannot help thinking, however, that
the generous and trusting hand of Steele is very visible
throughout this portrait ; and in the touch just mentioned, in
particular.

The engaging manners of Mrs. Bracegirdle gave rise to a
tragical circumstance in Howard Street—the death of Mountford her fellow-player. Mrs. Bracegirdle, one of the most
popular actresses of that time, was a brunette, not remarkable
for her beauty, but so much so for the attractiveness superior
to beauty, that Cibber calls her the "darling of the stage,"
and says it was a kind of fashion for the young men about
town to have a tenderness for her. This general regard she
preserved by setting a value on herself, not so common with
actresses at that time as it has been since. Accordingly, some
made honourable proposals, which were then still more remarkable. In Rowe's poems, there is a bantering epistle to
an Earl of S——, advising him not to care for what people
might think, but to pursue his inclinations to that effect.
Among others a Captain Hill made desperate love, professing
the same intentions ; but he was a man of bad character,
and the lady would have nóthing to say to him. The captain,
like a proper coxcomb, took it into his head that nothing
could have prevented his success, but some other person ; and
he fixed upon Mountford as the happy man. Mountford was
the best lover and finest gentleman then on the stage, as
Mrs. Bracegirdle was the most charming heroine ; but it does
not appear that Hill had any greater ground for his suspicion
than their frequent performance in the same play, which,
however, to a jealous man, must have been extremely provoking. They used to act Alexander and Statira together. In
Mountford's Alexander, according to Cibber, there were seen
" the great, the tender, the penitent, the despairing, the transported, and the amiable, in the highest perfection ;" and " if
anything," he said, " could excuse that desperate extravagance
of love, that almost frantic passion," it was when Mrs.
Bracegirdle was the Statira. Imagine a dark-souled fellow in
the pit thinking himself in love with this Statira, and that
the passion between her and the Alexander was real. This
play was acted a few nights before the catastrophe which we
are about to relate.

Hill was intimate with another man of bad character, Lord Mohun; who agreed to assist him in carrying off Mrs. Bracegirdle. The captain had often said that he would be "revenged" upon Mountford; and dining with Lord Mohun on the day when they attempted the execution of their plot, he said, further, that he would " stab " him " if he resisted;" upon which Mohun said that he would "stand by his friend."

Mohun and Hill met at the playhouse at six o'clock, changed clothes there, and waited some time for Mrs. Bracegirdle; but not finding her come, they took a coach which they had ordered to be ready, drove towards her lodgings in Howard Street, and then back to Drury Lane, where they directed the coach to stop near Lord Clare's house (by the present Craven Buildings). Mrs. Bracegirdle had been supping at a Mr. Page's, in Princess Street, Drury Lane. She came out, accompanied by her mother, brother, and Mr. Page, and was seized by Hill, who, with the aid of a number of soldiers, endeavoured to force her into the coach. In the coach was Lord Mohun, with seven or eight pistols. Old Mrs. Bracegirdle threw her arms round her daughter's waist; her ₍other friends, and at length the passengers, interfered; and our heroine succeeded in getting into her lodgings in Howard Street, Hill and Mohun following them on foot. When they all came to the door, Hill would have spoken with Page, but the latter refused; and the door was shut. A witness, at the trial of Lord Mohun, deposed, that they knocked several times at the door, and then the captain entreated to beg pardon of Mrs. Bracegirdle for having affronted her, but in vain.

Hill and Mohun remained in the street. They sent to a tavern for a bottle of wine, and perambulated before the door with drawn swords. Mrs. Browne, the mistress of the house, came out to know what they did there; upon which Hill said that he would light upon Mountford some day or other, and that he would be revenged on him. The people in-doors, upon this, sent to Mountford's house in Norfolk Street, to inform his wife; and she despatched messengers to all the places where he was likely to be found, to warn him of his danger, but they could not meet with him. Meanwhile the constables and watchmen come up and ask the strangers what they mean. They say they are drinking a bottle of wine. Lord Mohun adds that he is ready to put up his

sword, remarking, withal, that he is a "peer of the realm."
Upon asking why the other gentleman did not put up his,
his lordship tells them, that his friend had lost the scabbard.
The watchmen, like "ancient and quiet watchmen," go away
to the tavern to "examine who they are;" and in the
meantime Mountford makes his appearance coming up the
street.   Mountford lived in Norfolk Street, but he turned out
of the path that led to his own house, and was coming
towards Mrs. Bracegirdle's—whether to her house, or to any
other, does not appear.   By this time two hours had elapsed.
Mrs. Browne, who seems to have remained watching at the
door, caught sight of Mountford, and hastened to warn him
how he advanced.   She was either not quick enough, or
Mountford (which appears most likely) pressed on in spite of
what she said, and, according to her statement, the following
dialogue took place between him and Lord Mohun :—

"Your humble servant, my lord."
"Your servant, Mr. Mountford.   I have a great respect for you,
Mr. Mountford, and would have no difference between us; but there
is a thing fallen out between Mr. Hill and Mrs. Bracegirdle."
"My lord, has my wife disobliged your lordship? if she has, she
shall ask your pardon.   But Mrs. Bracegirdle is no concern of mine:
I know nothing of this matter; I come here by accident.   But I hope
your lordship will not vindicate Hill in such actions as these are."

Upon this, according to Mrs. Browne's statement, Hill bade
Mountford draw; which the other said he would; but whether
he received his wound before or after she could not tell, owing
to its being night-time.

Another female witness, who lived next door, gives the
dialogue as follows.   Lord Mohun begins:—

"Mr. Mountford, your humble servant.   I am glad to see you"
(embracing him).
"Who is this? my Lord Mohun?"
"Yes, it is."
"What bringeth your lordship here at this time of night?"
"I suppose you were sent for, Mr. Mountford?"
"No, indeed; I came by chance."
"You have heard of the business of Mrs. Bracegirdle?"
Hill (interfering).   "Pray, my lord, hold your tongue.   This is
not a convenient time to discuss this business."   (On saying which,
the witness adds, that he would have drawn Mohun away.)
Mountford.   "I am very sorry, my lord, to see that your lordship
should assist Captain Hill in so ill an action as this: pray let me
desire your lordship to forbear."

As soon as he had uttered these words Hill, according to
the witness, came up and struck Mountford a box on the ear;

upon which the latter demanded with an oath, "what that was for;" and then she gives a confused account of the result, which was the receipt of a mortal wound by the poor actor. It was agreed that Mountford's sword was not drawn in the first instance, and that Hill's was; and the question was settled by the dying deposition of Mountford, who stated several times over, that Lord Mohun offered him no violence, but that Hill struck him with his left hand, and then ran him through the body, before he had time to draw in defence.

Mountford died next day. Hill fled at the time, and we hear no more of him. Mohun was tried for his life, but acquitted, for want of evidence, of malice prepense. The truth is, he was a great fool, and Hill appears to have been another. The captain himself, probably, did not know what he intended, though his words would have hung him had he been caught. They were a couple of box-lobby swaggerers, who had heated themselves with wine; and Hill, who told the constables "they might knock him down if they liked," and was for drawing Mohun away on Mountford's appearance, was most likely overcome with rage and jealousy at hearing the latter speak of him with rebuke. Mohun was at that time very young. He never ceased, however, hankering after this sort of excitement to his dulness, till he got killed in a duel about an estate with the Duke of Hamilton, who was at the same time mortally wounded. Swift, in a letter about it, calls Mohun a "dog." Pennant says, that when his body was taken home bleeding (to his house in Gerrard Street), Lady Mohun was very angry at its being flung upon the best bed."*

In front of the spot now occupied by St. Mary-le-Strand, commonly called the New Church, anciently stood a cross, at which, says Stowe, "in the year 1294, and other times, the justices itinerant sat without London." In the place of this cross was set up a May-pole, by a blacksmith named John Clarges, whose daughter Ann became the wife of Monk, Duke of Albemarle. It was for a long time in a state of decay, and having been taken down in 1713, a new one was erected opposite Somerset House. This second May-pole had two gilt balls and a vane on the summit, and was decorated on

* Pennant's London, *ut supra*, p. 124. Swift's Letters to Stella. The particulars of the case are taken from Howell's State Trials. vol. xii., p. 947.

holidays with flags and garlands. The races in the "Dunciad" take place

> "Where the tall May-pole overlook'd the Strand."

It was removed in 1718, probably being thought in the way of the new church, which was then being finished. Sir Isaac Newton begged it of the parish, and afterwards sent it to the Rector of Wanstead, who set it up in Wanstead Park to support the then largest telescope in Europe. The gift of John Clarges came a day too late. In old times, May had been a great holiday in the streets of London. We shall speak further of it when we come to the parish of St. Andrew Undershaft, so called from a May-pole higher than the church. But though the holiday returned with the Restoration, it never properly recovered the disuse occasioned by the civil wars, and the contempt thrown on it by the spirit of puritanism. We gained too many advantages by the thoughtfulness generated in those times to quarrel with their mistakes ; and have no doubt that the progress of knowledge to which they gave an impulse, will bring back the advantages they omitted by the way."*

The New Church, or, more properly, the Church of St. Mary - le - Strand, was built by Gibbs, the architect of St. Martin-in-the-Fields. It was one of the "fifty," improperly so called, that are said to have been built in the reign of Queen Anne; for though fifty were ordered, the number was not completed. The old church in this quarter, which stood at a little distance to the south, was removed by the Protector Somerset, to make way for Somerset House, and has never been restored. The parishioners went to the neighbouring churches. The New Church is in the pretty, over-ornamented style, very different from that of St. Martin's with its noble front : and though far better than St. Clement's, and as superior to many places of worship built lately† as art is

---

* "Captain Baily, said to have accompanied Raleigh in his last expedition to Guiana, employed four hackney coaches, with drivers in liveries, to ply at the May-pole in the Strand, fixing his own rates, about the year 1634.   Baily's coaches seem to have been the first of what are now called hackney-coaches ; a term at that time applied indiscriminately to all coaches let for hire."   The favourite Buckingham, about the year 1619, introduced the sedan. The post-chaise, invented in France, was introduced by Mr. Tull, son of the well-known writer on husbandry.   The stage first came in about the year 1775 ; and mail-coaches appeared in 1785.—See a note to the *Tatler*, as above, vol. iv., p. 415.

† This was written in 1834.

superior to ignorance, yet it surely is not worthy of its advantageous situation. It is one of those toys of architecture which have been said to require glass cases. For the superfluous height of the steeple, Gibbs offered an excuse. A column was to have been erected near the church in honour of Queen Anne, but, as the Queen died, she was no longer thought deserving the column, and the architect was ordered to make a steeple with the materials, whereas he had intended only a belfry. Now, to render the steeple fitting, the church should have had a wider base ; but the structure was already begun, and there was no changing the plan of it. It might be still argued, that the steeple should not have been made so high: but then, what was to be done with the stones? This, in the mouth of parish virtù, was a triumphant reply. After all, however, the artist need not have spoilt his church with ornament. He said, that being situated in a very public place, " the parishioners" spared no cost to beautify it; but to beautify a church is not to make it a piece of confectionery."*

Somerset House occupies the site of a princely mansion built by Somerset the Protector, brother of Lady Jane Seymour, and uncle to King Edward VI. His character is not sufficiently marked to give any additional interest to the spot. He was great by accident ; lost and gained his greatness, according as others acted upon it; and ultimately resigned it on the scaffold. The house he left became the property of the Crown, and was successively in possession of Queen Elizabeth and of the queens of James I., Charles I., and Charles II.

The rooms in this house witnessed many joyous scenes and many anxious ones. Somerset had not long inhabited it when he was taken to the scaffold. Elizabeth, in her wise economy, lent it to her cousin Lord Hunsdon, whom she frequently visited within its walls.

During its occupation by James's queen, Anne of Denmark (from whose family it was called Denmark House), Wilson says, that a constant masquerade was going on, the Queen and

---

* The faults of the New Church are, that it is too small for the steeple; that it is divided into two stories, which make it still smaller; that the entablature on the north and south parts is too frequently interrupted; that pediments are "affectedly put over each projection;" in a word, that a little object is cut up into too many little parts, and rendered fantastic with embellishment. See the opinions of Gwynn, Ralph, and Malton, quoted in Brayley's London and Middlesex, vol. iv., p. 199.

her ladies, "like so many sea-nymphs, or nereids," appearing in various dresses, "to the ravishment of the beholders."*

Here began the struggle for mastery between Charles I. and Henrietta Maria, which terminated in favour of the latter, though the King behaved himself manfully at first. Henrietta had brought over with her a meddling French household which, after repeated grievances, his Majesty was obliged to send "packing." He summoned them all together one evening in the house, and addressed them as follows:—

"Gentlemen and ladies,

"I am driven to that extremity, as I am personally come to acquaint you, that I very earnestly desire your return into France. True it is, the deportment of some amongst you hath been very inoffensive to me; but others again have so dallied with my patience, and so highly affronted me, as I cannot, and will not, longer endure it."†

"The King's address, implicating no one, was immediately followed by a volley of protestations of innocence. An hour after he had delivered his commands, Lord Conway announced to the foreigners, that early in the morning carriages and carts and horses would be ready for them and their baggage. Amidst a scene of confusion, the young Bishop (he was scarcely of age) protested that this was impossible; that they owed debts in London, and that much was due to them. On the following day, the *procureur-general* of the Queen flew to the keeper of the great seal at the privy council, requiring an admission to address his Majesty, then present at his council, on matters important to himself and the Queen. This being denied, he exhorted them to maintain the Queen in all her royal prerogatives; and he was answered, 'So we do.'

"Their prayers and disputes served to postpone their departure. Their conduct during this time was not very decorous. It appears, by a contemporary letter-writer, that they flew to take possession of the Queen's wardrobe and jewels. They did not leave her a change of linen, since it was with difficulty her Majesty procured one. Everyone now looked to lay his hand on what he might call his own. Everything he could touch was a perquisite. One extraordinary expedient was that of inventing bills to the amount of ten thousand pounds, for articles and other engagements in which they had entered for the service of the Queen, which her Majesty acknowledged, but afterwards confessed that the debts were fictitious."‡

"In truth," continues the writer, "the breaking up of this French establishment was ruinous to the individuals who had purchased their places at the rate of life annuities." Charles now grew indignant, and sent the following letter to Buckingham:—

---

* Life of James I. quoted in Pennant, p. 155.

† L'Estrange's Life of Charles I., quoted in D'Israeli's Commentaries on the Life and Reign of Charles I, vol. ii., p. 218.

‡ L'Estrange's Life of Charles I.

" Steenie.*

" I have receaved your letter by Dic Greame (Sir Richard Grahame). This is my answer : I command you to send all the French away to-morrow out of the towne, if you can by fair meanes (but stike not long in disputing), otherways force them away, dryving them away lyke so manie wilde beastes, until ye have shipped them, and so the devil goe with them. Let me heare no answer, but of the performance of my command.   So I rest,

" Your faithful, constant, loving friend,

"Oaking,   " C. R."

" The seventh of August, 1626."

" This order put an end to the delay, but the King paid the debts, the fictitious ones and all—at the cost, as it appears, of fifty thousand pounds. Even the haughty beauty, Madame St. George, was pre-sented by the king on her dismission with several thousand pounds and jewels."

Still the French could not go quietly.   " The French bishop," says D'Israeli, " and the whole party having con-trived all sorts of delays to avoid the expulsion, the yeomen of the guard were sent to turn them out of Somerset House, whence the juvenile prelate, at the same time making his protest and mounting the steps of the coach, took his depar-ture ' head and shoulders.'   In a long procession of near forty coaches, *after four days' tedious travelling*, they reached *Dover;* but the spectacle of these impatient foreigners so reluctantly quitting England, gesticulating their sorrows or their quarrels, exposed them to the derision, and stirred up the prejudices, of the common people. As Madame St. George, whose vivacity is always described as extremely French, was stepping into the boat, one of the mob could not resist the satisfaction of flinging a stone at her French cap.   An English courtier who was conducting her, instantly quitted his charge, ran the fellow through the body, and quietly returned to the boat. The man died on the spot, but no further notice appears to have been taken of the inconsiderate gallantry of the English courtier."

Henrietta had a magnificent Catholic chapel in Somerset House, and a cloister of Capuchins.   The former has given occasion to some interesting descriptions of papal show and spectacle in the commentaries just quoted.†

* Steenie—a familiarisation of Stephen.   The name was given Buckingham by James I., in reference to the beauty of St. Stephen, whose face, during his martyrdom, is described in the New Testament as shining like that of an angel.

† See the account of the Paradise of Glory, in vol. ii., p. 225.

Cromwell's body lay in state at Somerset House, as Monk's did afterwards, probably on that account.

Pepys, the prince of gossips, gives an edifying picture of the presence chamber in this palace, when the queens of the two Charleses were there together, a little after the Restoration :

"Meeting Mr. Pierce the chyrurgeon," says he, "he took me into Somerset House, and there carried me into the Queene-mother's presence chamber, where she was with our own queene sitting on her left hand, whom I did never see before, and though she be not very charming, yet she hath a good, modest, and innocent look, which is pleasing. Here I also saw Madame Castlemaine; and, which pleased me most, Mr. Crofts, the King's bastard, a most pretty sparke of about fifteen years old, who, I perceive, do hang much upon my Lady Castlemaine, and is always with her; and, I hear, the queenes both are mighty kind to him. By and by, in comes the King, and anon the duke and his duchesse; so that they being all together, was such a sight, as I never could almost have happened to see, with so much ease and leisure. They staid till it was dark and then went away; the King and his Queene, and my Lady Castlemaine and young Crofts, in one coach, and the rest in other coaches. Here were great stores of great ladies, but very few handsome. The King and Queene were very merry; and he would have made the Queene-mother believe that his Queene was with child, and said that she said so, and the young Queene answered, 'You lye;' which was the first English word that I ever heard her say: which made the King good sport."*

After this we shall not wonder at the following:—

"30th (Dec., 1662). Visited Mrs. Ferrer and staid talking with her a good while, there being a little proud, ugly, talking little lady there, that was much crying up the Queene-mother's court at Somerset House above our own Queene's; there being before her no allowance of laughing and the mirth that is at others; and, indeed, it is observed that the greatest court now-a-days is there."†

The following print represents Old Somerset House, as it appeared in the reign of Charles II. We have seen, but in vain endeavoured to procure for this book, a scarce one by Hollar, in which the towers in the back ground mark out the front in the Strand, and a tall May-pole to the right was the May-pole of John Clarges. The front, looking on the river, was added by Charles II. Inigo Jones was the architect. In Hollar's print it gives us a taste of the banqueting room at Whitehall in its elevation, and in the harmonies of the windows and pilasters, Below is a portico; and there is another to the right. The chapel, with an enclosure to the left, was the Catholic one; the houses by it, the cloisters of

---

* Memoirs of Samuel Pepys, Esq., 2nd edition, vol. i., p. 309.
† Id., p. 357.

the Capuchins. There was a figure walking in the chapel garden, whom, by his gesticulating arm, we might imagine to be the queen's confessor, studying his to-morrow's sermon, or thinking how he shall get the start of the king's chaplain in saying grace. A curious scene of this kind is worth extracting. "Once," Mr. D'Israeli informs us, "when the king and queen were dining together in the presence, Hacket being to say grace, the queen's confessor would have antici-

pated him, and an indecorous race was run between the Catholic priest and the Protestant chaplain, till the latter shoved him aside, and the king pulling the dishes to him, the carvers performed their office. Still the confessor, standing by the queen, was on the watch to be before Hacket for the after-grace, but Hacket again got the start. The confessor, however, resounded the grace louder than the chaplain, and the king, in great passion, instantly rose, taking the queen by the hand." The bowling-green that we read of is probably between the two rows of trees to the right, in front of the right portico (the left, if considered from the house). The garden is in the most formal style of the parterre, where

    —— "each alley has its brother,
    And half the platform just reflects the other;"

a style, however, not without its merits, particularly in admitting so many walks among the flowers, and inviting a pace up and down between the trees. Milton, though he made a different garden for his Eden, spoke of "trim gardens," as enjoyed by "retired leisure." In this back

front were the apartments of the court. The scene we have
just been reading in Pepys must have passed in one of them.
Here Charles the First's widow lived with her supposed
husband, the Earl of St. Albans; though she was not so
constant to the place as Waller prophesied she would be.
She had been used to too much power as a queen, and found
she had too little as a dowager. Poor Catherine remained as
long as she could. She lived here till she returned to
Portugal, in the reign of William III. Speaking of Waller,
we must not quit the premises without noticing a catastrophe
that befel him at the water-gate, or Somerset-stairs (also, by
the way, the work of Inigo Jones). Waller, according to
Aubrey, had but " a tender weak body, but was always very
temperate." —— (we know not who this is) "made him
damnable drunk at Somerset House, where, at the water
stayres, he fell down, and had a cruel fall. 'Twas a pity to
use such a sweet swan so inhumanly."* Waller, who, notwithstanding his weak body, lived to be old, was a water-
drinker; but he had a poet's wine in his veins, and was
excellent company. Saville said, " that nobody should keep
him company without drinking, but Ned Waller."

Subsequently to Catherine's departure, old Somerset House
was chiefly used as a residence for princes from other countries
when on a visit. It was pulled down towards the end of the
last century, and the present structure erected by Sir William
Chambers, but left unfinished. The unfinished part, which
is towards the east, is now in a state of completion, as the
King's College. The only memorial remaining of the old
palace and its outhouses is in the wall of a house in the Strand,
where the sign of a lion still survives a number of other
signs, noticed in a list made at the time, and common at that
period to houses of all descriptions.

The area of New Somerset House occupies a large space
of ground, the basement of the back-front being in the river.
Three sides of it are appropriated to a variety of public offices,
connected with trade, commerce, and civil economy; and the
front was lately dignified by the occupancy of the Royal and
Antiquarian Societies and the Royal Academy of Painting.
The structure was an ambitious one on the part of the
architect, and upon the whole is elegant but timid. There is
a look of fragility in it. It has the extent, but not the

* Lives and Letters, as above.

majesty, of a national emporium.   Rules are violated in some
instances for the sake of trifles, as is the case of pillars
"standing on nothing and supporting nothing;" and in
others, it would seem out of a dread of the result, as in the
instance of the huge basement over the water, supporting a
cupola, which is petty in the comparison.   Sir William did
well in wishing to have an imposing front towards the river;
but he might have had another towards the Strand, nobler
than the present one.   The lower part is nothing better than
a pillared coachway.   However, the front of the story is,
perhaps, the best part of the whole building.   It present a
graceful harmony in the proportions.

The Royal Society, which originated in the college rooms
of Dr. Wilkins, afterwards bishop of Chester, met, when it
was incorporated, at Old Gresham College in Aldersgate
Street; then at Arundel House (on account of the fire); then
returned to Gresham College; and, after a variety of other
experiments upon lodging, was settled by the late king in
New Somerset House.   This society, on its foundation, was
much ridiculed by the wits.   Though its ends were great, it
naturally busied itself with little things; pragmatical and
pedantic persons naturally enough got mixed up with it;
some of its members had foibles of enthusiasm and pedantry,
which were easily confounded with their capacities; and the
jokes were most likely encouraged by the king (Charles II.),
who, though fond of scientific experiments, and wearing a
grave face in presence of the learned body (of which he
declared himself a member), was not a man to forego such an
opportunity of jesting.   Wilkins wrote a book to show that
a man might go to the moon; and the ethical common-places
of Boyle (who was as great a natural philosopher as he was a
poor moralist) were the origin of Swift's *Essays on the Tritical
Faculties of the Mind.*   Then there was the good Evelyn
with his hard words, wondering sentimentally at every thing;
and jolly Pepys marvelling like Sancho Panza.   The readers
of Pepy's *Diary* have been surprised at his not liking
Hudibras.   Perhaps one reason was, that Butler was the
greatest of the jesters against the society.   It was impossible
not to laugh at the jokes, in which he charges them with
attempting to

"Search the moon by her own light;
To take an inventory of all
Her real estate and personal;—

> To measure wind, and weigh the air,
>   And turn a circle to a square;
>   And in the braying of an ass,
>   Find out the treble and the bass ;
>   If mares neigh *alto*, and a cow
>   In double diapason low." *

Evelyn got angry, and pretended to be calm.   Cowley expressed his anger with a generous indignation.   The following passage in his *Ode to the Society* concludes with a fine,
appropriate simile.   " Mischief and true dishonour," says he,

> —— "fall on those
> Who would to laughter and to scorn expose
> So virtuous and so noble a design,
> So human for its use, for knowledge so divine.
> The things which these proud men despise and call
> Impertinent, and vain, and small,
> Those smallest things of Nature let me know,
> Rather than all their greatest actions do !
> Whoever would deposed Truth advance
>   Into the throne usurped from it,
> Must feel at first the blows of Ignorance,
>   And the sharp points of envious Wit.
> So, when, by various turns of the celestial dance
>   In many thousand years
>   A star, so long unknown, appears,
> Though Heaven itself more beauteous by it grow,
> It troubles and alarms the world below,
> Does to the wise a star, to fools a meteor, show." †

Perhaps a part of the jealousy against the Royal Society
arose from a notion which has since become not uncommon,
that bodies of this nature, incorporated by kings, are calculated rather to limit inquiry, than to enlarge it.   Without
stopping to discuss this point, we shall merely observe, that
the real greatness of all such bodies, like those of nations
themselves, must arise from the greatness of individuals ; and
that whether the bodies give any lustre to them or not, there
is no denying that the individuals give lustre to the bodies.
When Sir Isaac Newton became president, jesting ceased.

It is pleasant to think, while passing Somerset House, in
the midst of the noise of a great thoroughfare, that philosophical speculation is, perhaps, going on within those graceful
walls ; that in the midst of all sorts of new things, sight is not
lost of the venerable beauties of old ; and that art, as well as
philosophy, is considering what it shall do for 'our use and

---

* See three Poems in his Genuine Remains.—*Chalmers's British
Poets*, vol. viii., p. 187.
    † British Pocts, vol. vii., p. 101.

entertainment.   The Antiquarian Society originated as far
back as the sixteenth century (about the year 1580), and held
its first sittings in a room in the Herald's College ; but it did
not receive a charter till the year 1751.   Neither Elizabeth
nor James would give it one, fearful, perhaps, of bringing up
discussions on matters connected with politics and religion
Elizabeth has now become one of the most interesting of its
heroines.   There is no society, we think, more likely to increase with age, and to outgrow half-witted objection.   The
growth of time adds daily to its stock ; and as reflecting men
become interested in behalf of ages to come, they naturally
turn with double sympathy towards the periods that have
gone by, and to the multitudes of beating hearts that have
become dust. We should like to see the society in a venerable
building of its own, raised in some quiet spot, with trees
about it, and with painted windows reflecting light through
old heraldry.

The Royal Academy of Painters, now removed to Trafalgar
Square, first met in Saint Martin's Lane, under the title of
the Society of Artists of Great Britain.   They had a division
among them, which gave rise to the establishment as it now
stands ; and are a flourishing body, we believe, in point of
funds. Of the deceased members who have done them honour,
we shall speak when we come to their abodes.

The Turk's Head Coffeehouse, near Somerset House, was
frequented by Dr. Johnson.

In a lodging opposite Somerset House, died the facetious
Dr. King, whom we have mentioned in speaking of Doctors'
Commons.   He had been residing in the house of a friend in
the garden-grounds between Lambeth and Vauxhall, where
he stuck so close to his books and bottle, that he began to
decline with the autumn, and shut himself up from his friends.
Lord Clarendon, who resided in Somerset House, and was his
relation, sent his sister to fetch him to a lodging he had prepared for him over the way, where he died before the lapse of
many hours, while all the world were busy with the meats
and mince-pies he had so often celebrated ; for it was
Christmas-day. Dr. King was the author of an *Art of Cookery*,
in which he pleasantly bantered a learned Kitchener of his
time ; though no man had a livelier relish of their subjects
than he.   But he wished the relish to be lively in others.   At
least, he wished them to be *leviter in modo*, if *graviter in re*.
Though occasionally coarse, he had the right style of banter,

and was of use to the Tories. In return, they would have
been of use to him, if his habits would have let them. Swift
procured him the place of Gazetteer; but he soon got rid
of it.

The precinct called the Savoy was anciently the seat of
Peter, Earl of Savoy, who came into England to visit his niece
Eleanor, Queen to Henry III. It is not known whether the
house was built or appointed for him, but on his death it
became the property of the queen, who gave it to her second
son Edmund, afterwards Earl of Lancaster; and from his
time the Savoy was reckoned part and parcel of the earldom
and honour of Lancaster, afterwards the duchy. Henry VII.

converted the palace into an hospital for the poor; and it
remained so till the time of Charles II.; though the master
and other officers, by an abuse which grew into a custom,
appear to have had no regular inmates, except themselves.
The poor were to apply, as it might happen; and what they
got depended on the generosity of the master. In answer to a
question put by Government in the reign of Queen Anne, it
was stated by the lawyer and four chaplains, that "the statutes
relating to the reception of the poor had not been observed
within the memory of man."* Charles II. put wounded
soldiers and sailors into the hospital; and since his time it
appears to have been used for the reception of soldiers and
prisoners. Latterly, it was a prison for deserters.

The Savoy was the scene of a conference in Charles II.'s

* Londinium Redivivum, vol. iv., p. 410.

reign, between the Church and the Presbyterians, in which possession was proved to be nine points of the Gospel, as well as law. The Presbyterians thought so when it was their turn to rule, and would have thought so again; and the progress of genuine Christianity has been a gainer by the mild sway of the Church of England.

In the chapel was buried old Gawen Douglas, the Chaucer of Scotland; and Anne Killegrew, celebrated by Dryden's ode for her poetry and painting. She was the daughter of one of the masters, Dr. Henry Killegrew, brother of the famous jester, and himself a man of talent.

Mrs. Anne Killegrew,

> A grace for beauty, and a muse for wit,

had probably the honour, some day, of dining with her washerwoman's daughter, in the guise of Duchess of Albemarle; for John Clarges, the blacksmith, who lived in the Savoy, had a wife who was a washerwoman, and the washerwoman had a daughter, who took linen to Monk, when he was in the Tower, and married him. It is not commonly known that the validity of this marriage was contested. Upon the trial of an action at law between the representatives of Monk and Clarges, some curious particulars, says an article in the *Gentleman's Magazine*, came out respecting the family of the duchess.

"It appeared that she was the daughter of John Clarges, a farrier, in the Savoy, and farrier to Colonel Monk, in 1632. She was married in the church of St. Lawrence Pountney, to Thomas Ratford, son of Thomas Ratford, late a farrier, servant to Prince Charles, and resident in the Mews. She had a daughter who was born in 1634, and died in 1638. Her husband and she 'lived at the Three Spanish Gypsies, in the New Exchange, and sold wash-balls, powder, gloves, and such things, and she taught girls plain work. About 1647, she, being a sempstress to Colonel Monk, used to carry him linen.' In 1648 her father and mother died. In 1649, she and her husband 'fell out and parted.' But no certificate from any parish register appears, reciting his burial. In 1652, she was married in the church of St. George, Southwark, to 'General George Monk;' and in the following year was delivered of a son, Christopher, (afterwards the second and last Duke of Albemarle), who was suckled by Honour Mills, who sold apples, herbs, oysters, &c. One of the plaintiff's witnesses swore, 'that a little before the sickness, Thomas Ratford demanded and received of him the sum of twenty shillings; that his wife saw Ratford again after the sickness, and a second time after the Duke and Duchess of Albemarle were dead.' A woman swore, 'she saw him on the day his wife (then called Duchess of Albemarle) was put into her coffin, which was after the death of the duke her second husband, who died the 3rd of January, 1669-70.' And a third witness swore,

that he saw Ratford about July, 1660.' In opposition to this evidence,
it was alleged, that 'all along, during the lives of Duke George and
Duke Christopher, this matter was never questioned,' that the latter
was universally received as only son of the former, and that 'this
matter had been thrice before tried at the bar of the King's Bench,
and the defendant had three verdicts.' A witness swore that he
owed Ratford five or six pounds, which he had never demanded.
And a man, who had married a cousin to the Duke of Albemarle,
had been told by his wife, that Ratford *died five or six years* before the
duke married. Lord Chief Justice Holt told the jury, 'If you are
certain that Duke Christopher was born while Thomas Ratford was
living, you must find for the plaintiff. If you believe he was born
after Ratford was dead, or that nothing appears what became of him
after Duke George married his wife, you must find for the defendant.'
A verdict was given for the defendant, who was only son to Sir
Thomas Clarges, knight, brother to the illustrious duchess in question,
who was created a baronet October 30, 1674, and was ancestor to the
baronets of his name."*

It does not appear on which of these accounts the jury
found a verdict for the defendant—whether because Ratford
was dead, or because nothing had been heard of him ; so that
the duchess, after all, might have been no duchess. However,
she carried it with as high a hand as if she had never been
anything else, and Monk had been a blacksmith. There are
some amusing notices of her in Pepys.

"8th (March, 1661-2). At noon, Sir W. Batten, Col. Slingsby,
and I, by coach to the Tower, to Sir John Robinson's, to dinner,
where great good cheer. High company, and among others the
Duchess of Albemarle, who is ever a plain homely dowdy."†

"9th (Dec. 1665). My Lord Brouncker and I dined with the
Duke of Albemarle. At table, the duchess, a very ill-looked woman,
complaining of her lord's going to sea next year, said these cursed
words:—' If my lord had been a coward, he had gone to sea no more;
it may be then he might have been excused, and made an ambassador,'
(meaning my Lord Sandwich). This made me mad, and I believe
she perceived my countenance change, and blushed herself very
much. I was in hopes others had not minded it, but my Lord
Brouncker, after we came away, took notice of the words to me with
displeasure." ‡

Lord Sandwich, the famous admiral, who has such light
repute with posterity, was a relation of Pepys, and much connected with him in affairs. There does not appear to have
been the least foundation for the duchess's charge ; except,
perhaps, that Sandwich had brains enough to know the
danger which he braved, while Monk knew nothing but how
to fight and lie.

* Gentleman's Magazine for 1793, p. 88.
† Memoirs and Correspondence, as above, vol. i., p. 182.
‡ Vol. ii., p. 348.

"4th (Nov. 1666)." Pepys says that Mr. Cooling tells him, "the Duke of Albemarle is grown a drunken sot, and drinks with nobody but Troutbecke, whom nobody else will keep company with. Of whom he told me this story; that once the Duke of Albemarle in his drink taking notice, as of a wonder, that Nan Hide should ever come to be Duchess of York: 'Nay,' says Troutbecke, 'ne'er wonder at that, for if you will give me another bottle of wine, I will tell you as great, if not greater, miracle.' And what was that, but that our dirty Besse (meaning his duchess) should come to be Duchess of Albemarle."*

"4th (April, 1667). I find the Duke of Albemarle at dinner with sorry company, some of his officers of the army; dirty dishes and a nasty wife at table, and bad meat, of which I made but an ill dinner. Colonel Howard asking how the Prince (Rupert) did (in the last fight); the Duke of Albemarle answering, 'Pretty well,' the other replied, 'but not so well as to go to sea again.'—'How!' says the duchess, 'what should he go for, if he were well, for there are no ships for him to command? And so you have brought your hogs to a fair market,' said she."†

"29th (March 1667-8). I do hear by several, that Sir W. Pen's going to sea do dislike the Parliament mightily, and that they have revived the Committee of Miscarriages, to find something to prevent it; and that he being the other day with the Duke of Albemarle, to ask his opinion touching his going to sea, the duchess overheard and came into him; and asked W. Pen how he durst have the confidence to go to sea again to the endangering of the nation, when he knew himself such a coward as he was; which, if true, is very severe."‡

The habit of charging cowardice against the first officers of the time, which was not confined to the Duchess, is characteristic of the grossness of that period, the refinements of which were entirely artificial and modish. No people talked or acted more grossly than the finest gentlemen of the day, or believed more ill of one another; and it was not to be expected that the uneducated should be behindhand with them.

The Duchess of Albemarle is supposed to have had a considerable hand in the Restoration. She was a great loyalist, and Monk was afraid of her; so that it is likely enough she influenced his gross understanding, when it did not exactly know what to be at. Aubrey says, that her mother was one of the "five women barbers." How these awful personages came up we know not—but he has quoted a ballad upon them :—

> "Did you ever hear the like,
> Or ever hear the fame,
> Of five women barbers,
> That lived in Drury Lane?"§

---

* Memoirs and Correspondence, as above, vol. iii., p. 75.
† Id., p. 185.　　　　　　　‡ Vol. iv., p. 81.
§ Granger's Biographical History of England, 1824, vol. v., p. 356.

After all, the father, John Clarges, must have been a man
of substance in his trade, to be enabled to set up the enormous May-pole which we see in the picture. But this did
not prevent the daughter from growing up vulgar and foul-
mouthed, and a very different person from the *Belles Ferro-
nières* of old.

The Savoy, on the one side, with its Gothic gate and flint
wall, and the splendid mansion called Exeter House on the
other, appear in former times to have narrowed the highway
hereabouts, as much as Exeter 'Change did lately.

At the corner of Beaufort Buildings flourished Mr. Lillie,
the perfumer so often mentioned in the *Tatler*. He was secretary to Mr. Bickerstaff's Court of Honour, in Shire Lane,
where people had actions brought against them for pulling out
their watches while their superiors were talking; and for
brushing feathers off a gentleman's coat, with a cane "value
fivepence." Lillie published two volumes of Contributions,
of which the *Tatler* had made no use. We believe they had
no merit. In Beaufort Buildings lived Aaron Hill, and at
one time Fielding.

Southampton Street, a little to the west, on the other side of
the way, has been much inhabited by wits' and theatrical
people. Congreve once lived there, Mrs. Bracegirdle, and
Garrick. It was called Southampton Street from the noble
family of that title, who are allied to the Bedford family, the
proprietors.

On the ground of Cecil and Salisbury Streets, opposite
Southampton Street, stood the mansion of Robert Cecil, first
Earl of Salisbury, the cunning son of a wise father. It was
he who, contriving to keep up to the last his interest with the
queen Elizabeth, and to oust his rivals, Essex and others,
was the first to make secret terms with her successor James,
and to prepare the way for his reception in England: of which,
perhaps, Elizabeth was aware, when she lay moaning on the
ground.

Where the Adelphi now stands, was Durham Place, originally a palace of the Bishops of Durham, who resigned it to
Henry VIII. Henry made it the scene of magnificent tournaments. The Lord High Admiral Seymour caused the Mint
to be established in this house, with a view to coin money for
his designs on the throne. It was afterwards inhabited by
Dudley, Earl of Northumberland, who here married his son
to Lady Jane Grey. But its most illustrious tenant was

Raleigh, to whom it was lent by Queen Elizabeth, and who lived in it during the attempt made at Essex House. The four turrets of the mansion, under the roof of which lived and speculated that romantic but equivocal person, have been marked out in an engraving from Hollar. Durham Place, though it got into royal hands during the fluctuation of religious opinions, never seems to have been reckoned out of the pale of the bishopric of Durham; for Lord Pembroke bought it of that see in 1640, and pulled it down for the erection of houses on its site.

"Be it known," says the lively Pennant, speaking of the word 'place,' as applied to great mansions, and interpreted by him to mean palace, "that the word is only applicable to the habitations of princes, or princely persons, and that it is with all the impropriety of vanity bestowed on the houses of those who have luckily acquired money enough to pile on one another a greater quantity of stones or bricks than their neighbours. How many imaginary *parks* have been formed within precincts where deer were never seen! And how many houses misnamed *halls*, which never had attached to them the privilege of a manor."*

This is true; but unless the words *palazzo* and *piazza* are traceable to the same root, palatium (as perhaps they are), *place* does not of necessity mean *palace;* and palace certainly does not mean exclusively the habitation of princes or princely persons (that is to say, supposing princeliness to exclude riches,) for in Italy, whence it comes, any large mansion may be called a palace; and many old palaces there were built by merchants. Palatium, it is true, with the old Romans, though it may have originally meant any house on Mount Palatine, yet in consequence of that place becoming the court end of the city, and containing the imperial palace, may have come ultimately to mean only a princely residence. Ovid uses it in that sense in his *Metamorphoses.*† But custom is everything in these matters. Place is now used as a variety of term, either for a large house or street. Perhaps in both

* Pennant, *ut supra*, p. 144.
† Where he likens Jupiter's house in the Milky Way to the palace of Augustus:—

> " Hic locus est, quem, si verbis audacia detur,
> Haud timeam magni dixisse Palatia cœli."
> Lib. i. v. 175.

Which Sandys, by a felicitous conceit in the taste of his age (and of Ovid too), has transferred to the palace of Charles the First, and rendered still more applicable to the Milky Way:—

> " This glorious roofe I would not doubt to call,
> Had I but boldness giv'n me, Heaven's *White-Hall.*"

N

cases it ought to imply something of the look of a palace, or
at least an openness of aspect analogous to that of a *square*—
square in England, corresponding with *place*, *piazza*, and *plaça*
on the Continent.   The Piazza in Covent Garden, properly
means the place itself, and not the portico.

"To the north of Durham Place, fronting the street," says Pennant,
"stood the *New Exchange*, which was built under the auspices of our
monarch in 1608, out of the rubbish of the old stables of *Durham
House*.   The King, Queen, and Royal Family, honoured the opening
with their presence, and named it Britaine's Burse.   It was built
somewhat on the model of the Royal Exchange, with cellars beneath,
a walk above, and rows of shops over that, filled chiefly with milliners,
sempstresses, and the like.   This was a fashionable place of resort.
In 1654, a fatal affair happened here.   Mr. Gerard, a young gentleman, at that time engaged in a plot against Cromwell, was amusing
himself in a walk beneath, when he was insulted by *Don Pantaleon
de Saa*, brother to the Ambassador of Portugal, who, disliking the
return he met with, determined on revenge.   He came there the next
day with a set of bravoes, who, mistaking another gentleman for
Mr. Gerard, instantly put him to death, as he was walking with his
sister in one hand and his mistress in the other.   *Don Pantaleon* was
tried, and with impartial justice condemned to the axe.   Mr. Gerard,
who about the same time was detected in the conspiracy, was likewise
condemned to die.   By singular chance, both the rivals suffered on the
scaffold, within a few hours of each other : Mr. Gerard with intrepid
dignity ; the *Portuguese* with all the pusillanimity of an assassin.

"Above stairs," continues Pennant, "sat, in the character of a
milliner, the reduced Duchess of Tyrconnel, wife to Richard Talbot,
Lord Deputy of Ireland, under James II.; a bigoted Papist, and fit
instrument of the designs of the infatuated prince, who had created
him Earl before his abdication, and after that, Duke of Tyrconnel.
A female, suspected to have been his duchess, after his death, supported herself for a few days (till she was known and otherwise
provided for) by the little trade of this place; but had delicacy
enough to wish not to be detected.   She sat in a white mask, and a
white dress, and was known by the name of the White Widow.   This
Exchange has long since given way to a row of good houses, with
uniform front, engraved in Mr. Nichols's *Progresses of Queen Elizabeth*,
which form a part of the street."*

The houses in the quarter behind these, built by the Earl
of Pembroke, made way, sixty years back, for the present
handsome set of buildings called the Adelphi, from the Messrs.
Adam, brothers, who built it.†   The principal front faces the

---

* Pennant, p. 147.

† It was a joke, probably invented, against a late festive alderman,
that some lover of Terence, at a public dinner, having toasted two
royal brothers, who were present, under the title of the Adelphi (the
Greek word for "brothers"), the Alderman said, that as they were
on the subject of streets, "he would beg leave to propose "Finsbury
Square.'"

Thames, and is almost the only public walk left for the inhabitants of London on the river side. The centre house was purchased when new, by Garrick in 1771, and was his town house for the rest of his life. He died there about nine years after; but Mrs. Garrick possessed it till a late period. Mrs. Garrick had been a dancer in her youth, with a name as vernal as need be—Mademoiselle Violette : she died a venerable old lady, at the age of ninety odd. Boswell has recorded a delightful day spent with Johnson and others at her house, the first time she re-opened it after Garrick's death. Sir Joshua Reynolds was there, Mrs. Carter, Mrs. Boscawen, and others. "She looked well," says Boswell; "talked of her husband with complacency; and while she cast her eyes at his portrait, which was hung over the chimney-piece, said, that 'death was now the most agreeable object to her.'"* It is no dishonour to her, that her constitution was too good for her melancholy. She spoke enthusiastically of her husband to the last, and used to decide on theatrical subjects, by right of being his representative.

On the same terrace had lived their common friend Beauclerc. On coming away after the party just mentioned, Boswell tells us that Johnson and he stopped a little while by the rails of the Adelphi, looking on the Thames; "and I said to him," says Boswell, "with some emotion, that I was now thinking of two friends we had lost, who once lived in the buildings behind us, Beauclerc and Garrick." "Ay, sir," said he tenderly, "and two such friends as cannot be supplied."*

When Beauclerc was labouring under the illness that carried him off, Johnson said to Boswell, in a faltering voice, that he "would walk to the extent of the diameter of the earth to save him." It does not appear what Beauclerc had in his nature to excite this tenderness ; but it is observable, that Johnson had a kind of speculative regard for rakes and men of the town, if he thought them not essentially vicious. He seemed willing to regard them as evidences of the natural virtue of all men, bad as well as good, and of the excuse furnished for irregularity by animal spirits. It is not impossible even that he might have thought them rather conventionally than abstractedly vicious. He had a similar regard for Hervey, a great rake, who was very kind to him. "Sir," said he, "if you call a dog 'Hervey,' I shall love him." At

* Boswell, iv., p. 102.   † Id., p. 106.

the same time it is not to be forgotten, that these rakes were fine gentlemen and men of birth ; representatives, in some respect, of the license assumed by authority. Beauclerc, however, like Hervey, had a taste for better things than he practised, and could love scrupulous men. Boswell has given an interesting account of his first intimacy with Johnson. Langton and Beauclerc had become intimate at Oxford. " Their opinions and mode of life," we are told, "were so different, that it seemed utterly impossible they should at all agree ;" but Beauclerc " had so ardent a love of literature, so acute an understanding, such elegance of manners, and so well discerned the excellent qualities of Mr. Langton, a gentleman eminent not only for worth and learning, but for an inexhaustible fund of entertaining conversation, that they became intimate friends."

" Johnson, soon after this acquaintance began, passed a considerable time at Oxford. He at first thought it strange that Langton should associate so much with one who had the character of being loose, both in his principles and practice, but by degrees, he himself was fascinated. Mr. Beauclerc's being of the St. Albans family, and having, in some particulars, a resemblance to Charles the Second, contributed, in Johnson's imagination, to throw a lustre upon his other qualities; and, in a short time, the moral, pious Johnson, and the gay, dissipated Beauclerc were companions. 'What a coalition!' said Garrick, when he heard of this: 'I shall have my old friend to bail out of the round-house.' But I can bear testimony that it was a very agreeable association. Beauclerc was too polite, and valued learning and wit too much, to offend Johnson by sallies of infidelity or licentiousness ; and Johnson delighted in the good qualities of Beauclerc, and hoped to correct the evil. Innumerable were the scenes in which Johnson was amused by these young men. Beauclerc could take more liberty with him than any body with whom I ever saw him; but, on the other hand, Beauclerc was not spared by his respectable companion, when reproof was proper. Beauclerc had such a propensity to satire, that at one time, Johnson said to him, 'You never open your mouth but with intention to give pain, and you have often given me pain, not from the power of what you said, but from seeing your intention.' At another time, applying to him, with a slight alteration, a line of Pope, he said—
  'Thy love of folly, and thy scorn of fools'—
Every thing thou dost shows the one, and every thing thou say'st the other.' At another time he said to him, 'Thy body is all vice, and thy mind all virtue.' Beauclerc not seeming to relish the compliment, Johnson said, 'Nay, sir, Alexander the Great, marching in triumph into Babylon, could not have desired to have had more said to him.' "*

The streets in the Adelphi—John, Robert, Adam, &c.—are

* Boswell, vol. i., p. 225.

named from the builders. In this instance, the names are well
bestowed; but the "fond attempt," on the part of bricklayers
and builders in general to give a "deathless lot" to their
names in the same way, is very idle. Wherever we go now-
a-days, among the new buildings, especially in the suburbs,
we meet with names that nobody knows anything about, nor
ever will know. Probably, as knowledge increases, this custom
will go out. With this exception, streets in the British metropolis have hitherto been named after royalty or nobility, or
from local circumstances, or from saints. Saints went out
with popery. The reader of the *Spectator* will recollect the
dilemma which Sir Roger de Coverley underwent in his youth,
from not knowing whether to ask for Marylebone or Saint
Marylebone. In Paris they have streets named after men of
letters. There is the *Quai de Voltaire* ; and one of the most
frequented thoroughfares in that metropolis, for it contains the
Post-Office, is *Jean Jacques Rousseau Street*. It is not unlikely
that a similar custom will take place in England before long.
A nobleman, eminent for his zeal in behalf of the advancement of society, has called a road in his neighbourhood,
Addison Road.*

In John Street, Adelphi, are the rooms of the Society for the
Encouragement of Arts, Manufactures, and Commerce. This
society originated in 1753, at the suggestion of Mr. Shipley,
an artist, and, as the title implies, is very miscellaneous in its
object; perhaps too much so to make sufficient impression. It
gives rewards for discoveries of all sorts, and for performances
of youth in the fine arts. It is, however, one of those combi-
nations of zealous and intelligent men, which have marked the
progress of latter times, and which will have an incalculable
effect on posterity. Its great room is adorned with the celebrated pictures of Mr. Barry, which he painted in order to
refute the opinion that Englishmen had no genius for the
higher department of art, no love of music, &c., nor a proper
relish of anything, "even life itself." The statement of these
positions was not so discreet as the paintings were clever.
Mr. Barry was one of those impatient, self-willed men who,
with a portion of genuine power, think it greater than it is,
and will not take the pains to make themselves masters of
their own weapons. His pictures in the Adelphi, which are
illustrations of the progress of society, are striking, ingenious,
with great elegance here and there, and now and then an

* Near Holland House, Kensington. Addison died in that house.

evidence of the highest feeling ; as in the awful pity of the
retributive angel who presides over the downfall of the wicked
and tyrannical.   But the colouring is bad and "foxy ;" his
Elysium is deformed with the heterogeneous dresses of all ages,
William Penn talking in a wig and hat with Lycurgus, &c.
(which, however philosophically such things might be regarded in another world, are not fitly presented to the eye in
this); and by way of disproving the bad taste of the English
in music, he has put Dr. Burney in a coat and toupee, floating
among the water nymphs! The consequence is, that although
these pictures are, perhaps, the best ever exhibited together
in England by one artist, they fall short of what he intended
to establish by them, as far as England is concerned.

Between Adam Street and George Street, on the other side
of the Strand, is Bedford Street, the site of an old mansion of
the Earls and Dukes of Bedford.

With George Street commence the precincts of an ancient
"Inn," or palace, originally belonging to the Bishops of
Norwich; then to Charles Brandon, Duke of Suffolk; then to
the Archbishops of York, from whom it was called York
House ; then to the Crown, who let it to Lord Chancellor
Egerton and to Bacon ; then to the Duke of Buckingham,
the favourite, who rebuilt it with great magnificence, and at
whose death it was let to the Earl of Northumberland; and
finally to the second Duke of Buckingham, who pulled it
down and converted it into the present streets and alleys, the
names of which contain his designation at full length, even to
the sign of the genitive case, for there is an " *Of* Alley :" so
that we have George, Villiers, Duke, Of, Buckingham.

Brandon, Duke of Suffolk, was the man who, on his
marriage with Henry VIII.'s sister, appeared at a tournament on a horse that had a cloth half frieze and half gold,
with that touching motto—

> Cloth of gold, do not thou despise,
> Though thou be matched with cloth of frize:
> Cloth of frize, be not thou too bold,
> Though thou be matched with cloth of gold.

Bacon belongs to Gray's Inn, and the second Duke of
Buckingham to Wallingford House, where he chiefly resided (on the site of the present Admiralty) : but the reader,
who should go down Buckingham Street, and contemplate the
spot which Inigo Jones and the trees have beautified, will not
fail to be struck with the many different spirits that have

passed through this spot—the romantic Suffolk ; the correct
Egerton; the earth-moving Bacon; the first Buckingham with
a spirit equal to his fortunes; the second, witty but selfish,
who lavished them away ; and all the visitors, of so many
different qualities, which these men must have had, crowding
or calmly moving to the gate across the water, in quiet or
in jollity, clients, philosophers, poets, courtiers, mistresses,
gallant masques, the romance of Charles the First's reign,
and the gaudy revelry of Charles II. A little spot remains,
with a few trees, and a graceful piece of art, and the river
flowing as calmly as meditation.

WATER-GATE OF YORK HOUSE.

The only vestige now remaining of the splendid mansion of
the Buckinghams is the Water-Gate at the end of Buckingham
Street, called York Stairs,* and built by Inigo Jones. It has

* "York Stairs," says the author of the ' Critical Reviews of Public
Buildings,' quoted in ' Brayley's London and Middlesex,' "form unquestionably the most perfect piece of building that does honour to
Inigo Jones : it is planned in so exquisite a taste, formed of such equal
and harmonious parts, and adorned with such proper and elegant
decorations, that nothing can be censured or added. It is at once
happy in its situation beyond comparison, and fancied in a style exactly
suited to that situation. The rock-work, or rustic, can never be
better introduced than in buildings by the side of water; and, indeed,

been much admired, and must have admitted, in its time, the entrance of many extraordinary persons.

York Buildings affords us another name, not unworthy to be added to the most useful and delightful of these, Richard Steele, who lived here just before he retired into Wales. The place in his time was celebrated for a concert-room. We must not omit the termination of a curious dispute at the gate of York House, to which Pepys was a witness.

" 30th (September 1661). This morning up *by moonshine*, at five o'clock," (here was one of the great secrets of the animal spirits of those times), " to Whitehall, to meet Mr. More at the Privy Seale, and there I heard of a fray between the two embassadors of Spaine and France, and that this day being the day of the entrance of an embassador from Sweeden, they intended to fight for the precedence. Our King, I heard, ordered that no Englishman should meddle in the business, but let them do what they would. And to that end, all the soldiers in town were in arms all the day long, and some of the train bands in the city, and a great bustle through the city all the day. Then we took coach (which was the business I came for) to Chelsey, to my Lord Privy Seale, and there got him to seal the business. Here I saw by daylight two very fine pictures in the gallery, that a little while ago I saw by night; and did also go all over the house, and found it to be the prettiest contrived house that ever I saw in my life. So back again; and at Whitehall light, and saw the soldiers and people running up and down the streets. So I went to the Spanish embassador's and the French, and there saw great preparations on both sides; but the French made the most noise and ranted most, but the other made no stir almost at all; so that I was afraid the other would have too great a conquest over them. Then to the wardrobe and dined there; and then abroad, and in Cheapside hear, that the Spanish hath got the best of it, and killed three of the French coach-horses and several men, and is gone through the city next to our King's coach; at which, it is strange to see how all the city did rejoice. And, indeed, we do naturally all love the Spanish and hate the French. But I, as I am in all things curious, presently got to the water side, and there took oars to Westminster Palace, and ran after them through all the dirt, and the streets full of people; till at last, in the Mews, I saw the Spanish coach go with fifty drawn swords at least to guard it, and our soldiers shouting for joy And so I followed the coach, and then met it at York House, where the embassador lies; and there it went in with great state. So then I went to the French house, where I observe still, that there is no men in the world of a more insolent spirit where they do well, nor before they begin a matter, and

---

it is a great question whether it ought to have been made use of anywhere else. On the side next the river appear the arms of the Villiers family; and on the north front is inscribed their motto: *Fidei Coticula Crux*,—The Cross is the touch-stone of faith. On this side is a small terrace, planted with lime-trees; the whole supported by a rate raised upon the houses in the neighbouring streets; and being inclosed from the public, forms an agreeable promenade for the inhabitants."

more abject if they do miscarry, than these people are ; for they all look like dead men, and not a word among them, but shake their heads. The truth is, the Spaniards were not only observed to fight more desperately, but also they did outwitt them; first in lining their own harnesse with chains of iron that they could not be cut, then in setting their coach in the most advantageous place, and to appoint men to guard every one of their horses, and others for to guard the coach, and others the coachman. And, above all, in setting upon the French horses and killing them, for by that means the French were not able to stir. There were several men slaine of the French, and one or two of the Spaniards, and one Englishman by a bullet. Which is very observable, the French were at least four to one in number, and had near one hundred cases of pistols among them, and the Spaniards had not one gun among them, which is for their honour for ever, and the others' disgrace. So having been very much daubed with dirt, I got a coach and home; where I vexed my wife in telling her of this story, and pleading for the Spaniards against the French."[*]

In James the Second's time, the French embassy had the house of their rival, and drew the town to see Popish devices in wax-work.

" The fourth of April," says Evelyn (1672), " I went to see the fopperies of the Papists at Somerset House and York House, where now the French ambassador had caused to be represented our Blessed Saviour at the Pascal Supper with his disciples, in figures and puppets made as big as the life, of wax-work, curiously clad and sitting round a large table, the room nobly hung, and shining with innumerable lamps and candles ; this was exposed to all the world ; all the city came to see it: such liberty had the Roman Catholicks at this time obtained."[†]

They have obtained more liberty since, and can dispense with these " fopperies." At least they would do well to think so.

Hungerford Market takes its name from an old Wiltshire family, who had a mansion here in the time of Charles II., which they parted with, like others, to the encroachments of trade. It used to be an inconvenient and disagreeable place, little frequented, but has lately been converted into a handsome market, and put an end to the monopoly of Billingsgate.

No. 7 in Craven Street is celebrated as having been, at one time, the residence of Franklin. What a change along the shore of the Thames in a few years (for two centuries are less than a few in the lapse of time), from the residence of a set of haughty nobles, who never dreamt that a tradesman could be anything but a tradesman, to that of a yeoman's son, and a printer, who was one of the founders of a great state!

[*] Diary, vol. i., p. 221.
[†] " Memoirs of John Evelyn, Esq." Second edit. vol. ii., p. 364.

Northumberland House is the only one remaining of all the great mansions which lorded it on the river side. It was built by Henry Howard, Earl of Northampton, son of the famous Henry Howard, Earl of Surrey, the poet; but a very unworthy son, except in point of capacity. He was one of those men, who, wanting a sense of moral beauty, are in every other respect wise in vain, and succeed only to become despised and unhappy. He was the grossest of flatterers; paid court to the most opposite rivals, in the worst manner; and seems to have stuck at nothing to obtain his ends. His

OLD NORTHUMBERLAND HOUSE.

perception of what was great, extrinsically, led him to build this princely abode; and his worship of success and court favour degraded him into an accomplice of Carr, Earl of Somerset. It is thought by the historians, that he died just in time to save him from the disgraceful consequences of the murder of Sir Thomas Overbury.*

* In 1596, Northampton writes thus to Lord Burghley (Essex's great enemy), upon presenting to him a *devotional* composition. "The weight of your lordship's piercing judgment held me in so reverend an awe, as before I were encouraged by two or three of my friends, who had a taste, I durst not present this treatise to your view: but since their partiality hath made me thus bold, my own affection to sanctify this labour to yourself hath made me impudent."

Yet in the year succeeding, our authority observes, he has the fol-

Northumberland House was built upon the site of the old hospital of St. Mary Roncesvaux—Osborne says, with Spanish gold. "Part of the present mansion," says the *Londinium Redivivum*, "is from the designs of Bernard Jansen, and the frontispiece or gateway from those of Gerard Christmas. This gateway cannot possibly be described correctly, as the ornaments are scattered in the utmost profusion, from the base to the attic, which supports a copy of Michael Angelo's celebrated lion. Double ranges of grotesque pilasters inclose eight niches on the sides, and there are a bow window and an open arch above the gate. The basement of the whole front contains fourteen niches, with ancient weapons crossed within them; and the upper stories have twenty-four windows, in two ranges, with pierce battlements. Each wing terminates in a cupola, and the angles have rustic quoins. The quadrangle within the gate is in a better style of building, but rather distinguished by simplicity than grandeur; and the garden next the Thames, with many trees, serves to screen the mansion from those disagreeable objects which generally bound the shores of the river in this vast trading city."

"Northumberland House was discovered to be on fire, March 18, 1780, at five o'clock in the morning, which raged from that hour till eight, when the whole front next the Strand was completely destroyed. Dr. Percy's apartments were consumed; but great part of his library escaped the general ruin."[*]

We have been the more particular in laying this extract before our readers, because, though the house still exists, the public see little of it. All they behold, indeed, is the screen or advanced guard, which is no very fine sight, and only serves to narrow the way. Of the quadrangle inside the public know nothing; and thousands pass every day without

lowing passage in a letter to Essex:—"Some friend of mine means this day, before night, to merit my devotion and uttermost gratitude by seeking to do good to you; the success whereof my prayers in the meantime shall recommend to that best gale of wind that may favour it. Your lordship, by your last purchase, hath almost enraged the dromedary that would have won the Queen of Sheba's favour by bringing pearls. If you could once be as fortunate in dragging old Leviathan (Burghley) and his cub, *tortuosum colubrum* (Sir Robert Cecil), as the prophet termeth them, out of this den of mischievous device, the better part of the world would prefer your virtue to that of Hercules." See "Memoirs of the Peers of James I." p. 240. Such "wise men" are the worst of fools. And here he was acting, as such men are apt to do, like one of the commonest fools, in saying such contradictory things under his own hand.

[*] Vol. iv., p. 308.

suspecting that there is such a thing as a tree on the premises.

The Percys had this house in consequence of a marriage with the daughter of the Earl of Suffolk, who was Northampton's nephew. During the Earl's possession it was called Suffolk House, and furnished an escape to a person of the name of Emerson from one of the mad pranks of Lord Herbert of Cherbury, who was for fighting everybody. His lordship had had sundry fits of ague, which brought him at last to be "so lean and yellow, that scarce any man," he says, " did know him."

"It happened," he continues, "during this sickness, that I walked abroad one day towards Whitehall, where, meeting with one Emerson, who spoke very disgraceful words of Sir Robert Harley, being then my dear friend, my weakness could not hinder me to be sensible of my friend's dishonour; shaking him, therefore, by a long beard he wore, I stept a little aside, and drew my sword in the street; Captain Thomas Scrivan, a friend of mine, not being far off on one side, and divers friends of his on the other side. All that saw me wondered how I could go, being so weak and consumed as I was, but much more that I would offer to fight; howsoever, Emerson, instead of drawing his sword, ran away into Suffolk House, and afterwards informed the Lords of the Council of what I had done; who, not long after sending for me, did not so much reprehend my taking part with my friend, as that I would adventure to fight, being in such a bad condition of health."*

The disgraceful words spoken by Emerson were very likely nothing at all, except to his lordship's ultra-chivalrous fancy ; but this is a curious scene to imagine at the entrance of the present quiet Northumberland House—Emerson slipping into the gate with horror in his looks, and the lean and yellow ghost of the knight-errant behind him, sword in hand.

Mr. Malcolm has spoken of the apartments of Dr. Percy. This was Dr. Percy, Bishop of Dromore, who gave an impulse to the spirit of the modern muse by his *Reliques of Ancient English Poetry.* He was a kinsman of the Northumberland family. We believe it was in Northumberland House that his friend Goldsmith, stammering out a fine speech of thanks to a personage in a splendid dress whom he took for the Duke, was informed, when he had done, that it was his Grace's " gentleman."

A little way up Catherine Street is Exeter Street, where Johnson first lodged when he came to town.   His lodgings

* "Life of Edward Lord Herbert of Cherbury," in the " Autobiography," p. 110.

were at the house of Mr. Morris, a stay-maker. He dined at the Pine-apple in New Street, "for eightpence, with very good company." Several of them, he told Boswell, had travelled. "They expected to meet every day; but did not know one another's names." The rest of his information is a curious and interesting specimen of his disposition. "It used," said he, "to cost the rest a shilling, for they drank wine: but I had a cut of meat for sixpence, and bread for a penny, and gave the waiter a penny; so that I was quite as well served, nay, better than the rest, for they gave the waiter nothing." Johnson drank at this time no fermented liquors. Boswell supposes that he had gained a knowledge of the art of living in London from an Irish painter, whom he knew at Birmingham, and of whom he gave this account.

"Thirty pounds a year," according to this economical philosopher, "was enough to enable a man to live there without being contemptible. He allowed ten pounds for clothes and linen. He said a man might live in a garret at eighteen pence a week; few people would inquire where he lodged: and if they did, it was easy to say, 'Sir, I am to be found at such a place.' By spending three pence at a coffee-house, he might be for some hours every day in very good company; he might dine for sixpence, breakfast on bread and milk for a penny, and do without supper. *On clean shirt day* he went abroad and paid visits."[*]

The Strand end of Catherine Street is mentioned in Gay's " Trivia " for a notoriety which it now unfortunately shares with too many places to render it remarkable. His picture of one of the women he speaks of possesses a literal truth, the characteristic of the whole of this curious poem.

"'Tis she who nightly strolls with sauntering pace;
No stubborn stays her yielding shape embrace;
Beneath the lamp her tawdry ribands glare,
The new scower'd manteau, and the slattern air;
High draggled petticoats her travels show,
And hollow cheeks with artful blushes glow.
In riding-hood, near tavern door she plies,
Or muffled pinners hide her livid eyes.
With empty band-box she delights to range,
And feigns a distant errand from the 'Change."

Gay contents himself with a picture, and a warning. In our times, we have learnt to pity the human beings, and to think what can be done to remedy the first causes of the evil. The houses between Catherine Street and Burleigh Street stand upon ground formerly occupied by Wimbledon House, a mansion built by Sir Edward Cecil, whom Charles I. created

* Boswell, vol. i., p. 81.

Viscount Wimbledon. It was burnt down; and Stow says, that the day before, his lordship's country house at Wimbledon was blown up.

The late Lyceum was built about the year 1765, as an academy and exhibition-room, in anticipation of the royal one then contemplated. It did not succeed; and part of it was converted into a theatre for musical performances. It then became a place of exhibition for large panoramic pictures, among which we remember with pleasure the battle pieces of Robert Ker Porter (Seringapatam, Acre, &c.) A species of entertainment then took place in it, which has justly been called "useful and liberal," presenting, on a regular stage, pictures or scenes of famous places, while a person read accounts of them from a desk. We remember the Ægyptiana, or description of Ægypt, and, if we mistake not, an attempt, not quite so well founded, to illustrate the scenes of Milton's Allegro and Penseroso. Neither of the attempts met with success; but the former, perhaps, might be tried again with advantage, now that information and the thirst for it have so wonderfully increased. The panorama, however, may have realised all that can be done in this way. Visitors to those admirable contrivances may be almost said to become travellers; and a reader at hand might disturb them, like an impertinence. We recollect being so early one morning at a panorama, that we had the place to ouselves. The room was without a sound, and the scene Florence; and when we came out, the noise and crowd of the streets had an effect on us, as if we had been suddenly transported out of an Italian solitude. The Lyceum has since been handsomely rebuilt as a new English Opera House, under the management of Mr. Arnold, who has done much to cultivate a love of music in this country. Over the former theatre, we believe, was a room built by him for the members of the famous Beef-Steak Club, equally celebrated for loving their steaks and roasting one another.*

* The author of a "History of the Clubs of London" (vol. ii. p. 3.), says that this is not the Beef-Steak Club of which Estcourt, the comedian, was steward, and Mrs. Woffington president. He derives its origin from an accidental dinner taken by Lord Peterborough in the scenic room of Rich the Harlequin, over Covent Garden Theatre. The original gridiron, on which Rich broiled the Peer's beef-steak, is still preserved, as the palladium of the club; and the members have it engraved on their buttons. It has generally, we believe, admitted the leading men of the day, of whatever description,

The little crowded nest of shop-counters and wild beasts, called Exeter Change, which has lately been pulled down, took its name from a mansion belonging to the Bishop of Exeter, whether on the south or north side of the street does not appear. It is not necessary that the spot should have been the same. Any connection with a large mansion, or its neighbourhood, is sufficient to give name to a new house. Pennant thinks, we know not on what authority, that the great Lord Burleigh had a mansion on the spot; and he adds, that he died here. Exeter Change was supposed to have been built in the reign of William and Mary, as a speculation. The lower story, at the beginning of the last century, was appropriated to the shops of milliners; and upholsterers had the upper. In the year 1721, the town were invited to this place to look at a *bed*.

" Mr. Normond Cony," saith the historian, "exhibited a singular bed for two shillings and sixpence each person, the product of his own ingenuity; the curtains of which were woven in the most ingenious manner, with feathers of the greatest variety and beauty he could procure; the ground represented white damask, mixed with silver and ornaments of various descriptions, supporting vases of flowers and fruits. Each curtain had a purple border a foot in breadth, branched with flowers shaded with scarlet, the valence and bases the same. The bed was eighteen feet in height; and from the description must have been a superior effort of genius, equally original with the works of the South Sea Islanders, whose cloaks, mantles, and caps, grace the collection formed by Captain Cook, now preserved in the British Museum."*

This was a gentle exhibition enough. Sixty years ago, instead of the bed, was presented the right honourable body of Lord Baltimore, a personage who ran away with young ladies against their will. The body lay " in state," previously to its interment at Epsom. Lord Baltimore was succeeded by the wild beasts, who kept possession in their narrow unhealthy cages till the death of the poor elephant in 1826, which conspiring with the new spirit of improvement to call final attention to this excresence in the Strand, it was adjudged to be rooted out. The death of this unfortunate animal, who seems to have had just reason enough to grow mad, had its proper effect, in exciting the public to guard against similar evils; nor is it likely that these intelligent and noble creatures, nor

provided they can joke and bear joking. The author just mentioned says, that Lord Sandwich's and Wilkes's days are generally quoted as the golden period of the society.
* Londinium Redivivum, vol. iv., p. 302.

indeed any others, will undergo such a monstrous state of existence again.

Passing one day by Exeter Change, we beheld a sight strange enough to witness in a great thoroughfare— a fine horse startled, and pawing the ground, at the roar of lions and tigers. It was at the time, we suppose, when the beasts were being fed.

CHAPTER V.

LINCOLN'S INN, AND THE NEIGHBOURHOOD.

Lincoln's Inn — Ben Jonson's Bricklaying — Enactments against Beards—Oliver Cromwell, More, Hale, and other eminent Students of Lincoln's Inn—Lincoln's Inn Fields, or Square—Houses there built by Inigo Jones—Pepys's Admiration of the Comforts of Mr. Povey—Surgeons' College—Sir Richard and Lady Fanshawe, and Lord Sandwich—Execution of the patriotic Lord Russell, with an Account of the Circumstances that led to and accompanied it, and some Remarks on his Character—Affecting Passages from the Letters of his Widow—Ludicrous Story connected with Newcastle House.

INCOLN'S INN, upon the side of Chancery Lane, presents a long, old front of brick, more simple than clean. It is saturated with the London smoke. Within is a handsome row of buildings, and a garden, in which Bickerstaff describes himself as walking, by favour of the Benchers, who had grown old with him.*

It will be recollected that Bickerstaff lived in Shire Lane, which leads into this inn from Temple-bar. The garden-

* Tatler, No. 100.

wall on the side next Chancery Lane is said by Aubrey to
have been the scene of Ben Jonson's performance as a bricklayer. We have spoken of it in our remarks on that lane ;
but shall now add the particulars. " His mother, after his
father's death," says Aubrey, " married a bricklayer ; and 'tis
generally said that he wrought for some time with his father-
in-law, and particularly on the garden-wall of Lincoln's Inn,
next to Chancery Lane." Aubrey's report adds, that " a
knight, or bencher, walking through and hearing him repeat
some Greek names out of Homer, discoursing with him, and
finding him to have a wit extraordinary, gave him some
exhibition to maintain him at Trinity College in Cambridge." *
Fuller says, that he had been there before at St. John's, and
that he was obliged by the family poverty to return to the
bricklaying.† " And let them not blush," says this good-
hearted writer, " that have, but those who have not a lawful
calling. He helped in the building of the new structure of
Lincoln's Inn, where, having a trowell in his hand, he had a
book in his pocket." A late editor of Ben Jonson rejects these
literary accounts of the poet's bricklaying as " figments."‡
And he brings his author's own representations to prove that
he left the business, not for the University, but the continent.
As this writer has nothing, however, to oppose to what Aubrey
and Fuller believed respecting the rest, the reports, so far, are
worth as much as they were before. Nobody was more likely
than Ben Jonson to carry a Greek or Latin book with him on
such occasions : nor, as far as that matter goes, to let others
become aware of it.

Pennant's sketch of Lincoln's Inn continues to be the best,
notwithstanding all that has been said of it since his time.
He begins with observing, that " the gate is of brick, but of
no small ornament to the street." This is the gate in Chancery
Lane.

"It was built," he continues, "by Sir Thomas Lovel, once a
member of this inn, and afterwards treasurer of the household to
Henry VII. The other parts were rebuilt at different times, but
much about the same period. None of the original building is left,
for it was formed out of the house of the Black Friars, which fronted
Holborn end of the palace of Ralph Nevil, Chancellor of England, and
Bishop of Chichester, built by him in the reign of Henry III., on a
piece of ground granted to him by the king. It continued to be in-

---

* "Lives and Letters," *ut supra.*
† " Worthies of England," *ut supra.*
‡ Gifford's " Works of Ben Jonson," vol. i., p. ix.

o

habited by some of the successors in the see. This was the original site of the Dominicans or Black Friars, before they removed to the spot now known by that name. On part of the ground, now covered with buildings, Henry Lacy, Earl of Lincoln, built an Inne, as it was in those days called, for himself, in which he died in 1312. The ground did belong to the Black Friars; and was granted by Edward I. to that great Earl. The whole has retained his name. One of the Bishops of Chichester, in after times, did grant leases of the buildings to certain students of the law, reserving to themselves a rent, and lodgings for themselves whenever they came to town. This seems to have taken place about the time of Henry VII."

"The chapel," continues our author, "was designed by Inigo Jones; it is built upon massy pillars, and affords, under its shelter, an excellent walk. This work evinces that Inigo never was designed for a Gothic architect. The Lord Chancellor holds his sittings in the great hall. This, like that of the Temple, had its revels, and great Christmasses. Instead of the Lord of Misrule, it had its King of the Cocknies. They had also a Jack Straw; but in the time of Queen Elizabeth he, and all his adherents, were utterly banished. I must not omit, that in the same reign sumptuary laws were made to regulate the dress of the members of the house; who were forbidden to wear long hair, or great ruffs, cloaks, boots, or spurs. In the reign of Henry VIII. beards were prohibited at the great table, under pain of paying double commons. His daughter, Elizabeth, in the first year of her reign, confined them to a fortnight's growth, under penalty of 3s. 4d.: but the fashion prevailed so strongly, that the prohibition was repealed, and no manner of size limited to that venerable excrescence."[*]

> 'Tis merry in the hall,
> When beards wag all,

says the proverb; but the lawyers in those days had already so many refreshments to their solemnity, in masks and revels, that it was thought necessary to provide for decency of mastication in ordinary. Attempts to regulate trifles of this sort, however, have always been found more difficult than any others, the impertinence of the interference being in proportion. Think of the officers watching the illegal growth of the beard; the vexation of the "dandies," who wanted their beards out of doors; and the resentment of the unservile part of the elders! He that parted with his beard, rather than his three and fourpence, would be looked upon as an alien.

In the hall of Lincoln's Inn is Hogarth's celebrated failure of "Paul preaching before Felix." It seems hard upon a great man to exhibit a specimen of what he could not do. However, the subject does not appear to have been of the society's choosing. A bequest had been made them which produced a commission to Hogarth, probably in expectation

---

[*] Pennant, *ut supra*, p. 176.

that he would illustrate some of the consequences of good laws in his usual manner.

Old Fortescue was of Lincoln's Inn ; Spelman, the great antiquary ; Sir Thomas More ; Cromwell ; Sir Mathew Hale; Lord Chancellor Egerton, otherwise known by his title of Lord Ellesmere ; Shaftesbury, the statesman ; and Lord Mansfield. Dr. Donne also studied there for a short time, but left the Inn to enjoy an inheritance, and became a clergyman. However, he returned to it in after life as preacher of the lecture; which office he held about two years, to the great satisfaction of his hearers. Tillotson was another preacher. It is difficult to present to one's imagination the venerable judges in their younger days ; to think of Hale as a gay fellow (which he was till an accident made him otherwise); or fancy that Sir Thomas More had any other face but the profound and ponderous one in his pictures. His face, indeed, must have been full of meaning enough at all times ; for at twenty-one he was a stirring youth in Parliament ; and at twenty he took to wearing a hair-shirt, as an aid to his meditations. It is interesting to fancy him passing us in the Inn square, with a glance of his deep eye ; we (of posterity) being in the secret of his hair-shirt, which the less informed passengers are not.

The account of Hale's change of character, on his entrance into Lincoln's Inn, merits to be repeated.

" At Oxford," says his biographer, " he fell into many levities and extravagances, and was preparing to go along with his tutor, who went chaplain to Lord Vere, into the Low Countries, with a resolution of entering himself into the Prince of Orange's army, when he was diverted from his design by being engaged in a lawsuit with Sir William Whitmore, who laid claim to part of his estate. Afterwards, by the persuasions of Serjeant Glanville, who happened to be his counsel in this case, and had an opportunity of observing his capacity, he resolved upon the study of the law, and was admitted of Lincoln's Inn, November 8, 1629. Sensible of the time he had lost in frivolous pursuits, he now studied at the rate of sixteen hours a-day, and threw aside all appearance of vanity in his apparel. He is said, indeed, to have neglected his dress so much, that, being a strong and well-built man, he was once taken by a press-gang, as a person very fit for sea-service, which pleasant mistake made him regard more decency in his clothes for the future, though never to any degree of extravagant finery. What confirmed him still more in a serious and regular way of life was an accident, which is related to have befallen one of his companions. Hale, with other young students of the Inn, being invited out of town, one of the company called for so much wine, that notwithstanding all Hale could do to prevent it, he went on in his excess till he fell down in a fit, seemingly dead, and was with some difficulty recovered. This particularly affected Hale, in whom the principles of religion had been early implanted; and, therefore, retiring into another room, and falling down upon his knees, he prayed earnestly to God, both for his friend, that he might be restored to life again, and for himself, that he might be forgiven for being present and countenancing so much excess; and he vowed to God, that he would never again keep company in that manner, nor drink a health while he lived. His friend recovered; and from this time Mr. Hale forsook all his gay acquaintance, and divided his whole time between the duties of religion, and the studies of his profession."

Cromwell is supposed to have been about two years in Lincoln's Inn, and while he was there attended to anything but the law, the future devout Protector being, in fact, nothing more or less than a gambler and debauchee. However, he is supposed to have run all his round of dissipation in that time. Mansfield's residence in Lincoln's Inn, when Mr. Murray, gave rise to a singular reference in Pope. It is in the translation of Horace's ode, "Intermissa Venus diu," where the poet says to the goddess—

> " I am not now, alas! the man
> As in the gentle reign of my Queen Anne.
> To *number five* direct your doves,
> There spread round Murray all your blooming loves;
> Noble and young, who strikes the heart
> With every sprightly, every decent part;
> Equal the injured to defend,
> To charm the mistress, or to fix the friend."

This *number five* to which Venus is to go with her doves, points out Murray's apartments in Lincoln's Inn. Pope, as we have mentioned elsewhere, thought that nature intended his noble acquaintance for an Ovid; a notion partly suggested, perhaps, by Ovid's having been a lawyer. It was during his residence in Lincoln's Inn, that the future Lord Chief Justice is said to have drunk the Pretender's health on his knees; which he very likely did. The charge was brought up twenty years afterwards, to ruin his prospects under the Hanover succession; but it came to nothing. One dynasty has no dislike to a strong prejudice in favour of a preceding dynasty, when the latter has ceased to be formidable. The propensity to adhere to royalty is looked upon as a good symptom; and the event generally answers the expectation. The favourite courtiers under the house of Brunswick have come of Jacobite families.

A century ago, according to a passage in Gay, Lincoln's Inn and the neighbourhood were dangerous places to walk through at night.

" Where Lincoln's Inn, wide space, is railed around,
Cross not with venturous step; there oft is found
The lurking thief, who while the daylight shone,
Made the wall echo with his begging tone:
That crutch, which late compassion moved, shall wound
Thy bleeding head, and fell thee to the ground.
Though thou art tempted by the linkman's call,
Yet trust him not along the lonely wall;
In the midway he'll quench the flaming brand,
And share the booty with the pilfering band.
Still keep the public streets, where oily rays,
Shot from the crystal lamp, o'erspread the ways."

The wall here mentioned is probably that which was not
long since displaced by the new one, and the elegant structure
that now adorns the east side of Lincoln's Inn Fields.

Lincoln's Inn Fields, now a handsome square, set more
agreeably than most others, with grass plat and underwood,
were first disposed into their present regular appearance by
Inigo Jones, under the auspices of a committee of gentry and
nobility, one of whom was Bacon. Inigo built some of the
houses, and gave to the ground-plot of the square the exact
dimensions of the base of one of the pyramids of Egypt. He
could not have hit upon a better mode of conveying to the
imagination a sense of those enormous structures. If the
passenger stops and pictures to himself one of the huge
slanting sides of the pyramid, as wide as the whole length of
the square, leaning away up into the atmosphere, with an
apex we know not how high, it will indeed seem to him a
kind of stone mountain.

The houses in Lincoln's Inn Fields built by Inigo Jones
are in Arch Row (the western side), and may still be distinguished. Pennant speaks of one of them as being " Lindesey
House, once the seat of the Earls of Lindesey, and of their
descendants, the Dukes of Ancaster." They are probably still
a great deal more handsome inside, and more convenient,
than any of the flimsy modern houses preferred to them; but
London has grown so large, that everybody who can afford it
lives at the fashionable outskirts for the fresh air. It is probable that Inigo's houses created an ambition of good building
in this quarter. Pepys speaks of a Mr. Povey's house in Lincoln's Inn Fields as a miracle of elegance and comfort. His
description of it is characteristic of the snug and wondering
Pepys.

" Thence (that is to say, from chapel and the ladies) with **Mr.**
Povey home to dinner; where extraordinary cheer. And after **dinner**

up and down to see his house.   And in a word, methinks, for his per-
spective in the little closet; his room floored above with woods of
several colours, like, but above the best cabinet-work I ever saw; his
grotto and vault, with his bottles of wine, and a well therein to keep
them cool; his furniture of all sorts; his bath at the top of the house,
good pictures, and his manners of eating and drinking; do surpass all
that ever I did see of one man in all my life." *

The Country and City Mouse, in Pope's imitation of Horace,
go

> To a tall house near Lincoln's Inn,

which had

> Palladian walls, Venetian doors,
> Grotesco roofs, and stucco floors.   •

The house of a late architect (Sir John Soane) is observable
in Holborn Row (the north side of the square), and has a
singular but pleasing effect, though not quite desirable perhaps
in this northern climate, where light and sun are in request.
It presents a case of stone, added to the original front, and
comprising a balcony and arcade.   Shrubs and plate-glass
complete the taste of its appearance.   On the opposite side of
the way (called Portugal Row, most likely from our connection with Portugal in Charles the Second's time), the inhabitant of the above house had the pleasure, we believe, of
contemplating his own work in the handsome front and
portico of Surgeon's College.   This mode of giving a new
front to a house, and fetching it out into a portico, is an
ingenious way of getting up an ornament to the metropolis at
little expense.   Surgeons' College, instead of being two or
three old houses with a new face, looks like a separate building.   In Portugal Row sometime lived Sir Richard Fanshawe,
in whose quaint translation of the Camoens there is occasionally more genuine poetry, than in the less unequal version
of Mickle.   This accomplished person was recalled from an
embassy in Spain, on the ground that he had signed a treaty
without authority; which was fact; but the suspicious necessity of finding some honourable way of removing Lord Sandwich from his command in the navy, induced Lady Fanshawe
and others to conclude that he was sacrificed to that convenience.   He died on the intended day of his return, of a
violent fever, aggravated, not improbably, perhaps caused, by
this awkward close of his mission: for such things have been,
with men of sensitive imaginations.   His wife, a very frank
and cordial woman, has left interesting memoirs of him, in

* Diary, *ut supra*, vol. ii., p. 185.

which she countenances a clamour of that day, that Lord Sandwich was a coward. She adds, " He neither understood the custom of the (Spanish) court, nor the language, nor indeed anything but a vicious life ; and thus (addressing her children) was he shuffled into your father's employment, to reap the benefit of his five years' negotiation."* We quote this passage here, because Lord Sandwich was himself an inhabitant of Lincoln's Inn Fields. His want of courage (a charge shamefully bandied to and fro between officers at that time) is surely not to be taken for granted upon the word of his enemies, considering the testimonies borne in his favour by the Duke of York and others, and his numerous successes against the enemy. It is possible, however, that the pleasures of Charles's court might have done him no good. Sandwich had been one of Cromwell's council. He appears afterwards to have been a gallant of Lady Castlemain's ; was a great courtier ; and probably had as little principle as most public men of that age. Pepys, who was his relation, describes him as being a lute-player.

On Lady Fanshawe's return to England, she took a house for twenty-one years in Holborn Row (the north side of the Fields), where the contemplation of the houses opposite must have been very sad. Her account of the circumstances under which she returned is of a melancholy interest.

"I had not," she says, "God is my witness, above twenty-five doubloons by me at my husband's death, to bring home a family of three score servants, but was forced to sell one thousand pounds' worth of our own plate, and to spend the Queen's present of two thousand doubloons in my journey to England, not owing nor leaving one shilling debt in Spain, I thank God ; nor did my husband leave any debt at home, which every ambassador cannot say. Neither did these circumstances following prevail to mend my condition, much less found I that compassion I expected upon the view of myself, that had lost at once my husband, and fortune in him, with my son, but twelve months old, in my arms, four daughters, the eldest but thirteen years of age, with the body of my dear husband daily in my sight for near six months together, and a distressed family, all to be by me in honour and honesty provided for ; and, to add to my afflictions, neither persons sent to conduct me, nor pass, nor ship, nor money to carry me one thousand miles, but some few letters of compliment from the chief ministers, bidding 'God help me!' as they do to beggars, and they might have added, 'they had nothing for me,' with great truth. But God did hear, and see, and help me, and brought my soul out of trouble ; and, by his blessed providence, I and you live, move, and

---

* "Memoires of Lady Fanshawe, &c., written by herself." 1729, p. 267.

have our being, and I humbly pray God that that blessed providence may ever relieve our wants, Amen."*

Lady Fanshawe was no coward, whatever her foes may have been. During a former voyage with her husband to Spain, when she had been married about six years, the vessel was attacked by a Turkish galley, on which occasion she has left the following touching account of her behaviour:—

" When we had just passed the straits, we saw coming towards us, with full sails, a Turkish galley well manned, and we believed we should be all carried away slaves, for this man had so laden his ship with goods from Spain, that his guns were useless, though the ship carried sixty guns ; he called for brandy, and after he had well drunken, and all his men, which were near two hundred, he called for arms, and cleared the deck as well as he could, resolving to fight rather than lose his ship, which was worth thirty thousand pounds ; this was sad for us passengers, but my husband bid us be sure to keep in the cabin, and not appear—the women—which would make the Turks think we were a man-of-war, but if they saw women they would take us for merchants and board us. He went upon the deck, and took a gun and bandoliers, and sword, and, with the rest of the ship's company, stood upon deck, expecting the arrival of the Turkish man-of-war. This beast, the captain, had locked me up in the cabin ; I knocked and called long to no purpose, until at length the cabin-boy came and opened the door ; I, all in tears, desired him to be so good as to give me his blue thrum cap he wore, and his tarred coat, which he did, and I gave him half-a-crown, and putting them on, and flinging away my night-clothes, I crept up softly, and stood upon the deck by my husband's side, as free from sickness and fear, as, I confess, from discretion ; but it was the effect of that passion which I could never master.

" By this time the two vessels were engaged in parley, and so well satisfied with speech and sight of each other's forces, that the Turks' man-of-war tacked about, and we continued our course. But when your father saw it convenient to retreat, looking upon me, he blessed himself, and snatched me up in his arms, saying, 'Good God, that love can make this change!' and though he seemingly chid me, he would laugh at it as often as he remembered that voyage."

We now come to an event, uniting the most touching circumstances of private life with the loftiest utility of public, and the benefits of which we are this day enjoying, perhaps in every one of our comforts. In this square, now possessed by inhabitants who can think and write as they please on all subjects, and the centre of which is adorned with roses and lilacs, was executed the celebrated patriot, Lord Russell. We should ill perform any part of the object of this work, if we did not dwell at some length upon a scene so interesting, and upon the circumstances that led to it.

* "Memoires of Lady Fanshawe, &c., written by herself." 1729, p. 298,

Lord Russell (sometimes improperly called Lord William Russell, for he had succeeded to the courtesy-title by the decease of his elder brothers,) was son of William, Earl of Bedford, by Lady Ann Carr, daughter of Carr, Earl of Somerset; and he was beheaded in the year 1683, the last year but two of the reign of King Charles II., for an alleged conspiracy to seize the King's guards and put him to death. The conspiracy was called the Rye House Plot, but incorrectly as far as Lord Russell was concerned; for it is not proved that he ever heard of the house which occasioned the name; and he was condemned upon allegations which would have destroyed him, had no such place existed. The Rye House was a farm near Hoddesdon, in Hertfordshire, belonging to one of the alleged conspirators, and it had a bye-road near it through which Charles was accustomed to pass in returning from the races at Newmarket. It was said that the King was to have been assassinated in this road, but that a fire at Newmarket, which put the town into confusion, hastened his return to London before the conspirators had time to assemble.

Charles II., and his brother, the Duke of York, afterwards James II., in the prosecution of those designs against the liberty and religion of the state, which are now acknowledged by all historians, had lately succeeded in producing a strong re-action against the party opposed to them. This party, the Whigs, in their dread of arbitrary power and popery, had attempted with great pertinacity to exclude the Duke of York, an avowed papist, from the succession. They had indicted him as a popish recusant: they had listened, with too great credulity, to the story of a Popish Plot, for which several persons were executed: and while these strong measures were going forward, to which the general dread of popery encouraged them, they were inquiring into the King's illegal connections with France, and putting the last sting to his vexation by refusing him money. Charles's gambling and debaucheries kept him in a perpetual state of poverty. He was always endeavouring to raise money upon every shift he could devise, and misappropriating all he obtained, which completed the ingloriousness of his reign by rendering him a pensioner of France. He had a strong party of corruptionists in the House of Commons; but the public feeling against the Duke gave the elections a balance the other way; and the poor King was compelled, from time to time, to purchase what money he wanted, by the surrender of a popular right.

Driven thus from loss to loss, and not knowing where the diminution of his resources would end, Charles at length expressed himself willing to limit the powers of a Popish successor, though he would not consent to exclude him. The Whigs, strong in their vantage-ground, and backed by the voice of the country, rejected what they would formerly have agreed to, and insisted on the exclusion. And here the reaction commenced in Charles's favour. The Whigs had allied themselves to the dissenters, whose toleration they advocated in proportion as they opposed that of the Catholics. It was a contradiction natural enough at that time, when the remembrance of Protestant martyrdom was still lively, and the growth of philosophy had not neutralised the papal spirit, or, at least, was not yet understood to have done so; but by means of this alliance between the Whigs and Presbyterians Charles succeeded in awakening the fears of the orthodox. A secret treaty with the French King enabled him to reckon for a time on being able to dispense with the contributions of Parliament; and when the latter again pressed the exclusion bill, he dissolved them, with high complaints of their inveteracy against government, and artful insinuations of the favour they showed the dissenters. This declaration was read in all the churches and chapels, and produced the reaction he looked for. The Whig leaders, withdrawing into retirement, seemed to give up the contest for the present; but this was no signal to power to abstain from pursuing them. Charles, to secure himself a Parliament that should give him money without inquiry, and to indulge his brother in his love of revenge (not omitting a portion on his own account), set himself heartily about influencing the elections for a new House of Commons. The dissenters were persecuted all over the country; the Whig newspapers put down; one man, for his noisy zeal against Popery, put to death by means of the most infamous witnesses, who had sworn on the other side; and Shaftesbury's life was aimed at, but saved by the contrivances of the city authorities. The liberties of the city were then assailed, with but too great success, by means of judges placed on the bench for that purpose. Other corrupt law officers were brought into action; a servile lord-mayor was induced to force two sheriffs upon the city, in open defiance of law and a majority; in short, every obstacle was removed which accompanied the existence of properly constituted authorities, and of that late anti-popery spirit of the nation, which was now comparatively silent, for fear of being confounded with disaffection to the church.

For an account of what took place upon this corruption of church and bench, and neutralisation of the popular spirit, we shall now have recourse to the pages of the latest writer on the subject; who, though a descendant of Lord Russell, has stated it with a truth and moderation worthy of the best spirit of his ancestor. The narrative of the execution we shall take from an eye-witness, and intersperse such remarks as a diligent inquiry into the conduct and character of Lord Russell has suggested to our own love of truth.

"The election of the sheriffs," says our author, "seemed to complete the victory of the throne over the people. It was evident, from the past conduct of the court, that they would now select whom they pleased for condemnation.

"Lord Russell received the news with the regret which, in a person of his temper, it was most likely to produce. Lord Shaftesbury, on other hand, who was provoked at the apathy of his party, received with joy the news of the appointment of the sheriffs, thinking that his London friends, seeing their necks in danger, would join with him in raising an insurrection. He hoped at first to make use of the names of the Duke of Monmouth and Lord Russell, to catch the idle and unwary by the respect paid to their characters; but when he found them too cautious to compromise themselves, he endeavoured to ruin their credit with the citizens. He said that the Duke of Monmouth was a tool of the court; that Lord Essex had also made his bargain, and was to go to Ireland; and that, between them, Lord Russell was deceived. It is a strong testimony to the real worth of Lord Russell, that, when he made himself obnoxious, either to the court or to the more violent of his own party, the only charge they ever brought against him was, that of being deceived, either by a vain air of popularity or too great a confidence in his friends.

"Lord Shaftesbury, finding himself deserted, then attempted to raise an insurrection, by means of his own partisans in the city. The Duke of Monmouth, at various times, discouraged these attempts. On one of these occasions, he prevailed on Lord Russell, who had come to town on private affairs, to go with him to a meeting, at the house of Sheppard, a wine-merchant.

"Lord Shaftesbury, being concealed in the city at this time, did not dare to appear himself at this meeting, but sent two of his creatures, Rumsey and Ferguson. Lord Grey and Sir Thomas Armstrong were also there; but nothing was determined at this meeting.

"Soon after this, Lord Shaftesbury, finding he could not bring his friends to rise with the speed he wished, and being in fear of being discovered if he remained in London any longer, went over to Holland. He died in January, 1683.

*   *   *   *

"After Shaftesbury was gone, there were held meetings of his former creatures in the chambers of one West, an active, talking man, who had got the name of being an atheist. Colonel Rumsey, who had served under Cromwell, and afterwards in Portugal; Ferguson, who had a general propensity for plots; Goodenough, who had been under-sheriff; and one Holloway, of Bristol, were the chief persons at these meetings. Lord Howard was, at one time, among them. Their discourse seems to have extended itself to the worst species of treason and murder; but whether they had any concerted plan for assassinating the King is still a mystery. Amongst those who were sounded in this business was one Keeling, a vintner, sinking in business, to whom Goodenough often spoke of their designs. This man went to Legge, then made Lord Dartmouth, and discovered all he knew. Lord Dartmouth took him to Secretary Jenkins, who told him he could not proceed without more witnesses. It would also seem that some promises were made to him, for he said in a tavern, in the hearing of many persons, that 'he had considerable proffers made him of money, and a place worth 100*l*. or 80*l*. per annum, to do something for them;' and he afterwards obtained a place in the Victualling office, by means of Lord Halifax. The method he took of procuring another witness was, by taking his brother into the company of Goodenough, and afterwards persuading him to go and tell what he had heard at Whitehall.

"The substance of the information given by Josiah Keeling, in his first examination, was, that a plot had been formed for enlisting forty men, to intercept the King and Duke on their return from Newmarket, at a farm-house called Rye, belonging to one Rumbold, a maltster; that this plan being defeated by a fire at Newmarket, which caused the King's return sooner than was expected, the design of an insurrection was laid; and, as the means of carrying this project into effect, they said that Goodenough had spoken of 4,000 men and 20,000*l*. to be raised by the Duke of Monmouth and other great men. The following day, the two brothers made oath, that Goodenough had told them, that Lord Russell had promised to engage in the design, and to use all his interest to accomplish the killing of the King and the Duke. When the Council found that the Duke of Monmouth and Lord Russell were named, they wrote to the King to come to London, for they would not venture to go farther without his presence and leave. In the meantime, warrants were issued for the apprehension of several of the conspirators. Hearing of this, and having had private information from the brother of Keeling, they had a meeting, on the 18th of June, at Captain Walcot's lodging. At this meeting were present Walcot, Wade, Rumsey, Norton, the two Goodenoughs, Nelthrop, West, and Ferguson. Finding they had no means either of opposing the King or flying into Holland, they agreed to separate, and shift each man for himself.

"A proclamation was now issued for seizing on some who could not be found; and amongst these, Rumsey and West were named. The next day West delivered himself, and Rumsey came in a day after him. Their confessions, especially concerning the assassinations at the Rye-house, were very ample. Burnet says, they had concerted a story to be brought out on such an emergency.

"In this critical situation, Lord Russell, though perfectly sensible of his danger, acted with the greatest composure. He had long before told Mr. Johnson, that 'he was very sensible he should fall a sacrifice; arbitrary government could not be set up in England without wading through his blood.' The day before the King arrived, a messenger of the Council was sent to wait at his gate, to stop him if he had offered to go out; yet his back-gate was not watched, so that he might have gone away, if he had chosen it. He had heard that he was named by Rumsey; but forgetting the meeting at Sheppard's, he feared no danger from a man he had always disliked, and never trusted. Yet he thought proper to send his wife amongst his friends for advice. They were at first of different minds; but as he said he apprehended nothing from Rumsey, they agreed that his flight would look too like a confession of guilt. This advice coinciding with his own opinion, he determined to stay where he was. As soon as the King arrived, a messenger was sent to bring him before the Council. When he appeared there, the King told him, that nobody suspected him of any design against his person; but that he had good evidence of his being in designs against his government. He was examined upon the information of Rumsey, concerning the meeting at Sheppard's, to which Rumsey pretended to have carried a message, requiring a speedy resolution, and to have received for answer that Mr. Trenchard had failed them at Taunton. Lord Russell totally denied all knowledge of this message. When the examination was finished, Lord Russell was sent a close prisoner to the Tower. Upon his going in, he told his servant Taunton that he was sworn against, and they would have his life. Taunton said, he hoped it would not be in the power of his enemies to take it. Lord Russell answered, ' Yes; the devil is loose!'

"From this moment he looked upon himself as a dying man, and turned his thoughts wholly upon another world. He read much in the Scriptures, particularly in the Psalms; but whilst he behaved with the serenity of a man prepared for death, his friends exhibited an honourable anxiety to preserve his life. Lord Essex would not leave his house, lest his absconding might incline a jury to give more credit to the evidence against Lord Russell. The Duke of Monmouth sent to let him know he would come in and run fortunes with him, if he thought it could do him any service. He answered, it would be of no advantage to him to have his friends die with him.

"A committee of the Privy Council came to examine him. Their inquiries related to the meeting at Sheppard's, the rising at Taunton, the seizing of the guards, and a design for a rising in Scotland. In answer to the questions put to him, he acknowledged he had been at Sheppard's house divers times, and that he went there with the Duke of Monmouth; but he denied all knowledge of any consultation tending to an insurrection, or to surprise the guards. He remembered no discourse concerning any rising in Taunton ; and knew of no design for a rising in Scotland. He answered his examiners in a civil manner, but declined making any defence till his trial, when he had no doubt of being able to prove his innocence. The charge of treating with the Scots, as a thing the council were positively assured of, alarmed his friends; and Lady Russell desired Dr. Burnet to examine who it could be that had charged him ; but upon inquiry, it appeared to be only an artifice to draw confession from him ; and notwithstanding the power which the court possessed to obtain the condemnation of their enemies, by the perversion of law, the servility of judges, and the submission of juries, Lord Russell might still have contested his life with some prospect of success, had not a new circumstance occurred to cloud his declining prospects. This was the

apprehension and confession of Lord Howard. At first, he had talked
of the whole matter with scorn and contempt; and solemnly professed
that he knew nothing which could hurt Lord Russell. The King
himself said, he found Lord Howard was not amongst them, and he
supposed it was for the same reason which some of themselves had
given for not admitting Oates into their secrets, namely, that he was
such a rogue they could not trust him. But when the news was
brought to Lord Howard that West had delivered himself, Lord
Russell, who was with him, observed him change colour, and asked
him if he apprehended any thing from him? He replied that he had
been as free with him as any man. Hampden saw him afterwards
under great fears, and desired him to go out of the way, if he thought
there was matter against him, and he had not strength of mind to
meet the occasion. A warrant was now issued against him on the
evidence of West, and he was taken, after a long search, concealed in
a chimney of his own house. He immediately confessed all he knew
and more.

      *   *   *   *

" Hampden and Lord Russell were imprisoned upon Lord Howard's
information; and, four days afterwards, Lord Russell was brought to
trial: but, in order to possess the public mind with a sense of the
blackness of the plot, Walcot, Hone, and Rouse were first brought to
trial, and condemned upon the evidence of Keeling, Lee, and West,
of a design to assassinate the King."*

It is not necessary to enter at large into the trial. We
shall give the main points of it, on which sentence was
founded; but when it is considered that the bench had lately
had an accession of accommodating judges; that Jeffries was
one of the counsel for the prosecution; that the jury, illegally
returned, were not allowed to be challenged; that the witnesses were perjured, contradicted themselves, and swore to
save their lives; that one of them (Lord Howard) was a man
of such infamous character, that the King said, " he would not
hang the worst dog he had, upon his evidence;" that nevertheless the testimonies of the most honourable men against him
were not held to injure his evidence, and that a crowd of them
in Lord Russell's favour were of as little avail in giving the
prisoner the benefit of a totally different reputation, it will
be allowed, that our pages need not be occupied with details,
which in fact had nothing to do with his condemnation.

The ground on which Lord Russell was sentenced to death
was, that he had violated the law in conspiring the death of
the King. He argued, that granting the charge to be true
(which he denied), it was not that of conspiring the death of

* " Life of William Lord Russell, with some Account of the Times
in which he lived." By Lord John Russell, 3rd edition, 1820, vol. ii.,
p. 18, &c.

the King, but " a conspiracy to levy war;" that this was not treason within the statute (which it was not) ; and that if it had been, a statute of Charles II. made the accusation null and void, because the time had expired to which the operation of it was limited. The lawyers, who in fact had been compelled by their imperfect enactment to lay the charge on the ground of conspiring the King's death, had so worded the statute of Charles, that, like the oracles of old, it was capable of a double construction. But not to observe that the prisoner ought to have had the benefit of the doubt (and it has been generally thought that the statute was clearly the other way), they could never get rid of the necessity of assuming that the King's death was intended ; whereas, nothing can be more plain, not only from their own enactments, but from all history, that an insurrection, though against a King himself, may have no such object ; so that here was a man to be sacrificed to the *spirit* of the law (which by its very nature should have saved him,) while the court, in this and a thousand other instances, was violating the letter of it.

" Of the Rye House Plot," says Mr. Fox, " it may be said, much more truly than of the Popish, that there was in it some truth, mixed with much falsehood. It seems probable, that there was among some of the accused a notion of assassinating the King ; but whether this notion was ever ripened into what may be called a design, and much more, whether it were ever evinced by such an overt act as the law requires for conviction, is very doubtful. In regard to the conspirators of higher ranks, from whom all suspicion of participation in the intended assassination has been long since done away, there is unquestionable reason to believe that they had often met and consulted, as well for the purpose of ascertaining the means they actually possessed, as for that of devising others, for delivering their country from the dreadful servitude into which it had fallen ; and thus far their conduct appears clearly to have been laudable. If they went further, and did anything which could be really construed into an actual conspiracy to levy war against the King, they acted, considering the disposition of the nation at that time, very indiscreetly. But whether their proceedings had ever gone this length, is far from certain. Monmouth's communications with the King, when we reflect on all the circumstances of those communications, deserve not the smallest attention ; nor, indeed, if they did, does the letter which he afterwards withdrew prove anything upon this point. And it is an outrage to common-sense to call Lord Grey's narrative, written as he himself states in his letter to James II., while the question of his pardon was pending, an authentic account. That which is most certain in this affair is, that they had committed no overt act, indicating the imagining the King's death, even according to the most strained construction of the statute of Edward III. ; much less was any such act legally proved against them. And the conspiracy to levy war was not treason, except by a recent statute of Charles II., the prosecutions upon which were expressly limited to a certain time, which in these cases had elapsed; so that it is impossible not to assent to the opinion of those who have ever stigmatised the condemnation and execution of Russell as a most flagrant violation of law and justice." *

The truth respecting Lord Russell seems to be, that he was a man of the highest character and the best intentions, who suffered himself, not very discreetly, to listen to projects which he disapproved, in the hope of seeing better ones substituted. There can be no doubt that he wished to make changes in an illegal government, short of interfering with the King's possession of the throne. He had a right, by law, to endeavour it. He had openly shown himself anxious to do so; and the doubt can be as little, that the Duke of York, from that moment marked him out for his revenge. Russell implied as much in the paper he gave the sheriff; showing, indeed, such a strong sense of it, as (considering the truly Christian style of the paper in general) is very affecting. It has been justly said of him, that he was a man rather eminent for his virtues than his talents. We cannot help thinking that the paucity of words, to which he repeatedly alludes himself, and which was very evident during his trial, did him serious injury, both then and before. We mean, that if he had had a greater confidence, he might have advocated his cause to very solid advantage, perhaps to his entire acquittal. It is touching to observe, in the account of his behaviour after sentence, how the excitement of the occasion loosened his tongue, and inspired him with some turns of thought, more lively, perhaps, than he had been accustomed to. His character has been respectfully treated by all parties since the

---

* "History of the Reign of James the Second." Introductory Chapter. It is worth while, as a puzzle for the reader, to give here the contested point in the statute, which Lord Russell's enemies thought so clear against him, and his friends so much in his favour. 13 Car. II. "Provided always, that no person be prosecuted for any of the offences in this act mentioned, other than such as are made and declared to be high treason, unless it be by order of the King's Majesty, his heirs or successors, under his or their sign manual, or by order of the Council Table of his Majesty, his heirs or successors, directed unto the attorney-general for the time being: or some other counsel learned to his Majesty, his heirs or successors, for the time being: nor shall any person or persons, by virtue of this present act, incur any of the penalties herein before-mentioned, unless he or they be prosecuted within six months next after the offence committed, and indicted thereupon within three months after such prosecution; anything herein contained to the contrary notwithstanding."

Revolution, and his death lamented.   A startling charge, however, was brought against him and Sidney, in consequence of the discovery of a set of papers belonging to Barillon, the French Ambassador of that time, in which Sidney's name appears set down for five hundred pounds of secret service money from the French Government, and Russell is described as having interviews with Barillon's agent, Rouvigny, tending to prevent a war disagreeable both to Louis and the English patriots.   The vague allusions of some modern writers, together with an unsupported assertion of Ralph Montague, the intriguing English Ambassador in France, that money was to be distributed in Parliament " by means of William Russell, and other discontented people," have tended to lump together in the public mind the two charges occasioned by these documents.   But they are quite distinct.   Lord Russell had nothing to do with the money-list, in which the name of Sidney appears. The amount of the matter is this. Charles II. was always pretending to go to war with France, chiefly to get money for his debaucheries, and partly to raise an army which he might turn against the constitution.   The nation, in their hatred of Louis's anti-protestant bigotry, and their old and less warrantable propensity to fight with those whom they publicly considered as their natural enemies (a delusion, we trust, now going by), were always in a state to be deceived by Charles on this point ; and the patriots were as regularly perplexed how to agree to the wishes of the King and people, knowing as they did, the former's insincerity, loth to give him more money to squander, and yet anxious to show their dislike of an arbitrary neighbour, and afraid of his being in collision with their prince.   Their greatest fear, however, was upon this last point: it was very strong at the juncture in question; and therefore, when Louis gave them to understand, through his agent, that he himself was desirous of avoiding a war, Russell certainly does appear to have allowed the agent to talk with him on the subject, and to have expressed a willingness to influence the votes of Parliament accordingly.   There was a further understanding that Louis was to complete the mutual favour, by assisting to obtain a dissolution of Parliament, in case the peace should continue; for the patriots expected very different things from a dissolution at that time (1678), than what it produced afterwards.   Russell's noble biographer justly observes, that for the truth of these statements we are to trust Rouvigny's report, coming through the hands of

P

Barillon: but granting them to be true, he thinks there was nothing criminal in the intercourse.   He observes, that, in the first place, Russell was Rouvigny's kinsman by marriage, being first cousin to his wife, which accounts for the commencement of the intercourse; and, secondly,

" The imminent danger," he says, " which threatened us from the conduct of France abetting the designs of Charles, cannot, at this day, be properly estimated. At the very time when Parliament was giving money for a war, Lord Danby was writing, by his master's order, to beg for money as the price of peace. We shall presently see, that five days after the House of Commons had passed the act for a supply, Lord Danby wrote to Paris, that Charles expected six millions yearly from France. Had Louis been sincere in the project of making Charles absolute, there can be no doubt that it might have been easily accomplished. Was not this sufficient to justify the popular party in attempting to turn the battery the other way ? The question was not, whether to admit foreign interference, but whether to direct foreign interference, already admitted, to a good object. The conduct of Lord Russell, therefore, was not criminal; but it would be difficult to acquit him of the charge of imprudence.   The object of Louis must have been, by giving hopes to each party in turn, to obtain the command of both. Charles, on the other hand, was ready to debase himself to the lowest point, to maintain his alliance with France; any suspicion, therefore, of a connection between Louis and the popular party would have rendered him more and more dependent; till the liberties of England might at last have been set up to auction at Versailles."*

This is impartial.   But surely an imprudence so extremely dangerous, and an intercourse on any terms with an envoy's agent, the nature of which it must have been necessary to conceal, partook of a disingenuousness and selfwill that cannot be held innocent.   That Lord Russell had the best intentions is granted; but his principles were specially opposed by the doctrine of " doing evil, that good might come;" and if it be argued that good men are sometimes defeated in their intentions by not imitating the less scrupulous conduct of evil ones, it is to be replied, that there is no end of the re-actions consequent on such imitations, nor any bounds, on the other hand, to be put to the good consequences of a perfect example, even should its very perfection retard them. Good causes are not lost for want of passion and energy, but for that defect of faith and openness, which is the worst destroyer of both, and the loss of which is the worst hazard produced by a defect of example. We should be surprised that the patriots, while they were about it, did not denounce Charles's anti-constitutional behaviour more than they did, and openly demand their

* Life, as above, vol. i., p. 121.

rights as a matter of course; but it is easy to account for it upon the supposition that they were hampered with court connections, and not sure of one another.

The worst thing to be said of Lord Russell (for as to the letters he wrote for pardon, they must be considered as obtained from him by his friends and a tender wife) is, that when Lord Stafford, the victim of a plot charged on the papists, was sentenced to death, Russell opposed the King's privilege of dispensing with a barbarous part of the execution; so unworthy the rest of their character can men be rendered by party feeling, and so little do they foresee what they may themselves require in a day of adversity. When Charles II. was applied to on the same point in behalf of Lord Russell, he is reported to have said, "Lord Russell shall find I am possessed of that prerogative, which in the case of Lord Stafford he thought fit to deny me." The sarcasm (if made— for there is no real authority for it) was cruel; but it is not to be denied, that Lord Stafford, a man old and feeble, whose protestations of innocence called forth tears from the spectators when he was on the scaffold, might have thought Russell's conduct equally so. Let us congratulate ourselves, that the fiery trials which men of all parties have gone through, have enabled us to benefit by their experience, to be grateful for what was noble in them, and to learn (with modesty) how to avoid what was infirm.

Lord Russell, besides the general regard of posterity, has left two glorious testimonies to his honour—his behaviour in his last days, and the inextinguishable grief of one of the best of women. The latter, the celebrated Lady Rachael Russell, the daughter of Charles's best servant, Southampton, threw herself at the King's feet, "and pleaded," says Hume, "with many tears, the merit and loyalty of her father, as an atonement for those errors into which honest, however mistaken, principles had seduced her husband. These supplications were the last instance of female weakness (if they deserve the name) which she betrayed. Finding all applications vain, she collected courage, and not only fortified herself against the fatal blow, but endeavoured by her example to strengthen the resolution of her unfortunate lord."*

Echard says, that Charles refused her a reprieve of six weeks. If so, he probably feared some desperate attempt in Russell's favour; which, in fact, was proposed, as we shall

* Hume's History of England, vol. x. chap. 69.

see; and it is possible, that remembering what had happened
to Charles I., and conscious of his own deserts, he might really
have thought that Lord Russell would willingly have seen him
put to death ; for Rapin tells us that he said, in answer to
Lady Rachael, "How can I grant that man six weeks, who, if
it had been in his power, would not have granted me six
hours?"* And Lord Dartmouth in his notes upon Burnet, tells
us that when his (Dartmouth's) father represented to the King
the obligations which a pardon would lay upon a great family,
and the regard that was due to Southampton's daughter and
her children, the King answered, "All that is true ; but it is
as true, that if I do not take his life, he will soon have mine;"
"which," says Dartmouth, "would admit of no reply."†
Some, however, have said, that the King would have granted
Russell his life, if he had not been afraid of his brother, the
Duke of York; and as an instance of what was thought of the
characters of these two princes, whether the story is true or
not, it was added, that Charles did not like to hear any discourses about the pardon, because he could not grant it ;
whereas James would hear anything, though he resolved to
grant nothing.

Every other effort was made to save the live of Russell.

"Money," says Burnet, "was offered to the Lady Portsmouth, and to
all that had credit, and that without measure. He was pressed to
send petitions and submissions to the King and to the Duke ; but he
left it to his friends to consider how far these might go, and how they
were to be worded. All that he was brought to was, to offer to live
beyond sea, in any place that the King should name ; and never to
meddle any more in English affairs. But all was in vain. Both King
and Duke were fixed in their resolutions ; but with this difference, as
Lord Rochester afterwards told me, that the Duke suffered some,
among whom he was one, to argue the point with him, but the King
could not bear the discourse. Some said, that the Duke moved that
he might be executed in Southampton Square before his own house,
but that the King rejected that as indecent. So Lincoln's Inn Fields
was appointed for the place of his execution."‡

As a last resource Lord Cavendish offered to attack the
coach on either side with a troop of horse, and take his friend
out of it; but Russell would not consent to bring any one
into jeopardy on his behalf.

It has been said that Lincoln's Inn Fields was chosen, in
order that the people might witness the triumph of the Court,

* Rapin's History of England, 1731, vol. xiv., p. 333.
† Burnet's History of his Own Times.
‡ Burnet's History of his Own Times, 12mo., 1725, vol. ii., p. 260.

in seeing him led through the city; but others have reasonably observed upon this, that as he was to be taken from Newgate, the desire of making him a spectacle to the citizens would have been better gratified by his being carried to the old place of execution, the Tower. It is most probable, that Lincoln's Inn Fields was selected, as being the nearest feasible spot to the great town property of the Bedford family; Bloomsbury lying opposite, and Covent garden on one side.

The following is the letter addressed to the King by Russell's father, followed by that of Russell himself, which Burnet has mentioned as being drawn from him by his friends.

"To the King's most Excellent Majesty.

" The humble petition of William, Earl of Bedford:

" Humbly sheweth;

" That could your petitioner have been admitted into your presence, he would have laid himself at your royal feet, in behalf of his unfortunate son, himself, and his distressed and disconsolate family, to implore your royal mercy, which he never had the presumption to think could be obtained by any indirect means. But shall think himself, wife, and children, much happier to be left but with bread and water, than to lose his dear son for so foul a crime as treason against the best of princes ; for whose life he ever did, and ever shall pray, more than for his own.

" May God incline your Majesty's heart to the prayers of an afflicted old father, and not bring grey hairs with sorrow to my grave.
" BEDFORD."

" To the King's most Excellent Majesty.

" The humble petition of William Russell:

" Most humbly sheweth;

" That your petitioner does once more cast himself at your Majesty's feet, and implores, with all humility, your mercy and pardon, still avowing that he never had the least thought against your Majesty's life, nor any design to change the government; but humbly and sorrowfully confesses his having been present at those meetings, which he is convinced were unlawful, and justly provoking to your Majesty; but being betrayed by ignorance and inadvertence, he did not decline them as he ought to have done, for which he is truly and heartily sorry ; and, therefore, humbly offers himself to your Majesty, to be determined to live in any part of the world which you shall appoint, and never to meddle any more in the affairs of England, but as your Majesty shall be pleased to command me.

" May it therefore please your Majesty to extend your royal favour and mercy to your petitioner, by which he will be for ever engaged to pray for your Majesty, and to devote his life to your service.
" WILLIAM RUSSELL."

The third is to the Duke of York. It is certainly to be regretted, that these letters were drawn from a patriot, willing, there is no doubt, to have endured all extremities

without compromising the dignity of conscious right : but
the reader will bear in mind what has been said of them;
and we shall see presently what the writer said of the present
one.

"May it please your Highness;

"The opposition I have appeared in to your Highness's interest has
been such, as I have scarce the confidence to be a petitioner to you,
though in order to the saving of my life. Sir, God knows what I did
did not proceed from any personal ill-will, or animosity to your royal
Highness, but merely because I was of opinion, that it was the best
way for observing the religion established by law, in which, if I was
mistaken, yet I acted sincerely, without any ill end in it. And as for
any base design against your person, I hope your Royal Highness will
be so just to me as not to think me capable of so vile a thought. But
I am now resolved, and do faithfully engage myself, that if it shall
please the King to pardon me, and if your Royal Highness will inter-
pose in it, I will in no sort meddle any more, but will be readily
determined to live in any part of the world which his Majesty shall
prescribe, and will never fail in my daily prayers, both for his
Majesty's preservation and honour, and your Royal Highness's happiness, and will wholly withdraw myself from the affairs of England,
unless called by his Majesty's orders to serve him, which I shall never
be wanting to do, to the uttermost of my power. And if your Royal
Highness will be so gracious to me, as to move on my account, as it
will be an engagement upon me, beyond what I can in reason expect,
so it will make the deepest impressions on me possible ; for no fear of
death can work so much with me, as so great an obligation will for
ever do upon me. May it please your Royal Highness, your Royal
Highness's most humble and most obedient servant,

"W. RUSSELL."

"Newgate, July 16th, 1683."

Burnet says of this last letter, which he tells us was written
at the "earnest solicitations" of Lady Rachael, that as Russell
was folding it up, he said to him, " This will be printed, and
will be selling about the streets as my submission, when I am
led out to be hanged."

All efforts failed, and the patriot and husband composed
himself to die.   The touching particulars of his last days
we shall extract from the account of his friend Bishop Burnet.
It is one that, as it contains no disputed points, may be safely
relied on; and indeed, if we had not wished to show how
interested we are in the case of this advancer of public right,
and how anxious to spare no proper trouble for our readers,
we might safely have copied the whole case from the lively
pages of that historian, whose writings, whatever may have
been his faults of partizanship and complexion, have risen in
value, in proportion as documents come to light. A great

modern statesman, equally qualified to judge of it, both as a politician and a man, alludes with interesting emotion to Burnet's account of his last hours. Speaking of the dying behaviour of Russell and Sidney, he says, " In courage they are equal, but the fortitude of Russell, who was connected with the world by private and domestic ties, which Sidney was not, was put to the severer trial; and the story of the last days of this excellent man's life fills the mind with such a mixture of tenderness and admiration, that I know not any scene in history that more powerfully excites our sympathy, or goes more directly to the heart."*

" The last week of his life," says Burnet, " he was shut up all the morning as he himself desired. And about noon I came to him, and staid with him till night. All the while he expressed a very Christian temper, without sharpness or resentment, vanity or affectation. His whole behaviour looked like a triumph over death. Upon some occasions, as at table, or when his friends came to see him, he was decently cheerful. I was by him when the sheriffs came to show him the warrant for his execution. He read it with indifference; and when they were gone he told me it was not decent to be merry with such a matter, otherwise he was near telling Rich (who, though he was now on the other side, yet had been a member of the House of Commons, and had voted for the exclusion), that they should never sit together in that house any more to vote for the bill of exclusion. The day before his death he fell a bleeding at the nose; upon that he said to me pleasantly, I shall not now let blood to divert this: that will be done to-morrow. At night it rained hard, and he said, such a rain to-morrow will spoil a great show, which was a dull thing in a rainy day. He said, the sins of his youth lay heavy upon his mind; but he hoped God had forgiven them, for he was sure he had forsaken them, and for many years he had walked before God with a sincere heart. If in his public actings he had committed errors, they were only the errors of his understanding; for he had no private ends, nor ill designs of his own in them; he was still of opinion that the King was limited by law, and that when he broke through those limits, his subjects might defend themselves and restrain him. He thought a violent death was a very desirable way of ending one's life; it was only the being exposed to be a little gazed at, and to suffer the pain of one minute, which, he was confident, was not equal to the pain of drawing a tooth. He said he felt none of those transports that some good people felt; but he had a full calm in his mind, no palpitation at heart, nor trembling at the thoughts of death. He was much concerned at the cloud that seemed to be now over his country; but he hoped his death would do more service than his life could have done.

" This was the substance of the discourse between him and me. Tillotson was oft with him that last week. We thought the party had gone too quick in their consultations, and too far; and that resistance in the condition we were then in was not lawful. He said he

---

* Mr. Fox, in his history above-mentioned.

had leisure to enter into discourses of politics; but he thought a
government limited by law was only a name, if the subjects might
not maintain those limitations by force; otherwise all was at the discretion of the Prince: that was contrary to all the notions he had
lived in of our government.* But, he said, there was nothing among
them but the embryos of things that were never like to have any
effect, and they were now quite dissolved. He thought it was necessary for him to leave a paper behind him at his death; and, because
he had not been accustomed to draw such papers, he desired me to
give him a scheme of the heads fit to be spoken to, and of the order in
which they should be laid; which I did. And he was three days
employed for some time in the morning to write out his speech. He
ordered four copies to be made of it, all which he signed; and gave
the original with three of the copies to his lady, and kept the other to
give to the sheriffs on the scaffold. He writ it with great ease, and
the passages that were tender he writ in papers apart, and showed
them to his lady and to myself, before he writ them out fair. He was
very easy when this was ended. He also writ a letter to the King, in
which he asked pardon for every thing he had said or done contrary
to his duty, protesting he was innocent as to all designs against his
person or government, and that his heart was ever devoted to that
which he thought was his Majesty's true interest. He added that,
though he thought he had met with hard measures, yet he forgave all
concerned in it, from the highest to the lowest; and ended, hoping
that his Majesty's displeasure at him would cease with his own life,
and that no part of it should fall on his wife and children. The day
before his death he received the sacrament from Tillotson with much
devotion: and I preached two short sermons to him, which he heard
with great affection; and we were shut up till towards the evening.
Then he suffered his children that were very young, and some few of
his friends, to take leave of him; in which he maintained his con-
stancy of temper, though he was a very fond father. He also parted
from his lady with a composed silence; and as soon as she was gone,
he said to me, 'The bitterness of death is passed;' for he loved and
esteemed her beyond expression, as she well deserved it in all respects.
She had the command of herself so much that at parting she gave him
no disturbance. He went into his chamber about midnight, and I
stayed all night in the outward room. He went not to bed till about
two in the morning, and was fast asleep at four, when, according to
his order, we called him. He was quickly dressed, but would lose no
time in shaving, for, he said, he was not concerned in his good looks
that day."

    *   *   *   *   *

    "Lord Russell," continues Burnet, "seemed to have some satisfac-
tion to find that there was no truth in the whole contrivance of the
Rye Plot; so that he hoped that infamy, which now blasted their
party, would soon go off. He went into his chamber six or seven
times in the morning, and prayed by himself, and then came out to
Tillotson and me; he drank a little tea and some sherry. He wound
up his watch, and said, now he had done with time, and was going to

---

    * Burnet and Tillotson thought so too, when James II. afterwards
forced the church to declare one way or other.

eternity. He asked what he should give the executioner: I told him ten guineas: he said, with a smile, it was a pretty thing to give a fee to have his head cut off. When the sheriffs called him about ten o'clock, Lord Cavendish was waiting below to take leave of him. They embraced very tenderly. Lord Russell, after he had left him, upon a sudden thought came back to him, and pressed him earnestly to apply himself more to religion, and told him what great comfort and support he felt from it now in his extremity. Lord Cavendish had very generously offered to manage his escape, and to stay in prison for him while he should go away in his clothes; but he would not hearken to the motion. The Duke of Monmouth had also sent me word to let him know, that if he thought it could do him any service, he would come in and run fortunes with him. He answered, it would be of no advantage to him to have his friends die with him. Tillotson and I went in the coach with him to the place of execution. Some of the crowd that filled the streets wept, while others insulted; he was touched by the tenderness that the one gave him, but did not seem at all provoked by the other. He was singing psalms a great part of the way, and said, he hoped to sing better very soon.* As he observed the great crowds of people all the way, he said to us, 'I hope I shall quickly see a much better assembly.' When he came to the scaffold, he walked about it four or five times. Then he turned to the sheriffs, and delivered his paper. He protested that he had always been far from any designs against the King's life or government. He prayed God would preserve both, and the Protestant religion. He wished all Protestants might love one another, and not make way for Popery by their animosities."

Of the paper given by Russell to the sheriffs, Burnet has given the following honest abridgment. This testament to patriotism made a great sensation. To posterity, who have so benefited by its spirit, it is surely still of great interest.

"The substance of the paper he gave them," says Burnet, "was, first, a profession of his religion, and of his sincerity in it; that he was of the Church of England, but wished all would unite together against the common enemy; that churchmen would be less severe, and dissenters less scrupulous. He owned he had a great zeal against Popery, which he looked on as an idolatrous and bloody religion; but that, though he was at all times ready to venture his life for his religion or his country, yet that would never have carried him to a black or wicked design. No man ever had the impudence to move to

---

* In his Journal, Burnet says that he often sung "within himself," but that the words were not audible. When his companion asked him what he was singing, he said the beginning of the 119th Psalm. It is stated in the Life by his descendant (who has added some original passages from papers at Woburn), that "just as they were entering Lincoln's Inn Fields, he said, 'This has been to me a place of sinning, and God now makes it the place of my punishment.'" He had lived freely in his youth, though he is not the Russell spoken of in the Memoirs of Grammont, as many are led to believe by the engravings of him inserted in that work. The person there mentioned was a cousin.

him anything with relation to the King's life: he prayed heartily for him, that in his person and government he might be happy, both in this world and the next. He protested that in the prosecution of the Popish Plot he had gone on in the sincerity of his heart, and that he never knew of any practice with the witnesses. He owned he had been earnest in the matter of the exclusion, as the best way, in his opinion, to secure both the King's life and the Protestant religion, and to that he imputed his present sufferings; but he forgave all concerned in them, and charged his friends to think of no revenges. He thought his sentence was hard, upon which he gave an account of all that had passed at Shepherd's. From the heats that were in choosing the sheriffs, he concluded that matter would end as it now did, and he was not much surprised to find it fall upon himself; he wished it might end in him; killing by forms of law was the worst sort of murder. He concluded with some very devout ejaculations.

"After he had delivered this paper, he prayed by himself; then Tillotson prayed with him. After that he prayed again by himself, and then undressed himself and laid his head on the block, without the least change of countenance; and it was cut off at two strokes."

The following additional particulars are from Burnet's "Journal:"—

"When my lady went, he said he wished she would give over beating every bush, and running so about for his preservation. But when he considered that it would be some mitigation of her sorrow afterwards, that she left nothing undone that could have given any probable hopes, he acquiesced: and, indeed, I never saw his heart so near failing him, as when he spake of her. Sometimes I saw a tear in his eye, and he would turn about and presently change the discourse.

"At ten o'clock my lady left him. He kissed her four or five times; and she kept her sorrows so within herself, that she gave him no disturbance by their parting. After she was gone, he said, 'Now the bitterness of death is passed,' and ran out a long discourse concerning her—how great a blessing she had been to him; and said what a misery it would have been to him, if she had not had that magnanimity of spirit, joined to her tenderness, as never to have desired him to do a base thing for the saving of his life; whereas, otherwise, what a week should I have passed, if she had been crying on me to turn informer, and be a Lord Howard; though he then repeated what he often before said, that he knew of nothing whereby the peace of the nation was in danger; and that all that ever was, was either loose discourse, or at most embryos that never came to anything, so that there was nothing on foot to his knowledge.

"As we came to turn into Little Queen Street, he said, 'I have often turned to the other hand with great comfort, but now I turn to this with greater,' and looked towards his own house; and then, as the Dean of Canterbury, who sat over against him, told me, he saw a tear or two fall from him.

"When he had lain down, I looked once at him and saw no change in his looks; and though he was still lifting up his hands, there was no trembling, though, in the moment in which I looked, the executioner happened to be laying the axe to his neck to direct him to take aim. I thought it touched him, but I am sure he seemed not to mind it."

The widow of Lord Russell, daughter of the Lord South-ampton above mentioned, the most honest man ever known to have been in the service of Charles the Second, was grand-daughter of Shakspeare's Southampton, and appears to have united in her person the qualities of both. She was at once a pattern of good sense, and of romantic affection. Nor are the two things incompatible, when either of them exist in the highest degree, as she proved during the re-mainder of her life; for though she continued a widow all the rest of it, and it was a very long one, and though she never ceased regretting her lord's death, and had great troubles besides, yet the high sense she had of the duties of a human being enabled her to enjoy consolations that ordinary pleasure might have envied; first, in the education of her children, and secondly, in the tranquillity which health and temperance *forced* upon her. Her letters, with which the public are well acquainted, are not more remarkable for the fidelity they evince to her husband's memory, than for the fine sense they display in all matters upon which the pre-judices of education had left her a free judgment, and especially for their delightful candour. It has been thought that the blindness into which she fell in her old age was owing to weeping; but Mr. Howell, the judicious editor of the " State Trials," informs us, upon the authority of " a very learned, skilful, and experienced physiologist," " that a cataract, which seems," he says, " to have been the malady of Lady Rachael's eyes, is by no means likely to be produced by weeping."*

We will here insert a few of the most touching passages from the " Letters of Lady Russell" (seventh edition, 1819). On the 30th of September, she writes thus to her friend. Dr Fitzwilliam:—

"I endeavour to make the best use I can of both (a letter and prayer which the Doctor sent her); but I am so evil and unworthy a creature, that though I have desires, yet I have no disposition, or worthiness, towards receiving comfort." And again:—"I know I have deserved my punishment, and will be silent under it; but yet secretly my heart mourns, and cannot be comforted, because I have not the dear companion and sharer of all my joys and sorrows. I want

---

* For complete reports of all the trials connected with the Rye House Plot, and for several pamphlets written *pro* and *con* upon Lord Russell's case, see the " State Trials," vol. ix., beginning at p. 357.

him to talk with, to walk with, to eat and sleep with; all these things are irksome to me now; all company and meals I could avoid, if it might be.   Yet all this is, that I enjoy not the world in my own way, and this same hinders my comfort.   When I see my children before me. I remember the pleasure he took in them; this makes my heart shrink."

On the 21st July, 1685, the anniversary of her husband's death, two years after it, she writes thus:—

" My languishing weary spirit rises up slowly to all good; yet I hope by God's abundant grace, in time, your labours will work the same effect in my spirits: they will, indeed, in less time on others better disposed and prepared than I am, who in the day of affliction seem to have no remembrance with due thankfulness of prosperity."

In a letter written the 4th October, 1686, she says, speaking of a recovery of one of her children from sickness,—

" I hope this has been a sorrow I shall profit by; I shall, if God will strengthen my faith, resolve to return him a constant praise, and make this the season to chase all secret murmurs from grieving my soul for what is past, letting it rejoice in what it should rejoice, his favour to me, in the blessings I have left, which many of my betters want, and yet have lost their chiefest friend also.   But, oh, Doctor! the manner of my deprivation is yet astonishing."

The following is dated five years after her loss.   She is speaking of a letter she wrote once a week to Dr. Fitzwilliam. Her grief had now begun to taste the sweets of patience and temperance; but we see still how real it is:—

" I can't but own there is a sort of secret delight in the privacy of one of those mournful days; I think, besides a better reason, one is, that I do not tie myself up as I do on other days; for, God knows, my eyes are ever ready to pour out marks of a sorrowful heart, which I shall carry to the grave, that quiet bed of rest."

In 1692, Lady Russell writes less patiently, but shortly afterwards appears to have regained her composure; and in Letter 134, there is a remark on the blessings of health, and on the comfort of being able to do one's duty, if we aim at it. In 1711, she lost her only son, the Duke of Bedford, in his 31st year; and six months afterwards was deprived of one of her daughters, who died in childbed.   It was on this occasion that an affecting annecdote is told.   She had another daughter who happened to be in childbed also; and as it was necessary to conceal from her the death of her sister, this admirable woman assumed a cheerful air, and in answer to her daughter's anxious inquiries, said, with an extraordinary colouring of the fact, for which a martyr to truth could have loved her, " I have seen your sister out of bed to-day."

We intended not to omit the following charming passage from her letters, and therefore add it here. It is in the letter last quoted:—

"My friendships have made all the joys and troubles of my life; and yet who would live and not love? Those who have tried the insipidness of it would, I believe, never choose it. Mr. Waller says, 'tis (with singing) all we know they do above! And 'tis enough; for if there is so charming a delight in the love, and suitableness in humours, to creatures, what must it be to the clarified spirits to love in the presence of God!"

The passage from Waller is,—

"What know we of the blest above,
But that they sing and that they love?"

Certainly, if ever there was an angel upon earth this woman was one. Compare the above extracts with a letter from her to her husband, written in the year 1681, and published in the work of Lord John Russell, vol. ii., p. 2. It is a true, loving, happy wife's letter, and renders the contrast inexpressibly affecting.

The present ducal family of Bedford have the honour to be lineally descended from these two excellent persons, and to derive their very dukedom from public virtue—a rare patent. And they have shown that they estimate the honour. What must not Lady Russell have felt when James II., within six years after the destruction of her husband, was forced to give up his throne? And what, above all, must she not have felt, when she heard of the answer given by her aged father-in-law to the same prince, who had the meanness, or want of imagination, to apply to him in his distress? "My Lord," said James to the Earl of Bedford, "you are an honest man, have great credit, and can do me signal service." "Ah, sir," replied the Earl, "I am old and feeble, but I once had a son." The King is said to have been so struck with this reply, that he was silent for some minutes. With this anecdote we may well terminate our account of the patriot Russell.*

One remark, however, we must make. It has been asserted, that the great reason why the Whigs of those days wished to keep the Catholics out of power was the dread of losing their estates as well as political influence, and of being

* We quote the Earl of Bedford's reply from Granger's Biographical History of England, not being able to refer to Orrery, who we believe is the authority for it. Burnet's Journal is to be found at the end of Lord Russell's Life, by his descendants.

obliged to give up the Abbey lands. There may have been
a good deal of truth in this, and yet the rest of their feelings
have been very sincere. Men may be educated in undue
notions of the value of wealth and property, and yet prove
their possession of nobler thoughts, when brought to heroical
issues of life and death.

The house in this square (Lincoln's Inn,) at the corner of
Great Queen Street, with a passage under its side, was once
called Newcastle House, and was occupied by the well-known
fantastical duke of that name, Minister of George II. Pennant
says it was built about the year 1686, " by the Marquis of
Powis, and called Powis House, and afterwards sold to the
late noble owner. The architect was Captain William Winde.

NEWCASTLE HOUSE.

It is said," he adds, "that government had it once in contemplation to have bought and settled it officially on the
great seal. At that time it was inhabited by the lord keeper,
Sir Nathan Wright." It is at present occupied by the Society
for the diffusion of the Bible.

The Marquis of Powis, here mentioned, had scarcely built
his house in the square where Lord Russell was beheaded,
when he saw his lordship's destroyer forced to leave his

throne.   The Marquis followed his fortunes, and was created by him Duke of Powis.

A laughable, and, we believe, true story, connected with the Duke of Newcastle's residence in this house, is told in a curious miscellany intitled the "Lounger's Common-Place Book."

"This nobleman," says the writer, "with many good points, and described by a popular contemporary poet as almost eaten up by his zeal for the house of Hanover, was remarkable for being profuse of his promises on all occasions, and valued himself particularly on being able to anticipate the words or the wants of the various persons who attended his levees before they uttered a word.   This sometimes led him into ridiculous embarrassments; but it was his tendency to lavish promises, which gave occasion for the anecdote I am going to relate.

"At the election of a certain borough of Cornwall, where the opposite interests were almost equally poised, a single vote was of the highest importance; this object, the Duke, by *well-applied arguments*, and personal application, at length attained, and the gentleman *he* recommended gained his election.

"In the warmth of gratitude, his Grace poured forth acknowledgments and promises without ceasing, on the fortunate possessor of the casting vote; called him his best and dearest friend; protested that he should consider himself as for ever indebted; that he would serve him by night or by day.

"The Cornish voter, an honest fellow, as things go, and who would have thought himself sufficiently paid, but for such a torrent of acknowledgments, thanked the Duke for his kindness, and told him, 'The supervisor of excise was old and infirm, and if he would have the goodness to recommend his son-in-law to the commissioners in case of the old man's death, he should think himself and his family bound to render Government every assistance in his power, on any future occasion.'

"'My dear friend, why do you ask for such a trifling employment?' exclaimed his Grace, 'your relation shall have it at a word's speaking, the moment it is vacant.'—'But how shall I get admitted to you my Lord? for, in London, I understand, it is a very difficult business to get a sight of you great folks, though you are so kind and complaisant to us in the country.' — 'The instant the man dies,' replied the premier, used to and prepared for the freedom of a contested election,— 'the moment he dies, set out post-haste for London; drive directly to my house, by night or by day, sleeping or waking, dead or alive, thunder at the door; I will leave word with my porter to show you up-stairs directly, and the employment shall be disposed of according to your wishes.'

"The parties separated; the Duke drove to a friend's house in the neighbourhood, where he was visiting, without a wish or a design of seeing his new acquaintance till that day seven years; but the memory of a Cornish elector, not being loaded with such a variety of subjects, was more retentive.   The supervisor died a few months after, and the ministerial partisan relying on the word of a peer, was conveyed to London post-haste, and ascended with alacrity the steps of a large house, now divided into three, in Lincoln's Inn Fields, at the corner of Great Queen Street.

"The reader should be informed that precisely at the moment when the expectations of a considerable party of a borough in Cornwall were roused by the death of a supervisor, no less a person than the King of Spain was expected hourly to depart; an event in which the Minister of Great Britain was particularly concerned.

"The Duke of Newcastle, on the very night that the proprietor of the decisive vote was at his door, had sat up anxiously expecting despatches from Madrid: wearied by official business and agitated spirits, he retired to rest, having previously given particular instructions to his porter not to go to bed, as he expected every minute a messenger with advices of the greatest importance, and desired he might be shown up-stairs the moment of his arrival.

"His Grace was sound asleep; for, with a thousand singularities, of which the rascals about him did not forget to take advantage, his worst enemies could not deny him the merit of good design, that best solace in a solitary hour. The porter, settled for the night in his chair, had already commenced a sonorous nap, when the vigorous arm of the Cornish voter roused him from his slumbers.

"To his first question, 'Is the Duke at home?' the porter replied, 'Yes; and in bed, but has left particular orders that come when you will, you are to go up to him directly.'—'God for ever bless him, a worthy and honest gentleman,' cried our applier for the vacant post, smiling and nodding with approbation at a Prime Minister's so accurately keeping his promise; 'how punctual his Grace is! I knew he would not deceive me. Let me hear no more of lords and dukes not keeping their words. I believe, verily, they are as honest and mean as well as other folks, but I can't always say the same of those who are about them.' Repeating these words as he ascended the stairs, the burgess of —— was ushered into the Duke's bedchamber.

"'Is he dead?' exclaimed his Grace, rubbing his eyes, and scarcely awaked from dreaming of the King of Spain, 'Is he dead?' 'Yes, my lord,' replied the eager expectant, delighted to find that the election promise, with all its circumstances, was so fresh in the Minister's memory. 'When did he die?' 'The day before yesterday, exactly at half-past one o'clock, after being confined three weeks to his bed, and taking a *power of doctor's stuff*; and I hope your Grace will be as good as your word, and let my son-in-law succeed him.'

"The duke, by this time perfectly awake, was staggered at the impossibility of receiving intelligence from Madrid in so short a space of time, and perplexed at the absurdity of a king's messenger applying for his son-in-law to succeed the King of Spain: 'Is the man drunk or mad; where are your despatches?' exclaimed his Grace, hastily drawing back his curtain; when, instead of a royal courier, his eager eye recognised at the bedside the well-known countenance of his friend in Cornwall, making low bows, with hat in hand, and 'hoping my lord would not forget the gracious promise he was so good as to make in favour of his son-in-law at the last election at ——.'

"Vexed at so untimely a disturbance, and disappointed of news from Spain, he frowned for a few seconds, but chagrin soon gave way to mirth at so singular and ridiculous a combination of opposite circumstances. Yielding to the irritation, he sank on the bed in a violent fit of laughter, which, like the electrical fluid, was communicated in a moment to his attendants."*

---

* Lounger's Common-Place Book, 1805, 8vo. vol. i., p. 301.

OLD PALACE OF WHITEHALL, FROM THE RIVER.

CHAPTER VI.

Great Queen Street—Former fashionable Houses there—Lewis and Miss Pope, the Comedians—Martin Folkes—Sir Godfrey Kneller and his Vanity— Dr. Radcliffe—Lord Herbert of Cherbury—Nuisance of Whetstone Park—The Three Dukes and the Beadle—Rogues and Vagabonds in the Time of Charles II—Former Theatres in Vere Street and Portugal Street—First appearance of Actresses—Infamous deception of one of them by the Earl of Oxford—Appearance of an avowed Impostor on the Stage—Anecdotes of the Wits and fine Ladies of the Time of Charles, connected with the Theatre in this Quarter—Kynaston, Betterton, Nokes, Mrs. Barry, Mrs. Mountford, and other Performers—Rich—Joe Miller—Carey Street and Mrs. Chapone—Clare Market—History, and Specimens, of Orator Henley—Duke Street and Little Wild Street—Anecdotes of Dr. Franklin's Residence in those Streets while a Journeyman Printer.

REAT Queen Street, in the time of the Stuarts, was one of the grandest and most fashionable parts of the town. The famous Lord Herbert of Cherbury died there. Lord Bristol had a house in it, Lord Chancellor Finch, and the Conway and Paulet families. Some of the houses towards the west retain pilasters and other ornaments, probably indicating, as Pennant observes, the abodes in question. Little thought the noble lords that a time would come, when a player should occupy their rooms, and be able to entertain their descendants in them ; but in a house of this description, lately occupied by Messrs. Allman the booksellers, died Lewis, the comedian, one of the most delightful performers of his class, and famous to the last for his invincible airiness and juvenility. Mr. Lewis displayed a combination rarely to be found in acting, that of the fop and the real gentleman. With a voice, a manner, and a person, all equally graceful and light, and features at once whimsical and genteel, he played on the top of his profession like a plume. He was the Mercutio of the age, in every sense of the word mercurial. His airy, breathless voice, thrown to the audience before he appeared, was the signal of his winged animal spirits ; and when he gave a glance of his eye, or touched his finger at another's ribs, it was the very *punctum saliens* of playfulness and inuendo. We saw him take leave of the public, a man of

Q

sixty-five, looking not more than half the age, in the character
of the Copper Captain ; and heard him say, in a voice broken
by emotion, that " for the space of thirty years, he had not
once incurred their displeasure."

Next door but one to the Freemasons' Tavern (westward),
for many years lived another celebrated comic performer, Miss
Pope, one of a very different sort, and looking as heavy and
insipid as her taste was otherwise.   She was an actress of the
highest order for dry humour ; one of those who convey the
most laughable things with a grave face.   Churchill, in the
Rosciad, when she must have been very young, mentions her
as an actress of great vivacity, advancing in a " jig," and
performing the parts of Cherry and Polly Honeycomb.   There
was certainly nothing of the Cherry and Honeycomb about
her when older ; but she was an admirable Mrs. Malaprop.

Queen Street continued to be a place of fashionable resort
for a considerable period after the Revolution.   As we have
been speaking of the advancement of actors in social rank, we
will take occasion of the birth of Martin Folkes in this street,
the celebrated scholar and antiquary, to mention that he was
one of the earliest persons among the gentry to marry an
actress.   His wife was Lucretia Bradshaw.   It may be thought

OLD HOUSES IN GREAT QUEEN STREET.

worth observing by the romantic, that the ladies who were
first selected to give this rise to the profession, had all something peculiar in their Christian names.   Lord Peterborough
married Anastasia Robinson, and the Duke of Bolton, Lavinia
Fenton.

Sir Godfrey Kneller, and Radcliffe the physician, lived in this street. We mention them together because they were neighbours, and there is a pleasant anecdote of them in conjunction. The author of a book lately published, describes their neighbourhood as being in Bow Street; but Horace Walpole, the authority for the story, places it in the street before us; adding, in a note, that Kneller " first lived in Durham Yard (in the Strand), then twenty-one years in Covent Garden (we suppose in Bow Street), and lastly in Great Queen Street, Lincoln's Inn Fields." " Kneller," says Walpole, " was fond of flowers, and had a fine collection. As there was great intimacy between him and the physician, he permitted the latter to have a door into his garden ; but Radcliffe's servants gathering and destroying the flowers, Kneller sent him word he must shut up the door. Radcliffe replied peevishly, ' Tell him he may do anything with it but paint it.' ' And I,' answered Sir Godfrey, ' can take anything from him but physic.'"*

Kneller, besides being an admired painter (and it is supposed from one of his performances, the portrait of a Chinese, that he could have been admired by posterity, if he chose), was a man of wit; but so vain, that he is described as being the butt of all the wits of his acquaintances. They played upon him undoubtedly, and at a great rate ; but it has been suggested by a shrewd observer, that while he consented to have his vanity tickled at any price, he humoured the joke himself, and was quite aware of what they were at. Nor is this inconsistent with the vanity, which would always make large allowances for the matter of fact. The extravagance it would limit where it pleased ; the truth remained ; and Sir Godfrey, as Pope said, had a large appetite. With this probability a new interest is thrown upon the anecdotes related of his vanity, with the best of which the reader is accordingly presented. Kneller was a German, born at Lubec, so that his English is to be read with a foreign accent.

The younger Richardson tells us, that Gay read Sir Godfrey a copy of verses, in which he had pushed his flattery so far, that he was all the while in dread lest the knight should detect him. When Kneller had heard this through, he said, in his foreign style and accent, " Ay, Mr. Gay, all what you have said is very fine, and very true ; but you have forgot one thing, my good friend ; by G——, I should have been a

* Anecdotes of Painting, in his Works, 4to. vol. iii., p. 364.

general of an army; for when I was at Venice, there was a *girandole*, and all the place of St. Mark was in a smoke of gunpowder, and I did like the smell, Mr. Gay; should have been a great general, Mr. Gay!"

Perhaps it was this real or apparent obtuseness which induced Gay to add "engineering" to his other talents, in the verses describing Pope's welcome from Greece :—

> "Kneller amid the triumph bears his part,
> Who could (were mankind lost) a new create :
> What can the extent of his vast soul confine?
> A painter, critic, engineer, divine."

The following is related on the authority of Pope :—

"Old Jacob Tonson got a great many fine pictures, and two of himself, from him, by this means. Sir Godfrey was very covetous, but then he was very vain, and a great glutton; so he played these passions against the others ; besides telling him that he was the greatest master that ever was, sending him, every now and then, a haunch of venison, and dozens of excellent claret. 'O, my G—, man,' said he once to Vander Gucht, 'this old Jacob loves me; he is a very good man ; you see he loves me, he sends me good things; the venison was fat.' Old Geekie, the surgeon, got several fine pictures of him too, an l an excellent one of himself; but then he had them cheaper, for he gave nothing but praises; but then his praises were as fat as Jacob's venison; neither could be too fat for Sir Godfrey."

Pope related the following to Spence :—

"As I was sitting by Sir Godfrey Kneller one day, whilst he was drawing a picture, he stopt, and said, 'I can't do as well as I should do, unless you flatter me a little, Mr. Pope! You know I love to be flattered.' I was for once willing," continues Pope, "to try how far this vanity would carry him; and after considering a picture which he had just finished, for a good while very attentively, I said to him in French (for he had been talking for some time before in that language), 'On lit dans les Ecritures Saintes, que le bon Dieu faisoit l'homme après son image : mais, je crois, que s'il voudroit faire un autre à présent, qu'il le feroit après l'image que voilà.' Sir Godfrey turned round, and said very gravely, 'Vous avez raison, Monsieur Pope; par Dieu, je le crois aussi.'"

It must not be omitted that Kneller was a kind-hearted man. At Whitton, where he had a seat, he was justice of the peace, and,

"Was so much more swayed," says Walpole, "by equity than law, that his judgments, accompanied with humour, are said to have occasioned those lines by Pope:—

> "I think Sir Godfrey should decide the suit,
> Who sent the thief (that stole the cash) away,
> And punish'd him that put it in his way."

"This alluded to his dismissing a soldier who had stolen a joint of meat, and accused the butcher of having tempted him by it. Whenever Sir Godfrey was applied to, to determine what parish a poor man belonged to, he always inquired which parish was the richer, and settled the poor man there ; nor would he ever sign a warrant to distrain the goods of a poor man who could not pay a tax."*

Poor Radcliffe, after reigning as a physician so despotically, that Arbuthnot, in his projected map of diseases, was for putting him up at the corner of it disputing the empire of the world, became a less happy man than Sir Godfrey, by reason of his falling in love in his old age. He set up a coach, adorned with mythological paintings,—at least, Steele says so ; but soon had to put it in mourning for the death of his flame, who was a Miss Tempest, one of the maids of honour. Radcliffe was the Tory physician, and Steele, in the " Tatler," with a party spirit that was much oftener aggrieved than provoked in that good-natured writer, was induced, by some circumstance or other, perhaps Radcliffe's insolence, to make a ludicrous description of him, " as the mourning Esculapius, the languishing, hopeless lover of the divine Hebe." Steele accuses him of avarice. Others have said he was generous. He was the founder of the Radcliffe Library at Oxford, and made other magnificent bequests ; which prove nothing either way. But it is not favourable to a reputation for generosity, to own (as he did), that he was fond of spunging, and to avoid the paying of bills. However, when he lost 5,000l. in a speculation, he said " he had nothing to do but to go up so many pair of stairs to make himself whole again." He was undoubtedly a very clever physician, though he made little use of books. Like many men who go upon their own grounds in this way, he had an abrupt and clownish manner, which he probably thought of use. According to Richardson, he one day said to Dr. Mead, " Mead, I love you; now I will tell you a sure secret to make your fortune. Use all mankind ill." It is worth observing, that Mead acted on the reverse principle, and made double the fortune of his adviser. Radcliffe is is said have attended the lady of Judge Holt, in a bad illness, with unusual assiduity, " out of pique to her husband ; " a very new kind of satire. He used to send huffing messages to Queen Anne, telling her that he would not come, and that she only had the vapours ; and when King William consulted him on his swollen ankles and thin body, Radcliffe said he " would not have his Majesty's

* Walpole's Works, *ut supra*, vol iii., p. 364.

two legs for his three kingdoms ; " a speech which it was not
in the nature of royalty to forgive. His death is said to have
been hastened by his refusal to attend on Queen Anne in her
last illness ; which so exasperated the populace that he was
afraid to leave his country house at Carshalton, where he
died. He lived in Bow Street when he first came to London ;
and afterwards in Bloomsbury Square.

But the most remarkable inhabitant of Queen Street was
Lord Herbert of Cherbury, one of those extraordinary individuals who, with a touch of madness on the irascible side, and
subject to the greatest blindness of self-love, possess a profound
judgment on every other point. Such persons are supposed to
be victims of imagination ; but they are rather mechanical
enthusiasts (though of a high order), and, for want of an
acquaintance with the imaginative, become at the mercy of
the first notion which takes their will by suprise. Lord
Herbert, who in the intellectual part was intended for a
statist and a man of science, was unfortunately one of the
hottest of Welchmen in the physical. Becoming a Knight
of the Bath, he took himself for a knight-errant, and fancied
he was bound to fight everybody he met with, and to lie
under trees in the fields of Holland. He thought Revelation
a doubtful matter, and so he had recourse to the Deity for a
revelation in his particular favour to disprove it. We have
related an anecdote of him at Northumberland House, and
shall have more to tell ; but the account of his having
recourse to Heaven for the satisfaction of his doubts of its
interference, must not be omitted here. Perhaps it took
place in this very street. His Lordship was the first Deist
in England that has left an account of his opinions. Speaking of the work he wrote on this subject, he says :—

" My book ' De Veritate prout distinguitur à Revelatione verisimili,
possibili, et à falso,' having been begun by me in England, and formed
there in all its principal parts, was about this time finished; all the
spare hours which I could get from my visits and negotiations being
employed to perfect this work ; which was no sooner done, but that
I communicated it to Hugo Grotius—that great scholar, who, having
escaped his prison in the Low Countries, came into France, and was
much welcomed by me and Monsier Tieleners, also one of the greatest
scholars of his time; who, after they had perused it, and given it more
commendations than is fit for me to repeat, exhorted me earnestly to
print and publish it ; howbeit, as the frame of my whole work was
so different from anything which had been written heretofore, I found
I must either renounce the authority of all that I had written formerly, concerning the method of finding out truth, and consequently

insist upon my own way, or hazard myself to a general censure concerning the whole argument of my book ; I must confess it did not a
little animate me, that the two great persons above-mentioned did so
highly value it; yet, as I knew it would meet with much opposition,
I did consider whether it was not better for me for a while to suppress it.

"Being thus doubtful in my chamber one fair day in the summer,
my casement being open towards the south, the sun shining clear,
and no wind stirring, I took my book, 'De Veritate,' in my hand,
and kneeling on my knees, devoutly said these words:—

. "'Oh, thou eternal God, author of the light which now shines upon
me, and giver of all inward illuminations, I do beseech thee of thy
infinite goodness to pardon a greater request than a sinner ought to
make; I am not satisfied enough whether I shall publish this book
'De Veritate;' if it be for thy glory, I beseech thee give me some
sign from heaven; if not, I shall suppress it.'

"I had no sooner spoken these words, but a loud though gentle
noise came from the heavens (for it was like nothing on earth) which
did so comfort and cheer me, that I took my petition as granted, and
that I had the sign I demanded; whereupon also I resolved to print
my book. This (how strange soever it may seem) I protest, before
the eternal God, is true ; neither am I any way superstitiously
deceived herein ; since I did not only hear the noise, but, in the
serenest sky that ever I saw, being without all cloud, did to my
thinking see the place from whence it came."*

"How could a man," justly observes Walpole on this passage, "who doubted of partial, believe individual revelation !
What vanity to think his book of such importance to the
cause of truth, that it could extort a declaration of the Divine
will, when the interest of half mankind could not !" Yet the
same writer is full of admiration of him in other respects. It
is well observed by the editor of the *Autobiography* (in reply
to the doubts thrown on his lordship's veracity respecting his
chivalrous propensities, the consequences of which always fell
short of duels), that much of the secret might be owing "to
his commanding aspect and acknowledged reputation ; and a
little more to a certain perception of the Quixote in his
character, with which it might be deemed futile to contend.
His surprising defence of himself against the attack of Sir
John Ayres, forcibly exhibits his personal strength and mastery ; and his spirited treatment of the French Minister,
Luynes, and the general esteem of his contemporaries, suffi-

* Life of Edward Lord Herbert, of Cherbury, in the Autobiography
p. 145. It is an honour to Grotius, who wrote a book, De Veritate,
on the other side of the question, that he encouraged so renowned an
antagonist to publish : though, perhaps, he saw less danger in it than
singularity. At all events, he could anticipate no harm from the
close.

ciently attest his quick feeling of national and personal dignity, and general gallantry of bearing." There is no doubt, in short, that Lord Herbert of Cherbury was a brave, an honest, and an able man, though with some weaknesses, both of heat and vanity, sufficient to console the most commonplace.

With all this elegance of neighbourhood, Lincoln's Inn Fields, in the time of Charles II., had one eyesore of an enormous description, in a place behind Holborn row, entitled Whetstone Park. It is now a decent passage between Great and Little Turnstiles.

"It is scarcely necessary," says Mr. Malcolm, "to remind the reader of a well-known fact, that all sublunary things are subject to change :—he who passes through the Little Turnstile, Holborn, at present, will observe on the left hand, near Lincoln's Inn Fields, a narrow street, composed of small buildings, on the corner of which is inscribed Whetstone Park. The repose and quiet of the place seem to proclaim strong pretensions to regular and moral life in the inhabitants ; and well would it have been for the happiness of many a family, had the site always exhibited the same appearance. On the contrary, Whetstone Park contributed to increase the dissoluteness of manners which distinguished the period between 1660 and 1700. Being a place of low entertainment, numerous disturbances occurred there, and rendered it subject to the satire and reprehension even of 'Poor Robin's Intelligencer,' a paper almost infamous enough for the production of a keeper of this theatre of vice. The publication alluded to says, in 1676, 'Notwithstanding the discourses that have been to the contrary, the boarding-school is still continued here, where a set of women may be readily untaught all the studies of modesty or chastity; to which purpose they are provided with a two-handed volume of impudence, loosely bound up in greasy vellum, which is tied by the leg to a wicker chair (as you find authors chained in a library), and is always ready to give you plain instructions and directions in all matters relating to immorality or irreligion.'   *   *

"Incomprehensible as it certainly is," continues our author, "the brutal acts of a mob are sometimes the result of a just sense of the ill consequences attending vice; and, although almost every individual composing it is capable of performing deeds which deserve punishment from the police, they cannot collectively view long and deliberate offences against the laws of propriety, without assuming the right of reforming them. 'The Loyal and Impartial Mercury' of Sept. 1, 1682, has this paragraph:—'On Saturday last, about 500 apprentices, and such like, being got together in Smithfield, went into Lincoln's Inn Fields, where they drew up, and marching into Whetstone Park, fell upon the lewd houses there, where, having broken open the doors, they entered, and made great spoil of the goods; of which the constables and watchmen having notice, and not finding themselves strong enough to quell the tumult, procured a party of the King's guards who dispersed them, and took eleven, who were committed to New Prison; yet on Sunday night they came again, and made worse havoc than before, breaking down all the doors and windows, and cutting the featherbeds and goods in pieces.' Another newspaper explains the origin of the riot by saying, 'that a countryman who had been decoyed into one of the houses alluded to, and robbed, lodged a formal and public complaint against them to those he found willing to listen to him in Smithfield, and thus raised the ferment.'"*

In the "State Poems" is a doggrel set of verses on a tragical circumstance occasioned by a frolic of three of Charles's natural sons in this place. It is entitled "On the three Dukes killing the Beadle on Sunday morning, Feb. the 26th, 1671." A great sensation was made by this circumstance, which was naturally enough regarded as a signal instance of the consequences of Charles's mode of life. Our Grub Street writer selected his title well—the "Dukes," the "Beadle," and the "Sunday." His first four lines might have been put into Martinus Scriblerus, as a specimen of the Newgate style.

> "Near Holborn lies a park of great renown,
> The place, I do suppose, is not unknown:
> For brevity's sake the name I shall not tell,
> Because most genteel readers know it well."

The three Dukes pick a quarrel with one poor damsel, and "murder" was cried.

> "In came the watch, disturbed with sleep and ale,
> By noises shrill, but they could not prevail
> T' appease their Graces. Strait rose mortal jars,
> Betwixt the night blackguard and silver stars;
> Then fell the beadle by a ducal hand,
> For daring to pronounce the saucy stand.
>   *   *   *   *
> See what mishaps dare e'en invade Whitehall,
> This silly fellow's death puts off the ball,
> And disappoints the Queen, poor little chuck;
> I warrant t'would have danced it like a duck.
> The fiddlers, voices, entries, all the sport,
> And the gay show put off, where the brisk court
> Anticipates, in rich subsidy coats,
> All that is got by necessary votes.
> Yet shall Whitehall, the innocent, the good,
> See these men dance, all daubed with lace and blood."†

The "subsidy coats" allude to Charles's raising money for his profligate expenditure under pretence of the public service. The last couplet would have done credit to a better satire.

* Malcolm's Customs and Manners of London, from the Roman Invasion to the Year 1700, vol. i., p. 318.

† Poems on Affairs of State, from the Time of Oliver Cromwell to the Abdication of King James the Second, vol. i., p. 147.

As we are upon the subject of a neighbourhood to which they apply, we shall proceed to give a few more extracts from Mr. Malcolm, highly characteristic of the lower orders of desperadoes in Charles's reign.

" The various deceivers," he tells us, " who preyed upon the public at this time were exposed in a little filthy work called the ' Canting Academy,' which went through more than one edition (the second is dated 1674). I shall select from it enough to show the variety of villany practised under their various names. The *Ruffler* was a wretch who assumed the character of a maimed soldier, and begged from the claims of Naseby, Edgehill, Newbury, and Marston Moor. Those who were stationed in the city of London were generally found in Lincoln's Inn Fields and Covent Garden ; and their prey was people of fashion, whose coaches were attacked boldly ; and if denied, their owners were told, ' 'Tis a sad thing that an old crippled cavalier should be suffered to beg for a maintenance, and a young cavalier that had never heard the whistle of a bullet should ride in his coach.'

" There were people called *Anglers*, from the nature of their method of depredating, which was thus .—They had a rod or stick, with an iron hook affixed : this they introduced through a window, or any other aperture, where plunder might be procured, and helped themselves at pleasure ; the day was occupied by them in the character of beggars, when they made their observations for the angling of the night.

" *Wild Rogues* were the offspring of thieves and beggars, who received the rudiments of the art even before they left their mothers' backs : " To go into churches and great crowds, and to *nim* golden buttons off men's cloaks ; and being very little are shown how to creep into cellar windows, or other small entrances, and in the night to convey out thereat whatever they can find to the thievish receivers, who wait without for that purpose ; and sometimes do open the door to let in such who have designed to rob the house ; if taken, the tenderness of their age makes an apology or an excuse for their fault, and so are let alone to be hanged at riper years.'

" *Palliards* or *Clapperdogeons*, were those women who sat and reclined in the streets, with their own borrowed or stolen children hanging about them, crying through cold, pinching, or real disease, who begged relief as widows, and, in the name of their fatherless children, gaining by this artifice, ' a great deal of money, whilst her comrogue lies begging in the fields, with climes or artificial sores.' The way they commonly take to make them is by sperewort or arsenic, which will draw blisters ; or they take unslacked lime and soap, mingled with the rust of old iron : these being well tempered together, and spread thick upon two pieces of leather, they apply to the leg, binding it thereunto very hard, which in a very little time would fret the skin so that the flesh would appear all raw, &c. &c.

" *Fraters* were impostors who went through the country with forged patents for briefs, and thus diverted charity from its proper direction.

" *Abram men* were fellows whose occupations seem to have been forgotten. They are described in the ' Canting Academy' in these words :—' Abram men are otherwise called Tom of Bedlams ; they are very strangely and antickly garbed, with several coloured ribands or tape in their hats, it may be instead of a feather, a fox tail hanging down, a long stick with ribands streaming, and the like; yet for all their seeming madness they have wit enough to steal as they go.' *

" The *Whip-Jacks* have left us a specimen of their fraternity. They were counterfeit mariners, whose conversations were plentifully embellished with sea-terms, and falsehoods of their danger in the exercise of their profession. Instead of securing their arms and legs close to their bodies, and wrapping them in bandages (as the modern *whip-jack* is in the habit of doing, to excite compassion for the loss of limbs and severe wounds), the *ancients* merely pretended they had lost their all by shipwreck, and were reduced to beg their way to a sea-port, if in the country; or to some remote one, if in London.

" *Mumpers.*—The persons thus termed are described as being of both sexes: they were not solicitors for food, but money and cloathes. ' The male mumper, in the times of the late usurpation, was clothed in an old torn cassock, begirt with a girdle, with a black cap, and a white one peeping out underneath.' With a formal and studied countenance he stole up to a gentleman, and whispered him softly in the ear, that he was a poor sequestered parson, with a wife and many children. At other times, they would assume the habit of a decayed gentleman, and beg as if they had been ruined by their attachment to the royal cause. Sometimes the mumper appeared with an apron before him, and a cap on his head, and begs in the nature of a broken tradesman, who, having been a long time sick, hath spent all his remaining stock, and so weak he cannot work! The females of this class of miscreants generally attacked the ladies, and in a manner suited to make an impression on their finer feelings.

" *Domerars* are such as counterfeit themselves dumb, and have a notable art to roll their tongues up into the roof of their mouth, that you would verily believe their tongues were cut out; and, to make you have a stronger belief thereof, they will gape and show you where it was done, clapping in a sharp stick, and, touching the tongue, make it bleed—and then the ignorant dispute it no further.'

" *Patricos* are the strolling priests: every hedge is their parish, and every wandering rogue their parishioner. The service, he saith, is the marrying of couples, without the Gospel, or Book of Common Prayer, the solemnity whereof is thus: the parties to be married find out a dead horse, or any other beast, and standing the one on the one side and the other on the other, the patrico bids them to live together till death them part; and, so shaking hands, the wedding is ended.' " †

On the southern side of Lincoln's Inn Fields, at the back of Portugal Row, is Portugal Street, formerly containing a theatre, as celebrated as Covent Garden or Drury Lane is now. This was the Duke's Theatre, so called from the Duke of York, afterwards James II., who, at the Restoration, patronised one of the principal companies of players, as his brother Charles did the other. The latter was the Drury Lane company. Readers of theatrical history are generally

* It is still a phrase with the vulgar to say, a man " shams Abram."
† Manners and Customs, vol. i., p. 322.

led to conclude that there was only one theatre in the Lincoln's
Inn quarter ; but this is a mistake. There were at least two
successive houses in two different places, though usually con-
founded under the title of " the theatre in Lincoln's Inn Fields."
The first was in Gibbon's tennis-court, in Vere Street, Clare
Market, where the actors who had played at the Red Bull
opened their performances in the year of the Restoration,
under the direction of Killigrew, and with the title of King's
Company. These in 1663 removed to Drury Lane. The
Duke's, or Sir William Davenant's company, removed in 1662
from Salisbury Court (see Fleet Street) to a new theatre " in
Portugal Row," says Malone, " *near* Lincoln's Inn Fields." *
Malone is a correct inquirer : so that he makes us doubt
whether the name of Portugal Row did not formerly belong
to Portugal Street. The latter is certainly meant, or he

OLD THEATRE IN PORTUGAL STREET.

would describe it as *in* and not *near* the Fields. Davenant's
company performed here till 1671, when they quitted it to
return to the renovated theatre in Salisbury Court, under the
management of his son, Charles Davenant (the father being
dead), and the famous Betterton, who had been Sir William's
first actor. The two companies afterwards came together at
Drury Lane, but again fell apart ; and in 1695 the Duke's
company (if its altered composition could still warrant the
name), with Betterton remaining at its head, and Congreve

* Historical Account of the English Stage, p. 320.

for a partner, again opened " the theatre in Lincoln's Inn Fields," which was rebuilt for the purpose, and is described as being in " the Tennis-court." Was this the tennis-court theatre in Vere Street ? or were there two tennis-courts, one in Vere Street, and one in Lincoln's Inn Fields ? We confess ourselves, after a diligent examination, unable to determine. At all events, the latest theatre of which we hear in Lincoln's Inn Fields, was not in Vere Street. It stood in Portugal Street, on the east end of the present burial ground, just at the back of Surgeons' College, and was subsequently the china warehouse of Messrs. Spode and Copeland.*   This theatre, which was built of red brick, and had a front facing the market, is the one generally meant by the theatre in Lincoln's Inn Fields.   It finally became celebrated for the harlequinades of Rich; but, on his removal to Covent Garden, was deserted, and, after a short re-opening by Gifford from Goodman's Fields, finally ceased to be a theatre about the year 1737. Since that period Covent Garden and Drury Lane playhouses have had this part of the town to themselves.

It is conjectured, that the first appearance of an actress on the English stage, to the scandle of the Puritans, and with many apologies for the " indecorum" of giving up the performances of female characters by boys, took place in the theatre in Vere Street, on Saturday, Dec. 8, 1660.   The part first performed was certainly that of Desdemona ; a very fit one to introduce the claims of the sex.†

Mr. Malone has given us the prologue written for this occasion by Thomas Jordan ; which, as it shows the " sensation " that was made, sets us in a lively manner in the situation of the spectators, and gives a curious account of some of the male actors of gentle womanhood, we shall here repeat.   It is entitled " A Prologue, to introduce the first Woman that came to act on the Stage, in the Tragedy called the Moor of Venice : "

> " I came unknown to any of the rest,
> To tell the news ; I saw the lady drest :
> The woman plays to-day ; mistake me not,
> No man in gown, or page in petticoat :
> A woman to my knowledge, yet I can't,
> If I should die, make affidavit on't.
> Do you not twitter, gentlemen ?   I know
> You will be censuring : do it fairly, though ;

---

* It has recently been pulled down to make room for the enlargement of the museum of the College of Surgeons.

† See Malone, pp. 135, 136.

'Tis possible a virtuous woman may
Abhor all sorts of looseness, and yet play ;
Play on the stage—where all eyes are upon her :
Shall we count that a crime France counts an honour ?
In other kingdoms husbands safely trust 'em ;
The difference lies only in the custom.
And let it be our custom, I advise ;
I'm sure this custom's better than th' excise,
And may procure *us* custom : hearts of flint
Will melt in passion, when a woman's in't.
But, gentlemen, you that as judges sit
In the Star-chamber of the house—the pit,
Have modest thoughts of her ; pray, do not run
To give her visits when the play is done,
With ' *damn me, your most humble servant, lady* ;'
She knows these things as well as you, it may be ;
Not a bit there, dear gallants, she doth know
Her own deserts,—and your temptations too.
But to the point :—in this reforming age
We have intents to civilize the stage.
Our women are defective, and so sized,
You'd think they were some of the guard disguised ;
For to speak truth, men act, that are between
Forty and fifty, wenches of fifteen ;
With bone so large, and nerve so incompliant,
When you call Desdemona, enter giant.
We shall purge everything that is unclean,
Lascivious, scurrilous, impious, or obscene ;
And when we've put all things in this fair way,
Barebones himself may come to see a play." *

The epilogue, " which consists of but twelve lines, is in
the same strain of apology."

"And how do you like her ;   Come, what is't ye drive at ?
She's the same thing in public as in private,
As far from being what you call a whore,
As Desdemona injured by the Moor ;
Then he that censures her in such a case,
Hath a soul blacker than Othello's face.
But, ladies, what think *you* ? for if you tax
Her freedom with dishonour to your sex,
She means to act no more, and this shall be
No other play, but her own tragedy.
She will submit to none but your commands,
And take commission only from your hands."†

From the nature of this epilogue, and the permission accorded
by the ladies, the women actors appear to have met with all
the success they could wish ; yet a prologue to the second
part of Davenant's " Siege of Rhodes," acted in April, 1662,

* Malone, p. 135.   † Ibid. p. 136.

shows us that the matter was still considered a delicate one
upwards of a year afterwards.

> "Hope little from our poet's withered wit,
> From infant players scarce grown puppets yet;
> Hope from our women less, whose bashful fear
> Wondered to see me dare to enter here :
> Each took her leave, and wished my danger past,
> And though I came back safe and undisgraced,
> Yet when they spy the wits here, then I doubt
> No amazon can make them venture out,
> Though I advised them not to fear you much,
> For I presume not half of you are such."*

It was in the Theatre at Vere Street that Pepys first saw a
woman on the stage.† One of the earliest female performers
mentioned by him was an actress whose name is not ascertained, but who attained an unfortunate celebrity in the part
of Roxana in the " Siege of Rhodes." She was seduced by
Aubery de Vere, the last Earl of Oxford of that name, under
the guise of a private marriage—a species of villany which
made a great figure in works of fiction up to a late period.
The story is "got up" in detail by Madame Dunois, in her
" History of the Court of Charles II. ;" ‡ but it is told with
more brevity in Grammont ; and as the latter, though apocryphal enough, pretends to say nothing on the subject in which
he is not borne out by other writers, his lively account may
be laid before the reader.

" The Earl of Oxford," says one of his heroines, "fell in love with
a handsome, graceful actress, belonging to the Duke's theatre, who
performed to perfection, particularly the part of Roxana in a very
fashionable new play; insomuch that she ever after retained that
name. This creature being both very virtuous and very modest, or,
if you please, wonderfully obstinate, proudly rejected the presents
and addresses of the Earl of Oxford. The resistance inflamed his
passion; he had recourse to invectives and even spells; but all in
vain. This disappointment had such an effect- upon him, that he
could neither eat nor drink; this did not signify to him; but his
passion at length became so violent, that he could neither play nor
smoke. In this extremity, Love had recourse to Hymen; the Earl of
Oxford, one of the first peers of the realm, is, you know, a very handsome man: he is of the order of the Garter, which greatly adds to an
air naturally noble. In short, from his outward appearance, you
would suppose he was really possessed of some sense; but as soon as
ever you hear him speak, you are perfectly convinced to the contrary.
This passionate lover presented her with a promise of marriage, in
due form, signed with his own hand; she would not, however, rely

---

* Malone, p. 136.　　　　　　† Memoirs, *ut supra*, vol. i., p. 167.
‡ Memoirs of the English Court in the Reign of Charles II., &c.,
by the Countess of Dunois, part ii., p. 71.

upon this; but the next day she thought there could be no danger, when the Earl himself came to her lodgings attended by a clergy-man, and another man for a witness; the marriage was accordingly solemnized with all due ceremonics, in the presence of one of her fellow-players, who attended as a witness on her part. You will suppose, perhaps, that the new countess had nothing to do but to appear at court according to her rank, and to display the earl's arms upon her carriage. This was far from being the case. When exami-nation was made concerning the marriage, it was found to be a mere deception: it appeared that the pretended priest was one of my lord's trumpeters, and the witness his kettle-drummer. The parson and his companion never appeared after the ceremony was over; and as for the other witness, he endeavoured to persuade her that the Sultana Roxana might have supposed, in some part or other of a play, that she was really married. It was all to no purpose that the poor creature claimed the protection of the laws of God and man; both which were violated and abused, as well as herself, by this infamous imposition: in vain did she throw herself at the king's feet to demand justice; she had only to rise up again without redress; and happy might she think herself to receive an annuity of one thousand crowns, and to resume the name of Roxana, instead of Countess of Oxford."*

This scoundrel Earl (whose alleged want of sense is extremely probable, and was his best excuse, as well as the worst thing to say for the lady), died full of years and honours, and was buried in Westminster Abbey.

In 1664, Mr. Pepys witnessed a scene in the theatre in Portugal Street, which shows the extremity to which the speculation of managers and the curiosity of the British public can go. This was no other than the appearance of an imposter, called the German Princess, in the part of her own character, after having been tried for it at the Old Bailey. She was tried for bigamy, and acquitted; but she had inveigled a young citizen into marriage under pretence of being a German Princess, the citizen pretending at the same time to be a nobleman. The impudence of the thing was completed by the badness of her performance. Granger, however, who appears to have read a vindication of her, which she published, thinks she had great natural abilities.

The following is curious :—4th (Feb. 1666-7).

"Soon as dined,' says Pepys, "my wife and I out to the Duke's playhouse, and there saw Heraclius, an excellent play, to my extra-ordinary content; and the more from the house being very full, and great company; among others Mrs. Stuart,† very fine, with her locks done up in puffes, as my wife calls them: and several other

---

* Memoirs of Count Grammont, 8vo. 1811, vol. ii. p. 142.

† With whom Charles II. was in love—afterwards Duchess of Richmond.

great ladies had their hair so, though I do not like it, but my wife do mightily; but it is only because she sees it is the fashion. Here I saw my Lord Rochester* and his lady, Mrs. Mallet, who hath after all this ado married him; and, as I hear some say in the pit, it is a great act of charity, for he hath no estate. But it was pleasant to see how everybody rose up when my Lord John Butler, the Duke of Ormond's son, came into the pit, towards the end of the play, who was a servant to Mrs. Mallett, and now smiled upon her, and she on him."†

One little thinks, now-a-days, in turning into Portugal Street, that all the fashionable world, with the wits and poets, once thronged into that poor-looking thoroughfare, with its bailiffs at one end, and its butchers at the other. The difference, however, between beaux and butchers was not so great at that time as it became afterwards; though none arrogated the praise of high breeding more than the fine gentlemen of Charles II. Next year Pepys speaks of a fray at this house between Harry Killigrew and the Duke of Buckingham, in which the latter beat him, and took away his sword. Another time, according to his account, Rochester beat Tom Killigrew, at the Dutch Ambassador's, and in the King's presence. Blows from people of rank do not appear to have been resented as they would be now.

In the following passage we have an author's first night before us, and that author the gallant Etherege, with dukes and wits about him in the pit. He makes, however, a very different figure in our eyes from what we commonly conceive of him, for he is unsuccessful and complaining.

"My wife," says Pepys, "being gone before (6th Feb. 1667-8), I to the Duke of York's playhouse, where a new play of Etheridge's, called 'She would if she could;' and, though I was there by two o'clock, there was one thousand people put back that could not have room in the pit; and I at last, because my wife was there, made shift to get into the 18d. box, and there saw. But Lord! how full was the house, and how silly the play, there being nothing in the world good in it, and few people pleased in it. The King was there; but I sat mightily behind, and could see but little, and hear not at all. The play being done, I into the pit to look for my wife, it being dark and raining; but could not find her, and so staid, going between the two doors and through the pit, an hour and a half, I think, after the play was done, the people staying there till the rain was over, and to talk one with another. And among the rest here was the Duke of Buckingham to-day openly sat in the pit; and there I found him with my Lord Buckhurst, and Sedley, and Etheridge the poet; the last of whom I did hear mightily find fault with the actors, that they were

---

* The famous wit and debauchee.
† Pepys' Memoirs, vol. iii., p. 136.

out of humour and had not their parts perfect, and that Harris did do nothing, nor could so much as sing a catch in it; and so was mightily concerned; while all the rest did through the whole pit blame the play as a silly, dull thing, though there was something very roguish and witty; but the design of the play and end mighty insipid. At last I did find my wife."

The ensuing is a specimen of the manners of one of the fine ladies:—

"5th (May, 1668), Creed and I to the Duke of York's playhouse; and there, coming late, up to the balcony-box, where we find my Lady Castlemaine (the King's mistress) and several great ladies; and there we sat with them, and I saw the 'Impertinents' once more than yesterday! and I for that reason like it, I find, the better too. By Sir Positive At-all I understand is meant Sir Robert Howard. My lady pretty well pleased with it; but here I sat close to her fine woman, Wilson, who indeed is very handsome, but they say with child by the King. I asked, and she told me this was the first time her lady had seen it, I having a mind to say something to her. One thing of familiarity I observed in my Lady Castlemaine; she called to one of her women, another that sat by this, for a little patch off of her face, and put it into her mouth and wetted it, and so clapped it upon her own by the the side of her mouth; I suppose she feeling a pimple rising there."*

More manners of this gallant reign. Pepys says he went to see a woman with a great bushy beard, " which pleased him mightily."

"Thence to the Duke's playhouse, and saw 'Macbeth.' The King and Court there; and we sat just under them and my Lady Castlemaine, and close to a woman that comes into the pit, a kind of a loose gossip, that pretends to be like her, and is so something. And my wife, by my troth, appeared, I think, as pretty as any of them; I never thought so much before; and so did Talbot and W. Hewer, as they said, I heard, to one another. The King and Duke of York minded me, and smiled upon me, at the handsome woman near me; but it vexed me to see Moll Davies, in the box over the King and my Lady Castlemaine, look down upon the King and he up to her; and so did my Lady Castlemaine once to see who it was; but when she saw Moll Davies, she looked like fire; which troubled me."†

Modes of thinking. Mr. Pepys is of opinion that the "Tempest," which he saw at this house, is an "innocent" play; "no great wit, but yet good above ordinary plays." This appears to have been his general opinion of Shakspeare. That year he says,

"After dinner to the Duke of York's playhouse, and there saw 'Sir Martin Mar-all,' which I have seen so often, and yet am mightily pleased with it, and think it mighty witty, and the fullest of proper matter for mirth that was ever writ; and I do clearly see that they do improve in their acting of it. Here a mighty company of citizens, 'prentices, and others; and it makes me observe, that

* Pepys' Memoirs, vol. iv., p. 99.   † Id. p. 222.

when I began first to be able to bestow a play on myself, I do not remember that I saw so many by half of the ordinary 'prentices and mean people in the pit, at 2s. 6d. a piece, as now ; I going for several years no higher than the 12d. and then the 18d. places, though I strained hard to go in them when I did : so much the vanity and prodigality of the age is to be observed in this particular." *

What he calls the vanity of the age, was one of the best signs of its advancement. Plays, at the time above mentioned, began as early as they did before the civil wars ; and when they were over, people rode out in their coaches to take the air. Our author, when the King visited the theatre, speaks of being there by one o'clock to get a seat. Kynaston, a favourite actor at this house, used to be taken out airing by the ladies, in the dress which he wore as a female. Cibber mentions this particular among others in an entertaining account of Kynaston, whom the ladies do not appear to have spoiled :—

"Though women," he says, " were not admitted to the stage till the return of King Charles, yet it could not be so suddenly supplied with them, but that there was still a necessity, for some time, to put the handsomest young men into petticoats, which Kynaston was then said to have worn with success ; particularly in the part of Evadne, in the 'Maid's Tragedy,' which I have heard him speak of ; and which calls to my mind a ridiculous distress that arose from these sort of shifts, which the stage was then put to. The King, coming a little before his usual time to a tragedy, found the actors not ready to begin, when his Majesty, not choosing to have as much patience as his good subjects, sent to them to know the meaning of it; upon which the master of the company came to the box, and rightly judging that the best excuse for their default would be the true one, fairly told his Majesty that the queen was not *shaved* yet: the King, whose good humour loved to laugh at a jest as well as to make one, accepted the excuse, which served to divert him till the male queen could be effeminated. In a word, Kynaston, at that time, was so beautiful a youth, that the ladies of quality prided themselves in taking him with them in their coaches to Hyde Park in his theatrical habit, after the play; which in those days they might have sufficient time to do, because plays then were used to begin at four o'clock : the hour that people of the same rank are now going to dinner. Of this truth I had the curiosity to inquire, and had it confirmed from his own mouth, in his advanced age : and, indeed, to the last, of him, his handsomeness was very little abated; even at past sixty his teeth were sound, white and even, as one would wish to see in a reigning toast of twenty. He had something of a formal gravity in his mien, which was attributed to the stately step he had been so early confined to, in a female decency. But even that, in characters of superiority, had its proper graces; it misbecame him not in the part of Leon, in

* Pepys' Memoirs, vol. iv., p. 2.

R 2

Fletcher's 'Rule a Wife,' &c., which he executed with a determined manliness, and honest authority, well worth the best actor's imitation. He had a piercing eye, and, in characters of heroic life, a quick imperious vivacity in his tone of voice, that painted the tyrant truly terrible. There were two plays of Dryden in which he shone with uncommon lustre; in 'Aurengzebe' he played Morat, and in 'Don Sebastian,' Muley Moloch; in both these parts he had a fierce, lion-like majesty in his port and utterance, that gave the spectator a kind of trembling admiration." *

Pepys does not speak much of Betterton, the chief performer at the Portugal-street playhouse. The reason must be, either that Betterton played chiefly in tragedy, or that his comic talent (which is probable) was not equal to his tragic. He was the great actor of his time, as Garrick was of the last century, and Mr. Kean lately. His most admired character appears to have been that of Hamlet; though Steele, in a paper to his memory in the 'Tatler,' seems to have been most impressed by his performance of Othello. If an actor's Othello is really fine, perhaps it must be his best part, as in Mr. Kean's instance, owing to the nature of the character. Hamlet speaks to the reflecting part of us; Othello to the sensitive. We will not present the reader with extracts from Cibber which contain little respecting this actor that might not be said of others; only it may be observed, that in the better parts of the performances of the old players we have something perhaps handed down to us of the manner of these ancient ornaments of the stage. The liveliest idea remaining of the genius of Betterton is furnished by an anecdote of Booth, who, when he first performed the Ghost to Betterton's Hamlet, is said to have been so astonished at the other's look of surprise, that for some moments he was unable to speak. Betterton died old and poor, rather, it should seem, from misfortune than imprudence. The actors in those times, though much admired, were not rewarded as they have been since; nor received anything like the modern salaries. His death is said to have been hastened by tampering with the gout, in order to perform on his benefit night. His person was rather manly than graceful. He was a good-natured man; and, like Molière, would perform when he was ill, rather than hinder the profits of his brother actors.† At Caen Wood, Hampstead, the seat of Lord Mansfield, there is a portrait of him by Pope, who was an amateur in painting. They became acquainted when the latter was young, and the

* Cibber's Apology, chap. v., &c.　　† See Tatler, No. 167.

actor old; and took such a liking to one another, that Pope is supposed to have had a hand in a volume of pieces from 'Chaucer,' purporting to have been modernised by Betterton.

Another celebrated actor in Portugal Street during the reign of Charles II. was Nokes, who appears, from Cibber's account of him to have been something between Liston and Munden. By a line in one of Dryden's Epistles, the town seem to have thought a comedy deficient in which he did not make his appearance. The poet says to Southern on his play of the ' *Wives' Excuse* '—

> " The hearers may for want of Nokes repine,
> But rest secure, the readers will be thine."

Nokes was one of those actors who create a roar the moment they are seen, and make people ache with laughter.

These were among the older performers in Portugal Street. When Congreve took a share in the theatre, some others had joined it, and become celebrated, two of whom, Mr. Mountford and Mrs. Bracegirdle, we have already described. Another two, whose names remain familiar with posterity, are Mrs. Mountford and Mrs. Barry. Mrs. Mountford was a capital stage coquette; besides being able to act male coxcombs and country dowdies. Mrs. Barry was a fine tragedian, both of the heroic and tender cast. Dryden pronounced her the best actress he had seen. It is said she was a mistress of Lord Rochester's when young ; that it was to her his love-letters were addressed ; and that she owed her celebrity to his instructions. She was not handsome, and her mouth was a little awry, but her countenance was very expressive. This is the actress, who, in the delirium of her last moments, is said to have alluded in an extempore blank verse to a manœuvre played by Queen Anne's ministry some time before :—

> "Ha ! ha ! and so they make us lords by dozens !"

Cibber's sketch of Mrs. Mountford, in the character of Melantha is the masterpiece of his book, and presents a portrait sufficiently distinct to be extracted.

"Melantha," says our lively critic (himself a coxcomb of the first water), " is as finished an impertinent as ever fluttered in a drawing-room, and seems to contain the most complete system of female foppery that could possibly be crowded into the tortured form of a fine lady. Her language, dress, motion, manners, soul and body, are in a continual hurry to do something more than is necessary or commendable. And though I doubt it will be a vain labour to offer you

a just likeness of Mrs. Mountford's action, yet the fantastic impression
is still so strong in my memory, that I cannot help saying something,
though fantastically, about it. The first ridiculous airs that break
from her are upon a gallant, never seen before, who delivers her a
letter from her father, recommending him to her good graces, as an
honourable lover. Here now, one would think, she might naturally
show a little of the sex's decent reserve, though never so slightly
covered. No, sir, not a tittle of it; modesty is the virtue of a poor-
souled country gentlewoman; she is too much a court lady to be
under so vulgar a confusion; she reads the letter, therefore, with a
careless dropping lip, and an erected brow, humming it hastily over,
as if she were impatient to outgo her father's commands, by making
a complete conquest of him at once; and that the letter might not
embarrass her attack, crack! she scrambles it at once into her palm,
and pours upon him her whole artillery of airs, eyes, and motion;
down goes her dainty diving body to the ground, as if she were
sinking under the conscious load of her own attractions; then launches
into a flood of fine language and compliment, still playing her chest
forward in fifty falls and risings, like a swan upon waving water; and
to complete her impertinence, she is so rapidly fond of her own wit,
that she will not give her lover leave to praise it: silent assenting
bows, and vain endeavours to speak, are all the share of the conversation he is admitted to, which, at last, he is relieved from, by her
engagements to half-a-score visits, which she swims from him to
make, with a promise to return in a twinkling." *

Three of Congreve's plays, ' *Love for Love*,' the ' *Mourning
Bride*,' and the ' *Way of the World*,' came out at the theatre
in Portugal Street. In the first paper of the ' *Tatler*,' Steele
gives a criticism on the performance of ' *Love for Love*,' which
contains one or two curious points of information respecting
the customs of play-goers in the reign of Anne. The "article"
begins like that of a modern newspaper.

" On Thursday last was acted, for the benefit of Mr. Betterton, the
celebrated comedy called ' Love for Love.' Those excellent players,
Mrs. Barry, Mrs. Bracegirdle, and Mr. Dogget, though not at present
concerned in the house, acted on that occasion. There has not been
known so great a concourse of persons of distinction as at that time :
the stage itself was covered with gentlemen and ladies; and when the
curtain was drawn, it discovered even there a very splendid audience.
This unusual encouragement, which was given to a play for the
advantage of so great an actor, gives an undeniable instance that the
true relish for manly entertainments and rational pleasures is not
wholly lost. All the parts were acted to perfection : the actors were
careful of their carriage, and no one was guilty of the affectation to
insert witticism of his own; but a due respect was had to the audience
for encouraging this accomplished player. It is not now doubted but
plays will revive, and take their usual course in the opinion of persons
of wit and merit, notwithstanding their late apostacy in favour of
dress and sound. The place is very much altered since Mr. Dryden

---

* Cibber's Apology, 2d edit. p. 138.

frequented it; where you used to see songs, epigrams, and satires, in the hands of every man you met, you have now only a pack of cards; and instead of the cavils about the turn of the expression, the elegance of the style, and the like, the learned now dispute only about the truth of the game."

The last proprietor of this theatre was Rich, the famous harlequin, who, having, a poor company, unable to compete with Drury Lane, introduced that love of show and spectacle which has ever since been willing to forego the regular drama, however reproached by the critics. Pope has hitched him into the ' Dunciad,' (book iii.), as one of the ministers of Dulness.

> " Immortal Rich ! how calm he sits at ease,
> 'Midst snows of paper, and fierce hail of pease;
> And proud his mistress' order to perform,
> Rides in the whirlwind, and directs the storm."

He had the merit, however, of producing the 'Beggar's Opera,' which was acted scores of nights together all over England, and finally rendered its heroine a duchess, and is said to have made " Gay Rich, and Rich Gay." Rich had no education. He was in the habit, when conversing, of saying mister, instead of sir.

One of Rich's actors was Quin, of whom more by and by. Garrick was never at this theatre. It closed a little before his time, and was never reopened. The vulgar attributed its desertion to a supernumerary devil, who made his appearance in the pantomine of ' *Harlequin and Dr. Faustus*,' and took his exit through the roof instead of the door; which so frightened the manager that he had not the courage to open the theatre again. The only memorial now remaining in Portugal Street of theatres and play-goers, and all their lively generation, is a table set up in the burial-ground to the memory of the famous Joe Miller, author of so many posthumous good things. He was an actor in Congreve's time, and has the reputation of having been an honest, as well as a pleasant fellow. The jest-book, which passes for his publication, was collected by a companion of his, who is thought to have owed to him nothing but his name. It is but reasonable to conclude, however, that many of the jests were of the comedian's relating.

In Carey Street, when she was first married, lived Mrs. Chapone. She afterwards resided in Arundel Street. When we have no greater names to mention, we think it our duty to avail ourselves of those of any intelligent and amiable persons who are really worth mention, though they may not be of the first order. They will be welcome to the inhabitants of the street, and perhaps serve to throw a grace over neighbourhoods that want it. It is better to think of Mrs. Chapone in going along Carey Street, than of bailiffs and lock-up houses—unless, indeed the latter should make us zealous to reform the debtor and creditor laws; and even then we might be glad of the refreshment. Mrs. Chapone was one of the disciples of Richardson, and is well known for her '*Letters on the Improvement of the Mind.*' Ten months after her marriage she lost her husband, to whom she was greatly attached, and then she left Carey Street; so that the pleasantest part of her life was probably spent there.

Clare Market stands on a spot formerly called Clement's Inn Fields, the property of the Earls of Clare, one of whom built the market about the year 1657. He is said to have lived close by, in a style of magnificence. The names of the family, Denzel, Holles, &c., are retained in some of the neighbouring streets.

Clare Market became notorious in the time of Pope, for the extravagance of Orator Henley, a clever, but irregular-minded man, who overrated himself, and became, it may be said, mad with impudence. Some describe his Oratory as being in the Market, others in Duke Street, which is the street going out of the western side of Lincoln's Inn Square through the archway. Another writer says it was the old theatre of Sir William Davenant, in Gibbon's Tennis Court, of which we have just spoken, and which is said to have been in Vere Street. Most likely all these accounts are to be reconciled. A tenement is often described as existing in a certain street, when the street presents nothing but a passage to it; and we take Henley's Oratory to have been the old theatre, with a passage to it from the market, from Vere Street, and from Duke Street. Having settled this magnificent point, we proceed with the no less magnificent orator.

He was a native of Melton Mowbray, in the county of Leicester, the son of a clergyman, and after going to St. John's College, Cambridge, returned to his native place, and became master of the school there.

"Feeling, or fancying," says the author of the 'Lounger's Common-Place Book,' "that a genius like his ought not to be buried in so obscure a situation, having been long convinced that many gross errors and impostures prevailed in the various institutions and establishments of mankind; being also ambitious of restoring ancient eloquence, but as his enemies asserted, to avoid the scandalous embarrassments of illicit love, he repaired to the metropolis, and for a short time performed clerical functions at St. John's Chapel, near Bedford Row, with the prospect of succeeding to the lectureship of an adjoining parish (Bloomsbury), which soon became vacant.

"Several candidates offering for this situation, a warm contest ensued; probation sermons were preached; and Henley's predominating vanity made him expect an easy victory.

"We may guess at his disappointment, when this disciple of Demosthenes and Cicero was informed that the congregation had no objection to his language or his doctrine, but that he threw himself about too much in the pulpit, and that another person was chosen.

"Losing his temper as well as his election, he rushed into a room where the principal parishioners were assembled, and thus addressed them, in all the vehemence of outrageous passion:—

"'Blockheads! are *you* qualified to judge of the degree of action necessary for a preacher of God's word? Were you able to read, or had you sufficient sense, you sorry knaves, to understand the renowned orator of antiquity, he would tell you, almost the only requisite of a public speaker was action, action, action.

"'But I despise and defy you; *provoco ad populum;* the public shall decide between us.' He then hastily retired, and, to vindicate his injured fame, published the probationary discourse he had delivered.

"Thus disappointed in the regular routine of his profession, he became a quack divine; for this character he was eminently qualified, possessing a strong voice, fluent language, an imposing magisterial air, and a countenance, which no violation of propriety, reproach, or self-correction, was ever known to embarrass or discompose.

"He immediately advertised that he should hold forth publicly, two days in the week, and hired for this purpose, a large room in or near Newport Market, which he called the Oratory; but previous to the commencement of his 'academical discourses,' he chose to consult Mr. Whiston, a learned clergyman of considerable mathematical and astronomical research, but who had rendered himself remarkable by eccentric simplicity of heart, and the whimsical heterodoxy of his creed.

"In a letter to this gentleman he desired to be informed, whether he should incur any legal penalties by officiating as a separatist from the Church of England. Mr. Whiston did not encourage Henley's project, and a correspondence took place, which, ending in virulence and ill-language, produced, a few years after, the following letter:—

"'To Mr. William Whiston,
'Take notice, that I give you warning not to enter my room in Newport Market, at your peril. 'JOHN HENLEY.'"*

Henley succeeded in his speculation, by lecturing, in the most important manner, on all sorts of subjects, from the origin of evil down to a shoe. He also published a variety of pamphlets, and a periodical farrago called the 'Hyp Doctor,' for which he is said to have had pay from Sir

* "Lounger's Common Place Book," vol. ii., p. 137.

Robert Walpole ; and as his popularity rapidly increased in consequence of his addressing himself to uneducated understandings, he removed from his Oratory in Newport Market to the more capacious room in Clare Market ; for he seems to have had a natural propensity to the society of butchers, and they were fond of his trenchant style. He sometimes threatened his enemies with them. Pope, in answering the assertions of those who charged him with depriving people of their bread, asks whether Colley Cibber had not " still his lord," and Henley his butchers.

> "And has not Colley still his lord——
> His butchers Henley, his freemasons Moore."

Pope had been attacked by him. The poet speaks of him again, several times, in the 'Dunciad :'

> "Imbrown'd with native bronze, lo! Henley stands,
> Tuning his voice, and balancing his hands.
> How fluent nonsense trickles from his tongue!
> How sweet the periods, neither said nor sung!
> Still break the benches, Henley! with thy strain,
> While Sherlock, Hare, and Gibson preach in vain.
> O great restorer of the good old stage,
> Preacher at once and zany of the age!
> O worthy thou of Egypt's wise abodes,
> A decent priest where monkeys were the gods."
>
> Book iii., v. 199.

Pope says he had a "gilt tub," and insinuates that he sometimes got drunk. Among the sleeping worthies in the 'Dunciad,'

> "——Henley lay inspired beside a sink,
> And to mere mortals seemed a priest in drink."

A contemporary journalist, who says that the fame of Henley induced him to be present at one of the lectures in Newport Market, describes him as entering like a harlequin by a door behind the pulpit, and " at one large leap jumping into it, and falling to work." " His notions," he says, " the orator beat into the audience with hands, arms, legs, and head, as if people's understandings were to be courted and knocked down with blows." The price of admission was a shilling. The following are samples of Henley's extraordinary advertisements :—

"At the Oratory in Newport Market, to-morrow, at half-an-hour after ten, the sermon will be on the Witch of Endor. At half-an-hour after five, the theological lecture will be on the conversion and original of the Scottish nation, and of the Picts and Caledonians ; St. Andrew's relics and panegyric, and the character and mission of the Apostles.

' " On Wednesday, at six, or near the matter, take your chance, will be a medley oration on the history, merits, and praise of confusion, and of confounders, in the road and out of the way.

" On Friday, will be that on Dr. Faustus and Fortunatus, and conjuration; after each, the Chimes of the Times, No. 23 and 24. N.B. Whenever the prices of the seats are occasionally raised in the week days, notice will be given of it in the prints. An account of the performances of the Oratory from the 1st of August is published, with the Discourse on Nonsense; and if any bishop, clergyman, or other subject of his Majesty, or the subject of any foreign prince or state, can at my years, and in my circumstances and opportunities, without the least assistance or any patron in the world, parallel the study, choice, variety, and discharge of the said performances of the Oratory by his own or any others, I will engage forthwith to quit the said Oratory.

" J. HENLEY."*

In the bill of fare issued for Sunday, September 28, 1729, the most extraordinary theological speculations are followed by a list of the fashions in dress.

" At the Oratory, the corner of Lincoln's Inn Fields, near Clare Market, to-morrow, at half-an-hour after ten : 1. The postil will be on the turning of Lot's wife into a pillar of salt. 2. The sermon will be on the necessary power and attractive force which religion gives the spirit of a man with God and good spirits.

" II. At five : 1. The postil will be on this point: in what language our Saviour will speak the last sentence on mankind. 2. The lecture will be on Jesus Christ's sitting at the right hand of God ; where that is ; the honours and lustre of his inauguration ; the learning, criticism, and piety of that glorious article.

" The Monday's orations will shortly be resumed. On Wednesday, the oration will be on the skits of the fashions, or a live gallery of family pictures in all ages ; ruffs, muffs, puffs manifold ; shoes, wedding-shoes, two-shoes, slip-shoes, heels, clocks, pantofles, buskins, pantaloons, garters, shoulder-knots, periwigs, head-dresses, modesties, tuckers, farthingales, corkins, minikins, slammakins, ruffles, round robins, tollets, fans, patches ; dame, forsooth, madam, my lady, the wit and beauty of my grannum ; Winnifred, Joan, Bridget, compared with our Winny, Jenny, and Biddy ; fine ladies, and pretty gentlewomen ; being a general view of the *beau monde*, from before Noah's flood to the year 29. On Friday will be something better than last Tuesday. After each, a bob at the times."†

Henley must have lectured a long while ; for one of his " bobs at the times" was occasioned by the dismissal of Dr. Cobden, a chaplain to George II. in the year 1748, for preaching from the following text : " Take away the wicked from before the king, and his throne shall be established in righteousness." The wicked, we believe, meant the king's

* Malcolm's Anecdotes of the Manners and Customs of London during the Eighteenth Century, vol. i., p. 417.

† Malcolm, *et seq.*, p. 421.

mistresses. Next Saturday, Henley's advertisement appeared with an epigram on this text for a motto :—

> "Away with the wicked before the king,
> And away with the wicked behind him ;
> His throne it will bless
> With righteousness,
> And we shall know where to find him."

This must be what the reviewers call a "favourable specimen."

"Sometimes," says the 'Lounger's Common-Place Book,' "one of his old Bloomsbury friends caught the speaker's eye; on these occasions, he could not resist the temptation to gratify his vanity and resentment ; after a short pause he would address the unfortunate interloper in words to the following effect : 'You see, sir, all mankind are not exactly of your opinion; there are, you perceive, a few sensible people in the world, who consider me as not wholly unqualified for the office I have undertaken.'

"His abashed and confounded adversaries, thus attacked in a public company, a most awkward species of distress, were glad to retire precipitately, and sometimes were pushed out of the room by Henley's partizans." *

It is probable that Henley's partizans were sometimes necessary to secure him from the results of his imprudence, though his boldness appears to have been on a par with it. He once attracted an audience of shoemakers by announcing that he could teach them a method of making shoes with wonderful celerity. The secret consisted in cutting off the tops of old boots. His motto to the advertisement (*omne majus continet in se minus*, the greater includes the less) had a pleasantry in it, which makes the disappointment of the poor shoemakers doubly ludicrous.

Henley, on one occasion, was for several days in the custody of the King's messenger, having incurred the displeasure of the House of Lords. "Lord Chesterfield, at that time secretary of state," says the 'Lounger,' "amused himself and his associates in office by sporting with the hopes and fears of our restorer of ancient eloquence ; during his examination before the privy council, he requested permission to sit, on account of a real, or, as it was supposed, pretended rheumatism. Occasioning considerable merriment by his eccentric answers, and sometimes by the oddity of his questions, he was observed to join heartily and loudly in the laugh he had himself created.

* Lounger's Common-Place Book, vol. ii., p. 139.

"The Earl having expostulated with him on the impropriety of ridiculing the exertions of his native country, at the moment rebellion raged in the heart of the kingdom, Henley replied, 'I thought there was no harm, my Lord, in *cracking a joke on a red-herring :*' alluding to the worthy primate of that name, who proposed, and, I believe, had actually commenced, arming and arraying the clergy.

" Many disrespectful and unwarrantable expressions he had applied to persons high in office, being mentioned to him, he answered, without embarrassment, ' My Lords, I must live.'

"' I see no kind of reason for that,' said Lord Chesterfield, 'but many against it.' The council were pleased, and laughed at the retort ; the prisoner, somewhat irritated, observed, ' That is a good thing, but it has been said before.'

" A few days after, being reprimanded for his improper conduct, and cautioned against repeating it, he was dismissed, as an impudent, but entertaining fellow."*

To complete the history of this man, he struck medals for his tickets, with a star rising to the meridian ; over it the motto, *Ad summa* (to the height), and below, *Inveniam viam aut faciam* (I will find a way or make one). As might be expected, he found no way at last, but that of falling into contempt. He appears to have been too imprudent to make money by his vagaries ; and his manners, probably in consequence, became gross and ferocious. He died in 1756. His person makes a principal figure in two humorous plates, attributed to Hogarth.

Duke Street and Little Wild Street have had an inhabitant, as illustrious afterwards as he was then obscure, in the person of Benjamin Franklin, who, when he was first in England, worked in the printing office of Mr. Watts, in the latter street, and lodged in the former. When he came to England afterwards, as the agent of Massachusetts, he went into this office, " and going up," says his biography, " to a particular press [now in America], thus addressed the two workmen : ' Come, my friends, we will drink together : it is now forty years since I worked like you at this press, as a journeyman printer.'" The same publication gives an account of him during this period, which, besides containing more than one curious local particular, is highly worth the attention of those who confound stimulus with vigour.

"After the completion," says the writer, "of twelve months at Palmer's " (in Bartholomew Close), " Franklin removed to the printing-office of Mr. Watts, in Lincoln's Inn Fields, where he continued during the whole of his subsequent stay in the British metropolis. He found a contiguous lodging with a widow lady in

* Lounger's Common-Place Book, vol. ii., p. 141.

Duke Street, opposite the Catholic chapel, for which he paid at his old rate of three and sixpence weekly, and received no new impressions in favour of Christians from his occasional notices of the Romish superstitions in this family and neighbourhood. His landlady was a clergyman's daughter, who, marrying a Catholic, had abjured Protestantism, and became acquainted with several distinguished families of that persuasion. She and Franklin found mutual pleasure in each other's society. He kept good hours, and she was too lame generally to leave her room; frugality was the habit of both; half an anchovy, a small slice of bread and butter each, with half a pint of ale between them, furnished commonly their supper. So well pleased was the widow with her inmate, that when Franklin talked of removing to another house, where he could obtain the same accommodation as with her for two shillings per week, she became generous in his favour, and abated her charge for his room to that sum. He never paid her more during the rest of his stay with her, which was the whole time he continued in London. In the attic, was a maiden Catholic lady, by choice and habit a nun. She had been sent early in life to the Continent to take the veil; but the climate disagreeing with her health, she returned home; devoted her small estate to charitable purposes, with the exception of about 12l. a-year; practised confession daily; and lived entirely on water-gruel. Her presence was thought a blessing to the house, and several of its tenants in succession had charged her no rent. Her room contained a mattress, table, crucifix, and stool, as its only furniture. She admitted the occasional visits of Franklin and her landlady; was cheerful, he says, and healthful: and while her superstition moved his compassion, he felt confirmed in his frugality by her example, and exhibits it in his journal as another proof of the possibiblity of supporting life, health, and cheerfulness on very small means.

"During the first weeks of his engagement with Mr. Watts, he worked as a pressman, drinking only water, while his companions had their five pints of porter each, per day; and his strength was superior to theirs. He ridiculed the verbal logic of strong beer being necessary for strong work; contending that the strength yielded by malt liquor could only be in proportion to the quantity of flour or actual grain dissolved in the liquor, and that a pennyworth of bread must have more of this than a pot of porter. The Water-American, as he was called, had some converts to his system; his example, in this case, being clearly better than his philosophy.*

---

* "For," says the note, "while the mucilaginous qualities of porter may form one criterion of the nourishment it yields, it does not follow that mere nourishment is or ought to be the only consideration in a labouring man's use of malt liquor, or any other aliment. It is well known that flesh-meats yield chyle in greater abundance than any production of the vegetable kingdom; but Franklin would not have considered this any argument for living wholly upon meat. The fact is, that the stimulating quality of all fermented liquors (when moderately taken) is an essential part of the refreshment, and therefore of the strength they yield.

'We curse not wine—the vile excess we blame.' "

[To this Franklin might have answered, that the want of stimulus is

"Franklin was born to be a revolutionist, in many good senses of the word. He now proposed and carried several alterations in the so-called *chapel*-laws of the printing office; resisted what he thought the impositions, while he conciliated the respect of his fellow-workmen; and always had cash and credit in the neighbourhood at command, to which the sottish part of his brethren were occasionally, and sometimes largely indebted. He thus depicts this part of his prosperous life:—'On my entrance, I worked at first as a pressman, conceiving that I had need of bodily exercise, to which I had been accustomed in America, where the printers work alternately, as compositors and at the press. I drank nothing but water. The other workmen, to the number of about fifty, were great drinkers of beer. I carried occasionally a large form of letters in each hand, up and down stairs, while the rest employed both hands to carry one. They were surprised to see by this and many other examples, that the *American aquatic*, as they used to call me, was stronger than those that drank porter. The beer-boy had sufficient employment during the whole day in serving that house alone. My fellow-pressman drank every day a pint of beer before breakfast, a pint with bread and cheese for breakfast, one between breakfast and dinner, one at dinner, one again about six o'clock in the afternoon, and another after he had finished his day's work. This custom appeared to me abominable; but he had need, he said, of all this beer, in order to acquire strength to work.

"'I endeavoured to convince him, that the bodily strength furnished by the beer could only be in proportion to the solid part of the barley dissolved in the water of which the beer was composed; that there was a larger portion of flour in a penny-loaf, and that, consequently, if he ate this loaf, and drank a pint of water, he would derive more strength from it than from a pint of beer. This reasoning, however, did not prevent him from drinking his accustomed quantity of beer, and paying every Saturday night a score of four or five shillings a-week for this cursed beverage; an expense from which I was wholly exempt. Thus do these poor devils continue all their lives in a state of voluntary wretchedness and poverty.

"'My example prevailed with several of them to renounce their abominable practice of bread and cheese with beer; and they procured, like me, from a neighbouring house, a good basin of warm gruel, in which was a small slice of butter, with toasted bread and nutmeg. This was a much better breakfast, which did not cost more than a pint of beer, namely, three halfpence, and at the same time

---

generally produced by a previous abuse of it, and that the having recourse to fermented liquors is likely to continue the abuse, whatever may be said about moderation. The moderation is so difficult, that it is better to abstain than to hazard it. It is true (not to quote the words irreverently) "man does not live by bread alone," but by sociality and good-humour; and that even a little excess occasionally is not to be narrowly considered; but for the purposes of labour we may surely gather from the recorded experience of those who have laboured most, whether physically or mentally, first, that the more temperate our *habits*, the more we can perform; and, secondly, that an habitual abstinence from some kinds of refreshment is the only way to secure them.]

preserved the head clearer. Those who continued to gorge themselves with beer, often lost their credit with the publican, from
neglecting to pay their score. They had then recourse to me to
become security for them, *their light*, as they used to call it, *being out*.
I attended at the table every Saturday evening to take up the little
sums which I had made myself answerable for, and which sometimes
amounted to near thirty shillings a-week.

"'This circumstance, added to the reputation of my being a
tolerable good *gabber*, or, in other words, skilful in the art of burlesque, kept up my importance in the chapel. I had, besides, recommended myself to the esteem of my master by my assiduous application
to business, never observing Saint Monday. My extraordinary
quickness in composing always procured me such work as was most
urgent, and which is commonly best paid; and thus my time passed
away in a very pleasant manner.'" *

---

* Life of Benjamin Franklin, 1826, p. 31.

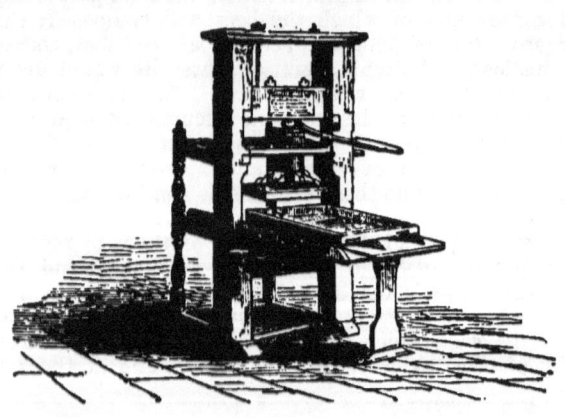

THE PRINTING PRESS AT WHICH FRANKLIN WORKED.

CHAPTER VII.

DRURY LANE, AND THE TWO THEATRES IN DRURY LANE AND COVENT GARDEN.

Craven House—Donne and his vision—Lord Craven and the Queen of Bohemia—Nell Gwynn—Drury Lane Theatre—Its antiquity, different eras, and rebuildings—The principal theatre of Dryden, Wycherley, Farquhar, Steele, Garrick, and Sheridan—Old Drury in the time of Charles II.—A visit to it—Pepys and his theatrical gossip, with notes—Hart and Mohun—Goodman—Nell Gwynn—Dramatic taste of that age—Booth—Artificial tragedy—Wilks and Cibber—Bullock and Penkethman—A Colonel enamoured of Cibber's wig—Mrs. Oldfield—Her singular position in society—Not the Flavia of the Tatler—Pope's account of her last words pro·bably not true—Declamatory acting—Lively account of Garrick and Quin by Mr. Cumberland—Improvement of stage costume—King—Mrs. Pritchard—Mrs. Clive—Mrs. Woffington—Covent Garden—Barry—Contradictory characters of him by Davies and Churchill—Macklin—Woodward—Pantomime—English taste in music—Cooke—Rise of actors and actresses in social rank—Improvement of the audience—Dr. Johnston at the theatre—Churchill a great pit critic—His Rosciad—His picture of Mossop—Mrs. Jordan and Mr. Suett—Early recollections of a play-goer.

RURY LANE takes its name from "the habitation of the great family of the Druries," built, "I believe," says Pennant, "by Sir William Drury, knight of the garter, a most able commander in the Irish wars, who unfortunately fell in a duel with Sir John Burroughs, in a foolish quarrel about precedency. Sir Robert, his son, was a great patron of Dr. Donne, and assigned to him apartments in his house. I cannot learn into whose hands it passed afterwards. During the time of the fatal discontents of the favourite, Essex, it was the place where his imprudent advisers resolved on such counsels as terminated in the destruction of him and his adherents." *

Drury House stood at the corner of Drury Lane and Wych Street, upon the ground now included in Craven Buildings in the one thoroughfare, and the Olympic Pavilion in the other.

Pennant proceeds to say, that it was occupied in the next century by "the heroic William Lord Craven, afterwards

* P. 160.

Earl Craven," who rebuilt it in the form standing in his time. He describes it as "a large brick pile,"—a public-

CRAVEN HOUSE.

house with the sign of the Queen of Bohemia,—a head which still mystifies people in some parts of the country. The remains were taken down in 1809, and the Olympic Pavilion built on part of the site. But the public-house was only a portion of it.

Who would suppose, in going by the place now, that it was once the habitation of wit and elegance, of a lord and a queen, and of more than one "romance of real life?" Yet the passenger acquainted with the facts can never fail to be impressed by them, especially by the romantic history of Donne. This master of profound fancies (whom Dryden pronounced "the greatest wit, though not the best poet," of our nation) had in his youth led a gay imprudent life, which left him poor. He became secretary to Lord Chancellor Ellesmere, and fell in love with his lordship's niece, then residing in the house, daughter to a Sir George Moor or More, who, though Donne was of an ancient family, was very angry, and took the young lady away into the country. The step, however, was too late; for, the passion being mutual, a private marriage had taken place. The upshot was, that Sir George would have nothing to say to the young couple, and that they fell into great distress. After a time, Sir Robert Drury, a man of large fortune, who possessed the mansion above described, invited Donne and his wife to live with him, and this too in a spirit that enabled all parties to be the better for it. But for this, and the curious story connected with it, we shall have recourse to the pages of our angling friend Walton, who was a good fellow enough when he was not " handling a worm as if he loved him."

" Sir Robert Drury," says Walton, " a gentleman of a very noble estate, and a more liberal mind, assigned him and his wife an useful apartment in his own large house in Drury Lane, and not only rent free, but was also a cherisher of his studies, and such a friend as sympathised with him and his, in all their joy and sorrows.

" At this time of Mr. Donne's and his wife's living in Sir Robert's house, the Lord Hay was, by King James, sent upon a glorious embassy to the then French King, Henry IV., and Sir Robert put on a sudden resolution to accompany him to the French Court, and to be present at his audience there. And Sir Robert put on a sudden resolution to solicit Mr. Donne to be his companion in that journey. And this desire was suddenly made known to his wife, who was then with child, and otherwise under so dangerous a habit of body as to her health, that she professed an unwillingness to allow him any absence from her; saying, ' her divining soul boded her some ill in his absence;' and, therefore, desired him not to leave her. This made Mr. Donne lay aside all thoughts of his journey, and really to resolve against it. But Sir Robert became restless in his persuasions for it, and Mr. Donne was so generous as to think he had sold his liberty when he received so many charitable kindnesses from him, and told his wife so; who did, therefore, with an unwilling-willingness, give a faint consent to the journey, which was proposed to be but for two months; for about that time they determined their return. Within a few days after this resolve, the ambassador, Sir Robert, and Mr. Donne, left London; and were the twelfth day got all safe to Paris. Two days after their arrival there, Mr. Donne was left alone in that room, in which Sir Robert, and he, and some other friends had dined together. To this place Sir Robert returned within half an hour; and as he left, so he found Mr. Donne alone; but in such an ecstacy and so altered in his looks, as amazed Sir Robert to behold him; insomuch that he earnestly desired Mr. Donne to declare what had befallen him in the short time of his absence. To which Mr. Donne was not able to make a present answer; but, after a long and perplexed pause, did at last say, ' I have seen a dreadful vision since I saw you: I have seen my dear wife pass twice by me in this room, with her hair hanging about her shoulders, and a dead child in her arms: this I have seen since I saw you.' To which Sir Robert replied, ' Sure, sir, you have slept since I saw you; and this is the result of some melancholy dream, which I desire you to forget, for you are now awake.' To which Mr. Donne's reply was, ' I cannot be surer that I now live, than that I have not slept since I saw you; and am as sure, that at her second appearing she stopped and looked me in the face, and vanished.' Rest and sleep had not altered Mr. Donne's opinion the next day; for he then affirmed this vision with a more deliberate, and so confirmed a confidence, that he inclined Sir Robert to a faint belief that the vision was true. It is truly said, that desire and doubt have no rest; and it proved so with Sir Robert; for he immediately sent a servant to Drewry House, with a charge to

s 2

hasten back, and bring him word, whether Mrs. Donne were alive; and, if alive, in what condition she was in as to her health. The twelfth day the messenger returned with this account:—That he found and left Mrs. Donne very sad, and sick in her bed; and that, after a long and painful labour, she had been delivered of a dead child. And, upon examination, the abortion proved to be the same day, and about the very hour, that Mr. Donne affirmed he saw her pass by him in his chamber.

"This is a relation," continues Walton, "that will beget some wonder, and it well may; for most of our world are at present possessed with an opinion, that visions and miracles are ceased. And, though it is most certain, that two lutes being both strung and tuned to an equal pitch, and then one played upon, the other that is not touched, being laid upon a table at a fit distance will—like an echo to a trumpet—warble a faint audible harmony in answer to the same tune; yet many will not believe that there is any such thing as the sympathy of souls; and I am well pleased that every reader do enjoy his own opinion. But if the unbelieving will not allow the believing reader of this story a liberty to believe that it may be true, then I wish him to consider, that many wise men have believed that the ghost of Julius Cæsar did appear to Brutus, and that both St. Austin, and Monica his mother, had visions in order to his conversion. And though these, and many others—too many to name—have but the authority of human story, yet the *incredible* reader may find in the sacred story, that Samuel, &c." *

We may here break off with the observation of Mr. Chalmers, that " the whole may be safely left to the judgment of the reader."† Walton says he had not this story from Donne himself, but from a " Person of Honour," who " knew more of the secrets of his heart than any person then living," and who related it " with such circumstance and asseveration," that not to say anything of his hearer's belief, Walton did " verily believe," that the gentleman " himself believed it."

The biographer then presents us with some verses which " were given by Mr. Donne to his wife at the time he then parted from her," and which he " begs leave to tell us " that he has heard some critics, learned both in languages and poetry, say, that " none of the Greek or Latin poets did ever equal."

These lines are full of the wit that Dryden speaks of, horribly misused to obscure the most beautiful feelings. Some of them are among the passages quoted in Dr. Johnson to illustrate the faults of the metaphysical school. Mr. Chalmers and others have thought it probable, that it was upon

* Lives of Dr. John Donne, Sir Henry Wotton, Hooker, &c. by Izaac Walton, 1825, p. 22.
† Life of Donne, in Chalmers's " British Poets."

this occasion Donne wrote a set of verses, which he addressed to his wife, on her proposing to accompany him abroad as a page ; but as the writer speaks of going to Italy, which appears to have been out of the question in this two months' visit to Paris, they most probably belong to some other journey or intended journey, the period of which is unknown. The numbers of these verses are sometimes rugged, but they are full of as much nature and real feeling, as sincerity ever put into a true passion. There is an awfulness in the commencing adjuration :—

> " By our first strange and fatal interview,
> By all desires which thereof did ensue;
> By our long striving hopes; by that remorse
> Which my words' masculine persuasive force
> Begot in thee, and by the memory
> Of hurts which spies and rivals threaten me,
> I calmly beg: but by thy father's wrath,
> By all pains which want and divorcement hath,
> I conjure thee, and all the oaths which I
> And thou have sworn to seal joint constancy,
> I here unswear, and overswear them thus:
> Thou shalt not love by means so dangerous.
> Temper, O fair Love! love's impetuous rage;
> Be my true mistress, not my feigned page.
> I 'll go; and by thy kind leave, leave behind
> Thee, only worthy to nurse in my mind
> Thirst to come back. O! if thou die before,
> My soul from other lands to thee shall soar:
> Thy (else almighty) beauty cannot move
> Rage from the seas, nor thy love teach them love,
> Nor tame wild Boreas' harshness: thou hast read
> How roughly he in pieces shiverèd
> Fair Orithea, whom he swore he loved.
> Fall ill or good, 'tis madness to have proved
> Dangers unurged: feed on this flattery,
> That absent lovers one in the other be;
> Dissemble nothing, not a boy, nor change
> Thy body's habit, nor mind; be not strange
> To thyself only: all will spy in thy face
> A blushing womanly discovering grace.
>   *   *   *   *   *
> When I am gone dream me some happiness,
> Nor let thy looks our long-hid love confess;
> Nor praise nor dispraise me, nor bless nor curse
> Openly love's force; nor in bed fright thy nurse
> With midnight's startings, crying out, Oh! oh!
> Nurse! oh, my love is slain! I saw him go
> O'er the white Alps alone; I saw him, I,
> Assailed, taken, fight, stabbed, bleed, fall, and die.
> Augur me better chance; except dread Jove
> Think it enough for me to have had thy love."

Drury House, when rebuilt by Lord Craven, took the name of Craven House. To this abode, at the restoration of Charles II., his lordship brought his royal mistress, the Queen of Bohemia, to whose interest he had devoted his fortunes, and to whom he is supposed to have been secretly wedded. She was daughter to James I., and, with the reluctant consent of her parents (particularly of her mother, who used to twit her with the title of Goody Palsgrave), was married to Frederick, the Elector Palatine, for whom the Protestant interest in Germany erected Bohemia into a kingdom, in the vain hope, with the assistance of his father-in-law, of competing with the Catholic Emperor. Frederic lost everything, and his widow became a dependent on the bounty of this Lord Craven, a nobleman of wealthy commercial stock, who had fought in her husband's cause, and helped to bring up her children. It is through her that the family of Brunswick succeeded to the throne of this kingdom, as the next Protestant heirs of James I. James's daughter, being a woman of lively manners, a queen, and a Protestant leader, excited great interest in her time, and received more than the usual portion of flattery from the romantic. Donne wrote an epithalamium on her marriage, in which are those preposterous lines beginning—

"Here lies a she sun, and a he moon there."

Sir Henry Wotton had permission to call her his " royal mistress," which he was as proud of as if he had been a knight of old. And when she lost her Bohemian kingdom, it was said that she retained a better one, for that she was still the " Queen of Hearts." Sir Henry wrote upon her his elegant verses beginning—

"You meaner beauties of the night,"

in which he gives a new turn to the commonplaces of stars and roses, and calls her

"Th' eclipse and glory of her kind."

It is doubtful, nevertheless, whether she was ever handsome. None of the Stuarts appear to have been so, with the exception of Henrietta, Duchess of Orleans, who resembled, perhaps, her mother. Pepys, who saw the Queen of Bohemia at the Restoration, " thought her a very debonaire, but plain lady." This, it is true, was near her death; but Pepys was given to admire, and royalty did not diminish the inclination. Had her charms ever been as great as reported, he would have discovered the remains of them. It has been beautifully said by Drayton, that

"Even in the aged'st face, where beauty once did dwell,
And nature, in the least, but seemèd to excel,
Time cannot make such waste, but something will appear
To show some little tract of delicacy there."

Pepys saw the queen afterwards two or three times at the play, and does not record any alteration of his opinion. Her Majesty did not survive the Restoration many months. She quitted Craven House for Leicester House (afterwards Norfolk House, in the Strand,) seemingly for no other purpose than to die there; which she did in February 1661-2. Whether Lord Craven attended her at this period does not appear; but she left him her books, pictures, and papers. Sometimes he accompanied her to the play. She and her husband, King Frederick, appear to have been lively, good-humoured persons, a little vain of the royalty which proved such a misfortune to them. The queen had the better sense, though it seems to have been almost as much over-rated as her beauty. But all the Stuarts were more or less clever, with the exception of James II.

The author of a *History and Antiquities of the Deanery of Craven in Yorkshire*, gives it as a tradition, that Lord Craven's father, a lord-mayor, was born of such poor parents that they sent him when a boy by a common carrier to London, where he became a mercer or draper. His son was a distinguished officer under Gustavus Adolphus, was ennobled, attached himself to the King and Queen of Bohemia, and is supposed, as we have seen, to have married the king's widow. He was her junior by twelve years. He long resided in Craven House, became Colonel of the Coldstream Regiment of Foot Guards, and was famed for his bustling activity. He so constantly made his appearance at a fire, that his horse is said to have "smelt one as soon as it happened." Pepys, during a riot against houses of ill-fame (probably the houses in Whetstone Park, as well as in Moorfields, for he talks of going to Lincoln's Inn Fields to see the 'prentices,) describes his lordship as riding up and down the fields, "like a madman," giving orders to the soldiery. It was probably in allusion to this military vivacity that Lord Dorset says, in his ballad on a mistress,—

" The people's hearts leap, wherever she comes,
And beat day and night, like my Lord Craven's drums."

When there was a talk in his old age of giving his regiment
to somebody else, Craven said, that "if they took away his
regiment they had as good take away his life, since he had
nothing else to divert himself with." The next king, however, William III., gave it to General Talmash; yet the old
lord is said to have gone on, busy to the last. He died in
1697, aged nearly 89 years. He was intimate with Evelyn,
Ray, and other naturalists, and delighted in gardening. The
garden of Craven House ran in the direction of the present
Drury Lane; so that where there is now a bustle of a very
different sort, we may fancy the old soldier busying himself
with his flower-beds, and Mr. Evelyn discoursing upon the
blessings of peace and privacy."*

The only other personage of celebrity whom we know of as
living in Drury Lane, is one of another sort; to wit, Nell
Gwynn. The ubiquitous Pepys speaks of his seeing her there
on a May-morning.

"May 1st, 1667. To Westminster, in the way meeting many milkmaids with garlands upon their pails, dancing with a fiddler before
them; and saw pretty Nelly standing at her lodging's door in Drury
Lane in her smock sleeves and boddice, looking upon one. She seemed
a mighty pretty creature."

Lodgings in this quarter, though Nell lived there, must
have been of more decent reputation than they became afterwards. It is curious that the old English word Drury, or
Druerie, should be applicable to the fame we allude to. It has
more or less deserved it for a long period, though we believe
the purlieus rather warrant it now, than the lane itself. Pope
and Gay speak of it. Pope describes the lane also as a place
of residence for poor authors:—

> "'Keep your piece nine years.'
> 'Nine years!' cries he, who high in Drury Lane,
> Lull'd by soft zephyrs through the broken pane,
> Rhymes ere he wakes, and prints before term ends,
> Obliged by hunger and request of friends."

The existence of a theatre in Drury Lane is as old as the
time of Shakspeare. It was then called the Phœnix; was
"a private," or more select house, like that of Blackfriars;
and had been a cock-pit, by which name it was also desig-

---

* For complete particulars of the history of James's daughter and
son-in-law, and their gallant adherents, see "Memoirs of Elizabeth
Stuart, Queen of Bohemia," by Miss Benger, and "Collins's Peerage,"
by Sir Egerton Brydges, vol. v., p. 446. Miss Benger is as romantic
as if she had lived in the queen's time, but she is diligent and amusing.
The facts can easily be separated from her colouring.

nated. Phœnix generally implies that a place has been destroyed by fire, a common fate with theatres; but the first occasion on which we hear of the present one is the destruction of it by a Puritan mob. This took place in the year 1617, in the time of James; and was doubtless caused by the same motives that led to the demolition of certain other houses, which it was thought to resemble in fame. In Howe's Continuation of Stowe, it was called a " new play-house;" so that it had lately been either built or rebuilt. This theatre stood opposite the Castle tavern. There is still in existence a passage, called Cockpit Alley, into Great Wild Street; and there is a Phœnix Alley, leading from Long Acre into Hart Street.

The Phœnix was soon rebuilt: and the performances continued till 1648, when they were again stopped by the Puritans who then swayed England, and who put an end to playhouses for some time. In the interval, some of the most admired of our old dramas were produced there, such as Marlowe's *Jew of Malta;* Heywood's *Woman killed with Kindness; The Witch of Edmonton*, by Rowley, Decker, and Ford ; Webster's *White Devil,* or *Vittoria Colombona,* Massinger's *New Way to Pay Old Debts,* and indeed many others.* It does not appear that Shakspeare or his immediate friends had any pieces performed there. He was a performer in other theatres; and the pressure of court, as well as city, lay almost exclusively in their direction, till the growth of the western part of the metropolis divided it. The Phœnix known in his time was probably nearly as select a house as the Blackfriars. The company had the title of Queen's Servants (James's Queen), and the servants of the Lady Elizabeth (Queen of Bohemia).

A few years before the Restoration, Davenant, supported by some of the less scrupulous authorities, ventured to smuggle back something like the old entertainments, under the pretence of accompanying them with music; a trick understood in our times where a license is to be encroached upon. In 1656, he removed with them from Aldersgate Street to this house; and, after the fluctuation of different companies hither and thither, the Cockpit finally resumed its rank as a royal theatre, under the direction of the famous Killigrew, whose set of players were called the King's company, as those under Sir William Davenant had the title of the Duke's.

* See Baker's Biographia Dramatica, vol. ii.

Killigrew, dissatisfied with the old theatre at the Cockpit, built a new one nearly on the site of the present, and opened it in 1663. This may be called the parent of Drury Lane theatre as it now stands. It was burnt in 1671-2, rebuilt by Sir Christopher Wren, and opened in 1674, with a prologue, from the pen of Dryden, from which time it stood till the year 1741. There had been some alterations in the structure of this theatre, which are said to have hurt the effect contemplated by Sir Christopher Wren, and perhaps assisted its destruction; for seventy years is no great age for a public

ENTRANCE FRONT OF DRURY LANE THEATRE, ERECTED BY GARRICK.

building. Yet old Drury, as it was called, was said to have died of a "gradual decline." It was rebuilt, and became Old Drury the second; underwent the usual fate of theatres, in the year 1809; and was succeeded by the one now standing.

It is customary to divide the eras of theatres according to their management; but, as managers become of little consequence to posterity, we shall confine ourselves in this as in other respects to names, with which posterity is familiar. In Shakspeare's time, Drury Lane appears to have been celebrated for the best productions of the second-rate order of dramatists, a set of men who would have been first in any other age. We have little to say of the particulars of Drury

Lane at this period, no memorandums having come down to us as they did afterwards. All we can imagine is, that, the Phœnix being much out of the way, with fields and country roads in the interval between court and city, and the performances taking place in the day time, the company probably consisted of the richer orders, the poorer being occupied in their labours. The court and the rich citizens went on horseback; the Duke of Buckingham in his newly-invented sedan. In the time of the Puritans we may fancy the visitors stealing in, as they would into a gambling-house.

The era of the Restoration, or second era of the Stuarts, is that of the popularity of Ben Jonson's and Beaumont and Fletcher's plays, compared with Shakspeare's, though Davenant tried hard to revive him; of the plays of Dryden, Lee, and Otway; and finally of the rise of comedy, strictly so called, in those of Wycherly, Congreve, Farquhar, and Vanbrugh. All these writers had to do with Drury Lane Theatre, some of them almost exclusively. Nineteen out of Dryden's twenty-seven plays were produced there; seven out of Lee's eleven; all the good ones of Wycherly (that is to say, all except the ' Gentleman Dancing-Master'); two of Congreve's (the ' Old Bachelor' and ' Double Dealer '), and all Farquhar's, except the ' Beaux' Stratagem.' Otway's best pieces came out at the Duke's Theatre; and Vanbrugh's in the Haymarket.* This may be called the second era of Drury Lane, or rather the second and third; the former, which is Dryden's and Lee's, having for its principal performers Hart, Mohun, Lacy, Goodman, Nell Gwynn, and others; the latter, which was that of Congreve and Farquhar, presenting us with Cibber, Wilks, Booth, Mrs. Barry, and Mrs. Bracegirdle. The two, taken together, began with the Restoration and ended with George II.

Sir Richard Steele and the sentimental comedy came in at the close of the third era, and may be said to constitute the fourth; which, in his person, did not last long. Steele, admirable as an essayist, and occasionally as humorous as any dramatist in a scene or two, was hampered in his plays by the new moral ambition now coming up, which induced him to show, not so much what people are, as his notions of what they ought to be. This has never been held a legitimate business of the stage, which, in fact, is nothing else than what its favourite metaphor declares it, a glass of men and

* See Baker, *passim.*

manners, in which they are to see themselves as they actually exist. It is the essence of the wit and dialogue of society brought into a focus. Steele was manager of Drury Lane Theatre, and made as bad a one as improvidence and animal spirits could produce.

The sentimental comedy continued into the next or fifth Drury Lane era, which was that of Garrick, famous for his great reputation as an actor, and for his triumphant revival of Shakspeare's plays, which have increased in popularity ever since. Not that he revived them in the strictest sense of the word; for the attempt was making when he came to town; but he hastened and exalted the success of it.

The last era before the present one was that of Sheridan, who, though he began with Covent Garden, produced four out of his seven pieces at this theatre; where he showed himself a far better dramatist, and a still worse manager than Steele.

We shall now endeavour to possess our readers with such a sense of these different periods, as may enable them to " live o'er each scene," not indeed of the plays, but of the general epochs of Old Drury; to go into the green-room with Hart and Nell Gwyn; to see Mrs. Oldfield swim on the stage as Lady Betty Modish; to revive the electrical shock of Garrick's leap upon it, as the lively Lothario;—in short, to be his grandfather and great-grandfather before him, and make one of the successive generations of play-goers, now in his peruke *à la Charles II.*, and now in his Ramillie wig, or the bobs of Hogarth. Did we introduce him to all this ourselves, we should speak with less confidence; but we have a successsion of play-goers for his acquaintance, who shall make him doubt whether he really is or is not his own ancestor, so surely shall they place him beside them in the pit.

And first, for the immortal and most play-going Pepys. To the society of this jolliest of government officers, we shall consign our reader and ourselves during the reign of Charles II.; and if we are not all three equally intimate with old Drury at that time, there is no faith in good company. By old Drury, we understand both the theatres; the Cockpit or Phœnix and the new one built by Killigrew, which took the title of " King's Theatre." There was a cockpit at White-hall, or court theatre, to which Pepys occasionally alludes; but after trying in vain to draw a line between such of his memorandums as might be retained and omitted, we here give up the task as undesirable, the whole harmonizing in one mass of theatrical gossip, and making us acquainted collaterally, even with what he is not speaking of. We have not, indeed, retained everything, but we have almost.

We now, therefore, pass Drury House, proceed up the lane by my Lord Craven's garden, and turn into Russell Street amongst a throng of cavaliers in flowing locks, and ladies with curls *à la Valliere.* Some of them are in masks, but others have not put theirs on. We shall see them masquing as the house grows full. It is early in the afternoon. There press a crowd of gallants, who have already got enough wine. Here, as fast as the lumbering coaches of that period can do it, dashes up to the door my lord Duke of Buckingham, bringing with him Buckhurst and Sedley. There comes a greater, though at that time a humbler man, to wit, John Dryden, in a coat of plain drugget, which by and by his fame converted into black velvet. He is somewhat short and stout, with a roundish dimpled face and a sparkling eye; and, if scandal says true, by his side is "Madam" Reeves, a beautiful actress; for the ladies of the stage were so entitled at that time. Horses and coaches throng the place, with here and there a sedan; and, by the pulling off of hats, we find that the king and his brother James have arrived. The former nods to his people as if he anticipated their mutual enjoyment of the play; the latter affects a graciousness to match, but does not do it very well. As soon as the king passes in, there is a squeeze and a scuffle ; and some blood is drawn, and more oaths uttered, from which we hasten to escape. Another scuffle is silenced on the king's entrance, which also makes the gods quiet; otherwise, at no period were they so loud. The house is not very large, nor very well appointed. Most of the ladies masque themselves in the pit and boxes, and all parties prepare for a play that shall render it proper for the remainder to do so. The king applauds a new French tune played by the musicians. Gallants, not very sober, are bowing on all sides of us to ladies not very nice; or talking to the orange girls, who are ranged in front of the pit with their backs to the stage. We hear criticisms on the last new piece, on the latest panegyric, libel, or new mode. Our friend Pepys listens and looks everywhere, tells all who is who, or asks it ; and his neighbours think him a most agreeable fat little gentleman. The curtain rises : enter Mistress Marshall, a pretty woman, and speaks a prologue which makes all the ladies hurry on their masks, and convulses the house with laughter. Mr. Pepys " do own " that he cannot help laughing too, and calls the actress " a merry jade;" " but, lord!" he says, " to see the difference of the times, and but two years gone." And then he utters something between a sigh and a chuckle, at the recollection of his Presbyterian breeding, compared with the jollity of his expectations.

But let us hear our friend's memorandums:—

" 29th (September 1662). To the King's Theatre, where we saw ' Midsummer's Night's Dream,' which I had never seen before, nor shall ever again, for it is the most insipid, ridiculous play that ever I saw in my life. [The gods certainly had not made Pepys poetical, except on the substantial side of things.]

" 5th (January 1662-3). To the Cockpit, where we saw ' Claracilla,' a poor play, done by the King's house; but neither the king nor queen were there, but only the duke and duchess.

" 23d (February, 1662-3). We took coach and to court, and there we saw ' The Wilde Gallant,' performed by the King's house, but it was ill acted. The king did not seem pleased at all, the whole play, nor anybody else. My Lady Castlemaine was all worth seeing to-night, and little Stewart. [This is Miss, or as the designation then was, Mrs. Stewart, afterwards Duchess of Richmond. ' The Wild Gallant ' was Dryden's first play, and was patronised by Lady Castlemaine, afterwards not less notorious as Duchess of Cleveland. Miss Stewart and she were rival beauties.]

" 1st (February, 1663-4). To the King's Theatre, and there saw the ' Indian Queen ' (by Sir Robert Howard and Dryden); which indeed is a most pleasant show, and beyond my expectation the play good, but spoiled with the rhyme, which breaks the sense. But above my expectation most, the eldest Marshall did do her part most excellently well as I have heard a woman in my life; but her voice is not so sweet as Ianthe's: but, however, we come home mightily contented.

" 1st (January, 1664). To the King's house, and saw ' The Silent Woman ' (Ben Jonson's); but methought not so well done or so good a play as I formerly thought it to be. Before the play was done, it fell such a storm of hayle, that we in the middle of the pit were fain to rise, and all the house in a disorder.

" 2nd (August, 1664). To the King's playhouse, and there saw ' Bartholomew Fayre' (Ben Jonson's), which do still please me; and is, as it is acted, the best comedy in the world, I believe. I chanced to sit by Tom Killigrew, who tells me that he is setting up a nursery; that is, is going to build a house in Moorfields, wherein we will have common plays acted. But four operas it shall have in the year, to act six weeks at a time: where we shall have the best scenes and machines, the best musique, and everything as magnificent as in Christendome, and to that end hath sent for voices and painters, and other persons from Italy.

" 4th (August, 1664). To play at the King's house, ' The Rivall

Ladies' (Dryden's), a very innocent and most pretty witty play. I was much pleased with it, and it being given me, I look upon it as no breach of my oath. [Pepys means that he had made a vow not to spend money on theatres, but that he was now treated to a play.] Here we hear that Clun, one of their best actors, was, the last night, going out of town after he had acted the Alchymist (wherein was one of his best parts that he acts), to his country house, set upon and murdered; one of the rogues taken, an Irish fellow. It seems most cruelly butchered and bound. The house will have a great miss of him. [Clun's body was found at Kentish Town in a ditch. Pepys went to see the place.]

"11th (October, 1664). Luellin tells me what an obscene loose play this 'Parson's Wedding' is (by Tom Killigrew), that is acted by nothing but women at the King's house.

"14th (January, 1664-5). To the King's house, there to see 'Vulpone,' a most excellent play (Ben Jonson's); the best, I think, I ever saw, and well acted.

"19th (March, 1666). After dinner we walked to the King's playhouse, all in dirt, they being altering of the stage to make it wider. But God knows when they will begin to act again; but my business here was to see the inside of the stage, and all the tiring-rooms and machines; and, indeed, it was a sight worthy seeing. But to see their clothes, and the various sorts, and what a mixture of things there was; here a wooden leg, there a ruff, here a hobby-horse, there a crown, would make a man split himself to see with laughing; and particularly Lacy's wardrobe and Shotrell's. But then again to think how fine they show on the stage by candlelight, and how poor things they are to look at too near hand, is not pleasant at all. The machines are fine, and the paintings very pretty.

"7th (December, 1666). To the King's playhouse, where two acts were almost done when I came in; and there I sat with my cloak about my face, and saw the remainder of 'The Mayd's Tragedy;' a good play, and well acted, especially by the younger Marshall, who is become a pretty good actor; and is the first play I have seen in either of the houses, since before the great plague, they having acted now about fourteen days publickly. But I was in mighty pain, lest I should be seen by anybody to be at the play. [The plague seems to have made it an indecorum to resume visits to the theatre very speedily. Pepys had been educated among the Commonwealth-men, for whom he never seems to have got rid of a respect. The contrast aggravated his festivity.]

"8th (December, 1666). To the King's playhouse, and there did see a good part of 'The English Monsieur' (by James Howard), which is a mighty pretty play, very witty and pleasant. And the women do very well; but above all, little Nelly. [Nell Gwynn, not long entered upon the stage.]

"27th (December, 1666). By coach to the King's playhouse, and there saw 'The Scornful Lady' (Beaumont and Fletcher's), well acted; Doll Common doing Abigail most excellently, and Knipp the widow very well (and will be an excellent actor, I think). In other parts the play not so well done as need be by the old actors.

"3rd (January, 1666-7). Alone to the King's house, and there saw 'The Custome of the Country' (Beaumont and Fletcher's), the second time of its being acted, wherein Knipp does the widow well; but if

all the plays that ever I did see, the worst, having neither plot, language nor anything on the earth that is acceptable; only Knipp sings
a song admirably. [Mistress Knipp was a particular acquaintance of
our friend's.]

"23rd (January, 1666-7). To the King's house, and there saw the
'Humourous Lieutenant' (Beaumont and Fletcher's), a silly play, I
think; only the spirit in it that grows very tall, and then sinks again
to nothing, having two heads breeding upon one, and then Knipp's
singing did please us. Here in a box above we spied Mrs. Pierse;
and going out they called us; and so we staid for them; and Knipp
took us all in and brought us to Nelly (Nell Gwynn), a most pretty
woman, who acted the great part of Cœlia to-day very fine, and did it
pretty well: I kissed her, and so did my wife; and a mighty pretty
soul she is. We also saw Mrs. Ball, which is my little Roman-nose
black girl, that is mighty pretty; she is usually called Betty. Knipp
made us stay in the box, and see the dancing preparatory to to-
morrow for the 'Goblins,' a play of Suckling's, not acted these twenty
years; which was pretty.

"5th (February, 1666-7). To the King's house to see 'The Chances'
(Beaumont and Fletcher's). A good play I find it, and the actors
most good in it. And pretty to hear Knipp sing in the play very
properly, 'All night I weepe;' and sung it admirably. The whole
play pleases me well: and most of all, the sight of many fine ladies;
among others, my lady Castlemaine and Mrs. Middleton: the latter of
the two hath also a very excellent face and body, I think. And so
home in the dark over the ruins with a link. [The ruins are those of
the city, occasioned by the fire. Mr. Pepys lived in Creed Lane, where
the Navy Office then was, in which he had an appointment.]

"18th (February, 1666-7). To the King's house, to 'The Mayd's
Tragedy' (Beaumont and Fletcher's); but vexed all the while with
two talking ladies and Sir Charles Sedley; yet pleased to hear the
discourse, he being a stranger. And one of the ladies would and did
sit with her mask on all the play, and being exceedingly witty as ever
I heard a woman, did talk most pleasantly with him; but was, I
believe, a virtuous woman and of quality. He would fain know who
she was, but she would not tell; yet did give him many pleasant hints
of her knowledge of him, by that means setting his brains at work to
find out who she was, and did give him leave to use all means to find
out who she was, but pulling off her mask. He was mighty witty,
and she also making sport with him mighty inoffensively, that more
pleasant rencontre I never heard. But by that means lost the pleasure of the play wholly, to which now and then Sir Charles Sedley's
exceptions against both words and pronouncing were very pretty.
[This is the famous wit and man of pleasure. We have him before
us, as if we were present, together with a curious specimen of the
manners of these times. The pit, though subject to violent scuffles,
greatly occasioned by the wearing of swords, seems to have contained
as good company as the opera pit does now.]

"2nd (March, 1666-7). After dinner with my wife to the King's
house, to see 'The Mayden Queen,' a new play of Dryden's, mighty
commended for the regularity of it, and the strain and wit: and the
truth is, there is a comical part, played by Nell, which is Florimell,
that I never can hope to see the like done again by man or woman.
The King and Duke of York were at the play. But so great per-

formance of a comical part was never, I believe, in the world before as Nell do this, both as a mad girl, then most and best of all when she comes in like a young gallante; and hath the motions and carriage of a spark the most that ever I saw any man have. It makes me, I confess, admire her.

"25th (March, 1666-7). To the King's playhouse, and by and by comes Mr. Lowther and his wife and mine, and into a box, forsooth, neither of them being dressed, which I was almost ashamed of. Sir W. Pen and I in the pit, and here saw the 'Mayden Queen' again; which, indeed, the more I see the more I like, and is an excellent play, and so done by Nell her merry part, as cannot be better done in nature.

"9th (April, 1667). To the King's house, and there saw the 'Taming of the Shrew,' which hath some very good pieces in it, but generally is but a mean play; and the best part 'Sawny,' done by Lacy; and hath not half its life, by reason of the words, I suppose, not being understood, at least by me. [This was one of the *rifacimentos* of Shakspeare, by which he was to be rendered palatable.]

"15th (April, 1667). To the King's house, by chance, where a new play: so full as I never saw it; I forced to stand all the while close to the very door till I took cold, and many people went away for want of room. The King and Queene and Duke of York and Duchesse there, and all the court, and Sir W. Coventry. The play called 'The Change of Crownes;' a play of Ned Howard's, the best that I ever saw at that house, being a great play and serious; only Lacy did act the country gentleman come up to court with all the imaginable wit and plainness about the selling of places, and doing everything for money. The play took very much.

"16th (April, 1667). Knipp tells me the King was so angry at the liberty taken by Lacy's part to abuse him to his face, that he commanded they should act no more, till Moone (Mohun) went and got leave for them to act again, but not in this play. The King mighty angry; and it was bitter indeed, but very fine and witty. I never was more taken with a play than I am with this 'Silent Woman' (Ben Johnson's) as old as it is, and as often as I have seen it. [Ned Howard, the author of 'The Change of Crownes,' was one of the sons of the Earl of Berkshire, and though of a family who helped to bring in the King, was probably connected with the Presbyterians, and disgusted, like many of the royalists on that side, by the disappoinments they had experienced in church and state. Dryden, who married one of his sisters, was of a Presbyterian stock. Ned, however, who afterwards became the butt of the wits, was not very nice, and might have 'committed himself,' as the modern phrase is, in his mode of conducting his satire].

"20th (April, 1667). Met Mr. Rolt, who tells me the reason of no play to-day at the King's house—that Lacy had been committed to the porter's lodge, for his acting his part in the late new play; and being thence released to come to the King's house, he there met with Ned Howard, the poet of the play, who congratulated his release; upon which Lacy cursed him, as that it was the fault of his nonsensical play that was the cause of his ill-usage. Mr. Howard did give him some reply, to which Lacy answered him that he was more a fool than a poet; upon which Howard did give him a blow on the

T

face with his glove; on which Lacy, having a cane in his hand, did give him a blow over the pate. Here Rolt and others, that discoursed of it in the pit, did wonder that Howard did not run him through, he being too mean a fellow to fight with. But Howard did not do anything but complain to the King; so the whole house is silenced: and the gentry seem to rejoice much at it, the house being become too insolent.

"1st (May, 1667). Thence away to the King's playhouse, and saw 'Love in a Maze:' but a sorry play; only Lacy's clown's part, which he did most admirably indeed; and I am glad to find the rogue at liberty again. Here was but little, and that ordinary company. We sat at the upper bench, next the boxes; and I find it do pretty well, and have the advantage of seeing and hearing the great people, which may be pleasant when there is good store.

"15th (August, 1667). And so we went to the King's house, and there saw 'The Merry Wives of Windsor;' which did not please me at all, in no part of it.

"17th (August, 1667). To the King's playhouse, where the house extraordinary full; and there the King and Duke of York to see the new play, 'Queene Elizabeth's Troubles, and the History of Eighty-eight.' I confess I have sucked in so much of the sad story of Queene Elizabeth from my cradle, that I was ready to weep for her sometimes; but the play is the most ridiculous that sure ever came upon stage, and, indeed, is merely a show, only shows the true garb of the Queene in those days, just as we see Queene Mary and Queene Elizabeth painted; but the play is merely a puppet play, acted by living puppets. Neither the design nor language better; and one stands by and tells us the meaning of things: only I was pleased to see Knipp dance among the milkmaids, and to hear her sing a song to Queene Elizabeth, and to see her come out in her nighte-gown with no lockes on, but her bare face, and hair only tied up in a knot behind; which is the comeliest dress that ever I saw her in to her advantage.

"22nd (August, 1667). With my lord Brouncker and his mistress to the King's playhouse, and there saw 'The Indian Emperour;' where I find Nell come again, which I am glad of; but was most infinitely displeased with her being put to act the Emperour's daughter, which is a great and serious part, which she does most basely.

"14th (September, 1667). To the King's playhouse, to see 'The Northerne Castle, (quære Lasse, by Richard Brome?) which I think I never did see before. Knipp acted in it, and did her part very extraordinary well; but the play is but a mean sorry play.

"——, my wife, and Mercer, and I, away to the King's playhouse, to see 'The Scornful Lady' (Beaumont and Fletcher's), but it being now three o'clock, there was not one soul in the pit; whereupon, for shame, we could not go in; but against our wills, went all to see 'Tu Quoque' again (by John Cooke), where there was pretty store of company. Here we saw Madame Morland, who is grown mighty fat, but is very comely. Thence to the King's house, upon a wager of mine with my wife, that there would be no acting there to-day, there being no company: so I went in and found a pretty good company there, and saw their dance at the end of the play. [There is a confusion in the memorandum under this date.]

"20th (September, 1667). By coach to the King's playhouse, and there saw 'The Mad Couple' (by Richard Brome), my wife having been at the same play with Jane in the 18d. seat.

"25th (September, 1667). I to the King's playhouse, my eyes being so bad since last night's straining of them, that I am hardly able to see, besides the pain that I have in them. The play was a new play; and infinitely full; the King and all the court almost there. It is 'The Storme,' a play of Fletcher's; which is but so-so, methinks; only there is a most admirable dance at the end, of the ladies, in a military manner, which indeed did please me mightily.

" 5th (October 1667.) To the King's house; and there going in met with Knipp, and she took us up into the tireing-rooms; and to the women's shift, where Nell was dressing herself, and was all unready, and is very pretty, prettier than I thought. And into the scene-room, and there sat down, and she gave us fruit; and here I read the questions to Knipp, while she answered me, through all her part of 'Flora's Figarys,' which was acted to-day. But, lord! to see how they were both painted, would make a man mad, and did make me loath them, and what base company of men comes among them, and how lewdly they talk. And how poor the men are in clothes, and yet what a show they make on the stage by candle-light, is very observable. But to see how Nell cursed, for having so few people in the pit, was strange; the other house carrying away all the people at the new play, and is said now-a-days to have generally most company, as having better players. By and by into the pit, and there saw the play, which is pretty good.

" 19th (October 1667). Full of my desire of seeing my Lord Orrery's new play this afternoon at the King's house, 'The Black Prince,' the first time it is acted; where, though we came by two o'clock, yet there was no room in the pit, but were forced to go into one of the upper boxes at 4s. a piece, which is the first time I ever sat in a box in my life. And in the same box came by and by, behind me, my Lord Barkely and his lady; but I did not turn my face to them to be known, so that I was excused from giving my seat. And this pleasure I had, that from this place the scenes do appear very fine indeed, and much better than in the pit. The house infinite full, and the King and Duke of York there. The whole house was mightily pleased all along till the reading of a letter, which was so long and so unnecessary, that they frequently began to laugh, and to hiss twenty times, that had it not been for the King's being there, they had certainly hissed it off the stage.

" 23d (October 1667). To the King's playhouse, and saw 'The Black Prince;' which is now mightily bettered by that long letter being printed, and so delivered to everybody at their going in, and some short reference made to it in the play. [This is in the style of what Buckingham called "insinuating the plot into the boxes."]

" 1st (November 1667). To the King's playhouse, and there saw a silly play and an old one, 'The Taming of the Shrew.'

" 2d (November 1667). To the King's playhouse, and there saw 'Henry the Fourth;' and, contrary to expectation, was pleased in nothing more than in Cartwright's speaking of Falstaffe's speech about 'What is honour?' The house full of parliament-men, it being holyday with them: and it was observable how a gentleman of good habit sitting just before us, eating of some fruit in the midst of

T 2

play, did drop down as dead, being choked; but with much ado
Orange Moll did thrust her finger down his throat, and brought him
to life again.

"26th (December 1667). With my wife to the King's playhouse,
and there saw 'The Surprizall' by Sir Robert Howard, brother of
Ned); which did not please me to-day, the actors not pleasing me ;
and especially Nell's acting of a serious part which she spoils.

"28th (December 1667). To the King's house, and there saw
'The Mad Couple,' which is but an ordinary play; but only Nell's
and Hart's mad parts are most excellent done, but especially hers:
which makes it a miracle to me to think how ill she do any serious
part, as, the other day, just like a fool or changeling; and, in a mad
part, do beyond all imitation almost. It pleased us mightily to see
the natural affection of a poor woman, the mother of one of the children brought on the stage; the child crying, she by force got upon
the stage, and took up her child, and carried it away off the stage
from Hart. Many fine faces here to-day.

"7th (January 1667-8). To the Nursery [qy. in Barbican, for
children performers?], but the house did not act to-day; and so I to
the other two playhouses, into the pit to gaze up and down, and there
did, by this means, for nothing, see an act in 'The Schoole of Compliments' at the Duke of York's house, and 'Henry the Fourth' at
the King's house; but not liking either of the plays, I took my coach
again, and home. [It would here seem, that a man who did not
choose to pay for a *seat*, might witness a play for nothing.]

"11th (January 1667-8). To the King's house, to see 'The Wild-
Goose Chase' (Beaumont and Fletcher's). In this play I met with
nothing extraordinary at all, but very dull inventions and designs.
Knipp came and sat by us, and her talk pleased me a little, she telling me how Miss Davies is for certain going away from the Duke's
house, the King being in love with her; and a house is taken for her,
and furnishing; and she hath a ring given her already worth 600*l*.:
that the King did send several times for Nelly, and she was with him;
and I am sorry for it, and can hope for no good to the state from
having a prince so devoted to his pleasure. She told me also of a play
shortly coming upon the stage, of Sir Charles Sedley's, which, she
thinks, will be called 'The Wandering Lady's,' a comedy that she
thinks will be most pleasant; and also another play called 'The
Duke of Lorane;' besides 'Cataline,' which she thinks, for want of the
clothes which the King promised them, will not be acted for a good
while.

"20th (February 1667-8). Dined, and by one o'clock to the King's
house; a new play, 'The Duke of Lerma,' of Sir Robert Howard's;
where the King and court was; and Knipp and Nell spoke the prologue most excellently, especially Knipp, who spoke beyond any
creature I ever heard. The play designed to reproach our King with
his mistresses, that I was troubled for it, and expected it should be
interrupted; but it ended all well; which salved me.

"27th (February 1667-8.) With my wife to the King's house, to
see 'The Virgin Martyr' by (Massinger), the first time it hath been
acted a great while: and it is mighty pleasant; not that the play is
worth much, but it is finely acted by Beck Marshall. But that which
did please me beyond anything in the world, was the wind-musique
when the angel comes down; which is so sweet that it ravished me,

and, indeed, in a word, did wrap up my soul so that it made me really sick, just as I have formerly been when in love with my wife; that neither then, nor all the evening going home, and at home, I was able to think of anything, but remained all night transported, so as I could not believe that ever any musique hath that real command over the soul of a man, as this did upon me; and makes me resolve to practise wind-musique, and to make my wife do the like. [Pepys's use of the word " sick," and his resolution to make his wife practise the hautboy, are very ludicrous. His love of music, however, is genuine. He was an amateur composer. On the 23d Feb. 1666, he has the following memorandum : " Comes Mrs. Knipp to see my wife, and I spent all the night talking with this baggage, and teaching her my song of 'Beauty retire,' which she sings and makes go most rarely, and a very fine song it seems to be."]

" 6th (March 1667-8.)   After dinner to the King's house, and there saw part of the 'Discontented Colonell' (Sir John Suckling's ' Brennoralt').

" 7th (April 1668). To the King's house, and there saw ' The English Monsieur,' (sitting for privacy sake in an upper box): the play hath much mirth in it, as to that particular humour. After the play done, I down to Knipp, and did stay her undressing herself ; and there saw the several players, men and women, go by; and pretty to see how strange they are all, one to another, after the play is done. Here I hear Sir W. Davenant is just now dead, and so, who will succeed him in the mastership of the house is not yet known. The eldest Davenport is, it seems, gone from this house to be kept by somebody; which I am glad of, she being a very bad actor. Mrs. Knipp tells me that my Lady Castlemaine is mighty in love with Hart of their house, and he is much with her in private, and she goes to him and do give him many presents; and that the thing is most certain, and Beck Marshall only privy to it, and the means of bringing them together: which is a very odd thing; and by this means she is even with the King's love to Mrs. Davies.

" 28th (April 1668). To the King's house, and there did see ' Love in a Maze,' (the author is not mentioned in Baker); wherein very good mirth of Lacy the clown, and Wintershell, the country-knight, his master.

" 1st (May 1668). To the King's playhouse, and there saw the ' Surprizall;' and a disorder in the pit by its raining in from the cupola at top.

" 7th (May 1668). To the King's house; where going in for Knipp, the play being done, I did see Beck Marshall come dressed off of the stage, and look mighty fine, and pretty and noble; and also Nell in her boy's clothes mighty pretty. But lord ! their confidence, and how many men do hover about them as soon as they come off the stage, and how confident they are in their talk. Here was also Haynes, the incomparable dancer of the King's house.

" 16th (May 1668). To the King's playhouse, and there saw the best part of ' The Sea Voyage' (Beaumont and Fletcher), where Knipp did her part of sorrow very well.

" 18th (May 1668). It being almost twelve o'clock, or little more, to the King's playhouse, where the doors were not then open ; but presently they did open, and we in, and find many people already come in by private ways into the pit, it being the first day of Sir

Charles Sedley's new play so long expected 'The Mulberry Garden,'
of whom, being so reputed a wit, all the world do expect great matters.   I having sat here a while and eat nothing to-day, did slip out,
getting a boy to keep my place; and to the Rose Tavern (Will's, in
Russell Street), and there got half a breast of mutton off the spit, and
dined all alone.   And so to the playhouse again, where the King and
Queene by and by come, and all the court, and the house infinitely
full.   But the play, when it come, though there was here and there a
pretty saying, and that not very many neither, yet the whole of the
play had nothing extraordinary in it at all, neither of language nor
design; insomuch that the King I did not see laugh nor pleased from
the beginning to the end, nor the company; insomuch that I have not
been less pleased at a new play in my life, I think.

"30th (May 1668).   To the King's playhouse, and there saw
'Philaster;' where it is pretty to see how I could remember almost
all along, ever since I was a boy, Arethusa, the part which I was to
have acted at Sir Robert Cooke's; and it was very pleasant to me,
but more to think what a ridiculous thing it would have been for me
to have acted a beautiful woman.

"22nd (June 1668).   To the King's playhouse, and saw an act
or two of the new play, 'Evening Love' again (Dryden's) but like it
not.

"11th (July 1668).   To the King's playhouse, to see an old play of
Shirley's, called ' Hyde Parke,' the first day acted ; where horses are
brought upon the stage; but it is but a very moderate play, only an
excellent epilogue spoken by Beck Marshall.

"31st (July 1668).   To the King's house, to see the first day of
Lacy's ' Monsieur Ragou,' now new acted.   The King and court all
there, and mighty merry : a farce.

"15th (September 1668).   To the King's playhouse to see a new
play, acted but yesterday, a translation out of French by Dryden,
called 'The Ladys à la Mode' [probably the Precieuses, but not
translated by Dryden] : so mean a thing as when they came to say it
would be acted again to-morrow, both he that said it (Beeston) and
the pit fell a-laughing.

"19th (September 1668).   To the King's playhouse, and there saw
the ' Silent Woman ;' the best comedy, I think, that ever was wrote :
and sitting by Shadwell the poet, he was big with admiration of it.
Here was my Lord Brouncker and W. Pen and their ladies in the box,
being grown mighty kind of a sudden; but, God knows, it will
last but a little while, I dare swear.   Knipp did her part mighty
well.

"28th (September 1668).   To the King's playhouse, and there saw
'The City Match' (by Jasper Maine), not acted these thirty years,
and but a silly play; the King and court there; the house, for the
women's sake, mighty full.

"14th (October 1668).   To the King's playhouse, and there saw
' The Faithful Shepherdess' (Fletcher's), that I might hear the French
eunuch sing; which I did to my great content; though I do admire
his actions as much as his acting, being both beyond all I ever saw
or heard.

"2nd (December 1678).   So she (Mrs. Pepys) and I to the King's
playhouse, and there saw 'The Usurper;' a pretty good play in all
but what is designed to resemble Cromwell and Hugh Peters, which is

mighty silly. [The Usurper was by Ned Howard, who seems to have wished to show how impartial he could be.]

" 19th (December 1678). My wife and I by hackney to the King's playhouse, and there, the pit being full, sat in the box above, and saw ' Cataline's Conspiracy' (Ben Jonson's), yesterday being the first day. a play of much good sense and words to read, but that do appear the worst upon the stage, I mean the least diverting, that ever I saw any, though most fine in clothes; and a fine scene of the senate and of a fight as ever I saw in my life. We sat next to Betty Hall, that did belong to this house, and was Sir Philip Howard's mistress; a mighty pretty wench.

" 7th (January 1668-9). My wife and I to the King's pla͟ house, and there saw ' The Island Princesse' (Beaumont and Fletcher's), the first time I ever saw it; and it is a pretty good play, many good things being in it, and a good scene of a town on fire. We sat in an upper box, and the merry Jade Nell came in and sat in the next box; a bold slut, who lay laughing there upon people, and with a comrade of hers, of the Duke's house, that came to see the play.

" 11th (January 1668-9). Abroad with my wife to the King's playhouse, and there saw ' The Joviall Crew' (by Richard Brome), ill acted to what it was in Clun's time, and when Lacy could dance.

" 19th (January 1668-9). To the King's house to see ' Horace' (translated from Corneille by Charles Cotton); this is the third day of its acting; a silly tragedy; but Lacy hath made a farce of several dances—between each act one; but his words are but silly, and invention not extraordinary as to the dances. [Pepys adds, with seeming approbation, an instance of satire on the Dutch, too gross to extract, and highly disgraceful to that age of "fine ladies and gentlemen."]

" 2nd (February 1668-9). To dinner at noon, where I find Mr. Sheres; and there made a short dinner, and carried him with us to the King's playhouse, where ' The Heyresse,' notwithstanding Kynaston's being beaten, is acted; and they say the King is very angry with Sir Charles Sedley for his being beaten, but he do deny it. But his part is done by Beetson, who is fain to read it out of a book all the while, and thereby spoils the part, and almost the play, it being one of the best parts in it: and though the design is, in the first conception of it, pretty good, yet it is but an indifferent play; wrote, they say, by my Lord Newcastle. But it was pleasant to see Beeston come in with others, supposing it to be dark, and yet forced to read his part by the light of the candles; and this I observing to a gentle-man, that sat by me, he was mightily pleased therewith and spread it, up and down. But that that pleased me most in the play, is the first song that Knipp sings (she sings three or four); and indeed it was very finely sung, so as to make the whole house clap her.

" 6th (February 1668-9). To the King's playhouse, and there in an upper box (where come in Colonel Poynton and Doll Stacey, who is, very fine, and by her wedding-ring I suppose he hath married her at last), did see the ' Moor of Venice:' but ill acted in most parts, Moon (which did a little surprise me) not acting Iago's part by much so well as Clun used to do: nor another Hart's, which was Cassio's; nor indeed Burt doing the Moor's so well as I once thought he did.

" 9th (February 1668-9). To the King's playhouse, and there saw the ' Island Princesse,' which I like mighty well as an excellent play;

and here we find Kynaston to be well enough to act again; which he do very well, after his beating by Sir Charles Sedley's appointment. [Kynaston is generally supposed to have been taken for Sedley, and beaten for some offence of the baronet's. He affected to be Sedley's double.]

"26th (February 1668-9). To the King's playhouse, and saw the 'Faithful Shepherdesse.' But, lord! what an empty house, there not being, as I could see the people, so many as to make up above 10l. in the whole house! But I plainly discern the musick is the better, by how much the house the emptier." [The same thing was said by the great Handel, to console himself once, when he found a spare audience.]

Of the performers mentioned in this curious theatrical gossip, one of them, Hart, had been a captain in the civil wars; another, Mohun, a major; and there was a third a quarter-master; all on the royal side. Hart and Mohun were old actors, when Betterton was young; and they lived to see him reckoned superior to either. The two were accustomed to act together, Hart generally in the superior character, as Brutus to the other's Cassius; and both, like Betterton, acted in comedy as well as tragedy. They performed, for instance, Manly and Horner in 'The Country Wife,' and there appears to have been less distinction in their styles of acting than is customary. If Hart shone in the Dorimant of 'Sir Fopling Flutter,' Mohun was highly applauded in Davenant's Valentine, in 'Wit without Money.' Mohun, however, appears to have excelled in the more ferocious parts of tragedy, as Catiline; and Hart in the mixture of gaity with boldness, as in Hotspur and Alexander. His Alexander was particularly famous. Upon the whole, we should conclude, Mohun's to have the more artifical acting of the two, more like "the actor," in Partridge's sense of the word, but very fine nevertheless, otherwise Rochester would hardly have admired him, as he is said to have done; unless, indeed, it was out of spite to some other actor; for he was much influenced by feelings of that kind. Perhaps, however, it was out of some chance predilection, The Duke of Buckingham is said to have preferred Ben Jonson to Shakspeare, for no other reason than his having been introduced to him when a boy. The best compliment ever known to have been paid to Hart, is an anecdote recorded of Betterton. Betterton acted Alexander after Hart's time; and "being at a loss," says Davies, "to recover a particular emphasis of that performer, which gave a force to some interesting situation of the part, he applied for information to the players who stood near him. At last,

one of the lowest of the company repeated the line exactly in
Hart's key. Betterton thanked him heartily, and put a piece
of money into his hand, as a reward for so acceptable a
service."* Hart had the reputation of being the first lover
of Nell Gwyn, and one of the hundreds of the Duchess of
Cleveland.

Goodman was another of the favoured many. He was one
of the Alexanders of his time, but does not appear to have
been a great actor. He was a dashing impudent fellow, who
boasted of his having taken "an airing" on the road to
recruit his purse. He was expelled from Cambridge for
cutting and defacing the portrait of the Duke of Monmouth,
Chancellor of the University, but not loyal enough to his
father to please Goodman. James II. pardoned the loyal
highwayman, which Goodman (in Cibber's hearing) said
"was doing him so particular an honour, that no man could
wonder if his acknowledgement had carried him a little
further than ordinary into the interest of that prince. But
as he had lately been out of luck in backing his old master,
he had now no way to get home the life he was out, upon his
account, but by being under the same obligations to King
William."† The meaning of this is understood to be, that
Goodman offered to assassinate William, in consequence of his
having had a pardon from James ; but the plot not succeeding, he turned king's evidence against James, in order to
secure a pardon from William. This "pretty fellow" was
latterly so easy in his circumstances, owing, it is supposed, to
the delicate Cleveland, that he used to say he would never
act Alexander the Great, but when he was certain that "his
duchess" would be in the boxes to see him.

The stage in that day was certainly not behind-hand with
the court ; and as it had less conventional respectability in
the eyes of the world, its private character was never so low.
But we must do justice and not confound even the disreputable. Poor Nell Gwynn, in a quarrel with one of the
Marshalls, who reproached her with being the mistress of
Lord Buckhurst, said she was mistress but of one man at a
time, though she had been brought up in a bad house "to fill
strong waters to the gentlemen ;" whereas her rebuker,

---

* Dramatic Miscellanies, vol. iii., chap. 24. Most of the above
particulars respecting Hart and Mohun have been gathered from that
work. There are scarcely any records of them elsewhere.

† Cibber's 'Apology,' *ut supra*, p. 226.

though a clergyman's daughter, was the mistress of three. This celebrated actress, who was as excellent in certain giddy parts of comedy as she was inferior in tragedy, was small of person, but very pretty, with a good-humoured face, and eyes that winked when she laughed.   She is the ancestress of the ducal family of St. Albans, who are thought to have retained more of the look and complexion of Charles II. than any other of his descendants.   Beauclerc, Johnson's friend, was like him ; and the black complexion is still in vigour.   The King recommended her to his brother with his last breath, begging him "not to let poor Nelly starve."   Burnet says she was introduced to the King by Buckingham, to supplant the Duchess of Cleveland ; but others tell us, he first noticed her in consequence of a hat of the circumference of a coach-wheel, in which Dryden made her deliver a prologue, as a set-off to an enormous hat of Pistol's at the other house, and which convulsed the spectators with laughter.   If Nelly retained a habit of swearing, which was probably taught her when a child (and it is clear enough from Pepys that she did), the poets did not discourage her.   One of her epilogues by Dryden began in the following startling manner.   It is entitled " An Epilogue spoken by Mrs. Ellen, when she was to be carried off dead by the Bearers."

> "Hold, are you mad, you damn'd confounded dog ?
> I am to rise and speak the epilogue."

The poet makes her say of herself, in the course of the lines, that she was "a harmless little devil," and that she was slatternly in her dress.   Lely painted her with a lamb under her arm.   Mr. Pegge discovered that Charles made her a lady of the chamber to his queen.   Pennant seems to think this was only a title ; but it is plain from Evelyn's Memoirs that she had apartments in Whitehall.*   She died a few years after the King, at her house in Pall Mall.   Nell was much libelled in her time, and among others by Sir George

---

* "March 1st (1671).   I thence walked with him through St. James's Parke to the garden, where I both saw and heard a very familiar discourse between . . . . and Mrs. Nellie, as they called an impudent comedian, she looking out of her garden on a terrace at the top of the wall, and . . . . standing on ye greene walke under it.   I was heartily sorry at this scene.   Thence the King walked to the Duchess of Cleveland, another lady of pleasure, and curse of our nation."—Evelyn's ' Memoirs,' ut supra, vol. ii., p. 339.   It would be curious to know how Mr. Evelyn conducted himself during this time, if he and the King saw one another.

Etherege ;* very likely out of some personal pique or rejection, for such revenges were quite compatible with the " loves " of that age.† But she was a general favourite, nevertheless, owing to a natural good-heartedness which no course of life could overcome. Burnet's character of her is well known. " Guin," says he, " the indiscreetest and wildest creature that ever was in a court, continued, to the end of that king's life, in great favour and was maintained at a vast expense. The Duke of Buckingham told me that when she was first brought to the King, she asked only five hundred pounds a year ; and the King refused it. But when he told me this, about four years after, he said, she had got of the King above sixty thousand pounds. She acted all persons in so lively a manner, and was such a constant diversion to the King, that even a new mistress could not drive her away. But after all he never treated her with the decencies of a mistress."‡ Nell Gwynn is said to have suggested to her royal lover the building of Chelsea Hospital, and to have made him a present of the ground for it.

Upon the whole the dramatic taste during the greater part of Charles's reign was false and artificial, particularly in tragedy. Etherege produced one good comedy, the precursor of Wycherly and Congreve ; but Dryden, the reigning favourite, was not as great in dramatic as he was in other writing ; his heroic plays, and Lee's " Alexander," were admired, not so much for the beauties mixed with their absurdity, as for the improbable air they gave to a serious passion ; and the favourite plays of deceased authors were those of the most equivocal writers of the time of James, not the pure and profound nature of Shakspeare and his fellows. Otway flourished, but was not thought so great as he is now ; and even in Otway there is a hot bullying smack of the tavern, very different from the voluptuousness in Shakspeare. Towards the close of this reign comedy came to its height with Wycherly, who, almost as profligate in point of dialogue as any of his contemporaries, nevertheless hit the right vein of satire. Wycherly lived at the other end of Russell Street, in Bow Street, where we shall see him shortly.

* Miscellaneous Works of the Duke of Buckingham and others. 1704, vol. i., p. 34.

† The verses are attributed to Etherege ; but, from a Scotch rhyme in them of *trull* and *will*, are perhaps not his.

‡ History of His own Times, Edin. 1753, vol. i., p. 387.

We are now come to the time of Congreve, Mrs. Bracegirdle, and others ; Betterton remaining. Of these indivi-
dually we have spoken before ; and therefore shall only
observe that by the more serious examples of James II. and
King William, the manners of the day were reforming, and
those of the stage with them.   We now find ourselves among
audiences more composed, and witness plays less coarse, though
with an abundance of double meaning and exuberantly witty.
Coquetry and fashion are now the reigning stage goddesses, as
mere wantonness was that of the age preceding.

Farquhar and Vanbrugh succeeded, together with Cibber,
Wilkes, Booth, and latterly Steele and Mrs. Oldfield.   Vanbrugh does not belong to Drury Lane, but Farquhar does,
with the rest ; and a lively place he made of it.   He is *Captain* Farquhar, has a plume in his hat, and prodigious animal
spirits, with invention at will, and great good nature.   Captains abounded among the wits and adventurers of those days
down to Captains Macheath and Gibbet.   Vanbrugh was a
captain; Steele at one time was Captain Steele; and Mrs. Oldfield's father, though the son of a vinter, became Captain
Oldfield, and genteelly ran out an estate.   This is still the
age of genuine comedy, and the stage is worthy of it.   The
tragedy was proportionably bad.   Booth, indeed, was a good
tragic actor, but he suited the age in being declamatory.   He
was the hero of Addison's Cato, once the favourite tragedy of
the critics, now of nobody.

Rowe was another artificial writer of tragedy, but not without a vein of feeling.   It seems to have been thought in those
times, as we may see by these authors, and by the tragedies of
Banks and Lillo, that to be natural, an author was to be
prosaical ; while, if he had any pretensions to be poetical, it
was his business to—

    "—— wake the soul by tender strokes of *art*."

The gradual approach, also, of this period to our own times,
which are more critical in costume, and the pictures left to us
of favourite performers in Hamlet and Hermione, dressed in
wigs and hoop petticoats, render those outrages upon propriety
still stranger to one's imagination.   They set tragedy in a
mock-heroical light.   Cato wore a long peruke ; Alexander
the Great a wig and jack-boots ; and it was customary, down
to Garrick's time, to dress Macbeth and other tragic genera'-

officers in a suit of brick-dust. "Booth enters," says
Pope:—

—— "Hark, the universal peal!
But has he spoken? Not a syllable.
What shook the stage and made the people stare?
Cato's long wig, flowered gown, and lackered chair.'

The stare was not that of ridicule, but of admiration. All
this makes the comedy of that period shine out the more as
the only truth extant. Cherry, and Archer, and Sir Harry
Wildair, and Sir John Brute, and my Lady Betty Modish,
were like the age, and like the performers.

To return to these. Wilks was the fine gentleman of that
period. He was a friend of Farquhar's, and came to London
with him from Dublin. Cibber, though he wrote a good
comedy, would appear, by some accounts of him, to have been
little more on the stage than a mimic of past actors. Steele,
however, has a criticism on him and Wilks, in which he speaks
of them both as perfect actors in their kinds.

"Wilks," he tells us, "has a singular talent in representing the
graces of nature; Cibber the deformity in the affectation of them.
Were I a writer of plays, I should never employ either of them in parts
which had not their bents this way. This is seen in the inimitable
strain and run of good humour which is kept up in the character of
Wildair, and in the nice and delicate abuse of understanding in that
of Sir Novelty. Cibber, in another light, hits exquisitely the *flat*
civility of an affected gentleman usher, and Wilks the easy frankness
of a gentleman. . . . . . To beseech gracefully, to approach respectfully, to pity, to mourn, to love, are the places wherein Wilks may be
made to shine with the utmost beauty. To rally pleasantly, to scorn
artfully, to flatter, to ridicule, and to neglect, are what Cibber would
perform with no less excellence." *

This criticism produced a letter to Steele from two inferior
actors of that time, Bullock and Penkethman, who, rather
than not be noticed at all, were willing to be bantered. They
knew it would be done good-naturedly. Accordingly the
"Tatler" says,

"For the information of posterity I shall comply with this letter,
and set these two great men in such a light as Sallust has placed his
Cato and Cæsar. Mr. William Bullock and Mr. William Penkethman
are of the same age, profession, and sex. They both distinguish themselves in a very particular manner under the discipline of the crab
tree, with this only difference, that Mr. Bullock has the more agreeable
squall, and Mr. Penkethman the more graceful shrug. Penkethman
devours cold chick with great applause; Bullock's talent lies chiefly
in asparagus. Penkethman is very dexterous at conveying himself

* Tatler, No. 182.

under a table; Bullock is no less active at jumping over a stick. Mr. Penkethman has a great deal of money; but Mr. Bullock is the taller man."*

Off the stage, and behind the scenes, Cibber performed the part of a coxcomb of the first order. We shall not be properly acquainted with Drury Lane at this period if we do not repeat his story of the wig.

This was a peruke of his, famous in the part of Sir Fopling Flutter. It was so much admired, that Cibber used to have it brought upon the stage in a sedan, and put it on publicly, to the great content of the beholders. A set of curls so applauded was the next thing to a toast; and accordingly Colonel, then Mr. Brett, whom the toasts admired, could not rest till he had taken possession of it.

"The first view," says Colley, "that fires the head of a young gentleman of this modish ambition, just broke loose from business, is to cut a figure (as they call it) in a side box at the play, from whence their next step is to the green-room behind the scenes, sometimes their *non ultra*. Hither at last, then, in this hopeful quest of his fortune, came this gentleman-errant, not doubting but the fickle dame, while he was thus qualified to receive her, might be tempted to fall into his lap. And though, possibly, the charms of our theatrical nymphs might have their share in drawing him thither; yet, in my observation, the most visible cause of his first coming was a more sincere passion he had conceived for a fair full-bottomed periwig, which I then wore in my first play of the 'Fool in Fashion,' in the year 1695. For it is to be noted that the *beaux* of those days were of a quite different cast to the modern stamp, and had more of the stateliness of the peacock in their mien, than (which now seems to be their highest emulation) the pert of a lapwing. Now, whatever contempt philosophers may have for a fine periwig, my friend, who was not to despise the world, but to live in it, knew very well, that so material an article of dress upon the head of a man of sense, if it became him, could never fail of drawing to him a more partial regard and benevolence than could possibly be hoped for in an ill-made one. This, perhaps, may soften the grave censure which so youthful a purchase might otherwise have laid upon him. In a word, he made his attack upon this periwig, as your young fellows generally do for a lady of pleasure; first, by a few familiar praises of her person, and then a civil inquiry into the price of it. But on his observing me a little surprised at the levity of his question about a fop's periwig, he began to rally himself with so much wit and humour upon the folly of his fondness for it, that he struck me with an equal desire of granting anything in my power to oblige so facetious a customer. This singular beginning of our conversation, and the mutual laughs that ensued upon it, ended in an agreement to finish our bargain that night over a bottle."†

* Tatler, No. 188. See also No. 7.
† Apology, p. 303.

Colonel Brett, being a man of "*bonnes fortunes,*" married Savage's mother!

Mrs. Oldfield made such an impression in her day, and has been noticed by so many writers, that she must have a passage to herself. She was the daughter of Captain Oldfield above-mentioned, and went to live with her aunt, who kept the Mitre tavern in St. James's Market. Here, we are told, Captain Farquhar, overhearing Miss Nancy read a play behind the bar, was so struck "with the proper emphasis and agreeable turn she gave to each character, that he swore the girl was cut out for the stage." As she had always expressed an inclination for that way of life, and a desire of trying her fortune in it, her mother, on this encouragement, the next time she saw Captain Vanbrugh (afterwards Sir John), who had a great respect for the family, acquainted him with Captain Farquhar's opinion, on which he desired to know whether her bent was most tragedy or comedy. Miss, being called in, informed him that her principal inclination was to the latter, having at that time gone through all Beaumont and Fletcher's comedies ; and the play she was reading when Captain Farquhar dined there having been 'The Scornful Lady.' Captain Vanbrugh, shortly after, recommended her to Mr. Christopher Rich, who took her into the house at the allowance of fifteen shillings per week. However, her agreeable figure and sweetness of voice soon gave her the preference, in the opinion of the whole town, to all the young actresses of that time ; and the Duke of Bedford, in particular, being pleased to speak to Mr. Rich in her favour, he instantly raised her to twenty shillings per week. After which her fame and salary gradually increased, till at length they both attained that height which her merit entitled her to."[*]

The new actress had a silver voice, a beautiful face and person, great good-nature, sprightliness, and grace, and became the fine lady of the stage in the most agreeable sense of the word. She also acted heroines of the sentimental order, and had an original part in every play of Steele. But she was particularly famous in the part of Lady Betty Modish, in "*The Careless Husband.*" The name explains the character. Cibber tells us that he drew many of the strokes in it from her lively manner.

[*] Baker's Biographia Dramatica, Art. Farquhar, vol. i., p. 155. Faithful Memoirs, &c., of Mrs. Anne Oldfield, by Egerton, p. 76.

"Had her birth," he says, "placed her in a higher rank of life, she had certainly appeared in reality what in this play she only excellently acted, an agreeable gay woman of quality, a little too conscious of her natural attractions. I have often seen her in private societies, where women of the best rank might have borrowed some part of their behaviour, without the least diminution of their sense or dignity. And this very morning, where I am now writing, at the Bath, November 11th, 1738, the same words were said of her by a lady of condition, whose better judgment of her personal merit in that light has emboldened me to repeat them. After her success in this character of higher life, all that nature had given her of the actress seemed to have risen to its full perfection : but the variety of her power could not be known till she was seen in a variety of characters, which, as fast as they fell to her, she equally excelled in. Authors had much more from her performance than they had reason to hope for, from what they had written for her; and none had less than another, but as their genius, in the parts they allotted her, was more or less elevated.

"In the wearing of her person she was particularly fortunate; her figure was always improving to her thirty-sixth year; but her excellence in acting was never at a stand; and the last new character she shone in (Lady Townly) was a proof that she was still able to do more, if more could have been done for *her*. She had one mark of good sense, rarely known in any actor of either sex but herself. I have observed several, with promising dispositions, very desirous of instruction at their first setting out; but no sooner had they found their best account in it, than they were as desirous of being left to their own capacity, which they then thought would be disgraced by their seeming to want any farther assistance. But this was not Mrs. Oldfield's way of thinking; for to the last year of her life she never undertook any part she liked, without being importunately desirous of having all the helps in it that another could possibly give her. By knowing so much herself, she found how much more there was of nature yet needful to be known.

"Yet it was a hard matter to give her any hint, that she was not able to take or improve. With all this merit, she was tractable, and less presuming in her station than several that had not half her pretensions to be troublesome. But she lost nothing by her easy conduct; she had everything she asked, which she took care should be always reasonable, because she hated as much to be grudged as denied a civility. Upon her extraordinary action in the ' *Provoked Husband*,' the managers made her a present of fifty guineas more than her agreement, which never was more than a verbal one; for they knew she was above deserting them to engage upon any other stage, and she was conscious they would never think it their interest to give her cause of complaint. In the last two months of her illness, when she was no longer able to assist them, she declined receiving her salary, though by her agreement she was entitled to it. Upon the whole she was, to the last scene she acted, the delight of her spectators."*

This charming actress (Mrs. Oldfield) is said to have been the Flavia of "*The Tatler*" (No. 212). The catch-penny

* Apology, p. 250.

writer of her memoirs equivocally speaks of it as her "*vera effigies*," and on his authority the assertion has been repeated. But as a Flavia mentioned in the same work (No. 239) turns out to be Miss Osborne, afterwards the wife of Bishop Atterbury (upon whom he wrote the lines on a fan there inserted, beginning

> "Flavia the least and slightest toy
> Can with resistless art employ,")

and as the first Flavia is praised for her quality and the extreme simplicity of her manners (which, according to Cibber, was not exactly one of the charms of Mrs. Oldfield,) the supposition, we think, falls to the ground. We need have less hesitation in admitting that Steele, who knew her well, alludes to her in another paper under her favourite title of Lady Betty Modish. Speaking of the effects of love upon a generous temper, in refining the manners, he says, " There is Colonel Ranter, who never spoke without an oath until he saw the Lady Betty Modish, now never gives his man an order, but it is, ' Pray, Tom, do it.' The drawers where he drinks live in perfect happiness. He asked Will at the George the other day, how he did ? Where he used to say, ' Damn it, it is so ;' he now ' believes there is some mistake ; he must confess, he is of another opinion ; but, however, he will not insist.' "* This Colonel Ranter is supposed by the commentators to have been Brigadier-General Churchill, one of the Marlborough family, who lived with Mrs. Oldfield after the death of Mr. Maynwaring. Steele elsewhere speaks of a " General" (supposed to be the same) " weeping for her, in the character of Indiana in his ' *Conscious Lovers* ;' " upon which he said Mr. Wilks observed (for he had made all the fine gentlemen tender) that the General " would fight ne'er the worse for that."

Mrs. Oldfield's position in life was singular. With all her beauty and attraction, and the license of stage manners, she is understood to have attached herself but to two persons successively, and on the footing of a wife. The first was Mr. Maynwaring, a celebrated Whig writer, to whom one of the volumes of " The Spectator" is dedicated, and by whom she had a son ; and, after his death, she lived with General Churchill, by whom she had a son also. " She left," says ' *The General Biography*,' " the bulk of her substance to her son Maynwaring, from whose father she had received it ;

---

* Tatler, No. 10,

U

without neglecting, however, her other son Churchill, and her own relations."

During the period of these two connections, Mrs. Oldfield appears to have been received into the first circles, where she is described as being a pattern of good behaviour; and yet the feeling of Mr. Maynwaring's friends against the connection was so strong, that she herself, though she is understood to have had a sincere affection for him, is said to have often remonstrated with him against it as injurious to his interest. Marriage with an actress, though the example had been set by a duke, appears in neither case to have been thought of. The feeling of society seems to have been this :—" Here is a woman bred up to the stage, and passing her life upon it. It is therefore impossible she should marry a gentleman of family ; and yet, as her behaviour would otherwise deserve it, and the examples of actresses are of no authority for any one but themselves, some license may be allowed to a woman who diverts us so agreeably, who attracts the society of the wits, and is so capital a dresser. We will treat her profession with contempt, but herself with consideration." Upon these curious grounds Mrs. Oldfield lived in every respect like a woman of fashion, and as she became rich (which was, perhaps, not the least of her recommendations), she was admitted into the best society, and went to court. The pretence among her visitors during both her connections probably was, that she was privately married; but she was too sincere to warrant the deception. The Princess of Wales' (afterwards queen of George II.) asked her one day at a levee if her marriage with General Churchill was true. "So it is said, may it please your highness, but we have not owned it yet."—"It may appear singular," says Mr. Chalmers, who tells us this story, " to quote the late pious Sir James Stonhouse for anecdotes of Mrs. Oldfield ; yet in one of his letters we are informed, that she always went to the house in the same dress she had worn at dinner in her visits to the houses of great people ; for she was much caressed on account of her professional merit and her connection with Mr. Churchill, the Duke of Marlborough's brother ; that she used to go to the playhouse in a chair, attended by two footmen ; that she seldom spoke to any one of the actors ; and was allowed a sum of money to buy her own clothes."* Mrs. Oldfield's

* Letters from the Rev. J. Orton and the Rev. Sir John Stonhouse, quoted in the " General Biographical Dictionary," vol. xxiii. p. 326.

generosity was much admired in giving a pension to Savage, which he received regularly as long as she lived. This is what has given posterity a liking for her. When she died she lay in state in the Jerusalem Chamber, and her funeral in Westminster Abbey was attended by several noblemen, among others, as pall-bearers. Mr. Chalmers has repeated, with other biographers, that, " at her own desire," she was elegantly dressed in her coffin ; on which account, it is added, Pope introduced her in the character of Narcissa :

> " Odious ! in wollen ! 'twould a saint provoke,
> (Were the last words that poor Narcissa spoke) ;
> No, let a charming chintz and Brussels lace
> Wrap my cold limbs and shade my lifeless face :
> One would not sure be frightful when one's dead—
> And, Betty, give this cheek a little red."

But it does not appear that there is any authority for this speech, except the poet's. A letter written to her first biographer by an attendant during her last illness says, that " although she had no priest," she " prayed without ceasing," which does not look like an attention to dress ; but the biographer adds, that " as the nicety of dress was her delight when living, she was as nicely dressed after her decease ; being, by Mrs. Saunders' direction, thus laid in her coffin." The nicety here mentioned was, to be sure, " mortal fine."— " She had on," says the writer, " a very fine Brussels lace-head, a Holland shift with tucker, and double ruffles of the same lace ; a pair of new kid gloves, and her body wrapt up in a winding sheet."* Yet we are of Montaigne's opinion, and know not why death should be rendered more melancholy than it is. When a tomb was opened in Greece, supposed to be that of Aspasia, there was found in it a sprig of myrtle in gold.

The next batch of players, with Garrick at their head, are Quin, Macklin, Barry, King, Woodward, Gentleman Smith, and others ; with Mrs. Clive, Pritchard, Cibber, and Woffington. Garrick's later contemporaries are Parsons, Dodd, Quick, the Palmers, Miss Pope, Mrs. Abingdon, and others, who bring us down to Mrs. Siddons, Miss Farren, &c., the commencers of our own time. Of Steele and the sentimental comedy we need say no more. Goldsmith belongs to Covent Garden ; Foote to the Haymarket ; and Cumberland, though an elegant writer, does not call for any particular mention in an abstract like this.

* Memoirs, p. 144.

When Garrick first appeared, a declamatory grandeur
prevailed in tragedy, which we conceive to have arisen in the
time of Charles II.   It was probably handed down by Booth ;
and imitated, with the usual deterioration, from Betterton,
who, though a true genius and a universal one, may not have
been uncorrupted by the taste of the times ; not to mention
that it is doubtful, till Garrick appeared, whether the art of
acting was not identified with something too much of an art,
and the delicacy of verses expected to partake more of reci-
tation and musical accompaniment than we now look for.
Our suspicion to this effect arises from the traditional habits
of the stage, one generation handing down the manner of
another, and Betterton himself having been educated in the
school of those who were bred up in the recollection of Bur-
bage and Condell.   Shakspeare himself, from custom, or even
from some subtlety of reason, might have approved of something of this kind ; though, on the other hand, in the celebrated directions of Hamlet to the players, there appears to
be a secret dissatisfaction with the most applauded actors of
that time, as not being exactly what was desirable.   If this
notion is just, and the great poet of nature was as much
advanced beyond his time in this as in other respects, he
might indeed have hailed such an actor as Garrick, however
hyperbolically they have been sometimes put together.   The
best performers whom Garrick found in possession of public
applause, though some of them are described as excelling in
all the varieties of passion (as Mrs. Cibber, for instance, notwithstanding the different impression given of her in the following quotation), appear to have been more or less of the
old declamatory school.   Quin in particular, then at the head
of the profession, was an avowed declaimer, having the same
notions of tragedy in the delivery which his friend Thomson
had in the composition.   Posterity respects Quin as the
friend of Thomson, and laughs with him as an epicure and a
wit.   Garrick and he ultimately became friends.   Of the
first reception of the new style introduced by Garrick, its
electrical effects upon some, and the natural hesitation of
others to give up their old favourites, a lively picture has
been left us by Cumberland.

Speaking of himself, who was then at Westminster school,
he says,—

"I was once or twice allowed to go, under proper convoy, to the
play, where, for the first time in my life, I was treated by the sight

of Garrick in the character of Lothario. Quin played Horatio; Ryan, Altamont; Mrs. Cibber, Calista; and Mrs. Pritchard condescended to the humble part of Lavinia. I enjoyed a good view of the stage from the front row of the gallery, and my attention was rivetted to the scene. I have the spectacle even now, as it were, before my eyes. Quin presented himself, upon the rising of the curtain, in a green velvet coat, embroidered down the seams, an enormous full-bottomed periwig, rolled stockings, and high-heeled, square-toed shoes. With very little variation of cadence, and in a deep, full tone, accompanied by a sawing kind of action, which had more of the senate than of the stage in it, he rolled out his heroics with an air of dignified indifference, that seemed to disdain the plaudits that were bestowed upon him. Mrs. Cibber, in a key high pitched, but sweet withal, sung, or rather recitatived, Rowe's harmonious strain, something in the manner of the improvisatore's; it was so extremely wanting in contrast, that, though it did not wound the ear, it wearied it; when she had once recited two or three speeches, I could anticipate the manner of every succeeding one; it was like a long, old, legendary ballad of innumerable stanzas, every one of which is sung to the same tune, eternally chiming in the ear without variation or relief. Mrs. Pritchard was an actress of a different cast, had more nature, and, of course, more change of tone, and variety both of action and expression: in my opinion the comparison was decidedly in her favour; but when, after long and eager expectation, I first beheld little Garrick, then young and light and alive in every muscle and in every feature, come bounding on the stage, and pointing at the wittol Altamont and heavy-paced Horatio—heavens, what a transition!—it seemed as if a whole century had been swept over in the transition of a single scene; old things were done away and a new order at once brought forward, bright and luminous, and clearly destined to dispel the barbarisms and bigotry of a tasteless age, too long attached to the prejudices of custom, and superstitiously devoted to the illusions of imposing declamation. This heaven-born actor was then struggling to emancipate his audience from the slavery they were resigned to; and though, at times, he succeeded in throwing in some gleams of new-born light upon them, yet, in general they seemed to *love darkness better than light,* and, in the dialogue of altercation between Horatio and Lothario, bestowed far the greater *show of hands* upon the master of the old school than upon the founder of the new. I thank my stars, my feelings in those moments led me right; they were those of nature, and therefore could not err." *

----

* Memoirs of Richard Cumberland, written by himself, 4to. p. 59. Davies, in his "Life of Garrick," vol. i. p. 136, gives us a different idea of the preference awarded by the audience. To be sure, upon his knowledge, he says only that Quin was defeated "in the opinion of the best judges;" but he adds, from report, an anecdote that looks as if the general feeling also was against him. "When Lothario," he says, "gave Horatio the challenge, Quin, instead of accepting it instantaneously, with the determined and unembarrassed brow of superior bravery, made a long pause, and dragged out the words,

'I'll meet thee there!'

in such a manner as to make it appear absolutely ludicrous. He

It is needless to add that Garrick excelled in comedy as
well as tragedy, and in the lowest comedy too—in Abel
Drugger as well as Hamlet. He was first at Goodman's
Fields; then appeared both at Covent Garden and Drury
Lane; but in a short time settled for life at Drury Lane as
actor, manager, and author. He was a sprightly dramatist,
a man of wit, and no doubt a generous man, though the
endless matters of business in which he was concerned, and
the refusals of all kinds which he must have been often
forced into, got him, with many, a character for the reverse.
Johnson, who did not spare him, pronounced him generous.
Fine as his tragedy must have been, we suspect his comedy
must have been finer; because his own nature was one of
greater sprightliness than sentiment.   We hear nothing
serious of him throughout his life; and his face, with a great
deal of acuteness, has nothing in it profound or romantic.

Garrick has the reputation of improving the stage costume:
but it was Macklin that did it.   The late Mr. West, who was
the first (in his picture of the " Death of Wolfe ") to omit the
absurdity of putting a piece of armour instead of a waistcoat
upon a general officer, told us, that he himself once asked
Garrick why he did not reform the stage in that particular.
Garrick said the spectators would not allow it ; " they would
throw a bottle at his head."   Macklin, however, persevered,
and the thing was done.   The other, with all his nature,
seems to have had a hankering after the old dresses.   He had
first triumphed in them, and they suited his propensity to the
airy and popular.   Garrick had a particular dislike to
appearing in the Roman costume.   Probably in this there
was a consciousness of his small person.   There are many
engravings of him extant, in which his tragic characters are
seen in coats and toupees.   His appearance as Hotspur, in a
laced frock and Ramillie wig, was objected to, not as being
unsuitable to the time, but as " too insignificant for the
character." *

Of Barry, the most celebrated antagonist of Garrick, we
shall speak at Covent Garden.   King, according to Churchill,
by the force of natural impudence as well as genius, excelled
in "Brass;" and Churchill's opinions are worth attending to,

paused so long before he spoke, that somebody, it was said, called out
from the gallery, ' Why don't you tell the gentleman whether you
will meet him or not ? ' "

  * Davis's Miscellanies, *ut supra*, vol. i., p. 126.

though he expresses them with vehemence, and by wholesale. *Gentleman* Smith explains his character by his title. We should entertain a very high opinion of Mrs. Pritchard, even had she left us nothing but the face in her portraits. She seems to have been a really great genius, equally capable of the highest and lowest parts. The fault objected to her was, that her figure was not genteel; and we can imagine this well enough in an actress who could pass from Lady Macbeth to Doll Common. She seems to have thrown herself into the arms of sincerity and passion, not, perhaps, the most refined, but as tragic and comic as need be. As Churchill says,

> " Before such merits all objections fly,
> Pritchard's genteel, and Garrick six feet high."

Clive was an admirable comic actress, of the wilful and fantastic order, and a wit and virago in private life. She became the neighbour and intimate of Horace Walpole, and always seems to us to have been the *man* of the two. Mrs. Woffington was an actress of all work, but of greater talents than the phrase generally implies. Davies says she was the handsomest woman that ever appeared on the stage, and that Garrick was at one time in doubt whether he should not marry her. She was famous for performing in male attire, and openly preferred the conversation of men to women—the latter she said, talking of " nothing but silks and scandal." She was the only woman admitted into one of the beef-steak clubs, and is said to have been president of it. These humours, perhaps, though Davies praises her for feminine manners, as contrasted with her antagonist Mrs. Clive, frightened Garrick out of his matrimony.

We now pass at once to Covent Garden Theatre, which lies close by. Many old play-goers who are in the habit of associating the two theatres in their fancy, like twins, will be surprised to hear that the Covent Garden establishment is very young, compared with her sister, being little more than a hundred years old. It was first built by Rich, the harlequin, and opened in 1733 under the patent granted to the Duke's company. The Covent Garden company may therefore be considered as the representatives of the old companies of Davenant and Betterton; while those at Drury Lane are the successors of Killigrew, and more emphatically the King's actors. Indeed, they exclusively designate themselves as " his Majesty's servants ; " and, we believe, claim some privileges on that account. Covent Garden theatre was partly rebuilt in 1772, and wholly so in 1809, having undergone the usual death by conflagration. The new edifice was a structure in classical taste, by Mr. Smirke, the portico being a copy from the Parthenon of Athens.*

Actors have seldom been confined to any one house ; and those whom we are about to mention performed at Drury Lane as well as Covent Garden; but as they were rivals or opponents of Garrick, and may be supposed to have made the greatest efforts when they acted on a different stage, we shall speak of them apart under the present head. The first of them is Barry, who at one time almost divided the favour of of the town with Garrick, and in some characters is said to have excelled him, especially in love parts. How far this was owing to superiority of figure, and to a reputation for gallantry, it is impossible to say; and never were judgments more discordant than those which have been left us on the subject of Barry's merits. For instance, his character is thus summed up by Davies:—

"Of all the tragic actors who have trod the English stage for these last fifty years, Mr. Barry was unquestionably the most pleasing. Since Booth and Wilks, no actor had shown the public a just idea of the hero or the lover; Barry gave dignity to the one and passion to the other: in his person he was tall without awkwardness; in his countenance, handsome without effeminacy; in his uttering of passion, the language of nature alone was communicated to the feelings of an audience."

Davies proceeds to tell us, that Barry could not perform such characters as Richard and Macbeth, though he made a capital Alexander. "He charmed the ladies by the soft melody of his love-complaints, and the noble ardour of his courtship. There was no passion of the tender kind so truly pathetic and forcible in any actor as in Barry, except in Mrs. Cibber, who, indeed, excelled, in the expression of love, grief, tenderness, and jealous rage, all I ever knew. Happy it was for the frequenters of the theatre, when these two genuine children of nature united their efforts to charm an attentive audience. Mrs. Cibber, indeed, might be styled the daughter or sister of Mr. Garrick, but could be only the mistress or wife of Barry." † Our author afterwards calls him the

* Since this was written, Covent Garden has been converted into an Italian Opera House, has been a second time burnt, and a third time rebuilt; the architect being Mr. Barry, a son of Sir Charles Barry, who designed and erected the New Houses of Parliament.

† Alluding to her performance of Cordelia, &c., with the one, and of Juliet, Belvidera, &c., with the other.

"Mark Antony of the stage," whether his amorous disposition was considered, or his love of expense. He delighted in giving magnificent entertainments, and treated Mr. Pelham, who once invited himself to sup with him, in a style so princely, that the Minister rebuked him for it; which was not very civil. An actor has surely as much right to do absurd things as a statesman.

Now, as a contrast to this romantic portrait by Davies, take the following from the severer but masterly hand of Churchill:—

> "In person taller than the common size,
>   Behold where Barry draws admiring eyes;
>   When lab'ring passions in his bosom pent,
>   Convulsive rage, and struggling heave for vent,
>   Spectators, with imagined terrors warm,
>   Anxious expect the bursting of the storm:
>   But, all unfit in such a pile to dwell,
>   His voice comes forth like Echo from her cell;
>   To swell the tempest needful aid denies,
>   And all a-down the stage in feeble murmur dies.
>   What man, like Barry, with such pains, can err
>   In elocution, action, character?
>   What man could give, if Barry was not here,
>   Such well-applauded tenderness to Lear?
>   Who else can speak so very, very fine,
>   That sense may kindly end with every line?
>   Some dozen lines, before the ghost is there,
>   Behold him for the solemn scene prepare.
>   See how he frames his eyes, poises each limb,
>   Puts the whole body into proper trim,—
>   From whence we learn, with no great stretch of art,
>   Five lines hence comes a ghost, and lo! a start.
>   When he appears most perfect, still we find
>   Something which jars upon and hurts the mind.
>   Whatever lights upon a part are thrown,
>   We see too plainly they are not his own:
>   No flame from nature ever yet he caught,
>   Nor knew a feeling which he was not taught;
>   He raised his trophies on the base of art,
>   And conn'd his passions, as he conn'd his part."*

The probability, we fear, is that Barry was one of the old artificial school, who made his way more by person than by genius. Davies, who was a better gossip than critic, though he affected literature, was an actor himself of the mouthing order, if we are to believe Churchill; and his criticisms show him enough inclined to lean favourably to that side.

We have spoken of Quin, who acted much at this house in opposition to Garrick. It was here that he delivered the pro-

* The Rosciad.

logue to the memory of his friend Thomson; and affected the
audience by shedding real tears.*

Macklin was celebrated in Shylock; and in some other
sarcastic parts, particularly that of Sir Archy, in his comedy
of "Love-à-la-Mode." We take him to have been one of
those actors whose performances are confined to the reflection
of their own personal peculiarities. The merits of Shuter,
Edwin, Quick, and others who succeeded one another as
buffoons, were perhaps a good deal of this sort; but pleasant
humours are rare and acceptable. Macklin was a clever
satirist in his writing, and embroiled himself, not so cleverly,
with a variety of his acquaintances. He foolishly attempted
to run down Garrick; and once, in a sudden quarrel, poked
out a man's eye with his stick and killed him; for which he
narrowly escaped hanging. However, he was sorry for it;
and he is spoken of, by the stage historians, as kind in his
private relations, and liberal of his purse. A curious specimen of his latter moments we reserve for our mention of the
house where he died.

Woodward seems to have been a caricature anticipation of
Lewis, and was a capital harlequin. But nobody in harlequins
beat Rich, the manager of this theatre. His pantomimes and
spectacles produced a re-action against Garrick, when nothing
else could; and Covent Garden ever since has been reckoned
the superior house in that kind of merit,—"the wit," as Mr.
Ludlow Holt called it, "of goods and chattels." However, a
considerable degree of fancy and observation may be developed
in patomime: it is the triumph of animal spirits at Christmas,
for the little children; and for the men there is occasionally
some excellent satire on the times, reminding one, in its
spirit, of what we read of the comic buffoonery of the
ancients. Grimaldi, in his broad and fugitive sketches, often
showed himself a shrewder observer than many a comic actor
who can repeat only what is set down for him. Covent Garden
has, perhaps, been superior also in music, at least since

* "He (Thomson) left behind him the tragedy of ' Coriolanus,'
which was, by the zeal of his patron, Sir George Lyttleton, brought
upon the stage for the benefit of his family, and recommended by a
prologue, which Quin, who had long lived with Thomsom in fond
intimacy, spoke in such a manner as showed him ' to be,' on that
occasion, ' no actor.' The commencement of this benevolence is very
honourable to Quin; who is reported to have delivered Thomson,
then known to him only for his genius, from an arrest, by a very
considerable present; and its continuance is honourable to both, for
friendship is not always the sequel of obligation." Life, by Dr.
Johnson, in Chalmers's ' Poets,' p. 409.

the existence of the two houses together: for Purcell was before its time. Many of Arne's pieces came out here; and the famous Beard, a singer as manly as his name, the delight both of public and private life, was one of the managers.

Among the Covent Garden actors must not be forgotten Cooke, who came out there in Richard III. For some time he was the greatest performer of this and a few other characters. He was a new kind of Macklin, and like him, excelled in Shylock and Sir Archy M'Sarcasm; a confined actor, and a wayward man, but highly impressive in what he could do. His artful villains have been found fault with for looking too artful and villanous; but men of that stamp are apt to look so. The art of hiding is a considerable one; but habit will betray it after all, and stand foremost in the countenance. They who think otherwise are only too dull to see it. Besides, Cooke had generally to represent bold-faced, aspiring art; and to hug himself in its triumph. This he did with such a gloating countenance, as if villany was pure luxury in him, and with such a soft inward retreating of his voice—a wrapping up of himself, as it were, in velvet—so different from his ordinary rough way, that sometimes one could almost have wished to abuse him.

John Kemble, who, like the whole respectable family of that name, contributed much to maintain the rising character of the profession, may be considered the last popular actor of the declamatory school. His sister was a far greater performer, a true theatrical genius, especially for the stately and dominant; and had a great effect in raising the character of the profession. The growth of liberal opinion is nowhere more visible than in the different estimation in which actors and actresses are now held, compared with what it was. Individuals, it is true, always made their way into society by dint of the interest they excited; but still they were upon sufferance. Anybody could insult an actor, could even beat him, without its being dreamt that he had a right to retaliate; and the most amiable and lady-like actresses were thought unfit for wives, as we have seen in the case of Mrs. Oldfield. Things are now upon a different footing. Talent is allowed its just pretensions, whether coming from author or performer, and actresses have taken such a step, in ascension, that nobility almost seems to look out for a wife among them, as in a school that will inevitably furnish it with some kind of grace and intellect. The famous Lord Peterborough, who was the first nobleman that married an actress, kept the union concealed as long as he could, and only owned it just before his death. The Duke of Bolton, who married Miss Fenton, the Polly of Gay's opera, had first had several children by her as his mistress; so that this is hardly a case in point; and the marriage of Beard, the singer, with a lady of the Waldegrave family, though he was one of the most excellent of men, was looked upon as such a degradation, that they have contrived to omit the circumstance in the peerage-books to this day! Martin Folkes's marriage with Mrs. Bradshaw probably made the world consider the case a little more rationally, as he was a clever man; but Lord Derby's marriage with Miss Farren, who was eminently the gentlewoman, as well as of spotless character, seems to have been the first that rendered such unions compatible with public opinion. Lord Craven's with Miss Brunton followed, though at a considerable interval; and since that time, the town are so far from being surprised at the marriages of actresses with people of rank or fashion, that they seem to look for them. Lord Thurlow, not long afterwards, married Miss Bolton; another noble lord was lately the husband of an eminent singer; and several other favourites of the town, Miss Tree, Miss O'Neill, &c., have become the wives of men of fortune. We remember even a dancer, Miss Searle (but she was of great elegance, and had an air of delicate self-possession), who married into a family of rank.

The whole entertainment of a theatre has been rising in point of accommodation and propriety for the last fifty years. The scenery is better, the music better—we mean the orchestra—and last, not least, the audiences are better. They are better behaved. Garrick put an end to one great nuisance—the occupation, by the audience, of part of the stage. Till his time, people often sat about a stage as at the sides of a room, and the actor had to make his way among them, sometimes with the chance of being insulted; and scuffles took place among themselves. Dr. Johnson, at Lichfield, is said to have pushed a man into the orchestra who had taken possession of his chair. The pit, also, from about Garrick's time, seems to have left to the galleries the vulgarity attributed to it by Pope. There still remains, says he—

> ————" to mortify a wit,
> The many-headed monster of the pit,
> A senseless, worthless, and unhonoured crowd,
> Who, to disturb their betters mighty proud,
> Clattering their sticks before ten lines are spoke,
> Call for the farce, the bear, or the black-joke."

This would now be hardly a fair description of the galleries; and yet modern audiences are not reckoned to be of quite so high a cast as they used, in point of rank and wealth; so that this is another evidence of the general improvement of manners. Boswell, in an ebullition of vivacity, while sitting one night in the pit by his friend Dr. Blair, gave an extempore imitation of a cow! The house applauded, and he ventured upon some attempts of the same kind which did not succeed. Blair advised him in future to "stick to the cow." No gentleman now-a-days would think of a freak like this. There is one thing, however, in which the pit have much to amend. Their destitution of gallantry is extraordinary, especially for a body so ready to accept the clap-traps of the stage, in praise of their "manly hearts," and their "guardianship of the fair." Nothing is more common than to see women standing at the sides of the pit benches, while no one thinks of offering them a seat. Room even is not made, though it often might be. Nay, we have heard women rebuked for coming without securing a seat, while the reprover complimented himself on his better wisdom, and the hearers laughed. On the other hand, a considerate gentleman one night, who went out to stretch his legs, told a lady in our hearing that she might occupy his seat "till he returned!"

A friend of ours knew a lady who remembered Dr. Johnson in the pit taking snuff out of his waistcoat pocket. He used to go into the green-room to his friend Garrick, till he honestly confessed that the actresses excited too much of his admiration. Garrick did not much like to be seen by him when playing any buffoonery. It is said that the actor once complained to his friend that he talked too loud in the stage box, and interrupted his feelings: upon which the doctor said, "Feelings! Punch has no feelings." It was Johnson's opinion (speaking of a common cant of critics), that an actor who really "took himself" for Richard III., deserved to be hanged; and it is easy enough to agree with him; except that an actor who did so would be out of his senses. Too great a sensibility seems almost as hurtful to acting as too little. It would soon wear out the performer. There must be a quickness of conception, sufficient to seize the truth of the character, with a coolness of judgment to take all advantages; but as the actor is to represent as well as conceive, and to be the character in his own person, he could not with impunity give way to his emotions in any degree equal to what the spectators suppose. At least, if he did, he would

fall into fits, or run his head against the wall. As to the
amount of talent requisite to make a great actor, we must not
enter upon a discussion which would lead us too far from our
main object; but we shall merely express our opinion, that
there is a great deal more of it among the community than
they are aware.

Goldsmith was a frequenter of the theatre: Fielding and
Smollett, Sterne, but particularly Churchill. "His obser-
vatory," says Davies, "was generally the first row of the pit,
next the orchestra." His "Rosciad," a criticism on the most
known performers of the day, made a great sensation among
a body of persons who, as they are in the habit of receiving
applause to their faces, and in the most victorious manner,
may be allowed a greater stock of self-love than most people
—a circumstance which renders an unexacting member of
their profession doubly delightful. "The writer," says Davies,
"very warmly, as well as justly, celebrated the various and
peculiar excellencies of Mrs. Pritchard, Mrs. Cibber, and Clive;
but no one has, except Garrick, escaped his satirical lash."
Poor Davies is glad to say this, because of the well-known
passage in which he himself is mentioned:—

> "With him came mighty Davies! On my life
> That Davies hath a very pretty wife."

We will make one more quotation from this poem, because
it describes a class of actors, who are now extinct, and who
carried the artificial school to its height:—

> "Mossop, attached to military plan,
> Still kept his eye fixed on his right-hand man.
> Whilst the mouth measures words with seeming skill,
> The right hand labours, and the left lies still;
> For he resolved on scripture grounds to go,
> What the right doth, the left hand shall not know.
> With studied impropriety of speech,
> He soars beyond the hackney critic's reach;
> To epithets allots emphatic state,
> Whilst principals, ungraced, like lackeys, wait;
> In ways first trodden by himself excels,
> And stands alone in indeclinables;
> Conjunction, preposition, adverb join,
> To stamp new vigour on the nervous line:
> In monosyllables his thunders roll;
> He, she, it, and we, ye, they, fright the soul."

Mr. Barrymore (of whom we have no unpleasing recollection) had something of this manner with him; but the extremity of the style is now quite gone out.

The only capital performers we remember, that are now
dead and gone, with the exception of two or three already

mentioned, were Mrs. Jordan, a charming cordial actress, on
the homely side of the agreeable, with a delightful voice;
and Suett, who was the very personification of weak whim-
sicality, with a laugh like a peal of giggles. Mathews gives
him to the life.

We shall conclude this chapter with some delightful play-
going recollections of the best theatrical critic now living *—
the best, indeed, as far as we know, that this country ever
saw. He is one who does not respect criticism a jot too
much, nor any of the feelings connected with humanity, or
the imitation of it, too little. We here have him giving us
an account of the impression made upon him by the first
sight of a play, and concluding with a good hint to those older
children, who, because they have cut their drums open,
think nothing remains in life to be pleased with. A child
may like a theatre, because he is not thoroughly acquainted
with it; but if he become a wise man, he will find reason to
like it, because he is.

Life always flows with a certain freshness in these quarters;
nor, with all their drawbacks, have we more agreeable impressions from any neighbourhood in London, than what we receive
from the district containing the great theatres. It is one of
the most social and the least sordid.

"At the north end of Cross Court," says Mr. Lamb, "there yet
stands a portal, of some architectural pretensions, though reduced to
humble use, serving at present for an entrance to a printing-office.
This old door-way, if you are young, reader, you may not know
was the identical pit entrance to old Drury—Garrick's Drury—all
of it that is left. I never pass it without shaking some forty years
from off my shoulders, recurring to the evening when I passed
through it to see *my first play*. The afternoon had been wet, and
the condition of our going (the elder folks and myself) was, that
the rain should cease. With what a beating heart did I watch
from the window the puddles, from the stillness of which I was
taught to prognosticate the desired cessation. I seem to remember
the last spurt, and the glee with which I ran to announce it.
          *   *   *   *   *

"In those days were pit orders. Beshrew the uncomfortable
manager who abolished them!—with one of these we went. I
remember the waiting at the door—not that which is left—but
between that and an inner door, in shelter. Oh, when shall I be
such an expectant again!—with the cry of nonpareils, an indispen-
sable playhouse accompaniment in those days. As near as I can
recollect, the fashionable pronunciation of the theatrical fruiteresses
was, '*chase* some oranges, *chase* some nonpareils, *chase* a bill of the
play:' chase *pro* chuse. But when we got in and I beheld the green

* Alas! now dead. This passage was written before the departure
of our admirable friend.

curtain that veiled a heaven to my imagination, which was soon to be disclosed—the breathless anticipations I endured! I had seen something like it in the plate prefixed to 'Troilus and Cressida,' in Rowe's 'Shakspeare,'—the tent scene with Diomede; and a sight of that plate can always bring back, in a measure, the feeling of that evening. The boxes at that time full of well-dressed women of quality, projected over the pit; and the pilasters, reaching down, were adorned with a glittering substance (I know not what) under glass (as it seemed), resembling—a homely fancy—but I judged it to be sugar-candy—yet, to my raised imagination, divested of its homelier qualities, it appeared a glorified candy! The orchestra lights at length arose, those 'fair Auroras!' Once the bell sounded. It was to ring out yet once again; and, incapable of the anticipation, I reposed my shut eyes in a sort of resignation upon the maternal lap. It rang the second time. The curtain drew up—I was not past six years old—and the play was 'Artaxerxes!'

"I had dabbled a little in the 'Universal History'—the ancient part of it—and here was the court of Persia. It was being admitted to a sight of the past. I took no proper interest in the action going on, for I understood not its import; but I heard the word Darius, and I was in the midst of Daniel. All feeling was absorbed in vision. Gorgeous vests, gardens, palaces, princes, passed before me—I knew not players. I was in Persepolis for the time, and the burning idol of their devotion almost converted me into a worshipper. I was awe-struck, and believed those significations to be something more than elemental fires. It was all enchantment and a dream. No such pleasure has ever since visited me but in dreams. Harlequin's invasion followed; where, I remember, the transformation of the magistrates into reverend beldames seemed to me a piece of grave historic justice, and the tailor carrying his own head to be as sober a verity as the legend of St. Denys.

"The next play to which I was taken, was the 'Lady of the Manor,' of which, with the exception of some scenery, very faint traces are left in my memory. It was followed by a pantomime called 'Lun's Ghost'—a satiric touch, I apprehend, upon Rich, not long since dead —but to my apprehension (too sincere for satire) Lun was as remote a piece of antiquity as Lud—the father of a line of harlequins—transmitting his dagger of lath (the wooden sceptre) through countless ages. I saw the primeval Motley come from his silent tomb in a ghastly vest of white patch-work, like the apparition of a dead rainbow. So harlequins (thought I) look when they are dead.

"My third play followed in quick succession. It was 'The Way of the World.' I think I must have sat at it as grave as a judge; for, I remember, the hysteric affectations of good Lady Wishfort affected me like some solemn tragic passion. 'Robinson Crusoe' followed, in which Crusoe, Man Friday, and the Parrot were as good and authentic as in the story. The clownery and pantaloonery of these pantomimes have clean passed out of my head. I believe I no more laughed at them, than at the same age I should have been disposed to laugh at the grotesque gothic heads (seeming to me then replete with devout meaning) that gape and grin, in stone, around the inside of the old round church (my church) of the Templars.

"I saw these plays in the season of 1781-2, when I was from six to seven years old. After the intervention of six or seven years (for at school all play-going was inhibited) I again entered the doors of a theatre. That old Artaxerxes' evening had never done ringing in my fancy. I expected the same feelings to come again with the same occasion. But we differ from ourselves less at sixty and sixteen, than the latter does from six. In that interval what had I not lost! At the first period I knew nothing, understood nothing, discriminated nothing. I felt all, loved all, wondered all—

'Was nourished I could not tell how.'

I had left the temple a devotee, and was returned a rationalist. The same things were there materially; but the emblem, the reverence was gone! The green curtain was no longer a veil drawn between two worlds, the unfolding of which was to bring back past ages, to present a 'royal ghost,' but a certain quantity of green baize, which was to separate the audience for a given time from certain of their fellow-men who were to come forward and pretend those parts. The lights—the orchestra lights—came up, a clumsy machinery. The first ring, and the second ring, was now but a trick of the prompter's bell, which had been like the note of the cuckoo, a phantom of a voice, no hand seen or guessed at, which ministered to its warning. The actors were men and women painted. I thought the fault was in them; but it was in myself, and the alteration which those many centuries—of six short twelvemonths—had wrought in me. Perhaps it was fortunate for me that the play of the evening was but an indifferent comedy, as it gave me time to crop some unreasonable expectations, which might have interfered with the genuine emo· tions with which I was soon after enabled to enter upon the first appearance, to me, of Mrs. Siddons in Isabella. Comparison and retrospection soon yielded to the present attraction of the scene; and the theatre became to me, *upon a new stock*, the most delightful of recreations."—ELIA, p. 221.

ENTRANCE DOOR, OLD COVENT GARDEN.

CHAPTER VIII.

COVENT GARDEN CONTINUED AND LEICESTER SQUARE.

Bow Street once the Bond Street of London—Fashions at that time—
Infamous frolic of Sir Charles Sedley and others—Wycherly and
the Countess of Drogheda—Tonson the Bookseller—Fielding—
Russell Street—Dryden beaten by hired ruffians in Rose Street—
His Presidency at Will's Coffee-House—Character of that Place—
Addison and Button's Coffee-House—Pope, Philips, and Garth—
Armstrong—Boswell's introduction to Johnson—The Hummums—
Ghost Story there—Covent Garden—The Church—Car, Earl of
Somerset — Butler, Southern, Eastcourt, Sir Robert Strange—
Macklin—Curious Dialogue with him when past a century—
Dr. Walcot—Covent Garden Market—Story of Lord Sandwich,
Hackman, and Miss Ray—Henrietta Street—Mrs. Clive—James
Street—Partridge, the almanack-maker—Mysterious lady—King
Street — Arne and his Father — The four Indian Kings —
Southampton Row—Maiden Lane—Voltaire—Long Acre and its
Mug-Houses—Prior's resort there—Newport Street—St. Martin's
Lane, and Leicester Square—Sir Joshua Reynolds—Hogarth—Sir
Isaac Newton.

OW STREET was once the Bond Street
of London. Mrs. Bracegirdle began an
epilogue of Dryden's with saying—

"I've had to-day a dozen billet-doux
From fops, and wits, and cits, and Bow-
street beaux;
Some from Whitehall, but from the Temple
more:
A Covent-garden porter brought me four."

Sir Walter Scott says, in a note on the passage, "With a
slight alteration in spelling, a modern poet would have written
Bond Street beaux. A billet-doux from Bow Street would
now be more alarming than flattering."[*]

Mrs. Bracegirdle spoke this epilogue at Drury Lane.
There was no Covent Garden theatre then. People of fashion
occupied the houses in Bow Street, and mantuas floated up
and down the pavement. This was towards the end of the
Stuart's reign, and the beginning of the next century—the
times of Dryden, Wycherly, and the Spectator. The beau of
Charles's time is well-known. He wore, when in full flower,
a peruke to imitate the flowing locks of youth, a Spanish hat,
clothes of slashed silk or velvet, the slashes tied with ribands,

* Scott's 'Dryden,' vol. viii., p. 178.

a coat resembling a vest rather than the modern coat, and silk stockings, with roses in his shoes. The Spanish was afterwards changed for the cocked hat, the flowing peruke for one more compact; the coat began to stiffen into the modern shape, and when in full dress, the beau wore his hat under his arm. His grimaces have been described by Dryden—

> " His various modes from various fathers follow;
> One taught the toss, and one the new French wallow;
> His sword-knot this, his cravat that designed;
> And this the yard-long snake that twirls behind.
> From one the sacred periwig he gained,
> Which wind ne'er blew, nor touch of hat profaned.
> Another's diving bow he did adore,
> Which with a shog casts all the hair before,
> Till he, with full decorum, brings it back,
> And rises with a water-spaniel shake." *

One of these perukes would sometimes cost forty or fifty pounds. The fair sex at this time waxed and waned through all the varieties of dishabilles, hoop-petticoats, and stomachers. We must not enter upon this boundless sphere, especially as we have to treat upon it from time to time. We shall content ourselves with describing a set of lady's clothes, advertised as stolen in the year 1709, and which would appear to have belonged to a belle resolved to strike even Bow Street with astonishment. They consisted of "a black silk petticoat, with a red-and-white calico border; cherry-coloured stays, trimmed with blue and silver; a red and dove-coloured damask gown, flowered with large trees; a yellow satin apron, trimmed with white Persian; muslin head-cloths, with crow-foot edging; double ruffles with fine edging; a black silk furbelowed scarf, and a spotted hood!" † It is probable, however, the lady did not wear all these colours at once.

A tavern in Bow Street, the Cock, became notorious for a frolic of Sir Charles Sedley, Lord Buckhurst, and others, frequently mentioned in the biographies, but too disgusting to be told. There was an account of it in Pepy's manuscript, but it was obliged to be omitted in the printing. Anthony à Wood found it out, and first gave it to the public. It was not commonly dissolute, there was a filthiness in it, which would have been incredible if told of any other period than that of

* In the prologue to Etherege's play of the 'Man of Mode.' Scott's 'Dryden,' vol. x., p. 340.

† Manners and Customs of London during the Eighteenth Century, vol. ii., p. 317.

the fine gentlemen of the court of Charles. What can be repeated has been told by Johnson in his life of Sackville, Lord Dorset.

"Sackville, who was then Lord Buckhurst, with Sir Charles Sedley, and Sir Thomas Ogle, got drunk at the Cock, in Bow Street, by Covent Garden, and going into the balcony, exposed themselves to the company in very indecent postures. At last, as they grew warmer, Sedley stood forth naked, and harangued the populace in such profane language, that the public indignation was awakened; the crowd attempted to force the door, and being repulsed, drove in the performers with stones, and broke the windows of the house. For this misdemeanour they were indicted, and Sedley was fined five hundred pounds; what was the sentence of the others is not known. Sedley employed Killegrew and another to procure a remission of the King, but (mark the friendship of the dissolute!) they begged the fine for themselves, and exacted it to the last groat."

Opposite this tavern lived Wycherly, with his wife, the Countess of Drogheda. Charles paid him a visit there, before Wycherly knew the lady; and showed him a kindness which his marriage is said to have interrupted. The story begins and ends with Bow Street, and, as far as concerns the lady, is curious.

"Mr. Wycherly," says the biographer, "happened to be ill of a fever at his lodgings in Bow Street, Covent Garden: during his sickness, the King did him the honour of a visit: when, finding his fever indeed abated, but his body extremely weakened, and his spirits miserably shattered, he commanded him to take a journey to the south of France, believing that nothing could contribute more to the restoring his former state of health than the gentle air of Montpelier during the winter season: at the same time, the King assured him, that as soon as he was able to undertake the journey, he would order five hundred pounds to be paid him to defray the expenses of it.

"Mr. Wycherly accordingly went to France, and returned to England the latter end of the spring following, with his health entirely restored. The King received him with the utmost marks of esteem, and shortly after told him he had a son, who he resolved should be educated like the son of a king, and that he could make choice of no man so proper to be his governor as Mr. Wycherly; and that, for this service, he should have fifteen hundred pounds a-year allotted to him; the King also added, that when the time came that his office should cease, he would take care to make such a provision for him as should set him above the malice of the world and fortune. These were golden prospects for Mr. Wycherly, but they were soon by a cross accident dashed to pieces.

"Soon after this promise of his Majesty's, Mr. Dennis tells us that Mr. Wycherly went down to Tunbridge, to take either the benefit of the waters or the diversions of the place, when, walking one day upon the Wells-walk with his friend, Mr. Fairbeard, of Gray's Inn, just as he came up to the bookseller's, the Countess of Drogheda, a young widow, rich, noble, and beautiful, came up to the bookseller and inquired for the 'Plain Dealer.' 'Madam,' says Mr. Fairbeard, 'since you are for the "Plain Dealer," there he is for you,' pushing Mr. Wycherly towards her. 'Yes,' says Mr. Wycherly, 'thi• lady can bear plain-dealing, for she appears to be so accomplished, that what would be a compliment to others, when said to her would be plain-dealing.' 'No, truly, sir,' said the lady, 'I am not without my faults more than the rest of my sex : and yet, notwithstanding all my faults, I love plain-dealing, and am never more fond of it than when it tells me of a fault.' 'Then, Madam,' says Mr. Fairbeard, "you and the plain dealer seem designed by heaven for each other.' In short, Mr. Wycherly accompanied her upon the walks, waited upon her home, visited her daily at her lodgings whilst she stayed at Tunbridge; and after she went to London, at her lodgings in Hatton Garden: where, in a little time, he obtained her consent to marry her. This he did, by his father's command, without acquainting the King ; for it was reasonably supposed, that the lady's having a great independent estate, and noble and powerful relations, the acquainting the King with the intended match would be the likeliest way to prevent it. As soon as the news was known at court, it was looked upon as an affront to the King, and a contempt of his Majesty's orders ; and Mr. Wycherly's conduct after marrying made the resentment fall heavier upon him: for being conscious he had given offence, and seldom going near the court, his absence was construed into ingratitude.

"The Countess, though a splendid wife, was not formed to make a husband happy; she was in her nature extremely jealous; and indulged in it to such a degree, that she could not endure her husband should be one moment out of her sight. Their lodgings were in Bow Street, Covent Garden, over against the Cock Tavern, whither, if Mr. Wycherly at any time went, he was obliged to leave the windows open, that his lady might see there was no woman in the company."*

"The Countess," says another writer, "made him some amends by dying in a reasonable time." His title to her fortune, however, was disputed, and his circumstances, though he had property, were always constrained. He was rich enough however to marry a young woman a few days before he died, in order to disappoint a troublesome heir. In his old age he became acquainted with Pope, then a youth, who vexed him by taking him at his word, when asked to correct his poetry. Wycherly showed a candid horror at growing old, natural enough to a man who had been one of the gayest of the gay, very handsome, and a " Captain." He was captain in the regiment of which Buckingham was colonel. We have mentioned the Duchess of Cleveland's visits to him when a student in the Temple. Wycherly is the greatest of all our comic dramatists for truth of detection in what is ill, as Congreve is the greatest painter of artificial life, and Farquhar and

* Cibber's 'Lives of the Poets ' vol. iii., p. 252.

Hoadley the best discoverers of what is pleasant and good-
humoured. When the profligacy of writers like Wycherly is
spoken of, we should not forget that much of it is not only
confined to certain characters, but that the detection of these
characters leaves an impression on the mind highly favourable to genuine morals. A modern critic, as excellent in his
remarks on the drama as the one quoted at the conclusion of
our last chapter is upon the stage, says on this point, speaking
of the comedy of the "Plain Dealer,"—"The character of
Manly is violent, repulsive, and uncouth, which is a fault,
though one that seems to have been intended for the sake of
contrast; for the portrait of consummate, artful hypocrisy
in Olivia, is, perhaps, rendered more striking by it. The
indignation excited against this odious and pernicious quality
by the masterly exposure to which it is here subjected, is
'a discipline of humanity.' No one can read this play attentively without being the better for it as long as he lives. It
penetrates to the core; it shows the immorality and hateful
effects of duplicity, by showing it fixing its harpy fangs in
the heart of an honest and worthy man. It is worth ten
volumes of sermons. The scenes between Manly, after his
return, Olivia, Plausible, and Norel, are instructive examples
of unblushing impudence, of shallow pretensions to principle,
and of the most mortifying reflections on his own situation,
and bitter sense of female injustice and ingratitude on the
part of Manly. The devil of hypocrisy and hardened assurance seems worked up to the highest pitch of conceivable
effrontery in Olivia, when, after confiding to her cousin
the story of her infamy, she, in a moment, turns round upon
her for some sudden purpose, and affecting not to know the
meaning of the other's allusions to what she had just told her,
reproaches her with forging insinuations to the prejudice of
her character, and in violation of their friendship. 'Go!
you're a censorious woman.' This is more trying to the
patience than anything in the Tartuffe."

Tonson, the great bookseller of his time, had a private
house in Bow Street. Rowe, in an amusing parody of Horace's
dialogue with Lydia, has left an account of old Jacob's visitors
here, and of his style of language.

Tonson got rich, but he was penurious; and his want of
generosity towards Dryden (to say the least of it) has done
him no honour with posterity. It may be said that he cared
little for posterity or for anything else, provided he got his

money; but a man who cares for money (unless he is a pure miser) only cares for power and consideration in another shape; and no man chooses to be disliked by his fellow-creatures, living, or to come. In the correspondence between Tonson and Dryden, we see the usual painful picture (when the bookseller is of this description) of the tradesman taking all the advantages, and the author made to suffer for being a gentleman and a man of delicacy. This is the common, and, perhaps, the natural order of things, till society see better throughout; though there have been, and still are, some handsome exceptions, as in the instances of Dodsley, the late Mr. Johnson, and others. The bookseller generally behaves well, in proportion to his intelligence; nothing being so eager to catch all petty advantages as the consciousness of having no other ground to go upon. It may be answered that Dryden's patience with Tonson sometimes got exhausted, and he became "captious and irritable:" and it is always to be remembered that the bookseller need not pretend to be anything more than a tradesman seeking his allowed profits; but he should not on every occasion retreat into the strongholds of trade, and yet claim the merit of acting otherwise; and Tonson, who undertook to be the familiar friend of Rowe and Congreve, ought not to have been able to insult the man whom they both respected, because he was not so well off as they. The following passage of mingled amusement and painfulness is out of Sir Walter Scott:—

"Dryden," says Sir Walter, in his life of the poet, "seems to have been particularly affronted at a presumptuous plan of that publisher (a keen whig, and Secretary to the Kit-Cat Club) to drive him into inscribing the translation of 'Virgil' to King William. With this view Tonson had an especial care to make the engraver aggravate the nose of Eneas in the plates into a sufficient resemblance of the hooked promontory of the Deliverer's countenance, and foreseeing Dryden's repugnance to his favourite plan, he had recourse, it would seem, to more unjustifiable means to further it; for the poet expresses himself as convinced that, through Tonson's means, his correspondence with his sons, then at Rome, was intercepted. I suppose Jacob, having fairly laid siege to his author's conscience, had no scruple to intercept all foreign supplies, which might have confirmed him in his pertinacity. But Dryden, although thus closely beleaguered, held fast his integrity; and no prospect of personal advantage, or importunity on the part of Tonson, could induce him to take a step inconsistent with his religious and political sentiments. It was probably during the course of these bickerings with his publisher, that Dryden, incensed at some refusal of accommodation on the part of Tonson, sent him three well-known coarse and forcible satirical lines descriptive of his personal appearance:—

> 'With leering looks, bull-faced, and freckled fair,
> With two left legs, and Judas-coloured hair,
> And frouzy pores, that taint the ambient air.'

" 'Tell the dog,' said the poet to the messenger, 'that he who wrote these can write more.' But Tonson, perfectly satisfied with this single triplet, hastened to comply with the author's request, without requiring any further specimen of his poetical powers. It would seem, on the other hand, that when Dryden neglected his stipulated labour, Tonson possessed powers of animadversion, which, though exercised in plain prose, were not a little dreaded by the poet. Lord Bolingbroke, already a votary of the Muses, and admitted to visit their high-priest, was wont to relate, that one day he heard another person enter the house. 'This,' said Dryden, 'is Tonson; you will take care not to depart before he goes away, for I have not completed the sheet which I promised him; and if you leave me unprotected, I shall suffer all the rudeness to which his resentment can prompt his tongue.' " *

Fielding lived some time in Bow Street, probably during his magistracy.

We turn out of Bow Street into Russell Street, so called from the noble family of that name, who possess great property in this quarter. It is pleasant to think that the name is accordant with the reputation of the place, for we are more than ever in the thick of wits and men of letters, especially of a race which was long peculiar to this country, literary politicians. At the north-east corner of the two streets was the famous Will's coffee-house, formerly the Rose, where Dryden presided over the literature of the town; and on the other side of the way, on a part of the site of the present Hummums, stood Button's coffee-house, no less

---

* Works of Dryden, vol. i., p. 387. Sir Walter thus notices a letter of Tonson's on the subject of Dryden's contribution to one of the volumes known under the title of his Miscellanies:—" The contribution, although ample, was not satisfactory to old Jacob Tonson, who wrote on the subject a most mercantile expostulatory letter to Dryden, which is fortunately still preserved, as a curious specimen of the minutiæ of a literary bargain in the seventeenth century. Tonson, with reference to Dryden, having offered a strange bookseller six hundred lines for twenty guineas, enters into a question in the rule of three, by which he discovers and proves, that for fifty guineas he has only 1,446 lines, which he seems to take more unkindly, as he had not counted the lines until he had paid the money; from all which Jacob infers, that Dryden ought, out of generosity, at least to throw him in something to the bargain, especially as he had used him more kindly in Juvenal, which, saith old Jacob, is not reckoned so easy to translate as Ovid."—Vol. i., p. 379.

celebrated as the resort of the wits and poets of the time of Queen Anne.

Dryden is identified with the neighbourhood of Covent Garden. He presided in the chair at Russell Street; his plays came out in the theatre at the other end of it; he lived in Gerrard Street, which is not far off; and, alas! for the anti-climax! he was beaten by hired bravos in Rose Street, now called Rose Alley. Great men come down to posterity with their proper aspects of calmness and dignity ; and we do not easily fancy that they received anything from their contem-poraries but the grateful homage which is paid them by our-selves. " But the life of a wit," says Steele, " is a warfare upon earth." Sir Walter Scott, speaking of the beautiful description given by Dryden of the Attic nights he enjoyed with Sir Charles Sedley and others, observes, " He had not yet experienced the disadvantages attendant on such society, or learned how soon literary eminence becomes the object of detraction, of envy, of injury, even from those who can best feel its merit, if they are discouraged by dissipated habits from emulating its flight, or hardened by perverted feeling against loving its possessors." *

The outrage perpetrated upon the sacred shoulders of the poet was the work of Lord Rochester, and originated in a mistake not creditable to that would-be great man and das-tardly debauchee. The following is Sir Walter's account of the matter.

" The 'Essay on Satire' (by Lord Mulgrave, afterwards Duke of Buckinghamshire), though written, as appears from the title-page of the last edition, in 1675, was not made public until 1679, with this observation :—I have sent you herewith a libel, in which my own share is not the least. The king having perused it, is no way dis-satisfied with his. The author is apparently Mr. Dr [yden], his patron Lord M [ulgrave], having a panegyric in the midst. From hence it is evident that Dryden obtained the reputation of being the author ; in consequence of which, Rochester meditated the base and cowardly revenge which he afterwards executed ; and he thus coolly expressed his intention in another of his letters :—' You write me word that I am out of favour with a certain poet, whom I have admired for the disproportion of him and his attributes. He is a rarity which I cannot but be fond of, as one would be of a hog that could fiddle, or a singing owl. If he falls on me at the blunt, which is his very good weapon in wit, I will forgive him if you please, and leave the repartee to black Will with a cudgel.'

" In pursuance of this infamous resolution, upon the night of the 18th December, 1679, Dryden was waylaid by hired ruffians, and

---

* Dryden, vol. i., p. 114.

severely beaten, as he passed through Rose Street, Covent Garden, returning from Will's coffee-house to his own house in Gerrard Street. A reward of fifty pounds was in vain offered in the 'London Gazette' and other newspapers, for the discoverers of the perpetrators of this outrage. The town was, however, at no loss to pitch upon Rochester as the employer of the bravos, with whom the public suspicion joined the Duchess of Portsmouth, equally concerned in the supposed affront thus avenged. In our time, were a nobleman to have recourse to hired bravos to avenge his personal quarrels against any one, more especially a person holding the rank of a gentleman, he might lay his account with being hunted out of society. But in the age of Charles, the ancient high and chivalrous sense of honour was esteemed Quixotic, and the civil war had left traces of ferocity in the manners and sentiments of the people. Encounters, where the assailants took all advantages of number and weapons, were as frequent, and held as honourable, as regular duels. Some of these approached closely to assassination; as in the famous case of Sir John Coventry, who was waylaid and had his nose slit by some young men of rank, for a reflection upon the King's theatrical amours. This occasioned the famous statute against maiming and wounding, called the Coventry Act, an Act highly necessary, for so far did our ancestors' ideas of manly forbearance differ from ours, that Killegrew introduces the hero of one of his comedies, a cavalier, and the fine gentleman of the piece, lying in wait for, and slashing the face of a poor courtezan, who had cheated him.

"It will certainly be admitted, that a man, surprised in the dark, and beaten by ruffians, loses no honour by such a misfortune. But if Dryden had received the same discipline from Rochester's own hand, without resenting it, his drubbing could not have been more frequently made a matter of reproach to him: a sign, surely, of the penury of subjects for satire in his life and character, since an accident, which might have happened to the greatest hero that ever lived, was resorted to as an imputation on his honour. The Rose Alley ambuscade became almost proverbial; and even Mulgrave, the real author of the satire, and upon whose shoulders the blows ought in justice to have descended, mentions the circumstance in his 'Art of Poetry,' with a cold and self-sufficient sneer:—

'Though praised and punished for another's rhymes,
His own deserve as great applause *sometimes.*'

To which is added in a note, 'A libel for which he was both applauded and wounded, though entirely ignorant of the whole matter.' This flat and conceited couplet, and note, the noble author judged it proper to omit in the corrected edition of his poem. Otway alone, no longer the friend of Rochester, and, perhaps, no longer the enemy of Dryden, has spoken of the author of this dastardly outrage with the contempt it deserved:—

'Poets in honour of the truth should write,
With the same spirit brave men for it fight;
And though against him causeless hatreds rise,
And daily where he goes of late, he spies
The scowls of sudden and revengeful eyes;
'Tis what he knows with much contempt to bear,
And serves a cause too good to let him fear,

> He fears no poison from incensed drab,
> No ruffian's five-foot sword, nor rascal's stab ;
> Nor any other snares of mischief laid,
> *Not a Rose-alley cudgel ambuscade;*
> From any private cause where malice reigns,
> Or general pique all blockheads have to brains.' "*

We dismiss this specimen of the times, that we may enjoy the look of Dryden as posterity sees it,—that is to say, as that of the first poet of his class, presiding over the tastes and aspirations of the town. Milton sat in his suburban bower, equally removed from outrage and compliment, and contemplating a still greater futurity. In the following passage from the ' Country and City Mouse,' by Prior and Montagu, Dryden, it is true, is spoken of with hostility, but his acknowledged predominance shines through it. Prior's instinct misgave him in writing against his natural master.

> "Then on they jogg'd; and since an hour of talk
> Might cut a banter on the tedious walk,
> As I remember, said the sober mouse,
> I've heard much talk of the Wits' Coffee-house;
> Thither, says Brindle, thou shalt go and see
> Priests supping coffee, sparks and poets tea;
> Here rugged frieze, there quality well drest,
> These baffling the grand Senior, those the Test,
> And there shrewd guesses made, and reasons given,
> That human laws were never made in heaven;
> But, above all, what shall oblige thy sight,
> And fill thy eye-balls with a vast delight,
> Is the poetic judge of sacred wit,
> Who does i' th' darkness of his glory sit;
> And as the moon who first receives the light,
> With which she makes these nether regions bright,
> So does he shine, reflecting from afar
> The rays he borrowed from a better star;
> For rules, which from Corneille and Rapin flow,
> Admired by all the scribbling herd below,
> From French tradition while he does dispense
> Unerring truths, 'tis schism, a damned offence,
> To question his, or trust your private sense." †

Will's Coffee-house was at the western corner of Bow Street. It first had the title of the Red Cow, then of the Rose; and we believe is the same house alluded to in the pleasant story in the second number of the ' Tatler:'—

> "Supper and friends expect we at the Rose."

The Rose, however, was a common sign for houses of public entertainment. The company, of which our poet was

* Dryden, vol. i., p. 203. † Poems on State Affairs, vol. i., p. 99.

the arbiter, sat up-stairs in what was then called the dining,
but now the drawing-room; and there was a balcony, to which
his chair was removed in summer from its prescriptive corner
by the fire-side in winter. " The appeal," says Malcolm,
" was made to him upon every literary dispute. The company did not sit in boxes, as at present, but at various tables
which were dispersed through the room. Smoking was permitted in the public room : it was then so much in vogue that
it does not seem to have been considered a nuisance. Here,
as in other similar places of meeting, the visitors divided
themselves into parties; and we are told by Ward, that the
young beaux and wits, who seldom approached the principal
table, thought it a great honour to have a pinch out of
Dryden's snuff-box." *

A lively specimen of a scene with Dryden in this coffee-
house has been afforded us by Dean Lockier. " I was about
seventeen when I first came up to town," says the Dean, " an
odd-looking boy, with short rough hair, and that sort of
awkwardness which one always brings up at first out of the
country with one. However, in spite of my bashfulness and
appearance, I used, now and then, to thrust myself into Will's,
to have the pleasure of seeing the most celelebrated wits of
that time, who then resorted thither. The second time that
ever I was there, Mr. Dryden was speaking of his own things,
as he frequently did, especially of such as had been lately
published. 'If anything of mine is good,' says he, ' 'tis
" Mac-Flecno;" and I value myself the more upon it, because
it is the first piece of ridicule written in heroics.' On hearing this I plucked up my spirit so far as to say, in a voice
but just loud enough to be heard, ' that " Mac-Flecno " was a
very fine poem, but that I had not imagined it to be the first
that was ever writ that way.' On this, Dryden turned short
upon me, as surprised at my interposing; asked me how long
' I had been a dealer in poetry; and added, with a smile,
' Pray, sir, what is it that you did imagine to have been writ
so before ? ' — I named Boileau's ' Lutrin,' and Tassoni's
' Secchia Rapita,' which I had read, and knew Dryden had
borrowed some strokes from each. ' 'Tis true,' said Dryden,
' I had forgot them.' A little after, Dryden went out, and in
going, spoke to me again, and desired me to come and see
him the next day. I was highly delighted with the invitation;

* Spence's ' Anecdotes,' p. 263.

went to see him accordingly; and was well acquainted with him after, as long as he lived."*

Dryden's mixture of simplicity, good-nature, and good opinion of himself, is here seen in a very agreeable manner. It must not be omitted, that it was to this house Pope was taken when a boy, by his own desire, on purpose to get a sight of the great man; which he did. According to Pope, he was plump, with a fresh colour and a down look, and not very conversable. It appears, however, that what he did say was much to the purpose; and a contemporary mentions his conversation on that account as one of the few things for which the town was desirable. He was a temperate man; though, for the last ten years of his life, Davies informs us that he drank with Addison a great deal more than he used to do, " probably so far as to hasten his end."

It is curious, considering his peculiar sort of reputation with posterity, that Addison's name should be found so connected in his own time with this species of irregularity. The same cause is supposed to have hastened his own end; and it is related by Pope, that he was obliged to avoid the Russell Street Coffee-house, and the bad hours of Addison, otherwise they might have hastened his.

Will's Coffee-house was the great emporium of libels and scandal. The channels that have since abounded for the dregs of literature had scarcely then begun to exist; and, instead of purveying for periodical publications, the retailers of obloquy attended among the minor wits of this place, and distributed the last new lampoon in manuscript. There was a drunken fellow of that time, named Julian, who acquired an infamous celebrity in this way. Sir Walter Scott, in his edition of Dryden, has given the following account of him and his vocation.

" The extremity of license in manners necessarily leads to equal license in personal satire, and there never was an age in which both were carried to such excess as in that of Charles II. These personal and scandalous libels acquired the name of lampoons, from the established burden formerly sung to them:—

> 'Lampone lampone, camerada lampone.'

"Dryden suffered under these violent and invisible assaults, as much as any of his age; to which his own words in several places of his writing, and also the existence of many of the pasquils themselves in the Luttrel Collection, bear ample witness. In many of his prologues and epilogues, he alludes to this rage for personal satire, and

---

* Spence's ' Anecdotes,' p. 59.

to the employment which it found for the half and three-quarter wits
and courtiers of the time!

> 'Yet these are pearls to your lampooning rhymes;
> Ye abuse yourselves more dully than the times;
> Scandal, the glory of the English nation,
> Is worn to rags, and scribbled out of fashion:
> Such harmless thrusts, as if, like fencers wise,
> They had agreed their play before their prize.
> Faith, they may hang their harp upon the willows;
> 'Tis just like children when they box their pillows.'

"Upon the general practice of writing lampoons, and the necessity
of finding some mode of dispersing them, which should diffuse the
scandal widely while the authors remained concealed, was founded
the self-erected office of Julian, Secretary, as he calls himself, to the
Muses. This person attended Will's, the Wits' Coffee-house, as it was
called; and dispersed among the crowds who frequented that place of
gay resort copies of the lampoons which had been privately communicated to him by their authors. 'He is described,' says Mr. Malone,
'as a very drunken fellow, and at one time was confined for a libel.'
Several satires were written, in the form of addresses to him as well
as the following. There is one among the 'State Poems,' beginning—

> 'Julian, in verse, to ease thy wants I write,
> Not moved by envy, malice or by spite,
> Or pleased with the empty names of wit and sense,
> But merely to supply thy want of pence:
> This did inspire my muse, when out at heel,
> She saw her needy secretary reel;
> Grieved that a man, so useful to the age,
> Should foot it in so mean an equipage;
> A crying scandal that the fees of sense
> Should not be able to support the expense
> Of a poor scribe, who never thought of wants,
> When able to procure a cup of Nantz.'

"Another, called a 'Consoling Epistle to Julian,' is said to have been
written by the Duke of Buckingham.

"From a passage in one of the letters from the 'Dead to the Living,'
we learn, that after Julian's death, and the madness of his successor,
called Summerton, lampoon felt a sensible decay; and there was no
more that 'brisk spirit of verse, that used to watch the follies and
vices of the men and women of figure, that they could not start new
ones faster than lampoons exposed them.'"*

These "brisk spirits" have still their descendants, and
always will have till their betters cease to set the example of
railing, or to encourage it. There is a difference, indeed,
between the lampoons of such men and those of Dryden, or
the literary personalities to which some ingenious minds will
give way, before they well know what they are about, out
of mere emulation, perhaps, of the names of Pope and
Boileau. But it is not to be expected that the others will

* Vol. xv., p. 218.

stop where they do, or refine with the progress of their years and knowledge. The most generous sometimes find it difficult to leave off saying ill-natured things of one another, out of shame of yielding, or the habit of indulging their irritability. They endeavour to reconcile themselves to it by trying to think that the abuse has a utility ; but when they come to this point, the doubt is a proof that they ought to forego it, and help to teach the world better. Honest contention, however, is one thing, and scandal is another. The dealer in the latter has always a petty mind and inferior understanding, most likely accompanied with conscious unworthiness ; the great secret of the love of scandal lying in the wish to level others with the calumniators.

"Will's continued to be the resort of the wits at least till 1710," says Mr. Malcolm. "Probably Addison established his servant [Button] in a new house about 1712, and his fame after the production of 'Cato,' drew many of the Whigs thither."*

"Addison," says Pope, "passed each day alike ; and much in the manner that Dryden did. Dryden employed his mornings in writing, dined *en famille*, and then went to Will's : only he came home earlier a'nights." And again : "Addison usually studied all the morning ; then met his party at Button's ; dined, and staid there five or six hours ; and sometimes far into the night. I was of the company for about a year, but found it too much for me: it hurt my health, and so I quitted it."†

Button had been a servant of the Countess of Warwick, whom Addison married. It is said that when the latter was dissatisfied with the Countess (we believe during the period of his courtship), he used to withdraw the company from her servant's coffee-house. Unfortunately it is as easy to believe a petty story of Addison as a careless one of Steele. Addison, intellectually a great man, was complexionally a little one. He was timid, bashful, and reserved, and instinctively sought success by private channels and disingenous measures.

Under the influence of these eminent persons, Button's became the head-quarters of the Whig literati, as Will's had been that of the Tory. Steele, however, dated his poetical papers in the ' Tatler ' from Will's, as the old haunt of the town muse. Perhaps the Whiggery of Button's was one of the reasons why Pope left off going there, as he did not wish to indentify himself with either party. Ambrose Philips is said to have hung up a rod at that coffee-house, as an intimation of what Pope should receive at his hands, in case the

* Spence, p. 263.   † Ibid, p. 286.

satirist chose to hazard it.   A similar threat is related of
Cibber.   The behaviour of both has been cried out against
as unhandsome, considering the little person and bodily infirmities of the illustrious offender : but as the threateners
were so much his inferiors in wit, and he exercised his great
powers at their expense, it might not be difficult to show that
their conduct was as good as his.   Why attack a man, if he
is to be allowed no equality of retaliation ?   The truth is, that
personal satire is itself an unhandsome thing, and a childish
one, and there will be no end to childish retorts, till the more
grown understandings reform.   Pope accused Philips of pilfering his pastorals, and of "turning a Persian tale for half-
a-crown ;" the one an offence not very likely, unless, indeed,
all common-places may be said to be stolen ; the other no
offence at all, though it might have been a misfortune.
These littlenesses in great men are a part of the childhood of
society.   They show us how young it still is, and what a
parcel of wrangling schoolboys (in that respect) a future
period may consider us.

One of the most agreeable memories connected with
Button's is that of Garth, a man whom, for the sprightliness
and generosity of his nature, it is a pleasure to name.   He
was one of the most amiable and intelligent of a most amiable
and intelligent class of men — the physicians.

Armstrong, another poet and physician and not unworthy
of either class, for genius and goodness of heart, though he
had the weakness of affecting a bluntness of manners, and of
swearing, drew his last breath in this street.   He is well
known as the author of the most elegant didactic poem in
the language,—the 'Art of Preserving Health.'   The affectations of men of genius are sometimes in direct contradiction
to their best qualities, and assumed to avoid a show of pretending what they feel.   Armstrong, who had bad health, and
was afraid perhaps of being thought effeminate, affected
the bully in his prose writings ; and he was such a swearer,
that the late Mr. Fuseli's indulgence in that infirmity has
been attributed to his keeping company with the Doctor when
a youth.   We never met with a habitual swearer in whom
the habit could not be traced to some feeling of conscious
weakness.   Fuseli swore as he painted, in the hope of making
up for the defects of his genius by the violence of his style.

At No. 8, Russell Street, Boswell was introduced to his
formidable friend of whom he became the biographer.   The

house then belonged to Davies the bookseller.   The account given us of his first interview is highly characteristic of both parties.   Boswell had a thorough specimen of his future acquaintance at once, and Johnson evidently saw completely through Boswell.

"Mr. Thomas Davies, the actor," saith the particular Boswell, "who then kept a bookseller's shop in Russell Street, Covent Garden, told me that Johnson was very much his friend, and came frequently to his house, where he more than once invited me to meet him; but by some unlucky accident or other he was prevented from coming to us.

"Mr. Thomas Davies was a man of good understanding and talents, with the advantage of a liberal education.   Though somewhat pompous, he was an entertaining companion; and his literary performances have no inconsiderable share of merit.   He was a friendly and very hospitable man.   Both he and his wife (who had been celebrated for her beauty), though upon the stage for many years, maintained an uniform decency of character, and Johnson esteemed them, and lived in as easy an intimacy with them as any family which he used to visit.   Mr. Davies recollected several of Johnson's remarkable sayings, and was one of the best of the many imitators of his voice and manner, while relating them.   He increased my impatience more and more to see the extraordinary man whose works I highly valued, and whose conversation was reported to be so peculiarly excellent.

"At last," continues Mr. Boswell, "on the 16th of May, when I was sitting in Mr. Davies's back parlour, after having drank tea with him and Mrs. Davies, Johnson unexpectdly came into the shop, and Mr. Davies having perceived him through the glass-door in the room in which we were sitting, advancing towards us—he announced his awful approach somewhat as an actor in the part of Horatio, when he addresses Hamlet on the appearance of his father's ghost, 'Look, my lord, it comes.' I found that I had a very perfect idea of Johnson's figure, from the portrait of him painted by Sir Joshua Reynolds soon after he had published his 'Dictionary,' in the attitude of sitting in his easy chair in deep meditation; which was the first picture his friend did for him, which Sir Joshua very kindly presented to me, and from which an engraving has been made for this work. Mr. Davies mentioned my name, and respectfully introduced me to him; I was much agitated, and recollecting his prejudice against the Scotch, of which I had heard much, I said to Davies, 'Don't tell where I come from.'—'From Scotland,' cried Davies, roguishly. 'Mr. Johnson,' said I, 'I do indeed come from Scotland, but I cannot help it.' I am willing to flatter myself that I meant this as light pleasantry to soothe and conciliate him, and not as a humiliating abasement at the expense of my country.   But however that might be, this speech was somewhat unlucky; for with that quickness of wit for which he was so remarkable, he seized the expression 'come from Scotland!' which I used in the sense of being of that country; and, as if I had come away from it, or left it, retorted, 'That, sir, I find, is what a great many of your countrymen cannot help.'   This stroke stunned me a good deal; and when we had sat down, I felt myself not a little embarrassed, and apprehensive of what might come next.   He then addressed him-

Y

self to Davies': 'What do you think of Garrick? he has refused me an order for the play for Miss Williams, because he knows the house will be full, and that an order will be worth three shillings.' Eager to take any opening to get into conversation with him, I ventured to say, 'O, sir, I cannot think Mr. Garrick would grudge such a trifle to you.' 'Sir (said he, with a stern look,) I have known David Garrick longer than you have done; and I know no right you have to talk to me on the subject.' Perhaps I deserved this check; for it was rather presumptuous in me, an entire stranger, to express any doubt of the justice of his animadversion upon his old acquaintance and pupil. I now felt myself much mortified, and began to think that the hope I had long indulged of obtaining his acquaintance was blasted. And, in truth, had not my ardour been uncommonly strong, and my resolution uncommonly persevering, so rough a reception might have deterred me for ever from making any further attempts. Fortunately, however, I remained upon the field, not wholly discomfited." * * * "I was highly pleased with the extraordinary vigour of his conversation, and regretted that I was drawn away from it by an engagement at another place. I had, for a part of the evening, been left alone with him, and had ventured to make an observation now and then, which he received very civilly; so that I was satisfied that, though there was a roughness in his manner, there was no ill-nature in his disposition. Davies followed me to the door, and when I complained to him a little of the hard blows which the great man had given me, he kindly took upon him to console me by saying, 'Don't be uneasy. I can see he likes you very well.'"*

The Hummums Hotel and Coffee-house which occupies the south-west corner of this street, and stretches round into Covent Garden market, is so called from an eastern word signifying baths. It was one of the earliest houses set up in England of that kind, and thence called bagnios; and one of the few that retained their respectability. The generality were so much the reverse, that the word bagnio came to mean a brothel. It appears from a story we are about to relate, that people went to the Hummums not only to bathe, but to get themselves cupped. Bathing is too much neglected in this country; but the consequences of our sedentary habits have forced upon us a greater degree of attention to it, and the imitation of the Turkish system of cleanliness has been carried further in vapour baths and the startling luxury of shampooing, which makes people discover that they have in general two or three skins too many. Englishmen, in the pride of their greater freedom, often wonder how Eastern nations can endure their servitude. This is one of the secrets by which they endure it. A free man in a dirty skin is not in so fit a state to endure existence as a slave with a clean one; because nature insists, that a due attention to the clay which

* Boswell, vol. i., p. 373.

our souls inhabit, shall be the first requisite to the comfort of the inhabitant. Let us not get rid of our freedom; let us teach it rather to those that want it; but let such of us as have them, by all means get rid of our dirty skins. There is now a moral and intellectual commerce among mankind, as well as an interchange of inferior goods; we should send freedom to Turkey as well as clocks and watches, and import not only figs, but a fine state of the pores.

Of the Hummums there is a ghost-story in Boswell, a thing we should as little dream of in this centre of the metropolis, as look for a ghost at noonday. The reader will see how much credit is to be given it, by the style of the narrator, who, with all his good-will towards superstition (and it is no less a person that speaks than Dr. Johnson), had an inveterate love of truth, which led him to defeat his own object.

"Amongst the numerous prints," says Boswell. "pasted on the walls of the dining-room at Streatham, was 'Hogarth's Modern Midnight Conversation.' I asked him what he knew of Parson Ford, who makes a conspicuous figure in the riotous group. *Johnson.* 'Sir, he was my acquaintance and relation,—my mother's nephew. He had purchased a living in the country, but not simoniacally. I never saw him but in the country. I have been told that he was a man of great parts, very profligate, but I never heard he was impious.' *Boswell.* 'Was there not a story of his ghost having appeared?' *Johnson.* 'Sir, it was believed. A waiter at the Hummums, in which house Ford died, had been absent some time, and returned, not knowing that Ford was dead. Going down to the cellar, according to the story, he met him; going down again he met him a second time. When he came up, he asked some people of the house what Ford could be doing there. They told him Ford was dead. The waiter took a fever, in which he lay for some time. When he recovered he said he had a message to deliver to some women from Ford; but he was not to tell what, or to whom. He walked out; he was followed; but somewhere about St. Paul's they lost him. He came back, and said he had delivered the message, and the women exclaimed, 'Then we are all undone!' Dr. Pellett, who was not a credulous man, inquired into the truth of this story, and he said, the evidence was irresistible. My wife went to the Hummums (it is a place where people get themselves cupped). I believe she went with intention to hear about this story of Ford. At first they were unwilling to tell her; but after they had talked to her, she came away satisfied that it was true. To be sure the man had a fever; and this vision may have been the beginning of it. But if the message to the women, and their behaviour upon it, were true as related, there was something supernatural. That rests upon his word: and there it remains.' "*

At the beginning of the reign of Elizabeth, Covent Garden (or, as it would be more properly spelt, *Convent* Garden†)

* Boswell, vol. iii., p. 378.
† It is still so called by many of the poorer orders, who are oftener

extended from Drury Lane to St. Martin's Lane, and was
surrounded by a brick wall. It had lately belonged to the
abbots of Westminster, whom it supplied, doubtless, with
fruit and vegetables, as it has since done the metropolis, and
hence its appellation. The reader will see it in the old print
of London by Aggas. There was a break into it on the
south-west, made by the garden of Bedford House, which stood
facing the Strand between the present Bedford and Southampton Streets. On the dissolution of the monasteries, Covent
Garden was given to the Duke of Somerset, and on his fall, to
John, Earl of Bedford, whose family converted it into a
pasture ground, including Long Acre, then part of the fields
leading to St. Giles's. His descendant Francis, about seventy
years afterwards, let the whole pasture on a building lease,
and built the old church for the intended inhabitants. The
architect was Inigo Jones. To the same hand we are indebted
for the portico of the north-eastern quarter, which still
remains. There was a continuation of it on the south-east,
which was burnt down. It was to have been carried all round
the square, and the absence of it might be regretted on the
score of beauty ; but porticoes are not fit for this climate,
unless where the object is to furnish a walk during the rain.
Covered walks devoted to that purpose, and conveniently distributed, might be temptations to out-of-door exercise in bad
weather. If they succeeded, they would effect a very desirable end. But covered walks, however beautiful, which are
not used in that way, are rather to be deprecated in this cold
and humid climate. In Italy, where the summer sun at
noon-day burns like a cauldron, they are much to the purpose ; but the more sun we can get in England the better.
Luckily, there is a convenience in this portico, as far as the
theatre is concerned ; otherwise the circuit would be more
agreeable without it, and the coffee-houses of the place more
light and cheerful.

Of the style of building observed in the church there is a
well-known story. " The Earl is said to have told Inigo
Jones he wished to have as plain and convenient a structure
as possible, and but little better than a barn ; to which the
architect replied, he would build a barn, but that it should
be the handsomest in England."*

in the right in their old English than is suspected. Some of them call
it Common Garden, which is a better corruption than its present one.

* Londinium Redivivum, vol. iv., p. 213.

Inigo Jones's church was burnt down in the year 1795, owing to the carelessness of some plumbers who were mending the roof. " When the flames were at their height," says Malcolm, " the portico and massy pillars made a grand scene, projected before a back-ground of liquid fire, which raged with so much uncontrolled fury, that not a fragment of wood, in or near the walls, escaped destruction."*

INIGO JONES'S CHURCH, AND OLD COVENT GARDEN.

The barn-like taste, or in other words the Grecian (for usefulness and simplicity are the secrets of it, and the Temple of Theseus and a common barn have the same principles of structure), was copied in the new edifice. By a passage quoted in the *Londinium Redivium* from the *Weekly Journal* of April 22, 1727, it appears that the portico of the old church had been altered by the inhabitants, and restored by the Earl of Burlington, " out of regard to the memory of the celebrated Inigo Jones, and to prevent our countrymen being exposed for their ignorance." The spirit of this portico has been retained, and the church of St. Paul's Covent garden is one of the most pleasing structures in the metropolis.

A great many actors have been buried in this spot; among them, Eastcourt the famous mimic, Edwin, Macklin, and King. We shall speak of one or two of them presently, but it is desirable, especially in a work of this kind, to observe a chronological order. The mere observance itself conveys in-

* Londinium Redivivum, vol. iv., p. 219.

formation. Among the variety of persons buried here may be mentioned, first:

Car, Earl of Somerset, in the old church. His burial in Covent Garden was, doubtless, owing to his connection with the family of Russell, his daughter having married William, afterwards Earl and Duke of Bedford, father of the famous patriot. It is said that his lady was bred up in such ignorance of the dishonour of her parents, that having met by accident with a book giving an account of it, she fainted away, and was found in that condition by her domestics. Her lover's family were very averse to the match, but wisely allowed it upon due trial, and had no reason to repent their generosity. To read the history of the foolish and unprincipled Countess of Somerset, who would suppose that her daughter was to give birth to the conscientious martyr for liberty? But the blood which folly makes wicked, a good education may render noble.

Butler in the church-yard. The popular notion that he was starved is unfounded ; but he was very ill-treated by a court whom his wit materially served. It is said that Charles, once and away, gave him a hundred pounds. This is possible ; but it is at least as possible that he gave him nothing, though he would willingly have done it, perhaps, had his debaucheries left him the means. Charles, in his way, was as poor as Butler, though not as honourably so, for it does not appear that the poet was unwilling to labour for his subsistence. There is a mystery, however, in Butler's private affairs. He once appears to have had some office in the family of the Countess of Kent. Perhaps he was not a very good man of business, though the learning exhibited in ' Hudibras' showed how he could work on a favourite subject. When men succeed to this extent in what nature evidently designs them for, great allowance is to be made for their disinclination to other tasks ; and Butler had no children to render the neglect of his fortune criminal. The Duke of Buckingham, who once undertook to "do something for him," and had a meeting for the purpose at a coffee-house, saw a pander of his go by the window with a " brace of ladies," and going after him, we hear no more of his Grace. Luckily, to prevent him from starvation, Butler found a friend in the excellent Mr. Longueville of the Temple, a scholar and a real gentleman, who did not confine his generosity to an admiration of him in books. The poet is understood to have been indebted to him for support during the latter part of his life ; and it was he who buried him in this church-yard. It is to Mr. Longueville that we are indebted for the publication of Butler's " Remains," which are quite worthy of the wit of " Hudibras," and deserve to be more generally known. Butler was the greatest wit that ever wrote in verse; perhaps the greatest that ever wrote at all, meaning by wit the union of remote ideas. He was undoubtedly the most learned. His political poem is out of date ; and much of the humour that delighted the cavaliers must, of necessity, be lost to us ; but passages of it will always be repeated ; and it is difficult to hear his name mentioned, without quoting some of his rhymes. He was the first man that gave rhyme itself an air of wit. His couplets are not only witty themselves, but seem to add a new idea to their imagery in the very sounds at the end of them. His startling turns of thought are accompanied by as surprising a turn in the cadence, as if the echo itself could not help laughing. Thus his doctor's shop is

> "—— stored with deletery medicines,
> Which whosoever took is dead since : "

his sour religionists

> " Compound for sins they are inclined to,
> By damning those they have no mind to : "

and again,

> " Synods are mystical bear-gardens,
> Where elders, deputies, church-wardens,
> And other members of the court,
> Manage the Babylonish sport;
> For prolocutor, scribe, and bear-ward,
> Do differ only in a mere word:
> Both are but several synagogues
> Of carnal men, and bears, and dogs;
> Both antichristian assemblies
> To mischief bent, as far 's in them lies."

His most quoted rhyme, when

> " —— Pulpit, drum ecclesiastic,
> Was beat with fist instead of a stick,

is, singularly enough, no rhyme at all ; but the surprise of the echo, and the truth conveyed in it, affect us as if it were perfect. Here are one or two more of the wilful order, very ludicrous : —

> " —— The captive knight
> And pensive squire, both bruised in body
> And conjured into safe custody.

> ——— in all the fabrick
> You could not see one stone or a brick.
>
> Who deals in destiny's dark counsels,
> And sage opinions of the moon sells.
>
> Those wholesale critics that in coffee-
> Houses cry down all philosophy."

Mrs. Pilkington tells us that Swift took down a "Hudibras"
one day, and ordered her to examine him in the book, when,
to her great suprise, she found he remembered " every line,
from beginning to end of it."* Mrs. Pilkington is a lady whose
word is to be taken *cum multis granis ;* nor is it very likely
she should ever have heard the Dean repeat a whole volume
through ; but if Swift knew any author entire, Butler is
likely to have been the man.   Butler had the same politics,
the same love of learning, the same wit, the same apparent
contempt of mankind, the same charity underneath it, and
the same impatient wish to see them wiser.   His style of
writing is evidently the origin of Swift's.   If the reader is
not yet acquainted with his ' Remains,' the following sample
or two will give him a desire to be so : —

> " The truest characters of ignorance
> Are vanity, and pride, and arrogance ;
> As blind men use to bear their noses higher,
> Than those who have their eyes and sight intire."
> *   *   *   *   *

> " There needs no other charm, nor conjuror,
> To raise infernal spirits up, but fear ;
> That makes men pull their horns in like a snail,
> That 's both a prisoner to itself, and jail ;
> Draws more fantastic shapes than in the grains
> Of knotted wood, in some men's crazy brains,
> When all the cocks they think they see, and bulls,
> Are only in the inside of their skulls."

Sir Peter Lely, the painter of the meretricious beauties
of the court of Charles II.—Pope's couplet on him is well
known : —

> " Lely on animated canvass stole
> The sleepy eye that spoke the melting soul."

The canvass is more sleepy than animated, and the ladies
more like what they were in inclination than in features.
However, there is a great likeness on that very account.
They are all of a sisterhood ;—*qualem* non *decet esse sororum.*
A master of pictorial criticism has said of the collection of
them at Windsor Castle, that " they look just like what they

* Memoirs of Mrs. Letitia Pilkington. Dublin, 1748, vol. i., p. 136.

were, a set of kept-mistresses, painted, tawdry, showing off their theatrical or meretricious airs and graces, without one trace of real elegance or refinement, or one spark of sentiment to touch the heart. Lady Grammont is the handsomest of them ; and though the most voluptuous in her attire and attitude, the most decent. The Duchess of Portsmouth (Cleveland), in her helmet and plumes, looks quite like a heroine of romance, or modern Amazon ; but for an air of easy assurance, inviting admiration, and alarmed at nothing but being thought coy, commend us to my Lady—— above, in the sky-blue drapery, thrown carelessly over her shoulders. As paintings, these celebrated portraits cannot rank very high. They have an affected ease, but a real hardness of manner and execution ; and they have that contortion of attitude and setness of features, which we afterwards find carried to so disgusting and insipid an excess in Kneller's portraits. Sir Peter Lely was, however, a better painter than Sir Godfrey Kneller—that is the highest praise that can be accorded to him. He had more spirit, more originalty, and was the livelier coxcomb of the two! Both these painters possessed considerable mechanical dexterity, but it is not of a refined kind. Neither of them could be ranked among great painters, yet they were thought by their contemporaries and themselves superior to every one. At the distance of a hundred years we see the thing plainly enough." * Sir Peter was a Westphalian, of a family named Vander Vaas. His father was an officer in the army, who, having been born in a perfumer's house which had a lily for its sign, got the name of Captain Du Lys, or Lely, and the cognomen was retained by his son. He aimed at magnificence in his style of living, probably in imitation of his predecessor at the English court, Vandyke ; but there was a certain coarseness about him which showed the inferiority of his taste in that particular, as well as in the rest.

Wycherly in the Church. See Bow Street.

Southern, one of those dramatic writers who, without much genius, succeed in obtaining a considerable name, and justly, by dint of genuine feeling for common nature. He began in Dryden's time, who knew and respected his talents, was known and respected by Pope, and lived to enjoy a similar regard from Gray. "I remember," says Oldys, "this venerable old gentleman, when he lived in Covent Garden, and used to

* Hazlitt's 'Picture Galleries of England,' p. 80.

frequent the evening prayers in the church there. He was always neat and decently dressed, commonly in black, with his silver sword, and silver locks." Gray, in a letter to Walpole, dated Burnham, in Buckinghamshire, 1737, says, "We have old Mr. Southern at a gentleman's house, a little way off, who often comes to see us; he is now seventy-seven years old, and has almost wholly lost his memory; but is as agreeable an old man as can be; at least I persuade myself so when I look at him, and think of Isabella and Oroonoko." Southern died about nine years after this period, aged about eighty-five. With all the respect he obtained, probably a great deal more by the decency and civility of his habits than by his genius, Southern, it appears, was not above making application to the nobility and others to buy tickets for his plays.

Joe Haines, the comedian. See Drury Lane.

Eastcourt, the comedian—or mimic, rather—for, like most players who devote themselves to mimicry, which is a kind of caricature portrait-painting, his comedy or general humour was inferior to it. He was, however, a man of wit as well as a mimic; and, in spite of a talent which seldom renders men favourites in private, was so much regarded, that, when the Beef-steak Club was set up (which a late author says must not be confounded with the Beef-steak Club held in Covent Garden Theatre and the Lyceum), Eastcourt was appointed *provveditore* or *caterer*, and presented as a badge of distinction with a small gridiron of gold, which he wore about his neck fastened to a green ribbon. He is said at one time to have been a tavern-keeper, in which quality (unless it was in the other) Parnell speaks of him in the beginning of one of his poems:—

> Gay Bacchus liking Estcourt's wine
> A noble meal bespoke us,
> And for the guests that were to dine
> Brought Comus, Love, and Jocus.*

---

* The best account we are acquainted with of the various Beef-steak Clubs has been given us by the good-humoured author of 'Wine and Walnuts.' His book is an antiquarian fiction, but not entirely such; and the present account, among others, may be taken as fact. George Lambert, Rich's scene-painter at Covent Garden, says he, "being a man of wit, and of repute as an artist, was frequently visited by persons of note while at his work in the scene-room. In those days it was customary for men of fashion to visit the green-room, and to indulge in a morning lounge behind the curtain of the theatre. Lambert, when preparing his designs for a pantomime or new spectacle

But his greatest honour is the following remarkable testimony borne to his merits by Sir Richard Steele, whose own fineness of nature was never more beautifully evinced in any part of his writings :—

"Poor Eastcourt! the last time I saw him we were plotting to show the town his great capacity for acting in his full light, by introducing

(for which exhibitions the manager, Rich, was much renowned), would often take his chop or steak cooked on the German stove, rather than quit his occupation for the superior accommodation of a neighbouring tavern. Certain of his visitors, men of taste, struck with the novelty of the thing perhaps, or tempted by the savoury dish, took a knife and fork with Lambert, and enjoyed the treat. Hence the origin of the Beef-steak Club, whose social feasts were long held in the painting-room of this theatre, which, from its commencement, has enrolled among its members persons of the highest rank and fortune, and many eminent professional men and distinguished wits. The Club subsequently met in an apartment of the late theatre ; then it moved to the Shakspeare Tavern; thence again to the theatre; until, being burnt out in 1812, the meetings adjourned to the Bedford. At present the celebrated convives assemble at an apartment at the English Opera House in the Strand.

"At the same time this social club flourished in England, and about the year 1749, a Beef-steak Club was established at the Theatre Royal, Dublin, of which the celebrated Mrs. Margaret Woffington was president. It was begun by Mr. Sheridan, but on a very different plan to that in London, no theatrical performer, save one *female*, being admitted; and though called a Club, the manager alone bore all the expenses. The plan was, by making a list of about fifty or sixty persons, chiefly noblemen and members of Parliament, who were invited. Usually about half that number attended, and dined in the manager's apartment in the theatre. There was no female admitted but this *Peg Woffington*, so denominated by all her contemporaries, who was seated in a great chair at the head of the table, and elected president for the season.

"'It will readily be believed,' says Mr. Victor, who was joint proprietor of the house. 'that a club where there were good accommodations, such a *lovely president*, full of wit and spirit, and *nothing to pay*, must soon grow remarkably fashionable.' It did so—but we find it subsequently caused the theatre to be pulled to pieces about the manager's head.

"Mr. Victor says of Mrs. Margaret, 'she possessed captivating charms as a jovial, witty bottle companion, but few remaining as a mere female.' We have Dr. Johnson's testimony, however, who had often gossipped with Mrs. Margaret in the green-room at old Drury, more in the lady's favour.

"This author (Victor) says, speaking of the Beaf-steak Club, 'It was a club of ancient institution in every theatre; when the principal performers dined one day in the week together (generally Saturday), and authors and other geniuses were admitted members.'

"The *club* in Ivy Lane, celebrated by Dr. Johnson, was originally a *Beef-steak.*"

him as dictating to a set of young players, in what manner to speak this sentence and utter t'other passion. He had so exquisite a discerning of what was defective in any object before him, that in an instant he could shew you the ridiculous side of what would pass for beautiful and just, even to men of no ill judgment, before he had pointed at the failure. He was no less skilful in the knowledge of beauty; and, I dare say, there is no one who knew him well, but can repeat more well-turned compliments, as well as smart repartees of Mr. Eastcourt's, than of any other man in England. This was easily to be observed in his inimitable faculty of telling a story, in which he would throw in natural and unexpected incidents to make his court to one part, and rally the other part of the company. Then he would vary the usage he gave them, according as he saw them bear kind or sharp language. He had the knack to raise up a pensive temper and mortify an impertinently gay one, as he saw them bear kind or sharp language.

"It is an insolence natural to the wealthy, to affix, as much as in them lies, the character of a man to his circumstances. Thus it is ordinary with them to praise faintly the good qualities of those below them, and say, it is very extraordinary in such a man as he is, or the like, when they are forced to acknowledge the value of him whose lowness upbraids their exaltation. It is to this humour only that it is to be ascribed, that a quick wit in conversation, a nice judgment upon any emergency that could arise, and a most blameless inoffensive behaviour, could not raise this man above being received only upon the foot of contributing to mirth and diversion. But he was as easy under that condition as a man of so excellent talents was capable; and since they would have it that to divert was his business, he did it with all the seeming alacrity imaginable, though it stung him to the heart that it was his business. Men of sense, who could taste his excellencies, were well satisfied to let him lead the way in conversation, and play after his own manner; but fools, who provoked him to mimicry, found he had the indignation to let it be at their expense who called for it; and he would show the form of conceited heavy fellows as jests to the company at their own request, in revenge for interrupting him from being a companion, to put on the character of a jester.

"What was peculiarly excellent in this memorable companion was, that in the accounts he gave of persons and sentiments, he did not only hit the figure of their faces, and manner of their gestures, but he would in his narration fall into their very way of thinking, and this when he recounted passages wherein men of the best wit were concerned, as well as such wherein were represented men of the lowest rank of understanding. It is certainly as great an instance of self-love to a weakness, to be impatient of being mimicked, as any can be imagined. There were none but the vain, the formal, the proud, or those who were incapable of mending their faults, that dreaded him; to others he was in the highest degree pleasing, and I do not know any satisfaction of any indifferent kind I ever tasted so much as having got over an impatience of seeing myself in the air he could put me when I have displeased him. *It is indeed to his exquisite talent this way, more than any philosophy I could read on the subject, that my person is very little of my care; and it is indifferent to me what is said of my shape, my air, my manner, my speech, or my address. It is to poor East-*

court I chiefly owe that I am arrived at the happiness of thinking nothing a diminution to me, BUT WHAT ARGUES A DEPRAVITY OF MY WILL.

"I have been present with him among men of the most delicate taste a whole night, and have known him (for he saw it was desired) keep the discourse to himself the most part of it, and maintain his good humour with a countenance and in a language so delightful, without offence to any person or thing upon earth, still preserving the distance his circumstances obliged him to; I say, I have seen him do all this in such a charming manner, that I am sure none of those I hint at will read this without giving him some sorrow for their abundant mirth, and one gush of tears for so many bursts of laughter I wish it were any honour to the pleasant creature's memory that my eyes are too much suffused to let me go on."*

Closterman in the church-yard. He was an indifferent, but once popular artist, whom we mention on account of his painful domestic end. He had a mistress, whom he thought devoted to him. She robbed him of everything she could lay her hands on, money, plate, jewels, and moveables, and fled out of the kingdom. He pined away with an impaired understanding, and was soon brought to the grave. Closterman was once set in competition with Sir Godfrey Kneller. He painted the family of the Duke of Marlborough, and had so many disputes about the picture with the Duchess, that Marlborough said to him, "It has given me more trouble to reconcile my wife and you, than to fight a battle."

Arne, the celebrated musician, in the church-yard. See King Street.

Sir Robert Strange, the greatest engraver, perhaps, this country has seen; that is to say, supposing the merits of an engraver to be in proportion to his relish for and imitation of his originals. Other men may have drawn a finer mechanical line, but none have surpassed Strange in giving the proper diversity of surfaces, or equalled him in transferring to hard copper the roundness and delicacy of flesh. His engravings from Titian almost convey something of the colours of that great painter. Like all true masters, Strange took pains with whatever he did, and bestowed attention on every part of it; so much indeed, that his love for his art appears to have been an exhausting one, and he was anxious to keep the burin out of the hands of his children. He had seen a great deal of the world, and was a very amiable as well as intelligent man. When young he was a great Jacobite, and fought sword-in-hand for the Pretender; though it is said that a main cause of his ardour was the hope of attaining the hand of a fair friend,

* From a paper of Steele's in the 'Spectator,' No. 468.

equally devoted to the cause. It is pleasant to add, that he did attain it, and that she made him a good wife. Sir Robert was a Scotchman of a good family ; but his knighthood came from George the Third, a few years before the artist's death.

Macklin, the comedian, in the church-yard, at the age of one hundred and seven, and upwards. We have spoken of him before in his stage character. His long age in the midst of cities and theatres is very remarkable. It seems to have been owing to the inheritance of a robust constitution—the great cause of longevity next to temperance, perhaps the greatest, unless contradicted by the reverse. Most persons who have been long-lived have had long-lived progenitors; but somebody must begin. The foundation is always temperance. Macklin must have been very lucky in his physical advantages, for he did not keep any very strict rein over his temper; nor does he appear to have followed any regimen, till latterly, and then he consulted the immediate ease of his stomach, and not the quality of what he took. However, his habits, whatever they were, were most likely regular. "It had been his constant rule," says his biographer, "for a period of thirty years and upwards, to visit a public-house called the Antelope, in White Hart Yard, Covent Garden, where his usual beverage was a pint of beer called *stout*, which was made hot and sweetened with moist sugar, almost to a syrup. This, he said, balmed his stomach, and kept him from having any inward pains."* The same writer, in a report of a conversation he had with Mr. Macklin, has left us an affecting but not unpleasing picture of the decay of faculties, remarkable to the very last for their shrewdness and vivacity. It is the liveliest picture of old mortality we ever met with.

Question. "Well, Mr. Macklin, how do you do to-day ?"
Answer. "Why, I hardly know, sir ; I think I am a little better than I was in the morning."
Q. "Why, sir, did you feel any pain in the morning ?"
A. "Yes, sir, a good deal."
Q. "In what part ?"
A. "Why, I feel a sort of a—a—a—" (shaking his head), "I forget everything ; I forget the word : I felt a kind of pain here" (putting his hand upon his left breast),—"but it is gone away, and I am better now."
Q. "How do you sleep, sir ?"
A. "Not so well as I could wish ; I am becoming more wakeful

---

* Memoirs of the Life of Charles Macklin, Esq., &c., by James Thomas Kirkman, vol. ii., p. 419.

than usual; I awoke last night two or three times: I got up twice, walked about my room here, and then went to bed again."

Q. "Do you always get up when you awake, sir?"

A. "No, sir, not always; but I get up and walk about as soon as I feel myself—there, now, it is all gone" (putting his hand upon his forehead).

Q. "You get up, sir, I suppose, as soon as you feel yourself uneasy in bed?"

A. "Yes, sir, when I begin to be troublesome to myself."

Q. "Do not you, sir, find it unpleasant to walk about here alone, and to have nobody to converse with?"

A. "Not at all, sir, I get up when I am tired abed, and I walk about till I am tired, and then I go to bed again; and so forth."

Q. "But does it not afford you great pleasure when any person comes to see you?"

A. "Why, not so much as one would expect, sir."

Q. "Are you not pleased when your friends come and converse with you?"

A. "I am always very happy to see my friends, and I should be very happy to hold a—a—a, see there now . . . . ."

Q. "A conversation you mean, sir?"

A. "Ay, a conversation. Alas! sir, you see the wretched state of my memory—see there now, I could not recollect that common word—but I cannot converse. I used to go to a house very near this where my friends assemble . . . . it was a—a—a [a company] no, that's not the word, a—a—club, I mean. I was the father of it, but I could not hear all; and what I did hear, I did not—a—a—under—under—understand; they were all very attentive to me, but I could ot be one of them. I always feel an uneasiness, when I don't know what the people are talking about. Indeed, I found, sir, that I was not fit to keep company—so I stay away."

Q. "Have you been reading this morning, sir?"

A. "Yes, sir."

Q. "What book?"

A. "I forget:—here, look at it;"—handing the book.

Q. "I see, it is Milton's 'Paradise Lost.'"

[He then took the book out of my hand and said:—"I have only read this much" (about four pages) "these two days—but what I read yesterday, I have forgot to-day." He next read a few lines of the beginning inimitably well, and laying down the book, said] "I understand all that, but if I read any farther, I forget that passage which I understood before."

Q. "But I perceive with satisfaction, sir, that your sight is very good."

A. "Oh, sir, my sight, like everything else, begins to fail too; about two days ago I felt—a—a—there now . . . . I have lost it—a pain just above my left eye, and heard something give a crack, and ever since, this eye (pointing to the left) has been painful."

Q. "I think, sir, it would be advisable for you to refrain from reading a little time."

A. "I believe you are in the right, sir."

Q. "I think you appear at present free from pain?"

A. "Yes, sir, I am pretty comfortable now: but I find my—my—my strength is all gone. I feel myself going gradually."

Q. " But you are not afraid to die ?"

A. " Not in the least, sir—I never did any person any serious mis-chief in my life :—even when I gambled, I never cheated :—I know that a—a—a—see, now—death, I mean, must come, and I am ready to give it up" (meaning the ghost).

Q. " I understand you were at Drury Lane theatre last night ?"

A. " Yes, sir, I was there."

Q. " Yes, sir, the newspapers of this morning take notice of it."

A. " Do they ?"

Y. " Yes, sir ;—the paragraph runs thus :—' Among the numerous visitors at Drury Lane Theatre last night, we observed the Duke of Queensbury and the veteran Macklin, whose ages together amount to one hundred and ninety-six."

Mr. Macklin. " The Duke of who ?"

A. " The Duke of Queensbury, sir."

Mr. Macklin. " I don't know that man. The Duke of Queensbury! The Duke of Queensbury! Oh! ay, I remember him now very well : —The Duke of Queensbury old! Why, sir, I might be his father! ha! ha! ha!"

Q. " Well, sir, I understand that you went to the Haymarket Theatre to see the ' Merchant of Venice ?' "

A. " I did, sir."

Q. " What is your opinion of Mr. Palmer's Shylock ?"

[This question was answered by a shake of the head. Being de-sirous of hearing his opinion I asked him the second time.]

Mr. Macklin.—" Why, sir, my opinion is, that Mr. Palmer played the character of Shylock in *one style*. In this scene there was a sameness, in that scene a sameness, and in every scene a sameness : it was all same! same! same!—no variation. He did not look the character, nor laugh the character, nor speak the character of Shaks-peare's Jew. In the trial scene, where he comes to cut the pound of flesh, he was no Jew. Indeed, sir, he did *not hit* the *part*, nor the *part* did *not hit* him."*

This conversation took place in September 1796 : in July 1797 he died.

Dr. Walcot, better known by the name of Peter Pindar. He was a coarse and virulent satirist, and content to write so many common-places, that they will stifle his works with posterity, with the exception of a few pieces. His humour, however, was genuine of its kind. His caricatures are strik-ing likenesses ; and the innocent simplicity which he is fond of affecting makes a ludicrous contrast with his impudence. Dr. Walcot's largest poems are worth little, and his serious worth nothing. What we think likely to last in the collec-tions, are his " Bozzy and Piozzi," his ' Royal visit to Whitbread's Brewhouse,' one or two more of that stamp, some of his " Odes to Academicians," and the immortal

* Memoirs of the Life of Charles Macklin, Esq., by James Thomas Kirkman, vol. ii., p. 416.

"Pilgrims and the Peas," the hero of which is assuredly hobbling to this day, and will never arrive. Dr. Walcot was a man of taste in the fine arts, and produced some landscapes, which we believe do credit to his pencil. We have never seen them. His critical good taste is not to be disputed, though the Academicians, at one time, would have given a great deal to find it wanting. He was latterly blind, but maintained his spirits to the last. He had a fine skull, which he was not displeased to be called upon to exhibit, taking his wig off, and saying "There," with a lusty voice; which formed a singular contrast with the pathos attached to the look of blind eyes.

Covent Garden market has always been the most agreeable in the metropolis, because it is devoted exclusively to fruit, flowers, and vegetables. A few crockery-ware shops make no exceptions to this "bloodless" character. The seasons here regularly present themselves in their most gifted looks, — with evergreens in winter, the fresh verdure of spring, all the hues of summer, and whole loads of desserts in autumn. The country girls who bring the things to market at early dawn are a sight themselves worthy of the apples and roses; the good-natured Irish women who attend to carry baskets for purchasers are not to be despised, with the half-humorous, half pathetic tone of their petitions to be employed; and the ladies who come to purchase, crown all. No walk in London, on a fine summer's day, is more ageeeable than the passage through the flowers here at noon, when the roses and green leaves are newly watered, and blooming faces come to look at them in those cool and shady avenues, while the hot sun is basking in the streets. On these occasions we were very well satisfied with the market in its old state. The old sheds, and irregular avenues, when dry, assorted well with the presence of leaves and fruits. They had a careless picturesque look, as if a bit of an old suburban garden had survived from ancient times.

Nothing, however, but approbation can be bestowed on the convenient and elegant state into which the market has been raised by the magnificence of the noble proprietor, whose arms we are glad to see on the side next James Street. They are a real grace to the building and to the owner, for they are a stamp of liberality. In time we hope to see the roofs of the new market covered with shrubs and flowers, nodding over the balustrades, and fruits and red berries sparkling in

z

the sun.* As an ornament, nothing is more beautiful in combination than the fluctuating grace of foliage and the stability of architecture. And, as a utility, the more air and sun the better. There is never too much sun in this country, and every occasion should be seized to take advantage of it.

The space between the church and the market is the scene of Hogarth's picture of the 'Frosty Morning.' Here in general take place the elections for Westminster. Sheridan has poured forth his good things in this spot, and Charles Fox won the hearts of multitudes. It would be an endless task to trace the recollections connected with the coffee-houses under the portico. Perhaps there is not a name of celebrity in the annals of wit or the stage, between the reigns of Charles II. and the present sovereign, which might not be found concerned in the clubs or other meetings which they have witnessed, particularly those of Garrick, Hogarth, and their contemporaries. *Sir Roger de Coverley* has been there, a person more real to us than nine-tenths of them. When in town he lodged in Bow Street.

Opposite the Bedford Coffee-house a tragical scene took place, the particulars of which are interesting. The Earl of Sandwich, grandson of Charles II.'s Earl of Sandwich, and first Lord of the Admiralty during the North administration, had for his mistress a Miss Ray, whom he had rendered as accomplished as she was handsome. Some say that she was the daughter of a labourer at Elstree, others of a stay-maker in Covent Garden. Her father is said to have had a shop in that way of business in Holywell Street in the Strand. Miss Ray was apprenticed at an early age to a mantua-maker in Clerkenwell Close, with whom she served her time out and obtained a character that did her honour. A year or two after the expiration of this period she was taken notice of by Lord Sandwich, who gave her a liberal education; rendered her a proficient in his favourite arts of music and singing; and made her his mistress. He was old enough to be her father.

Lord Sandwich was in the habit of having plays and music at his house, particularly the latter. At Christmas the musical performance was an oratorio, for, "to speak seriously," says Mr. Cradock, "no man was more careful than Lord Sandwich not to trespass on public decorum." This gentleman, in his

* A few days after writing this passage, we saw the shrubs making their appearance.

Memoirs, has furnished us with accounts which will give a livelier idea of the situation of Miss Ray in his Lordship's house than any formal abstract of them.

"Plays at Hinchinbrook had ceased before I had ever been in company with Lord Sandwich, and oratorios for a week at Christmas had been substituted. Miss Ray, who was the first attraction, was instructed in music both by Mr. Bates and Signor Giardini. Norris and Champness regularly attended the meetings, and there were many excellent amateur performers; the Duke of Manchester's military band assisted, and his Lordship himself took the kettle-drums to animate the whole. 'Non nobis, Domine,' was sung after dinner, and then catches and glees succeeded; all was well conducted, for whatever his Lordship undertook he generally accomplished, and seemed to have adopted the emphatic advice of Longinus, 'always to excel.' Miss Ray, in her situation, was a pattern of discretion; for when a lady of rank, between one of the acts of the oratorio, advanced to converse with her, she expressed her embarrassment; and Lord Sandwich, turning privately to a friend, said, 'As you are well acquainted with that lady, I wish you would give her a hint, that there is a boundary line in my family I do not wish to see exceeded; such a trespass might occasion the overthrow of all our music meetings.'

"From what I have collected, Miss Ray was born in Hertfordshire, in 1742, and that his lordship first saw her in a shop in Tavistock Street where he was purchasing some neckcloths. This was all that Mr. Bates seemed to have ascertained, for both his lordship and the lady were equally cautious of communicating anything on the subject. From that time her education was particularly attended to, and she proved worthy of all the pains that were taken with her. Her voice was powerful and pleasing, and she has never been excelled in that fine air of Jephtha, 'Brighter scenes I seek above;' nor was she less admired when she executed an Italian bravura of the most difficult description."*

Again:—"I did not know his lordship in early life; but this I can attest, and call any contemporary to ratify who might have been present, that we never heard an oath, or the least profligate conversation at his lordship's table in our lives. Miss Ray's behaviour was particularly circumspect. Dr. Green, Bishop of Lincoln, always said, 'I never knew so cautious a man as Lord Sandwich.' The Bishop came too soon once to an oratorio; we went to receive him in the dining-room, but he said, 'No; the drawing-room is full of company, and I will go up and take tea there.' Lord Sandwich was embarrassed, as he had previously objected to Lady Blake speaking to Miss Ray between the acts; and as the Bishop would go up, a consequence ensued just as I expected. Some severe verses were sent, which Mr. Bates intercepted. * * * * *

"The elegant Mrs. Hinchcliffe, lady of the Bishop, attended one night with a party. She had never seen Miss Ray before, and she feelingly remarked afterwards, 'I was really hurt to sit directly opposite to her, and mark her discreet conduct, and yet to find it improper to notice her. She was so assiduous to please, was so very

* Literary and Miscellaneous Memoirs, by J. Cradock, Esq., M.A., F.S.A., vol. i., p. 117.

excellent, yet so unassuming, I was quite charmed with her; yet a seeming cruelty to her took off the pleasure of my evening.'"*

While Miss Ray was thus situated, his lordship, through the medium of a neighbour, Major Reynolds, became acquainted with a brother officer of the major's, a Captain Hackman, and invited him to his house. The Captain fell in love with Miss Ray, and Miss Ray is understood not to have been insensible to his passion. He was her junior by several years, though the disparity was nothing like the reverse one on the part of Lord Sandwich. Sir Herbert Croft, who wrote a history of their intimacy and correspondence, under the title of "Love and Madness," represents the attachment as mutual. According to his statement, Hackman urged her to marry him, and Miss Ray was desirous of doing so, but fearful of hurting the feelings of the man who had educated her, and who is represented as a sort of Old Robin Gray. In this sentiment, Hackman with all his passion is represented as partaking. Sir Herbert's book, though founded on fact, and probably containing more truth than can now be ascertained, is considered apocryphal; and Mr. Cradock, who is as cautious in his way as his noble acquaintance, doubts whether any man was really acquainted with the particulars. All that he could call to mind relative to either party was, that for three weeks after the Captain's introduction, till his military pursuits led him to Ireland, he was observed to bow to Miss Ray whenever she went out; and that Miss Ray, during the latter part of her time at the Admiralty, did not continue to speak of her situation as before. "She complained," he says, "of being greatly alarmed by ballads that had been sung, or cries that had been made, directly under the windows that looked into the park; and that such was the fury of the mob, that she did not think either herself or Lord Sandwich was safe whenever they went out; and I must own that I heard some strange insults offered; and that I with some of the servants once suddenly rushed out, but the offenders instantly ran away and escaped. One evening afterwards, when sitting with Miss Ray in the great room above stairs, she appeared to be much agitated, and at last said, ' she had a particular favour to ask of me; that, as her situation was very precarious, and no settlement had been made upon her, she wished I would hint something of the kind to Lord Sandwich.' I

* Literary and Miscellaneous Memoirs, by J. Cradock, Esq., M.A., F.S.A., vol. iv., p. 166.

need not express my surprise, but I instantly assured her, 'that no one but herself could make such a proposal, as I knew Lord Sandwich never gave any one an opportunity of interfering with him on so delicate a subject.' She urged that her wish was merely to relieve Lord Sandwich as to great expense about her ; for as her voice was then at the best, and Italian music was particularly her forte, she was given to understand she might succeed at the Opera-house, and as Mr. Giardini then led, and I was intimate with Mrs. Brooke and Mrs. Yates, she was certain of a most advantageous engagement. I then instantly conjectured who one of the advisers must have been ; and afterwards found that three thousand pounds and a free benefit had been absolutely held out to her, though not by the two ladies who managed the stage department. Whether any proposals of marriage at that time or afterwards were made by Mr. Hackman, I know not."* Be this as it may, Hackman's passion was undoubted. He was originally an apprentice to a merchant at Gosport ; was impatient of serving at the counter ; entered the army at nineteen, but during his acquaintance with Miss Ray, exchanged the army for the church, " as a readier road to independence ;" and was presented to the living of Wyverton in Norfolk.

Whatever was the nature of the intimacy between these unfortunate persons, a sudden stop appears to have been put to Hackman's final expectations, and he became desperate. By what we can gather from the accounts, Lord Sandwich, either to preserve her from her lover or herself, thought proper to put Miss Ray under the charge of a duenna. Hackman grew jealous either of him or of some other person; he was induced to believe that Miss Ray had no longer a regard for him, and he resolved to put himself to death. In this resolution a sudden impulse of frenzy included the unfortunate object of his passion.

On the evening of the fatal day, Miss Ray went with her female attendant to Covent Garden Theatre to see " Love in a Village." Mr. Cradock thinks she had declined to inform Hackman how she was engaged that evening. Hackman, who appears to have suspected her intentions, watched her, and saw the carriage pass by the Cannon Coffee-house (Cockspur Street, Charing Cross), in which he had posted

* Literary and Miscellaneous Memoirs, by J. Cradock, Esq., M.A., F.S.A., vol. i., p. 143.

himself. Singularly enough, Mr. Cradock happened to be in the same coffee-house, and says that he wondered to see the carriage go by without Lord Sandwich. This looks as if there was more in Hackman's suspicion than can now be shown. Hackman followed them.

"The ladies sat in a front box," says Mr. Cradock; "and three gentlemen, all connected with the Admiralty, occasionally paid their compliments to them; Mr. Hackman was sometimes in the lobby, sometimes in an upper side box, and more than once at the Bedford coffee-house to take brandy and water, but still seemed unable to gain any information; and I can add, as a slight circumstance, that in the afternoon I had myself been at the coffee-house (Cockspur Street, Charing Cross), and, observing the carriage pass by, had remarked to my friend that I wondered at seeing the ladies on their way to the theatre without Lord Sandwich; that I meant to have dined at the Admiralty, but had been prevented; so that it appears now that most of the circumstances must have been accidental. The dreadful consummation, however, was, that at the door of the theatre, directly opposite the Bedford coffee-house, Mr. Hackman suddenly rushed out, and as a gentleman was handing Miss Ray into the carriage, with a pistol he first destroyed this most unfortunate victim, and, though not at the time, fell a most dreadful sacrifice himself."*

"Miss Ray," says the Introduction to 'Love and Madness,' "was coming out of Covent Garden Theatre in order to take her coach, accompanied by two friends, a gentleman and a lady, between whom she walked in the piazza. Mr. Hackman stepped up to her without the smallest previous menace or address, put a pistol to her head, and shot her instantly dead. He then fired another at himself, which, however, did not prove equally effectual. The ball grazed upon the upper part of the head, but did not penetrate sufficiently to produce any fatal effect; he fell, however, and so firmly was he bent on the entire completion of the destruction he had meditated, that he was found beating his head with the utmost violence with the butt-end of the pistol, by Mr. Mahon, apothecary, of Covent Garden, who wrenched the pistol from his hand. He was carried to the Shakspeare, where his wound was dressed. In his pocket were found two letters; the one a copy of a letter which he had written to Miss Ray, and the other to Frederic Booth, Esq., Craven Street, Strand. When he had so far recovered his faculties as to be capable of speech, he inquired with great anxiety concerning Miss Ray; and being told she was dead, he desired her poor remains might not be exposed to the observation of the curious multitude. About five o'clock in the morning, Sir John Fielding came to the Shakspeare, and not finding his wounds of a dangerous nature, ordered him to Tothill Fields Bridewell.

"The body of the unhappy lady was carried into the Shakspeare Tavern for the inspection of the coroner."†

---

* Cradock, as above, p. 144.

† Love and Madness, a Story too True, in a series of Letters, &c. 1822, p. 11.

The whole of the circumstances connected with this catastrophe are painfully dramatic.

"The next morning," says Mr. Cradock, "I made several efforts before I had resolution enough to see any one of the Admiralty; at last old James, the black, overwhelmed with grief, came down to me, and endeavoured to inform me, that when he had mentioned what had occurred, Lord Sandwich hastily replied, 'You know that I forbad you to plague me any more about those ballads: let them sing or say whatever they please about me!' 'Indeed, my lord,' I said, 'I am not speaking of any ballads; it is all too true.' Others then came in, and all was a scene of the utmost horror and distress. His lordship for a while stood, as it were, petrified, till, suddenly seizing a candle, he ran up-stairs and threw himself on the bed; and in an agony exclaimed, 'Leave me for a while to myself—I could have borne anything but this!' The attendants remained for a considerable time at the top of the staircase, till his lordship rang the bell and ordered that they should all go to bed. They assured me that at that time they believed fewer particulars were known at the Admiralty than over half the town besides; indeed all was confusion and astonishment; and even now I am doubtful whether Lord Sandwich was ever aware that there was any connection between Mr. Hackman and Miss Ray. His lordship continued for a day or two at the Admiralty, till, at the earnest request of those about him, he at last retired for a short time to a friend's house in the neighbourhood of Richmond."*

Hackman was executed at Tyburn. He confessed at the bar that he had intended to kill himself, but he protested that but for a momentary frenzy he should not have destroyed her, "who was more dear to him than life." It appears, however, that he was furnished with two pistols; which told against him on that point.

"On Friday," says Boswell, "I had been present at the trial of the unfortunate Mr. Hackman, who, in a fit of frantic jealous love, had shot Miss Ray, the favourite of a nobleman. Johnson, in whose company I dined to-day, with some other friends, was much interested by my account of what passed, and particularly with his prayer for mercy of heaven. He said in a solemn, fervent tone, 'I hope he *shall* find mercy.' In talking of Hackman, Johnson argued as Judge Blackstone had done, that his being furnished with two pistols was a proof that he meant to shoot two persons. Mr. Beauclerk said, 'No; for that every wise man who intended to shoot himself, took two pistols, that he might be sure of doing it at once. Lord ——'s cook shot himself with one pistol, and lived ten days in great agony. Mr. ——, who loved buttered muffins, but durst not eat them because they disagreed with his stomach, resolved to shoot himself, and then he ate three buttered muffins for breakfast before shooting himself, knowing that he should not be troubled with indigestion; *he* had two charged pistols: one was found lying charged upon the table by him, after he had shot himself with the other.' 'Well (said Johnson with

----

* Cradock's Memoirs, vol. iv., p. 166.

an air of triumph). you see here one pistol was sufficient.' Beauclerk replied smartly, ' Because it happened to kill him.' "*

It is impossible to settle this point.   The general impression will be against Hackman ; but, perhaps, the second pistol, though not designed for himself, might have been for Miss Ray.   His victim was buried at Elstree, where she had been a lowly and happy child, running about with her blooming face, and little thinking what trouble it was to cost her.

In Mr. Cradock's book we hear again of Lord Sandwich on whom this story has thrown an interest.   On his return from Richmond, Mr. Cradock went to see him, and was admitted into the study where the portrait of Miss Ray, an exact resemblance, still hung over the chimney-piece.   "I fear," says Mr. Cradock, "I rather started on seeing it, which Lord Sandwich perceiving, he instantly endeavoured to speak of some unconnected subject ; but he looked so ill, and I felt so much embarrassed, that as soon as I possibly could, I most respectfully took my leave."

"His lordship rarely dined out anywhere; but after a great length of time he was persuaded by our open-hearted friend, Lord Walsingham, to meet a select party at his house.   All passed off exceedingly well for a while, and his lordship appeared more cheerful than could have been expected; but after coffee, as Mr. and Mrs. Bates were present, something was mentioned about music, and one of the company requested that Mrs. Bates would favour them with, ' Shepherds, I have lost my love.'   This was, unfortunately, the very air that had been introduced by Miss Ray at Hinchinbrook, and had been always called for by Lord Sandwich.   Mr. Bates immediately endeavoured to prevent its being sung, and by his anxiety increased the distress, but it was too late to pause. Lord Sandwich for a while struggled to overcome his feelings, but they were so apparent that at last he went up Mrs. Walsingham, and in a very confused manner said, he hoped she would excuse his not staying longer at that time; but that he had just recollected some pressing business, which required his return to the Admiralty, and bowing to all the company, rather hastily left the room.   Some other endeavours to amuse him afterwards did not prove much more successful."†

His lordship afterwards lived in retirement, and died in 1792.
    It does not appear that Lord Sandwich's disinclination to be amused arose from excessive sensibility.   Mr. Cradock represents him in his political character as bearing "daily insults and misrepresentations as a stoic rather than an injured and feeling man," and he describes his calmness of

* Boswell, vol. iii., p. 414.
† Cradock's Memoirs, vol. i., p. 146.

mind in retirement, and his enjoyment of solitude. The same writer who calls him "a steady friend," speaks highly of his classical attainments, and his accomplishments as a modern linguist and an amateur, to which he added great caution (as the Bishop said), a love of "badgering," and an incompetency for the personal graces. When he played his part in the oratorios, it was on the kettle-drum. He related the following anecdote of himself.

"When I was in Paris, I had a dancing-master; the man was very civil, and on taking leave of him, I offered him any service in London. 'Then,' said the man, bowing, 'I should take it as a particular favour, if your lordship would never tell any one of whom you have learned to dance.'"

"Hurd once said to me," adds Mr. Cradock, "there is a line in the Heroic Epistle that I do not at all comprehend the meaning of ; but you can, perhaps, acquaint me. It alludes to Lord Sandwich, I suppose; but one word, *shambles*, I cannot guess at,—

'See Jemmy Twitcher *shambles*—stop, stop, thief.'

'That, sir,' said I, 'alludes to his lordship's shambling gait.' "*

Upon the whole we have no doubt that he was a cold and superficial person, and that Miss Ray would not have been sorry had Hackman succeeded in retaining her heart ; for, as to Hackman, the great cause of his mischance, according to the passage in Boswell, appears to have been the violence of his temper, — the common secret of most of these outrageous love stories. He was not a bad-hearted man, merely selfish and passionate, otherwise he would have meditated no mischief against himself.

> "He that beats or knocks out brains,
> The devil's in him, if he feigns,"

says the poet. But he was weak, wilful, and, by his readiness to become a clergyman from a Captain, perhaps not very principled. The truest love is the truest benevolence; it acquires an infinite patience out of the very excess of its suffering, and is content to merge its egotism in the idea of the beloved object. He that does not know this, does not know what love is, whatever he may know of passion.

In Henrietta Street Mrs. Clive once resided. She was the favourite Nell of the stage in the "Devil to Pay," and similar characters ; and, according to Garrick, there was something of the Devil to Pay in all her stage life. She might have been Macklin's sister for humour, judgment, and a sturdiness of purpose amounting to violence, not unmixed with gene-

* Cradock's Memoirs, vol. iv., p. 166.

rosity. The latter part of her life she spent in retirement at Strawberry Hill, where she was a neighbour and friend to Horace Walpole, whose effeminacy she helped to keep on the alert. It always seems to us, as if she had been the man of the two, and he the woman.

Henrietta Street was most probably named after the queen of Charles I., and James Street after her father-in-law. In both these streets lived the egregious almanack-maker, and quack doctor, the butt of the wits of his time. He died in Salisbury Street, Strand, which is the scene of his posthumous behaviour, — his pretending to be alive, when Bickerstaff had declared him dead. Partridge had foretold the death of the French king. Swift, under the name of Bickerstaff, foretold Partridge's, and, when the time came, insisted he was dead. Partridge gravely insisted that he was alive. The wits, the friends of Swift, maintained the contrary, wondering at the dead man's impudence : and the whole affair was hawked about the streets, to the ludicrous distress of poor Partridge, who not only highly resented it, and repeatedly advertised his existence, but was fairly obliged to give up almanack-making. "He persisted, indeed, sturdily in his refusal to be buried till 1715 : but he actually died as an almanack-maker in 1709, his almanack for that year being the last, and the only one he wrote after this odd misfortune befell him." *

The following are specimens of the way in which Partridge resisted his death and burial. In the almanack for 1709, he says,

"You may remember there was a paper published predicting my death on the 29th of March at night, 1708, and after that day was passed the same villain told the world I was dead, and how I died, and that he was with me at the time of my death. I thank God, by whose mercy I have my being, that I am still alive, and, excepting my age, as well as ever I was in my life, as I was on that 29th of March. And that paper was said to be done by one Bickerstaff, Esq., but that was a sham name, it was done by an impudent lying fellow. But his prediction did not prove true. What will he say to excuse that? for the fool had considered the star of my nativity, as he said. Why, the truth is, he will be hard put to it to find a salvo for his honour. It was a bold touch, and he did not know but it might prove true.

"Feb. 1709. Much lying news dispersed about this time, and also scandalous pamphlets; perhaps we may have some knavish scribbler,

---

* Account of John Partridge, in the Appendix to the Tatler, vol. iv., p. 613.

a second Bickerstaff, or a rascal under that name for that villain, &c. It is a cheat, and he a knave that did it, &c.

"Whereas, it has been industriously given out by Bickerstaff, Esq., and others, to prevent the sale of this year's almanack, that John Partridge is dead; this may inform all his loving countrymen, that, blessed be God, he is still living in health, and they are knaves who reported otherwise. 'Merlinus Liberatus, with an almanack [printed by allowance for 1710]. By John Partridge, student in Physic and Astrology.'"

In James Street, towards the begining of the last century, lived a mysterious lady, who will remind the reader of the Catholic lady in the " Fortunes of Nigel."

"In the month of March 1720," says Mr. Malcolm, "an unknown lady died at her lodgings in James Street, Covent Garden. She is represented to have been a middle-sized person, with dark-brown hair, and very beautiful features, and mistress of every accomplishment peculiar to ladies of the first fashion and respectability. Her age appeared to be between thirty and forty. Her circumstances were affluent, and she possessed the richest trinkets of her sex, generally set with diamonds. A John Ward, Esq., of Hackney, published many particulars relating to her in the papers; and amongst others, that a servant had been directed by her to deliver him a letter after her death; but as no servant appeared, he felt himself required to notice those circumstances, in order to acquaint her relations of her decease, which occurred suddenly after a masquerade, where she declared she had conversed with the King, and it was remembered that she had been seen in the private apartments of Queen Anne; though after the Queen's demise she had lived in obscurity. This unknown arrived in London from Mansfield, in 1714, drawn by six horses. She frequently said that her father was a nobleman, but that, her elder brother dying unmarried, the title was extinct; adding, that she had an uncle then living, whose title was his least recommendation.

"It was conjectured that she might be the daughter of a Roman Catholic, who had consigned her to a convent, whence a brother had released her and supported her in privacy. She was buried at St. Paul's, Covent Garden."*

Perhaps she had some connection with Queen Anne's brother, the Pretender.

In King Street lived the father of Arne and Mrs. Cibber. He was an upholsterer, and is said to have been the original of the Quid-nunc in the *Tatler,* and the hero of Murphy's farce of the *Upholsterer, or, What News?* His name is connected also with that of the four "Indian Kings," as they were called, who came into this country in Queen Anne's time, to ask her assistance against the French in Canada.

---

* Anecdotes, Manners, and Customs of London during the Eighteenth Century, vol. i., p. 407.

" They were clothed and entertained," says a note in the 'Tatler,
" at the public expense, being lodged, while they continued in London,
in an handsome apartment," perhaps in the house of Mr. Arne, as
may be inferred from ' Tatler,' 155, and note. Certainly their landlord was an upholsterer in Covent Garden, in a new street, which
seems at that time to have received the name of King Street, which
it retains to this day, in common with many other streets so called, in
honour of Charles II. The figures of these four Indian kings or chiefs
are still preserved in the British Museum. The names and titles of
their Majesties are recorded there and in the ' Annals of Queen Anne,'
but with the following differences from the account of them in this
paper : *Tee Yee Neen Ho Ga Prow*, and *Su Ga Yean Qua Prah Ion*,
of the *Maquas ;—Elow Oh Kaom*, and *Oh Nee Yeath Ion No Prow*, of
the river *Sachem*, and the *Ganajoh-hore Sachem*. On the 18th of
April 1710, according to Salmon, on the 19th according to Boyer,
these four illustrious personages were conveyed in two of the Queen's
coaches to St. James's, by Sir Charles Cotterel, master of the ceremonies, and introduced to their public audience by the Duke of
Shrewsbury, then Lord Chamberlain. They made a speech by an
interpreter, which Major Pidgeon, an officer who came over with them
from America, read in English to her Majesty. " They had (they
said) with one consent hung up the kettle and taken up the hatchet,
in token of their friendship to their great queen and her children, and
had been, on the other side of the great water, a strong wall of security to their great queen's children, even to the loss of their best men.
For the truth of what they affirmed, and their written proposals, they
referred to Colonel Scuyder and Colonel Nicholson, whom they
called, in their language, Brother Queder, and Anadgargaux, and,
speaking of Colonel Vetch, they named him Anadiasia. They said
they always considered the French as men of falsehood, and rejoiced
in the prospect of the reduction of Canada; after which they should
have free hunting, and a great trade with their great queen's chil-
children; and as a token of the sincerity of the six nations, in the
name of all, they presented their great queen with the belts of
wampum. They concluded their speech with recommending their
very hard case to their great queen's gracious consideration, expressing their hopes of her favour, and requesting the mission of more of
her children to reinforce and to instruct, for they had got, as they
said, since their alliance with her children, some knowledge of the
Saviour of the world. The curious may see this speech at full length
in the ' Annals of Queen Anne,' year 9th, p. 191, *et seq.*, 8vo. On
the same day, according to Boyer, a royal messenger of the Emperor of
Morocco, Elhadge Guzman, was likewise introduced by the Duke of
Shrewsbury to a private audience, and delivered letters to the Queen
from Mula Ishmael, his master; the same emperor, probably, who
sent an ambassador to our court in 1706, mentioned in the 'Tatler,'
No. 130, and note, vol. iii., p. 44. The Indian Kings continued about
a fortnight longer in London, during which time they were hospi-
tably entertained by some of the lords commissioners of the Admiralty,
by the Duke of Ormond, and several persons of distinction. They
were carried to see Dr. Flamstead's house and the mathematical
instruments in Greenwich Park, and entertained with the sight of the
principal curiosities in and about the metropolis ; then conveyed
to Portsmouth through Hampton Court and Windsor, and embarked

with Colonel Frances Nicholson, commander-in-chief of the forces appointed to the American service, on board the Dragon, Captain Martin, Commodore, who, with about eighteen sail under his convoy, sailed from Spithead on the 18th of May, and landed their Majesties safe at Boston, in New England, July 15th, 1710."*

Their names are like a set of yawns and sneezes.

Young Arne, who was born in King Street, was a musician against his father's will, and practised in the garret, on a muffled spinnet, when the family had gone to bed. He was sent to Eton, which was probably of use to him in confirming his natural refinement, but nothing could hinder his devoting himself to the art. It is said the old man had no suspicion of his advancement in it, till, going to a concert one evening, he was astonished to see his son exalted, bow in hand, as the leader. Seeing the praises bestowed on him, he suffered him to become what nature designed him for. Arne was the most flowing, Italian-like musician of any we have had in England ; not capable of the grandeur and profound style of Purcell, but more sustained, continuous, and seductive. His " Water parted " is a stream of sweetness ; his song, " When Daisies pied " is truly Shaksperian, full of archness and originality. Like many of his profession, who feel much more than they reflect, he became, in some measure, the victim of his sense of beauty, being excessively addicted to women. His sister, Mrs. Cibber, whose charming performances on the stage we have before noticed, did not escape without the reputation of a like tendency ; but she had a bad husband (the notorious Theophilus Cibber) ; and on the occasion that gave rise to it, is understood to have been the victim of his mercenary designs.

Southampton Street we have noticed in speaking of the Strand. Godfrey's, the chemist's, in this street, is an establishment of old standing, as may be seen by the inscription over the door. A hundred years ago, Mr. Ambrose Godfrey, who lived here, proposed to extinguish fire by a new method of " explosion and suffocation ;" that is to say, a mixture of water and *gunpowder*. Tavistock Street (where Lord Sandwich first saw Miss Ray) was once the great emporium of millinery and mantua-making. Macklin died there. He lived many years in Wyld Street. In Maiden Lane, Voltaire lodged, when in England, at the sign of the White Peruke, probably the house of a fashionable French peruquier. In

* Tatler, *ut supra*, vol. iii., p. 397.

" Swift's Works" (vol. xx. of the duodecimo edition, p. 294),
there is a letter to him, in English, by Voltaire, and dated
from this house.   The English seems a little too perfect.
There is another following it which looks more authentic.
But there is no doubt that Voltaire, while in England, made
himself such a master of the language, as to be able to write
in it with singular correctness for a foreigner.   He was then
young.   He had been imprisoned in the Bastile for a libel ;
came over here, on his release ; procured many subscriptions
for the " Henriade ;" published in English " An Essay on
Epic Poetry," and remained some years, during which he
became acquainted with the principal men of letters—Pope,
Congreve, and Young.   He is said to have talked so inde-
cently at Pope's table (probably no more than was thought
decent by the belles in France), that the good old lady, the
poet's mother, was obliged to retire.   Objecting, at Lord
Chesterfield's table, to the allegories of Milton, Young is said
to have accosted him in the well-known couplet :—

> Thou art so witty, profligate, and thin,
> Thou seem'st a Milton, with his Death and Sin.

But this story has been doubted.   Young, though not so thin,
was as witty and profligate in his way as Voltaire : for, even
when affecting a hermit-like sense of religion, he was a servile
flatterer and preferment-hunter.   The secret of the gloomy
tone in his " Night-Thoughts" was his not having too much,
and his missing a bishopric.   This is the reason why the
" Night-Thoughts" are overdone, and have not stood their
ground.   Voltaire left England with such a mass of subscriptions for his " Henriade" as laid the foundation of his fortunes,
and with great admiration of English talent and genius, particularly that of Newton and Locke, which, with all his
insinuations against our poetry, he took warm pains to extend,
and never gave up.   He was fond to the last of showing he
had not forgotten his English.   Somebody telling him that
Johnson had spoken well of his talents, he said, in English,
" He is a clever fellow ;" but the gentleman observing that
the doctor did not think well of his religion, he added, " a
superstitious dog."

During his residence in Maiden Lane, there is a story of
Voltaire's having been beset, in one of his walks, by the
people, who ridiculed him as a Frenchman.   He got upon the
steps of a door-way and harangued them in their own language
in praise of English liberty and the nation ; upon which, the

story adds, they hailed him as a fine fellow, and carried him to his lodgings on their shoulders. The treatment of foreigners at this time in the streets of London (and every foreigner was a Frenchman) was very much the reverse of what the inhabitants took it for. Thanks to the progress of knowledge, nations have learnt to understand one another's common cause better, and to suspect that the most ridiculous thing they could do is to forget it.

Long Acre is a portion of the seven acres before mentioned. The great plague of London began there in some goods brought over from Holland ; but as that calamity made its principal ravages in the city, we shall speak of it under another head. During the battles of the Whigs and Tories, Long Acre was famous for its Mug-houses, where beer-drinking clubs were held, and politics " sung or said." Cheapside was another place of celebrity for these meetings. There is a description of them in a Journey through England in 1724, quoted by Mr. Malcolm in his "Manners and Customs of London during the Eighteenth Century." "Gentlemen, lawyers, and tradesmen," says the account, "used to meet in a great room, seldom under a hundred."

"They had a president, who sat in an arm-chair some steps higher than the rest of the company, to keep the whole room in order. A harp played all the time at the lower end of the room, and every now and then one or other of the company rose and entertained the rest with a song, and (by the by) some were good masters. Here was nothing drank but ale, and every gentleman had his separate mug, which he chalked on the table where he sat as it was brought in; and every one retired when he pleased, as from a coffee-house.

"The rooms were always so diverted with songs, and drinking from one table to another one another's healths, that there was no room for anything that could sour conversation.

" One was obliged to be there by seven to get room, and after ten the company were for the most part gone.

" This was a winter's amusement, agreeable enough to a stranger for once or twice, and he was well diverted with the different humours when the mugs overflow.

" On King George's accession to the throne, the Tories had so much the better of the friends to the Protestant succession, that they gained the mobs on all public days to their side. This induced this set of gentlemen to establish mug-houses in all the corners of this great city, for well-affected tradesmen to meet and keep up the spirit of loyalty to the Protestant succession, and to be ready upon all tumults to join their forces for the suppression of the Tory mobs. Many an encounter they had, and many were the riots, till at last the Parliament was obliged by law to put an end to this city strife, which had this good effect, that, on pulling down the mug-houses in Salisbury Court, for which some boys were hanged on this Act, the city has not been troubled with them since."*

One of the mistresses whom Prior celebrates, under the name of Chloe, and compares to Venus and Diana, lived in Long Acre, and was the wife, some say, of a common soldier, others of a cobbler, others of the keeper of an ale-house. Perhaps she was all these, or there were three mistresses whose alliances were confounded. Spence says that the ale-house keeper was the first husband, and the cobbler the second. "Everybody knows," says Pope, "what a wretch she was." And again:—"Prior was not a right good man. He used to bury himself, for whole days and nights together, with a poor mean creature, and often drank hard. He turned from a strong Whig (which he had been when most with Lord Halifax) to a violent Tory; and did not care to converse with any Whigs after, any more than Rowe did with Tories."† "I have been assured," says Pope's friend, Richardson, the painter, "that Prior, after having spent the evening with Oxford, Bolingbroke, Pope, and Swift, would go and smoke a pipe, and drink a bottle of ale, with a common soldier and his wife, in Long Acre, before he went to bed."‡ After the poet's death, Arbuthnot says something to the same effect; but we forget what.

None of the wits of that time seem to have known much about love as a sentiment. There is no end of the misconceptions of what is called love. Prior would probably have retorted upon Pope, that his own taste was not very delicate; and upon Arbuthnot, that the doctor was a sensualist in his way, and of a lower order.§ He would have quoted Propertius, Raphael, and others, for the impartiality of his taste; and the woman, though in low life, might have had wit and beauty. The secret of these inequalities has been explained by Fielding.‖

Sir Joshua Reynolds lived successively in St. Martin's Lane, and on the north side of Great Newport Street, before

* Anecdotes, Manners, &c. *ut supra*, vol. iii., p. 239.
† Spence, *ut supra*, pp. 2. and 49.
‡ Johnson's Life of Prior.
§ Arbuthnot was a lover of the table, and is understood to have embittered his end by it; a charge which has been brought against Pope. Perhaps there is not one that might be brought with more safety against ninety men out of a hundred.
‖ Journey to the Next World.

he settled finally in Leicester Square. In Newport Street was born the celebrated Horne Tooke, the son of a poulterer in the adjoining market ; which made him say, that his father was a "Turkey merchant." He was, perhaps, the hardest-headed man that ever figured in the union of literature and politics; meaning, by that epithet, the power to discuss, and impenetrability to objection. He died at his house at Wimbledon, and was buried at Ealing. His history trenches too closely on the politics of our own day, to allow us to expatiate upon it in a work expressly devoted to the past.

St. Martin's Lane (see Charing Cross, for a notice of the church,) was once as famous for artists as Newman Street has been since. In Salisbury Court and in St. Martin's Lane the Royal Academy may be said to have originated, for in those places successively its original members first came together as a society established by themselves. Perhaps there was not a single artist, contemporary with Sir Joshua, who was unconnected with St. Martin's Lane, either as a lodger, student, or visitor. Old Slaughter's coffee-house, in the same lane, became celebrated on the same account, and as a resort of the contemporary wits, especially Hogarth, who may be said to have amalgamated in his works the wit and the painter. St. Martin's Lane and Leicester Square are the head-quarters of the memory of English art. In the annals of the former we meet with the names of Wilson and Gainsborough : in the latter flourished and died Hogarth and Sir Joshua Reynolds.

Sir Joshua's house in Leicester Square was on the eastern side, four doors from Sydney's Alley.* It was there he kept a handsome table, and was visited by Johnson and Goldsmith, and had the whole round of the fashionable world fluttering before him, and steadying itself to become immortal in his pictures : if, indeed, immortal they are to be, in the ordinary meaning of that word ; for, out of certain misgivings, which perhaps argued a want of perfect claim to that destiny, he dabbled in experiments upon colours which have failed ; and his pictures, though but of yesterday, already look old and worn out, while Titian's are as blooming as Apollo.

Hogarth, the greatest name in English art, lived in one of the two houses which now form Sabloniere's hotel. It was the one to the north. He was a little bustling man, with a face more lively than refined, a sort of knowing jockey look ;

* The house was probably on the site now occupied by the south-east corner of New Coventry Street.

A A

and was irritable and egotistical, but not ungenerous As
a painter, he did what no man ever did before or since—
brought out the absurdities of artificial life,

　　"Showed vice her own features, scorn her own image,"

and fairly painted even goods and chattels with a meaning!
His intentions were less profound than his impulses; that is
to say, he sometimes had an avowed common-place in view,
as in the instance of the Industrious and Idle Apprentice,
while the execution of it was full of much higher things and
profounder humanities. As to the rest, if ever there was a
wit on canvass, it was he. To take one instance alone, his
spider's web over the poor's box is a union of remote ideas,
coalescing but too perfectly.*

　　Leicester Square, formerly Leicester Fields, was not built
upon till towards the restoration of Charles II. It took its
name from a family mansion of the Sydneys, Earls of Leicester,
which stood on the north side, on the site of the present houses
and of Leicester Place.

RESIDENCE OF SIR ISAAC NEWTON.

　　"It was for a short time," says Pennant, "the residence of Elizabeth,
daughter of James I., the titular Queen of Bohemia, who, on February
13th, 1661, here ended her unfortunate life. It has been tenanted for

* For masterly criticisms on Hogarth, see the "Works of Charles
Lamb," vol. ii., p. 88, and the "Picture Galleries of England," p. 181.

a great number of years. It was successively the pointing-place of princes. The late King [George II.], when Prince of Wales, after he had quarrelled with his father, lived here several years. His son Frederic followed his example, succeeded him in his house, and in it finished his days." ·

" Behind Leicester House," the same author informs us, " stood, in 1658, the Military-yard, founded by Henry Prince of Wales, the spirited son of our peaceful James. M. Faubert afterwards kept here his academy for riding and other gentlemanlike exercises, in the reign of Charles II., which, in later years, was removed to Swallow Street, opposite the end of Conduit Street. Part is retained for the purpose of a riding-house; the rest is converted into a workhouse for the parish of St. James's." *

But the glory of the neighbourhood of Leicester Fields is in St. Martin's Street, where the house is still remaining which was occupied by the great Newton.

CHAPTER IX.

CHARING CROSS AND WHITEHALL.

Old Charing Cross, and New St. Martin's Church—Statue of Charles I.—Execution of Regicides—Ben Jonson—Wallingford House, now the Admiralty—Villiers, Duke of Buckingham; Sir Walter Scott's Account of him—Misrepresentation of Pope respecting his Death—Charles's Horse a Satirist—Locket's Ordinary—Sir George Etherege.—Prior and his Uncle's Tavern—Thomson—Spring Gardens—Mrs. Centlivre—Dorset Place, and Whitcombe Street, &c., formerly Hedge Lane—The Wits and the Bailiffs—Suffolk Street—Swift aud Miss Vanhomrigh—Calves' Head Club, and the Riot it occasioned—Scotland Yard—Pleasant Advertisement—Beau Fielding, and his Eccentricities—Vanbrugh—Desperate Adventure of Lord Herbert of Cherbury.

IN the reign of Edward I., on the country road from London to Westminster, stood the hamlet of Charing; a rustic spot, containing a few houses, and the last cross set up by that Prince in honour of the resting-places of his wife's body on its way to interment in the Abbey. The Cross was originally of wood, but afterwards of stone. The reader may see it in the old map of London by Aggas. He will there observe, that towards the beginning of Elizabeth's reign Charing Cross was united with London on the Strand side, and at little intervals with Whitehall; but Spring Gar-

* Pennant, p. 120.

A A 2*

dens was then and long after what its name implies; and, in
the reign of Charles II., Hedge Lane (now Whitcomb Street)
and the Haymarket were still real lanes and passages into
the fields.   In Elizabeth's time, you might set out from the
site of the present Pall-mall, and, leaving St. Giles in the
Fields on the right hand, walk all the way to Hampstead
without encountering perhaps a dwelling-place.   Lovers
plucked flowers in Cranbourne Alley, and took moonlight
walks in St. James's market.

On this spot, in Dr. Johnson's opinion, is to be found the
fullest " tide of human existence" in the metropolis.   We
know not how that may be at present when the tide is so full
everywhere ; but Charing Cross has long been something the
reverse of a rural village, and is now exhibiting one of the
newest and grandest evidences of an improving metropolis.

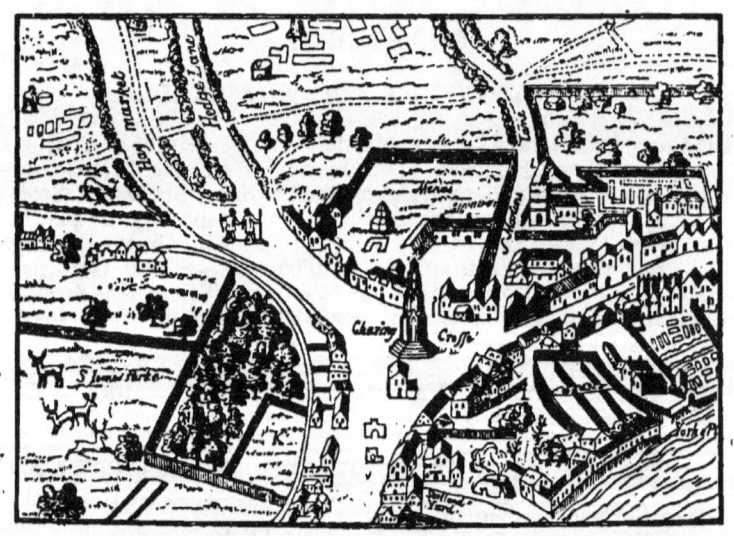

THE VILLAGE OF CHARING FROM AGGAS'S MAP.

By way of north front, the Mews (formerly the mews of the
King's falcons) has given way to a sorry palace for the Fine
Arts; on the west is a handsome edifice including the new
college of Physicians ; on the east St. Martin's church has
obtained its long desired opening : and in the midst of these
buildings and of the Strand-end is a new square, named after
the greatest of our naval victories, adorned with a column
surmounted by their hero, and disgraced by a couple of shabby

fountains. Here also is an equestrian statue of George the Fourth. What for? ·

"In the reign of Henry VIII.," says Pennant, "speaking of St Martin's, "a small church was built here at the King's expense, by reason of the poverty of the parishioners, who possibly were at that period very poor. In 1607 it was enlarged because of the increase of buildings. In 1721 it was found necessary to take the whole down, and in five years from that time this magnificent temple was completed at the expense of near thirty-seven thousand pounds. This is the best performance of Gibbs, the architect of the Radcliffe Library. The steeple is far the most elegant of any of that style which I named the *pepper-box*; and with which (I beg pardon of the good people of Glasgow) I marked their boasted steeple of St. Andrew."*

Our lively biographer seems chiefly to admire the steeple of this church. The Corinthian portico, we believe, is the usual object of praise. Both of them may deserve praise separately; nor, indeed, will their size and situation allow them to be regarded with indifference in conjunction; but the elevation of the steeple on the neck of the church, or without any apparent or proper base to rest upon, is a fault not to be denied; and Mr. Pennant perhaps would not have been in the wrong, had he found an ill name for steeples in general, as well as for the species which he "peppered." Steeples, however noble, and porticoes, however Greek, can never truly coalesce. The finest steeple with a portico to it is but an excrescence and an anomaly, a horn growing out of the church's neck. The Italians felt this absurdity so much, that they have often made a separate building of the steeple, converting it into a beautiful tower aloof from the church, as in the instances of the famous Hanging Tower in Pisa, and the Campanile in Florence. Suppose a shaft like the Monument, in a space near St. Martin's church, and the church itself a proper building with a portico, like St. Paul's Covent Garden, and you have an improvement in the Italian style. The best thing to say for

—— sharpèd steeples high shot up in air

(as Spenser calls them) is, that they seem to be pointing to heaven, or running up into space like an intimation of interminability. An idea of this kind is supposed to have given rise to them. But they always have a meagre, incongruous look, considered in their union with the body to which they are attached. Their best appearance is at a distance, and when they are numerous, as in the view of a great city; but

* Page 143.

even then, how inferior are they to the massive dignity of such towers as those of Westminster Abbey, or to a dome like that of St. Paul's!

The origin of the word Charing is unknown. The cross was destroyed during the Reformation. The spot where it stood is occupied by the statue of Charles I. originally the property of the Earl of Arundel, for whom it was cast by Le Sœur in 1633. It was not placed in its present situation till the decline of the reign of Charles II. The pedestal is the work of Grinling Gibbons. The statue had been condemned by Parliament to be sold and broken in pieces ; "but John River, the brazier, who purchased it," says Pennant, " having more taste or more loyalty than his masters, buried it unmutilated and showed to them some broken pieces of brass in token of his obedience. M. D'Archenholz gives a diverting anecdote of this brazier, and says that he cast a vast number of handles of knives and forks in brass, which he sold as made of the broken statue. They were bought with great eagerness by the royalists, from affection to their monarch; by the rebels as a mark of triumph over the murdered sovereign."[*] The sovereign now faces Whitehall as if in triumph : yet behind the Banquetting house lurks a statue of another of this unfortunate race, who lost his throne for attempting to renew the dictatorial spirit which cost his ancestor his head. The omission of the horse's girth in this statue his been thought a singular instance of forgetfulness in the artist. But it is hardly possible he could have forgotten it. Most likely he took a poetical license, and rejected what might have hurt the symmetry of his outline.

Charles's memory, like his life, was destined to be connected with tragedies. On this spot, before the statue was erected, a number of the regicides were executed with tortures ; and, till of late years, it was a place for the pillory. Harrison died there, Scrope, Colonel Jones, Hugh Peters, and others of those extraordinary men, who, in welcoming a bloody death, gave the last undoubted proofs that they were real patriots as well as bigots. The spirit in which they died (bold and invincible, though in the very glow and loquacity evincing that lingering love of life which is so affecting to one's own mortality,) had such an effect on the public, that the king was advised not to have any more such executions near the court,

* Pennant, p. 112. He quotes Archenholz's Tableau d'Angleterre, , 183.

and the scaffold was accordingly removed to Tyburn. A ghastly story is related of Harrison;—that after he was cut down alive (according to his sentence), and had his bowels removed and burnt before his face by the executioner, he rose up and gave the man a box on the ear. He had behaved with great patience before this half-death ; so that there appears to have been something of delirium in this action,— the action, perhaps, of a being feeling himself to be no longer under the ordinary condition of his species.

The particular sort of religious enthusiasm evinced by these men is now as obsolete as some of the absurdities which they fought against, and as others which they would have upheld ; but there are passages of lasting interest in the account of their last moments, which the reader will perhaps expect to see.

As Harrison was going to suffer, " one in derision called to him and said, ' Where is your Good Old Cause ?' He with a cheerful smile clapt his hand on his breast, and said ' Here it is, and I am going to seal it with my blood ?' And when he came to the sight of the gallows, he was transported with joy, and his servant asked him how he did ; he answered ' Never better in my life.' His servant told him, ' Sir, there is a crown of glory ready prepared for you.' ' O yes,' said he, ' I see.' When he was taken off the sledge, the hangman desired him to forgive him. ' I do forgive thee,' said he, ' with all my heart, as it is a sin against me;' and told him he wished him all happiness. And further said, ' Alas, poor man, thou dost it ignorantly; the Lord grant that this sin may not be laid to thy charge !' And putting his hand into his pocket gave him all the money he had, and so parting with his servant, hugging of him in his arms, he went up the ladder with an undaunted countenance.

" The people observing him to tremble in his hands and legs, he, taking notice of it, said :—

" ' Gentlemen, by reason of some scoffing that I do hear, I judge that some do think I am afraid to die, by the shaking I have in my hands and knees; I tell you no, but it is by reason of much blood I have lost in the wars, and many wounds I have received in my body, which caused this shaking and weakness in my nerves; I have had it this twelve years: I speak this to the praise and glory of God; he hath carried me above the fear of death ; and I value not my life, because I go to my Father, and am assured I shall take it again.

" ' Gentlemen, take notice, that for being instrumental in that cause and interest of the Son of God, which hath been pleaded amongst us, and which God hath witnessed to my appeals and wonderful victories I am brought to this place to suffer death this day, and if I had ten thousand lives, I could freely and cheerfully lay them down all, to witness to this matter.' "*

The time of Colonel Jones's departure being come "this aged gentleman," says the account, "was drawn in one sledge with his aged companion Scroope, whose grave and graceful countenances, accompanied with courage and cheerfulness, caused great admiration and compassion in the spectators, as they passed along the streets to Charing Cross, the place of their execution ; and, after the executioner had done his part upon three others that day he was so drunk with blood, that, like one surfeited, he grew sick at stomach ; and not being able himself, he set his boy to finish the tragedy upon Col. Jones." The night before he died he " told a friend he had no other temptation but this, lest he should be too much transported, and carried out to neglect and slight his life, so greatly was he satisfied to die in that cause."

"The day he suffered, he grasped a friend in his arms, and said to him with some expressions of endearment, 'Farewell: I could wish thee in the same condition with myself, that thou mightest share with me in my joys.' "†

The famous Hugh Peters, the commonwealth preacher, whom Burnet speaks of as an "enthusiastical buffoon," and a very "vicious man," is thought by a greater loyalist (Burke) to have had "hard measures dealt him at the Restoration." He calls him a "poor good man." Peters was afraid at first he should not behave himself with the proper courage, but rallied his spirits afterwards, and, according to the account published by his friends (and all the accounts, it should be observed, emanate from that side), no man appears to have behaved better. Burnet says otherwise, and that he was observed all the while to be drinking cordials to keep him from fainting, and Burnet's testimony is not to be slighted, though he seems too readily to have taken upon trust some evil reports of Peters' life and manners, which the "poor man," expressly contradicted in prison. Be this as it may, "Being carried," says the account, "upon the sledge to execution, and made to sit thereon within the rails at Charing Cross to behold the execution of Mr. Cook, one comes to him and upbraided him with the death of the King,

---

* State Trials, *ut supra*, vol. v., p. 1236.

† Id. pp. 1284, 1286.

bidding him (with opprobrious language) to repent ; he replied, 'Friend, you do not well to trample upon a dying man ; you are greatly mistaken, I had nothing to do in the death of the King.' "

"When Mr. Cook was cut down and brought to be quartered, one they called Colonel Turner called to the Sheriff's men to bring Mr. Peters near that he might see him ; and by and by the hangman came to him all besmeared in blood, and rubbing his bloody hands together, he tauntingly asked, ' Come, how do you like this, how do you like this work ?' To whom he replied, 'I am not, I thank God, terrified at it ; you may do your worst.'

" When he was going to his execution, he looked about and espied a man, to whom he gave a piece of gold (having bowed it first), and desired him to go to the place where his daughter lodged, and to carry that to her as a token from him, and to let her know that his heart was as full of comfort as it could be, and that before that piece should come into her hands he should be with God in glory.

" Being upon the ladder, he spake to the Sheriff, saying, ' Sir, you have here slain one of the servants of God before mine eyes, and have made me to behold it on purpose to terrify and discourage me ; but God hath made it an ordinance to me for my strengthening and encouragement.'

" When he was going to die, he said, ' What ! flesh, art thou unwilling to go to God through the fire and jaws of death ? Oh' (said he), ' this is a good day; he is come that I have long looked for,' and I shall be with him in glory ;' and so smiled when he went away.

" What Mr. Peters said farther at his execution, either in his speech or prayer, it could not be taken, in regard his voice was low at that time, and the people uncivil." *

Ben Jonson is supposed to have been born in Hartshorn Lane, Charing Cross, where he lived when a little child. " Though I cannot," says Fuller, " with all my industrious inquiry, find him in his cradle, I can fetch him from his long coats. When a little child he lived in Hartshorn Lane, Charing Cross, when his mother married a bricklayer for her second husband. He was first bred in a private school in St. Martin's Court ; then in Westminster school." But we shall have other occasions of speaking of him.

The famous reprobate Duke of Buckingham, Villiers, the second of that name, was born in Wallingford House, which stood on the site of the present Admiralty. " The Admiralty Office," says Pennant " stood originally in Duke Street, Westminster : but in the reign of King William was removed to the present spot, to the house then called Wallingford, I believe, from its having been inhabited by the Knollys, Viscounts Wallingford. From the roof the pious Usher,

* State Trials, vol. v., p. 1282.

Archbishop of Armagh, then living here with the Countess of Peterborough, was prevailed on to take the last sight of his beloved master Charles I., when brought on the scaffold before Whitehall. He sank at the horror of the sight, and was carried in a swoon to his apartment." Wallingford House was often used by Cromwell and others in their consultations.

" The present Admiralty Office," continues Pennant, " was rebuilt in the late reign, by Ripley ; it is a clumsy pile, but properly veiled from the street by Mr. Adam's handsome screen." Where the poor Archbishop sank in horror at the sight of the misguided Charles, telegraphs have since plied their dumb and far-seen discourses, like spirit in the guise of mechanism, telling news of the spread of liberty and know-ledge all over the world. Of the Villierses, Dukes of Buck-ingham, who have not heard ? The first one was a favourite not unworthy of his fortune, open, generous, and magnificent; the second, perhaps because he lost his father so soon, a spoiled child from his cradle, wilful, debauched, unprincipled, but witty and entertaining. Here, and at York House in the Strand, he turned night into day, and pursued his intrigues, his concerts, his dabblings in chemistry and the philosopher's stone, and his designs on the Crown: for Charles's character, and the devices of Buckingham's fellow quacks and astro-logers, persuaded him that he had a chance of being king. When a youth, he compounded with Cromwell, and married Fairfax's daughter; — he was afterwards all for the king, when he was not " all for rhyming" or ousting him; — when an old man, or near it (for these prodigious possessors of animal spirits have a trick of lasting a long while), he was still a youth in improvidence and dissipation, and his whole life was a dream of uneasy pleasure. He is now best known from Dryden's masterly portrait of him in the " Absalom and Achitophel."

> " A man so various, that he seemed to be,
> Not one, but all mankind's epitome ;
> Stiff in opinions, always in the wrong,
> Was everything by starts, and nothing long ;
> But in the course of one revolving moon,
> Was chemist, fiddler, statesman, and buffoon :
> Then all for women, painting, rhyming, drinking,
> Besides ten thousand freaks that died in thinking.
> Blest madman! who could every hour employ
> With something new to wish or to enjoy.
> Railing and praising were his usual themes ;
> And both, to show his judgment, in extremes ,

So very violent, or over civil,
That every man with him was God or devil.
In squandering wealth was his peculiar art;
Nothing went unrewarded but desert.
Beggar'd by fools, whom still he found too late,
He had his jest, and they had his estate.
He laugh'd himself from court; then sought relief
By forming parties, but could ne'er be chief;
For spite of him, the weight of business fell
On Absalom, or wise Achitophel;
Thus wicked but in will, of means bereft,
He left not faction, but of that was left."

"This inimitable description," observes Sir Walter Scott, in a note on the subject, "refers, as is well known, to the famous George Villiers, Duke of Buckingham, son of the favourite of Charles I., who was murdered by Felton. The Restoration put into the hands of the most lively, mercurial, ambitious, and licentious genius who ever lived, an estate of 20,000*l.* a year, to be squandered in every wild scheme which the lust of power, of pleasure, of license, or of whim, could dictate to an unrestrained imagination. Being refused the situation of President of the North. he was suspected of having favoured the disaffected in that part of England, and was disgraced accordingly. But in 1666 he regained the favour of the King, and became a member of the famous Administration called the Cabal, which first led Charles into unpopular and arbitrary measures, and laid the foundation for the troubles of his future reign. Buckingham changed sides about 1675, and becoming attached to the country party, made a most active figure in all proceedings which had relation to the Popish plot; intrigued deeply with Shaftesbury, and distinguished himself as a promoter of the bill of exclusion. Hence, he stood an eminent mark for Dryden's satire; which we may believe was not the less poignant, that the poet had sustained a personal affront, from being depicted by his grace under the character of Bayes in the "Rehearsal." As Dryden owed the Duke no favour, he has shown him none. Yet even here the ridiculous rather than the infamous part of his character is touched upon; and the unprincipled libertine, who slew the Earl of Shrewsbury while his adulterous countess held his horse in the disguise of a page, and who boasted of caressing her before he changed the bloody clothes in which he had murdered her husband, is not exposed to hatred, whilst the spendthrift and castle builder are held up to contempt. So just, however, is the picture drawn by Dryden, that it differs little from the following sober historical account.

"'The Duke of Buckingham was a man of great parts, and an infinite deal of wit and humour; but wanted judgment, and had no virtue, or principle of any kind. These essential defects made his whole life one train of inconsistencies. He was ambitious beyond measure, and implacable in his resentments; these qualities were the effects or different faces of his pride; which, whenever he pleased to lay aside, no man living could be more entertaining in conversation. He had a wonderful talent in turning all things into ridicule; but, by his own conduct, made a more ridiculous figure in the world than any which he could, with all his vivacity of wit and turn of imagination, draw of others. Frolic and pleasure took up the greatest part of his life: and in these he had neither any taste nor set himself any bounds: running into the wildest extravagances and pushing his debaucheries to a height, which even a libertine age could not help censuring as downright madness. He inherited the best estate which any subject had at that time in England; yet his profuseness made him always necessitous, as that necessity made him grasp at every thing that would help to support his expenses. He was lavish without generosity, and proud without magnanimity; and though he did not want some bright talents, yet no good one ever made part of his composition; for there was nothing so mean that he would not stoop to, nor anything so flagrantly impious but he was capable of undertaking.' "

"Buckingham's death," concludes the commentator, "was as awful a beacon as his life. He had dissipated a princely fortune, and lost both the means of procuring and the power of enjoying the pleasures to which he was devoted. He had fallen from the highest pinnacle of ambition into the last degree of contempt and disregard." His dying scene, in a paltry inn, in Yorkshire, has been immortalized by Pope's beautiful lines:—

> "In the worst inn's worst room, with mat half hung;
> The floors of plaister and the walls of dung;
> On once a flock bed, but repaired with straw,
> With tape-tied curtains never meant to draw,
> The George and Garter, dangling from that bed,
> Where tawdry yellow strove with dirty red,
> Great Villiers lies! Alas! how changed from him!
> That life of pleasure and that soul of whim;
> Gallant and gay in Cliefden's proud alcove,
> The bower of wanton Shrewsbury and love;
> Or just as gay at council, in a ring
> Of mimicked statesmen and a merry king;
> No wit to flatter left of all his store,
> No fool to laugh at, which he valued more;
> There victor of his health, of fortune, friends,
> And fame, this lord of useless thousands ends!"*

"The worst inn's worst room," however, is a poetical fiction. Buckingham died at the house of one of his tenants at Kirby Mallory, where he was overtaken with illness. He had wasted his fortune to a comparifive nothing; but was not reduced to such necessity as the poet would imply.†

Andrew Marvel makes the statue of Charing Cross the speaker in one of his witty libels on Charles and his brother. There was an equestrian statue of Charles II. at Woolchurch, the horse of which is made to hold a dialogue with this other. The poet fancies that the riders, "weary of sitting all day,"

---

* Scott's Edition of "Dryden," vol. ix., p. 270.
† See the life of him by his retainer Fairfax, and the account of him on his deathbed in the "Collection of Letters of several Persons of Quality and others."

stole off one evening, and the two horses came together. The readers at Will's must have been a little astonished at the boldness of such passages as the following :—

"Quoth the marble horse, It would make a stone speak,
To see a Lord Mayor and a Lombard Street beak,
Thy founder and mine, to cheat one another,
When both knaves agreed to be each other's brother.
Here Charing broke forth, and thus he went on—
My brass is provoked as much as thy stone
To see church and state bow down to a ——
And the King's chief ministers holding the door,
The money of widows and orphans employed,
And the bankers quite broke to maintain the ——'s pride.
WOOLCHURCH. To see *Dei Gratia* writ on the throne.
And the King's wicked life says God there is none.
CHARING. That he should be styled Defender of the Faith,
Who believes not a word what the Word of God saith.
WOOLCHURCH. That the Duke should turn Papist, and that church defy,
For which his own father a Martyr did die.
CHARING. Tho' he changed his religion, I hope he's so civil,
Not to think his own father has gone to the Devil.
    *   *   *   *   *

CHARING. Pause, brother, awhile, and calmly consider
What thou hast to say against my royal rider.
WOOLCHURCH. Thy priest-ridden King turned desperate fighter
For the surplice, lawn-sleeves, the cross, and the mitre;
Till at last on the scaffold he was left in the lurch,
By knaves, who cried themselves up for the church,
Archbishops and bishops, archdeacons and deans.
CHARING. Thy King will ne'er fight unless for his Queens.
WOOLCHURCH. He that dys for ceremonys, dys like a fool.
CHARING. The King on thy back is a lamentable tool.
WOOLCHURCH. The goat and the lion I equally hate,
And freemen alike value life and estate:
Tho' the father and son be different rods,
Between the two scourgers we find little odds;
Both infamous stand in three kingdoms' votes,
This for picking our pockets, that for cutting our throats.
    *   *   *   *   *

What is thy opinion of James Duke of York?
CHARING. The same that the frogs had of Jupiter's stork.
With the Turk in his head, and the Pope in his heart,
Father Patrick's disciples will make England smart.
If e'er he be king, I know Britain's doom,
We must all to a stake, or be converts to Rome.
Ah! Tudor, ah! Tudor, of Stuarts enough;
None ever reigned like old Bess in the ruff.
    *   *   *   *   *

WOOLCHURCH. But canst thou devise when things will be mended?
CHARING. When the reign of the line of the Stuarts is ended."

And these very lampoons had a hand in ending them.

In the days of Buckingham there was a famous house of entertainment in Charing Cross, called Locket's Ordinary. Where it exactly stood seems to be no longer known : we suspect by the great Northumberland Coffee-house. " It is often mentioned," says a manuscript in Birch's collection, "in the plays of Cibber, Vanbrugh, &c., where the scene sometimes is laid." It was much* frequented by Sir George Etherege, as appears from the following anecdotes, picked up at the British Museum. Sir George Etherege and his company, " provoked by something amiss in the entertainment or attendance, got into a violent passion and abused the waiters. This brought in Mrs. Locket : ' We are so provoked,' said Sir George, 'that even I could find in my heart to pull the nosegay out of your bosom, and throw the flowers in your face.' This turned all their anger into jest."

" Sir G. Etherege discontinued Locket's Ordinary, having run up a score which he could not conveniently discharge. Mrs. Locket sent one to dun him, and to threaten him with a prosecution. He bid the messenger tell her that he would kiss her if she stirred a step in it. When this answer was brought back, she called for her hood and scarf, and told her husband, who interposed, that ' she'd see if there was any fellow alive who had the impudence.' 'Pr'ythee, my dear, don't be so rash,' said her husband, 'you don't know what a man may do in his passion.' "*

The site of the tavern is now also unknown, where Prior was found, when a boy, reading Horace. It was called the Rummer. Mr. Nichols has found that, in the year 1685, it was kept by " Samuel Prior," and that the " annual feasts of the nobility and gentry living in the parish of St. Martin " were held there, October 14, in that year. " Prior," says Johnson, " is supposed to have fallen, by his father's death, into the hands of his uncle, a vintner near Charing Cross, who sent him for some time to Dr. Busby, at Westminster ; but, not intending to give him any education beyond that of the school, took him, when he was well educated in literature, to his own house, where the Earl of Dorset, celebrated for patronage of genius, found him by chance, as Burnet relates, reading Horace, and was so well pleased with his proficiency, that he undertook the care and cost of his academical education." †

* MSS. Birch, 4221, quoted in the Notes of the Tatler, *ut supra*, vol. i., p. 208.
† Life of Prior in the "Lives of the Poets."

It is doubtful, however, from one of Prior's epistles to Fleetwood Shepherd. whether the poet was more indebted to the Lord Dorset or to that gentleman for his first advancement in life, though the Earl finally became his great patron. He says to Shepherd,—

> "Now, as you took me up when little
> Gave me my learning and my vittle,
> Asked for me, from my lord, things fitting
> Kind, as I 'ad been your own begetting,
> Confirm what formerly you 've given,
> Nor leave me now at six and seven,
> As Sunderland has left Mun Stephen."

And again :—

> "My uncle, rest his soul! when living,
> Might have contrived me ways of thriving;
> Taught me with cider to replenish
> My vats, or ebbing tide of Rhenish;
> So, when for hock I drew pricked white-wine,
> Swear 't had the flavour, and was right-wine;
> Or sent me with ten pounds to Furni-
> Val's Inn, to some good rogue attorney;
> Where now, by forging deeds and cheating,
> I 'ad found some handsome ways of getting.
> All this you made me quit to follow
> That sneaking, whey-fac'd god Apollo;
> Sent me among a fiddling crew
> Of folks, I 'ad never seen nor knew,
> Calliope, and God knows who.
> I add no more invectives to it,
> You spoiled the youth to make a poet."

Johnson says " A survey of the life and writings of Prior may exemplify a sentence which he doubtless understood well when he read Horace at his uncle's ; ' the vessel long retains the scent which it first receives.'   In his private relaxation he revived the tavern, and in his amorous pedantry he exhibited the college.   But on higher occasions and nobler subjects, when habit was overpowered by the necessity of reflection, he wanted not wisdom as a statesman, or elegance as a poet."   It is doubtful whether the general colour of everybody's life and character might not be found in that of his childhood ; but there is no more reason to think that Prior's tavern propensities were owing to early habit than those of his patrician companions.   No man was fonder of his bottle than Lord Dorset, and of low company than many a lord has been.   According to Burke, who was a king's man, kings are naturally fond of low company.   Yet they are no nephews of tavern-keepers.   Nor does it appear that Prior did anything in his uncle's house but pass the time and read.

Thomson wrote part of his "Seasons" in the room over the shop of Mr. Egerton, bookseller, where he resided when he first came to London.   He was at that time a raw Scotchman, gaping about town, getting his pocket picked, and obliged to wait upon great men with his poem of "Winter."   Luckily his admiration of freedom did not hinder him from acquiring the highest patronage.   He obtained an easy place, which required no compromise with his principles, and passed the latter part of his life in a dwelling of his own at Richmond, writing in his garden, and listening to nightingales.   He was of an indolent constitution, and has been seen in his garden eating peaches off the trees, with his hands in his waistcoat pockets.   But his indolence did not hinder him from writing. He had the luck to have the occupation he was fond of ; and no man perhaps in his native country, with the exception of Shakspeare, has acquired a greater or more unenvied fame. His friends loved him, and his readers love his memory.

In Spring Gardens, originally a place of public entertainment, died Mrs. Centlivre, the sprightly authoress of the "Wonder," the "Busy Body," and the "Bold Stroke for a Wife."   She was buried at St. Martin's.   She is said to have been a beauty, an accomplished linguist, and a good-natured friendly woman.   Pope put her in his "Dunciad," for having written, it is said, a ballad against his "Homer" when she was a child ! But the probability is that she was too intimate with Steele and other friends of Addison while the irritable poet was at variance with them.   It is not impossible, also, that some raillery of hers might have been applied to him, not very pleasant from a beautiful woman against a man of his personal infirmities, who was naturally jealous of not being well with the sex.   Mrs. Centlivre is said to have been seduced when young by Anthony Hammond, father of the author of the "Love Elegies," who took her to Cambridge with him in boy's clothes.   This did not hinder her from marrying a nephew of Sir Stephen Fox, who died a year thereafter ; nor from having two husbands afterwards.   Her second was an officer in the army, of the name of Carrol, who, to her great sorrow, was killed in a duel.   Her third husband, Mr. Centlivre, who had the formidable title of Yeoman of the Mouth, being principal cook to Queen Anne, fell in love with her when she was performing the part of

Alexander the Great, at Windsor ; for she appears at one time to have been an actress, though she never performed in London.   Mrs. Centlivre's dramas are not in the taste of Mrs. Hannah More's, but the public still have a regard for them. All the plays above-mentioned are stock pieces.   The reason is, that, careless as they are in dialogue, and not very scrupulous in manners, they are full of action and good-humour.

Hedge Lane retained its name till lately, when, ceasing to be a heap of squalidity, it was new christened and received the appellation of Dorset Place.   Part of it is merged in Pall Mall East.   It is now the handsomest end of the thoroughfare which runs up into Oxford Road, and takes the successive names of Whitcomb, Princes, and Wardour Streets. Not long ago the whole thoroughfare appears to have been called Hedge Lane.   It is related of Steele, Budgel, and Philips, that, issuing from a tavern one day in Gerrard Street, they were about to turn into Hedge Lane, when they were told that some suspicious-looking persons were standing there as if in wait. "Thank ye," said the wits, and hurried three different ways.

It is not pleasant to have old places altered which are connected with interesting recollections, even if the place or recollection be none of the pleasantest.   When the houses in Suffolk Street were pulled down, we could not help regretting that the abode was among them in which poor Miss Vanhomrigh lived, who died for love of Swift. She resided there with her mother, the widow of a Dutch merchant, and had a small fortune.   Swift while in England, upon the affairs of the Irish Church, was introduced to them, and became so intimate as to leave his best gown and cassock there for convenience.   He found the coffee also very pleasant, and gradually became too much interested in the romantic spirit and flattering attentions of the young lady, whose studies he condescended to direct, and who, in short, fell in love with him at an age when he was old enough to be her father.   Unluckily he was married ; and most unluckily he did not say a word about the matter.   It is curious to observe in the letters which he sent over to Stella (his wife), with what an affected indifference he speaks of the Vanhomrighs and his visits to them, evidently thinking it necessary all the while to account for their frequency.   When he left England, Miss Vanhomrigh, after the death of her mother, followed him, and proposed that he should either marry or refuse her. He would do neither.

At length both the ladies, the married and unmarried, discovered their mutual secret : a discovery which is supposed
ultimately to have hastened the death of both. Miss Vanhomrigh's survival of it was short—not many weeks. For
what may remain to be said on this painful subject the
reader will allow us to quote a passage from one of the
magazines.

"There was a vanity, perhaps, on both sides, though it may be
wrong to attribute a passion wholly to that infirmity, where the
object of it is not only a person celebrated, but one full of wit and
entertainment.   The vanity was certainly not the less on his side.
Many conjectures have been made respecting the nature of this connection of Swift's, as well as another more mysterious.   The whole
truth, in the former instance, appears obvious enough.   Swift, partly
from vanity, and partly from a more excusable craving after some
recreation of his natural melancholy, had suffered himself to take a
pleasure, and exhibit an interest, in the conversation of an intelligent
young woman, beyond what he ought to have done.   An attachment
on her part ensued, not greater, perhaps, than he contemplated with
a culpable satisfaction as long as it threatened no very great disturbance of his peace, but which must have given him great remorse in
after-times, when he reflected upon his encouragement of it.   On the
occasion of its disclosure his self-love inspired him with one of his
most poetical fancies:—

> 'Cadenus many things had writ ;
> Vanessa much esteemed his wit,
> And called for his poetic works:
> Meanwhile the boy in secret lurks,
> And while the book was in her hand
> The urchin from his private stand,
> Took aim, and shot with all his strength
> A dart of such prodigious length,
> It pierced the feeble volume through,
> And deep transfixed her bosom too.
> Some lines more moving than the rest,
> Stuck to the point that pierced her breast,
> And borne directly to the heart,
> With pains unknown increased her smart.
> Vanessa, not in years a score,
> Dreams of a gown of forty-four,
> Imaginary charms can find
> In eyes with reading almost blind:
> Cadenus now no more appears
> Declined in health, advanced in years,
> She fancies music in his tongue,
> Nor farther looks, but thinks him young.'

"A reflection ensues which it is a pity he had not made before:—

> 'What mariner is not afraid
> To venture in a ship decayed ?
> What planter will attempt to yoke
> A sapling with a fallen oak ?

As years increase she brighter shines,
Cadenus with each day declines;
And he must fall a prey to time
While she continues in her prime.'

"If he had thought of this when he used to go to her mother's house in order to change his wig and gown and drink coffee, he would have avoided those encouragements of Miss Vanhomrigh's sympathy and admiration, which must have given rise to very bitter reflections when she read such passages as the lines that follow :—

' Cadenus, common forms apart,
In every scene had kept his heart;
Had sighed and languished, vowed and writ,
For pastime, or to show his wit.'

"It was sport to him, but death to her. His allegations of not being conscious of anything on her part, are not to be trusted. There are few men whose self-love is not very sharp-sighted on such occasions,—men of wit in particular; nor was Swift, notwithstanding the superiority he assumed over fopperies of all sorts, and the great powers which gave a passport to the assumption, exempt, perhaps, from any species of vanity. The more airs he gives himself on that point, the less we are to believe him. He was fond of lords and great ladies, and levees, and canonicals, and of having the verger to walk before him. He saw very well, we may be assured, the impression which he made on the young lady; but he hoped, as others have hoped, that it would accommodate itself to circumstances in cases of necessity; or he pretended to himself that he was too modest to believe it a great one; or sacrificing her ultimate good to her present pleasure and to his own, he put off the disagreeable day of alteration and self-denial till it was too late. There are many reasons why Swift should have acted otherwise, and why no man, at any time of life, should hazard the peace of another by involvements which he cannot handsomely follow up. If he does, he is bound to do what he can for it to the last."*

The famous Calves' Head Club (in ridicule of the memory of Charles I.) was held at a tavern in Suffolk Street ; at least the assembly of it was held there which made so much noise in the last century, and produced a riot. At this meeting it was said that a bleeding calf's head had been thrown out of the window, wrapt up in a napkin, and that the members drank damnation to the race of the Stuarts. This was believed till the other day, and has often been lamented as a disgusting instance of party spirit. To say the truth, the very name of the club was disgusting, and a dishonour to the men who invented it. It was more befitting their own heads. But the particulars above mentioned are untrue. The letter has been set right by the publication of " Spence's Anecdotes," at the end of which are some letters to Mr. Spence, including one from Lord Middlesex, giving the real account of the

* New Monthly Magazine, vol. xvii., p. 140.

affair. By the style of the letter the reader may judge what sort of heads the members had, and what was reckoned the polite way of speaking to a waiter in those days :—

Whitehall, Feb. yᵉ 9th, 1735.

" Dear *Spanco*,

" I don't in the least doubt but long before this time the noise of the riot on the 30 of Jan. has reached you at Oxford, and though there has been as many lies and false reports raised upon the occasion in this good city as any reasonable man could expect, yet I fancy even those may be improved or increased before they come to you. Now, that you may be able to defend your friends (as I don't in the least doubt you have an inclination to do), I'll send you the matter of fact literally and truly as it happened, upon my honour. Eight of us happened to meet together the 30th of January, it might have been the 10th of June, or any other day in the year, but the mixture of the company has convinced most reasonable people by this time that it was not a designed or premeditated affair. We met, then, as I told you before, by chance upon this day, and after dinner, having drunk very plentifully, especially some of the company, some of us going to the window unluckily saw a little nasty fire made by some boys in the street, of straw I think it was, and immediately cried out, ' Damn it, why should not we have a fire as well as anybody else?' Up comes the drawer, ' Damn you, you rascal, get us a bonfire.' Upon which the imprudent puppy runs down, and without making any difficulty (which he might have done by a thousand excuses, and which if he had, in all probability, some of us would have come more to our senses), sends for the faggots, and in an instant behold a large fire blazing before the door. Upon which some of us, wiser, or rather soberer, than the rest, bethinking themselves then, for the first time, what day it was, and fearing the consequences a bonfire on that day might have, proposed drinking loyal and popular healths to the mob (out of the window), which by this time was very great, in order to convince them we did not intend it as a ridicule upon that day. The healths that were drank out of the window were these, and these only: The King, Queen, and Royal Family, the Protestant Succession, Liberty and Property, the present Administration. Upon which the first stone was flung, and then began our siege: which, for the time it lasted, was at least as furious as that of Philipsbourgh; it was more than an hour before we got any assistance; the more sober part of us, doing this, had a fine time of it, fighting to prevent fighting; in danger of being knocked on the head by the stones that came in at the windows; in danger of being run through by our mad friends, who, sword in hand, swore they would go out, though they first made their way through us. At length the justice, attended by a strong body of guards, came and dispersed the populace. The person who first stirred up the mob is known; he first gave them money, and then harangued them in a most violent manner; I don't know if he did not fling the first stone himself. He is an Irishman and a priest, and belonging to Imberti, the Venetian Envoy. This is the whole story from which so many calves' heads, bloody napkins, and the Lord knows what has been made; it has been the talk of the town and the country, and small beer and bread and cheese to my friends the Gar-

retters in Grub Street, for these few days past. I, as well as your
friends, hope to see you soon in town. After so much prose, I can't
help ending with a few verses:—

O had I lived in merry Charles's days,
When dull the wise were called, and wit had praise ;
When deepest politics could never pass
For aught, but surer tokens of an ass;
When not the frolicks of one drunken night
Could touch your honour, make your fame less bright,
Tho' mob-form'd scandal rag'd, and Papal spight.
                                        "MIDDLESEX."

The author of a " Secret History of the Calves' Head Club,
or the Republicans Unmasked" (supposed to be Ned Ward, of
ale-house memory), attributes the origin to Milton and some
other friends of the Commonwealth, in opposition to Bishop
Juxon, Dr. Sanderson, and others, who met privately every
30th of January, and had compiled a private form of service
for the day, not very different from that now in use.

"After the Restoration," says the writer, "the eyes of the Government being upon the whole party, they were obliged to meet with a
great deal of precaution; but in the reign of King William they met
almost in a public manner, apprehending no danger." The writer
farther tells us, he was informed that it was kept in no fixed house,
but that they moved as they thought convenient. The place where
they met when his informant was with them was in a blind alley
near Moorfields, where an axe hung up in the club-room, and was
reverenced as a principal symbol in this diabolical sacrament. Their
bill of fare was a large dish of calves' heads, dressed several ways, by
which they represented the king and his friends who had suffered in his
cause; a large pike, with a small one in his mouth, as an emblem of
tyranny; a large cod's head by which they intended to represent the
person of the king singly ; a boar's head with an apple in its mouth,
to represent the king by this as bestial, as by their other hieroglyphics
they had done foolish and tyrannical. After the repast was over, one
of their elders presented an *Icon Basilike,* which was with great
solemnity burnt upon the table, whilst the other anthems were singing. After this, another produced Milton's *Defensio Populi Anglicani,*
upon which all laid their hands, and made a protestation in form of
an oath for ever to stand by and maintain the same. The company
only consisted of Independents and Anabaptists; and the famous
Jeremy White, formerly chaplain to Oliver Cromwell, who no doubt
came to sanctify with his pious exhortations the ribaldry of the day,
said grace. After the table-cloth was removed, the anniversary
anthem, as they impiously called it, was sung, and a calf's skull filled
with wine, or other liquor; and then a brimmer went about to the
pious memory of those worthy patriots who had killed the tyrant and
relieved their country from his arbitrary sway: and, lastly, a collection was made for the mercenary scribbler, to which every man contributed according to his zeal for the cause and ability of his purse."

"Although no great reliance," says Mr. Wilson, from whose life
of De Foe this passage is extracted, " is to be placed upon the faith-

fulness of Ward's narrative, yet, in the frighted mind of a high-flying churchman, which was continually haunted by such scenes, the caricature would easily pass for a likeness." "It is probable," adds the honest biographer of De Foe, "that the persons thus collected together to commemorate the triumph of their principles, although in a manner dictated by bad taste, and outrageous to humanity, would have confined themselves to the ordinary methods of eating and drinking, if it had not been for the ridiculous farce so generally acted by the royalists upon the same day. The trash that issued from the pulpit in this reign, upon the 30th of January, was such as to excite the worst passions in the hearers. Nothing can exceed the grossness of language employed upon these occasions. Forgetful even of common decorum, the speakers ransacked the vocabulary of the vulgar for terms of vituperation, and hurled their anathemas with wrath and fury against the objects of their hatred. The terms rebel and fanatic were so often upon their lips, that they became the reproach of honest men, who preferred the scandal to the slavery they attempted to establish. Those who could profane the pulpit with so much rancour in the support of senseless theories, and deal it out to the people for religion, had little reason to complain of a few absurd men who mixed politics and calves' heads at a tavern; and still less, to brand a whole religious community with their actions."*

Scotland Yard is so called from a palace built for the reception of the Kings of Scotland when they visited this

SCOTLAND YARD IN 1750.

country. Pennant tells us that it was originally given to King Edgar, by Kenneth, Prince of that country, for the purpose of his coming to pay him annual homage, as Lord Paramount of Scotland. Margaret, widow of James V. and sister of Henry VIII., resided there a considerable time after the death of her husband, and was magnificently entertained

.* Memoirs of the Life and Writings of De Foe, 1829, vol. ii., p. 116.

by her brother on his becoming reconciled to her second marriage with the Earl of Angus.* When the Crowns became united, James I. of course waived his right of abode in the homage-paying house, which was finally deserted as a royal residence. We know not when it was demolished. Probably it was devoted for some time to Government offices. Scotland Yard was the place of one of Milton's abodes during the time he served the Government of Cromwell. He lost an infant son there. The eccentric Beau Fielding died in it at the beginning of the last century, and Vanbrugh a little after him. There was a coffee-house in the yard, which seems, by the following pleasant advertisement, to have been frequented by good company :—

"Whereas six gentlemen (all of the same honourable profession), having been more than ordinarily put to it for a little pocket-money, did, on the 14th instant, in the evening, near Kentish Town, borrow of two persons (in a coach) a certain sum of money, without staying to give bond for the repayment: And whereas fancy was taken to the hat, peruke, cravat, sword, and cane, of one of the creditors, which were all lent as freely as the money: these are therefore to desire the said six worthies, how fond soever they may be of the other loans, to un-fancy the cane again and send it to Well's Coffee House in Scotland Yard; it being too short for any such proper gentlemen as they are to walk with, and too small for any of their important uses; and withal, only valuable as having been the gift of a friend."†

Beau Fielding was thought worthy of record by Sir Richard Steele, as an extraordinary instance of the effects of personal vanity upon a man not without wit. He was of the noble family of Fielding, and was remarkable for the beauty of his person, which was a mixture of the Hercules and the Adonis. It is described as having been a real model of perfection. He married to his first wife the dowager Countess of Purbeck ; followed the fortunes of James II., who is supposed to have made him a major-general and perhaps a count; returned and married a woman of the name of Wadsworth, under the impression that she was a lady of fortune ; and, discovering his error, addressed or accepted the addresses of the notorious Duchess of Cleveland, and married her, who, on discovering her mistake in turn, indicted him for bigamy and obtained a divorce. Before he left England to follow James, "Handsome Fielding," as he was called, appears to have been insane with

* Pennant, p. 110.
† Extracted from Salisbury's Flying Post, of October 27, 1696, in Malcolm's Manners and Customs of London to the year 1700, vol. i., p. 396.

vanity. On his return, he had added, to the natural absurdities
of that passion, the indecency of being old ; but this only
rendered him the more perverse in his folly.　He always
appeared in an extraordinary dress : sometimes rode in an
open tumbril, of less size than ordinary, the better to display
the nobleness of his person ; and his footmen appeared in
liveries of yellow, with black feathers in their hats, and black
sashes.　When people laughed at him, he refuted them, as
Steele says, " by only moving."　Sir Richard says he saw
him one day stop and call the boys about him, to whom he
spoke as follows :—

"Good youths,—Go to school, and do not lose your time in
following my wheels : I am loth to hurt you, because I know
not but you are all my own offspring.　Hark ye, you sirrah
with the white hair, I am sure you are mine, there is half-a-
crown for you.　Tell your mother, this, with the other half-
crown I gave her　.　.　.　. comes to five shillings.　Thou
hast cost me all that, and yet thou art good for nothing.
Why, you young dogs, did you never see a man before?"
"Never such a one as you, noble general," replied a truant
from Westminster.　"Sirrah, I believe thee: there is a crown
for thee.　Drive on, coachman."　Swift puts him in his list of
Mean Figures, as one who "at fifty years of age, when he was
wounded in a quarrel upon the stage, opened his breast and
showed the wound to the ladies, that he might move their love
and pity ; but they all fell a laughing."　His vanity, which
does not appear to have been assisted by courage, sometimes
got him into danger.　He is said to have been caned and
wounded by a Welsh gentleman, in the theatre in Lincoln's
Inn Fields; and pressing forward once at a benefit of Mrs. Oldfield's, 'to show himself,' he trod on Mr. Fulwood, a barrister,
who gave him a wound twelve inches deep.　His fortune,
which he ruined by early extravagance, he thought to have
repaired by his marriage with Mrs. Wadsworth, and endeavoured to do so by gambling ; but succeeded in neither
attempt, and after the short-lived splendour with the Duchess
of Cleveland, returned to his real wife, whom he pardoned,
and died under her care.　During the height of his magnificence, he carried his madness so far, according to Steele, as
to call for his tea by beat of drum ; his valet got ready to
shave him by a trumpet to horse; and water was brought for
his teeth, when the sound was changed to boots and saddle."
If this looks like a jest, there is no knowing how far vanity

might be carried, especially when the patient may cloak it from himself under the guise of giving way to a humour.*

Vanbrugh, comic poet, architect, and herald, was comptroller of the royal works. His house in Whitehall, built by himself, was remarkable for its smallness. Swift compared it to a goose-pie. On the other hand, his Blenheim and public buildings are ridiculed for their ponderous hugeness. The close of Dr. Evans's epitaph upon him is well known:—

> Lie heavy on him earth, for he
> Laid many a heavy load on thee.

When he was made Clarencieux king-at-arms, Swift said he might now " build houses." The secret of this ridicule was, that Vanbrugh was a Whig. Sir Joshua Reynolds has left the following high encomium on his merits as an architect. " In the buildings of Vanbrugh, who was a poet as well as an architect, there is a greater display of imagination than we shall find, perhaps, in any other ; and this is the ground of the effect we feel in many of his works, notwithstanding the faults with which many of them are charged. For this purpose, Vanbrugh appears to have had recourse to some principles of the Gothic architecture, which, though not so ancient as the Grecian, *is more so to our imagination*, with which the artist is more concerned than with absolute truth." " To speak of Vanbrugh (adds Sir Joshua), in the language of a painter, he had originality of invention; he understood light and shadow, and had great skill in composition. To support his principal object, he produced his second and third groups or masses. He perfectly understood in his art, what is the most difficult in ours, the conduct of the back-ground, by which the design and invention are set off to the greatest advantage. What the back-ground is in painting, in architecture is the real ground on which the building is erected ; and no architect took greater care that his work should not appear crude and hard ; that is, that it did not abruptly start out of the ground without expectation or preparation. This is a tribute which a painter owes to an architect who com-

---

* See State Trials, *ut supra*, " Egerton's Memoirs of Mrs. Oldfield;" " Swift's Great and Mean Figures," vol. xvii., 1765 ; and the " History of Orlando the Fair, in the Tatler," as above, Nos. 50 and 51. " The author of Memoirs of Fielding in the Select Trials," says a note on the latter number, " admits, that for all the ludicrous air and pleasantry of this narration (Steele's), the truth of facts and character is in general fairly represented."

posed like a painter, and was defrauded of the due reward of his merit by the wits of his time, *who did not understand the principles of composition in poetry better than he, and who knew little or nothing of what he understood perfectly—the general ruling principles of architecture and painting.* Vanbrugh's fate was that of the great Perrault. Both were the objects of the petulant sarcasms of factious men of letters, and both have left some of the fairest monuments which, to this day, decorate their several countries;—the façade of the Louvre; Blenheim, and Castle Howard."[*] Perrault, however, had a worse fate than Vanbrugh, for the Frenchman was ridiculed not only as an architect but as a man of letters, whereas our author's pretensions that way were acknowledged.

In the front of Scotland Yard an extraordinary adventure befell Lord Herbert of Cherbury—(*see* Queen Street, Lincoln's Inn Fields), who relates it in a strain of coxcombry (particularly about the ladies) which would have brought discredit upon such a story from any other pen. There is no doubt, however, that the story is true.

"There was a lady," says his lordship, "wife to Sir John Ayres, knight, who finding some means to get a copy of my picture from Larkin, gave it to Mr. Isaac, the painter, in Blackfriars, and desired him to draw it in little, after his manner; which being done, she caused it to be set in gold and enamelled, and so wore it about her neck so low that she hid it under her breasts, which I conceive, coming afterwards to the knowledge of Sir John Ayres, gave him more cause of jealousie than needed, had he known how innocent I was from pretending to anything that might wrong him or his lady, since I could not so much as imagine that either she had my picture, or that she bare more than ordinary affection to me. It is true, that as she had a place in court, and attended Queen Anne, and was beside of an excellent wit and discourse, she had made herself a considerable person. Howbeit, little more than a common civility ever passed betwixt us; though I confess I think no man was welcomer to her when I came, for which I shall allege this passage:—

"Coming one day into her chamber, I saw her through the curtains lying upon her bed with a wax candle in one hand, and the picture I formerly mentioned in the other. I coming thereupon somewhat boldly to her, she blew out the candle and hid the picture from me: myself thereupon being curious to know what that was she held in her hand, got the candle to be lighted again, by means whereof I found it was my picture she looked upon with more earnestness and passion than I could easily have believed, especially since myself was not engaged in any affection towards her. I could willingly have omitted this passage, but that it was the beginning of a bloody history which followed: howsoever, yet I must before the eternal God clear

---

[*] Discourses delivered at the Royal Academy. Sharpe's Edition, vol. ii., pp. 113, 115.

her honour. And now in court a great person sent for me divers times to attend her; which summons, though I obeyed, yet God knows I declined coming to her as much as conveniently I could without incurring her displeasure; and this I did, not only for very honest reasons, but, to speak ingenuously, because that affection passed between me and another lady (who I believe was the fairest of her time) as nothing could divert it. I had not been long in London, when a violent burning fever seized upon me, which brought me almost to my death, though at last I did by slow degrees recover my health. Being thus upon my amendment, the Lord Lisle, afterwards Earl of Leicester, sent me word, that Sir John Ayres intended to kill me in my bed; and wished me to keep guard upon my chamber and person. The same advertisement was confirmed by Lucy, Countess of Bedford, and the Lady Hobby, shortly after. Hereupon I thought fit to entreat Sir William Herbert, now Lord Powis, to go to Sir John Ayres, and tell him that I marvelled much at the information given me by these great persons, and that I could not imagine any sufficient ground hereof; howbeit, if he had anything to say to me in a fair and noble way, I would give him the meeting as soon as I had got strength enough to stand on my legs. Sir William hereupon brought me so ambiguous and doubtful an answer from him, that, whatsoever he meant, he would not declare yet his intention, which was really, as I found afterwards, to kill me any way that he could." The reason, Lord Herbert tells us, was, that Sir John, though falsely, accused him of having seduced his wife. "Finding no means thus to surprise me," continues the noble lord, "he sent me a letter to this effect; that he desired to meet me somewhere, and that it might so fall out as I might return quietly again. To this I replied, that if he desired to fight with me on equal terms, I should, upon assurance of the field and fair play, give him meeting when he did any way specify the cause, and that I did not think fit to come to him upon any other terms, having been sufficiently informed of his plots to assassinate me.

" After this, finding he could take no advantage against me, then in a treacherous way he resolved to assassinate me in this manner; —hearing I was to come to Whitehall on horseback with two lacqueys only, he attended my coming back in a place called Scotland Yard, at the hither end of Whitehall, as you come to it from the Strand, hiding himself here with four men armed to kill me. I took horse at Whitehall Gate, and, passing by that place, he being armed with a sword and dagger, without giving me so much as the least warning, ran at me furiously, but instead of me, wounded my horse in the brisket, as far as his sword could enter for the bone; my horse hereupon starting aside, he ran him again in the shoulder, which, though it made the horse more timorous, yet gave me time to draw my sword: his men thereupon encompassed me, and wounded my horse in three places more; this made my horse kick and fling in that manner, as his men durst not come near me, which advantage I took to strike at Sir John Ayres with all my force, but he warded the blow both with his sword and dagger; instead of doing him harm, I broke my sword within a foot of the hilt; hereupon, some passenger that knew me, observing my horse wounded in so many places, and so many men assaulting me, and my sword broken, cried to me several times, 'Ride away, ride away;' but I scorning a base flight upon what terms soever,

instead thereof alighted as well I could from my horse; I had no
sooner put one foot upon the ground than Sir John Ayres, pursuing
me, made at my horse again, which the horse perceiving, pressed on
me on the side I alighted, in that manner, that he threw me down, so
that I remained flat upon the ground, only one foot hanging in the
stirrup, with that piece of a sword in my right hand. Sir John Ayres
hereupon ran about the horse, and was thrusting his sword into me,
when I, finding myself in this danger, did with both my arms reaching at his legs pull them towards me, till he fell down backwards on
his head; one of my footmen hereupon, who was a little Shropshire
boy, freed my foot out of the stirrup, the other, who was a great fellow,
having run away as soon as he saw the first assault; this gave me
time to get upon my legs and to put myself in the best posture I
could with that poor remnant of a weapon; Sir John Ayres by this
time likewise was got up, standing betwixt me and some part of
Whitehall, with two men on each side of him, and his brother behind
him, with at least twenty or thirty persons of his friends, or attendants
on the Earl of Suffolk; observing thus a body of men standing in opposition against me, though to speak truly I saw no swords drawn but Sir
John Ayres' and his men, I ran violently against Sir John Ayres,
but he, knowing my sword had no point, held his sword and dagger
over his head, as believing I could strike rather than thrust, which I
no sooner perceived but I put a home thrust to the middle of his
breast, that I threw him down with so much force, that his head fell
first to the ground and his heels upwards; his men hereupon assaulted
me, when one Mr. Mansel, a Glamorganshire gentleman, finding so
many set against me alone, closed with one of them; a Scotch gentleman also, closing with another, took him off also: all I could well do
to those that remained was to ward their thrusts, which I did with
that resolution that I got ground upon them. Sir John Ayres was
now got up a third time, when I making towards him with intention
to close thinking, that there was otherwise no safety for me, put by
a thrust of his with my left hand, and so coming within him, received
a stab with his dagger on my right side, which ran down my ribs as
far as my hips, which I feeling, did with my right elbow force his
hand, together with the hilt of the dagger, so near the upper part of
my right side, that I made him leave hold. The dagger now sticking
in me, Sir Henry Carey, afterwards Lord of Faulkland, and Lord
Deputy of Ireland, finding the dagger thus in my body, snatched it
out; this while I, being closed with Sir John Ayres, hurt him on the
head and threw him down a third time, when kneeling on the ground
and bestriding him, I struck at him as hard as I could with my piece
of a sword, and wounded him in four several places, and did almost
cut off his left hand; his two men this while struck at me, but it
pleased God even miraculously to defend me, for when I lifted up my
sword to strike at Sir John Ayres, I bore off their blows half a dozen
times; his friends now finding him in this danger, took him by the
head and shoulders and drew him from betwixt my legs, and carrying
him along with them through Whitehall, at the stairs whereof he took
boat, Sir Herbert Croft (as he told me afterwards) met him upon the
water vomiting all the way, which I believe was caused by the
violence of the first thrust I gave him; his servants, brother, and
friends, being now retired also, I remained master of the place and his

weapons, having first wrested his dagger from him, and afterwards struck his sword out of his hand.

" This being done, I retired to a friend's house in the Strand, where I sent for a surgeon, who, searching my wound on the right side, and finding it not to be mortal, cured me in the space of some ten days, during which time I received many noble visits and messages from some of the best in the kingdom. Being now fully recovered of my hurts, I desired Sir Robert Harley to go to Sir John Ayres, and tell him, that though I thought he had not so much honour left in him, that I could be in any way ambitious to get it, yet that I desired to see him in the field with his sword in his hand; the answer that he sent me was (repeating the charge above mentioned) ' that he would kill me with a musket out of a window.'

" The Lords of the Privy Council, who had at first sent for my sword, that they might see the little fragment of a weapon with which I had so behaved myself, as perchance the like had not been heard in any credible way, did afterwards command both him and me to appear before them; but I, absenting myself on purpose, sent one Humphrey Hill with a challenge to him in an ordinary, which he refusing to receive, Humphrey Hill put it upon the point of his sword, and so let it fall before him and the company then present.

" The Lords of the Privy Council had now taken order to apprehend Sir John Ayres, when I, finding nothing else to be done, submitted myself likewise to them. Sir John Ayres had now published everywhere that the ground of his jealousie, and consequently of his assaulting me, was drawn from the confession of his wife, the Lady Ayres. She, to vindicate her honour, as well as free me from this accusation, sent a letter to her aunt, the Lady Crook, to this purpose: that her husband, Sir John Ayres, did lie falsely, ... but most falsely of all did lie when he said he had it from her confession, for she had never said any such thing.

" This letter the Lady Crook presented to me most opportunely, as I was going to the Counsell table before the Lords, who, having examined Sir John Ayres concerning the cause of his quarrel with me, found him still to persist on his wife's confession of the fact; and now, he being withdrawn, I was sent for, when the Duke of Lennox, afterwards of Richmond, telling me that was the ground of his quarrel, and the only excuse he had for assaulting me in that manner, I desired his lordship to peruse the letter, which I told him was given me as I came into the room; this letter being publicly read by a clerk of the Counsell, the Duke of Lennox then said, that he thought Sir John Ayres the most miserable man living, for his wife had not only given him the lie, as he found by the letter, but his father had disinherited him for attempting to kill me in that barbarous fashion, which was most true, as I found afterwards;—for the rest, that I might content myself with what I had done, it being more almost than could be believed, but that I had so many witnesses thereof; for all which reasons, he commanded me in the name of his Majesty, and all their lordships, not to send any more to Sir John Ayres, nor to receive any message from him, in the way of fighting, which commandment I observed: howbeit, I must not omit to tell, that some years afterwards Sir John Ayres, returning from Ireland by Beaumaris, where I then was, some of my servants and followers broke open the doors of the house where he was, and would, I believe, have cut him into pieces, but that I, hearing thereof, came suddenly to the house and recalled them, sending him word also that I scorned to give him the usage he gave me, and that I would set him free of the town, which courtesie of mine (as I was told afterwards) he did thankfully acknowledge."*

CHAPTER X.

WOLSEY AND WHITEHALL.

Regal Character of Whitehall—York Place—Personal and Moral Character of Wolsey—Comparison of him with his Master, Henry —His Pomp and Popularity—Humorous Account of his Flatterers by Sir Thomas More—Importance of his Hat—Cavendish's Account of his household State, his goings forth in Public, and his entertainments of the King.

HE whole district containing all that collection of streets and houses, which extends from Scotland Yard to Parliament Street, and from the river side, with its wharfs, to St. James's Park, and which is still known by the general appellation of Whitehall, was formerly occupied by a sumptuous palace and its appurtenances, the only relics of which, perhaps the noblest specimen, is the beautiful edifice built by Inigo Jones, and retaining its old name of the Banqueting House.

* Life of Lord Herbert of Cherbury, in the "Autobiography," p. 79.

As this palace was the abode of a series of English sovereigns, beginning with Henry the Eighth, who took it from
Wolsey, and terminating with James the Second, on whose
downfall it was destroyed by fire, we are now in the very
thick of the air of royalty ; and so being, we mean to lead
a princely life with the reader for a couple of chapters,—
whether he take the word "princely" in a good or ill sense,
as first in magnificence and authority, or in wilfulness and
profusion.   Cavendish, Holinshed, and the poets, will enable
us to live with Wolsey, with Henry, and with Elizabeth ;
Wilson and the poets, with James the First; Clarendon, Pepys,
and others with Charles the First, Cromwell, Charles the
Second, and his brother.   We shall eat and drink, and swell
into most unapostolical pomp, with the great Cardinal ; shall
huff and fume with Henry, and marry pretty Anne Bullen in
a closet (Lingard says in a "garret") ; send her to have her
head cut off as if nothing had happened ; be an everlasting
young old gentlewoman with Queen Elizabeth, enamouring
people's eyes at seventy ; drink and splutter, and be a great
baby, with King James; have a taste, and be henpecked, and
not very sincere, yet melancholy and much to be pitied, with
poor Charles the First; be uneasy, secret, and energetic, and
like a crowned Methodist preacher, or an old dreary piece of
English oak (choose which you will) with Oliver Cromwell ;
saunter, squander, and be gay, and periwigged, and laughing,
and ungrateful, and liked, and despised, and have twenty mistresses, and look as grim and swarthy, and with a face as full
of lines, as if we were full of melancholy and black bile,
with Charles the Second ; and, finally, have all his melancholy,
and none of his wit and mirth, with his poor, dreary, bigoted
brother James.

"Now, this is worshipful society."

Whether it be happy or not, or enviable by the least peasant
who can pay his way and sleep heartily, will be left to the
judgment of the reader.

The site of Whitehall was originally occupied by a mansion
built by Hubert de Burgh, Earl of Kent, and Chief Justice of
England in the reign of Henry the Third, one of the ancestors
of the present Marquess of Clanricarde. De Burgh bequeathed
it to the Brotherhood of the Black Friars, near "Oldborne," in
whose church he was buried ; the Brotherhood sold it to
Walter Gray, Archbishop of York, who left it to his successors in that see as the archiepiscopal residence, which pro-

cured it the name of York Place; and under that name, two
centuries and a half afterwards, it became celebrated for the
pomp and festal splendour of the " full-blown" priest, Wolsey,
the magnificent butcher's son.   Wolsey, on highly probable
evidence, is thought to have so improved and enlarged the
mansion of his predecessors, as to have in a manner rebuilt
it, and given it its first royalty of aspect: but, as we shall see
by and by, it was not called Whitehall, nor occupied anything
like the space it did afterwards, till its seizure by the Cardinal's master.

We have always thought the epithet of "full-blown," as
applied to Wolsey, the happiest poetical hit ever made by
Dr. Johnson :

> " In full-blown dignity see Wolsey stand,
> Law in his voice, and fortune in his hand."

His ostentation, his clerical robes, his very corpulence, and
his subsequent *fading*, all conspire to render the image felicitous. Wolsey is the very flower of priestly prosperity—fat,
full-blown, gorgeous, called into life by sunshine ; the very
odours he was fond of carrying in his hand, become a part of
his efflorescence; one imagines his cheek florid, and his huge,
silken vestments expanding about him, like bloated petals.
Anon, the blast blows from the horrid royal mouth : the
round flower hangs its head ; it lays its dead neck on the
earth ; and in its room, is a loathed weed.

Wolsey, however, did not grow to be what he was with the
indolence of a flower. He began his career with as much
personal as mental activity, rendered himself necessary to the
indolence of a young and luxurious Sovereign,—in fact,
became his Sovereign's will in another shape, relieving the
royal person of all trouble, and at the same time securing all
his wishes, from a treaty down to a mistress; and hence, as
he himself intimated, the whole secret of his prosperity. He
had industry, address, eloquence, the power of pleasing, the
art (till success spoilt him) of avoiding whatever was unpleasant. He could set his master at ease with himself, in the
smallest points of discourse, as well as on greater occasions.
Henry felt no misgiving in his presence. He beheld in his
lordly and luxurious agent a second self, with a superior
intellect, artfully subjected to his own, so as to imply intellectual as well as royal superiority ; and he loved the priestly
splendour of Wolsey, because, in setting the church so high,
and at the same time carrying himself so loyally, the church-

man only the more elevated the Prince. The moment the great servant appeared as if he could do without the greater master, by a fortune superior to failure in his projects, Henry's favour began to give way; and when the princely churchman, partly in the heedlessness arising from long habits of security, and partly in the natural resentment of a superior mind, expressed a doubt whether his Sovereign was acting with perfect justice towards him, his doom was sealed. Kings never forgive a wound to their self-love. They have been set so high above fellowship by their fellow-creatures, that they feel, and in some measure they have a right to feel, the least intimation of equality, much more of superiority, as an offence, especially when it is aggravated by a secret sense of the justice of the pretension; and all Wolsey's subsequent self-abasements could not do away with that stinging recollection, pleased as Henry was to widen the distance between them, and recover his own attitude of self-possession by airs of princely pity. Wolsey was a sort of Henry, himself— wilful, worldly, and fat, but with more talents and good-nature; for he appears to have been a man of rare colloquial abilities, and, where he was not opposed in large matters, of a considerate kindliness. He was an attached as well as affable master; and his consciousness of greater merit in himself would never have suffered him to send a couple of poor light-hearted girls to the scaffold, for bringing the royal marriage-bed into some shadow of a doubt of its sacredness. He would have sent them to a nunnery, and had a new marriage, without a tragedy in it, like a proper Christian Sultan! Had Henry been in Wolsey's place, he would have proposed to set up the Inquisition; and King Thomas would have reproved him, and told him that such severities did not become two such fat and jolly believers as they.

The people appear to have liked Wolsey much. They enjoyed his pomp as a spectacle, and pitied his fall. They did not grudge his pomp to one who was so generous. Besides, they had a secret complacency in the humbleness of his origin, seeing that he rose from it by real merit. Those that quarrelled with him for his pride, were proud nobles and grudging fellow-divines. It is pretty clear that Shakspeare, who was such a " good fellow " himself, had a regard for Wolsey as another. He takes opportunities of echoing his praises, and dresses his fall in robes of pathos and eloquence. As to a true feeling of religion, it is out of the question in

considering Wolsey's history and times. It was not expected
of him. It was not the fashion or the morality of the day.
It was sufficient that the Church made its way in the world,
and secretly elevated the interests of literature and scholarship along with it. A king in those times was regarded as a
visible God upon earth, not thoroughly well behaved, but
much to be believed in ; and if the Church could compete
with the State, it was hoped that more perfect times would
somehow or other ensue. A good deal of license was allowed
it on behalf of the interests of better things—a singular
arrangement, and, as the event turned out, not likely to better
itself quite so peaceably as was hoped for ; but it was making
the best, under the circumstances, of the old perplexity
between " the shows of things, and the desires of the mind."
Wolsey (as the prosperous and the upper classes are apt to
do in all ages) probably worshipped success itself as the final
proof of all which the divine Governor of the world intended,
in his dealings with individuals or society. Hence his proud
swelling while possessed of it, and his undisguised tears and
lamentations during his decline. He talks with his confidants
about the King and good fortune, like a boy crying for a cake,
and they respectfully echo his groans, and evidently think
them not at all inconsistent, either with manliness or wisdom.
There was a breadth of character in all that Wolsey thought,
did, and suffered—in his strength and in his weakness. In
his prosperity he set no bounds to his pomp ; in adversity he
cries out and calls upon the gods, not affecting to be a
philosopher. When he was angry he huffed and used big
words, like his master ; when in good humour, he loaded
people with praise ; and he loved a large measure of it himself.
He issued forth, with his goodly bulk and huge garments,
and expected a worship analogous to his amplitudes. There
is a passage written with great humour by Sir Thomas More,
which, according to Dr. Wordsworth (the poet's brother), is
intended, " no doubt, to represent the Cardinal at the head of
his table." What reasons the doctor has for not doubting the
application, we cannot say, and therefore do not think ourselves any more justified than inclined to dispute them. The
supposition is hghly probable. Wolsey must have offered a
fine dramatic spectacle to the eyes of a genius like More. We
shall therefore copy the passage for the reader's entertainment,
from a note in Mr. Singer's excellent edition of the Cardinal's
Life by Cavendish :—

"*Anthony.* I praye you, Cosyn, tell on.   *Vincent.* Whan I was fyrste in Almaine, Uncle, it happed me to be somewhat favoured *with a great manne of the churche, and a great state,* one of the greatest in all that country there.   And in dede whosoever might spende as muche as hee mighte in one thinge and other, were a ryght great estate in anye countrey of Christendom.   But *glorious* was hee verye farre above all measure, and that was great pitie, for it dyd harme, and made him abuse many great gyftes that God hadde given him.   Never was he saciate of hearinge his owne prayse.

"So happed it one daye, that he had in a great audience made an oracion in a certayne matter, wherein he liked himselfe so well, that at his dinner he sat, him thought, on thornes, tyll he might here how they that sat with hym at his borde, woulde commende it.   And whan hee had sitte musing a while, devysing, as I thought after, uppon some pretty proper waye to bring it in withal, at the laste for lacke of a better, lest he should have letted the matter too long, he brought it even blontly forth, and asked us al that satte at his bordes end (for at his owne messe in the middes there sat but himself alone) how well we lyked his oracion that he hadde made that daye.   But in fayth, Uncle, whan that probleme was once proponed, till it was full answered, *no manne (I wene) eate one morsell of meate more.*   Every manne was fallen in so depe a studye, for the fyndynge of *some exquisite prayse.*   For he that shoulde have broughte out but a vulgare and a common commendacion, woulde have thoughte himself shamed for ever.   Then sayde we our sentences by rowe as wee sat, from the lowest unto the hyghest in good order, *as it had bene a great matter of the common weale, in a right solemne counsayle.*   Whan it came to my parte, I wyll not say it, Uncle, for no boaste, mee thoughte, by oure Ladye, for my parte, I quytte my selfe metelye wel.   And I lyked my selfe the better because mee thoughte my words beeinge but a straungyer, wente yet with some grace in the Almain tong; wherein lettyng my latin alone me listed to shewe my cunnyng, and I hoped to be lyked the better, because I sawe that he that sate next mee, and should saie his sentence after mee, was an unlearned Prieste, for he could speake no latin at all.   But whan he came furth for hys part with my Lordes commendation, the wyly fox hadde be so well accustomed in courte with the crafte of flattry, that he wente beyonde me to farre.

"And then might I see by hym, what excellence a right meane witte may come to in one crafte, that in al his whole life studyeth and busyeth his witte about no mo but that one.   But I made after a solempne vowe unto my selfe, that if ever he and I were matched together at that boarde agayne, whan we should fall to our flattrye, I would flatter in latin, that he should not contende with me no more.   For though I could be contente to be out runne by an horse, yet would I no more abyde it to be out runne of an asse.   But, Uncle, here beganne nowe the game; he that sate hyghest, and was to speake, was a great beneficed man, and not a Doctour only, but also somewhat learned in dede in the lawes of the Churche.   A worlde it was to see howe he marked every mannes worde that spake before him.   And it seemed that every worde *the more proper it was, the worse he liked it, for the cumbrance that he had to study out a better to passe it.*   The manne even swette with the laboure, so that he was faine in the while now and than to wipe his face.   Howbeit in conclusion whan it came to his course, we that had spoken before him, hadde so taken up al among us before, that we hadde not lefte him one wye worde to speake after.

"*Anthony*. Alas good manne! amonge so manye of you, some good felow shold have lente hym one. *Vincent*. It needed not, as happe was, Uncle. For he found out such a shift, that in hys flatterying *he passed us all the many*. *Anthony*. Why, what sayde he, Cosyn? *Vincent*. By our Ladye, Uncle, *not one worde*. But lyke as I trow Plinius telleth, that when Appelles the Paynter in the table that he paynted of the sacryfyce and the death of Iphigenia, hadde in the makynge of the sorrowefull countenances of the other noble menne of Greece that beehelde it, spente out so much of his craft and hys cunnynge, that whan he came to make the countenance of King Agamemnon her father, which hee reserved for the laste . . . . . he could devise no maner of newe heavy chere and countenance—but to the intent that no man should see what maner countenance it was, that her father hadde, the paynter was fayne to paynte him, holdyng his face in his handkercher—the like pageant in a maner plaide us there *this good aunciente honourable flatterer*. For whan he sawe that he coulde fynde no woordes of prayse, that woulde passe al that hadde bene spoken before all readye, the wyly Fox woulde speake never a worde, *but as he that were ravished unto heavenwarde with the wonder of the wisdom and eloquence that my Lordes Grace had uttered in that oracyon, he fette a long syghe with an Oh! from the bottome of his breste, and helde uppe bothe hys handes, and lyfte uppe both his handes, and lyfte uppe his head, and caste up his eyen into the welkin and wept.*"

But if Wolsey set store by his fine speaking, he knew also what belonged to his *hat*; he was quite alive to the effect produced by his office, and knew how to *get up* and pamper a ceremony—to cook up a raw material of dignity for the public relish. It should be no fault of his, that any toy of his rank should not be looked up to with awe. Accordingly, a most curious story is told of the way in which he contrived that the Cardinal's hat, which was sent him during his residence in York Place, should make its first appearance in public. Cavendish says, that the hat having been sent by the Pope through the hands of an ordinary messenger, without any state, Wolsey caused him to be " stayed by the way," newly dressed in rich apparel, and met by a gorgeous cavalcade of prelates and gentry. But a note in Mr. Singer's edition, referring to Tindal and Fox, tells us that the messenger actually reached him in York Place, was clothed by him as aforesaid, *and sent back with the hat to Dover*, from whence the cavalcade went and fetched him. The hat was then set on a sideboard full of plate, with tapers round about it, " and the greatest Duke in the lande must make curtesie thereto."

Cavendish has given a minute account of the household at York Place, from which the following are extracts. Compare them with the recollection of " the disciples plucking ears of corn :"—

" He had in his hall, daily, three especial tables furnished with three principal officers ; that is to say, a Steward, which was always a dean or a priest ; a Treasurer, a knight ; and a Comptroller, an esquire; which bore always within his house their white staves. Then had he a cofferer, three marshals, two yeoman ushers, two grooms, and an almoner," &c., &c., &c. . . . . . " In his privy kitchen, he had a master-cook, who went daily in damask, satin, or velvet, with a chain of gold about his neck." . . . . In his chapel, he had "a Dean, who was always a great clerk and a divine ; a Sub-dean ; a Repeater of the quire ; a Gospeller, a Pisteller (separate men to read the Gospels and the Epistles), and twelve singing Priests ; of Scholars, he had first, a Master of the children ; twelve singing children ; sixteen singing men ; with a servant to attend upon the said children. In the Revestry, a yeoman and two grooms : then were there divers retainers of cunning singing men, that came thither at divers sundry principal feasts. But to speak of the furniture of this chapel passeth my capacity to declare the number of the costly ornaments and rich jewels, that were occupied in the same continually. For I have seen there, in a procession, worn forty-four copes of one suit, very rich, besides the sumptuous crosses, candlesticks, and other necessary ornaments to the comely furniture of the same. Now shall ye understand that he had two cross-bearers, and two pillar-bearers ; and in his chamber, all these persons ; that is to say : his High Chamberlain; his Vice-Chamberlain ; twelve Gentlemen Ushers, daily waiters; besides two in his Privy Chamber ; and of Gentlemen waiters in his Privy Chamber he had six; and also he had of Lords nine or ten, who had each of them allowed two servants ; and the Earl of Derby had allowed five men. Then had he of Gentlemen, as cup-bearers, carvers, sewers, and Gentlemen daily waiters, forty persons; of yeomen ushers he had six; of grooms in his chamber he had eight; of yeomen of his chamber he had forty-six daily to attend upon his person ; he had also a priest there which was his Almoner, to attend upon his table at dinner. Of doctors and chaplains attending in his closet to say daily mass before him, he had sixteen persons : and a clerk of his closet. Also he had two secretaries, and two clerks of his signet : and four counsellors learned in the laws of the realm.

" And, for as much as he was Chancellor of England, it was necessary for him to have divers officers of the Chancery, to attend daily upon him, for the better furniture of the same. That is to say, first, he had the Clerk of the Crown, a Riding Clerk, a Clerk of the Hanaper, a Chafer of Wax. Then had he a Clerk of the Check, as well to check his chaplains, as his yeomen of the chamber; he had also four Footmen, which were apparelled in rich running coats, whensoever he rode any journey. Then had he an Herald at Arms, and a Serjeant at Arms; a Physician; an Apothecary; four Minstrels; a Keeper of his Tents ; an Armourer ; an Instructor of his Wards; two Yeomen in his Wardrobe ; and a Keeper of his chamber in the court. He had also daily in his house the Surveyor of York, a Clerk of the Green Cloth; and an auditor. All this number of persons were daily attendant upon him in his house, down-lying and up-rising.

And at meals, there was continually in his chamber a board kept for his Chamberlains, and Gentlemen Ushers, having with them a mess of the young Lords, and another for gentlemen. Besides all these, there was never an officer and gentleman, or any other worthy person in his house, but he was allowed some three, some two servants; and all other one at the least; which amounted to a great number of persons."

Such was the style in which Wolsey grew fat, in-doors. When he went out of doors, to Westminster Hall for instance, as Chancellor, or merely came into an anteroom, to speak with his suitors, the following was the state which he always kept up. Think of Lord Brougham or Lord Lyndhurst in our own times, modestly eschewing notice, and going down to the House in a plain hat and trowsers, and then look on the following picture :—

"Now will I declare unto you," says the worthy Cavendish, striking up a right gentleman-usher note (and out of this very gentleman-usher's family came the princely house of Devonshire, which has lasted with so much height and refinement ever since,)—"Now will I declare unto you his order in going to Westminster Hall, *daily* in the term season. First, before his coming out of his privy chamber, he heard most commonly every day two masses in his private closet ; and there then said his daily service with his chaplain; and, as I heard his chaplain say, being a man of credence and of excellent learning, that the Cardinal, what business or weighty matters soever he had in the day, he never went to his bed with any part of his divine service unsaid, yea, not so much as one collect; wherein I doubt not but he deceived the opinion of divers persons. And after mass he would return in his privy chamber again, and being advertised of the furniture of his chambers without, with noblemen, gentlemen, and other persons, would issue out into them, apparelled all in red, in the habit of a cardinal; which was either of fine scarlet, or else of crimson satin, taffety, damask, or caffa, the best that he could get for money; and upon his head a round pillion, with a noble of black velvet set to the same in the inner side; he had also a tippet of fine sables about his neck; holding in his hand a very fair orange, whereof the meat or substance within was taken out, and filled up again with the part of a sponge, wherein was vinegar, and other confections against the pestilent airs ; the which he most commonly smelt unto, passing among the press, or else when he was pestered with many suitors. There was also borne before him, first, the great seal of England, *and then his cardinal's hat, by a nobleman or some worthy gentleman, right solemnly, bareheaded.* And as soon as he was entered into his chamber of presence, where there was attending his coming to await upon him to Westminster Hall, as well noblemen and other worthy gentlemen, as noblemen and gentlemen of his own family ; thus passing forth with two great crosses of silver borne before him ; with also two great pillars of silver, and his pursuivant at arms with a great mace of silver gilt. Then his gentlemen ushers cried, and said : ' On, my lords and masters, on before; make way for my Lord's Grace !' Thus passed he down from his chamber through the hall; and when he came to the hall door, there was attendant for him his mule, trapped altogether in crimson velvet, and gilt stirrups. When he was mounted, with his cross bearers, and pillow bearers, also upon great horses trapped with [fine] scarlet, then marched he forward, with his train and furniture in manner as I have declared, having about him four footmen, with gilt poll-axes in their hands; and thus he went until he came to Westminster Hall door. And there alighted and went after this manner, up through the hall into the chancery; howbeit he would most commonly stay awhile at a bar, made for him, a little beneath the chancery [on the right hand], and there commune some time with the judges, and some time with other persons. And that done he would repair into the chancery, sitting there till eleven of the clock, hearing suitors, and determining on divers matters. And from thence, he would divers times go into the star chamber, as occasion did serve; where he spared neither high nor low, but judged every estate according to their merits and demerits."

But this style of riding abroad was not merely for official occasions. He went through Thames Street every Sunday, in his way to the court at Greenwich, with his crosses, his pillars, his hat, and his great seal. He was as fond of his pomp out of doors, as a child is of its new clothes.

The description of the way in which he used to receive the visits of the King at York Place, has acquired a double interest from the use made of it by Shakspeare, by whom it has been, in a manner, copied, in his play of "Henry the Eighth:"

"Thus in great honour, triumph, and glory," says Cavendish, "he reigned a long season, ruling all things within this realm, appertaining unto the King, by his wisdom, and also all other weighty matters of foreign regions with which the King of this realm had any occasion to intermeddle. All Ambassadors of foreign potentates were always dispatched by his discretion, to whom they had always access for their dispatch. His house was also always resorted and furnished with noblemen, gentlemen, and other persons, with going and coming in and out, feasting and banqueting all Ambassadors divers times, and other strangers right nobly.

"And when it pleased the King's Majesty, for his recreation, to repair unto the Cardinal's house, as he did divers times in the year, at which time there wanted no preparations, or goodly furniture, with viands of the finest sort that might be provided for money or friendship, such pleasures were then devised for the King's comfort and consolation, as might be invented, or by man's wit imagined. The banquets were set forth, with masks and mummeries, in so gorgeous a sort, and costly a manner, that it was a heaven to behold. *There wanted no dames, or damsels, meet or apt to dance with the maskers, or to garnish the place for the time, with other goodly disports.* Then was there all kind of music and harmony set forth, with excellent voices both of men and children. I have seen the King suddenly come in thither in a mask, with a dozen of other maskers, all in garments like shepherds, made of fine cloth of gold and fine crimson satin paned, and caps of the same, with visors of good proportion of visnomy; their hairs, and beards, either of fine gold wire, or else of silver, and some being of black silk; having sixteen torch-bearers, besides their drums, and other persons attending upon them, with visors, and clothed all in satin, of the same colours. And at his coming, and before he came into the hall, ye shall understand, that he came by water to the water gate, without any noise: where, against his coming, were laid charged, many chambers*, and at his landing they were all shot off, which made such a rumble in the air, that it was like thunder.   It made all the noblemen, ladies, and gentlewomen, to muse what it should mean coming so suddenly, they sitting quietly at a solemn banquet; under this sort: First, ye shall perceive that the tables were set in the chamber of presence, banquet-wise covered, my Lord Cardinal sitting under the cloth of estate, and there having his service all alone; and then was there set a lady and a nobleman, or a gentleman and gentlewoman, throughout all the tables in the chamber on the one side, which were made and joined as it were but one table. All which order and device was done and devised by the Lord Sands, Lord Chamberlain to the King; and also by Sir Henry Guildford, Comptroller to the King.   Then immediately after this great shot of guns, the Cardinal desired the Lord Chamberlain and Comptroller to look what this sudden shot should mean, as though he knew nothing of the matter. They thereupon looking out of the windows into Thames, returned again, and showed him that it seemed to them there should be some noblemen and strangers arrived at his bridge, as ambassadors from some foreign prince. With that, quoth the Cardinal, 'I shall desire you, because ye can speak French, to take the pains to go down into the hall to encounter and to receive them, according to their estates, and to conduct them into this chamber, where they shall see us, and all these noble personages sitting merrily at our banquet, desiring them to sit down with us, and to take part of our fare and pastime.'   Then [they] went incontinent down into the hall, where they received them with near twenty new torches, and conveyed them up into the chamber, with such a number of drums and fifes as I have seldom seen together at one time, in any masque. At their arrival into the chamber, two and two together, they went directly before the Cardinal where he sat, saluting him very reverently; to whom the Lord Chamberlain for them said ; 'Sir, for as much as they be strangers, and can speak no English, they have desired me to declare unto your Grace thus : they, having understanding of this your triumphant banquet, where was assembled such a number of excellent fair dames, could do no less, under the supportation of your good Grace, but to repair hither to view as well as their incomparable beauty, as for to accompany them at mumchance†,

* *Chambers*, short guns, or cannon, standing upon their breaching without carriages, chiefly used for festive occasions; and having their name most probably from being little more than *chambers* for powder. It was by the discharge of these *chambers* in the play of Henry VIIIth. that the Globe Theatre was burnt in 1613. Shakspeare followed pretty closely the narrative of Cavendish.—*Singer*.

† *Mumchance* appears to have been a game played with dice, at which silence was to be observed.—*Singer*.

and then after to dance with them, and so to have of them acquaintance. And, sir, they furthermore require of your Grace license to
accomplish the cause of their repair.' To whom the Cardinal answered, that he was very well contented that they should do so. Then
the maskers went first and saluted all the dames as they sat, and then
returned to the most worthiest, and there opened a cup full of gold,
with crowns and other pieces of coin, to whom they set divers pieces
to cast at. Thus in this manner perusing all the ladies and gentlewomen, and to some they lost, and of some they won. And this done,
they returned unto the Cardinal, with great reverence, pouring down
all the crowns into the cup, which was about two hundred crowns.
' At all,' quoth the Cardinal, and so cast the dice, and won them all
at a cast ; whereat was great joy made. Then quoth the Cardinal
to my Lord Chamberlain, 'I pray you,' quoth he, ' show them that it
seemeth me that there should be among them some noble man, whom
I suppose to be much more worthy of honour to sit and occupy this
room and place than I; to whom I would most gladly, if I knew him,
surrender my place, according to my duty.' Then spake my Lord
Chamberlain unto them in French, declaring my Lord Cardinal's
mind, and they rounding him again in the ear, my Lord Chamberlain
said to my Lord Cardinal, ' Sir, they confess,' quoth he, ' that among
them there is such a noble personage, whom, if your Grace can
appoint him from the other, he is contented to disclose himself, and to
accept your place most worthily.' With that the Cardinal, taking a
good advisement among them, at the last, quoth he, ' me seemeth the
gentleman with the black beard should be even he.' And with that
he arose out of his chair, and offered the same to the gentleman in the
black beard, with his cap in his hand. The person to whom he
offered then his chair was Sir Edward Neville, *a comely knight of a
goodly personage,** that much more resembled the King's person in that
mask than any other. The King, hearing and perceiving the Cardinal
so deceived in his estimation and choice, could not forbear laughing;
but plucked down his visor, and Master Neville's also, *and dashed†
out with such a plesant countenance and cheer*, that all noble estates
there assembled, seeing the King to be there amongst them, rejoiced
very much. The Cardinal eftsoons desired his highness to take the
place of estate, to whom the King answered, that he would go first
and shift his apparel; and so departed, and went straight into my
lord's bedchamber, where was a great fire made and prepared for
him; and there new apparelled him with rich and princely garments.
And in the time of the King's absence the dishes of the banquet were
clean taken up, and the tables spread again with new and sweet per-
fumed clothes; every man sitting still until the King and his maskers
came in among them again, every man being newly apparelled. Then
the King took his seat under the cloth of state, commanding no man
to remove, but sit still, as they did before. Then in came a new
banquet before the King's majesty, and to all the rest through the
tables, wherein, I suppose, were served two hundred dishes or above,

---

* Probably a handsomer figure than the King. This (though not the
subtlest imaginable) would be likely to be among Wolsey's court-
tricks, and modes of gaining favour.

† This "dashed out" is in the best style of bluff King Hal, and
capitally well said by Cavendish.

of wondrous costly meats and devices, subtilly devised. Thus passed they forth the whole night with banqueting, dancing, and other triumphant devices, to the great comfort of the King, and pleasant regard of the nobility there assembled.

" All this matter I have declared at large, because ye shall understand what joy and delight the Cardinal had to see his Prince and sovereign Lord in his house so nobly entertained and pleased, which was always his only study, to devise things to his comfort, not passing of the charges or expenses. It delighted him so much, to have the King's pleasant princely presence, that nothing was to him more delectable than to cheer his sovereign lord, to whom he owed so much obedience and loyalty, as reason required no less, all things well considered.

" Thus passed the Cardinal his life and time, from day to day, and year to year, in such great wealth, joy, and triumph, and glory, having always on his side the King's especial favour; until Fortune, of whose favour no man is longer assured than she is disposed, began to wax something wroth with his prosperous estate [and] thought she would devise a mean to abate his high port; wherefore she procured Venus, the insatiate Goddess, to be her instrument. To work her purpose, she brought the King in love with a gentlewoman, that, after she perceived and felt the King's goodwill towards her, and how diligent he was both to please her, and to grant all her requests, she wrought the Cardinal much displeasure ; as hereafter shall be more at large declared."

Pretty Anne Bullen completed the ruin of Wolsey for having thwarted her, and not long afterwards was sent out of this very house from which she ousted him, to the scaffold, herself ruined by another rival.   On the Cardinal's downfall, Henry seized his house and goods, and converted York Place into a royal residence, under the title of Westminster Place, then, for the first time, called also Whitehall.

" It is not impossible," says Mr. Brayley (Londiniana, vol. ii., p. 27.) " that the Whitehall, properly so called, was erected by Wolsey, and obtained its name from the newness and freshness of its appearance, when compared with the ancient buildings of York Place. Shakspeare, in his play of King Henry VIII., makes one of the interlocutors say, in describing the coronation of Queen Anne Boleyn:—

' So she parted,
And with the same full state paced back again
To York Place, where the feast is held.'

To this is replied—

' Sir, you
Must no more call it York Place—that is past.
For since the Cardinal fell, that title's lost.
'Tis now the King's, and called Whitehall.' "

It is curious to observe the links between ancient names and their modern representatives, and the extraordinary contrast sometimes exhibited between the two. The "Judge," who by

Henry's orders went to turn Wolsey out of his house, without any other form of law—a proceeding which excited even the fallen slave to a remonstrance—was named Shelly, and was one of the ancestors of the *poet!* the most independent-minded and generous of men.

CHAPTER XI.

Henry the Eighth—His Person and Character—Modern Qualifications of it considered—Passages respecting him from Lingard, Sir Thomas Wyatt, and others—His additions to Whitehall—A Retrospect at Elizabeth—Court of James resumed—Its gross Habits—Letter of Sir John Harrington respecting them—James's Drunkenness—Testimonies of Welldon, Sully, and Roger Coke—Curious Omission in the Invective of Churchill the Poet—Welldon's Portrait of James—Buckingham, the Favourite—Frightful Story of Somerset—Masques—Banqueting House—Inigo Jones and Ben Jonson—Court of Charles the First—Cromwell—Charles the Second—James the Second.

E have said more about Wolsey than we intend to say of Henry the Eighth; for the son of the butcher was a great man, and his master was only a king. Henry, born a prince, became a butcher; Wolsey, a butcher, became a prince. And we are not playing upon the word as applied to the king; for Henry was not only a butcher of his wives, he resembled a brother of the trade in its better and more ordinary course. His pleasures were of the same order; his lan-

guage was coarse and jovial; he had the very straddle of a
fat butcner, as he stands in his doorway.   Take any picture
or statue of Henry the Eighth—fancy its cap off, and a knife
in its girdle, and it seems in the very act of saying, " What
d'ye buy ? What d'ye buy ?"   There is even the petty complacency in the mouth, after the phrase is uttered.

And how formidable is that petty unfeeling mouth, in the
midst of those wide and wilful cheeks !   Disturb the self-
satisfaction of that man, derange his bile for an instant, make
him suppose that you do not quite think him

" Wisest, virtuousest, discreetest, best,"

and what hope have you from the sentence of that mass of
pampered egotism?

Let us not do injustice, however, even to the doers of it.
What better was to be looked for, in those times, from the
circumstances under which Henry was born and bred—from
the son of a wilful father, and an unfeeling state marriage—
from the educated combiner of church and state, instinctively
led to entertain the worldliest notions of both, and of heaven
itself—from the inheritor of the greatest wealth, and power,
and irresponsibility, ever yet concentrated in an English
sovereign ?   It has been attempted of late by various writers
(and the attempt is a good symptom, being on the charitable
side,) to make out a case for Henry the Eighth, as if he were a
sort of rough but honest fellow, a kind of John Bull of that
age, who meant well upon the whole, and thought himself
bound to keep up the conventionalities of his country.   We
know not what compliment is intended to be implied by this,
either to Henry or his countrymen ; but really when a man
sends his wives, one after the other, to the scaffold, evidently
as much to enable him to marry another as to vindicate any
propriety—when he "cuts" and sacrifices his best friends and
servants, and pounces upon their goods—when he takes every
license himself, though he will not allow others even to be
suspected of it—when he grows a brute beast in size as well
as in habits, and dies shedding superfluous blood to the last—
we cannot, for our parts, as Englishmen, but be glad of some
better excuses for him of the kind above stated, than such as
are to be found in the roots of the national character, however
jovial.   Imagine only the endearments that must have passed
between this man and Anne Bullen, and then fancy the heart
that could have sent the poor little, hysterical, half-laughing,

half-crying thing to the scaffold! The man was *mad* with power and vanity. That is his real excuse.

It has been said, that all which he did was done by law, or at least under the forms of it, and by the consent, sometimes by the recommendation, of his statesmen. The assertion is not true in all instances; and where it is, what does it prove but that his tyrannical spirit had helped to make his statesmen slaves? They knew what he wished, and notoriously played the game into his hands. When they did not, their heads went off. That circumstances had spoilt them altogether, and that society, with all its gaudiness, was but in a half-barbarous state, is granted; but it is no less true, that his office, his breeding, and his natural temper, conspired to make Henry the worst and most insolent of a violent set of men; and he stands straddling out accordingly in history, as he does in his pictures, an image of sovereign brutality.

Excessive vanity, aggravated by all the habits of despotism and luxury, and accompanied, nevertheless, by that unconscious misgiving which is natural to inequalities between a man's own powers and those which he derives from his position, is the clue to the character of Henry the Eighth. Accordingly, no man gave greater ear to tale-bearers and sowers of suspicion, nor resented more cruelly or meanly the wounds inflicted on his self-love, even by those who least intended them, or to whom he had shown the greatest fondness. The latter, indeed, he treated the worst, out of a frenzy of egotistical disappointment; for his love arose, not from any real regard for their merits, but from what he had taken for a flattery to his own. Sir Thomas More knew him well, when, in observation to some one who had congratulated him on the King's having walked up and down with his arm around his neck, he said that he would have that neck cut in two next day, if the head belonging to it opposed his will. He not only took back without scruple all that he had given to Wolsey, but he went to live in the houses of his fallen friend and servant—places which a man of any feeling and kindly remembrance would have avoided. He was very near picking a murderous quarrel with his last wife, Catherine Parr, on one of his theological questions. And how did he conduct himself to the memory of poor Anne Bullen, even on the day of her execution? Hear Lingard, who, though no partizan of his, thinks he must have had some heinous cause of provocation, to induce him to behave so roughly:—

"Thus fell," says the historian, "this unfortunate Queen within four months after the death of Catherine. To have expressed a doubt of her guilt during the reign of Henry, or of her innocence during that of Elizabeth, would have been deemed a proof of disaffection. The question soon became one of religious feeling, rather than of historical disquisition. Though she had departed no farther than her husband from the ancient doctrine, yet, as her marriage with Henry led to the separation from the communion of Rome, the Catholic writers were eager to condemn, the Protestant to exculpate her memory. In the absence of those documents which alone could enable us to decide with truth, I will only observe that the King must have been impelled by some powerful motive to exercise against her such extraordinary, and, in one supposition, such superfluous vigour. Had his object been (we are sometimes told that it was) to place Jane Seymour by his side on the throne, the divorce of Anne without execution, or the execution without the divorce, would have effected his purpose. But he seemed to have pursued her with insatiable hatred. Not content with taking her life, he made her feel in every way in which a wife and a mother could feel. He stamped on her character the infamy of adultery and incest; he deprived her of the name and right of wife and Queen; and he even bastardized her daughter, though he acknowledged that daughter to be his own. If then he were not assured of her guilt, he must have discovered in her conduct some most heinous cause of provocation, which he never disclosed. He had wept at the death of Catherine (of Arragon); but, as if he sought to display his contempt for the character of Anne, he dressed himself in white on the day of her execution, and was married to Jane Seymour the next morning."*

Now, nothing could be more indecent and unmanly than such conduct as this, let Anne have been guilty as she might; and nothing, in such a man, but mortified self-love could account for it. Probably he had discovered, that in some of her moments of levity she had laughed at him. But not to love him would have been offence enough. It would have been the first time he had discovered the possibility of such an impiety towards his barbarous divinityship: and his rage must needs have been unbounded.

What Providence may intend by such instruments, is one thing: what we are constituted to think of them, is another: charitably, no doubt, when we think our utmost; but still with a discrimination, for fear of consequences. As to what was thought of Henry in his own time or afterwards, we must not rely on the opinion of Baker, Holinshed, and other servile chroniclers, of mean understanding and time-serving habits, who were the least honourable kind of "waiters upon Providence," taking the commonest appearances of adversity and prosperity (so to speak) for vice and virtue, and flattering

* Lingard, vol. iv., p. 246. (Quarto Edit.)

every arbitrary and conventional opinion, as though it were
not to perish in its turn. We are to recollect what More said
of him (as above) in his confidential moments and Wolsey in
his agony, and Pole and others, when, having got to a safe
distance, they returned him foul language for his own
bullying, and blustered out what was thought of him by
those who knew him thoroughly. Observe also the manifest
allusions in what was written upon the court of those days,
by one of the wisest and best of its ornaments, Sir Thomas
Wyat—a friend of Anne Bullen's. The verses are entitled,
" Of a Courtier's Life," and it may be observed, by the way,
that they furnish the second example, in the English language, of the use of the Italian *rime terzette*, or triplets, in
which Dante's poem is written, and which had been first
introduced among us by Sir Thomas's friend, the Earl of
Surrey (another of Henry's victims):—

> Mine owne John Poynes, sins ye delight to know
>   The causes why that homeward I me draw
>   And flee the prease of courtes whereso they goe,
> Rather than to live thrall *under the awe*
>   *Of lordly lookes,* wrapped within my cloke,
>   *To will and lust* learning to set a law,
> It is not, that because I storme or mocke
>   The power of those whom fortune here hath lent
>   Charge over us, of right to strike the stroke ;
> But true it is, that I have alway ment
>   Less to esteeme them, than the common sort
>   Of outward thinges that judge in their entent ;
>   *   *   *   *
> My Poynes, I cannot frame my tong to fayn,
>   To cloke the truth, for praise, without desert,
>   Of them that list all vice for to retayne ;
> I cannot *honour* them that set theyr part
>   *With Venus and with Bacchus their life long,*
>   Nor hold my peace of them although I smart
> I cannot crouch, nor *kneele* to such a wrong,
>   TO WORSHIP THEM LIKE GOD ON EARTH ALONE,
>   *That are as wolves these sely lambs among.*

(Here was a sigh perhaps to the memory of his poor friend
Anne):—

> I cannot wrest the law to fyll the coffer   ·
>   With innocent blood to feed myselfe *fat,*

> Call him pitiefull, *and him true and playne*
> *That raylest reckless unto each man's shame;*
> Say he is rude, that cannot lye and fayne,
> *The lecher a lover,* AND TYRANNY
> TO BE RIGHT OF A PRINCE'S RAIGNE;
> I cannot, I;—no, no;—it will not be;
> This is the cause that I could never yet
> Hang on their sleeves, that weigh, as thou maist see,
> A chippe of chaunce more than a pound of wit;
> This makes me at home to hunt and hawke,
> And in foul weather at my book to sit;
> In frost and snowe, then with my bowe stalke;
> No man doth marke whereso I ryde or goe;
> In lustie leas at libertie I walke.

Towards the conclusion, he says he does not spend his time among those who have their wits *taken away* with *Flanders cheer and " beastliness :"*—

> Nor I am not, where truth is given in prey
> For money, and prison and treason of some
> A common practice used night and day;
> But I am here in Kent and Christendom,
> Among the Muses, where I read and ryme;
> Where if thou list, mine owne John Poynes, to come,
> Thou shalt be judge how I do spend my time.

Among the poems of Surrey, is a sonnet in reproach of " Sardanapalus," which probably came to the knowledge of Henry, and may have been intended to do so.

It was in Whitehall that Henry made his ill-assorted marriage with Anne Bullen; Dr. Lingard says in a "garret;" Stowe says in the royal "closet." It is likely enough that the ceremony was hurried and sudden;—a fit of will, perhaps, during his wine; and if the closet was not ready, the garret was. The clergyman who officiated was shortly afterwards made a bishop.

Henry died in Whitehall; so fat, that he was lifted in and out his chamber and sitting-room by means of machinery.

He was " *somewhat* gross, or, as we tearme it, bourlie," says time-serving Holinshed.[*]

" He *laboured* under the *burden* of an extreme fat and un-wieldy body," says noble Herbert of Cherbury.[†]

" The king," says Lingard, " had long indulged without restraint in the pleasures of the table. At last he grew so *enormously corpulent*, that he could neither support the weight of his own body, nor remove without the aid of machinery into the different apartments of his palace. Even the fatigue of subscribing his name to the writings

---

[*] Vol. iii., p. 862, Edit. 1808.   [†] Folio edit ·

which required his signature, was more than he could bear; and to relieve him from this duty, three commissioners were appointed, of whom two had authority to apply to the paper a dry stamp, bearing the letters of the king's name, and the third to draw a pen furnished with ink over the blank impression. An inveterate ulcer in the thigh which had more than once threatened his life, and which now seemed to baffle all the skill of the surgeons, added to the irascibility of his temper."*

It was under this Prince (as already noticed) that the palace

HOLBEIN'S GATE OF WHITEHALL PALACE.

of the Archbishop of York first became the "King's Palace at Westminster," and expanded into that mass of houses which

* *Ut supra*, p. 347. Henry had been afflicted with this ulcer a long while. He was in danger from it during his marriage with Anne Bullen. It should be allowed him among his excuses of temperament; but then it should also have made him more considerate towards his wives. It never enters the heads, however, of such people that *their* faults or infirmities are to go for anything, except to make others considerate for them, and warrant whatever humours they choose to indulge.

stretched to St. James's Park.   He built a gate-house which
stood across what is now the open street, and a gallery connecting the two places, and overlooking a tilt-yard; and on
the park-side he built a cockpit, a tennis-court, and alleys for
bowling; for although he put women to death, he was fond of
manly sports.   He was also a patron of the fine arts; and
gave an annuity and rooms in the palace to the celebrated
Holbein, who is said to have designed the gate, as well as
decorated the interior.   It is to Holbein we are indebted for
our familiar acquaintance with his figure.

The reader is to bear in mind, that the street in front of the
modern Banqueting-house was always open, as it is now, from
Charing Cross to King Street, narrowing opposite to the south
end of the Banqueting-house, at which point the gate looked
up it towards the Cross.   Just opposite the Banqueting-house,
on the site of the present Horse Guards, was the Tilt-yard.
The whole mass of houses and gardens on the river side comprised the royal residence.   Down this open street then, just
as people walk now, we may picture to ourselves Henry
coming with his regal pomp, and Wolsey with his priestly;
Sir Thomas More strolling thoughtfully, perhaps talking with
quiet-faced Erasmus; Holbein, looking about him with an
artist's eyes; Surrey coming gallantly in his cloak and
feather, as Holbein has painted him; and a succession of
Henry's wives, with their flitting groups on horseback or
under canopy;—handsome, stately Catherine of Arragon;
laughing Anne Bullen; quiet Jane Seymour; gross-bodied
but sensible Anne of Cleves; demure Catherine Howard, who
played such pranks before marriage; and disputatious yet
buxom Catherine Parr, who survived one tyrant, to become
the broken-hearted wife of a smaller one.   Down this road,
also, came gallant companies of knights and squires, to the
tilting-yard; but of them we shall have more to say in the
time of Elizabeth.

We see little of Edward the Sixth, and less of Lady Jane
Grey and Queen Mary, in connection with Whitehall.   Edward
once held the Parliament there, on account of his sickly condition; and he used to hear Latimer preach in the Privy
garden (still so called), where a pulpit was erected for him on
purpose.   As there are gardens there still to the houses erected
on the spot, one may stand by the rails, and fancy we hear
the voice of the rustical but eloquent and honest prelate, rising
through the trees.

Edward has the reputation usually belonging to young and untried sovereigns, and very likely deserves some of it; certainly not all—as Mr. Sharon Turner, one of the most considerate of historians, has shown. He partook of the obstinacy of his father, which was formalised in him by weak health and a precise education; and though he shed tears when prevailed upon to assign poor Joan of Kent to what he thought her eternity of torment, his faults assuredly did not lie on the side of an excess of feeling, as may be seen by the cool way in which he suffered his uncles to go to the scaffold, one after another, and recorded it in the journal which he kept. He would probably have turned out a respectable, but not an admirable sovereign, nor one of an engaging character. Years do not improve a temperament like his.

Even poor Lady Jane Grey's character does not improve upon inspection. The Tudor blood (she was grand-daughter of Henry's sister) manifested itself in her by her sudden love of supremacy the moment she felt a crown on her head, and her preferring to squabble with her husband and his relations (who got it her), rather than let him partake her throne. She insisted he should be only a Duke, and suspected that his family had given her poison for it. This undoes the usual romance of "Lady Jane Grey and Lord Guildford Dudley;"—and thus it is that the possession of too much power spoils almost every human being, practical or theoretical. Lady Jane came out of the elegancies and tranquillities of the schools, and of her Greek and Latin, to find her Platonisms vanish before a dream of royalty. She rediscovered them, however, when it was over; and that is something. She was brought up a slave, and therefore bred to be despotic in her turn; but habit, vanity, and good sense alike contributed to restore her to the better part of herself at the last moment.

We confess we pity "Bloody Mary," as she has been called, almost as much as any unfortunate sovereign on record. She caused horrible and odious suffering, but she also suffered horribly herself, and became odious where she would fain have been loved. She had a bigoted education and a complexional melancholy; was stunted in person, plain in face, with impressive but gloomy eyes; a wife with affections unrequited; and a persecuting, unpopular, but conscientious sovereign. She derived little pleasure apparently from having her way, even in religious matters; but acted as she did out of a narrow sense of duty; and she proved her honesty, however perverted, by a perpetual anxiety and uneasiness. When did a charitable set of opinions ever inflict upon honest natures these miseries of an intolerant one ?

It was under Elizabeth that Whitehall shone out in all its romantic splendour. It was no longer the splendour of Wolsey alone, nor of Henry alone, or with a great name by his side now and then ; but of a Queen, surrounded and worshipped through a long reign by a galaxy of the brightest minds and most chivalrous persons ever assembled in English history.

Here she comes, turning round the corner from the Strand, under a canopy of state, leaving the noisier, huzzaing multi-tude behind the barriers that mark the precincts of the palace, and bending her eyes hither and thither, in acknowledgment of the kneeling obeisances of the courtiers. Beside her are Cecil and Knolles, and Northampton, and Bacon's father ; or, later in life, Leicester, and Burleigh, and Sir Philip Sidney, and Greville, and Sir Francis Drake (and Spenser is looking on) ; or, later still, Essex, and Raleigh, and Bacon himself, and Southampton, Shakspeare's friend, with Shakspeare among the spectators. We shall see her by and by, at that period, as brought to life to us in the description of Heutzner the traveller. At present (as we have her at this moment in our eye) she is younger, of a large and tall, but well-made figure, with fine eyes, and finer hands, which she is fond of displaying. We are too apt to think of Elizabeth as thin and elderly, and patched up ; but for a good period of her life she was plump and personable, warranting the history of the robust romps of the Lord Admiral, Seymour ; and till her latter days (and even then, as far as her powers went), we are always to fancy her at once spirited and stately of car-riage, impulsive (except on occasions of ordinary ceremony), and ready to manifest her emotions in look and voice, whether as woman or Queen ; in a word, a sort of Henry the Eighth corrected by a female nature and a better under-standing—or perhaps an Anne Bullen, enlarged, and made less feminine, by the father's grossness. The Protestants have represented her as too staid, and the Catholics as too violent and sensual. According to the latter, Whitehall was a mere sink of iniquity. It was not likely to be so, for many reasons ; but neither, on the other hand, do we take it to have been anything like the pattern of self-denial which some fond writers have supposed. Where there is power, and leisure, and luxury, though of the most legitimate kind, and refine-

ment, though of the most intellectual, self-denial on the side
of enjoyment is not apt to be the reigning philosophy ; nor
would it reasonably be looked for in any court, at all living
in wealth and splendour.

Imagine the sensations of Elizabeth, when she first set
down in the palace at Whitehall, after escaping the perils of
imputed illegitimacy, of confinement for party's sake and for
religion's, and all the other terrors of her father's reign and
of Mary's, danger of death itself not excepted. She was a
young Queen of twenty-five years of age, healthy, sprightly,
good-looking, with plenty of will, power, and imagination ;
and the gallantest spirits of the age were at her feet. How
pitiable, and how respectable, become almost all sovereigns,
when we consider them as human beings put in possession of
almost superhuman power; and when we reflect in general
how they have been brought up, and what a provocative to
abuse at all events becomes the possession of a throne! We
in general spoil them first;—we always tempt them to take
every advantage, by worshipping them as if they were different creatures from ourselves ;—and then we are astonished
that they should take us at our word. How much better
would it be to be astonished at the likeness they retain to us,
even in the kindlier part of our weaknesses.

By a very natural process, considering the great and
chivalrous men of that day, Elizabeth became at once one of
the greatest of Queens and one of the most flattered and vain
of women. Nor were the courtiers so entirely insincere as
they are supposed to have been, when they worshipped her as
they did, and gave her credit for all the beauty and virtue
under heaven. On the contrary, the power to benefit them
went hand-in-hand with their self-love to give them a sincere
though extravagant notion of their mistress ; and the romantic
turn of the age and its literature, its exploits, its poetry, all conspired to warm and sanction the enthusiasm on both sides, and
to blind the admiration to those little outward defects, and inward defects too, which love at all periods is famous for overlooking—nay, for converting into noble grounds of denial, and
of subjection to a sentiment. Thus Elizabeth's hook nose,
her red hair, nay, her very age and crookedness at last, did
not stand in the way of raptures at her " beauty" and " divine
perfections," any more than a flaw in the casket that held a
jewel. The spirit of love and beauty was there; the appre-
ciation of the soul of both; the glory of exciting, and of

giving, the glorification ;—and all the rest was a trifle, an accident, a mortal show of things, which no gentleman and lady can help. The Queen might even swear a good round oath or so occasionally; and what did it signify? It was a pleasant ebullition of the authority which is above taxation ; the Queen swore, and not the woman; or if the woman did, it was only an excess of feeling proper to balance the account, and to bring her royalty down to a level with good hearty human nature.

It has been said, that as Elizabeth advanced in life, the courtiers dropped the mention of her beauty; but this is a mistake. They were more sparing in the mention of it, but when they spoke they were conscious that the matter was not to be minced. When her Majesty was in her sixty-second year, the famous Earl of Essex gave her an entertainment, in the course of which she was complimented on her " *beauty* " and *dazzling outside*, in speeches written for the occasion by Lord, then " Mr. Francis, Bacon."* Sir John Davies, another lawyer, who was not born till she was near forty, and could not have written his acrostical " Hymns " upon her till she was elderly, celebrates her as awakening " thoughts of young love," and being " beauty's rose indeed ;"† and it is well known that she was at a reverend time of life when Sir Walter Raleigh wrote upon her like a despairing lover, calling her " Venus" and " Diana," and saying he could not exist out of her presence.

At the entrance from Whitehall to St. James's Park, where deer were kept, was the following inscription, recorded by Heutzner, the German traveller :—

" The fisherman who has been wounded learns, though late, to
    beware :
But the unfortunate Actæon always presses on.
The chaste Virgin naturally pitied ;
    But the powerful Goddess revenged the wrong.
Let Actæon fall a prey to his dogs,
    An example to youth,
A disgrace to those that belong to him !
    May Diana live the care of Heaven,
The delight of mortals,
    The security of those that belong to her."

Walpole thinks that this inscription alluded to Philip the

---

* Nicholls's " Progresses and Public Processions of Queen Elizabeth," year 1595, pp. 4-8. "He will ever bear in his heart the picture of her beauty." " He now looks on his mistress's outside with the eyes of sense, which are dazzled and amased."

† See the poems in Anderson's Edition, vol. ii., p. 706.

Second, who courted Elizabeth after her sister's death, and to the destruction of his Armada. It might ; but it implied also a pretty admonition to youth in general, and to those who ventured to pry into the goddess's retreats.

It was about the time of Essex's entertainment that the same traveller gives the following minute and interesting account of her Majesty's appearance, and of the superhuman way in which her very dinner-table was worshipped. He is describing the manner in which she went to chapel at Greenwich :—

" First went Gentlemen, Barons, Earls, Knights of the Garter, all richly dressed and bare-headed; next came the Chancellor, bearing the seals in a silk purse, between two, one of which carried the royal sceptre, the other the sword of state in a red scabbard, studded with golden fleurs-de-lis, the point upwards; next came the Queen, in the fifty-sixth year of her age (as we were told), very majestic; her face oblong, fair but wrinkled; her eyes small, yet black and pleasant; her nose a little hooked, her lips narrow, and her teeth black (a defect the English seem subject to, from their too great use of sugar); she had in her ears two very rich pearls with drops ; she wore false hair, and that red : upon her head she had a small crown, reported to have been made of some of the gold of the celebrated Lunebourg table; her bosom was uncovered, as all the English ladies have it till they marry; and she had on a necklace of exceeding fine jewels; her hands were small, her fingers long ; and her stature neither tall nor low; her air was stately ; her manner of speaking mild and obliging. The day she was dressed in white silk, bordered with pearls of the size of beans, and over it a mantle of black silk shot with silver threads; her train was very long, the end of it borne by a Marchioness; instead of a chain, she had on an oblong collar of gold and jewels. As she went along in all this state and magnificence, she spoke very graciously, first to one and then to another (whether foreign ministers, or those who attended on different reasons), in English, French, or Italian; for besides being very well skilled in Greek and Latin, and the languages I have mentioned, she is mistress of Spanish, Scotch, and Dutch. Whoever speaks to her, it is kneeling ; now and then she raises some with her hand. While we were there, William Slawater, a Bohemian Baron, had letters to present to her, and she, after pulling off her glove, gave him her right hand to kiss, sparkling with rings and jewels, a mark of particular favour. Whenever she turned her face as she was going along, everybody fell down on their knees. The ladies of the court followed next to her, very handsome and well shaped, and for the most part dressed in white. She was guarded on each side by the Gentlemen Pensioners, fifty in number, with gilt battle-axes. In the ante-chamber next the hall, where we were, petitions were presented to her, and she received them most graciously, which occasioned the acclamation of 'God Save the Queen Elizabeth!' She answered it with 'I thanke youe, myne good peuple.' In the chapel was excellent music; as soon as it and the service was over, which scarce exceeded half an hour, the Queen returned in the same state by water, and prepared to go to dinner

"A gentleman entered the room bearing a rod, and along with him another bearing a table-cloth, which, after they had both kneeled three times with the utmost veneration, he spread upon the table, and after kneeling again they both retired; then came two others, one with the rod again, the other with a salt-cellar, a plate, and bread; when they had kneeled as the others had done, and placed what was brought upon the table, they too retired with the same ceremonies performed by the first: at last came an unmarried lady, (we were told she was a Countess), and along with her a married one, bearing a tasting knife; the former was dressed in white silk, who when she had prostrated herself three times in the most graceful manner, approached the table, and rubbed the table with bread and salt, with as much awe as if the Queen had been present. When they had waited there a little while, the Yeoman of the Guard entered, bare headed, clothed in scarlet with golden roses upon their backs, bringing in each turn a course of dishes, served in plate, most of it gilt. These dishes were received by a gentleman in the same order they were brought, and placed upon the table, while the lady taster gave to each guard a mouthful to eat of the particular dish he had brought, for fear of any poison. During the time that this guard (which consist of the tallest and stoutest men that can be found in all England, being carefully selected for this service), were bringing dinner, twelve trumpets and two kettle drums made the hall ring for half an hour together. At the end of all this ceremonial a number of unmarried ladies appeared, who with particular solemnity lifted the meat from the table and conveyed it to the Queen's inner and more private chamber, where after she had chosen for herself, the next goes to the ladies of the court.

"The queen dines and sups alone, with very few attendants; and it is very seldom that anybody, foreigner or native, is admitted at that time, and then only at the intercession of somebody in power." *

A "Character of Queen Elizabeth,' written by Edmund Bohun, Esq., published in " Nichols's Progresses," has given the following account of her daily habits:—

"Before day, every morning, she heard the petitions of those that had any business with her, and, calling her secretaries of state, and masters of requests, she caused the order of councils, proclamations, patents, and all other papers relating to the public, to be read, which were then depending; and gave such order in each affair as she thought fit, which was set down in short notes, either by herself, or her secretaries. As often as anything happened that was difficult, she called her great and wise men to her; and proposing the diversity of opinions, she very attentively considered and weighed on which side the strongest reason lay, ever preferring that way which seemed most to promote the public safety and welfare. When she was thus wearied with her morning work, she would take a walk, if the sun shined, into her garden, or otherwise in her galleries, especially in windy or rainy weather. She would then cause —— Stanhop, or Sir

---

* From an article in the second volume of that elegant and interesting publication, the " Retrospective Review;" the discontinuance of which, some years back, was regretted by every lover of literature.

Henry Savill, or some other learned man, to be called to walk with her, and entertain her with some learned subject; the rest of the day she spent in private, reading history, or some other learning, with great care and attention ; not out of ostentation, and a vain ambition of being always learning something, but out of a diligent care to enable herself thereby to live the better, and to avoid sin; and she would commonly have some learned man with her, or near her, to assist her ; whose labour and industry she would well reward.   Thus she spent her winter.

"In the summer time, when she was hungry, she would eat some-- thing that was of light and easy digestion, in her chamber, with the windows open to admit the gentle breezes of wind from the gardens or pleasant hills.   Sometimes she would do this alone, but more commonly she would have her friends with her then.   When she had thus satisfied her hunger and thirst with a moderate repast, she would rest awhile upon an Indian couch, curiously and richly covered.   In the winter time she observed the same order; but she omitted her noon sleep.   When her day was thus spent, she went late to supper, which was ever sparing, and very moderate.   At supper she would divert herself with her friends and attendants; and if they made her no answer, she would put them upon mirth and pleasant discourse with great civility.   She would also then admit Tarleton, a famous comedian and a pleasant talker, and other such like men, to divert her with stories of the town, and the common jests or accidents; but so that they kept within the bounds of modesty and chastity.   In the winter time, after supper, she would sometimes hear a song, or a lesson or two played upon the lute; but she would be much offended if there was any rudeness to any person, any reproach or licentious reflection used.   Tarleton, who was then the best comedian in England, had made a pleasant play; and when it was acted before the Queen, he pointed at Sir Walter Rawleigh, and said, —'See, the knave commands the Queen;' for which he was corrected by a frown from the Queen; yet he had the confidence to add, that he was of too much and too intolerable a power ; and going on with the same liberty was so universally applauded by all that were present, that she thought fit for the present to bear these reflections with a seeming unconcernedness.   But yet she was so offended, that she forbad Tarleton and all her jesters from coming near her table, being inwardly displeased with this impudent and unreasonable liberty.   She would talk with learned men that had travelled, in the presence of many, and ask them many questions concerning the government, customs, and discipline used abroad.   She loved a natural jester, that would tell a story pleasantly, and humour it with his countenance, and gesture, and voice ; but she hated all those praters who made bold with other men's reputation, or defamed them.   She detested, as ominous and unfortunate, all dwarfs and monstrous births.   She loved little dogs, singing birds, parrots, and apes; and when she was in private, she would recreate herself with various discourses, a game at chess, dancing, or singing.   Then she would retire into her bedchamber, where she was attended by married ladies of the nobility, the Marchioness of Winchester, then a widow, the Countess of Warwick, and the Lord Scroop's Lady, whose husband was governor of the West Marshes.   She would seldom suffer any one to wait upon her there, except Leicester, Hatton, Essex, Nottingham, and Sir Walter Rawleigh, who were more intimately conversant with her than any other of the courtiers. She frequently mixed serious things with her jests and her mirth; and upon festival-days, and especially in Christmas time, she would play at cards and tables, which was one of her usual pastimes; and if any time she happened to win, she would be sure to demand the money. When she found herself sleepy, she would take her leave of them that were present with much kindness and gravity, and so betake her to her rest; some lady of good quality, and of her intimate acquaintance, always lying in the same chamber. And besides her guards, that were always upon duty, there was a gentleman of good quality, and some others, up in the next chamber, who were to wake her in case anything extraordinary happened.

"Though she was endowed with all the goods of nature and fortune, and adorned with all those things which are valuable and to be desired, yet there were some things in her that were capable of amendment, nor was there any mortal, whose virtues were not eclipsed by the neighbourhood of some vices or imperfections. She was subject to be vehemently transported with anger; and when she was so, she would show it by her voice, her countenance, and her hands. She would chide her familiar servants so loud, that they that stood afar off might sometimes hear her voice. And it was reported, that for small offences she would strike her maids of honour with her hand: but then her anger was short, and very innocent; and she learned from Xenophon's book of the Institution of Cyrus, the method of curbing and correcting this unruly and uneasy passion. And when her friends acknowledged their offences, she with an appeased mind easily forgave them many things. She was also of opinion, that severity was safe, and too much clemency was destructive; and, therefore, in her punishments and justice, she was the more severe.

Some of the panegyric in this account must be taken with allowance ; as, for instance, in what is said of the maiden modesty of Elizabeth's ears. It would be far easier than pleasant to bring proofs to the contrary from plays and other entertainments performed in her presence, and honoured with her thanks. Some of the licenses in them would be held much too gross for the lowest theatre in our days. Allowance, however, is to be made for difference of times ; and considering the grave assumptions that must have been practised at court in more than one respect, and made most likely a matter of conscience towards the community, it may have been none of the least exquisite of them, that what was understood to all the masculine ears present, was unintelligible to those of "Diana," even though she had a goddess's knowledge as well as beauty.

Of one thing, it surprises us that there could ever have

been a question; namely, that Elizabeth was a great as well as fortunate sovereign,—a woman of extraordinary intellect. To the undervaluing remark that she had wise Ministers, it was well answered that she chose them; and if, like most other people, she was less wise and less correct in her conduct than she had the reputation of being, nothing, on that very account, can surely be thought too highly of the wonderful address with which she succeeded in sitting upon the top of the Protestant world as she did throughout her whole reign, supreme over her favourites as well as her Ministers—the refuge of struggling opinion, and the idol of romance.

Enter James I., on horseback, fresh from hunting, clad all in grass green, with a green feather, shambling limbs, thick features, a spare beard, and a tongue too big for his mouth. He looks about him at the by-standers, half frightened; yet he has ridden boldly, and been " in at the death."

The sensations of James the First on getting snugly nestled in the luxurious magnificence of Whitehall must, if possible, have been still more prodigious than those of Elizabeth in her triumphant safety. Coming from a land comparatively destitute, and a people whose contentiousness at that time was equal to their valour, and suddenly becoming rich, easy, and possessor of the homage of Elizabeth's sages and cavaliers, the lavish and timid dogmatist must have felt himself in heaven. There are points about the character of this prince, which it is not pleasant to canvass ; but we think the whole of it (like that of other men, if their history were equally known,) traceable to the circumstances of his birth and breeding. He was the son of the accomplished and voluptuous Mary, and the silly and debauched Darnley; his mother, during her pregnancy, saw Rizzio assassinated before her face; Buchanan was his tutor, and made ·him a pedant, " which was all," he said, " that he could make of him ; " he was a king while yet a child;—and from all these circumstances it is not to be wondered at that he was at once clever and foolish—confident, and, in some respects, of no courage—the son of handsome people, and yet disjointedly put together—and that he continued to be a child as long as he existed.

Granger, a shrewd man up to a certain pitch, makes a shallow remark upon what Sir Kenelm Digby has said on one of these points in James's history. " Sir Kenelm Digby," says he, " imputes the strong aversion James had to a drawn sword, to the fright his mother was in, during her pregnancy,

at the sight of the sword with which David Rizzio, her
secretary, was assassinated in her presence. 'Hence it came,'
says this author, 'that her son, King James, had such an
aversion, all his life-time, to a naked sword, that he could not
see one without a great emotion of the spirits, although otherwise courageous enough; yet he could not over-master his
passion in this particular. I remember, when he dubbed me
knight, in the ceremony of putting the point of a naked sword
upon my shoulder, he could not endure to look upon it, but
turned his face another way; insomuch, that, in lieu of
touching my shoulder, he had almost thrust the point into
my eyes, had not the Duke of Buckingham guided his hand
aright.' 'I shall only add," continues Granger, "to what
Sir Kenelm has observed, that James discovered so many
marks of pusillanimity, when the sword was at a distance
from him, that it is needless in this case to allege that an impression was made upon his tender frame before he saw the
light."* And then he makes another objection, which,
though not so obviously unfounded, is perhaps equally so; for
effects must have causes of some sort; and among the mysteries
of our birth and being, what is more probable, than that the
same wonders by which we exist at all, should cause the peculiarities of our existence? The same "tender frame" would
produce the general pusillanimity, as well as the particular.

Before we continue our remarks on the court of James the
First, we must look back a moment at that of Elizabeth, to
say, that Tallis, Bird, and others, gave dignity to the service
of Elizabeth's chapel at Whitehall, by their noble psalmody
and organ-playing. Her Majesty, one day, not in quite so
appropriate a strain, looked out of her closet in the chapel,
and lectured a preacher out loud, for talking indiscreetly of
people's age and dress in a sermon!

The Court of James the First was a great falling off from
that of Elizabeth, in point of decency. It was Sir Toby keeping
house after the death of Olivia; or a fox-hunting squire succeeding to the estate of some courtly dame, and mingling
low life with high. The open habit of drinking to intoxication, so long the disgrace of England, seems first to have come
up in this reign; yet James, who indulged in it, was remarkable for his edicts against drunkenness. Perhaps he issued
them during his fits of penitence; or out of a piece of his
boasted "kingcraft," as a blind to his subjects; or, at best, as

* Biographical History of England. Vol. ii., p. 7. Fifth Edition.

intimations to them, that the vulgar were not to take liberties like the gods. James's court was as great in inconsistency as himself. His father's grossness, his mother's refinement, and the faults common to both, were equally to be seen in it—drunkenness and poetry, dirt and splendour, impiety with claims to religion, favouritism without principle, the coarsest and most childish buffoonery, and the exquisite fancies of the masque.

When Christian IV. of Denmark, brother of James's queen, came into England to visit him, both the kings got drunk together. Sir John Harrington the wit, translator of Ariosto (the best English version of that poet, till Mr. Stewart Rose's appeared), has left a letter on the subject of the court revels of those days, which makes mention of these royal elegancies, and is on every account worth repeating :—

[From London] 1606.

" My good Friend,

" In compliance with your asking, now shall you accept my poor accounte of rich doings. I came here a day or two before the Danish King came, and from the day he did come till this hour, I have been well nigh overwhelmed with carousal and sports of all kinds. The sports began each day in such manner and such sorte, as well nigh persuaded me of Mahomet's paradise. We had women, and indeed wine too, of such plenty, as would have astonished each beholder. Our feasts were magnificent, and the two royal guests did most lovingly embrace each other at table. I think the Dane hath strangely wrought on our good English nobles; for those whom I could never get to taste good liquor, now follow the fashion, and wallow in beastly delights. The ladies abandon their sobriety, and are seen to roll about in intoxication. In good sooth, the parliament did kindly to provide his Majestie so seasonably with money, for there have been no lack of good livinge, shews, sights, and banquetings from morn to eve.

" One day a great feast was held, and after dinner the representation of Solomon, his temple, and the coming of the Queen of Sheba was made, or (as I may better say) was meant to have been made before their Majesties, by device of the Earl of Salisbury and others. But, alas! as all earthly things do fail to poor mortals in enjoyment, so did prove our presentment thereof. The lady who did play the Queen's part did carry most precious gifts to both their Majesties; but forgetting the steppes arising to the canopy, overset her caskets into his Danish Majestie's lap, and fell at his feet, though I think it was rather in his face. Much was the hurry and confusion; cloths and napkins were at hand to make all clean. His Majestie then got up, and would dance with the Queen of Sheba; but he fell down and humbled himself before her, and was carried to an inner chamber, and laid on a bed of state, which was not a little defiled with the presents of the Queen, which had been bestowed on his garments;

such as wine, cream, jelly, beverage, cakes, spices, and other good matters. The entertainment and show went foward, and most of the presenters went backward or fell down; wine did so occupy their upper chambers. Now did appear, in rich dress, Hope, Faith, and Charity. Hope did essay to speak, but wine rendered her endeavours so feeble that she withdrew, and hoped the king would excuse her brevity. Faith was then all alone, for I am certain she was not joyned to good works, and left the court in a staggering condition. Charity came to the King's feet, and seemed to cover the multitude of sins her sisters had committed; in some sorte she made obeyance, and brought giftes, but said she would return home again, as there was no gift which heaven had not already given his Majesty. She then returned to Hope and Faith, who were both sick . . . . in the lower hall. Next came Victory, in bright armour, and presented a rich sword to the King, who did not accept it, but put it by with his hand; and by a strange medley of versification, did endeavour to make suit to the King. But Victory did not triumph long; for, after much lamentable utterance, she was led away like a silly captive, and laid to sleep in the outer steps of the anti-chamber. Now did Peace make entry, and strive to get foremoste to the King; but I grieve to tell how great wrath she did discover unto those of her attendants; and much contrary to her semblance, made rudely war with her olive-branch, and laid on the pates of those who did oppose her coming."*

We suspect that some excuse might be found for James's tendency to drinking, in the same lax and ricketty constitution which made him timid and idle. His love of field sports might indeed have given him strength enough to counteract it, had he been forced into greater economy of living; but the sportsman is seldom famous for eschewing the pleasures of the table; he thinks he has earned, and can afford, excess; and so he can, more than most men. James would have died of idleness and repletion at half the age he did, had he not been a lover of horseback; but when he got to his table he loved it too well; one excess produced another; the nerves required steadying; and the poor disjointed, "ill-contrived" son of Mary (to use a popular, but truly philosophic epithet,) felt himself too stout and valiant by the help of the bottle, not to become overfond of it when he saw it return. All his feelings were of the same incontinent maudlin kind, easily flowing into temptation, and subjecting themselves to a ruler. The bottle governed him; the favourite governed him; his horse and dogs governed him; pedantry governed him; passion governed him; and when the fit was over, repentance governed him as absolutely.

* *Nugæ Antiquæ*, Ed. 1804, vol i., p. 348, *et seq.* (Quoted in a note to Peyton's "Catastrophe of the Stuarts," in "Secret History of the Court of James I." Vol. ii., p. 387.)

Sir Anthony Welldon (a discharged servant of James's for writing a banter upon Scotland, and therefore of doubtful authority concerning him, but credible from collateral evidence, and in some respects manifestly impartial,) says that there was an organised system of buffoonery for the King's amusement, at the head of which were Sir Edward Souch, singer and relater of indecent stories, Sir John Finet, composer of ditto, and Sir George Goring, master of the practical jokes! Sir George sometimes brought two fools riding on people's shoulders, and tilting at one another till they fell together by the ears. The same writer says that James was *not* addicted to drinking; but in this he is contradicted by every other authority, and indeed a different conclusion may be drawn from what Sir Anthony himself subsequently remarks. Sully (Henry the Fourth's Sully, who was at one time ambassador to James, and who tells us that the English monarch usually spent part of the afternoon in bed, "sometimes the whole of it,") says that his custom was "never to mix water with his wine;"* and Sir Roger Coke says he was—

"Excessively addicted to hunting and drinking, not ordinary French and Spanish wines, but strong Greek wines; and though he would *divide* his hunting from drinking those wines (that is to say, have set times for them, apart), yet he would *compound* his hunting with drinking those wines; and to that purpose he was attended with a special officer, who was, as much as could be, always at hand to fill the King's cup in his hunting when he called for it. I have heard my father say that, being hunting with the King, after the King had drank of the wine, he also drank of it, and though he was young and of a healthful constitution, it so disordered his head that it spoiled his pleasure, and disordered him for three days after. Whether it was from drinking these wines, or from some other cause, the King became so lazy and unwieldy, that he was thrust on horseback, and as he was set, so he would ride, without otherwise poising himself on his saddle; nay, when his hat was set on his head, he would not take the pains to alter it, but it sat as it was upon him."†

Perhaps Sir Anthony was fond of the bottle himself, and thought the King drank no more than a gentleman should. It is curious, that Churchill, in his long and laboured invective against James,‡ does not even allude to this propensity. The poet drank himself; probably wrote the very invective with the bottle at his side. However, it is strange, nevertheless, he did not turn the habit itself against the Scottish monarch, as a virtue which failed to redeem him and make him a good fellow.

* Harris, vol. i., p. 17.   † Harris, vol. i., p. 79.
‡ See the Poem of "Gotham" in Churchill's works.

Sir Anthony Welldon's account of James's person and demeanour is so well painted that we must not omit it. It carries with it its own proofs of authenticity, and is one of those animal likenesses which, in certain people, convey the best evidence of the likeness moral:—

"He was of a middle stature, more corpulent through his clothes than in his body, yet fat enough, his clothes being made large and easie, the doublets quilted for steletto proofe, his breeches in great pleits and full stuffed. He was naturally of a timorous disposition, which was the reason of his quilted doublets; his eyes large, ever rolling after any stranger that came in his presence, insomuch as many for shame have left the roome, as being out of countenance; his beard was very thin; his tongue too large for his mouth, which ever made him speak full in the mouth, and made him drink very uncomely, as if eating his drink, which came out into the cup of each side of his mouth; his skin was as soft as taffeta sarsnet, which felt so because he never washt his hands, onely rubb'd his fingers' ends slightly with the wet end of a napkin; his legs were very weake, having had (as was thought) some foul play in his youth, or rather before he was born, that he was not able to stand at seven years of age, that weaknesse made him ever leaning on other men's shoulders. His walke was ever circular, his fingers ever in that walke fiddling about."—"In his dyet, apparell, and journeys, he was very constant; in his apparell so constant, as by his good-will he would never change his clothes, until worn out to ragges; his fashion never—insomuch, as one bringing to him a hat of a Spanish block, he cast it from him, swearing he neither loved them nor their fashions, Another time, bringing him roses on his shooes, he asked, If they would make him a ruffe-footed dove? One yard of sixpenny ribbon served that turn. His diet and journeys were so constant, that the best observing courtier of our time was wont to say, were he asleep seven yeares, and then awakened, he would tell where the King every day had been, and every dish he had had at his table."[*]

Sir Anthony tells us, that James could be as pleasant in speech, and "witty," as any man, though with a grave face; and that he never forsook a favourite, not even Somerset, till the "poisoning" stories about the latter forced him. It may be added, that he did not even then forsake Somerset, as far as he could abide by him; for he gave a pardon to him and his wife for the murder of Sir Thomas Overbury, though he hanged their agents. This is the greatest blot on James's character; for though it was a very mean thing in him to put Raleigh to death, we really believe Raleigh "frightened" him; and as to his discountenance of the "mourning" for Queen Elizabeth, it appears to us, that, instead of telling against him, and being a thing "ungrateful," it was the least evidence he could give of something like a feeling for his own

* Secret History, &c., as above, vol. ii., p. 1.

mother whom Elizabeth had put to death. James owed no " gratitude " to Elizabeth. She would manifestly have hindered him from succeeding her, could she in common policy, or regal feeling, have helped it; and she kept him, or tried to keep him, in doubt of his succession to the last.

James's style of evincing his regard for his favourites was of a maudlin and doating description, not necessary to be dwelt upon; and it was traceable perhaps to the same causes as his other morbid imperfections; but the horrible injustice which he would allow these favourites to perpetrate, and his open violation of his own solemn oaths and imprecations of himself to the contrary, deepen the suffocating shadow which is thrown over this part of the history of Whitehall by the perfumes of effeminacy and the poisons of murderous incontinence. James's lavish bestowal of other people's money upon his favourites (for it was all money of the State which he gave away, not his own; though, indeed, he might have bestowed it in a less generous style upon himself) was the fault of those who let him give it. There was something hearty and open in the character of Buckingham, though he was a " man of violence " after his fashion, and made Whitehall the scene of his " abductions." But the sternest and most formidable testimony we know against the spirit of this prince's favouritism, and the horrors with which it became mixed up, probably against his will, but still with a connivance most weak and guilty, is in the verses entitled the " Five Senses," the production of his countryman, admirer, and panegyrist, and one of the most loyal of men to his house—Drummond of Hawthornden, who had formerly written a beautiful eulogium upon him, in a poem which Ben Jonson wished had been his own, the " River of Forth Feasting." It is clear by these verses that Drummond believed in the worst stories related of Somerset and the Court. The history of that unhappy favourite is well known. The Countess of Essex, the young and beautiful wife of the subsequent parliamentary general, fell in love with him, and got divorced from her husband under circumstances of the most revolting indelicacy. Sir Thomas Overbury, an agent of Somerset's, and one of those natures that puzzle us by the extreme inconsistency of a fine and tender genius, combined with a violent worldliness (with such at least is he charged), was to be got rid of for stopping short in his furtherance of their connection after the divorce. He was

E E

poisoned, and Somerset and his new wife were tried for the
murder.   Somerset denied it, but was found guilty; the
Countess confessed it; yet both were pardoned, while other
agents of theirs were hung.   There is no rescuing James,
after this, from the imputation of the last degree of criminal
weakness, to say the least of it.   It is said that the other
guilty parties (the victims, most likely, of a bad bringing-up,)
grew at last as hateful to one another, as they had been the
reverse—the dreadfulest punishment of affections destitute of
all real regard, and furthered by hateful means.

We gladly escape from these subjects into the poetical
atmosphere of the Masque, the only glory of King James's
reign, and the greatest glory of Whitehall.

But the Masque, in which James's Queen was a performer,
reminds us that we must first say a word or two of herself
and the other princely inmates of Whitehall during this reign.
The Queen, Anne of Denmark, has been represented by some
as a woman given to love intrigues, and by others to intrigues
political.   We take her to have been a common-place woman,
given as much perhaps to both as her position and the
surrounding example induced;—the good-natured wife (after
her fashion) of a good-natured husband, sympathising with
him in his pleasures of the table, and dying of a dropsy.
She danced and performed in the Masques at court, not,
we should guess, with any exquisite grace.   Her daughter
Elizabeth, who married the Elector Palatine, afterwards
struggling King of Bohemia, and who has found an agreeable
biographer and panegyrist in the late Miss Benger, appears to
have partaken of her good nature, with more levity, and was
very popular with the gentry for her affable manners and her
misfortunes.   When she accompanied the Elector to the altar,
in the chapel at Whitehall, she could not help laughing out
loud, at something which struck her fancy.   Her brother
Henry, Prince of Wales, who died in the flower of his youth,
and who, like all princes who die early, has been extolled as
a person of wonderful promise, obtained admiration in his
day for frequenting the tilt-yard while his father was lying in
bed, and for announcing himself as the opponent of his anti-
warlike disposition.   There was probably quite as much of
the opposition of heirs apparent in this, as anything more
substantial; for Henry seems to have exhited his father's
levity and inconsistency of character.   He was thought to be
no adorer of the fair sex, yet has the credit of an intrigue

with the Countess of Essex; and though he reprobated his father's swearing, made no scruple of taunting his brother Charles for his priestly education, and "quizzing" him for not being straight in the legs. As to poor Charles ("Baby Charles," as his father called him, for he was a fond parent, though not a wise one), he became at once the ornament of his family, and the most unfortunate of its members; but he seems from an early age to have partaken of the weakness of character, and the consequent mixture of easiness and obstinacy, common to the family. Buckingham lorded it over him like a petulant elder brother. He once rebuked him publicly, in language unbefitting a gentleman; and at another time, threatened to give him a knock on the head.

We have seen court mummeries in the time of Henry the Eighth, and pageants in that of Elizabeth. In the time of James, the masquings of the one, and the gorgeous shows of the other, combined to produce the Masque, in its latest and best acceptation; that is, a dramatic exhibition of some brief fable or allegory, uniting the most fanciful poetry and scenery, and generally heightened with a contrast of humour, or an anti-masque. Ben Jonson was their great poetical master in the court of James; and Inigo Jones claimed to be their no less masterly and important setter-forth in scene and show.

BANQUETING HOUSE, WHITEHALL.

The poet and artist had a quarrel upon this issue, and Inigo's memory suffers from divers biting libels in the works of his adversary. The noble Banqueting-house remains to show that the architect might have had some right to dispute pre-

tensions, even with the author of the "Alchemist" and the
"Sad Shepherd;" for it is a piece of the very music of his
art (if we may so speak)—the harmony of proportion.
Within these walls, as we now see them, rose, "like a steam
of rich distilled perfumes," the elegant lines of Ben Jonson,
breathing court flowers,—the clouds and painted columns of
Jones—and the fair faces, gorgeous dresses, and dances, of
the beauties that dazzled the young eyesight of the Miltons
and Wallers. Ben's burly body would then break out, as it
were, after his more refined soul, in some burlesque anti-
masque, now and then not a little coarse; and the sovereign
and the poet most probably concluded the night in the same
manner, though not at the same table, in filling their skins
full of wine.

The Court of Charles I. was decorum and virtue itself in
comparison with that of James. Drunkenness disappeared;
there were no scandalous favourites ; Buckingham alone
retained his ascendency as the friend and assistant; and the
King manifested his notions of the royal dignity by a stately
reserve. Little remained externally of the old Court but its
splendour; and to this a new lustre was given by a taste for
painting, and the patronage of Rubens and Vandyke. Charles
was a great collector of pictures. He was still fonder of
poetry than his father, retained Ben Jonson as his laureate,
encouraged Sandys, and May, and Carew, and was a fond
reader of Spenser and Shakspeare; the last of whom is styled
by Milton (not in reproach, as Warton strangely supposed;
for how could a poet reproach a King with loving a poet?)
the "closet companion" of the royal "solitudes." Walpole,
as Mr. Jesse observes, was of opinion, that—

" The celebrated festivals of Louis XIV. were copied from the
shows exhibited at Whitehall, in its time the most polite court in
Europe." Bassompierre, in mentioning his state introduction to
Charles and Henrietta, says, " I found the King on a stage raised
two steps, the Queen and he on two chairs, who rose on the first bow
I made them on coming in. The company was magnificent, and the
order exquisite." " I never knew a duller Christmas than we have
had this year," writes Mr. Gerrard to the Earl of Strafford: " but
one play all the time at Whitehall, and no dancing at all. The
Queen had some little infirmity, the bile or some such thing, which
made her keep in; only on Twelfth Night she feasted the King at
Somerset House, and presented him with a play newly studied, the
Faithful Shepherdess (Fletcher's) which the King's players acted in
the robes she and her ladies acted their pastoral in last year. I had
almost forgot to tell your Lordship, that the dicing night, the King
carried away in James Palmer's hat 1,850*l.* The Queen was his help,

and brought him that luck; she shared presently 900*l.* There are two masques in hand; first, the Inns of Court, which is to be presented on Candlemas-day; the other, the King presents the Queen with on Shrove Tuesday, at night : high expenses; they speak of 20,000*l.* that it will cost the men of the law." *

"Charles was not only well informed," says Mr. Jesse, "in all matters of court etiquette, and in the particular duties of each individual of his household, but enjoined their performance with remarkable strictness. Ferdinand Masham, one of the esquires of his body, has recorded a curious anecdote relative to the King's nice exaction of such observances. 'I remember,' he says, 'that coming to the King's bedchamber door, which was bolted in the inside, the Earl of Bristol, then being in waiting and lying there, he unbolted the door upon my knocking, and asked me "What news ?" I told him I had a letter for the King. The earl then demanded the letter of me, which I told him I could deliver to none but to the King himself; upon which the King said, "The esquire is in the right: for he ought not to deliver any letter or message to any but myself, he being at this time the chief officer of my house; and if he had delivered the letter to any other, I should not have thought him fit for his place."' It seems, that after a certain hour, when the guard was set, and the 'all right' served up, the royal household was considered under the sole command of the esquire in waiting. 'The King,' says Lord Clarendon, 'kept state to the full, which made his court very orderly, no man presuming to be seen where he had no pretence to be.'" †

The truth is, that both from greater virtue and a less jovial temperament, Charles carried his improvement upon the levity of his father's court too far. Public opinion had long been quitting the old track of an undiscerning submission; and, though it was the King's interest to avoid scandal, it was not so to provoke dislike. It was on the side of manner in which he failed. His reformations, the more scandalous ones excepted, appear to have been rather external than otherwise. Mrs. Hutchinson, while she speaks of them highly, intimates that there was still a good deal of private licence; and though it is asserted that Charles discountenanced swearing, perhaps even this was only by comparison. It is reported of Charles II., that in answer to a remonstrance made to him on the oaths in which he indulged, he exclaimed in a very irreverent and unfilial manner, "Oaths ! why, your Martyr was a greater swearer than I am." It has been questioned also, whether in other respects Charles's private conduct was so "immaculate," to use Mr. Jesse's phrase, as the solemnity of his latter years and his fate has led most people

* Jesse's Memoirs of the Court of England during the Reign of the Stuarts, vol. ii., p. 91.
† Ibid., p. 94.

to conclude. Indeed, it is a little surprising how anybody, partisans excepted, could have supposed, that a prince, brought up as he was, and the friend of Buckingham, should be entirely free from the licence of the time. His manners and speeches to women, though not gross for that age, would be thought coarse now; and, at all events, were proofs of a habit of thinking quite in unison with custom. But the present age has been far stricter in its judgment on these points than any which preceded it—at least up to the time of George III. It was not the question of his gallantries, or of his freedom with them, that had anything to do with Charles's unpopularity. The people will pardon a hundred gallantries sooner than one want of sympathy. Charles I. would not have been unpopular in the midst of court elegancies, if he had not been stiff and repulsive in his manners. Unfortunately he wanted address; he had a hesitation in his speech; and his consciousness of a delicate organization and of infirmity of purpose, with the addition of a good deal of the will common to most people, and particularly encouraged in princes, made him afraid of being thought weak and easy. He therefore, in what he thought self-defence, took to an offensive coldness and dryness of behaviour, and gradually became not unwilling even to wreak upon other people the irritability occasioned by it to himself. He got into unseemly passions with ambassadors, and neither knew how to refuse a petition gracefully, nor to repel an undue assumption with real superiority. Even his troubles did not teach him wisdom in these respects till the very last. He was riding out one day during the wars, when a "Dr. Wykes, dean of Burian in Cornwall," says Mr. Jesse, " an inveterate punster, happened to be near him, extremely well mounted. 'Doctor,' said the King, 'you have a pretty nag under you; I pray, how old is he?' Wykes, unable to repress, even in the presence of majesty, the indifferent conceit which presented itself, 'If it please your Majesty' he said, 'he is in the second year of his reign' (rein). Charles discovered some displeasure at this unlicensed ribaldry. 'Go,' he replied, ' you are a fool!' " Now that the dean was a fool there can be no doubt; but that this blunt, offensive, and never-to-be-forgotten word was the only one which a king in a state of war with his subjects could find, in order to discountenance his folly, shows a lamentable habit of subjecting the greater consideration to the less.

Unluckily for Charles's dignity in the eyes of his attendants, and for his ultimate welfare with the people, there was a contest of irritability too often going forward between him and his consort Henrietta; in which the latter, by dint perhaps of being really the weaker of the two, generally contrived to remain conqueror. Swift has recorded an extraordinary instance of her violence in his list of *Mean and Great Fortunes*. He says, that one day Charles made a present to his wife of a handsome brooch, and gallantly endeavouring to fix it in her bosom, happened unfortunately to wound the skin, upon which her Majesty, in a fit of passion, and in the presence of the whole court, took the brooch out and dashed and trampled it on the floor. The trouble that Charles had to get rid of Henrietta's noisy and meddling French attendants, not long after his marriage, is well known; but not so, that, having contrived to turn the key upon her in order that she might not behold their departure, " she fell into a rage beyond all bounds, tore the hair from her head, and cut her hands severely by dashing them through the glass windows." *

When not offended, however, the Queen's manners were lively and agreeable. We are to imagine the time of the court divided between her Majesty's coquetries, and accomplishments, and Catholic confessors, and the King's books, and huntings, and political anxieties; Buckingham, as long as he lived, being the foremost figure next to himself; and Laud and Strafford domineering after Buckingham. In the morning the ladies embroidered and read huge romances, or practised their music and dancing (the latter sometimes with great noise in the Queen's apartments), or they went forth to steal a visit to a fortune-teller, or to see a picture by Rubens, or to sit for a portrait to Vandyke, who married one of them. In the evening there was a masque, or a ball, or a concert, or gaming; the Sucklings, the Wallers, and Carews repeated their soft things, or their verses; and " Sacharissa " (Lady Dorothy Sydney) doubted Mr. Waller's love, and glanced towards sincere-looking Henry Spencer; Lady Carlisle flirted with the Riches and Herberts ; Lady Morton looked grave; the Queen threw round the circle bright glances and French *mots*; and the King criticised a picture with Vandyke or Lord Pembroke, or a poem with Mr. Sandys (who, besides being a poet, was gentleman of his Majesty's chamber); or

* Jesse, vol. ii., p. 79.

perhaps he took Hamilton or Strafford into a corner, and talked, not so wisely, against the House of Commons. It was, upon the whole, a grave and a graceful court, not without an under-current of intrigue.

It seems ridiculous to talk of the court of Oliver Cromwell, who had so many severe matters to attend to in order to keep himself on his throne; but he had a court, nevertheless; and, however jealously it was watched by the most influential of his adherents, it grew more courtly as his protectorate advanced; and it must always have been attended with a respect which Charles knew not sufficiently how to insure, and James not at all. Its dinners were not very luxurious, and the dishes appear to have been brought in by the heavy gentlemen of his guard. In April, 1654, we read of the "grey coats" of these gentlemen, with "black velvet collars, and silver lace and trimmings"—a very sober effort at elegance. Here his daughters would pay him visits of a morning, fluttering betwixt pride and anxiety; and his mother sit with greater feelings of both, starting whenever she heard a noise: flocks of officers came to a daily table, at which he would cheerfully converse; and now and then ambassadors or the Parliament were feasted; and in the evening, perhaps after a portion of a sermon from his Highness, there would be the consciousness of a princely presence, and something like a courtly joy. In the circle Waller himself was to be found (making good the doubts of "Sacharissa"), and Lord Broghill, the friend of Suckling, who refused to join him; and Lady Carlisle, growing old, but still setting her beauty-spots at the saints; and Richard Cromwell, heir-apparent, whom Dick Ingoldsby is forcing to die with laughter, though severe Fleetwood is looking that way; and the future author of Paradise Lost talking Italian with the envoys from the Apennines; and Marvel, his brother secretary, chuckling to hear from the Swedish ambassador the proposal of a visit from Queen Christina; and young Dryden, bashfully venturing in under the wing of his uncle Sir Gilbert Pickering, the chamberlain. There was sometimes even a concert; Cromwell's love of music prevailing against the un-angelical denouncements of it from the pulpit. The Protector would also talk of his morning's princely diversion of hunting; or converse with his daughters and the foreign ambassadors, some of which latter had that day paid their respects to the former, as to royal personages, on their arrival in England;

or if the evening were that of a christening or a marriage, or other festive solemnity, his Highness, not choosing to forget the rough pleasures of his youth, and combining, perhaps, with the recollection something of an hysterical sense of his present wondrous condition, would think it not unbecoming his dignity to recall the days of King James, and bedaub the ladies with sweetmeats, or pelt the heads of his brother generals with the chair cushions. Nevertheless, he could resume his state with an air that inspired the pencil of Peter Lely beyond its fopperies ; and Mazarin at Paris trembled in his chair to think of it.

But how shall we speak of the court of Charles II.? of that unblushing seminary for the misdirection of young ladies, which, occupying the ground now inhabited by all which is proper, rendered the mass of buildings by the water's side, from Charing Cross to the Parliament, one vast—what are we to call it?—

"Chi mi darà le voci e le parole
Convenienti a sì nobil soggetto?"

Let Mr. Pepys explain. Let Clarendon explain. Let all the world explain, who equally reprobate the place and its master, and yet somehow are so willing to hear it reprobated, that they read endless accounts of it, old and new, from the not very bashful *exposé* of the Count de Grammont, down to the blushing deprecations of Mrs. Jameson. Mr. Jesse himself begins with emphatically observing, that " a professed apology either for the character or conduct of Charles II. might almost be considered as an insult to public rectitude and female virtue ;" yet he proceeds to say, that there is a charm nevertheless in " all that concerns the 'merry monarch,' which has served to rescue him from entire reprobation ;" and accordingly he proceeds to devote to him the largest portion given to any of his princes, not omitting particulars of all his natural children ; and winding up with separate memoirs of the maids of honour, the mistresses, and those confidential gentlemen — Messrs. Chiffinch, Prodgers, and Brouncker.

Upon the reason of this apparent contradiction between the morals and toleration of the reading world, we have touched before ; and we think it will not be expected of us to enter further into its metaphysics. The court is before us, and we must paint it, whatever we may think of the matter. We shall only observe in the outset, that the

"merry monarch," besides not being handsome, had the most
serious face, perhaps, of any man in his dominions. It was
as full of hard lines as it was swarthy. If the assembled
world could have called out to have a specimen of a "man of
pleasure" brought before it, and Charles could have been
presented, we know not which would have been greater, the
laughter or the groans. However, "merry monarch" he is
called ; and merry doubtless he was, as far as his numerous
cares and headaches would let him be. Nor should it be
forgotten that cares, necessities, and bad example, conspired,
from early youth, to make him the man he was. We know
not which did him the more harm—the jovial despair of his
fellow exiles, or the sour and repulsive reputation which
morals and good conduct had acquired from the gloominess of
the Puritans.

Charles was of good height as well as figure, and not
ungraceful. Andrew Marvel has at once painted and intimated an excuse for him, in an exordium touching upon the
associates of his banishment. His allusion to the filial occupation of Saul is very witty :—

> " Of a tall stature and a sable hue,
>   Much like the son of Kish, that lofty Jew ;
>   Ten years of need he suffer'd in exile,
>   And kept his father's asses all the while."

He was a rapid and a constant walker, to settle his nerves ;
talked affably with his subjects ; had a parcel of little dogs
about him, which did not improve the apartments at Whitehall ; hated business ; delighted to saunter from one person's
rooms at court to another's, in order to pass the time ; was
fond of wit, and not without it himself ; drank and gamed,
and was in constant want of money for his mistresses, which
ultimately rendered him a scandalous pensioner upon the
King of France ; in short, was a selfish man, partly by temperament, and partly from his early experience of others ; but
was not ill-natured ; and, like his grandfather James, would
live and let live, provided his pleasures were untouched. His
swarthiness he got from the Italian stock of the Medici, and
his animal spirits from Italy or France, or both : they were
certainly not inherited from his father.

The man thus constituted was suddenly transferred from
an exile full of straits and mortifications into the rich and
glorious throne of England. The people, sick of gloom and
disappointment, were as mad to receive him as he was to
come. It was May, and all England dressed itself in garlands

and finery. Crowds shouted at him; music floated around
his steps; young females strewed flowers at his feet; gold
was poured into his pockets; and clergymen blessed him.
He receives the homage of Church and State; and goes the
same night to sup with Mrs. Barbara Palmer, at a house in
Lambeth.

Such was the event which, by an epithet that has since
acquired a twofold significancy, has been called the "blessed
Restoration." Orthodoxy and loyalty had obtained an awkward champion.

Mrs. Palmer soon restored the King to Whitehall by coming
there herself, where she became in due time Countess of
Castlemain, Duchess of Cleveland, and mother of three dukes
and as many daughters. This was for the benefit of the
peerage. But Charles, for the benefit of royalty, was unfortunately compelled to have a wife; though, as an alleviation
of the misfortune, his wife, he reflected, would have an establishment, with ladies of the bedchamber; nay, with a pleasing
addition of maids of honour. He therefore put what face he
could on the matter, and wedded Catharine of Braganza.
When Lady Castlemain was presented to her as one of the
ladies, the poor Queen burst out a-bleeding at the nose. It
took a good while to reconcile the royal lady to the "other
lady" (Clarendon's constant term for her), but it was done in
time, to the astonishment of most, and disgust of some.
Clarendon was one of the instruments that effected the good
work. From thenceforth the Queen was contented to get
what amusement she could, and was as merry as the rest.
She was not an ill-looking woman; was as fond of dancing as
her husband; and he used good-naturedly to try to make her
talk improper broken English, and would not let her be
persecuted.

Whitehall now adjusted itself to the system which prevailed through this reign, and which may be described as
follows: we do not paint it at one point of time only, but
through the whole period.

Charles walked a good deal in the morning, perhaps
played at ball or tennis, chatted with those he met, fed his
dogs and his ducks, looked in at the cockpit, sometimes did
a little business, then sauntered in-doors about Whitehall;
chatted in Miss Wells' room, in Miss Price's room, in
Miss Stuart's room, or Miss Hamilton's; chatted in Mr.
Chiffinch's room, or with Mr. Prodgers; then dined, and took

enough of wine ; had a ball or a concert, where he devoted
himself to Lady Castlemain, the Duchess of Portsmouth, or
whoever the reigning lady was, the Queen talking all the
while as fast as she could to some other lady ; then, perhaps,
played at riddles, or joked with Buckingham and Killigrew,
or talked of the intrigues of the court—the great topic of the
day.   Sometimes the ladies rode out with him in the morning,
perhaps in men's hats and feathers ; sometimes they went to
the play, where the favourite was jealous of the actresses ;
sometimes an actress is introduced at court and becomes a
" madam" herself—Madam Davis, or Madam Eleanor Gwyn.
Sometimes the Queen treats them with a cup of the precious
and unpurchasable beverage called tea, or even ventures
abroad with them in a frolicsome disguise.   Sometimes the
courtiers are at Hampton, playing at hide-and-seek in a
labyrinth ; sometimes at Windsor, the ladies sitting half-
dressed for Sir Peter Lely's voluptuous portraits.

Lady Castlemain, the Duchess of Portsmouth, and Nell
Gwyn, all have their respective lodgings in Whitehall, looking
out upon gardens, elegant with balconies and trellises.   By
degrees the little dukes grow bigger, and there is in particular
a great romping boy, very handsome, called Master Crofts,
afterwards Duke of Monmouth, who is the protégé of Lady
Castlemain, though his mother was Mrs. Walters, and who
takes the most unimaginable liberties in all quarters.   He
annoys exceedingly the solemn Duke of York, the King's
brother, who heavily imitates the reigning gallantries, stupidly
following some lady about without uttering a word, and who
afterwards cut off the said young gentleman's head.   The
concerts are French, partly got up by St. Evremond and the
Duchess of Mazarin, who come to hear them ; and there, in
addition to the ladies before mentioned, come also the Duchess
of Buckingham, short and thick, (daughter of the old Parliamentary general, Fairfax,) and Lady Ossory, charming and
modest, and the Countess of Shrewsbury, who was neither,
and Lady Falmouth, with eyes at which Lord Dorset never
ceased to look, and the Duchess of York (Clarendon's daughter), eating something, and divine old Lady Fanshawe, who
crept out of the cabin in a sea-fight to stand by her husband's
side.   The Queen has brought her there, grateful for a new
set of sarabands, at which Mr. Waller is expressing his
rapture—Waller, the visitor of three courts, and admired and
despised in them all.   Behind him stands Dryden, with a

quiet and somewhat down-looking face, finishing a couplet of
satire. "Handsome Sydney" is among the ladies; and so is
Ralph Montague, who loved ugly dogs because nobody else
would; and Harry Jermyn, who got before all the gallants,
because he was in earnest. Rochester, thin and flushed, is
laughing in a corner at Charles's grim looks of fatigue and
exhaustion; Clarendon is vainly flattering himself that he is
diverting the king's ennui with a long story; Grammont is
shrugging his shoulders at not being able to get in a word;
and Buckingham is making Sedley and Etherege ready to die
of laughter by his mimicry of the poor Chancellor.

The following delicate morceaux from the pages of our
friend Pepys will illustrate the passages respecting my Lady
Castlemain and others.

"1660—Sept. 14.—To White Hall Chappell, where one Dr. Crofts
made an indifferent sermon, and after it an anthem, ill sung, which
made the King laugh. Here I first did see the Princesse Royall since
she came into England. Here I also observed, how the Duke of York
(James II.) and Mrs. Palmer (Lady Castlemaine) did talk to one
another very wantonly through the hangings that part the king's
closet and the closet where the ladies sit.

"May 21.—My wife and I to Lord's lodgings, where she and I staid
talking in White Hall Garden. And in the Privy-garden saw the
finest smocks and linnen petticoats of my Lady Castlemaine's, laced
with rich lace at the bottom, that ever I saw; and did me good to
look at them. Sarah told me how the King dined at my Lady Castlemaine's, and supped, every day and night the last week; and that the
night that the bonfires were made for joy of the Queene's arrival, the
King was there; but there was no fire at her door, though at all the
rest of the doors almost in the street; which was much observed;
and that the King and she did send for a pair of scales and weighed
one another; and she being with child, was said to be heaviest. But
she is now a most disconsolate creature, and comes not out of doors,
since the King's going (to meet his wife).

"August 23d.—Walked to White Hall, and through my Lord's
lodgings we got into White Hall Garden, and so to the Bowling-
greene, and up to the top of the new Banqueting House there, over
the Thames, which was a most pleasant place as any I could have
got; and all the show consisted chiefly in the number of boats and
barges; and two pageants, one of a king, and the other a queene,
with her maydes of honour sitting at her feet very prettily; and they
tell me the queene is Sir Richard Ford's daughter. Anon come the
King and Queene in a barge under a canopy with 1,000 barges and
boats I know, for they could see no water for them, nor discern the
King nor Queene. And so they landed at White Hall Bridge, and
the great guns on the other side went off. But that which pleased
me best was, that my Lady Castlemaine stood over against us upon a
piece of White Hall. But methought it was strange to see her lord
and her upon the same place walking up and down without taking
notice one of another, only at first entry he put off his hat, and she

made him a very civil salute, but afterwards took no notice one of another; but both of them now and then would take their child, which the nurse held in her armes, and dandle it. One thing more; there happened a scaffold below to fall, and we feared much hurt, but there was none, but she of all the great ladies only run down among the common rabble to see what hurt was done, and did take care of a child that received some little hurt, which methought was so noble. Anon, there come one there booted and spurred that she talked long with, and by and by, she being in her haire, she put on his hat, which was but an ordinary one, to keep the wind off. But it become her mightily, as everything else do."

What Pepys thought "noble" was probably nothing more than the consequence of a habit of doing what she pleased, in spite of appearances. The "hat" is a comment on it, to the same effect.

"December 25th. — Christmas Day. — Had a pleasant walk to White Hall, where I intended to have received the communion with the family, but I come a little too late. So I walked up into the house and spent my time looking over pictures, particularly the ships in King Henry the VIIIth's Voyage to Bullonn*, marking the great difference between those built then and now. By and by, down to the chapel again, where Bishop Morley preached upon the song of the angels, 'Glory to God on high, on earth peace, and good-will towards men.' Methought he made but a poor sermon, but long, and reprehending the common jollity of the court for the true joy that shall and ought to be on these days; particularized concerning their excess in playes and gaming, saying, that he whose office it is to keep the gamesters in order and within bounds, serves but for a second rather in a duell, meaning the groome-porter. Upon which it was worth observing how far they are come from taking the reprehensions of a bishop seriously, that they all laugh in the chapel when he reflected on their ill actions and courses. He did much press us to joy in these publick days of joy, and to hospitality. But one that stood by whispered in my ear that the bishop himself do not spend one groate to the poor himself. The sermon done, a good anthem followed with violls, and the King come down to receive the sacrament.

"1662-3—February 1st.—This day Creed and I walking in White Hall did see the King coming privately from my Lady Castlemaine's; which is a poor thing for a Prince to do: and so I expressed my sense of it to Creed in terms which I should not have done, but that I believe he is trusty in that point."

The court of James II. is hardly worth mention. It lasted less than four years, and was as dull as himself. The most remarkable circumstance attending it was the sight of friars and confessors, and the brief restoration of Popery. Waller, too, was once seen there; the *fourth* court of his visiting. There was a poetess also, who appears to have been attached

* Boulogne.

by regard as well as office to the court of James—Anne
Kingsmill, better known by her subsequent title of Countess
of Winchilsea. The attachment was most probably one of
feeling only and good-nature, for she had no bigotry of any
sort. Dryden, furthermore, was laureate to King James; and
in a fit of politic, perhaps real, regret, turned round upon
the late court in his famous comparison of it with its predecessor.

James fled from England in December, 1688, and the
history of Whitehall terminates with its conflagration, ten
years afterwards.

CHAPTER XII.

St. James's Park and its associations.—Unhealthiness of the Place
and neighbourhood.—Leper Hospital of St. James.—Henry the
Eighth builds St. James's Palace and the Tilt Yard.—Original
State and Progressive Character of the Park.—Charles the First.—
Cromwell.—Charles the Second; his Walks, Amusements, and
Mistresses.—The Mulberry Gardens.—Swift, Prior, Richardson,
Beau Tibbs, Soldiers, and Syllabubs.—Character of the Park at
present.—St. James's Palace during the Reigns of the Stuarts and
two first Georges.—Anecdotes of Lord Craven and Prince George
of Denmark.—Characters of Queen Anne and of George the First
and Second.—George the First and his Carp.—Lady Mary Wortley
Montagu and the Sack of Wheat.—Horace Walpole's Portrait of
George the First.—The Mistresses of that King, and of his Son.—
Mistake of Lord Chesterfield.—Queen Caroline's Ladies in Waiting.
—Miss Bellenden and the Guineas.—George the Second's Rupture
with his Father, and with his Son.—Character of that Son.—Buckingham House.—Sheffield and his Duchess.—Character of Queen
Charlotte.—Advantages of Queen Victoria over her predecessors.

T. JAMES'S PARK is associated in con-
temporary minds with nothing but amusing recollections of bands of music
marching soldiers, maid-servants and
children, drinkings of "milk from the
cow," the hoop-petticoats of the court
days of George the Third, and fading
images of passages in novels, or of shabby-
genteel debtors sitting lounging on the
benches. A little further back in point of time we see a novelist
himself, Richardson, walking in it, with other invalids, for his
health; then Swift crossing it from Suffolk Street in his way

to Chelsea, or thinking of the *Spectator* and *Rosamond's Pond*;
then the gallants of the time of Charles the Second, with
Charles himself feeding his ducks and playing at mall; then
his unhappy father led through it from St. James's Palace on
his way to the scaffold at Whitehall; and then the chival-
resque sports of the Tudors in the famous tilt-yard, which
occupied the site of the Horse Guards. To all these points
we shall return for the purpose of entering into a few particulars; but as geographers begin their accounts of a place
with the soil, we shall first make a few remarks of a like
nature.

The site of this park, which must always have been low
and wet, is said in the days before the Conquest to have been
a swamp. Yet so little understood, not only at that time but
any time till within these few years, were those vitalest arts
of life which have been disclosed to us by the Southwood
Smiths and others, that the good citizens of London in those
days built a hospital upon it for lepers (by way of purifying
their skins), and people of rank and fashion have been
clustering about it more and more ever since, especially of late
years. "If a merry-meeting is to be wished," says the man
in Shakspeare, "may God prohibit it." If our health is to be
injured while in town by luxury and late nights, say the men
of State and Parliament, let us all go and make it worse in
the bad air of Belgravia. Nay, let us sit with our feet in the
water, while in Parliament itself, and then let us aggravate
our agues in Pimlico and the park.—There is no use in
mincing the matter, even though the property of a great
lord be doubled by the mistake. The fashionable world
should have stuck to Marylebone and the good old dry parts
of the metropolis, or gone up hill to Kensington gravel-pits, or
into any other wholesome quarter of the town or suburbs,
rather than have descended to the water-side, and built in
the *mush* of Pimlico. Building and house-warming doubtless
make a difference; and wealth has the usual advantages compared with poverty: but the malaria is not done away. A
professional authority on the subject gave the warning five
and twenty years ago in the *Edinburgh Review;* but what are
warnings to house-building and fashion? "It is not suspected,"
he says (vol. xxxvi. p. 341) " that St. James's Park is a perpetual source of malaria, producing frequent intermittents,
autumnal dysenteries, and various derangements of health,
in all the inhabitants who are subject to its influence. The

cause being unsuspected, the evil is endured, and no further inquiries are made." The malaria (he tells us in another passage of the same article) " spreads even to Bridge Street and Whitehall. Nay, in making use of the most delicate *miasmometer* (if we may coin such a word) that we ever possessed, an officer who had suffered at Walcheren, we have found it reaching up to St. James's Street even to Bruton Street, although the rise of ground is here considerable, and the whole space from the nearest water is crowded with houses."

This statement, corroborated as it is by the obvious nature of the soil and air in the park, where the people to any eye coming from higher ground seem walking about only in a thinner kind of water—a perpetual haze and *mugginess*— ought to settle the question respecting the doom of Buckingham Palace. Her Majesty, whose life and comfort are precious to her subjects, should have her town residence in quite another sort of place. Almost everything indeed, artificial as well as natural, conspires to render the spot unwholesome. See what the royal lungs receive on all sides of the present abode whichever way the windows are opened. In front of it is the steam of the mushy ground and the canal; on the left comes draining down the wet of Constitution Hill; and on the right and at the back are the vapours of the river and the pestilential smokes of the manufactories. What an air in which to set forth the colours of the royal flag and refresh the anxieties of the owner! We never look down on the flag from Piccadilly, but we long to see it announcing the royal presence on higher ground and in a healthy breeze.

The Leper Hospital, being the ancientest known domicile in the spot before us, stood on the site of the present St. James's Palace; so that where state and fashion have congregated, and blooming beauties come laughing through the trees, was once heard the dismal sound of the " cup and clapper," which solicited charity for the most revolting of diseases. The spot was probably selected for the hospital, not only as being at the greatest convenient distance from the habitations of the good citizens its founders (lepers being always put as far as possible out of the way), but because it suggested itself to the imagination as possessed of an analogous dreariness and squalidity. Unfavourable circumstances in those days were only thought fit for one another, not for

F F

the super-induction of favourable ones. The lunatic was to be exasperated by whips and dark-keeping, and the leper thrust into the ditch. The world had not yet found out that light, cleanliness, and consolation were good for all. Imagine this " lake of the dismal swamp," now St. James's Park, with not another house nearer to it than the walls at Ludgate, presenting to the timid eyes of the Sunday pedestrian its lonely spital, which at once attracted his charity and repelled his presence (for leprosy was thought infectious), the wind sighing through the trees, and the rain mingling with the pestilential-looking mud.

The endowment of St. James's Hospital is said to have been originally for women only, fourteen in number, to whom were subsequently added eight brethren " to administer divine service." They were probably, however, in a good condition of life—" leper ladies," as an old poem styles the companions of Cressida; but ladies, according to the poem, were not exempt from the duty of asking alms with the " cup and clapper; " and as it was probably a part of their business and humiliation to watch for the appearance of wayfarers, and accost them with cries and clamour, scenes of that kind may have taken place in the walk now constituting the Mall.

The hospital was exchanged with Henry the Eighth for " a consideration; " and upon its site, or near it, that soul of leprosy built a manor, and transferred into it his own bloated and corrupted body. He was then in the forty-third year of his age, and in the same year (1532) he married poor Anne Boleyn. The town-residences (as they would now be called) of the kings of England had hitherto been at Kensington, or on the banks of the Thames at London and Westminster (such as the Tower, Westminster Hall, &c.) What it was that attracted Henry to the Leper Hospital it is difficult to conceive; though the neighbourhood, no doubt, had become a little cleansed and refined by the growth of Westminster and Whitehall. Much neatness was not required by a state of manners, which, according to Erasmus, must have been one of the dirtiest in Europe, and which allowed the refuse of meats and drinks, in gentlemen's houses, to collect under the rushes in the dining-rooms. Perhaps the new palace was to be a place of retirement for the King and his thoughtless victim, whom four years afterwards he put to death. Most likely, however, his great object was to grasp all he could, and add to the number of his parks and amusements; for the whole of the St. James's Fields (as they were called) fell into his hands with the house, and he stocked them with game, built a tilt-yard in front of Whitehall, on the site of the present Horse Guards, together with a cock-pit in its neighbourhood; and on the downfall of Wolsey took possession of Whitehall itself, which thenceforth became added to the list of royal abodes. The new palace could never have been handsome. It had the homely look which it retains to

ST. JAMES'S PALACE. 1650.

this day, as the reader will see in the print before him ; the gateway looking up St. James's Street being evidently a remnant of it.

The Tilt Yard, as its name implies, was the chief scene of knightly amusement in the reigns of the Tudors. Here Henry jousted till he grew too fat ; and here Elizabeth sat at the receipt of chivalrous adulation. The spot is full of life and colour in the eyes of one's imagination, with heralds and coats of arms, plumed champions, caparisoned steeds, and courts looking on from draperied galleries. The present tranquil exercises on parade may be considered as a remnant of the old military shows. But the people had no admittance within the court grounds, except on favour.

The new park seems to have remained strictly enclosed as a nursery for game till the period of the civil wars of the Commonwealth. A new palace by Inigo Jones was intended to overlook it at Whitehall, of which only the Banqueting House was erected. Charles the First was brought to this house across the Park, from St. James's Palace, in order to

suffer death. Cromwell is then discerned in the park grounds
taking the air in a sedan; but its popular history does not
commence till the Restoration, when Charles the Second, who
seems not to have known what to do with the quantity of life
and animal spirits that had been suppressed during his exile,
took to improving and enjoying it with great vivacity.   The
walks with him became real walks, for he was a great pedestrian.   He had got the habit, perhaps, when he could not
afford a horse.   He let the people in to see him feed his ducks
in the canal, a branch of which, called Duck Island, he
pleasantly erected into a "Government" for the French wit
and refugee, St. Evremond.   He made an aviary on the
south-east side of the park, thence called Birdcage Walk;
turned the north side into a mall for the enjoyment of the
pastimes so called, in which he excelled; introduced skating
from Holland on the canal and Rosamond's Pond (which was
another branch of it on the south-west); had mistresses in
lodgings east and west of him (Cleveland at Whitehall and
Nell Gwyn in Pall Mall); and saw, in the course of his reign,
new streets rising and old places of entertainment flourishing
in other quarters of his favourite district; Spring Gardens
(which became famous for the tavern called "Lockett's"), at
Charing Cross, and the Mulberry Gardens and noblemen's
mansions between Pimlico and Piccadilly.   It has been a
question whether the site of the Mulberry Gardens was on
the spot now occupied by Arlington Street, or on that of the
Queen's Palace.   We suspect it is difficult to say which, and
that they extended along the whole space between the two.
Particular sites are too often confounded with places near
them; and houses are said to displace one another, which only
occupied successive neighbourhoods.   By some writers, for
instance, the sites of Arlington and Old Buckingham Houses
are considered as identical, while others represent them in one
another's vicinity.   At all events, the Mulberry Gardens
appear to have included the site of both those houses.   Ladies
came there in masks to eat syllabubs, and converse with their
lovers.   Sedley made them the scene of a play.   The whole
park, indeed, in Charles's reign, may be said to have been the
scene of a play, especially towards evening, when the meetings
took place which Sedley and Etherege dramatised.   In the
morning all was duck-feeding and dog-playing and playing at
mall; in the evening all intrigue and assignation.   At one
time Waller is admiring the King's masterly use of the small

stick; at another Pepys is asking questions of the park-keepers, or transported at sight of the court ladies on horseback; at another Evelyn is horrified (though he seems to have sought occasions for such horrors) at overhearing a "very familiar discourse" between his Majesty and that "impudent comedian," Nelly Gwyn, who is standing at her garden-wall at the back of Pall Mall (near the present Marlborough House).

Matters in this respect mended, though not suddenly, at the Revolution. Whitehall Palace was then accidentally burnt down, and that of St. James's becomes one of the chief residences of the sovereign, which it remains till the reign of the present. Swift and Prior are now seen walking for their health in the park,—Swift to get thin, and Prior to get fat. The heroes and hungry debtors of the novelists (for the park was privileged from arrest) make their appearance, the former with their wives or friends, the latter sitting starving on the benches. Staid ladies have Sunday promenades under the eye of staid sovereigns. Something of a new license returns with the first and second Georges; but it comes from Germany, is discreet, and makes little impression. The greatest assignation we read of is an innocent one of Richardson with a Lady Bradshaigh, who is "mighty curious" to know what sort of man he is, and accordingly moves him to describe himself in the formal terms of an advertisement, in order that he may be recognised when she meets him. Goldsmith's Beau Tibbs, who "blasts himself with an air of vivacity" at seeing "nobody in town," is now the pleasantest fellow we encounter in the park for many a day. The ducks, and the dogs, and the birdcages, and Rosamond's Pond, dismal for drowning lovers, have long vanished; and the place begins to look as it used to do forty years ago. The gayest entertainment in it is "the soldiers," with their bands of music; and the most sensual pleasure a glass of milk from the cow. A mad woman (Margaret Nicholson) makes a sensation, by attempting to stab George the Third at the palace door; but all is quiet again, sedate and orderly, even when court-days bring together a crowd of beauties. George the Fourth just lives long enough to turn Buckingham Palace into a toy, and the site of Carlton Gardens into something better. With his successors comes the greatest of all the park improvements— the conversion of the poor fields and canal into a public pleasure-ground and an ornamental piece of water. Upon this King Charles's ducks have returned, equally improved;

and if it did but possess a good atmosphere, St. James's Park would now be as complete a place of recreation for the promenaders of its neighbourhood, as it is handsome and well-intended.

One of the most popular aspects of St. James's Park is that of a military and music-playing and milk-drinking spot. The milk-drinkings, and the bands of music, and the parades, are the same as they used to be in our boyish days; and, we were going to add, may they be immortal. But though it is good to make the best of war as long as war cannot be helped, and though music and gold lace, &c., are wonderful helps to that end, yet conscience will not allow us to blink all we know of a very different sort respecting battlefields and days after the battle. We say, therefore, may war turn out to be as mortal, and speedily so, as railroads and growing good-sense can make it; though in the meantime, and the more for that hope, we may be allowed to indulge ourselves as we did when children, in admiring the pretty figures which it cuts in this place—the harmlessness of its glitter and the transports of its beholders. Will anybody who has beheld it when a boy ever forget how his heart leaped within him when, having heard the music before he saw the musicians, he issued hastily from Whitehall on to the parade, and beheld the serene and stately regiment assembled before the colonel, the band playing some noble march, and the officers stepping forwards to the measure with their saluting swords? Will he ever forget the mystical dignity of the band-major, who made signs with his staff; the barbaric, and as it were, Othello-like height and lustre of the turbaned black who tossed the cymbals; the dapper juvenility of the drummers and fifers; and the astounding prematureness of the little boy who played on the triangle? Is it in the nature of human self-respect to forget how this little boy, dressed in a "right earnest" suit of regimentals, and with his hair as veritably powdered and plastered as the best, fetched those amazing strides by the side of Othello, which absolutely "kept up" with his lofty shanks, and made the schoolboy think the higher of his own nature for the possibility? Furthermore, will he ever forget how some regiment of horse used to come over the Park to Whitehall, in the midst of this parade, and pass the foot-soldiers with a sound of clustering magnificence and dancing trumpets? Will he ever forget how the foot then divided itself into companies, and turning about and deploying before the colonel, marched off in the opposite direction, carrying away the school-boy himself and the crowd of spectators with it ; and so, now with the brisk drums and fifes, and now with the deeper glories of the band, marched gallantly off for the court-yard of the palace, where it again set up its music-book, and enchanted the crowd with Haydn or Mozart ?   What a strange mixture, too, was the crowd itself—boys and grown men, gentlemen, vagabonds, maid-servants—there they all went listening, idling, gazing on the ensign or the band-major, keeping pace with the march, and all of them more or less, particularly the maid-servants, doting on the " sogers."   We, for one, confess to having drunk deep of the attraction, or the infection, or the balmy reconcilement (whichever the reader pleases to call it).   Many a holiday morning have we hastened from our cloisters in the city to go and hear " the music in the park," delighted to make one in the motley crowd, and attending upon the last flourish of the hautboys and clarionets.   There we first became acquainted with feelings which we afterwards put into verse (if the recollection be not thought an impertinence); and there, without knowing what it was called, or who it was that wrote it, we carried back with us to school the theme of a glorious composition, which afterwards became a favourite with opera-goers under the title of *Non più andrai*, the delightful march in *Figaro*.   We suppose it is now, and has ever since been played there, to the martialisation of hundreds of little boys, and the puzzlement of philosophy.   Everything in respect to military parade takes place, we believe, in the park just as it used to do, or with little variation.   The objects also which you behold, if you look at the parade and its edifices, are the same.   The Admiralty, the Treasury, the back of the Minister's house in Downing Street, and the back-front of the solid and not inappropriate building, called the Horse Guards, look as they did fifty years ago ; and there also continue to stand the slender Egyptian piece of cannon, and the dumpy Spanish mortar, trophies of the late war with France.   The inscriptions, however, on those triumphant memorials contain no account of the sums we are still paying for having waged it.

" The soldiers" and the " milk from the cow" do not at all clash in the minds of boyhood.   The juvenile imagination ignores what it pleases, especially as its knowledge is not very great.   It no more connects the idea of village massacre with guns and trumpets, than it supposes the fine scarlet coat

capable of being ragged and dirty. Virgil may say something about ruined fields, and people compelled to fly for their
lives; but this is only part of a "lesson," and the calamities
but so many nouns and verbs. The maid-servants, and
indeed the fair sex in general, till they become wives and
mothers, enjoy the like happy exemption from ugly associations of ideas; and the syllabub is taken under the trees, with
a delighted eye to the milk on one side, and the military show
on the other.

The late Mr. West, the painter, was so pleased with this
pastoral group of cows and milk-drinkers in the park, that he
went out of the line of his art to make a picture of it.

Saint James's Palace was not much occupied by the Tudor
and Stuart sovereigns. Their principal town residence was
Whitehall. The first of the Stuarts may have intended to
make St. James's the residence of the Princes of Wales; for
he gave it his son Henry, who died there. We have spoken
of this prince and his doubtful "promise" already. The best
thing known of him is the astonishment he expressed at his
father's keeping "such a bird" as Walter Raleigh locked up
in a cage.

Charles the First spent the three last days of his life in this
palace, occupying himself in devotion, and preparing to fall with
dignity;—happy if he had but known how to value the dignity
of truth, which would have saved him from the necessity. The
Stuarts, unfortunate everywhere in proportion to the gravity
of their pretensions, had their customary bad fortune in this
palace; at least the male portion of them. James the Second's
daughters, who got his throne, were born and married there;
but here also was born his son, the first Pretender, whose
mother's chamber being situate near some backstairs gave
colour to the ridiculous story of his having been a spurious
child smuggled into the palace in a warming pan; and here
his unlucky and narrow-minded father partly resided when he
per force invited his ouster and son-in-law William to take up
his abode in it, and received in return notice to quit his
throne. The old romantic Lord Craven, who was supposed
to have been privately married to James the First's daughter,
the luckless Queen of Bohemia, and who was thus destined
to witness the whole of the troubles of the English dynasty of
the Stuarts, happened to be on duty at St. James's when the
Dutch troops were coming across the park to take possession
of it. Agreeably to his chivalrous character, and to his habit

of taking warlike steps to no purpose, the gallant veteran
would have opposed their entrance; but his master forbade
him; and he marched away, says Pennant, "with sullen
dignity."

"*Est-il-possible*" got the house after James;—we mean his
daughter Anne's husband, George of Denmark, who being no
livelier a man than his father-in-law, made no other comment
than these three words (*Is it possible?*) on the accounts given
him by the poor King of every successive desertion from his
cause. In due time the man of one remark followed the
deserters; upon which James observed to one of the few
friends left him, "Who do you think is gone now? Little
Est-il-possible himself."

St. James's was given to Anne and her husband by the new
sovereign William the Third. She made it her chief palace
when she came to the throne, and such it continued to be
with the sovereigns of England till the reign of George the
Third, with whom its occupation was divided with Buckingham house. Lady Strafford, the wild daughter of Rochester,
who lived in France because England, she said, was "too
dull" for her, used to relate stories of the "orgies" in Anne's
palace. Palaces for the most part have been places of greater
license than the world supposes, owing to the natural results
of luxury, privilege, and the bringing of idle and agreeable
people together; but the orgies which the rattle-headed Lady
Strafford talked of, were probably never anything much
greater than a drinking-bout of her husband, who unluckily
taught his wife to drink too. Anne, between her Protestant
accession and her exiled Popish kindred, her imperious
favourite the Duchess of Marlborough, and her quarrelling
and fluctuating Administrations, had an anxious time of it.
There is an old French story of a sage but ugly cavalier,
who married a handsome fool, in the persuasion that his
children would inherit their mother's beauty and his own
wisdom. Unfortunately, they turned out to be specimens of
his own ugliness, combined with the mother's folly. We do
not say that Queen Anne was a fool, though she was not very
wise; but when her grandfather, Lord Clarendon, saw the
match between his clever daughter and the future James the
Second, he probably hoped that their offspring would possess
the father's figure combined with the mother's wit; whereas
neither Mary nor Anne possessed the latter, and Anne inherited the mother's fat with the father's dulness. She was a

well-meaning and fond, but sluggish-minded woman, with no force of character; her temperament was heavy and lax; she did not know what to do with her political perplexities; and the screw-up of her nerves with strong waters appears to have become irresistible. Swift gives a curious account of her levees, in which she would sit with a parcel of courtiers about her, silently giving glances at them, and putting the end of her fan in her mouth for want of address. She was glad to get the whole set away, that she might sink into her easy chair, and complain of the troubles of human life.

St. James's thus began with being a dull court, and dull for the most part it remained to the last—quite worthy of its external appearance. George the First and Second were both dull gentlemen, with a difference; the former a pale round-featured man, content to appear the insipid personage he was; the latter, aquiline-nosed, affecting spirit and gallantry, and attaining only to rudeness. They were people of the then German schools of breeding, very different from the present; and St. James's at that time combined a tasteless air of decorum with gallantries equally unengaging. George the First had two German mistresses, one as lean as the other was fat; and George the Second another, remarkable for nothing but making money. Lady Wortley Montagu and Horace Walpole have given some amusing notices of the palace in connection with their Majesties and the court.

" This is a strange country," said George the First on his coming to England. " The first morning after my arrival at St. James's, I looked out of the window and saw a park with walks, a canal, &c., which they told me were mine. The next day, Lord Chetwynd, the ranger of *my* park, sent me a fine brace of carp out of *my* canal; and I was told I must give five guineas to Lord Chetwynd's servant for bringing me *my own* carp out of *my own* canal in *my own* park."

We are not to suppose that the King delivered this speech in the smart good English of its reporter, or in any English; for he was not acquainted with the language. He and his Minister Sir Robert Walpole used to converse, even on the most important matters of state, in such Latin as their school recollections furnished, the Minister understanding German or French as little as the King did English.

His Majesty, in the first days of his new court, was more agreeably surprised one evening by the sudden return of Lady Mary Wortley to the party which were assembled in his rooms, and which she had somewhat strangely pleaded a previous engagement for quitting. She returned, borne in the arms of Mr. Secretary Craggs, junior, who had met her going away, and seized hold of the fugitive. He deposited her in the ante-room ; but the doors of the presence-chamber being hastily thrown open by the pages, she found herself so astonished and fluttered that she related the whole adventure to the no less astonished king ; who asked Mr. Craggs whether it was customary in England to carry ladies about " like sacks of wheat." " There is nothing," answered the adroit secretary, " which I would not do for your Majesty's satisfaction."

Towards the close of this monarch's reign, the future court historian, Horace Walpole, then a boy of ten years of age, had a longing " to see the King ; " and as he was the son of the Minister, his longing was gratified in a very particular manner. A meeting was arranged on purpose the day before his Majesty took his last journey to Hanover :—

"My mother," says Walpole, "carried me at ten at night to the apartments of the Countess of Walsingham, on the ground floor, towards the garden of St. James's, which opened into that of her aunt the Duchess of Kendal's ; apartments occupied by George the Second after his Queen's death, and by his successive mistresses, the Countesses of Suffolk and Yarmouth. Notice being given that the King was come down to supper, Lady Walsingham took me alone into the Duchess's ante-room, where we found alone the King and her. I knelt down and kissed his hand. He said a few words to me, and my conductress led me back to my mother. The person of the King is as perfect in my memory as if I saw him but yesterday. It was that of an elderly man, rather pale, and exactly like his pictures and coins, not tall, of an aspect rather good than august, with a dark tie-wig, a plain coat, waistcoat, and breeches, of snuff-coloured cloth, with stockings of the same colour, and a blue ribband over all. So entirely was he my object that I do not believe I once looked at the Duchess ; but as I could not avoid seeing her on entering the room, I remember that just beyond his Majesty stood a very tall, lean, ill-favoured old lady."

This lady, the Duchess of Kendal, a German, was the king's lean mistress. The fat one, another German, whom he made Countess of Darlington, was "as corpulent and ample as the duchess was long and emaciated." Walpole, who gives this account of her, adds, that he remembered being " terrified " in his infancy at her enormous figure. She had " two fierce black eyes, large and rolling between two lofty arched eyebrows, two acres of cheeks spread with crimson, an ocean of neck," &c., " and no part restrained by stays." " It was not,"

says Horace, "till the last year or two of his reign, that this
foreign sovereign paid the nation the compliment of taking
openly an English mistress." This was Miss Brett, daughter
of Savage's reputed mother the Countess of Macclesfield, by
her second husband, Colonel Brett, whom we have seen, in
our accounts of the Streets of London, keeping company with
Addison. Miss Brett was a very lively and aspiring damsel.
During the visit to Hanover just mentioned, she took it upon
herself to break out a door from her apartments in St. James's
Palace into the Royal garden. The eldest of the king's
grand-daughters, also a very spirited person, ordered it to be
closed up again. Miss Brett, more spirited, again broke it
open, and we hear of the matter no further. But the king
died on his journey, and the new mistress's empire was over.

The new King, George the Second, while Prince of Wales,
had quarrelled with his father, and had been ordered to quit
St. James's with all his household. Though a great formalist,
he was also a great, and indeed somewhat alarming, pretender
to gallantry, being of opinion, according to Lady Wortley
Montagu, that men and women were created solely to be
"kicked or kissed" by him at his pleasure. It is of him that
stories were told of the King's cuffing his ministers, and kick-
ing his hat about the room ; and he is understood to be the
King Arthur of Fielding's Tom Thumb. He had a wife,
however, of some real pretensions to liveliness of mind, afterwards Queen Caroline, the friend of men of letters, and a very
excellent wife too, for she was charitable to her husband's irre-
gularities, and is said to have even shortened her life by
putting her rheumatic legs into cold water in order to be able
to accompany him in his walks. Here, in St. James's Palace,
as well as at Kensington, she held her literary and philoso-
phico-religious levees (being fond of a little theological
inquiry); and here also she had brought together the handsomest and liveliest set of ladies in waiting ever seen on
these sober-looking premises before or since. For, though
Lady Winchelsea, the poetess, was among those of James the
Second, the ladies about that sombre personage and his Queen
seem, for the most part, to have been both dull and ugly.
His first Queen, Anne Hyde, had been a maid of honour herself, and did not encourage the sisterhood; and his second
Queen, the young and handsome Mary of Modena, who had
heard of the doings at Whitehall when her husband was
Duke of York, condescended to be jealous of him, in spite of

their difference of years; James being comparatively an old gentleman, while she was not out of her teens. Indeed, he gave cause for the jealousy, and added no hopes of amendment; for being a Papist as well as a solemn gallant, he divided his time between the ugly mistresses he was fond of, and the priests who absolved him from the offence; an absolution that was superfluous, according to his brother Charles; the "merry monarch" having been of opinion that the mistresses themselves were penance enough.

George the Second's German mistress was a Baroness de Walmoden. On the death of Queen Caroline, he brought her over from Germany, and created her Countess of Yarmouth. She had two sons, the younger of whom was supposed to be the King's; and a ludicrous anecdote connected with the supposition and with the abode before us, is related of the famous Lord Chesterfield. On the countess's settlement in her state apartments, his lordship found one day in the palace antechamber a fair young gentleman, whom he took for the son in question. He was accordingly very profuse in his compliments. The shrewd lad received them all with a grave face, and then delightfully remarked, " I suppose your lordship takes me for ' Master Louis;' but I am only Sir William Russell, one of the pages." Chesterfield piqued himself on his discernment, particularly in matters of intercourse; and it is pleasant to catch the heartless man of " the graces" at a disadvantage that must have extremely mortified him.

There is another St. James's anecdote of Chesterfield, which shows him in no very dignified light. Mrs. Howard, afterwards Countess of Suffolk, a very amiable woman, supposed to have been one of the mistresses of George the Second, was thought to have more influence with his Majesty than she possessed. Sir Robert Walpole told his son Horace that Queen Caroline saw Lord Chesterfield one night, after having won a large sum of money at court, steal along a dark passage under her window that was lighted only by a single lamp, in order to deposit it in Mrs. Howard's apartment, for fear of carrying it home in the dark. Sir Robert (his son adds) thought that this was the occasion of Chesterfield's losing his credit with the Queen; but the conclusion has shown it to be unfounded. Chesterfield, however, though really a very sharp-sighted man, was rendered liable by his bad principles to a failure in what he thought his acutest views; and Caroline's better nature may have seen through his lordship's character without the help of the lamp and the dark passage.

The Queen's ladies above alluded to were the famous bevy of the Howards, Lepells, and Bellendens, celebrated in the pages of Swift and Pope. They have become well known to the public by the appearance of the *Suffolk Correspondence*, and *Lady Hervey's Letters*. George the Second, when Prince of Wales, and living in this palace with his father, had probably made love to them all, fluttering more than flattering them, between his attentions as a prince and his unengaging qualities as a brusque and parsimonious man. Miss Bellenden, who became Duchess of Argyle, is said to have observed one day to him as he was counting his money in her presence (probably with an intimation of his peculiar sense of the worth of it), " Sir, I cannot bear it. If you count your money any more, I will go out of the room." Another version of the story says that she tilted the guineas over, and then ran out of the room while the Prince was picking them up. This is likely, for she had great animal spirits. When the Prince quarrelled with his father, and he and his household were ordered to quit St. James's, Miss Bellenden is described, in a ballad written on the occasion, as taking her way from the premises by jumping gaily down-stairs.

The occasion of this rupture between George the First and his son was curious. Palaces are very calm-looking things outside; but within, except in very wise and happy, or very dull reigns, are pampered passions, and too often violent scenes. George the First and his son, like most sovereigns and heirs apparent, were not on good terms. The Princess of Wales had been delivered of a second son, which was to be christened; and the Prince wished his uncle the Duke of York to stand godfather with his Majesty. His Majesty, on the other hand, peremptorily insisted on dividing the pious office with the officious Duke of Newcastle. The christening accordingly took place in the Princess's bed-chamber; and no sooner had the bishop shut the book than the Prince, furiously crossing the foot of the bed, and heedless of the King's presence, " held up his hand and forefinger to the Duke in a menacing attitude (as Lady Suffolk described the scene to Walpole) and said, ' You are a rascal, but I shall find you' (meaning in his broken English, ' I shall find a time to be revenged')." The next morning Lady Suffolk (then Mrs. Howard), while about to enter the Princess's apartment, was surprised to find her way barred by the yeomen with their halberds ; and the same night the Prince and Piincess were ordered to quit so unexpectedly, that they were obliged to go to the house of their chamberlain, the Earl of Grantham, in Albemarle Street.   The father and son were afterwards reconciled, but they never heartily agreed.

Nor was the case better between George the Second and the new Prince of Wales, his son Frederick.   If George the First was a common-place man of the quiet order, and George the Second of the bustling, Frederick was of an effeminate sort, pretending to taste and gallantry, and possessed of neither. He affected to patronise literature in order to court popularity, and because his father and grandfather had neglected it ; but he took no real interest in the literati, and would meanly stop their pensions when he got out of humour.   He passed his time in intriguing against his father, and hastening the ruin of a feeble constitution by sorry amours.

Not long after the marriage of George the Third, Bucking-ham House was settled on his young Queen in the event of her surviving him ; and the King took such a liking to it as to convert St. James's Palace wholly into a resort for state occasions, and confine his town residence to the new abode. Buckingham House was so called from John Sheffield, Duke of Buckinghamshire, who built it.   It was a dull though ornamented brick edifice, not unworthily representing the mediocre ability and stately assumptions of the owner, who was a small poet and a fastidious grandee, nearly as mad with pride as his duchess.   This lady was a natural daughter of James the Second (if indeed she was even that, for a Colonel Godfrey laid claim to the paternity), and she carried herself so loftily in consequence, as to be wish to be treated seriously as a princess, receiving visitors under a canopy, and going to the theatre in ermine.   She and the Duchess of Marlborough, who had a rival palace next door to St. James's, used to sit swelling at one another with neighbourly spite.   Sheffield, her husband, is said to have first made love to her sister Anne (afterwards Queen), for which her uncle, Charles the Second, has been accused of sending him on an expedition to Tangier in a "leaky vessel."   The duke wrote a long com-placent description of Buckingham House, that has often been reprinted, recording, among other things, the classical inscrip-tions which he put upon it and the princely chambers which it contained for the convenience of the births of his illustrious

house. The births came to nothing in consequence of the
death of his only legitimate child ; a natural son inherited
the property, and Government bought it for Queen Charlotte.
Henceforward it divided its old appellation of Buckingham
House with that of the " Queen's House ;" almost all the
Queen's children were born there ; and there, as at Kew and
Windsor, she may be said to have secreted her husband as
much as she could from the world, partly out of judicious
consideration for his infirmities, and partly in accordance
with the pride as well as penuriousnes that were at the
bottom of manners not ungentle, and a shrewd though narrow
understanding.   The spirit of this kind of life was very soon
announced to the fashionable world after her marriage by the
non-appearance of certain festivities; and it continued as long
as her husband lived, and as far as her own expenditure was
concerned ; though when her son came to the throne she
astonished the public by showing her willingness to partake
of festivities in an establishment not her own.   A deplorable
exhibition of her tyrannous and unfeeling habits of exaction
of the attentions of those about her is to be found in the
Diary of Madame d'Arblay (Miss Burney), whom they nearly
threw into a consumption.   It is clear that they would have
done so, had not the poor waiting-gentlewoman mustered up
courage enough to dare to save her life by persisting in her
request to be set free.   Queen Charlotte was a plain, penurious,
soft-spoken, decorous, bigoted, shrewd, over-weening personage,
"content" through a long life "to dwell on decencies for ever,"
inexorable "upon principle" to frailty, but not incapable of
being bribed out of it by German prepossessions, and whatever else might assist to effect the miracle, as was seen in the
instance of Mrs. Hastings, who had been Warren Hastings's
mistress, and who was, nevertheless received at court.   Pleasant as her Majesty might have been to Miss Burney, who
seems to have loved to be " persecuted," she was assuredly no
charmer in the eyes of the British nation; nor was she in the
slightest degree lamented when she died.   Nevertheless she
was a very good wife, for such we really believe her to have
been ; we mean not merely faithful, (for who would have
tempted her ?) but truly considerate, and anxious, and kind ;
and besides this she had another merit, not indeed of the same
voluntary description, but one for which the nation is strongly
indebted to her, though we are not aware that it has ever been
mentioned   We mean that her cool and calculating brain

turned out to be a most happy match for the warmer one of her husband, in ultimate as well as immediate respects; for it brought reason back into the blood of his race, and drew a remarkable line in consequence between him and his children; none of whom, however deficient in abilities, partook of their father's unreasonableness, while some went remarkably counter to his want of orderliness and self-government. The happy engraftment of the Cobourg family on the stock, completed this security in its most important quarter; and if ever a shade of more than ordinary sorrow for the necessity should have been brought across the memory in that quarter by a ridiculous pen, the sense of the security ought to fling it to the winds, with all the joy and comfort befitting the noblest brow and the wisest reign that have yet adorned the annals of its house.

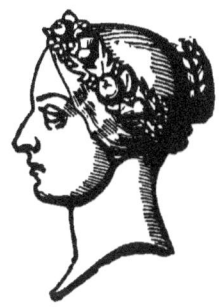

PRINTED BY

SPOTTISWOODE AND CO., NEW-STREET SQUARE

LONDON